READER'S DIGEST BOOKS

www.readersdigest.co.uk

The Reader's Digest Association Limited 11 Westferry Circus Canary Wharf London E14 4HE

For information as to ownership of copyright in the material of this book, and acknowledgments, see last page.

Printed in France
ISBN 0 276 42869 2

READER'S DIGEST BOOKS

*Selected and condensed
by Reader's Digest*

THE READER'S DIGEST ASSOCIATION LIMITED, LONDON

CONTENTS

THE LAST JUROR
page 9

John Grisham

In 1970, Willie Traynor arrives in Clanton, Mississippi and gets a job on the local paper—which usually reports nothing more exciting than obituaries. All that changes, however, when the town is rocked by its first major crime in decades. Suddenly, *The Ford County Times* is in the limelight, investigating the facts in the highly charged case. Grisham's best yet—an enthralling story and a fine portrait of a divided community.

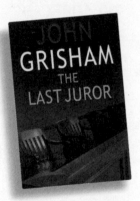

PUBLISHED BY CENTURY

THE VARIOUS HAUNTS OF MEN
page 159

Susan Hill

When a woman goes missing in Lafferton, the police show only mild concern—they know from experience that most people either turn up or have left of their own accord. But instinct tells DS Freya Graffham that something is wrong. Refusing to drop the case, she finds her suspicions well-founded when another woman vanishes and a sinister pattern starts to emerge. Superb crime-writing from the acclaimed author of *The Woman in Black*.

PUBLISHED BY CHATTO & WINDUS

THE CODEX

page 309

Douglas Preston

Notorious treasure-hunter Maxwell Broadbent has always tried to control the lives of his three sons. Now, close to death, he has set them a final challenge in a videotaped will: if they want to claim their inheritance—a fabulous collection of priceless artefacts— they must first find out where he has hidden them. It is a quest that will take the brothers into grave danger as they battle for survival in the Honduran jungle.

PUBLISHED BY FORGE, USA

LIFE AND LIMB

page 441

Jamie Andrew

The weather looked perfect when the two experienced climbers set off to climb the formidable north face of Les Droites. But as they neared the summit, a ferocious storm blew up, trapping them on an exposed ridge for the next five nights. Jamie Andrew's story is a truly enthralling epic of survival, and a moving tribute to his unshakable determination to overcome disability and reclaim the full and active life that he loves.

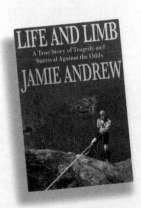

PUBLISHED BY PIATKUS

THE
LAST
JUROR

JOHN
GRISHAM

The Padgitts have long been the most powerful family in Ford County. Their criminal activities have made them immensely rich, and through bribery and intimidation they have always escaped the law.

So, when Danny Padgitt is arrested for murder, the trial is set to become one of the most explosive that the town of Clanton has ever known.

PART ONE

CHAPTER 1

After decades of patient mismanagement and loving neglect, *The Ford County Times* went bankrupt in 1970. The owner and publisher, Miss Emma Caudle, was ninety-three years old, blind and deaf, and strapped to a bed in a nursing home in Tupelo, Mississippi. The editor, her son Wilson Caudle, was in his seventies and had a plate in his head from the First War. A perfect circle of dark grafted skin covered the plate at the top of his long, sloping forehead, and throughout his adult life he had endured the nickname of Spot.

In his younger years, he had been a good reporter, thorough and intuitive. Evidently, the head wound did not affect his ability to write. But sometime after the Second War the plate apparently shifted, and Mr Caudle stopped writing everything but the obituaries. He loved obituaries. He spent hours on them. He filled paragraphs of eloquent prose detailing the lives of even the humblest of Ford Countians. He never missed a wake or a funeral, never wrote anything bad about anyone. Spot was a very popular man, even though he was crazy.

The only real crisis of his journalistic career happened in 1967, about the time the civil rights movement finally made it to Ford County. The paper had never shown the slightest hint of racial tolerance. No black faces appeared in its pages, except those belonging to known or suspected criminals. But one morning in 1967, Mr Caudle awoke to the realisation that black people were dying in Ford County, and their deaths were not being properly reported. There was a whole, new world of obituaries waiting out there, and Mr Caudle set sail in dangerous and uncharted waters. On Wednesday, March 8,

1967, the *Times* became the first white-owned weekly in Mississippi to run the obituary of a Negro. For the most part, it went unnoticed.

The following week, he ran three black obituaries, and people were beginning to talk. By the fourth week, a boycott was under way, with subscriptions being cancelled and advertisers holding their money. Mr Caudle knew what was happening, but he was too impressed with his new status as an integrationist to worry about such trivial matters as sales and profits. He explained to the public that he would publish whatever he damned well pleased, and if the white folks didn't like it, then he would simply cut back on their obituaries.

Now, dying properly is an important part of living in Mississippi, for whites and blacks, and the thought of being laid to rest without one of Spot's glorious send-offs was more than most whites could stand. And they knew he was crazy enough to carry out his threat.

The next edition was filled with all sorts of obituaries, blacks and whites. It sold out, and a brief period of prosperity followed.

The bankruptcy was called involuntary, as if others had eager volunteers. The pack was led by a print supplier from Memphis that was owed $60,000. Several creditors had not been paid in six months. The old Security Bank was calling in a loan.

I was new, but I'd heard the rumours. I was sitting on a desk in the front room of the *Times*'s offices reading a magazine, when a midget in a pair of pointed shoes strutted in the front door and asked for Wilson Caudle.

'He's at the funeral home,' I said.

'I need to serve these papers on him,' he said, waving an envelope.

'He's at the funeral home,' I repeated.

'Then I'll just leave them with you,' he declared.

Although I'd been around for less than two months, I had learned a few things. I knew that good papers were not served on people. The papers were trouble, and I wanted no part of them.

'I'm not taking the papers,' I said, looking down.

The midget glanced around the front office with a smirk, but he knew the situation was hopeless. He stuffed the envelope back into his pocket and demanded, 'Where's the funeral home?'

I pointed this way and that, and he left. An hour later, Spot stumbled through the door, waving the papers and bawling hysterically. 'It's over! It's over!' he kept wailing. Margaret Wright, the secretary, and Hardy, the pressman, came from the back and tried to console him. He sat in a chair, face in hands, elbows on knees. I read the petition aloud for the benefit of the others.

It said Mr Caudle had to appear in court in a week over in Oxford to meet the creditors and the judge, when a decision would be made as to whether the paper would continue to operate while a trustee sorted things out. Mr Caudle started crying and left. Six months later I would write his obituary.

Because I had attended college, and because I was holding the papers, Hardy and Margaret looked hopefully at me for advice. I was a journalist, not a lawyer, but I said that I would take the papers to the Caudle family lawyer. They smiled weakly and returned to work.

At noon, I bought a six-pack at Quincy's One Stop in Lowtown, the black section of Clanton, and went for a long drive in my Triumph Spitfire. It was late in February, unseasonably warm, so I put the top down and headed for the lake, wondering, not for the first time, just exactly what I was doing in Ford County, Mississippi.

I GREW UP in Memphis and studied journalism at Syracuse for five years before my grandmother got tired of paying for what was becoming an extended education. My grades were unremarkable, and I was a year away from a degree. Maybe a year and a half. She, BeeBee, had plenty of money, but after five years she figured my opportunity had been sufficiently funded. When she cut me off I was very disappointed, but I did not complain, to her anyway. I was her only grandchild and her estate would be a delight.

In the early days at Syracuse, I aspired to be an investigative reporter with the *New York Times* or the *Washington Post*. I wanted to save the world by uncovering corruption and injustice. But when my grades began their steady decline to the bottom of the class, I became captivated by the idea of working for a small-town newspaper. I cannot explain this attraction, except that it was at about this time that I met Nick Diener. He was from rural Indiana, and his family owned a rather prosperous county newspaper. He drove a fancy little Alfa Romeo and always had plenty of cash. We became close friends.

Nick was a bright student who could have handled medicine, law or engineering. His only goal, however, was to return to Indiana and run the family business. This baffled me until we got drunk one night and he told me how much his father cleared each year off their small weekly—circulation 6,000. It was a gold mine, he said. Just laid-back, low-pressure journalism with money growing on trees.

This appealed to me. After my fourth year, which should've been my last but wasn't close, I spent the summer interning at a small weekly in the Ozark Mountains of Arkansas. The pay was peanuts but BeeBee was impressed because I was employed. Each week I mailed her the paper, at least half of which was written by me. The owner/editor/publisher was a wonderful old gentleman who was delighted to have a reporter who wanted to write.

After five years at Syracuse my grades were irreparable, and BeeBee told me to find a job. At the time Wilson Caudle's sister lived in Memphis and this lady met BeeBee at a party. After a few phone calls back and forth, I was packed and headed to Clanton, Mississippi, where Spot was eagerly waiting. After an hour of orientation, he turned me loose on Ford County.

In the next edition he ran a sweet little story with a photo of me announcing my 'internship' at the *Times*. It made the front page. News was slow in those days.

The announcement contained two horrendous errors that would haunt me for years. The first and less serious was the fact that Syracuse had now joined the Ivy League, at least according to Spot. The second misstatement changed my life. I was born Joyner William Traynor. Until I was twelve I hammered my parents with enquiries about why two supposedly intelligent people would stick Joyner on a newborn. The story finally leaked that they had chosen Joyner as an olive branch to some feuding relative who allegedly had money. When I enrolled at Syracuse I was J. William, a rather imposing name for an eighteen-year-old. But Vietnam and all the rebellion and social upheaval convinced me that J. William sounded too corporate, too establishment. I became Will.

Spot at various times called me Will, William, Bill, or even Billy, but in the announcement, under my smiling face, was my new name. Willie Traynor. I was horrified. What would I tell my fraternity brothers at Syracuse? What would I tell BeeBee? I went to a prep school in Memphis and then to college in New York, and I had never met a person named Willie. I wasn't a good ole boy. I drove a Triumph Spitfire and had long hair.

After hiding in my apartment for two days, I mustered the courage to confront Spot. I marched into the *Times* office and bumped into Davey Bigmouth Bass, the sports editor of the paper. 'Hey, cool name,' he said. I followed him into his office, seeking advice.

'My name's not Willie,' I said.

'It is now. Hell, folks'll think you're pretty cool. A smart-ass from up north with long hair and a little imported sports car, and with a name like Willie. Think of Joe Willie.'

'Who's Joe Willie?'

'Joe Willie Namath.'

'Oh, him.' I began to feel better. In 1970, Joe Namath was probably the most famous athlete in the country. I went for a drive and kept repeating 'Willie'. Within a couple of weeks the name was beginning to stick. Everybody called me Willie and seemed to feel more comfortable because I had such a down-to-earth name.

I told BeeBee it was just a temporary pseudonym.

THE *TIMES* was a very thin paper, and I knew immediately that it was in trouble. Heavy on the obits, light on news and advertising. The employees were disgruntled, but quiet and loyal. Jobs were scarce in Ford County in 1970. After a week it was obvious even to my novice eyes that the paper was operating at a loss. Obits are free—ads are not. Spot spent most of his time in his cluttered office, napping periodically and calling the funeral home. There was one other general reporter, Baggy Suggs, a pickled old goat who hung around the courthouse across the street sniffing for gossip and drinking bourbon with a small club of washed-up lawyers too drunk to practise any more.

Margaret, the secretary, was a fine Christian lady who ran the place, though she was smart enough to allow Spot to think he was the boss. She was in her early fifties and had worked there for twenty years. Everything at the *Times* revolved around her. She and I became gossiping pals, and after a week or so she confirmed what I already suspected—that Mr Caudle was indeed crazy, and that the newspaper was indeed in dire financial straits. But, she said, the Caudles have family money!

It would be years before I understood this mystery.

In Mississippi, family money was not to be confused with wealth. It had nothing to do with cash or other assets. Family money was a status, obtained by someone who was white, somewhat educated beyond high school, born in a large home with a verandah—preferably one surrounded by cotton fields—and partially reared by a beloved black maid named Bessie or Pearl. Mississippi was full of insolvent blue bloods who inherited the status of family money. It could not be earned. It had to be handed down at birth.

When I talked to the Caudle family lawyer, he explained, rather succinctly, the real value of their family money. 'They're as poor as Job's turkey,' he said as I sat deep in a worn leather chair and looked up at him across his wide mahogany desk. Walter Sullivan, of Sullivan & O'Hara, had represented the Caudles for thirty years. He studied the bankruptcy petition and rambled on about how foolish the

Caudles had been in running a once-profitable newspaper into the ground. Back when Miss Emma ran things the *Times* had 5,000 subscribers and pages filled with advertisements. She kept a $500,000 certificate of deposit at Security Bank, just for a rainy day.

Then her husband died, and she remarried a local alcoholic twenty years her junior. Miss Emma loved him dearly and installed him as coeditor. It was the beginning of the end. Spot hated his new stepfather, the feelings were mutual, and their relationship finally climaxed with a fistfight on the downtown square, in front of a large and stunned crowd. The locals believed that Spot's brain, already fragile, took additional damage that day. Shortly thereafter, he began writing nothing but those damned obituaries. The stepfather ran off with Miss Emma's money, and she, heartbroken, became a recluse.

'It was once a fine paper,' Mr Sullivan said. 'But look at it now. Less than twelve hundred subscriptions, heavily in debt. Bankrupt.'

'What will the court do?' I asked.

'Try and find a buyer. The county has to have a newspaper.'

I immediately thought of two people—Nick Diener and BeeBee. Nick's family had become rich off their county weekly. BeeBee was already loaded and she had only one beloved grandchild. My heart began pounding as I smelt opportunity.

Mr Sullivan watched me intently, and it was obvious he knew what I was thinking. 'It could be bought for a song,' he said.

'How much?' I asked.

'Probably fifty thousand. Most of the debts can be bankrupted, then renegotiated with the creditors you need.' He paused and leaned forwards, elbows on his desk, thick greyish eyebrows twitching as if his brain was working overtime. 'It could be a real gold mine, you know.'

BeeBee had never invested in a gold mine, but after three days of priming the pump I left Memphis with a cheque for $50,000. I gave it to Mr Sullivan, who then petitioned the court for the sale of the paper. The judge nodded benignly and scrawled his name on an order that made me the new owner of *The Ford County Times*.

It takes at least three generations to be accepted in Ford County. Regardless of money or breeding, any newcomer is regarded with suspicion. The people there are exceedingly warm and gracious but they don't really trust you unless they trusted your grandfather.

Once word spread that I, a young green alien from Memphis, had bought the paper, a wave of gossip shook the community. Margaret gave me the updates. Because I was single, there was a chance I was a homosexual. Because I went to Syracuse, wherever that was, then I was probably a Communist. Or worse, a liberal. Because I was from Memphis, I was a subversive intent on embarrassing Ford County.

Just the same, as they all conceded quietly among themselves, I now controlled the obituaries! I was somebody!

The new *Times* debuted on March 18, 1970, only three weeks after the midget arrived with his papers. It was almost an inch thick and loaded with photos. Cub Scout troops, Brownies, junior high basketball teams, garden clubs, Bible study groups, adult softball teams, civic clubs. I tried to include every living soul in the county. And the dead ones were exalted like never before. I'm sure Spot was proud of the obits, but I never heard from him.

The news was light and breezy. Absolutely no editorials. People love to read about crime, so on the bottom of the front page I launched the Crime Notes Section. Thankfully, two pick-ups had been stolen the week before, and I covered these heists as if Fort Knox had been looted.

In the centre of the front page there was a rather large group shot of the new regime—Margaret, Hardy, Baggy Suggs, me, our photographer, Wiley Meek, Davey Bigmouth Bass, and Melanie Dogan, a high-school student and part-time employee. I was proud of my staff. We had worked round the clock for ten days, and our first edition was a great success. We printed 5,000 copies and sold them all. I sent some to BeeBee and she was most impressed.

For the next month, the new *Times* slowly took shape as I struggled to determine what I wanted it to become. I had never been attracted to long hours, but since I was the owner I forgot about the clock. I was twenty-three, and through luck and timing and a rich grandmother, I was suddenly the owner of a weekly newspaper. I figured it would take a year to become profitable. And, at first, revenue increased slowly. Then Rhoda Kassellaw was murdered. I guess it's the nature of the business to sell more papers after a brutal crime when people want details. We sold 2,400 papers the week before her death, and almost 4,000 the week after.

It was no ordinary murder. Thirty years later, I still think about it every day.

RHODA KASSELLAW lived in the Beech Hill community, twelve miles north of Clanton, in a modest grey-brick house on a narrow, tarmacked country road. The flowerbeds along the front of the house were weedless and the long wide lawn was thick and well cut.

Scattered across it was a collection of scooters and balls and bikes. Her two small children were always outdoors, playing hard.

It was a pleasant little country house, a stone's throw from Mr and Mrs Deece next door. The young man who bought it was killed in a trucking accident and, at the age of twenty-eight, Rhoda became a widow. The insurance on his life paid off the house and the car. The balance was invested to provide a modest monthly income that allowed her to remain at home and dote on the children. She spent hours outside, tending her vegetable garden, potting flowers, pulling weeds, mulching the beds along the front of the house.

She kept to herself. The old ladies in Beech Hill considered her a model widow, staying at home, looking sad, limiting her social appearances to an occasional visit to church.

Rhoda Kassellaw was a beautiful woman when she wanted to be, which was not very often. Her shapely, thin figure was usually camouflaged under a bulky chambray workshirt. She wore little make-up and kept her long flaxen-coloured hair pulled back and stuck together on top of her head. Such an attractive young widow would normally have been a hot property in the county, but she kept to herself.

After three years of mourning, however, Rhoda became restless. She was too young and too pretty to sit at home every Saturday. So she hired a baby sitter, and drove north for an hour to the Tennessee line, where she'd heard there were some respectable lounges and dance clubs. No one would know her there. She enjoyed the dancing and the flirting, but she never drank and always came home early. It became a routine, two or three times a month.

Then the jeans got tighter, the dancing faster, the hours longer. She was getting talked about in the bars and clubs along the state line.

He followed her home twice before he killed her. It was March, a dark night, with no moon. Bear, the family mutt, sniffed him first as he crept behind a tree in the back yard. Bear was primed to growl and bark when he was forever silenced.

Rhoda's son Michael was five and her daughter Teresa was three. She read them the story of Jonah and the whale before she tucked them in and kissed them good night. When Rhoda turned off the light to their bedroom, he was already in the house.

An hour later she turned off the television, locked the doors, and waited for Bear, who did not appear. That was no surprise because he often chased rabbits and squirrels into the woods. In her bedroom, she slipped out of her dress and opened the dressing-room door. He was waiting in there, in the dark.

He snatched her from behind, covered her mouth with a thick and sweaty hand, and said, 'I have a knife. I'll cut you and your kids.' With the other hand he held up a blade and waved it before her eyes.

'Understand?' he hissed into her ear.

She trembled and managed to nod her head. She couldn't see what he looked like. He threw her to the floor, face down, and yanked her hands behind her. He took a brown scarf and wrapped it roughly round her face. 'Not one sound,' he kept growling at her. 'Or I'll cut your kids.' When the blindfold was finished he dragged her to her bed. He poked the tip of the blade into her chin and said, 'Don't fight me. The knife's right here.' He cut off her panties and the rape began.

He wanted to see her eyes, those beautiful eyes he'd seen in the clubs. And the long hair. He'd bought her drinks and danced with her twice, and when he'd finally made a move she had stiff-armed him.

'Try these moves, baby,' he mumbled just loud enough for her to hear.

The smell of whiskey and sweat nauseated her, but she was too frightened to throw up. It might anger him, cause him to use the knife. As she started to accept the horror of the moment, she began to think. Keep it quiet. Don't wake up the kids. And what will he do with the knife when he's finished?

His movements were faster, he was mumbling louder. 'Quiet, baby,' he hissed again and again. 'I'll use the knife.' The wrought-iron bed was squeaking but he didn't care.

The rattling of the bed woke Michael, who then got Teresa up. They eased from their room and crept down the dark hall to see what was happening. Michael opened the door to his mother's bedroom, saw the strange man on top of her, and said, 'Mommy!' For a second the man stopped and jerked his head towards the children.

The sound of the boy's voice horrified Rhoda, who bolted upwards and thrust both hands at her assailant, grabbing whatever she could. One small fist caught him in the left eye, a solid shot that stunned him. Then she yanked off her blindfold while kicking with both legs. He slapped her and tried to pin her down again.

'Danny Padgitt!' she shouted, still clawing. He hit her once more.

'Mommy!' Michael cried.

'Run, kids!' Rhoda tried to scream, but she was struck dumb by her assailant's blows.

'Shut up!' Padgitt yelled.

'Run!' Rhoda shouted again, and the children backed away, then darted down the hallway, into the kitchen, and outside to safety.

17

In the split second after she shouted his name, Padgitt realised he had no choice but to silence her. He took the knife and hacked twice, then scrambled from the bed and grabbed his clothing.

MR AND MRS AARON DEECE were watching television when they heard Michael's voice calling. Mr Deece met the boy at the front door. His teeth were chattering so violently he had trouble speaking. 'He hurt my mommy!' he kept saying. 'He hurt my mommy!'

Through the darkness between the two houses, Mr Deece saw Teresa running after her brother, sucking her thumb, unable to speak.

Mr Deece raced into his den and grabbed two shotguns, one for him, one for his wife. The children were in the kitchen, shocked to the point of being paralysed. 'He hurt Mommy,' Michael kept saying. Mrs Deece cuddled them, told them everything would be fine. She looked at her shotgun when her husband laid it on the table. 'Stay here,' he said as he rushed out of the house.

He did not go far. Rhoda almost made it to the Deece home before she collapsed in the grass. She was completely naked, and from the neck down covered in blood. Mr Deece picked her up and carried her to the verandah, then shouted at his wife to move the children towards the back of the house and lock them in a bedroom. He could not allow them to see their mother in her last moments.

As he placed her in the swing, Rhoda whispered, 'Danny Padgitt. It was Danny Padgitt.'

He covered her with a quilt, then called an ambulance.

DANNY PADGITT kept his pick-up in the centre of the road and drove ninety miles an hour. He was half-drunk and scared as hell but unwilling to admit it. He'd be home in ten minutes, secure in the family's kingdom known as Padgitt Island.

Those little faces had ruined everything. He'd think about it tomorrow. He took a long pull on his Jack Daniel's and felt better.

It was a rabbit or a small dog or some varmint, and when it darted from the shoulder he caught a glimpse of it and reacted badly. He instinctively hit the brake pedal, just for a split second, but he'd punched too hard. The rear tyres locked and the pick-up fish-tailed. Before he realised it Danny was in serious trouble. The truck spun like a stock car on the backstretch and slid into the ditch, crashing into a row of pine trees. If he'd been sober he would've been killed, but drunks walk away.

He crawled out through a shattered window, and for a long while leaned on the truck, counting his cuts and scratches and considering his options. A leg was suddenly stiff, and as he climbed up the bank to the road he realised he could not walk far. Not that he would need to. The blue lights were on him before he realised it. The deputy was out of the car, surveying the scene with a long black flashlight. He saw the blood, smelt the whiskey, and reached for the handcuffs.

THE BIG BROWN RIVER drops nonchalantly south from Tennessee and runs as straight as a hand-dug channel for thirty miles through the centre of Tyler County, Mississippi. Two miles above the Ford County line it begins twisting and looping, and by the time it leaves Tyler County it looks like a scared snake, curling desperately and going nowhere. A hundred backwaters and creeks feed it with an inexhaustible supply of slow-moving, muddy water.

Its journey through Ford County is brief. It dips and forms a wide circle round 2,000 acres in the northeasternmost corner of the county, then leaves and heads back towards Tennessee. The circle is almost perfect and an island is almost formed, but at the last moment the Big Brown turns away from itself and leaves a narrow strip of land between its banks. The circle is known as Padgitt Island, a deep, dense woodland covered in pine, gum, elm, oak, and a myriad of swamps and bayous.

On the thin strip of land between the banks of the Big Brown a tar-macked road entered and left, always with someone watching. Few of the locals ever dared to use it.

The entire island had been in the Padgitt family since Reconstruction, when Rudolph Padgitt, a carpetbagger from the north, arrived a bit late after the war and found all the prime land taken. He searched in vain until he stumbled upon the snake-infested island. He put together a band of newly freed slaves and, with guns and machetes, fought his way onto the island. No one else wanted it.

Rudolph married a local whore and began cutting timber. Since timber was in great demand after the war, he became prosperous. Soon there was a horde of little Padgitts on the island. One of his ex-slaves had learned the art of distillery. Rudolph used his corn crop to produce what was soon known as one of the finest whiskeys in the Deep South.

For thirty years Rudolph made moonshine until he died of cirrhosis in 1902. By then an entire clan of Padgitts inhabited the island, and were proficient at milling timber and producing illegal whiskey. Scattered about the island were half a dozen distilleries, all well-protected and concealed.

The Padgitts were famous for their whiskey, though fame was not something they sought. They were secretive and clannish, fiercely private and deathly afraid that someone might infiltrate their little kingdom and disrupt their considerable profits. They said they were loggers, and the Padgitt Lumber Company was very visible on the main highway near the river. They claimed to be legitimate people, taxpayers and such, with their children in the public schools.

During the 1920s and 1930s, when alcohol was illegal and the nation was thirsty, Padgitt whiskey could not be distilled fast enough. It was shipped in oak barrels across the Big Brown and hauled by trucks up north, as far away as Chicago. The patriarch, president and director of production and marketing was an old warrior named Clovis Padgitt, Rudolph's eldest son. Clovis was a hard-nosed cash and no-taxes man, and the Padgitts were rumoured to have more money than the Mississippi state treasury.

One night in 1938, three revenue agents sneaked across the Big Brown in a rented flatboat in search of the source of Old Padgitt whiskey. Their covert invasion of the island was flawed in many ways, the obvious being the original idea itself. They were dismembered and buried in deep graves.

In 1943, a strange event occurred in Ford County—an honest man was elected sheriff. His name was Koonce Lantrip, and he vowed to end corruption, to clean up county government, to put the bootleggers and moonshiners out of business.

His supporters waited and waited, and, finally, six months after taking office he organised his deputies and crossed the Big Brown on the only bridge. Two of the deputies were shot in the head, and Lantrip's body was never found.

The massacre was hot news in Mississippi for weeks, and the governor threatened to send in the National Guard. But the Second War was raging, and D-Day soon captured the attention of the country. For those who were able to fight, the beaches of Normandy were more inviting.

With the noble experiment of an honest sheriff behind them, the good people of Ford County elected one from the old school. His name was Mackey Don Coley and his father had been the high sheriff back in the twenties when Clovis was in charge of Padgitt Island. When Mackey Don announced his candidacy, Clovis's eldest son, Buford, sent him $50,000 in cash. Mackey Don won in a landslide.

After the Second War, the demand for moonshine began a steady decline. Buford and the family began to diversify into other forms of illicit commerce. They ran guns, stole cars, counterfeited, bought and burned buildings to collect insurance. For twenty years they operated a highly successful brothel on the county line, until it mysteriously burned down in 1966.

In 1967, a younger Padgitt fled to Canada to avoid the draft. He drifted to California where he tried marijuana and realised he had a taste for it. After a few months as a peacenik, he got homesick and sneaked back to Padgitt Island. He brought with him four pounds of pot, which he shared with all his cousins, and they, too, were quite taken with it. He explained that the rest of the country was toking like crazy. As usual, Mississippi was at least five years behind the trend.

The stuff could be grown cheaply, then hauled to the cities where there was demand. His father, Gill, grandson of Clovis, saw the opportunity, and soon many of the old cornfields were converted to cannabis. A 2,000-foot strip of land was cleared for a runway and within a year the Padgitts had established contacts in Miami and Mexico, and the cash was coming in by the truckload. For years, no one in Ford County had a hint that the Padgitts were trafficking in drugs. And they never got caught. No Padgitt was ever indicted for a drug-related offence.

In fact, not a single Padgitt had ever been arrested. A hundred years of moonshining, stealing, gunrunning, gambling, counterfeiting, whoring, bribing, even killing, and eventually drug manufacturing, and not a single arrest. They were smart people, careful, deliberate, patient. Not surprisingly, the Padgitts were the source of endless gossip in the cafés and coffee shops around the square in Clanton. They were never considered local heroes, but certainly legends.

Then Danny Padgitt, Gill's youngest son, was arrested for the rape and murder of Rhoda Kassellaw.

CHAPTER 2

Mr Deece told me the next day that when he was certain Rhoda was dead he left her in the swing on the verandah. He went to his bathroom, where he showered and changed into work clothes. Then he waited for the police and the ambulance, watching Rhoda's house with a loaded shotgun in his hand. In the distance he could hear a siren.

Before long Benning Road was alive with red and blue flashing lights. Rhoda's body was photographed at length before it was taken away. Her home was cordoned off by a squad of deputies, led by Sheriff Coley himself. Mr Deece, still holding his shotgun, gave his statement to an investigator, then to the sheriff. His wife kept the two traumatised children locked in the back bedroom, where she huddled with them in the bed, under a blanket. Later in the day an aunt arrived from Missouri and took them away.

My phone rang seconds before midnight. It was Wiley Meek, the paper's photographer. He'd picked up the story on the police scanner and was already hanging around the jail waiting to ambush the suspect. Hurry, he urged me. This could be the big one.

At the time I lived above an old garage next to a decaying but still grand Victorian mansion known as the Hocutt House. It was filled with elderly Hocutts, three sisters and a brother, and they took turns being my landlord. Their five-acre estate was a few blocks from the Clanton square and had been built a century earlier with family money. The four-room loft apartment was spacious and clean and cost me the ridiculous sum of fifty dollars a month.

The Hocutts' father, Miles Hocutt, had been an eccentric doctor in Clanton for decades. Their mother died during childbirth, and, according to local legend, Dr Hocutt became very possessive of the children after her death. To protect them from the world, he explained to his children that insanity ran deeply in the family, and thus they should never marry lest they produce some hideous strain of idiot offspring. His children believed him. They never married. The oldest, Max Hocutt, was eighty-one when he leased me the apartment. The twins, Wilma and Gilma, were seventy-seven, and Melberta, the baby, was seventy-three and completely out of her mind.

Two cars were parked in the garage. One was my Spitfire, and the other was a black Mercedes. It was ten years old and had been driven less than eight thousand miles. Their father had also preached to them the sinfulness of women driving, so Mr Max was the chauffeur.

I eased the Spitfire down the drive and waved at Gilma peeking from behind the curtain. She jerked her head away and disappeared. The jail was six blocks away. I had slept for about thirty minutes.

Danny Padgitt was being fingerprinted when I arrived at the sheriff's office. The place was packed with deputies and reserves and volunteer firemen and everybody with access to a uniform and a police scanner. Wiley Meek met me on the front sidewalk.

'It's Danny Padgitt!' he said with great excitement.

I stopped for a second and tried to think. 'Who?'

'Danny Padgitt, from the island.'

I'd been in Ford County less than three months and had yet to meet a single Padgitt. But I'd heard various instalments of their legend.

Wiley gushed on, 'I got some great shots just as they got him out of the car. Had blood all over him. Great pictures! The girl's dead!'

'What girl?'

'The one he killed. Raped her too, at least that's the rumour.'

Danny Padgitt, I mumbled to myself as the sensational story began to sink in. I had my first glimpse of the headline, no doubt the boldest one the *Times* had run in many years.

We pushed our way inside and looked around for Sheriff Coley. He'd been the sheriff since the massacre in 1943, so he was pushing seventy years of age. On the surface he was a gentleman, always polite, always smiling, and both times I'd met him I'd later wondered how such a nice man could be so corrupt.

'Sheriff, just a couple of questions,' I said as he emerged from a back room. There were no other reporters present and his boys all got quiet and gave me their sneers. I was still very much the brash new rich boy who'd somehow wrangled control of their newspaper.

Sheriff Coley smiled as usual, as if these encounters happened all the time around midnight. 'Yes, sir, Mr Traynor.' He had a slow rich drawl that was very soothing. This man couldn't tell a lie, could he?

'What can you tell us about the murder?'

With his arms folded across his chest, he gave a few of the basics in copspeak. 'White female, age thirty-one, was attacked in her home on Benning Road. Raped, stabbed, murdered. Can't give you her name until we talk to her kinfolks.'

'And you've made an arrest?'

'Yes, sir, but no details now. Just give us a couple of hours. We're investigatin'. That's all, Mr Traynor.'

'Rumour has it that you have Danny Padgitt in custody.'

'I don't deal in rumours, Mr Traynor. Not in my profession. Yours neither.'

Wiley and I drove to the hospital, sniffed around for an hour, heard nothing we could print, then drove to the scene on Benning Road. The cops had cordoned off the house and a few of the neighbours were huddled quietly near the mailbox. They seemed too stunned to talk. After a few minutes of gawking at the house, we crept away.

Wiley had a nephew who was a part-time deputy, and we found him guarding the Deece home where they were still inspecting the verandah and the swing where Rhoda took her last breath. We pulled him off to the side, behind a row of Mr Deece's crape myrtles, and he told us everything. All off the record, of course, as if the gory details would somehow be kept quiet in Ford County.

THERE WERE THREE small cafés around the square in Clanton, two for the whites, one for the blacks. Wiley suggested we get an early table at the Tea Shoppe and just listen.

I do not eat breakfast, and I'm usually not awake during the hours in which it is served. I don't mind working until midnight, but I prefer to sleep until the sun is overhead and in full view. As I quickly realised, one of the advantages of owning a small weekly was that I could work late and sleep late.

I'd been to the Tea Shoppe a couple of times for late-morning coffee and once for lunch. As the owner of the paper, I felt it necessary to circulate and be seen, at a reasonable hour. Wiley had said the cafés would be crowded early today and he was right, the place was packed when we walked in, just after 6 a.m. He offered some hellos, shook some hands, exchanged a couple of insults. He was from Ford County and knew everyone. I nodded and smiled and caught the odd looks. It would take years. The people were friendly, but also wary of outsiders.

We found two seats at the counter and I asked for coffee. Nothing else. The waitress did not approve of this. She warmed to Wiley, though, when he reconsidered and ordered scrambled eggs, ham, grits and a side of hash browns, enough cholesterol to choke a mule.

The talk was of the rape and murder and nothing else. The Padgitts had had the run of the county for a hundred years; it was time to send 'em all to jail. Surround the island with the National Guard if necessary. Mackey Don had to go; he'd been in their pockets for too long.

Not much was said about Rhoda. Someone knew she'd been hanging around the lounges on the state line. Someone said she'd been sleeping with a local lawyer. Didn't know his name.

The rumours roared round the Tea Shoppe. Too bad I couldn't print all the wonderful gossip we heard, but we did, however, print a lot.

The headline proclaimed that Rhoda Kassellaw had been raped and murdered, and that Danny Padgitt had been arrested for it.

Under it were two photos; one of Rhoda as a senior in high school, and one of Padgitt as he was led into the jail in handcuffs. Wiley had ambushed him all right. It was a perfect shot, with Padgitt sneering at the camera. There was blood on his forehead and on his shirt. He looked nasty, mean, drunk, and guilty as hell, and I knew the photo would cause a sensation. Wiley thought we'd better avoid it, but I was twenty-three years old and too young to be restrained. I wanted my readers to know the ugly truth. I wanted to sell newspapers.

The photo of Rhoda had been obtained from a sister in Missouri. The first time I talked to her, by phone, she had had almost nothing to say and quickly hung up. The second time she thawed just a little, said the children were being seen by a doctor, that the funeral would take place Tuesday afternoon in a small town near Springfield, and, as far as the family was concerned, the entire state of Mississippi could burn in hell.

I told her that I understood, that I was from Syracuse, that I was one of the good guys. She finally agreed to send me a photo.

Using a host of unnamed sources, I described in detail what happened the previous Saturday night on Benning Road. When I was sure of a fact, I drove it home. When I wasn't so sure, I nibbled around the edges with enough innuendo to convey what I thought happened. Baggy Suggs sobered up long enough to reread and edit the stories. He probably kept us from getting sued or shot.

On page two there was a map of the crime scene and a large photo of Rhoda's home, complete with cop cars and yellow police ribbon and the bikes and toys of Michael and Teresa scattered around the front yard. The photo stated plainly that children lived there, and that children were involved in a crime so brutal that most Ford Countians were still trying to believe it really happened.

How much did the children see? That was the burning question.

I didn't answer it in the *Times*, but I got as close as possible. I described the house and its interior layout. Using an unnamed source, I estimated that the children's beds were about thirty feet from their mother's. The children fled the house before Rhoda, they were in shock by the time they got next door and were undergoing therapy back home in Missouri, where Rhoda's family lived. They saw a lot.

Would they testify at a trial? Baggy said there was no way; they were simply too young. But I pulled the question out of the air and posed it anyway, to give the readers something else to argue over.

We went to press about 10 p.m. on Tuesday night; the paper was in the racks around the Clanton square by 7 a.m. on Wednesday. The circulation had dropped to fewer than 1,200 at the time of the bankruptcy, but after a month of my fearless leadership we had close to 2,500 subscribers.

For the Rhoda Kassellaw murder we printed 8,000 copies and put them everywhere—by the doors of the cafés around the square, in the halls of the courthouse, in the lobbies of the banks. We mailed 3,000 free copies to potential subscribers, as part of a sudden, one-off special promotion effort.

According to Wiley, it was the first murder in eight years. It was a Padgitt! Sure I went for the shock, for the sensational, for the bloodstains. Sure it was yellow journalism, but what did I care?

I had no idea the response would be so quick and unpleasant.

AT 9 A.M., Thursday morning, the main courtroom of the Ford County courthouse was full. It was the domain of the Honourable Reed Loopus, an ageing circuit court judge from Tyler County, who passed through Clanton eight times a year to dispense justice. He was a legendary old warrior who ruled with an iron fist and, according to Baggy, was a thoroughly honest judge who had somehow managed to avoid the tentacles of the Padgitt money.

Because I was a member of the press, indeed the owner of the local paper, I felt it was my duty to arrive early and get a good seat. Yes, I was a bit smug. The other spectators were there out of curiosity. I, however, had very important work to do. Baggy and I were sitting in the second row when the crowd began to assemble.

Danny Padgitt's principal lawyer was a character named Lucien Wilbanks, a man I would quickly learn to hate. He wore a beard, swore like a sailor, drank heavily, and preferred clients who were rapists and murderers and child molesters. He was abrasive and fearless and downright mean, and he waited until everyone was settled in the courtroom—just before Judge Loopus entered—to walk slowly over to me. He was holding a copy of the latest *Times*, which he began waving as he started swearing. 'You little son of a bitch!' he said, quite loudly, and the courtroom became perfectly still. 'Who in hell do you think you are?'

I was too mortified to attempt an answer. I felt Baggy inch away. Every single person in the courtroom was staring at me, and I knew I had to say something. 'Just telling the truth,' I managed to say with as much conviction as I could muster.

'It's yellow journalism!' he roared. 'Sensational tabloid garbage!'

'Thank you,' I said, like a real wise guy. There were at least five deputies in the courtroom, none of whom was showing any interest in breaking this up.

'We'll file suit tomorrow!' he said, his eyes glowing. 'A million dollars in damages!'

'I got lawyers,' I said, terrified that I was about to be as bankrupt as the Caudle family. Lucien tossed the paper into my lap, then turned and went back to his table. I could feel my cheeks burning from embarrassment and fear, but I managed to keep a stupid grin on my face. I couldn't show the locals that I, the editor/publisher of their paper, was afraid of anything. But a million dollars in damages!

There was a commotion up behind the bench and a bailiff opened a door. 'Everyone rise,' he announced. Judge Loopus crept through it and shuffled to his seat, his faded black robe trailing behind him. Once situated, he surveyed the crowd, and said, 'Good morning. A rather nice turnout for a bail hearing.' Such routine matters generally attracted no one, except for the accused, his lawyer, and perhaps his mother. There were 300 people watching this one.

Judge Loopus nodded at another bailiff and a side door opened. Danny Padgitt was escorted in, his hands cuffed at his waist. He was wearing a neatly pressed white shirt, khaki pants and loafers. His handsome face was clean shaven and free of any apparent injuries. He was twenty-four, a year older than me, but he looked much younger. He managed a slow strut, then the sneer as the bailiff removed the handcuffs. He looked around at the crowd, showing all the confidence of someone whose family had unlimited cash, which it would use to get him out of his little jam.

Seated directly behind him were his parents and various other Padgitts. His father Gill, grandson of Clovis, had a college degree and was rumoured to be the chief money launderer in the gang. His mother was well dressed and somewhat attractive, which I found unusual for someone dimwitted enough to marry into the Padgitt clan.

The State was represented by the county prosecutor, a part-timer named Rocky Childers. Judge Loopus addressed him: 'Mr Childers, I assume the State is opposed to bail.'

Childers stood and said, 'Yes, sir.'

'On what grounds?'

'The horrific nature of the crimes, Your Honour. A vicious rape in front of the victim's small children. A simultaneous murder caused by at least two knife wounds. The attempted flight of the accused, Mr Padgitt.' Childers's words cut through the hushed courtroom. 'The likelihood that if Mr Padgitt leaves jail we will never see him again.'

Lucien Wilbanks couldn't wait to stand up and start bickering. He was on his feet immediately. 'We object to that, Your Honour. My client has no criminal record whatsoever, never been arrested before.'

Judge Loopus looked calmly over his reading glasses and said,

'Mr Wilbanks, I do hope that is the first and last time you interrupt anyone in this proceeding. I suggest you sit down, and when the Court is ready to hear from you, then you will be so advised.' His words were icy, almost bitter, and I wondered how many times these two had tangled.

Nothing bothered Lucien Wilbanks; his skin was as thick as rawhide.

Childers continued. 'If this defendant is released on bail, Your Honour, we'll never see him again. It's that simple.' He sat down.

'Mr Wilbanks,' His Honour said. 'Does your client own real estate in this county?'

'No, he does not. He's only twenty-four.'

'Let's get to the bottom line, Mr Wilbanks. I know his family owns considerable acreage. The only way I'll grant bail is if it's all pledged to secure his appearance for trial.'

'That's outrageous,' Lucien growled.

'So are his alleged crimes.'

Lucien flung his legal pad onto the table. 'Give me a minute to consult with the family.'

This caused quite a stir among the Padgitts. They huddled behind the defence table with Wilbanks and there was disagreement from the very start.

Lucien sensed that an agreement was unlikely, and to avoid embarrassment he turned and addressed the Court. 'That's impossible, Your Honour,' he announced. 'The Padgitt land is owned by at least forty people, most of them absent from this courtroom.'

'Then bail is denied until the preliminary hearing.'

'We waive the preliminary.'

'As you wish,' Loopus said, taking notes.

'And we will be moving for a change of venue as soon as possible.' Lucien said this boldly, as if an important proclamation was needed.

'It's a bit early for that, don't you think?' Loopus said.

'It will be impossible for my client to get a fair trial in this county.' Wilbanks gazed around the courtroom as he continued. 'An effort is already under way to indict, try and convict my client before he has the chance to defend himself, and I think the Court should intervene immediately with a gag order.'

'Where are you going with this, Mr Wilbanks?' Loopus asked.

'Have you seen the local paper, Your Honour?'

'Not lately.'

All eyes seemed to settle upon me, and my heart stopped dead still.

Wilbanks glared at me as he continued. 'Front-page stories, bloody photographs, unnamed sources, enough half-truths and innuendoes to convict any innocent man!'

Baggy was inching away again, and I was very much alone.

Lucien stomped across the courtroom and tossed a copy up to the bench. 'Take a look at this,' he growled.

Loopus adjusted his reading glasses, pulled the *Times* up high, and sank back into his chair.

He was a slow reader. At some point my heart began functioning again, returning with the fury of a jackhammer. The courtroom was silent except for the rattle of pages turning. Finally His Honour was finished. Would he toss me into jail right there? He leaned slightly forwards to the microphone and uttered words that would instantly make my career. He said, 'It's very well written. Engaging, perhaps a bit macabre, but certainly nothing out of line.'

I started scribbling on my reporter's pad, as if I hadn't just heard that I had prevailed over the Padgitts and Lucien Wilbanks. 'Congratulations,' Baggy whispered.

Loopus refolded the newspaper and laid it down. He allowed Wilbanks to rant and rave for a few minutes about leaks from the cops, leaks from the prosecutor's office, potential leaks from the grand jury room. He had lost his attempt to get bail, so now he was trying to impress the Padgitts with his zealousness.

Loopus bought none of it.

As we would soon learn, Lucien's act had been nothing but a smoke-screen. He had no intention of moving the case from Ford County.

WHEN I BOUGHT the *Times*, its prehistoric building came with the deal. It was on the south side of the Clanton square, on three levels, with a basement. There were several offices in the front, all with stained and threadbare carpet and peeling walls.

In the rear, as far away as possible, was the printing press. Every Tuesday night, Hardy, our pressman, somehow coaxed the old letter-press to life and managed to produce yet another edition of our paper.

The room on the ground floor was lined with bookshelves sagging under the weight of dusty tomes that had not been opened in decades. Standing in the front window, and looking through dingy panes of glass, one could see the Ford County courthouse and the bronze Confederate sentry guarding it.

The sentry could also be seen from my office, which was on the first floor. The office was spacious, cluttered, filled with useless arte-facts and I loved it. When Spot left he took nothing, and no one seemed to want any of his junk. So it remained where it was, neglected as always, slowly becoming my property. I boxed up his personal things—letters, bank statements, notes—and stored them in one of the many unused rooms down the hall.

My office had French doors that opened onto a small verandah with a wrought-iron railing, and there was enough room out there for four people to sit in wicker chairs and watch the square. Not that there was much to see, but it was a pleasant way to pass the time, especially with a drink.

Baggy was always ready for a drink. He brought a bottle of bourbon after dinner, and we assumed our positions in the rockers. The town was still buzzing over the bail hearing. It had been widely assumed that Danny Padgitt would be sprung as soon as Lucien Wilbanks and Mackey Don Coley could get matters arranged. But Judge Loopus had other plans.

Baggy's wife was a nurse. She worked the night shift in the emergency room at the hospital. He worked days, so they rarely saw each other, which was evidently a good thing because they fought constantly. Baggy was fifty-two, but he looked at least seventy, and I suspected that the booze was the principal reason he was ageing badly and fighting at home.

'We kicked their butts,' he said proudly. 'Never before has a newspaper story been so clearly exonerated. Right there in open court.'

'What's a gag order?' I asked. No sense in pretending I knew something when I didn't.

'I've never seen one. I've heard of them, and I think they're used by judges to shut up the lawyers and the litigants.'

'So they don't apply to newspapers?'

'Never. There's no way a court can tell a newspaper not to print something. It was apparent to Wilbanks that his client was staying in jail, so he had to showboat. Typical manoeuvre by lawyers. They teach it in law school.'

'So you don't think we'll get sued?'

'Hell, no. Look, first of all, we didn't libel or defame anyone. Sure we got kinda loose with some of the facts, but it was all probably true. Second, if Wilbanks had a lawsuit he would have to file it in Ford County. Same courthouse, same judge. The Honourable Reed Loopus, who, this morning, declared our stories to be just fine. Brilliant.'

I certainly didn't feel brilliant. I'd been worrying about the million dollars in damages but now the bourbon was settling in and I relaxed.

Baggy, as usual, had been relaxed for a long time.

'I guess Mackey Don's got the boy in the suite,' Baggy said, his words starting to slur.

'The suite?' I asked.

'Yeah—have you seen the jail?'

'No.'

'It's not fit for animals. No heat, no air, plumbing works about half the time. Rotten food. And that's for the whites. The blacks are at the other end, all in one cell. Their only toilet is a hole in the floor.'

'I think I'll pass.'

'Anyway, there's one little cell with air conditioning and carpet on the floor, one clean bed, colour television, good food. It's called the suite and Mackey Don puts his favourites there.'

'You think Padgitt's in the suite?'

'Probably. He came to court in his own clothes.'

'As opposed to?'

'Those orange coveralls everybody else wears. You haven't seen them?'

Yes, I had seen them. I had been in court a month or so earlier, and I suddenly recalled seeing two or three defendants wearing different shades of faded orange coveralls with 'Ford County Jail' printed across the front and back.

Baggy took a sip and expounded. 'You see, for the preliminary hearings and such, the defendants, if they're still in jail, always come to court dressed like prisoners. It's kinda hard to convince a jury you're not guilty when you're dressed like an inmate.'

I marvelled once again at the backwardness of Mississippi. I could see a criminal defendant, especially a black one, facing a jury and expecting a fair trial, wearing jail garb designed to be spotted from half a mile away.

I decided to go to the jail the next day and speak to as many of the inmates as possible, maybe consult with Wiley's nephew again about conditions around the jail.

THE NEXT EDITION of the *Times* did much to solidify my reputation as a fearless, twenty-three-year-old fool. On the front page was a huge photo of Danny Padgitt being led into the courthouse for his bail hearing. He was handcuffed and wore street clothes. Just above the story was the massive headline: BAIL DENIED FOR DANNY PADGITT.

Alongside was another story, almost as long and much more scandalous. Quoting unnamed sources, I described at length the conditions of Mr Padgitt's incarceration. I mentioned every possible perk he was getting. I talked about his food and diet, colour television, unlimited phone use. Everything I could possibly verify. Then I compared this with how the other twenty-one inmates were living.

In the story, I detailed my efforts to chat with the sheriff. My phone calls had not been returned. I'd gone to the jail twice and he wouldn't meet with me. I'd left a list of questions for him, which he chose to ignore. I painted the picture of a reporter desperately searching for the truth and being stiff-armed by an elected official.

With a rapist/murderer, a corrupt sheriff and an unpopular lawyer on one side, and me standing alone on the other, I knew I couldn't lose the fight. The response to the story was astounding. Baggy and Wiley reported that the cafés were buzzing with admiration for the fearless young editor of the paper. The Padgitts and Lucien had been despised for a long time. Now it was time to get rid of Coley.

Margaret said we were swamped with phone calls from readers incensed with the soft treatment Danny was receiving. Subscriptions jumped to almost 3,000. Ad revenue doubled. Not only was I shining a new light into the county, I was making money at the same time.

THE BOMB WAS a rather basic incendiary device that, if detonated, would have quickly engulfed our printing room and then raced through the front offices and the upper two floors.

It was discovered sitting ominously, still intact, next to a pile of old papers in the printing room, by the village idiot. Or, I should say, one of the village idiots. Clanton had more than its share.

His name was Piston, and he, like the building and the ancient press, came with the deal. Piston was not an official employee of the *Times*, but he nonetheless showed up every Friday to collect his $50 in cash. For this fee he sometimes swept the floors and occasionally rearranged the dirt on the front windows, and he hauled out the trash when someone complained. He provided janitorial services for several businesses around the square, and somehow survived.

Piston was in early Thursday morning and said that he first heard something ticking. Upon closer examination he noticed three five-gallon plastic cans laced together with a wooden box sitting on the floor next to them. The ticking sound came from the box.

Piston walked to Margaret's office and called Hardy. Hardy called the police, and around 9 a.m. I was woken with the news.

Most of downtown was evacuated by the time I arrived. The chief of police explained to me that the *Times* office was off limits because the wooden box had not been opened and whatever was in there was still ticking. 'It might explode,' he said gravely. I doubted if he had much experience with bombs. An official from the state crime lab was being rushed in. It was decided that the four buildings in our row would remain unoccupied until this expert finished his business.

A bomb in downtown Clanton! The news spread faster than the fire would have, and all work stopped. The county offices emptied, as well as the banks and stores and cafés, and before long large groups of spectators were crowded across the street, under the huge oaks on the south side of the courthouse, a safe distance away.

The Clanton city police had been joined by the sheriff's deputies, and every uniform in the county was soon present, milling about on the sidewalks, doing absolutely nothing. It was obvious that the city and county had no bomb drills.

Baggy needed a drink. It was too early for me. I followed him into the rear of the courthouse, up a narrow flight of stairs I'd not seen before, through a cramped hallway, then up another twenty steps to a small room with a low ceiling. 'Used to be the old jury room,' he said.

'What is it now?' I asked.

'The Bar Room. Get it? Bar? Lawyers? Booze?'

'Got it.'

There was a beaten-up card table surrounded by half a dozen mismatched chairs. In one corner there was a small refrigerator with a padlock. Baggy, of course, had a key, and inside he found a bottle of bourbon. He poured a generous shot into a paper cup and said, 'Grab a chair.' We pulled two of them up to the window, and below was the scene we had just left.

'I guess they're losin' their touch,' he said, gazing down at the excitement.

'They?' I was almost afraid to ask.

'The Padgitts.' He said this with a certain smugness. 'They've been burnin' buildings for ever. It's one of their scams—insurance fraud.' He smirked and took a quick sip. 'Odd, though, that they would use gasoline. A good fire marshal can smell gasoline within minutes after the blaze is out. Gasoline means arson. Arson means no insurance payoffs.' Another sip. 'Of course, in this case, they probably wanted you to know it's arson. Makes sense, doesn't it?'

Nothing made sense at that moment to me.

Baggy was content to do the talking. He thought he knew everything and he was right about half the time. 'Come to think of it, that's probably the reason it wasn't detonated. It was a subtle act of intimidation.'

'Subtle?'

'Yes, compared to what could've been. Believe me, those guys know how to burn buildings. You were lucky.'

I noticed how he had quickly disassociated himself from the paper. It was 'I' who was lucky, not 'we'.

'Yep. The fact that the Padgitts have brought their little show on the road means they're ready for war. If they can intimidate the newspaper, then they'll try it with the jury. They already own the sheriff.'

'But Wilbanks said he wants a change of venue.'

He snorted and rediscovered his drink. 'Don't bet on it, son.'

I was his boss and didn't like to be referred to as son. 'Please call me Willie,' I said. Odd how I was now clinging to that name.

'Don't bet on it, Willie. The boy's guilty; his only chance is to have a jury that can be bought or scared. Ten to one odds the trial takes place right here, in this building.'

AFTER TWO HOURS of waiting in vain for the ground to shake, the town was ready for lunch. The crowd broke up and drifted away. The expert from the state crime lab arrived and went to work in the printing room. I wasn't allowed in the building, which was fine with me.

Margaret, Wiley and I had a sandwich in the gazebo on the courthouse lawn. We ate quietly, chatted briefly, the three of us keeping an eye on our office across the street. Occasionally someone would see us and stop to offer sympathy. Eventually Sheriff Coley ambled over and gave his report. The clock was of the wind-up alarm variety, available in stores everywhere. At first glance the expert thought there was a problem with the wiring. Very amateurish, he said.

'How will you investigate this?' I asked with an edge.

'We'll check for prints, see if we can find any witnesses. The usual.'

'Will you talk to the Padgitts?' I asked, even edgier. I was, after all, in the presence of my employees. And though I was scared to death, I wanted to impress them with how utterly fearless I was.

'You know somethin' I don't?' he shot back.

'I know they're the most experienced arsonists in the county. Their lawyer threatened me in court last week. We've had Danny Padgitt on the front page twice. If they're not suspects, then who is?'

'Just go ahead and write the story, son. Call 'em by name. You seem determined to get sued anyway.'

'I'll take care of the paper,' I said. 'You catch the criminals.'

He tipped his hat to Margaret and walked away.

'Next year's re-election year,' Wiley said as we watched Coley chat with two ladies near a drinking fountain. 'I hope he has an opponent.'

CHAPTER 3

Prior to the bankruptcy, and my unlikely rise in prominence in Ford County, I had heard a fascinating story about a local family. Now that the paper was mine, I decided to follow it up.

Over in Lowtown, the coloured section, there lived an extraordinary couple—Calia and Esau Ruffin. They had been married for over forty years and had raised eight children, seven of whom had earned PhD's and were now college professors. Details on the remaining one were sketchy, though, according to Margaret, his name was Sam and for whatever reason he was hiding from the law.

I called the house and Mrs Ruffin answered the phone. I explained who I was and that I'd like to meet and talk about her remarkable family. She was flattered and insisted that I come over for lunch the following Thursday. Thus began an unusual friendship that opened my eyes to many things, not the least of which was Southern cuisine.

THE RUFFIN HOME was in one of the nicer sections of Lowtown, in a row of neatly preserved and painted houses. When I rolled to a stop I was smiling at the white picket fence and flowers—peonies and irises—that lined the sidewalk. It was early April, I had the top down on my Spitfire, and as I turned off the ignition I smelt something delicious. Pork chops!

My mother had died when I was thirteen. She was anorexic, and food was simply not important around our house. I cannot remember a single hot meal that she prepared for me. Breakfast was a bowl of Cheerios, lunch a cold sandwich, dinner some frozen mess I usually ate in front of the television, alone. I was an only child and my father was never at home, which was a relief because his presence caused friction between them. After she died I existed on frozen dinners. At Syracuse it was beer and pizza. For the first twenty-three years of my life, I ate only when I was hungry. This was wrong, I soon learned. In the south, eating has little to do with hunger.

Calia Ruffin met me at the low swing-gate that opened into her immaculate front lawn. She was a stout woman, thick in the shoulders and trunk, with a handshake that was firm and felt like a man's. She had grey hair and was showing the effects of raising so many children, but when she smiled, which was constantly, she lit up the world with two rows of brilliant, perfect teeth. I had never seen such teeth.

'I'm so glad you came,' she said, halfway up the brick walkway. I was glad too. It was about noon. Typically, I had yet to eat a bite, and the aromas wafting from the verandah were making me dizzy.

'A lovely house,' I said, gazing at the front of it. It was clapboard, painted a sparkling white.

'Why, thank you. We've owned it for thirty years.'

I knew that most of the dwellings in Lowtown were owned by white slumlords. To own a home was an unusual accomplishment for blacks in 1970.

Up three steps and onto the verandah, and there it was—the spread! A small table next to the railing was prepared for two people—white cotton cloth, white napkins, flowers in a small vase, a large pitcher of iced tea, and at least four covered dishes.

'Who's coming?' I asked. 'There's enough food for an army.' I inhaled as deeply as possible and my stomach ached in anticipation.

'Oh, just the two of us. Let's eat now,' she said, 'before it gets cold.'

I restrained myself, walked casually to the table and pulled back a chair for her. She was delighted that I was such a gentleman. I sat across from her and was ready to yank off the lids when she took both my hands and lowered her head. She began to pray.

It would be a lengthy prayer and I was mesmerised by her voice as she thanked the Lord for everything good, including me, 'her new friend'. Her diction was perfect, every consonant treated equally, every comma and period honoured. I had to peek to make sure I wasn't dreaming. I had never heard such speech from a Southern black, or a Southern white for that matter. In the clutches of this very holy woman, I had never felt closer to God.

Finally, she ended with a flourish, a long burst in which she managed to appeal for the forgiveness of her sins, which I presumed were few and far between, and for my own, which, well, if she only knew.

She released me and began removing lids from bowls. The first contained a pile of pork chops smothered in a sauce that included onions and peppers. In the second there was a mound of yellow corn, sprinkled with green peppers, still hot from the stove. There was boiled okra and butter beans cooked with ham hocks and bacon. There was a platter of small red tomatoes covered with pepper and olive oil. She apologised because the tomatoes were store bought; hers were still on the vine and wouldn't be ready until summertime. The corn, okra and butter beans had been preserved from her garden the previous August.

A large black skillet was hidden in the centre of the table, and when she pulled the napkin off it there were at least four pounds of hot corn bread. She placed a huge wedge in the centre of my plate, and said, 'There. That will get you started.' The feast began.

I tried to eat slowly, but I was famished and it was impossible. She seemed content to do the talking. She told me how she and Esau grew four types of tomatoes, butter beans, string beans, black-eyed peas, cucumbers, aubergine, squash, collards, turnips, onions, cabbage, okra, new red potatoes, carrots, beets, corn, green peppers, and a few other things she couldn't recall at the moment. The pork chops were provided by her brother, who still lived on the old family place out in the country. He killed two hogs for them every winter and they stuffed their freezer. In return, they kept him in fresh vegetables.

'Would you like to see my garden?' she asked, watching me gorge myself.

I nodded, both jaws filled to capacity.

'Good. It's out back. I'll pick you some lettuce and greens. I figure a single man like you needs all the help he can get.'

'How'd you know I was single?' I took a gulp of tea.

'Folks are talking about you. There aren't many secrets in Clanton.'

'What else have you heard?'

'Let's see. You rent from the Hocutts. You come from up north.'

'Memphis.'

'That far?'

'It's an hour away.'

'Just joking. One of my daughters went to college there.'

I had many questions about her children, but I was not ready to take notes. Both hands were busy eating. At some point I called her Miss Calia, instead of Miss Ruffin.

'It's Callie,' she said. 'Miss Callie will do just fine.' One of the first habits I picked up in Clanton was to stick the word 'Miss' in front of a lady's name. Miss Brown, Miss Webster, for new acquaintances who had a few years on them. Miss Martha, Miss Sara, for the younger ones. It was a sign of chivalry and good breeding, and since I had neither it was important to seize as many local customs as possible.

'Where did Calia come from?' I asked.

'It's Italian,' she said, as if that would explain everything. She ate some butter beans. I carved up a pork chop. Then I said, 'Italian?'

'Yes, that was my first language. It's a long story, one of many. Did they really try to burn down the paper?'

'Yes, they did,' I said, wondering if I'd heard this black lady in rural Mississippi just say that her first language was Italian.

'And who is they?'

'We don't know yet. Sheriff Coley is investigating. What do you think of him?'

She drank some tea and contemplated. Miss Callie did not rush her answers, especially when talking about others. 'On this side of the tracks, a good sheriff is one who keeps the gamblers and the bootleggers and the whoremongers away from the rest of us. In that regard, Mr Coley has done a proper job.'

'Can I ask you something?'

'Certainly. You're a reporter.'

'Your speech is unusually articulate and precise. How much education did you receive?' It was a sensitive question. In 1970, Mississippi still had no mandatory school attendance laws.

She laughed. 'I finished the ninth grade, but my situation was unusual. I had a wonderful tutor. It's another long story, Mr Traynor.'

I began to realise that these wonderful stories Miss Callie was promising would take months, maybe years to develop. Perhaps they would evolve on the verandah, over a weekly banquet. 'Could you call me Willie? I'm only twenty-three,' I said.

'I prefer Mr Traynor.' And that issue was settled. It would take four years before she would use my first name. 'You have courage,' she announced. 'You seem to have no fear of the Padgitt family.'

That was news to me. 'It's just part of my job,' I said.

'Do you expect the intimidation to continue?'

'Probably so. They are accustomed to getting whatever they want. They are violent people, but a free press must endure.' Who was I kidding? One more bomb and I'd be back in Memphis before sunrise.

She stopped eating and her eyes turned towards the street, where she looked at nothing in particular, deep in thought. Finally, she said, 'Those poor little children. Seeing their mother like that.'

That image finally caused my fork to stop. The horror of the crime was left to everyone's imagination, and for days Clanton had whispered about little else.

'Have you ever met a Padgitt?' I asked.

'No. They stay on the island. Even their Negroes stay out there, making whiskey, doing their voodoo, all sorts of foolishness.'

'Voodoo?'

'Yes, it's common knowledge on this side of the tracks. Nobody here messes with the Padgitt Negroes, never have.'

'Do people here believe Danny Padgitt raped and killed her?'

'The ones who read your newspaper certainly do.'

That stung more than she would ever know. 'We just report the facts,' I said smugly. 'The boy has been charged. He's awaiting trial.'

'Isn't there a presumption of innocence?'

Another squirm on my side of the table. 'Of course.'

'Do you think it was fair to use a photograph of him handcuffed, with blood on his shirt?' I was struck by her sense of fairness. Why would she, or any other black in Ford County, care if Padgitt was treated fairly? Few people had ever worried about black defendants getting decent treatment by the police or the press.

'He had blood on his shirt when he arrived at the jail. We didn't put it there.' Neither one of us was enjoying this little debate. I took a sip of tea and decided to act like a journalist.

According to Baggy, Sam Ruffin had been the first black student to enrol in the white schools in Clanton. It happened in 1964 when Sam was a seventh grader, aged twelve, and the experience had been difficult for everyone. Especially Sam. In 1963, the courts ruled that a white school district could not deny admission to a black student. Forced integration was still years in the future. Sam was Callie's youngest and when she and Esau made the decision to take him to the white school they hoped they would be joined by other black families. They were not, and for two years Sam was the only black student at Clanton Junior High School. He was tormented and beaten, but he quickly learned to handle his fists and with time was left alone. He begged his parents to take him back to the Negro school, but they held their ground.

'It is hard to believe that it is now 1970 and the schools here are still segregated,' she said.

'Do you regret sending Sam to the white school?'

'Yes and no. Someone had to be courageous. It was painful knowing he was very unhappy, but we were not going to retreat.'

'How is he today?'

'Sam is another story, Mr Traynor, one I might talk about later, or not. Would you like to see my garden now?'

It was more of a command than an invitation. I followed her through the house to the back porch and from there the Garden of Eden stretched to the rear fence. It was a postcard of beautiful colours, neat rows of plants and vines.

'What do you do with all this food?' I asked in amazement.

'We eat some, sell a little, give most away. No one goes hungry around here.' I followed her into the garden, moving slowly along the footpaths as she commented on every plant, including an occasional weed, which she snatched almost with anger and flung back into some vines. The stroll was doing wonders for my digestive system.

After three hours, I left the Ruffin home with a bag of 'spring greens', which I had no idea what to do with, and precious few notes on which to write a story. I also had an invitation to return the following Thursday for another lunch. Lastly, I had Miss Callie's handwritten list of all the errors she'd found in that week's edition of the *Times*—twelve in all. Under Spot, the average had been about twenty. Now it was down to around ten. I vowed to proofread the copy with much more enthusiasm. I also left with the feeling that I had entered a new and rewarding friendship.

WE RAN ANOTHER large photo on the front page. It was Wiley's shot of the bomb before the police dismantled it. The headline above it screamed: BOMB PLANTED IN *TIMES* OFFICE.

My story began with Piston and his unlikely discovery. It included every detail I could substantiate, and a few I could not. No comment from the chief of police, a few meaningless sentences from Sheriff Coley. It ended with a summary of the findings by the state crime lab, and a prediction that, if detonated, the bomb would have caused 'massive' damage to the buildings on the south side of the square. I implied rather strongly that little was being done by the authorities, especially Sheriff Coley, to prevent further intimidation. I never named the Padgitts. I didn't have to. Everyone in the county knew they were bullying me and my newspaper.

My editorial for that issue began, 'A free and uninhibited press is crucial to sound democratic government.' Without being windy or preachy, I went on for four paragraphs extolling the importance of an energetic and inquisitive newspaper. I vowed that the *Times* would not be frightened away from reporting local crimes, whether they were rapes and murders or corrupt acts by public officials.

It was bold, gutsy and downright brilliant. The townsfolk were on my side. It was, after all, the *Times* versus the Padgitts and their sheriff. We were taking a mighty stand against bad people, and though they were dangerous they were evidently not intimidating me.

My staff was elated with the editorial. Margaret said it made her proud to work for the *Times*. Wiley now carried a gun and was looking for a fight. 'Give 'em hell, rookie,' he said.

Only Baggy was sceptical. 'You're gonna get yourself hurt,' he said.

And Miss Callie once again described me as courageous. During lunch the following Thursday with her and her husband, Esau, I actually began taking notes about her family. More important, she'd found only three errors in that week's edition.

I WAS ALONE in my office one afternoon when someone made a noisy entrance downstairs, then came clamouring up. He shoved my door open without so much as a 'Hello'. He looked vaguely familiar; we'd met somewhere around the square.

'You got one of these, boy?' he growled, yanking his right hand out and momentarily freezing my heart and lungs. He slid a shiny pistol across my desk as if it were a set of keys. It spun wildly for a few seconds before resting directly in front of me.

He thrust out a massive hand, and said, 'Harry Rex Vonner, a pleasure.' I was too stunned to speak or move, but eventually honoured him with a weak handshake. I was still watching the gun.

'It's a Smith and Wesson thirty-eight, six-shooter, damned fine firearm. You carry one?'

I shook my head no. The name alone sent chills to my feet.

Harry Rex kept a nasty black cigar tucked into the left side of his mouth. It gave the impression of having spent most of the day there, slowly disintegrating like a plug of chewing tobacco. No smoke because it wasn't lit. He dropped his massive body into a chair.

'You a crazy sumbitch, you know that?' He didn't speak as much as he growled. He was a local lawyer, once described by Baggy as the meanest divorce attorney in the county. He had a large fleshy face with short hair that shot in all directions like wind-blown straw. His ancient khaki suit was wrinkled and stained and said to the world that Harry Rex didn't give a damn about anything.

'What am I supposed to do with this?' I asked, pointing at the gun.

'First you load it, I'll give you some bullets, then you stick it in your pocket and carry it with you everywhere you go, and when one of them Padgitt thugs jumps out from behind the bushes you blast him right between the eyes,' he said.

'It's not loaded?'

'Hell, no. Don't you know anything about guns?'

'Afraid not.'

'Well, you'd better learn, boy, at the rate you're goin'.'

'That bad, huh?'

He nodded. 'Yeah, the Padgitts got all sorts of thugs who work for them. Leg breakers, bomb throwers, car stealers, hit men.'

He allowed the 'hit men' to hang in the air while he watched me flinch. 'You ever eat goat?' he asked.

'No. I didn't know it was edible.'

'We're roastin' one this afternoon. The first Friday of each month I throw a goat party at my cabin in the woods. Some music, cold beer, fun and games, about fifty folks, all carefully selected by me, the cream of society. No doctors, no bankers, no country-club assholes. A classy bunch. Why don't you stop by? I got a firin' range out behind the pond. I'll take the pistol and we'll figure out how to use the damned thing.'

HARRY REX'S ten-minute drive into the country took almost half an hour, and that was on the hard county road. When I crossed the 'third creek past Heck's old Union 76 station', I left the asphalt and turned onto a dirt road. My Spitfire wasn't designed for the terrain. By the time I saw his cabin, I'd been driving for forty-five minutes.

There was a barbed-wire fence with an open metal gate, and I stopped there because the young man with the shotgun wanted me to. He looked scornfully at my car. 'What kind is it?' he grunted.

'Triumph Spitfire. It's British.' I was smiling, trying not to offend him. Why did a goat party need armed security?

'What's your name?' he asked.

'Willie Traynor.'

I think the 'Willie' made him feel better, so he nodded at the gate. 'Nice car,' he said as I drove through.

Parking was haphazard in a field in front of the cabin. One group of guests huddled over a pit where smoke was rising and the goat was roasting. Harry Rex appeared and greeted me warmly.

'Who's the boy with the shotgun?' I asked.

'Oh, him. That's Duffy, my first wife's nephew. Don't worry about him. Duffy ain't all there, and the gun ain't loaded. He's been guardin' nothin' for years.'

I smiled as if this made perfect sense. He guided me to the pit where I saw my first goat, dead or alive. I was introduced to the many chefs. With each name I got an occupation—a lawyer, a bail bondsman, a car dealer, a farmer. As I watched the goat spin slowly on a spit, I soon learned that there were many competing theories on how to properly barbecue one. Harry Rex introduced me to his wife, handed me a beer and we moved on to the cabin.

The cabin sat on the edge of a muddy pond with a deck that protruded over the water. There we worked the crowd. Harry Rex took great delight in introducing me to his friends. 'He's a good boy, not your typical Ivy League asshole,' he said more than once. I didn't like to be referred to as a 'boy', but then I was getting used to it.

I settled into a small group that included two ladies who looked as though they'd spent years in the local honky-tonks. Heavy eye make-up, teased hair, tight clothing, and they immediately took an interest in me. The conversation began with the bomb and the prevailing cloud of fear the Padgitts had spread over the county. I acted as if it was just another routine episode in my long and colourful career in journalism, and did more talking than I wanted to.

Harry Rex rejoined us and handed me a suspicious-looking jar of clear liquid. 'Sip it slowly,' he said, much like a father.

'What is it?' I asked. I noticed that others were watching.

'Peach brandy.'

'Why is it in a fruit jar?' I asked.

'That's the way they make it,' he said.

'It's moonshine,' one of the ladies said. The voice of experience.

Not often would these rural folks see an 'Ivy Leaguer' take his first drink of moonshine, so the crowd drew closer. I was certain I had consumed more alcohol in the prior five years at Syracuse than anyone else present, so I threw caution to the wind, said, 'Cheers,' and took a small sip. I smiled, smacked my lips, and said, 'Not bad.'

The burning began at the lips, spread rapidly across the tongue and gums, and by the time it hit the back of my throat I thought I was on fire. Everyone was watching. Harry Rex took a sip from his jar.

'Where does it come from?' I asked, as nonchalantly as possible, flames escaping through my teeth.

'Not far from here,' someone said.

Scorched and numb, I took another sip, anxious for the crowd to ignore me for a while. Oddly enough, the third sip revealed a hint of peach flavouring, as if the taste buds had to be shocked before they could work.

Harry Rex, ever anxious to speed along my education, thrust forwards a plate of fried something. 'Have one of these,' he said.

'What is it?' I asked, suspicious.

Both of my painted ladies curled up their noses and turned away, as if the smell might make them ill. 'Chitterlings,' one of them said.

'What's that?'

Harry Rex popped one in his mouth to prove they weren't poison, then shoved the plate closer to me. 'Go ahead,' he said.

Folks were watching again, so I picked out the smallest piece and put it in my mouth. The texture was rubbery, the taste was foul. I chewed as hard as possible, choked it down, then followed with a gulp of moonshine. And for a few seconds I thought I might faint.

'Hog guts, boy,' Harry Rex said, slapping me on the back. He threw another one in his large mouth and offered me the plate. 'Where's the goat?' I managed to ask. Anything would be an improvement.

Whatever happened to beer and pizza? Why would these people eat and drink such disagreeable things?

Harry Rex walked away, the putrid smell of the chitterlings following him like smoke. I excused myself from the deck, said I needed to find a rest room. Harry Rex emerged from the back door of the cabin holding two pistols and a box of ammo. 'We'd better take a few shots before it gets dark,' he said. 'Follow me.'

We stopped at the goat spit where a cowboy named Rafe joined us. 'Rafe's my runner,' Harry Rex said as the three of us headed for the woods.

'What's a runner?' I asked.

'Runs cases.'

'I'm the ambulance chaser,' Rafe added helpfully. 'Although usually the ambulance is behind me.'

We walked a hundred yards or so through some woods, then came to a clearing. Between two magnificent oaks Harry Rex had constructed a semicircular wall of hay bales twenty feet high. In the centre was a white bedsheet, and in the middle of it was the crude outline of a man. The enemy. The target.

Not surprisingly, Rafe whipped out his own handgun. Harry Rex was handling mine. 'Here's the deal,' Rafe said, beginning the lesson. 'This is a double-action revolver with six cartridges. Press here and the cylinder pops out.' Rafe reached over and deftly loaded six bullets. 'Snap it back like this, and you're ready to fire.'

We were about fifty feet from the target. I could still hear the music from the cabin. What would the other guests think when they heard gunfire? Nothing. It happened all the time.

Rafe took my handgun and faced the target. 'For starters, spread your legs to shoulders' width, bend the knees slightly, use both hands like this, and squeeze the trigger with your right index finger.' I was standing less than five feet away when the gun fired, and the sharp crack jolted my nerves. Why did it have to be so loud?

The second shot hit the target square in the chest, and the next four landed around the midsection. He turned to me, opened the cylinder, spun out the empty cartridges, and said, 'Now you do it.'

My hands were shaking as I took the gun. I managed to shove in the six cartridges and snap the cylinder shut without hurting anyone. I faced the target, lifted the gun with both hands, crouched like someone in a bad movie, closed my eyes and pulled the trigger. It felt and sounded like a small bomb of some sort.

'You gotta keep your eyes open, dammit,' Harry Rex growled.

'What did I hit?'

'That hill beyond the oak trees.'

'Try it again,' Rafe said.

I tried to look down the gunsight but it was shaking too badly to be of any use. I squeezed the trigger again, this time with my eyes open.

'He missed the sheet,' Rafe mumbled behind me.

'Fire again,' Harry Rex said.

I did, and again couldn't see where the bullet landed. Rafe gently took my left arm and eased me forwards another ten feet. 'You're doin' fine,' he said. 'We got plenty of ammo.'

I missed the hay on the fourth shot, and Harry Rex said, 'I guess the Padgitts are safe after all.'

'It's the moonshine,' I said.

'It just takes practice,' Rafe said, moving me forwards yet again. 'Relax. You're too tense.' This time he squeezed my hands around the gun. 'Breathe deeply,' he said over my shoulder. 'Exhale right before you pull the trigger.' He steadied the gun as I looked down the sight, and when it fired the target took a hit in the groin.

'Now we're in business,' Harry Rex said.

After four rounds, I began to relax and enjoy the sport of it. Rafe was an excellent teacher, and as I progressed he passed on tips here and there. 'It just takes practice,' he kept saying.

When we finished, Harry Rex said, 'The gun's a gift. You can come out here anytime for target practice.'

'Thanks,' I said. I stuck the gun in my pocket like a real redneck, delighted that I had accomplished something that every other male in the county had experienced by his twelfth birthday. I didn't feel any safer. Any Padgitt who jumped from the bushes would have the advantage of surprise, and the benefit of years of target practice.

We walked back to the cabin and Harry Rex gave me a plate of goat. It had a distinctive taste; not good, but, after the chitterlings, not nearly as bad as I had feared. It was tough and smothered in sticky barbecue sauce, which, I suspected, was applied to counter the taste of the meat. I toyed with a slice of it and washed it down with beer. Some of the guests were dancing on the deck above the pond. Harry

Rex sat nearby, telling everyone how effective I'd been shooting squirrels and rabbits. His talent for storytelling was remarkable.

I was an oddity but every effort was made to include me. Driving the dark roads home, I asked myself the same question I posed every day. What was I doing in Ford County, Mississippi?

CHAPTER 4

The gun was too big for my pocket. For a few hours I tried walking around with it, but I was terrified the thing would discharge. So I decided to carry it in a ragged leather briefcase my father had given me. After three days I grew weary of that too. After a week I left the pistol under the seat of my car, and after three weeks I had pretty much forgotten about it. I did not go to the cabin for more target practice, though I did attend a few other goat parties in the quiet time before the frenzy of the trial. The Padgitts were still refusing to pledge their land for Danny's bail, so he remained a guest in Sheriff Coley's special cell, watching television, playing cards or checkers.

The first week in May, Judge Loopus was back in town.

Lucien Wilbanks had filed a motion requesting a change of venue, and the judge set the hearing for 9 a.m. on a Monday morning. Half the county was there, it seemed. Baggy and I got to the courtroom early and secured good seats.

Lucien Wilbanks entered the courtroom from behind the bench. As he walked to the defence table, he scanned the crowd and his eyes locked onto me. They narrowed and his jaws clenched, and I thought he might hop over the bar and attack. His client turned round and began looking too. Someone pointed, and Mr Danny Padgitt himself commenced glaring at me as if I might be his next victim. I was having trouble breathing, but I tried to keep calm.

In the front row behind the defence crowd were several Padgitts. They, too, joined the staring, and I had never felt so vulnerable.

A bailiff called us to order and everybody stood to acknowledge the entrance of His Honour. 'Please be seated,' he said.

Loopus scanned the papers while we waited, then he adjusted his reading glasses and said, 'This is a motion to change venue, filed by the defence. Mr Wilbanks, how many witnesses do you have?'

'Half a dozen, give or take. We'll see how things go.'

'And the State?'

A short round man with no hair and a black suit bounced to his feet and said, 'About the same.' His name was Ernie Gaddis, the long-time, part-time district attorney from up in Tyler County.

'I don't want to be here all day,' Loopus mumbled, as if he had an afternoon golf game. 'Call your first witness, Mr Wilbanks.'

'Mr Walter Pickard.'

The name was unknown to me, but during the preliminary questions it was established that he lived in Karaway, eighteen miles to the west of Clanton, he went to church every Sunday and the Rotary Club every Thursday. His wife was a schoolteacher. For a living he owned a small furniture factory.

'Must buy lumber from the Padgitts,' Baggy whispered.

'When did you first hear that Miss Kassellaw had been murdered?' Wilbanks asked.

'Couple of days after it happened,' Mr Pickard said.

'Who told you?'

'One of my employees came in with the story. She has a brother who lives around Beech Hill, where it happened.'

'Did you hear that someone had been arrested for the murder?' Lucien asked, prowling around the courtroom like a bored cat.

'Yes, I saw the story in *The Ford County Times* a few days later. There was a large photo of Danny Padgitt on the front page, right next to a large photo of Rhoda Kassellaw.'

'And from the reports in the *Times* did you form an opinion about Mr Padgitt's guilt or innocence?'

'He looked guilty to me. In the photo he had blood all over his shirt. His face was placed right next to that of the victim's, you know, side by side. The headline was huge and said something like, DANNY PADGITT ARRESTED FOR MURDER.'

'So you assumed he was guilty?'

'It was impossible not to.'

'In your opinion, can Mr Padgitt receive a fair trial in Ford County?'

'No. He's already been tried and convicted by the newspaper.'

'Do you think your opinion is shared by most of your friends and neighbours over in Karaway?'

'I do.'

'Thank you.'

Mr Ernie Gaddis was on his feet. 'You said that the photograph in the *Times* had much to do with your assumption that the boy is guilty, that right, Mr Pickard?'

'It made him look very suspicious.'

'Did you read the entire story?'

'I believe so.'

'Did you read where it says that Mr Danny Padgitt was involved in an auto accident, that he was injured, and that he was also charged with drunk driving?'

'I believe I read that, yes.'

'Good, then why were you so quick to assume the blood came from the victim and not from Mr Padgitt himself?'

Pickard shifted and looked frustrated. 'I simply said that the photos and the stories, when taken together, make him look guilty.'

'Do you understand what's meant by the presumption of innocence, Mr Pickard?'

'Yes.'

'Do you understand that the State of Mississippi must prove Mr Padgitt guilty beyond a reasonable doubt?'

'Yes.'

'Do you believe everyone accused of a crime is entitled to a fair trial?'

'Yes, of course.'

'Good. Let's say you got a summons for jury service in this case. You've read the newspaper reports, listened to all the gossip, all the rumours, and you arrive in this very courtroom for the trial. Let's say you're selected for the jury. Let's say that Mr Wilbanks attacks the State's case and raises serious doubts about our proof. Could you at that point vote not guilty, Mr Pickard?'

He nodded, then said, 'Yes, under those circumstances.'

'So you would be willing to listen to the evidence and weigh it fairly before you decide the case?'

Pickard had no choice but to say, 'Yes.'

'And what about your wife? She's a schoolteacher, right? She would be as open-minded as you, wouldn't she?'

'I think so. Yes.'

'No further questions, Your Honour.'

Mr Pickard hustled off the witness stand and hurried from the courtroom. Lucien Wilbanks stood and said, rather loudly, 'Your Honour, the defence calls Mr Willie Traynor.'

A brick to the nose could not have hit Mr Willie Traynor with more force. I gasped for air and heard Baggy say, too loudly, 'Oh shit.'

Harry Rex was sitting in the jury box with some other lawyers, taking in the festivities. I looked at him desperately for help.

'Your Honour,' he said, rising to his feet. 'I represent Mr Traynor, and he has not been notified that he would be a witness.'

The judge shrugged. 'So? He's here. What's the difference?'

'Preparation for one thing. A witness has a right to be prepped.'

Lucien Wilbanks said, 'Your Honour, he will not be a witness at trial. He wrote the stories. Let's hear from him.'

'It's an ambush, Judge,' Harry Rex said.

'Sit down, Mr Vonner,' His Honour said and, as I took a seat in the witness chair, I fired a look at Harry Rex as if to say, 'Nice work, lawyer.'

Wilbanks began pleasantly enough with some preliminary enquiries about me and my purchase of the paper, then he produced copies of the *Times* and passed them to me, Gaddis and Loopus. He looked at me and said, 'Just for the record, Mr Traynor, how many subscribers does the *Times* have now?'

'About forty-two hundred,' I answered with a little pride.

'And how many copies are sold at the newsstand?'

'Roughly a thousand.'

'What percentage of your newspapers are sold in Ford County, Mr Traynor?' he asked casually.

'Virtually all. I don't have the exact numbers.'

At this point Mr Gaddis stood and said, 'Your Honour, please, where is this going?'

'Good question. Mr Wilbanks.'

Wilbanks suddenly raised his voice. 'I will argue, Your Honour, that potential jurors in this county have been poisoned by the sensational coverage thrust upon us by *The Ford County Times*. Mercifully, this newspaper has not been seen in other parts of the state. A change of venue is not only fair, but mandatory.'

The word 'poisoned' changed the tone of the proceedings dramatically. Once again I asked myself if I had done something wrong.

'I'll decide what's fair and mandatory, Mr Wilbanks. Proceed,' Judge Loopus said sharply.

Mr Wilbanks held up the paper. 'I refer to the photograph of my client,' he said, pointing. 'Who took this photograph?'

'Mr Wiley Meek, our photographer.'

'And who made the decision to put it on the front page?'

'I did.'

'Did it occur to you that this might be considered sensational?'

Damned right. Sensational was what I was after. 'No,' I replied coolly. 'It happened to be the only photo we had of Danny Padgitt at the moment so we ran it. I'd run it again.'

My haughtiness surprised me. I glanced at Harry Rex and saw one of his nasty grins. He was nodding. Go get 'em, boy.

'So in your opinion it was fair to run this photo?'

'Yes, it was fair, and it was accurate.'

'Your report has a rather detailed description of the interior of the home of Rhoda Kassellaw. When did you inspect the home?'

'I have not.'

He flipped open the newspaper, scanned it for a moment, then said, 'You report that the bedroom of Miss Kassellaw's two small children was down a short hallway, approximately fifteen feet from her bedroom door, and you estimate that their beds were about thirty feet from hers. How do you know this?'

'I have a source.'

'A source. Has your source been in the house?'

'Yes.'

'Is your source a police officer or a deputy?'

'He will remain confidential.'

Wilbanks continued, 'You report that the children were in shock. How do you know this?'

'I spoke with Mr Deece, the next-door neighbour.'

'Did he use the word "shock"?'

'He did.'

'You report that the children are now undergoing some type of therapy back home in Missouri. Who told you that?'

'I talked to their aunt.'

He tossed the newspaper on the table. 'The truth is, Mr Traynor, that in an effort to sell papers you tried to paint the unmistakable picture that these two innocent children saw their mother get raped and murdered in her own bed, isn't that right?'

I took a deep breath and weighed my response. The courtroom was silent, waiting. 'I have reported the facts as accurately as possible,' I said, staring straight at Baggy, who was nodding at me.

Wilbanks snorted and said, 'Is that so?' He grabbed the newspaper again and said, 'I quote: "Will the children testify at trial?" Did you write that, Mr Traynor?'

I couldn't deny it. It was the last section of the reports that Baggy and I had haggled over. We'd both been a little squeamish, and, with hindsight, we should have followed our instincts.

Denial was not possible. 'Yes,' I said.

'Upon what accurate facts did you base that question?'

'It was a question I heard asked many times after the crime,' I said.

He flung the newspaper back on his table as if it were pure filth. He shook his head in mock bewilderment. 'There are two children, right, Mr Traynor? A boy and a girl aged five and three?'

'Yes.'

The bloodshot eyes narrowed and glared at me. 'And how old are you, Mr Traynor?'

'Twenty-three.'

'And in your twenty-three years, how many trials have you covered as a reporter?'

'None.'

'What type of legal research did you do in order to accurately prepare yourself for these stories?'

'Legal research?' I repeated blankly, as if he were speaking another language.

'Yes, Mr Traynor. How many cases did you find where children aged five or younger were allowed to testify in a criminal trial?'

'None,' I said.

'Perfect answer, Mr Traynor. None. No child under the age of eleven has ever testified in a criminal trial in this state. Please remember that the next time you attempt to inflame your readers with yellow journalism.'

'Enough, Mr Wilbanks,' Judge Loopus said, a little too gently for my liking. I think he and the other lawyers, probably including Harry Rex, were enjoying this quick butchering of someone who'd meddled in legal affairs and got it all wrong.

Lucien was wise enough to stop when the blood was flowing. He growled something like, 'I'm through with him.' Mr Gaddis had no questions. The bailiff motioned for me to step down. I tried desperately to walk upright back to the bench where Baggy was hunkering down, like a stray dog in a hailstorm.

I scribbled notes through the rest of the hearing, but it was a failing effort to look busy. I could feel the stares. I was humiliated.

Wilbanks ended things with an impassioned plea to move the case somewhere where no one had been 'poisoned' by the *Times*'s coverage of the crime. He railed against me and my newspaper, and he went overboard. Mr Gaddis, in his closing remarks, reminded the judge of the old saying, 'Strong and bitter words indicate a weak cause.'

I wrote that down. Then I hustled out of the courtroom as if I had an important deadline.

BAGGY RUSHED into my office late the following morning with the hot news that Lucien Wilbanks had just withdrawn his motion to change venue. As usual, he was full of analysis.

His first windy opinion was that the Padgitts didn't want the trial moved to another county. They knew Danny was guilty and that he would almost certainly be convicted by a properly selected jury anywhere. Their sole chance was to get a jury they could either buy or intimidate. Since all guilty verdicts must be unanimous, they needed only a single vote in Danny's favour and the judge would be required by law to declare a mistrial. It would certainly be retried, but with the same result. After three or four attempts, the State would give up.

Baggy explained gravely that the hearing the day before had been staged by Lucien Wilbanks because he wanted to get me on the witness stand to peel off some skin. 'He damned sure did that,' Baggy said.

'Thanks, Baggy,' I said.

Wilbanks was setting the stage for the trial, one that he knew all along would take place in Clanton, and he wanted the *Times* to tone down its coverage.

I'm not sure I followed all of Baggy's thinking, but at that moment nothing else made sense. It seemed such a waste of time and effort to put on a two-hour hearing, knowing full well it was all a show. I figured worse things have happened in courtrooms.

BAGGY HAD SOME RESERVATIONS about the Ruffin story I was about to print. 'It's really not news,' he said as he read it. In fact, the entire office was cool to the idea, even Margaret, but I didn't care. I was doing what I thought was right. In 1967, Mr Caudle had shown guts in running black obituaries, but in the three years since then the *Times* had taken little interest in anything in Lowtown.

And so, on Wednesday, May 20, 1970, the *Times* devoted more than half of its front page to the Ruffin family. It began with a large headline—RUFFIN FAMILY BOASTS SEVEN COLLEGE PROFESSORS. Under it was a large photo of Callie and Esau sitting on their front steps, smiling proudly at the camera. Below them were the senior portraits of all eight children. My story began:

> When Calia Harris was forced to drop out of school in the tenth grade, she promised herself her children would be able to finish not only high school but college as well. The year was 1926, and Calia, or Callie as she prefers to be called, was, at the age of fifteen, the oldest of four children. Education became a

luxury when her father died of tuberculosis. Callie worked for the DeJarnette family until 1929, when she married Esau Ruffin, a carpenter and part-time preacher.

In 1931, Alberto was born.

In 1970, Dr Alberto Ruffin (known to everybody these days as Al), was a professor of sociology at the University of Iowa. Dr Leonardo Ruffin (Leon) was a professor of biology at Purdue. Dr Massimo Ruffin (Max) was a professor of economics at the University of Toledo. Dr Roberto Ruffin (Bobby) was a professor of history at Marquette. Dr Gloria Ruffin Sanderford taught Italian at Duke. Dr Carlota Ruffin was a professor of urban studies at UCLA. Dr Mario Ruffin had just completed his PhD in medieval literature and was a professor at Grinnell College in Iowa. I mentioned Sam but didn't dwell on him because Callie never wanted to talk about him to me.

By phone I had talked to all seven of the professors, and I quoted liberally from them in my story. The themes were common—love, sacrifice, discipline, hard work, encouragement, faith in God, faith in family, ambition, perseverance; no tolerance for laziness or failure. Each had worked at least one full-time job while struggling through college and grad school. Most had worked two jobs. The older ones had helped the younger ones.

The five older ones had been so tenacious in their studies that they had postponed marriage until in their late twenties and early thirties. Carlota and Mario were still single. Leon had the oldest grandchild, aged five. There were a total of five. Max and his wife were expecting their second.

There was so much material on the Ruffins that I ran only Part One that week. Part Two would follow in a fortnight. When I went to Lowtown for lunch the next day, Miss Callie met me with tears in her eyes. Esau met me too, with a firm handshake and a stiff, awkward, manly hug. We devoured a lamb stew and compared notes on how the story was being received. Needless to say, it was the talk of Lowtown. I had mailed copies to each of the professors.

Over coffee and fried apple pies, their preacher, Reverend Thurston Small, stopped by. He accepted a dessert and began a lengthy summary of how important the Ruffin story was to the black community of Clanton and how it was a giant step for racial tolerance in the town. I didn't see it that way. It was just a good human interest story about Miss Callie Ruffin and her extraordinary family.

ERNIE GADDIS, the district attorney, filed a motion to enlarge the jury pool for the Padgitt trial. According to Baggy, who was becoming more of an expert each day, in the typical criminal trial the circuit court clerk summoned about forty people for jury duty. Gaddis argued in his motion that the increased notoriety of the Kassellaw murder would make it more difficult to find impartial jurors, so he asked the court to summon at least a hundred prospective jurors.

What he didn't say in writing, but what everybody knew, was that the Padgitts would have a harder time intimidating one hundred than forty. Although Lucien Wilbanks objected strenuously, Judge Loopus took the unusual step of sealing the list of prospective jurors, which was generally viewed as a major setback to the Padgitts. If they didn't know who was in the pool, then how could they bribe or frighten them?

It was becoming obvious that Judge Loopus was determined to preside over a secure and unbiased trial. He certainly appeared to have little concern for the Padgitts and their legacy of corruption. Plus, on paper (and certainly in my paper), the case against Danny Padgitt appeared to be airtight.

On Monday, June 15, amid great secrecy, the circuit court clerk mailed 100 summonses for jury duty to registered voters all over Ford County. One arrived in the mailbox of Miss Callie Ruffin.

According to Harry Rex, there had never been a black juror in Ford County. Since potential jurors were selected from the voter registration rolls and nowhere else, few showed up in a jury pool because so few blacks bothered to register. Registration could mean more taxes, more supervision, more surveillance, more intrusions. Registration could mean serving on juries. The registration drives in Lowtown were met with indifference.

Callie and Esau Ruffin had registered to vote in 1951 and they never missed an election. Miss Callie had always worried because so few of her friends bothered to register and vote, but she was too busy raising eight children to do much about it.

AT FIRST I couldn't tell if she was anxious or excited. I'm not sure she knew either. She had been the first black female voter and might now become the first black juror. She had never backed away from a challenge, but she had grave moral concerns about judging another person. "'Judge not, that ye be not judged,'" she said more than once, quoting Jesus.

In reply, I asked her, 'But if everyone followed that verse of

Scripture, our entire judicial system would fail, wouldn't it?'

'I don't know,' she said, gazing away. I had never seen Miss Callie so preoccupied. We were eating fried chicken with mashed potatoes and gravy. Esau had not made it home for lunch.

'What about the death penalty?' she asked. 'Will they want to put that boy in the gas chamber if he's found guilty?'

'Yes, ma'am. It's a capital murder case.'

'Who decides whether he is put to death?'

'The jury.'

'Oh, my.'

She was unable to eat after that. She said her blood pressure had been up since she received the jury summons. I helped her to the sofa in the den and took her a glass of iced water. Later, she rallied a bit and we sat on the verandah in the rockers, talking about anything but the trial.

I finally hit pay dirt when I asked her about the Italian influence in her life. Over our first lunch she had told me that she learned Italian before she learned English. Seven of her eight children had Italian names. She needed to tell me a long story. I had absolutely nothing else to do.

IN THE 1890s, the price of cotton rose dramatically as demand increased around the world. The fertile regions of the south were under pressure to produce more but there was a severe labour shortage. Many of the blacks had fled the land their ancestors toiled as slaves for better jobs and certainly better lives up north.

The landowners hit upon a scheme to import European immigrants to raise cotton. Through contacts with Italian labour agents in New York and New Orleans, connections were made, promises swapped, lies told, and in 1895 the first boatload of families arrived. They were from northern Italy, near Verona. For the most part they were poorly educated and spoke little English, though in any language they quickly realised they were on the bad end of a huge scam. They were given miserable living accommodation, in a subtropical climate, and while battling malaria and snakes and rotten drinking water they were told to raise cotton for wages no one could live on. They were forced to borrow money at scandalous rates from the landowners. Their food and supplies came from the company store, at steep prices. A system of peonage was fine-tuned, and the Italians were treated worse than most black farmworkers.

After twenty years of abuse, the Italians finally scattered and the experiment became history. Those who remained in the Delta were considered second-class citizens for decades. But because they worked hard and saved their money, they slowly accumulated land.

The Rossetti family, who came from a village near Bologna, landed near Leland, Mississippi, in 1902. Penniless when they arrived, after three years of peonage the family had racked up $6,000 in debts to the plantation with no possible way of paying them off. They fled the Delta in the middle of the night and rode a boxcar to Memphis, where a distant relative took them in.

At the age of fifteen, the Rossetti's eldest daughter, Nicola, was stunningly beautiful. Long dark hair, brown eyes—a classic Italian beauty. She looked older than her years and managed to get a job in a clothing store in Memphis.

In those days, the wealthy farming families in northern Mississippi did their shopping and socialising in Memphis. It was there that Mr Zachary DeJarnette of Clanton had the blind luck of bumping into Nicola Rossetti. Two weeks later they were married.

He was thirty-one, a widower with no children and in the midst of a serious search for a wife. He was also the largest landowner in Ford County, having inherited over 4,000 acres from his family. His grandfather had once owned the grandfather of Calia Ruffin.

The marriage was a package deal. Before Nicola agreed to marriage, Mr DeJarnette promised not only to employ her father as a farm supervisor but to provide her family with very comfortable housing. He agreed to educate her three younger sisters. He agreed to pay off the peonage debts from the Delta. So smitten was Mr DeJarnette that he would have agreed to anything.

The first Italians in Ford County arrived not in a broken ox cart, but rather by first-class passage on the Illinois Central Rail Line. The Rossettis were treated like royalty as they followed Mr DeJarnette from party to party in Clanton. The town was instantly abuzz with descriptions of how beautiful the bride was.

When the Rossettis first glimpsed Mr DeJarnette's stately antebellum mansion, they all broke into tears. It was decided that they would live there until an overseer's house could be made suitable. Nicola assumed her duties as the lady of the manor and tried her best to get pregnant. Her younger sisters were provided with private tutors, and within weeks were speaking good English. Mr Rossetti learned how to run the plantation. And Mrs Rossetti worked in the kitchen, where she met Callie's mother, India.

'My grandmother cooked for the DeJarnettes, so did my mother,'

Miss Callie was saying. 'I thought I would too, but it didn't work out that way.'

'Did Zack and Nicola have children?' I asked.

'No. It was very sad because they wanted children so badly. When I was born in 1911, Nicola practically took me away from my mother. She insisted I have an Italian name. She kept me in the big house with her. My mother didn't mind—she had plenty of other children, plus she was in the house all day long.'

'What did your father do?' I asked.

'Worked on the farm. It was a good place to work, and to live. We were very lucky because the DeJarnettes took care of us. They were good, fair people. Always. My father, grandfather and great-grand-father worked their land, and they were never mistreated.'

'And Nicola?'

She smiled for the first time in an hour. 'God blessed me. I had two mothers. She gave me an Italian name and dressed me in clothes she bought in Memphis. When I was a toddler she taught me to speak Italian while I was learning English. She taught me to read.'

'You still speak Italian?'

'No. It was a long time ago. She loved to tell me stories of being a little girl in Italy, and she promised me that one day she would take me to Venice and Rome. She loved to sing and she taught me about the opera.'

'Was she educated?'

'Her mother had made sure Nicola and her sisters could read and write. She promised me I would go to college somewhere up north, where folks were more tolerant. The notion of a black woman going to college in the 1920s was downright crazy.'

The story was running in many directions. The image of a young black girl living in an ante-bellum home speaking Italian and listen-ing to the opera in Mississippi fifty years earlier had to be unique.

'Did you work in the house?' I asked.

'Oh, yes, when I got older. I was a housekeeper, but I never had to work as hard as the others. Nicola wanted me close by. At least an hour every day we would sit in her parlour and practise speaking with a retired schoolteacher called Miss Tucker. Nicola was determined to lose her Italian accent, and she was just as determined that I would have perfect diction.'

'What happened to college?'

She was suddenly exhausted and story time was over. 'Ah, Mr Traynor, it was very sad. Mr DeJarnette lost everything back in the

1920s. He'd invested heavily in railroads and ships and stocks and such stuff, and went broke almost overnight. He shot himself, but that's another story.'

'What happened to Nicola?'

'She managed to hold on to the house until the Second War, then she moved back to Memphis with Mr and Mrs Rossetti. We swapped letters every week for years. I still have them. She died four years ago, at the age of seventy-six. How I loved that woman.' Her words trailed off and I knew from experience that she was ready for a nap.

Late that night I buried myself in the *Times* archives. On September 12, 1930, there was a front-page story about the suicide of Zachary DeJarnette. Despondent over the collapse of his businesses, he had left a new will and a farewell note for his wife Nicola, then, to make things easier for everyone, he had driven to the funeral home in Clanton. He walked in the rear door with a double-barrelled shotgun, found the embalming room, took a seat, took off a shoe, put the gun in his mouth and pulled the trigger with a big toe.

CHAPTER 5

On Monday, June 22, all but eight of the 100 jurors arrived for the trial of Danny Padgitt. As we soon found out, four were dead and four had simply vanished. The rest looked very anxious.

Few things draw a crowd in a small town like a good murder trial, and the courtroom was full long before 9 a.m. Baggy and I were in the front row. He had convinced the circuit court clerk that we were entitled to press credentials, thus special seating. As a show of strength, Sheriff Coley had every available uniformed body milling around. What a perfect time to pull a bank heist, I thought.

The Padgitts were there in full force. They sat in chairs pulled close to the defence table and huddled round Danny and Lucien Wilbanks like the den of thieves they really were. I had my pistol in my briefcase. I'm sure they had theirs close by. A false move here or there and an old-fashioned gunfight would erupt. Throw in Sheriff Coley and his poorly trained but trigger-happy boys, and half the town would get wiped out.

I caught a few stares from the Padgitts, but they were much more worried about the jurors than me. They watched them closely as they filed into the courtroom and took their instructions from the clerk. The Padgitts and their lawyers looked at lists and compared notes.

Danny was nicely dressed in a white shirt and a pair of starched khakis. As instructed by Wilbanks, he was smiling a lot, as if he were really a nice kid whose innocence was about to be revealed.

Across the aisle, Ernie Gaddis and his smaller crew were likewise observing the prospective jurors. Gaddis had two assistants, one a paralegal and one a part-time prosecutor named Hank Hooten. The paralegal carried the files and briefcases. Hooten seemed to do little but just be there so Ernie would have someone to confer with.

Baggy leaned over and whispered. 'That guy there, brown suit,' he said, nodding at Hooten. 'He was screwin' Rhoda Kassellaw.'

I was shocked and my face showed it. I jerked to the right and looked at Baggy. He nodded smugly and said what he always said when he had the scoop on something really nasty. 'That's what I'm tellin' you,' he whispered. This meant that he had no doubts. Baggy was often wrong but never in doubt.

Hooten appeared to be about forty with prematurely grey hair, nicely dressed, somewhat handsome. 'Where's he from?' I whispered.

'Here. He does some real estate law, low-pressure stuff. A real jerk. Been divorced a couple of times, always on the prowl.'

'Does Gaddis know his assistant was seeing the victim?'

'Hell, no. Ernie would pull him from the case.'

Miss Callie arrived a few minutes before nine and took a seat in the third row. She looked around for me but there were too many people between us. I counted four other blacks in the pool.

A bailiff bellowed for us to rise, and it sounded like a stampede. Judge Loopus told us to sit, and the floor shook. He went straight to work and appeared to be in good spirits. He had a courtroom full of voters and he was up for re-election in two years. Six jurors were excused because they were over the age of sixty-five. Five were excused for medical reasons. The morning began to drag. I couldn't take my eyes off Hank Hooten. He certainly had the look of a ladies' man.

When the preliminary questions were over, the panel was down to seventy-nine duly qualified jurors. Judge Loopus yielded the floor to Ernie Gaddis, who explained that he was there on behalf of the State of Mississippi to prosecute Mr Danny Padgitt, who had been indicted by a grand jury for the rape and murder of Rhoda Kassellaw. He asked if it was possible that anyone had not heard something about the murder. Not a single hand went up.

Ernie had been talking to juries for thirty years. He was friendly and smooth and gave the impression that you could discuss almost anything with him, even in open court. He moved slowly into the area of intimidation. Has anyone outside your family contacted you about this case? A stranger? Has a friend tried to influence your opinion? The courtroom was very quiet as Ernie led them through these questions. He finished with a question that cut through the air like a rifle shot. 'Do all of you folks understand that jury tampering is a crime? And that I, as the prosecutor, will do my utmost to convict any person involved with jury tampering? Do you understand this?'

They seemed to understand. When Ernie had finished we all felt as though anyone who'd talked about the case, which was every person in the county, was in danger of being hounded to the grave.

'He's effective,' whispered a reporter from Tupelo, who was in the seat next to me.

Lucien Wilbanks began with a lengthy and quite dull lecture about the presumption of innocence and how it is the foundation of American jurisprudence. Regardless of what they'd read in the local newspaper, and here he managed a scornful glance in my general direction, his client was an innocent man. And if anyone felt otherwise, then it was his duty to raise a hand and say so.

No hands. 'Good. Then by your silence you're telling the Court that you, all of you, can look at Danny Padgitt right now and say he is innocent. Can you do that?' He hammered them on this for far too long, then started a lecture on the State's monumental challenge to prove his client guilty beyond a reasonable doubt.

We were approaching noon and everybody was anxious for a break. Wilbanks seemed to miss this and he kept rattling on. When he sat down at twelve fifteen, Judge Loopus announced that he was starving. We would recess until two o'clock.

Baggy and I had a sandwich upstairs in the Bar Room with several of his cronies, three ageing, washed-up lawyers who hadn't missed a trial in years. The clerk had given us a list of jurors as they were currently seated. Miss Callie was number twenty-two, the first black and the third female. It was the general feeling that the defence would not challenge her because she was black. Blacks, according to the prevailing theory, were sympathetic to those accused of crimes, although I wasn't sure how a black person could be sympathetic to a white thug like Danny Padgitt.

After lunch, Judge Loopus moved into the most serious phase of questioning—the death penalty. He explained the nature of a capital offence then he yielded again to Ernie Gaddis.

Ernie singled out individual jurors and asked them questions about judging others and imposing the death sentence. He eventually made it to Miss Callie. 'Now, Mrs Ruffin, I've read about you in the paper, and you seem to be a very religious woman. Is this correct?'

'I do love the Lord, yes, sir,' she answered, as clear as always.

'Are you hesitant to sit in judgment of another human?'

'I am, yes, sir.'

'Do you want to be excused?'

'No, sir. It's my duty as a citizen to be here.'

'And if you're on the jury, and the jury finds Mr Padgitt guilty of these crimes, can you vote to put him to death?'

'I certainly wouldn't want to.'

'My question was, "Can you?"'

'I can follow the law, same as these other folks. If the law says that we should consider the death penalty, then I can follow the law.'

FOUR HOURS LATER, Calia H. Ruffin became the last juror chosen. The defence wanted her because she was black. The State wanted her because they knew her so well through my stories in the *Times*. She came across as a sensible, God-fearing patriot, who had raised her kids with a heavy hand if they screwed up. The ideal juror for the prosecution. Though I tried not to show it, I was deeply concerned that my long and generous stories about Miss Callie would somehow come back to haunt her.

ON TUESDAY MORNING, almost two hours were wasted as the lawyers wrangled over some hotly contested motions back in the judge's chambers. 'Probably the photographs,' Baggy kept saying. While we waited impatiently in the courtroom, I wrote pages of useless notes to keep me busy and my eyes away from the ever-present stares of the Padgitts. With the jury out of the room they turned their attention to the spectators, especially me.

The jurors were locked away in the deliberation room. I thought of Miss Callie and her blood pressure. I knew she was reading the Bible and maybe this was calming her. I had called Esau early that morning. He was very upset that she had been sequestered and hauled away to a motel in another town for the week.

Esau was in the back row, waiting with the rest of us.

When Judge Loopus and the lawyers finally appeared they looked as though they had all been fistfighting. The judge nodded at the bailiff and the jurors were led in.

Ernie Gaddis began his opening statement to the jury. With great efficiency, he rattled off the case the State would prove against Danny Padgitt. When all the witnesses were finished, it would be left to the jury to serve justice. There was no doubt in his mind that they would find Danny Padgitt guilty of rape and murder. He didn't waste a word, and every word found its mark. His confident tone and concise remarks conveyed the clear message that he had the facts, the case, and he would get his verdict.

Oddly, Lucien Wilbanks deferred his opening remarks until the defence put on its case, an option rarely exercised. 'He's up to something,' Baggy mumbled.

The first witness for the State was Sheriff Coley. In a few months he would be up for re-election. It was important for him to look good before the voters.

With Ernie's meticulous planning and prodding, they walked through the crime. There were large diagrams of the Kassellaw home, the Deece home, the exact spot where Danny Padgitt was arrested. There were photographs of the area. Then, there were photographs of Rhoda's corpse, a series of eight by tens that were handed to the jurors and passed around. Every face was shocked. Some winced. Miss Callie closed her eyes and appeared to pray. Another lady on the jury, Mrs Barbara Baldwin, gasped at first sight and turned to Danny Padgitt as if she could shoot him at point-blank range. The pictures were inflammatory, highly prejudicial, yet always admissible, and as they caused a commotion in the jury box I thought Danny Padgitt was as good as dead. Judge Loopus allowed only six as exhibits. One would have sufficed.

It was just after 1 p.m., and everyone needed a break. I doubted that the jurors had much of an appetite.

THE STATE'S SECOND WITNESS was one of Rhoda's sisters from Missouri. Her name was Ginger McClure. She was the sister I had talked to several times after the murder, who had reluctantly sent me a photo for the obituary. Later, she had called and asked if I could send her copies of the *Times* when it mentioned Rhoda's case.

Ginger was a slim redhead, very attractive and well dressed, and when she settled into the witness chair she had everyone's attention.

Ernie wanted Ginger to be viewed by the jury and arouse their sympathy. He also wanted to remind the jury that the mother of two small children had been taken from them in a premeditated murder. Ginger's testimony was brief. Wisely, Lucien Wilbanks had no questions on cross-examination. When she was excused, she walked to a reserved chair behind Ernie Gaddis, and assumed the position as representative of the family. Her every move was watched until the next witness was called.

Then it was back to the gore.

A forensic pathologist from the state crime lab was called to discuss the autopsy. In layman's terms, her cause of death was obvious—a loss of blood. There was a four-inch gash beginning just below her left ear and running almost straight down. It was almost two inches deep, and, in his opinion, it was caused by a rapid and powerful thrust from a blade that was approximately six inches long and an inch wide. The person using the knife was, more than likely, right-handed. The gash cut completely through the left jugular vein, and at that point the victim had only a few minutes to live. A second gash was six and a half inches long, one inch deep, and ran from the tip of the chin and to the right ear.

The pathologist described these wounds as if he were talking about a tick bite. In his business he saw this carnage every day and talked about it with juries. But for everyone else in the courtroom, the details were unsettling. At some point during his testimony, every single juror looked at Danny Padgitt and silently voted 'Guilty'.

Lucien Wilbanks began his cross-examination pleasantly enough. He made the pathologist admit that some of his opinions might possibly be wrong, such as the size of the murder weapon and whether the assailant was right-handed. 'I stated that these were probabilities,' the doctor said patiently, giving the impression that he'd been grilled so many times nothing rattled him.

A second pathologist followed. Concurrent with the autopsy, he had made a thorough examination of the body and found several clues as to the identity of the killer. In the vaginal area, he found semen that matched perfectly with Danny Padgitt's blood. Under the nail of Rhoda's right index finger he had found a tiny piece of human skin. It too matched the defendant's blood type.

On cross-examination, Lucien Wilbanks asked him if he had personally examined Mr Padgitt. No, he had not. Where on his body was Mr Padgitt scraped or scratched or clawed in such a way?

'I did not examine him,' the pathologist said.

'So if he lost some skin, you can't tell where it came from?'

'I'm afraid not.'

After four hours of graphic testimony, everybody in the courtroom was exhausted. Judge Loopus sent the jury away with stern warnings about avoiding outside contact. It seemed overkill in light of the fact that they were being hidden in another town and guarded by police.

Baggy and I raced back to the office and typed frantically until almost ten. It was Tuesday, and Hardy liked to have the presses running no later than 11 p.m. Baggy was hitting the sauce as we finished up and couldn't wait to leave. I was about to head for my apartment when Ginger McClure strolled in the front door and said hello as if we were old friends. She asked if I had anything to drink. Not at the office, but that wouldn't stop us.

We left the square in my Spitfire and drove to Quincy's, where I bought a six-pack of Schlitz. She wanted to see Rhoda's house one last time, from the road, not too close.

As we headed out that way I cautiously enquired about the two children. The report was mixed. Both were living with another sister—Ginger was quick to tell me she was recently divorced—and both were undergoing intense counselling. The little boy appeared to be almost normal, though he sometimes drifted off into prolonged periods of silence. The little girl was much worse. She had constant nightmares about her mother and had lost the ability to control her bladder. She was often found curled in a foetal position, sucking her fingers and groaning. The doctors were experimenting with various drugs.

Neither child would tell the family or the doctors how much they saw that night. 'They saw their mother get raped and stabbed,' she said, killing off the first beer. Mine was still half full.

The Deece home looked as if Mr and Mrs Deece had been asleep for days. We turned into the gravel driveway of what was once the happy little Kassellaw home. It was empty, dark, and had an abandoned look to it. There was a FOR SALE sign in the yard.

At Ginger's request, I cut the lights and turned off the engine. It was not a good idea because the neighbours were understandably jumpy. Ginger gently placed her hand on mine and said, 'How did he get in the house?'

'They found some footprints at the patio door. It was probably unlocked.' And during a long silence both of us replayed the attack, the rape, the knife, the children fleeing through the darkness, yelling for Mr Deece to come save their mother.

'Were you close to her?' I asked, then I heard the distant approach of a vehicle.

'When we were kids, but not recently. She left home ten years ago.'

'How often did you visit here?'

'Twice. I moved away to California. We sort of lost touch. After her husband died, we begged her to come back to Springfield, but she said she liked it here. Truth was, she and my mother never got along.'

A pick-up truck slowed on the road behind us. I tried to act unconcerned, but I knew how dangerous things could be in such a dark part of the county. Ginger was staring at the house, lost in some horrible image, and seemed not to hear. Thankfully, the truck did not stop.

'Let's go,' she said, squeezing my hand. 'I'm scared.'

When we drove away, I saw Mr Deece crouching in the shadows of his garage, holding a shotgun. He was scheduled to be the last witness called by the State.

Ginger was staying at a local motel, but she did not want to go there. It was after midnight, our options were thin, so we drove to the Hocutt place, where I led her up the stairs, and into my apartment.

'Don't get any ideas,' she said as she kicked off her shoes and sat on the sofa. 'I'm not in the mood.'

'Neither am I,' I lied, hoping her mood might change real soon.

I found colder beer in the kitchen and we settled into our places as if we might talk until sunrise. 'Tell me about your family,' she said.

It was not my best subject, but, for this lady, I could talk. 'I'm an only child. My mother died when I was thirteen. My father lives in Memphis, in an old family house that he never leaves because both he and the house have a few loose boards. He has an office in the attic, and he stays there all day and night trading stocks and bonds. I don't know how well he trades, but I have a hunch he loses more than he gains. We speak by phone once a month.'

'Are you wealthy?'

'No, my grandmother is wealthy. My mother's mother, BeeBee. She loaned me the money to buy the paper.'

She thought about this as she sipped her beer. 'There were three of us girls, two now. We were pretty wild growing up. My father went out for milk one night and never came home. I'm divorced. My older sister is divorced. Rhoda is dead.' She reached across with the bottle and tapped mine. 'Here's to a couple of screwed-up families.'

We drank to that.

Divorced, childless, wild and cute. I could spend time with Ginger.

She wanted to know about Ford County and its characters—Lucien Wilbanks, the Padgitts, Sheriff Coley, and so on. I talked and talked and kept waiting for her mood to change.

It did not. Sometime after 2 a.m. she stretched out on the sofa, and I went to bed alone.

AT PRECISELY 9 a.m. on Wednesday morning the jurors were led in and Ernie Gaddis called his next witness. His name was Chub Brooner, the long-time investigator for the sheriff's department. According to both Baggy and Harry Rex, Brooner was famous for his incompetence.

To wake up the jury, Ernie Gaddis produced the bloody white shirt Danny Padgitt was wearing the night he was arrested. It had not been washed; the splotches of blood were dark brown. Tests had revealed two types of blood—O positive and B positive. Further tests by the state crime lab matched the B positive with the blood of Rhoda Kassellaw.

I watched Ginger as she looked at the shirt. After a few minutes she looked away and began writing something. She looked even better her second day in the courtroom.

The shirt was ripped across the front. Danny had cut himself when he crawled out of his wrecked truck and had received twelve stitches. Brooner did a passable job of explaining this to the jury. Ernie then pulled out an easel and placed on it two photographs of the footprints found on the patio of Rhoda's home. On the exhibit table he picked up the shoes Padgitt had been wearing. Everything matched.

Brooner was terrified of Lucien Wilbanks and began stuttering at the first question. Lucien wisely ignored the fact that Rhoda's blood was found on Danny's shirt, and chose instead to hammer Brooner on the art and science of matching up footprints. Lucien zeroed in on a series of ridges on the heel of the right shoe, and Brooner couldn't locate them in the print. Lucien harangued him to the point of confusing everyone, and I had to admit that I was sceptical of the footprints. Not that it mattered. There was plenty of other evidence.

'Was Mr Padgitt wearing gloves when he was arrested?' Lucien asked.

'I don't know. I didn't arrest him.'

'Well, you took his shirt and his shoes. Did you take any gloves?'

'Not to my knowledge. No.'

'Did you dust the crime scene for fingerprints?'

'Yes.'

'And you fingerprinted Mr Padgitt when he was arrested, right?'

'Yes.'

'Good. How many of Mr Padgitt's fingerprints did you find at the crime scene?'

'None.'

With that, Lucien went to sit down. It was difficult to believe that the murderer could enter the house, rape and murder his victim, then escape without leaving behind fingerprints. But Chub Brooner did not inspire a lot of confidence. There seemed an excellent chance that fingerprints could have been missed.

Judge Loopus called for the morning recess, and as the jurors stood to leave I made eye contact with Miss Callie. Her face exploded into one huge grin. She nodded, as if to say, 'Don't worry about me.'

THE STATE'S LAST WITNESS was Mr Aaron Deece. He walked to the stand shortly before 11 a.m., and Ernie Gaddis led him through a series of questions designed to personalise Rhoda and her two children. They had lived next door for seven years, perfect neighbours, wonderful people. He missed them greatly. At one point Mr Deece wiped a tear from his eye.

This was completely irrelevant to the issues at hand, and Lucien gamely allowed it for a few minutes. Then he stood and politely said, 'Your Honour, this is very touching, but it's really not admissible.'

'Move along, Mr Gaddis,' Judge Loopus said.

Mr Deece described the night, the time, the weather. He heard the panicked voice of little Michael, aged five, calling his name, crying for help. He found the children outside, in their pyjamas, wet with dew, in shock from fear. He took them inside where his wife put blankets on them. He got his shoes and his gun and was flying out of the house when he saw Rhoda, stumbling towards him. She was naked and, except for her face, she was completely covered in blood. He picked her up, carried her to the porch, placed her on a swing.

'Did she say anything?' Ernie asked.

Lucien was on his feet. 'Your Honour, I object to this witness testifying to anything the victim said. It's clearly hearsay.'

'We've had our debate this morning in chambers, Mr Wilbanks, and your motion is on file. You may answer the question, Mr Deece.'

Mr Deece swallowed hard and looked at the jurors. 'Two or three times, she said, "It was Danny Padgitt. It was Danny Padgitt."'

For dramatic effect, Ernie let those bullets crack through the air, then ricochet around the courtroom while he pretended to look at some notes. 'You ever met Danny Padgitt, Mr Deece?'

'No, sir.'

'Had you ever heard his name before that night?'

'No, sir.'

'Did she say anything else?'

'The last thing she said was, "Take care of my babies."'

Ginger was touching her eyes with a tissue. Miss Callie was praying. Several of the jurors were looking at their feet.

He finished his story—he called the sheriff's department; his wife had the children in a bedroom behind a locked door; he took a shower because he was covered with blood; the deputies showed up, the ambulance came and took away the body; he and his wife looked after the children until a relative arrived from Missouri.

There was nothing in his testimony that could be challenged or impeached, so Lucien Wilbanks declined a cross-examination. The State rested, and we broke for lunch.

THAT AFTERNOON Lucien Wilbanks began his defence with a little pep talk about what a nice young man Danny Padgitt really was. He had finished high school with good grades, he worked long hours in the family's timber business, he dreamed of one day running his own company. He had no police record. His only brush with the law had been one, just one, speeding ticket when he was sixteen years old.

Lucien's persuasive skills were well honed, but it was impossible to make a Padgitt appear warm and cuddly. There was quite a bit of squirming in the courtroom, some smirks here and there.

However, Danny was not a saint. Like most handsome young men he enjoyed the company of ladies. He had met the wrong one, though, a woman who happened to be married to someone else. Danny was with her the night Rhoda Kassellaw was murdered.

'Listen to me!' Lucien bellowed at the jurors. 'My client did not kill Miss Kassellaw! At the time of this horrible murder, my client was with another woman, in her home not far from the Kassellaw place. He has an airtight alibi.'

This announcement sucked the air out of the courtroom, and for a long minute we waited for the next surprise. Lucien played the drama perfectly. 'This woman, his lover, will be our first witness,' he said.

Her name was Lydia Vince. I whispered to Baggy and he said he'd never heard of her; and gauging from the frowns and puzzled looks it appeared as though the woman was a complete unknown. Lucien's preliminary questions revealed that she was living in Tupelo, that she and her husband were going through a divorce, that she had one child, that she grew up in Tyler County, and that she was currently unemployed. She was about thirty years old, somewhat attractive in a cheap way, and she was utterly terrified of the proceedings.

She and Danny had been having an adulterous affair for about a year. I glanced at Miss Callie and was not surprised to see this was not sitting well.

On the night Rhoda was murdered, Danny was at her house. Malcolm Vince, her husband, was supposedly in Memphis, out with the boys. She and Danny had sex twice and sometime around midnight he was preparing to leave when her husband's truck turned into the driveway. Danny sneaked out of the rear door and disappeared.

The shock of a married woman admitting in open court that she had committed adultery was designed to convince the jury that she had to be telling the truth. No one, respectable or otherwise, would admit this. It would have an impact on her divorce, perhaps even jeopardise custody of her child.

Her answers to Lucien's questions were brief and very well rehearsed. She refused to look at the jurors or at her alleged former lover. Instead, she kept her eyes down and appeared to be looking at Lucien's shoes. 'She's lyin',' Baggy whispered loudly, and I agreed.

When the direct examination was over, Ernie Gaddis stood up and walked to the podium, staring with great suspicion at this self-confessed adulteress. He kept his reading glasses on the tip of his nose, and looked above them with wrinkled brow and narrow eyes.

'Miss Vince, where does your husband, Malcolm Vince, live now?'

'I'm not sure. He moves around a lot. Last I heard he was somewhere around Tupelo.'

'And y'all are getting a divorce now, right?'

'Yes.'

'When did you file for divorce?'

She glanced quickly at Lucien, who was listening hard but refusing to watch her. 'We haven't actually filed papers yet,' she said.

'I'm sorry, I thought you said you were going through a divorce.'

'We've split, and we've both hired lawyers.'

'And who is your attorney?'

'Mr Wilbanks.'

Lucien flinched, as if this was news to him. Ernie let it settle in, then continued, 'Who is your husband's lawyer?'

'I can't remember his name.'

'Is he suing you for divorce, or is it the other way round?'

'It's a mutual thing.'

'I see. And you live in Tupelo, right?'

'Right.'

'You say you're unemployed, right?'

'For now.'

'Where do you live over in Tupelo?'

'An apartment.'

'How much is the rent?'

'Two hundred a month.'

'And you live there with your child?'

'Yes.'

'And how do you pay the rent and utilities?'

'I get by.' No one could have possibly believed her answer.

'What kind of car do you drive?'

She hesitated. It was the kind of question that required an answer that could be verified with a few phone calls. 'A '68 Mustang.'

'That's a nice car. When did you get it?'

Again, there was a paper trail here, and even Lydia, who wasn't bright, could see the trap. 'Coupla months ago,' she said, defiantly.

'Is the car titled in your name?'

'It is.'

'Is the apartment lease in your name?'

'It is.'

Paperwork, paperwork. She couldn't lie about it, and she certainly couldn't afford it.

'How long did you sleep with Danny Padgitt?'

'Fifteen minutes, usually.'

In a tense courtroom, the answer provided scattered laughter. Ernie gave her a nasty grin, and rephrased the question. 'Your affair with Danny Padgitt, how long did it last?'

'Almost a year.'

'Where did you first meet him?'

'At the clubs, up at the state line.'

'Did someone introduce the two of you?'

'I really don't remember. He was there, I was there, we had a dance. One thing led to another.'

Ernie Gaddis asked a series of questions about her background and her husband's—birth, education, marriage, employment, family. Names and dates and events that could be verified as true or false. He needed just a few more lies that he could nail down.

She was for sale. The Padgitts had found a witness they could buy.

As we left the courtroom late that afternoon, I was uneasy. I was still convinced that Danny Padgitt killed Rhoda Kassellaw. But the jury suddenly had something to hang itself with. A sworn witness had committed a dreadful act of perjury, but it was possible that a juror could have a reasonable doubt.

GINGER WAS more depressed than me, so we decided to get drunk. We bought burgers and fries and a case of beer and went to her small motel room, where we ate and then drowned our fears and hatred of a corrupt judicial system. She said that her family, fractured as it was, could not hold up if Danny Padgitt were let go. Her mother was not stable anyway, and a not-guilty verdict would push her over the cliff. What would they tell Rhoda's children one day?

We tried watching television, but nothing held our interest. We grew weary of worrying about the trial. As I was about to fall asleep, Ginger walked out of the bathroom naked, and the night took a turn for the better. We made love until the alcohol prevailed and we fell asleep.

CHAPTER 6

Unknown to me a secret meeting took place shortly after adjournment on Wednesday. Ernie Gaddis went to Harry Rex's office for a post-trial drink and both admitted they were sick over Lydia's testimony. They began making phone calls, and within an hour they had rounded up a group of lawyers they could trust, and a couple of politicians as well.

The opinion was unanimous that the Padgitts were wriggling out of what appeared to be a solid case against them. They had managed to find a witness they could bribe and who had given the jury a reason, albeit a weak one, to second-guess the prosecution.

An acquittal in such an open-and-shut case would infuriate the town and mock the court system. A hung jury would send a similar message—justice could be bought in Ford County. To allow Lucien Wilbanks and the Padgitts to corrupt the process would cause irreparable damage.

There was a consensus among these lawyers that a hung jury was entirely possible. As a believable witness, Lydia Vince left much to be desired, but the jurors were not as savvy about fabricated testimony and crooked clients. After two full days and almost fifteen hours of watching the jurors, the lawyers felt they could read them.

The man they dubbed Mr John Deere after the farming vehicle manufacturer, had them worried. His real name was Mo Teale and he'd been a mechanic down at the tractor place for over twenty years. He was a simple man with a limited wardrobe. Late on Monday afternoon when the jury was finally selected and Judge Loopus sent them home to hurriedly pack for the bus, Mo had simply loaded up his week's supply of work uniforms. Each morning he marched into the jury box wearing a bright yellow shirt with green trim and green trousers with yellow trim, as if he was ready for another vigorous day of pulling wrenches.

Mo sat with his arms crossed and frowned whenever Ernie Gaddis was on his feet. His body language terrified the prosecution.

They were also worried about a crippled boy from out near Dumas. Fargarson. He had hurt his back in a sawmill owned by his uncle. The uncle sold timber to the Padgitts many years ago. Fargarson seemed hostile to the prosecution.

Harry Rex thought it was important to find Lydia's estranged husband. If they were in fact going through a divorce, it was more than likely not an amicable one. The husband might have testimony that could severely discredit hers.

The search for Malcolm Vince began with Harry Rex and two others calling every lawyer within five counties. Around 10 p.m. they found a lawyer in Corinth, two hours away, who said he had met with a Malcolm Vince once about a divorce, but had not been retained. Mr Vince was living in a trailer somewhere out in the boondocks near the Tishomingo County line. He could not remember where he worked, but he was sure he had written it down in his file at the office. The district attorney himself got on the phone and coaxed the lawyer back to the office.

At eight o'clock the next morning, about the time I was leaving Ginger at the motel, Judge Loopus agreed to order a subpoena for Malcolm Vince. Twenty minutes later, a Corinth city policeman stopped a forklift in a warehouse and informed its operator that a subpoena had just been issued for his appearance in a murder trial over in Ford County.

Ninety minutes later a thoroughly bewildered Malcolm Vince was called into the packed courtroom to testify. Ernie had spent less than ten minutes with him in a back room, so Vince was as unprepared as he was confused.

Ernie started slow, with the basics—name, address, employment, recent family history. Malcolm somewhat reluctantly admitted being married to Lydia and shared her desire to escape from the union. He said he had seen neither his wife nor his child in about a month. His recent employment history was spotty at best, but he tried to send her $50 a week to support the child.

'You're not paying for her apartment?' Ernie asked with great suspicion, glancing warily at the jury.

'No, sir, I am not.'

'Is her family paying for her apartment?'

'Her family couldn't pay for one night in a motel,' Malcolm said with no small amount of satisfaction.

Once excused, Lydia had left the courtroom and was probably in the process of fleeing the country. Her act was complete, her performance over, her fee collected. Her absence gave Malcolm free rein to take all the cheap shots he wanted.

'You're not close to her family?' Ernie asked, a throwaway question.

'Most of them are in jail.'

'I see. She testified yesterday that a couple of months ago she bought a 1968 Ford Mustang. Did you help her with this purchase?'

'I did not.'

'Any idea how this unemployed woman could make this purchase?' Ernie asked, glancing at Danny Padgitt.

'No.'

'Do you know if she's made any other unusual purchases lately?'

'Yeah, she bought a new colour television for herself and a new motorcycle for her brother.'

It appeared as if everyone at the defence table had stopped breathing. The strategy over there had been to sneak Lydia in quietly, let her tell her lies, verify the alibi, get her off the stand, then push the case to a verdict before she could be discredited. The strategy was unravelling, with disastrous results.

'Do you know a man by the name of Danny Padgitt?' Ernie asked.

'Never heard of him,' Malcolm said.

'Your wife testified yesterday that she had been having an affair with him for almost a year.'

It's rare to see an unsuspecting husband confronted with such news so publicly, but Malcolm handled it well. 'That so?' he said.

'Yes, sir.'

'Well, sir, I'll tell you—that's kinda hard to believe.'

'And why is that?'

Malcolm was squirming. 'Well, it's kinda personal,' he said.

'Yes, Mr Vince, I'm sure it is. But sometimes personal matters have to be discussed in open court. A man is on trial here, charged with murder. This is serious business, and we need to know the truth.'

Malcolm scratched his chin. 'Well, sir, it's like this. We stopped havin' sex about two years ago. That's why we're gettin' a divorce.'

'Any particular reason you stopped having sex?' Ernie asked.

'Yes, sir. She told me she hated sex with me, said it made her sick to her stomach. Said she preferred sex with, you know, other ladies.'

Though he knew what answer was coming, Ernie managed to appear sufficiently shocked. Along with everyone else. He backed away from the podium and said, 'No further questions, Your Honour.'

LUCIEN APPROACHED Malcolm Vince as if he were staring at a loaded gun. According to Baggy, a good trial lawyer never asks a question unless he knows the answer. Lucien was a good lawyer, and he had no idea what Malcolm might say.

He admitted he had no affection for Lydia, that he couldn't wait to get through with the divorce. Typical divorce chatter. He remembered hearing about the Kassellaw murder. He'd been out the night before and returned home very late. Lucien scored a very weak point by proving that Lydia was indeed alone that night, as she had testified.

But it mattered little. The jurors and the rest of us were still struggling with the enormity of Lydia's sins.

AFTER A LONG RECESS, Lucien rose slowly and addressed the Court. 'Your Honour, the defence has no other witnesses. However, my client wishes to testify. I want it stated clearly in the record that he testifies against my advice.'

'Duly noted,' Loopus said.

'A very stupid mistake. Unbelievable,' Baggy whispered loudly enough for half the courtroom to hear.

Danny Padgitt strutted to the witness stand. His attempt at smiling came across as a smirk. His attempt at confidence came across as cockiness. He swore to tell the truth, but no one expected to hear it.

'Why do you insist on testifying?' was Lucien's first question.

'Because I want these good people to hear what really happened,' he answered, looking at the jurors.

'Then tell them,' Lucien said, waving his hand at the jury.

His version of events was wonderfully creative because there was no one to rebut him. Lydia was gone, Rhoda was dead. He began by saying that he had spent a few hours with his girlfriend, Lydia Vince, who lived less than half a mile from Rhoda Kassellaw. He knew where Rhoda lived because he had visited her on several occasions. She wanted a serious romance but he'd been too preoccupied with Lydia. Yes, he and Rhoda had had intimate relations on two occasions. They'd met at the clubs at the state line and spent hours drinking and dancing. She was hot and loose and known to sleep around.

As insult was added to injury, Ginger lowered her head and covered her ears. It was not missed by the jury.

He didn't believe Lydia's husband's garbage about her homosexual tendencies; the woman enjoyed the intimacy of men. Malcolm was lying so he could win custody of their child.

Padgitt was not a bad witness, but then he was testifying for his life. Every answer was quick, there were too many fake smiles towards the jury box. I listened to him and watched the jurors and I didn't see much sympathy. Lucien kept it brief. His client had plenty of rope with which to hang himself, no sense making it easier for the State.

Cross-examining such a guilty criminal is a prosecutor's dream. Ernie deliberately walked to the exhibit table and lifted Danny's bloody shirt. 'Exhibit number eight,' he said to the court reporter, holding it up for the jury to see again.

'Where'd you buy this shirt, Mr Padgitt?'

Danny froze, uncertain as to whether he should deny it was his, or admit ownership, or try and recall where he bought it.

'You didn't steal it, did you?' Ernie roared at him.

'I did not.'

'Then answer my question, and please try to remember you're under oath. Where did you buy this shirt?' As Ernie talked he held the shirt in front of him with his fingertips, as if the blood were still wet.

'Over in Tupelo, I think. I really don't remember. It's just a shirt.'

'And when you were in bed with Lydia that night, had you removed this shirt?' Ernie asked.

A very cautious, 'Yes.'

'Where was it while the two of you were, uh, having relations?'

'On the floor, I guess.'

Now that it was firmly established that the shirt was Danny's, Ernie was free to slaughter the witness. He pulled out the report from the state crime lab, read it to Danny, and asked him how his own blood came to be stained on the shirt. This led to a discussion about his driving abilities, his tendency to speed, and the fact that he was legally drunk when he flipped his truck. Not surprisingly, Danny began to bristle at Ernie's pointed and sardonic questioning.

On to Rhoda's bloodstains. If he was in bed with Lydia, with the shirt on the floor, how in the world did Rhoda's blood find its way from her bedroom to Lydia's, half a mile away?

It was a conspiracy, Danny said, advancing a new theory and digging a hole he would never get out of. Someone either stained his shirt with Rhoda's blood, he said, or it was more likely that the person who examined the shirt was simply lying in an effort to convict him. Ernie had a field-day with both scenarios, but he landed his heaviest blows with a series of brutal questions about why Danny, who certainly had the money to hire the best lawyers around, didn't hire his own expert to explain the tainted blood samples to the court.

Perhaps no expert was found because no expert could reach the ridiculous conclusions Padgitt wanted. Same for the semen. If Danny had been producing it over at Lydia's, how could it arrive at Rhoda's? Ernie hammered him until we were all exhausted.

At twelve thirty, Lucien suggested a break for lunch. 'I'm not done!' Ernie yelled across the courtroom. Padgitt was on the ropes, battered and gasping for air, and Ernie was not going to a neutral corner.

'Continue,' Judge Loopus said, and Ernie suddenly shouted at Padgitt, 'What did you do with the knife?'

The question startled everyone, especially the witness, who jerked back and quickly said, 'I, uh,—' then went silent.

'You what! Come on, Mr Padgitt, tell us what you did with the knife, the murder weapon.'

Danny shook his head fiercely and looked too scared to speak. 'What knife?' he managed to say. He could not have looked guiltier if the knife had dropped out of his pocket onto the floor.

'The knife you used on Rhoda Kassellaw.'

'It wasn't me.'

Like a slow and cruel executioner, Ernie took a long pause and huddled with Hank Hooten. He then picked up the autopsy report and asked Danny if he remembered the testimony of the first pathologist. Was his report also a part of this conspiracy? Danny wasn't sure how to answer. All of the evidence was being used against him, so, yes, he figured it must be bogus as well. And the piece of his skin found under her fingernail, that was part of the conspiracy? And his own semen? And on and on; Ernie hammered away. Occasionally, Lucien would glance over his shoulder at Danny's father with a look that said, 'I told you so.'

Danny's presence on the stand allowed Ernie to once more trot out all the evidence, and the impact was devastating. His weak protests that everything was tainted by a conspiracy sounded ridiculous. Finally, Ernie glared at the witness, and said, 'Under oath, you're telling this jury you didn't rape and murder Rhoda Kassellaw?'

'I didn't do it.'

'You didn't follow her home that Saturday night?'

'No.'

'You didn't sneak in her patio door?'

'No.'

'And hide in her dressing room until she put her children to bed?'

'No.'

'And you didn't attack her when she came in to put on her night clothes?'

'No.'

Lucien stood and said angrily, 'Objection, Your Honour, Mr Gaddis is testifying here.'

'Overruled!' Loopus snapped. To counteract all the lying done by the defence, the prosecution was being allowed considerable freedom in describing the murder scene.

'You didn't blindfold her with a scarf? And rape her in her own bed, with her two little children asleep not far away?'

'I did not.'

'And you didn't wake them with your noise?'

'No.'

Ernie walked as close to the witness chair as the Judge would allow, and he looked sadly at his jury. Then he turned to Danny and said, 'Michael and Teresa ran to check on their mother, didn't they, Mr Padgitt? And they found you on top of her, didn't they?'

'I wasn't there.'

'Rhoda heard their voices, didn't she? And she did what any mother would—she yelled for them to run, didn't she, Mr Padgitt?'

'I wasn't there.'

'You weren't there!' Ernie bellowed, and the walls seemed to shake. 'Your shirt was there, your footprints were there, you left your semen there! You think this jury is stupid, Mr Padgitt?'

The witness kept shaking his head. Ernie walked slowly to his chair. As he was about to sit, he said, 'You're a rapist. You're a murderer. And you're a liar, aren't you, Mr Padgitt?'

Lucien was up and yelling. 'Objection, Your Honour. This is enough.'

'Sustained. Any further questions, Mr Gaddis?'

'No, Your Honour, the State is finished with this witness.'

'Any redirect, Mr Wilbanks?'

'No, Your Honour.'

'The witness may step down.' Danny slowly got to his feet. Long gone was the smirk, the swagger. His face was red with anger.

As he was about to step out of the witness box and return to the defence table, he suddenly turned to the jury and said something that stunned the courtroom. His face wrinkled into pure hatred and he jabbed his right index finger into the air. 'You convict me,' he said, 'and I'll get every damned one of you.'

'Bailiff!' Judge Loopus said as he grabbed for his gavel. 'That's enough, Mr Padgitt.'

'Every damned one of you!' Danny repeated, louder. Two deputies raced forwards and shoved Padgitt towards the defence table. As he walked away he glared at the jurors as if he might just throw a grenade right then.

When things settled, I realised my heart was pounding with excitement. Even Baggy was too stunned to speak.

'Let's break for lunch,' His Honour said, and we fled the courtroom.

THE TRIAL RESUMED at 3 p.m. Judge Loopus explained to the jury that it was now time for the closing arguments, after which they would have the case to decide. They listened carefully, but I'm sure they were still reeling from the shock of being so flagrantly intimidated.

Ernie went first, and within minutes the bloody shirt was back in play. He was careful, though, not to overdo it. As he made his last appeal for a verdict of guilty, we watched the faces of the jurors. I saw no sympathy for the defendant. Fargarson, the crippled boy, was actually nodding as he followed along with Ernie. Mr John Deere had uncrossed his arms and was listening to every word.

Lucien was even briefer. He began by addressing his client's final words to the jury. He apologised for his behaviour. He blamed it on the pressure of the moment. Imagine, he asked the jurors, being twenty-four years old and facing either life in prison or, worse, the gas chamber. The stress on his young client was so enormous that he was concerned about his mental stability.

Since he could not pursue the goofy conspiracy theory advanced by his client, he spent half an hour or so praising the heroes who'd written our Constitution and the Bill of Rights. The way Lucien interpreted the requirement that the State prove its case beyond a reasonable doubt made me wonder how any criminal ever got convicted.

The State had the chance for a rebuttal; the defence did not. So Ernie got the last word. He talked then about Rhoda. Her youth and beauty, her simple life out in Beech Hill, the death of her husband, and the challenge of raising two small children alone.

This was very effective, and the jurors were absorbing every word. 'Let's not forget about her,' was Ernie's refrain.

A polished orator, he saved the best for last. 'And let's not forget about her children,' he said, looking into the eyes of the jurors. 'What they saw was so horrible that they will be forever scarred. They have a voice here in this courtroom, and their voice belongs to you.'

Judge Loopus read his instructions to the jury, then sent them back to begin their deliberations. It was after 5 p.m.

Much of the crowd lingered on the courthouse lawn, smoking, gossiping, predicting how long a verdict would take. Others wandered into the cafés. Ginger followed me to my office, where we sat on the balcony and watched the activity round the courthouse.

'How well do you know Hank Hooten?' she asked at one point.

'Never met him. Why?'

'He caught me during lunch, said he knew Rhoda well, said he knew for a fact that she was not sleeping around, especially not with Danny Padgitt.'

'Did he say he dated her?' I asked.

'He wouldn't say, but I got the impression he did. When we were going through her things, a week or so after the funeral, I found his name and phone number in her address book.'

'You've met Baggy,' I said.

'Yes.'

'Well, Baggy thinks he knows it all. He told me on Monday that Rhoda and Hank were seeing each other. He said Hank's been through a couple of wives, likes to be known as a ladies' man.'

'So he's not married?'

'I don't think so. I'll ask Baggy.'

'I guess I should feel better knowing my sister was sleeping with a lawyer.'

'Why would that make you feel better?'

'I don't know.'

She'd kicked off her heels and her short skirt was even higher up her thighs. I began to rub them, and my thoughts drifted away from the trial. But only for a moment. There was a commotion around the front door of the courthouse, and I heard someone yell 'Verdict.'

AFTER DELIBERATING for less than one hour, the jury was ready. When the lawyers were in place, Judge Loopus told a bailiff, 'Bring 'em in.'

'Guilty as hell,' Baggy whispered to me as the door opened and Fargarson came limping out first. 'Quick verdicts are always guilty.'

The foreman handed a folded sheet of paper to the bailiff, who then gave it to the judge. Loopus examined it for a long time, then said, 'Would the defendant please rise.' Both Padgitt and Lucien stood up, slowly, as if the firing squad was taking aim.

Judge Loopus read, 'As to count one, the charge of rape, we the jury find the defendant, Danny Padgitt, guilty. As to count two, the charge of capital murder, we the jury find the defendant guilty.'

Padgitt looked at the jurors with as much venom as he could convey, but he was getting more of it in return.

Loopus turned to the jury. 'Ladies and gentlemen, thank you for your service so far. Now we move to the capital phase in which you will be asked to decide whether this defendant gets a death sentence or life in prison. You will now return to your hotel, and we will recess until nine in the morning. Thank you and good night.'

It was over so quickly that most of the spectators didn't move for a moment. They led Padgitt out in handcuffs.

Baggy and I went to the office, where he began typing with a fury. The deadline was days away, but we wanted to capture the moment. It was almost dark when Ginger returned, in tight jeans, tight shirt, hair down, a look that said 'Take me somewhere.'

We stopped at Quincy's again, where I bought another six-pack for the road, and with the top down and the warm muggy air blowing by us, we headed for Memphis, ninety minutes away.

She said little, and I didn't poke around. She had been forced by her family to attend the trial. She hadn't asked for this nightmare. Luckily, she'd found me for a little fun.

I'll never forget that night. Racing the dark empty backroads, drinking a cold beer, holding hands with a beautiful lady who'd come looking for me, one I'd already slept with and was sure to do so again. Our sweet little romance had but a few hours left. I could almost count them. Ginger couldn't wait to leave Clanton and something told me that she would vanish from my life as quickly as she had appeared. I squeezed her hand and vowed to make the most of those last few hours.

In Memphis, we headed for the tall buildings by the river. I parked in a garage and we hustled across an alley to the door of a rib place called the Rendezvous, which at that time was the most famous restaurant in town. We ordered ribs and beer and groped each other while we waited.

The guilty verdict was a huge relief. Anything else would've been a civic disaster. For Ginger it meant justice had indeed prevailed. For me, it meant that too, but it also gave us another night together. I was consumed with lust and anxious to get started. We drove out of the city, into the suburbs, and found a Holiday Inn next to the interstate.

ON FRIDAY MORNING, outside the courtroom, Esau Ruffin found me and had a pleasant surprise with him. Three of his sons, Al, Max and Bobby (Alberto, Massimo and Roberto), were with him, anxious to say hello to me. I had spoken to all three on the phone a month earlier when I was doing the feature on Miss Callie. We shook hands and exchanged pleasantries. They politely thanked me for my friendship with their mother, and for the kind words I'd written about their family. They were all as pleasant and as articulate as Miss Callie.

They had arrived late the night before to give her moral support. Esau had talked to her once all week—each juror had been given one phone call—and she was holding up well but worried about her blood pressure.

We chatted for a moment as the crowd pushed towards the courtroom and walked in together. They sat directly behind me. A few moments later when Miss Callie took her seat, she saw her three sons and her smile was like a bolt of lightning. The fatigue around her eyes vanished immediately. During the trial, I had seen in her face a certain amount of pride. She was sitting where no black person had ever sat, shoulder to shoulder with fellow citizens, judging a white person for the first time in Ford County. I'd also had hints of the anxiety that comes with venturing into untested waters.

Ernie Gaddis stood and thanked the jurors for their proper verdict of guilty and confessed that he felt no further testimony was necessary. The crime was so heinous that nothing could be added to it. He asked the jurors to remember the graphic photos of Rhoda in the swing on Mr Deece's front porch, and the pathologist's testimony about her vicious wounds and how she died. And her children, please don't forget her children. As if anybody could.

He delivered an impassioned plea for the death penalty and wrapped it up by reminding the jurors that each had been selected on Monday after promising that they could follow the law. 'You have found Danny Padgitt guilty of rape and murder. The law now calls for the death penalty. You are duty-bound to deliver it.'

Ernie's spellbinding performance lasted for fifty-one minutes—I was trying to record everything—and when he finished I knew the jury would hang Padgitt not once but twice.

Next it was up to the defence to offer mitigating proof. Lucien called to the witness stand Danny's mother, Lettie Padgitt. She was a fiftyish woman with pleasant features and short greying hair, and she wore a black dress as if she was already mourning the death of her son. Led by Lucien, she unsteadily began testimony that seemed scripted down to every pause. Danny was never any trouble. In fact he was a real joy. His two older brothers were always into something, but not Danny.

The testimony was so silly and self-serving that it bordered on ridiculous. But there were three mothers on the jury—Miss Callie, Mrs Barbara Baldwin and Maxine Root—and Lucien was aiming for one of them. He needed just one.

Not surprisingly, Mrs Padgitt was soon in tears. She would never believe that her son had committed such a terrible crime, but if the jury felt so, then she would try and accept it. But why take him away? Why kill her little boy? What would the world gain if he were put to death? Her pain was real. Her emotions were raw and difficult to sit through. Any human being would feel sympathy for a mother about to lose a child. What began as a stilted performance ended in a gut-wrenching plea that forced most of the jurors to lower their eyes and study the floor.

Lucien said he had no other witnesses. He and Ernie made brief final summations, and by 11 a.m. the jury once again had the case.

GINGER DISAPPEARED into the crowd. I went to the office and waited, and when she didn't show I walked across the square to Harry Rex's office. He sent his secretary out for sandwiches and we ate in his cluttered conference room. Like most lawyers in Clanton, he'd spent the entire week in the courtroom watching a case that meant nothing to him financially.

'Is your gal gonna stick?' he asked with a mouth full of turkey. 'She OK with the gas chamber?'

'Miss Callie? I have no idea. We haven't discussed it.'

'She's got us worried, along with that damned crippled boy. Jurors do strange things when it's time to sign a death warrant.'

'So? Then he'll get life. From what I hear about Parchman, life there would be worse than the gas chamber.'

'Life ain't life, Willie,' he said. 'It's ten years, maybe less.'

I put my sandwich down while he took another bite. 'You mean a life sentence in Mississippi is ten years?'

'You got it. After ten years, less with good time, a murderer sent to prison for life is eligible for parole. Insane, don't you think?'

'But why—'

'Don't try and understand it, Willie, it's the law. And what's worse is the jury doesn't know it, because the Supreme Court says that if the jury knows how light a life sentence really is, it might be more inclined to give the death penalty. Thus, it's unfair to the defendant.'

'Life is ten years,' I mumbled to myself.

'You got it,' Harry Rex said, then finished his sandwich with one huge bite.

AFTER THREE HOURS of deliberation, the jury slipped a note to Judge Loopus. They were deadlocked and making little progress. He called things to order, and we raced across the street.

If the jury could not reach a unanimous verdict for the death penalty, then, by law, the judge imposed a life sentence. Fear pervaded the crowd as we waited for the jurors. Something was going wrong back there. Had the Padgitts finally found their mark?

Miss Callie was stony-faced, a look I'd never seen. Mrs Barbara Baldwin had obviously been crying. Several of the men gave the impression that their fistfight had just been broken up, and that they were anxious to resume the brawl.

The foreman stood and very nervously explained that the jury was divided and he was not optimistic about a unanimous verdict.

Judge Loopus then asked each juror if he or she thought a unanimous verdict could be reached. They unanimously said no.

I could feel the anger rise among the crowd. People were fidgeting and whispering, and this certainly didn't help the jurors.

Judge Loopus then delivered a lecture about following the law and keeping promises made during jury selection. It was stern and lengthy and loaded with no small measure of desperation.

It didn't work. Two hours later, a stunned courtroom listened as Judge Loopus quizzed the jurors again, with the same result. He grudgingly thanked them and sent them home.

When they were gone, he called Danny Padgitt forward, and on the record, gave him a tongue lashing that made my skin crawl. He called him a rapist, murderer, coward, liar, and, worst of all, a thief for having taken from two small children the only parent they had. If he had the power, he would sentence him to death, and a rapid and painful one at that. But the law was the law, and he had to follow it. He sentenced him to life and ordered Sheriff Coley to immediately transport him to the state penitentiary. Coley slapped handcuffs on him and he was gone. Loopus banged his gavel and bolted from the courtroom, followed quickly by the Padgitts.

The crowd lingered for a while, as if the trial weren't finished, as if justice had not been completely served. There was anger and cursing, and I had a whiff of how lynch mobs got organised.

GINGER DIDN'T SHOW. She'd said she would stop by the office after she checked out and say goodbye, but she obviously changed her mind. Our three-day fling had come to an abrupt end the way both of us expected but neither had admitted. I could not even imagine our paths ever crossing again.

I began writing an editorial about the verdict. It would be a scathing attack on the criminal laws of the state. It would be honest and heartfelt, and it would also play well with the audience.

Esau called and interrupted me. He was at the hospital with Miss Callie and asked me to hurry down.

She had fainted as she was getting into the car outside the courthouse. Esau had rushed her in, and wisely so. Her blood pressure was dangerously high, and the doctor was worried about a stroke. After a couple of hours, though, she had stabilised and her outlook was better. I held her hand briefly, told her I was very proud of her, and so on. What I really wanted was the inside story on what happened in the jury room. It was a story I would never get.

I drank coffee and talked with Al, Max, Bobby and Esau until midnight in the hospital canteen and then went home.

ON SATURDAY AFTERNOON, I crossed the tracks and drove slowly through Lowtown. The streets were alive with kids on bikes, basketball games, crowded porches, music from the doors of the honky-tonks. People waved and stared, more amused at my car than my pale skin.

There was a crowd on Miss Callie's verandah. Al, Max and Bobby were there along with Reverend Thurston Small and another church deacon. Callie had been discharged that morning with strict instructions to stay in bed for three days. Max led me to her bedroom.

She was sitting in bed, propped up with pillows, reading the Bible. She flashed a smile when she saw me, and said, 'Mr Traynor, so nice of you to come. Please sit. Esau, fetch Mr Traynor some tea.' Esau, as always, jumped when she gave orders.

I sat in a stiff wooden chair close to her bed. 'I'm really concerned about lunch next Thursday,' I began, and we laughed.

'I'm cooking,' she said.

'No, you're not. I have a better idea. I'll bring the food.'

'Why does that worry me?' She stopped smiling and looked away for a moment. 'We didn't do a good job, did we, Mr Traynor?' she said sadly.

'It's not a popular verdict,' I said.

'It's not what I wanted,' she said.

And that was as close to the deliberations as she would get for many years. Esau told me later that the other eleven jurors had sworn on a Bible not to talk about their decision. Miss Callie wouldn't swear on the Bible, but she gave them her word that she would guard their secrets.

I left her there to rest and went to the verandah, where I spent several hours listening to her sons and their guests talk about life. I sat in a corner, sipping tea, trying to keep myself out of their conversations.

The talk eventually came around to the trial and the verdict, and how was it playing on the other side of the tracks?

'Did he really threaten the jury?' Max asked me. I told the story, with Esau adding emphasis when needed. They were as shocked as those of us who'd seen it.

'Thank God he's locked up for life,' Bobby said, and I didn't have the heart to tell them the truth.

I was tired of the trial. I drove slowly and aimlessly back through Lowtown, alone and missing Ginger.

Clanton seethed over the verdict for days. We received eighteen letters to the editor, six of which I ran in the next edition.

As the summer dragged on, I was beginning to think the town would never stop talking about Danny Padgitt and Rhoda Kassellaw.

Then, suddenly, the two became history. Instantly, in the blink of an eye, the trial was forgotten. Clanton, both sides of the tracks, had something much more important to fret over.

PART TWO

CHAPTER 7

In a sweeping ruling that left no room for doubt or delay, the Supreme Court ordered the immediate termination of the dual school system. No more stalling, no more lawsuits, no more promises. Instant integration, and Clanton was as shocked as every other town in the south.

On a sweltering night in mid-July, a public gathering took place in the gym of the high school. The stands were packed, the floor covered with concerned parents. Mr Walter Sullivan, the *Times*'s lawyer, also served as the attorney for the school board. He did most of the

talking because he wasn't elected in any way. The politicians preferred to hide behind him. He was blunt and said that in six weeks the
Ford County school system would open and be fully desegregated.

A smaller meeting was held at the black school on Burley Street.
Baggy and I were there, along with Wiley Meek, who took photos.
Again Mr Sullivan explained to the meeting what was about to
happen. Twice his remarks were interrupted by applause.

The difference in those two meetings was astounding. The white
parents were angry and frightened. At the black school there was an
air of victory. The parents were concerned, but they were also elated
that their children would finally be enrolled in the better schools.
Though they had miles to go in housing, employment and health
care, integration into the public schools was an enormous step forward in their battle for civil rights.

There was also a meeting in the sanctuary of the First Baptist
Church. Whites only, and the crowd was slightly upper middle class,
the country-club types. Its organisers had been raising money to
build a private academy, and now suddenly the fundraising was more
urgent. Their children were apparently too good to go to school with
black children.

I wrote long reports and ran bold headlines. Desegregation was
selling newspapers. In fact, by late July 1970 our circulation topped
5,000, a stunning turnaround. I was getting a glimpse of what my
friend Nick Diener had said back at Syracuse. 'A good small-town
weekly doesn't print newspapers. It prints money.'

I needed news, and in Clanton it was not always available. In a
slow week, I would run an overblown story on the Padgitt appeal,
making it sound as if the boy might walk out of Parchman any
minute. I'm not sure my readers cared much any more. In early
August, though, the paper got another boost when Davey Bigmouth
Bass explained to me the rituals of high-school football.

Wilson Caudle had no interest in sports, which was fine except that
everyone else in Clanton lived and died with the Cougars on Friday
night. He shoved sports to the back of the paper and rarely ran
photos. I smelt money, and the Cougars became front-page news.

When the Cougars assembled for their first practice of the new
season, Bigmouth and Wiley were there to cover it. We ran a large
front-page photo of four players, two white and two black. Bigmouth
wrote columns about the team and its players and prospects, and this
was only the first week of practice.

We covered the opening of school, including interviews with students, teachers and administrators, and our slant was openly positive. I don't know how many kids failed to make the pages of our paper, but there weren't many. In truth, Clanton had little of the racial unrest that was common throughout the Deep South when schools opened that August.

The first football game was an annual family brawl against Karaway, a much smaller town that had a much better coach. I sat with Harry Rex and we screamed until we were hoarse. The game was a sellout and the crowd was mostly white.

But those white folks who had been so adamantly opposed to accepting black students were suddenly transformed that Friday night. In the first quarter of the first game, a star was born when Ricky Patterson, a pint-size black kid who could fly, ran eighty yards the first time he touched the ball. From then on, whenever they tossed it to him the entire crowd stood and yelled. Six weeks after the desegregation order hit the town, I saw narrow-minded, intolerant rednecks screaming like maniacs whenever Ricky got the ball.

Clanton won 34–30 in a cliffhanger, and our coverage of the game was shameless. We immediately initiated a Player-of-the-Week, with a $100 scholarship award, and Ricky was our first honouree.

When Clanton won its first four games, the *Times* was there to stir up the frenzy. Our circulation reached 5,500.

IN LATE SEPTEMBER there were two notable deaths in one week. The first was Mr Wilson Caudle. He died at home, alone, in the bedroom where he'd secluded himself since the day he walked out of the *Times*. It was odd that I had not spoken to him once in the six months I'd owned the paper, but I'd been too busy to fret over it. I certainly didn't want any advice from Spot. And, sadly, I knew of no one who'd either seen him or talked to him in the past six months.

He died on a Thursday and was buried on a Saturday. On Friday I hustled over to the menswear store and asked Mr Mitlo for advice about the proper funeral attire for someone of my stature. Mitlo was a Hungarian who had some colourful history of escaping from Europe while leaving behind a child or two. He was on my list of human-interest stories to pursue as soon as things quietened down.

He insisted on a black suit, and he had just the perfect bow tie. It was narrow, with black and maroon stripes, very dignified, very respectful, and when it was tied and I was properly turned out, I had to admit that the image was impressive. He pulled out a black felt fedora from his personal collection and proudly loaned it to me for the funeral; he said it was a shame American men didn't wear hats any more.

The final touch was a shiny black wooden cane. When he produced it I just stared. 'I don't need a cane,' I said. It seemed quite foolish.

'It's a walking stick,' he said, thrusting it at me, and launching into a baffling history of the crucial role walking sticks had played in the evolution of modern European male fashion. He felt passionately about it, and the more worked up he got, the thicker his accent became, and the less I understood. To shut him up I took the stick.

The following day, when I walked into the Methodist church for Spot's funeral, the ladies stared at me. Some of the men did too, most of them wondering what the hell I was doing with a black hat and a cane. In a whisper just loud enough for me to hear, Stan Atcavage, my banker, said behind me, 'I guess he's gonna sing and dance for us.'

'Been hangin' around Mitlo's again,' someone whispered back.

Within a month Clanton was accustomed to having a new character around the square. Gone were the jeans and crumpled button-down shirts. The new owner of *The Ford County Times* looked distinguished but a bit unconventional. I ordered another three suits—a blue seersucker and two light grey ones. I was getting noticed, especially by the opposite sex. Harry Rex laughed at me, but then his own outfits were comical.

The ladies loved it.

THE SECOND DEATH occurred on the night of Spot's funeral. When I heard about it on Monday I went straight to my apartment and found my pistol.

Malcolm Vince was shot twice in the head as he left a honky-tonk in a very remote part of Tishomingo County. Tishomingo was dry, the tonk was illegal, and that's why it was hidden so deep in the sticks.

There were no witnesses to the killing. Malcolm had been drinking beer and shooting pool, behaving himself generally and causing no trouble. Two acquaintances told the police that Malcolm left by himself around 11 p.m. He was in good spirits and was not drunk. He said goodbye to them, walked outside, and within seconds they heard gunfire. They were almost certain he was not armed.

I went and talked to the sheriff of Tishomingo County. He was of the opinion that someone was after Malcolm. It certainly wasn't a common-or-garden honky-tonk flare-up.

'Any idea who might be after Mr Vince?' I asked the sheriff, desperately hoping that Malcolm had made some enemies around Tishomingo County.

'No idea,' he said. 'The boy hadn't lived here long.'

For two days I carried the pistol in my pocket, then, again, grew weary of that. If the Padgitts wanted to get me or one of the jurors, or Judge Loopus or Ernie Gaddis or anyone they deemed guilty of helping send Danny away, then there was little we could do to stop them.

THE PAPER THAT WEEK was devoted to Mr Wilson Caudle. I pulled out some old photos from the archives and plastered them all over the front page. We ran testimonials, stories, and lots of paid announcements of sympathy from his many friends. It was the longest obituary in the history of the newspaper. Spot deserved it.

I wasn't sure what to do with the story about Malcolm Vince. If I exaggerated the story, the Padgitts would get the satisfaction of further intimidating the county. They would frighten us again. (Of those who'd heard of the killing, no one thought it might be the work of anyone other than the Padgitts.) But if I ignored the story, then I would be running scared and shirking my responsibility as a journalist. Baggy thought it was front-page material, but there was no room when I was finished with our farewell to Mr Caudle. I ran it at the top of page three, with the headline PADGITT WITNESS MURDERED IN TISHOMINGO COUNTY. The story was 300 words.

I drove to Corinth to snoop around. Harry Rex gave me the name of Malcolm's divorce lawyer, a local act who went by the name of Pud Perryman. His office was on Main Street, and when I opened the door I immediately knew that Mr Perryman was the least successful lawyer I would ever meet. The place reeked of lost cases, dissatisfied clients and unpaid bills.

Mr Perryman told me he hadn't seen Malcolm in a month. The divorce had never been filed. His efforts to work out an agreement with Lydia's lawyer had gone nowhere. 'She flew the coop,' he said. 'Packed up after the trial and hit the road. Took the kid, vanished.'

I really didn't care what happened to Lydia. I was much more concerned with who shot Malcolm. Pud offered a couple of vague theories, but they broke down after a few basic questions. When I finally left the lawyer's office I drove over to Iuka, the Tishomingo County seat. I found Sheriff Spinner just in time to buy him lunch. Over barbecued chicken, he brought me up to date on the murder. It was a clean hit by someone who knew the area well. They had found nothing—no footprints, no shell casings, nothing. The weapon had been a .44 magnum, and the two shots had practically blown off Malcolm's head. I lost what little appetite I had.

They had talked to all his acquaintances. Malcolm had lived in the area for about five months. He had no criminal record, no reports of fistfights, no dice shooting, disturbances or drunken brawls. There appeared to be no illicit affairs or jealous husbands.

'I can't find a motive,' the sheriff said. 'It doesn't make sense.'

I told him about Malcolm's testimony in the Padgitt trial, and about how Danny threatened the jury. 'That could be your motive,' I said.

He thought about it for a while. 'Guess we're lucky we weren't on that jury then, huh?' he said finally.

Driving back to Clanton, I could not erase the image of the sheriff's face when he said that. Spinner was truly grateful he was two counties away, and had nothing to do with the Padgitts.

His investigation was dead. Case closed.

THE ONLY JEW in Clanton was Mr Harvey Kohn, a dapper little man who'd been selling shoes and handbags to ladies for decades. His store was on the square, next door to the Sullivan law firm. He was a widower and his children had fled Clanton after high school. Once a month Mr Kohn drove to Tupelo to worship in the nearest synagogue.

Kohn ran the store himself, usually with the help of a part-time student. Two years before I arrived in Clanton he hired a sixteen-year-old black kid named Sam Ruffin to unpack inventory, move stock, clean the place, answer the phone. Sam proved to be bright and industrious. He was courteous, mannerly, well dressed, and before long he could be trusted to run the store while Mr Kohn went home every day at precisely eleven forty-five for a quick lunch and a long nap.

A lady by the name of Iris Durant dropped in around noon one day and found Sam all alone. Iris was forty-one years old, the mother of two teenage boys, one in Sam's class at Clanton High. She was mildly attractive, liked to flirt and wear miniskirts. She tried about two dozen of Mr Kohn's more exotic shoes, bought nothing, and took her time about it.

She was back the next day, same time, shorter skirt, heavier make-up. Barefoot, she seduced Sam on Mr Kohn's desk in his small office just behind the cash register. Thus began a torrid affair that would change both their lives.

Iris's husband was a sergeant in the Mississippi Highway Patrol. Alarmed at the number of new shoes in her closet, he became suspicious. Suspicion had been a way of life with Iris.

He hired Harry Rex to investigate. A Cub Scout could've caught the lovers. Three straight days she walked into Kohn's at the same time; three straight days Sam quickly locked the front door, eyes darting in all directions; three straight days the lights went off, etc. On the fourth day, Harry Rex and Rafe sneaked in the back of the store. They heard noises upstairs. Rafe barged into the love nest above the shop and in five seconds gathered enough evidence to send both of them packing.

Mr Kohn fired Sam an hour later. Harry Rex filed the divorce that afternoon. Iris was later admitted to the hospital with cuts, abrasions and a broken nose. After dark, three state troopers knocked on the door of Sam's home in Lowtown. They explained to his parents that he was wanted by the police in connection with some vague embezzling charge at Kohn's. If convicted he could be sentenced to twenty years in prison. They also told them, off the record of course, that Sam had been caught having sex with a white lady, another man's wife, and there was a contract on his head. Five thousand bucks.

Iris left town disgraced, divorced, without her children, and afraid to return.

It was old gossip by the time I arrived in Clanton, but it was still sensational enough to find its way into many conversations.

Miss Callie refused to talk about it. Sam was her youngest, and he couldn't come home. He had fled, dropped out of high school, and spent the past two years living off his brothers and sisters. Now he was calling me.

I went to the courthouse and dug through drawers of old files. I found no record of an indictment against Sam Ruffin. I asked Sheriff Coley if Sam would be arrested if he came home. He dodged the question. 'Be careful, Mr Traynor,' he warned, but would not elaborate.

I went to Harry Rex and asked about the now-legendary contract on Sam's head. He described his client, Sergeant Durant, as a former Marine, an expert marksman, a career cop, a hothead who was horribly embarrassed by Iris's indiscretion, and who felt the only honourable way out was to kill her lover. He had thought about killing her, but didn't want to go to prison. He felt safer killing a black kid. A Ford County jury would be more sympathetic.

'And he wants to do it himself,' Harry Rex explained. 'That way he can save the five grand.'

He enjoyed delivering such dire news to me, but he did admit that he hadn't seen his client in a year and a half, and he wasn't sure if Mr Durant hadn't already remarried.

On Thursday at noon we settled down at the table on the verandah and thanked the Lord for the meal we were about to receive. Esau was at work. The meal that day was chicken and dumplings. I was eating slowly, something Miss Callie had encouraged me to do. I was half through when I said, 'Sam called me, Miss Callie.'

She paused and swallowed, then said, 'How is he?'

'He's fine. He wants to come home this Christmas, said everybody else was coming back, and he wants to be here.'

'Do you know where he is?' she asked.

'He's in Memphis. We're supposed to meet tomorrow, up there.'

'Why are you meeting with Sam?' She seemed very suspicious of my involvement.

'He wants me to help him. Max and Bobby told him about our friendship. He said he thinks I'm a white person who can be trusted.'

'It could be dangerous,' she said.

'For who?'

'Both of you.'

She folded her napkin and began talking.

Sam left Clanton in the middle of the night on a bus headed for Memphis. He called Callie and Esau when he arrived there. The next day a friend drove up with some money and clothing. As the story about Iris broke fast around town, Callie and Esau were convinced their youngest son was about to be murdered by the cops. Highway patrol cars eased by their house at all hours of the day and night. There were anonymous phone calls with threats and abusive language.

Mr Kohn filed some papers in court. A hearing date came and went without Sam's appearance. Miss Callie never saw the indictment.

Memphis seemed too close, so Sam drifted to Milwaukee where he hid with Bobby for a few months. For two years now, he had drifted from one sibling to the next, always afraid that he was about to be caught. The older Ruffin children called home often and wrote once a week, but they never mentioned Sam. Someone might be listening.

'He was wrong to get involved with a woman like that,' Miss Callie said, sipping tea. 'But he was so young. He didn't chase her.'

I met Sam the next day in a coffee shop in south Memphis. From somewhere in the distance, he watched me wait for thirty minutes before he popped in from nowhere and sat across from me. Two years on the run had taught him a few tricks.

His youthful face was showing the strain of life on the run. Out of habit, he continually looked right and left. Not surprisingly, he was soft-spoken, articulate, very polite. And grateful that I had been willing to step forward and explore the possibility of helping him.

He thanked me for the courtesies and friendship I'd shown his mother. Bobby in Milwaukee had shown him the *Times* stories. He told me that he was desperate for a resolution to the mess at home so he could get on with a normal life. He wanted to finish high school, and planned eventually to go to law school. But he couldn't do it living like a fugitive.

'There's a fair amount of pressure on me, you know,' he said. 'Seven brothers and sisters, seven PhD's.'

I described my conversation with Harry Rex about Mr Durant's current mood, and my fruitless search for an indictment.

'There's no threat of being arrested,' I assured him. 'There is, however, the threat of catching a bullet.'

'He's a very scary man,' Sam said of Mr Durant. A story followed, one in which I did not get all the details. Seems as though Iris was now living in Memphis. Sam kept in touch. She had told him some horrible things about her ex-husband and her two teenage boys and the threats they'd made against her. She was not welcome anywhere in Ford County.

'And it's all my fault,' Sam said. 'I was raised better.'

Our meeting lasted an hour, and we promised to keep in touch. He handed me two thick letters he'd written to his parents, and we said goodbye. He disappeared in a crowd of shoppers.

I told Harry Rex about our meeting in Memphis. My lofty goal was to somehow convince Mr Durant to leave Sam alone. I would get Sam to agree to finish high school up north, then stay there for college and probably for the rest of his life. The kid simply wanted to be able to see his parents, to have short visits in Clanton, and to be able to live without looking over his shoulder.

Harry Rex reluctantly promised to relay the message to Mr Durant, but he wasn't optimistic his client would give it a sympathetic ear.

Trooper Durant had been quite pleased to learn that his threats were still hanging over the head of Sam Ruffin. Harry Rex had eventually delivered the word that Sam was still on the run but desperately wanted to come home and see his momma.

Durant had not remarried. He was very much alone and extremely bitter about his wife's affair. He ranted at Harry Rex about how his life had been destroyed, and how his two sons were subject to ridicule and abuse because of what their mother did. 'If that boy sneaks home at Christmastime, we'll be waitin',' he promised Harry Rex.

He also had some venom for me, and for my heart-warming stories about Miss Callie and her older children. He guessed correctly that I was the family's contact with Sam.

'You'd better get your nose outta this mess,' Harry Rex warned me after his meeting with Durant. 'This is a nasty character.'

ON CHRISTMAS EVE I drove to Memphis, to my childhood home. My father and I had dinner at a Chinese joint not far from the house. As I choked down bad wonton soup I couldn't help but think of the Ruffin family home, where the clan had been arriving for the past three days. There were more than twenty Ruffins staying in the house; I couldn't imagine where everyone slept, and I was certain no one really cared. Miss Callie had been cooking for a week and I let my mind wander to the chaos of her kitchen and all those wonderful dishes that would be being pulled from the oven.

My father worked hard to seem interested in my newspaper. I sent him a copy each week, but after a few minutes of chitchat I could tell he had never read a word. He was concerned with some ominous connection between the war in Southeast Asia and the bond market.

We ate quickly and went in different directions. Sadly, neither of us had given any thought to exchanging gifts.

Christmas lunch was with BeeBee, who, unlike my father, was delighted to see me. She invited three of her little blue-haired widow friends over for sherry and ham, and the five of us proceeded to get tipsy. I regaled them with stories from Ford County, some accurate, some highly embellished. Hanging around Baggy and Harry Rex, I was learning the art of storytelling.

By 3 p.m., we were all napping. Early the next morning, I raced back to Clanton.

ONE FRIGID DAY late in January, shots rang out somewhere around the square. I was sitting at my desk typing a story about Mr Lamar Farlowe and his recent reunion in Chicago with his battalion of army paratroopers, when a bullet shattered a windowpane less than twenty feet from my head. A slow news week thus came to a sudden end.

I hit the floor with all sorts of thoughts—Where was my pistol? Were the Padgitts assaulting the town? Were Trooper Durant and his boys after me? On my hands and knees I scrambled to my briefcase as shots continued to crack through the air; they sounded like they were coming from across the street.

I emptied the briefcase and then remembered I'd put the pistol in my car. I was unarmed and felt like such a weakling for not being able to defend myself. Harry Rex and Rafe had trained me better.

I was scared to the point of not being able to move. Then I remembered Bigmouth Bass was in his office downstairs, and like most real men in Clanton he had an arsenal close by. From somewhere below I heard Bigmouth yell, 'Stay in your offices!' I could almost see him down there, grabbing a 30.06 and a box of shells, ducking into a doorway in great anticipation. I couldn't imagine a worse place for some nut to start shooting. There were thousands of guns within arm's reach around the Clanton square. Every pick-up had two rifles in the window rack and a shotgun under the seat. These people couldn't wait to use their guns!

Then the shots resumed. They weren't getting any closer and I realised that the assault was not aimed at me. I just happened to own a nearby window. Sirens approached, then more shots, more shouting.

'Willie! You OK?' Bigmouth yelled from the bottom of the steps.

'Yeah!'

'There's a sniper on top of the courthouse! Stay low!'

'Don't worry!'

I relaxed a little and after a while I crawled towards one of the French doors and opened it. I'm not sure why I felt compelled to move closer to the sniper, but I knew that I would write a lengthy story about this dramatic episode. I needed details.

The verandah had a wrought-iron railing round it and when I finally looked out I saw the sniper. The courthouse had an oddly flattened dome, on top of which was a small cupola with four open windows. He'd made his nest there, and when I first saw him he was peeking just above the sill of one of the windows. He was reloading, and when he was ready he rose slightly and began shooting completely at random. He appeared to be shirtless, which, given the situation, seemed even stranger since it was around thirty degrees with a chance of light snow later in the afternoon. I was freezing and I was wearing a rather handsome wool suit from Mitlo's.

His body was white with black stripes, sort of like a zebra. It was a white man who'd painted his face and chest partially black.

All traffic was gone. The city police had blocked the streets and cops were darting about, squatting low and hiding behind their cars. The shooting stopped and the sniper disappeared for a while. Three county deputies dashed into the courthouse.

Wiley Meek bounded up to my office and was soon beside me. He was breathing so hard I thought he'd sprinted from his house out in the country. 'Where is he?' he asked as he moved a camera with a long-range lens into position.

'The cupola,' I said, pointing.

'Have you seen him?'

'Male, white, with black highlights.'

'Oh, one of those.'

'Keep your head down.'

We stayed crouched for several minutes. More cops scurried about, giving the distinct impression that they were thrilled to be there but had little idea what to do. Then more shots, very quick and startling. We peeked and saw him from the shoulders up, blazing away. Wiley focused and began taking pictures through the long-range lens.

Baggy and the boys were in the Bar Room on the second floor, not far from the cupola. After the shooting resumed for the tenth time, and they were convinced they were about to be slaughtered, they had decided to take matters into their own hands. Somehow they managed to prise open the intractable window of their little hideaway. We watched as an electrical cord was thrown out and fell almost to the ground, forty feet below. Baggy's right leg appeared next as he flung it over the brick sill and wiggled his portly body through the opening.

'Oh my God,' Wiley said, somewhat gleefully, and raised his camera. 'They're drunk as skunks.'

Clutching the electrical cord with all the grit he could muster, Baggy sprang free from the window and began his descent to safety. His strategy was not apparent. He appeared to give no slack on the cord, his hands frozen to it just above his head. Evidently there was plenty of cord left in the Bar Room, and his cohorts were supposed to ease him down.

As his hands rose higher above his head, his trousers became shorter. Soon they were just below his knees, leaving a long gap of pale white skin before his black socks bunched around his ankles.

The shooting stopped, and for a while Baggy just hung there, slowly twisting against the building, three feet below the window. Major, one of Baggy's Bar Room cronies, could be seen inside, clinging fiercely to the cord. He had only one leg though, and I worried that it would quickly give out. Behind him I could see two figures, probably Wobble Tackett and Chick Elliot, the usual poker gang.

Wiley began laughing, a low suppressed laugh that shook his entire body.

Two shots rang out. Baggy lurched as if he'd been hit—though in reality there was no possible way the sniper could even see him—and the suddenness evidently put too much pressure on Major's leg. It collapsed, the cord sprang free, and Baggy dropped like a cinder block into a row of thick boxwoods. The boxwoods absorbed the load, and, much like a trampoline, recoiled and sent Baggy to the sidewalk, where he landed like a melon and became the only casualty of the entire episode.

Without a trace of mercy, Wiley recorded the entire spectacle. The photos would be furtively passed around Clanton for years to come.

For a long time Baggy didn't move. 'Leave the sumbitch out there,' I heard a cop yell below us.

'You can't hurt a drunk,' Wiley said as he caught his breath.

Eventually, Baggy rose to all fours. Slowly and painfully, he crawled, like a dog hit by a truck, into the boxwoods that had saved his life, and there he rode out the storm.

A police car had been parked three doors down from the Tea Shoppe. The sniper fired a burst at it, and when the gas tank exploded we forgot about Baggy. The crisis stepped up to the next level as thick smoke poured out from under the car, then we saw flames. The sniper found this sporting, and for a few minutes he hit nothing but cars.

He lost his nerve when fire was eventually returned. Two of Sheriff Coley's men stationed themselves on roofs, and when they unloaded on the cupola the sniper ducked low and was out of business.

'I got him!' one of the deputies shouted down to Sheriff Coley.

We waited for twenty minutes; all was quiet. Then we saw a deputy in the cupola, and the town was safe again. I hurried over to the courthouse, along with the rest of downtown Clanton.

Court was not in session, so Sheriff Coley directed us to the courtroom, where he promised a quick briefing. As we were walking into the courtroom, I saw Major, Chick Elliot and Wobble Tackett being escorted down the hall by a deputy. They were obviously drunk and laughing so hard they had trouble staying on their feet.

Wiley went downstairs to sniff around. A body was about to be removed from the courthouse, and he wanted a shot of the sniper. The white hair, black face, painted stripes—there were a lot of questions.

THE DEPUTY SHARPSHOOTERS had evidently missed. The sniper was identified as Hank Hooten, the local lawyer who had assisted Ernie Gaddis in the prosecution of Danny Padgitt. He was in custody and unharmed. When Sheriff Coley announced this in the courtroom, we were shocked and bewildered. Our nerves were pretty raw anyway, but this was too much to believe. 'Mr Hooten did not resist arrest and is now in custody,' Coley said.

'What was he wearing?' someone asked.

'Nothing. He had what appeared to be black shoe polish on his face and chest, but other than that he was as naked as a newborn.'

'What type of weapons did he have?' I asked.

'We found two high-powered rifles, that's all I can say right now.'

'Did he say anything?'

'Not a word.'

Wiley said they wrapped Hank in some sheets and shoved him in the back seat of a patrol car. He shot some photos but was not optimistic. 'There were a dozen cops around him,' he said.

We drove to the hospital to check on Baggy. He was snoring when we got to his room. The medications he had been given had mixed with the whiskey and he appeared comatose. 'He will wish he could sleep for ever,' Wiley whispered.

And he was right. The legend of Bouncin' Baggy was told countless times in the years that followed and it was even rumoured that the three idiots Baggy left behind in the Bar Room had intentionally dropped him into the boxwoods.

ALL CHARGES against Hank Hooten were eventually dropped, and he was sent to the state mental hospital at Whitfield, where he would remain for several years. He allegedly told Ernie Gaddis that he had not been shooting at anyone in particular, didn't want to harm anyone, but was just upset because the town had failed to send Danny Padgitt to his death.

Word eventually drifted back to Clanton that he had been diagnosed as severely schizophrenic. 'Slap-ass crazy,' was the conclusion on the streets. Never in the history of Ford County had a person lost his mind in such a spectacular fashion.

CHAPTER 8

One year after I bought the newspaper, I sent BeeBee a cheque for $55,000—her loan plus interest at the rate of 10 per cent. She had not discussed the matter of interest when she gave me the money, nor had we signed a promissory note. Ten per cent was a bit high, and

I hoped it would prompt her to send the cheque back. Sure enough, about a week later there was a letter from Memphis.

Dear William,

I enclose your cheque, which I was not expecting and have no use for at this time. If, for some unlikely reason, I need the money in the future, then we shall at that time discuss this matter.

Your offer of payment makes me extremely proud of you and your integrity. What you have accomplished in one year is a source of great pride for me, and I delight in telling my friends about your success as a newspaper publisher and editor.

You're all I have, William, and I love you dearly. Please write me more often.

Love, BeeBee

I happily tore up the cheque, walked down to the bank, and borrowed another $50,000 from Stan Atcavage. Hardy had found a slightly used offset press in Atlanta, and I bought it for $108,000. We ditched our ancient letterpress and moved into the twentieth century. The *Times* took on a new look—much cleaner print, sharper photos, smarter designs. Our circulation was at 6,000 and I could see steady, profitable growth. The elections of 1971 certainly helped.

I WAS ASTOUNDED at the number of people who ran for public office in Mississippi. Each county was divided into five districts, and each district had an elected constable, who wore a badge and a gun. No training was required. No education. No supervision from the county sheriff or the city police chief, no one but the voters every four years.

Each county also had an elected sheriff, tax collector, tax assessor, chancery court clerk and coroner. The rural counties shared a state senator and state representative.

I thought this was a ridiculous and cumbersome system until the candidates for these positions began buying ads in the *Times*. By late February, the county was consumed with the August election. Sheriff Coley had two opponents with two more threatening. The deadline to file for office was June, and he had yet to do so. This fuelled speculation that he might not run. It took little to fuel speculation about anything when it came to local elections.

AT NOON on the Fourth of July the temperature was 101 degrees and the humidity felt even higher. The parade was led by the mayor, who sat on the rear seat of a 1962 Corvette and threw candy to the children packed along the sidewalks around the square. Behind him were two high-school bands, Clanton's and Karaway's, the Boy Scouts, a new fire truck, a dozen floats, a posse on horseback, veterans from every war that century, and three restored John Deere tractors. The rear was protected by a string of city and county police cars, all polished to perfection.

I watched the parade from the second-floor balcony of the Security Bank. Stan Atcavage threw an annual party up there. Since I now owed the bank a sizable sum, I was invited to watch the festivities.

For a reason no one could remember, the Rotarians were in charge of the speeches. They had parked a long flat-bed trailer next to the Confederate sentry and decorated it with bales of hay and red, white and blue bunting.

Mr Mervin Beets, president of the Rotary Club, stepped to the microphone and welcomed everyone. Prayer was required for any public event in Clanton, and in the new spirit of desegregation he had invited the Reverend Thurston Small, Miss Callie's minister, to properly get things going.

The first candidate was Timmy Joe Bullock, a terrified young man who wanted to serve as a constable. He walked across the flat-bed trailer as if it were a gangplank, and when he stood behind the mike and looked at the crowd he almost fainted.

Applause was light when he finished. But at least he showed up. There were twenty-two candidates for constable in the five districts, but only seven had the courage to face the crowd. When we finally finished with the constables, Woody Gates and the Country Boys played a few bluegrass tunes and the crowd appreciated the break.

At various places on the courthouse lawn, food and refreshments were being served. The ladies of the garden club were selling home-made ice cream. Others were barbecuing ribs. The crowd huddled under the ancient oak trees and hid from the sun.

Mackey Don Coley had entered the race for sheriff in late May. He had three opponents, including a Clanton city policeman named T. R. Meredith. When Mr Beets announced that it was time for the sheriff candidates, the voters swarmed round the trailer.

Freck Oswald had finished last three times previously and he appeared to be headed for the bottom again. Tryce McNatt was running for the second time. Tryce wanted harsher sentences for criminals and more prisons, even chain gangs and forced labour. 'Let's clean up the county!' was his refrain. The crowd was with him.

T. R. Meredith was a thirty-year veteran of law enforcement. He was an awful speaker but he was related to half the county, according to Stan. Stan knew about such things; he was related to the other half. 'Meredith'll win by a thousand votes in the run-off,' he predicted.

Mackey Don went last. He had been the sheriff since 1943, and wanted just one more term. 'He's been saying that for twenty years,' Stan said. Coley rambled on about his experience. When he finished, the applause was polite but certainly not encouraging.

The speeches continued throughout the afternoon. It was the summer of 1971, and by then at least 50,000 young Americans had been killed in Vietnam. A similar gathering of people in any other part of the country would have turned into a virulent antiwar rally. But Vietnam was never mentioned that Fourth of July.

I'd had great fun at Syracuse demonstrating on campus and marching in the streets, but such activity was unheard of in the Deep South. It was a war; therefore real patriots were supportive. We were stopping Communism; the hippies and radicals and peaceniks up north and in California were simply afraid to fight.

I bought a dish of strawberry ice cream from the garden ladies as I strolled around outside the courthouse for a while, then disappeared. I was tired of speeches and politics.

FOUR WEEKS LATER, on the first Tuesday in August, much of the same crowd gathered round the courthouse for the vote counting.

The polls closed at six, and an hour later the square was alive with anticipation. People formed little groups round their candidate. Two enormous black chalkboards were placed side by side near the front door of the courthouse, and there the returns were tallied.

'We have the results from North Karaway,' the clerk announced into a microphone. The festive mood was immediately serious.

'North Karaway's always first,' Baggy said. It was almost eight thirty. We were sitting on the verandah outside my office, waiting for the news. We planned to delay press time for twenty-four hours and publish our 'Election Special' on Thursday. When the clerk said, 'And in the sheriff's race—', several thousand people held their breath.

'Mackey Don Coley, eighty-four. Tryce McNatt, twenty-one. T. R. Meredith, sixty-two, and Freck Oswald, eleven.' A loud cheer went up on the far side of the lawn, where Coley's supporters were camped.

'Coley's beat,' Baggy said.

'He's beat?' I asked. The first of twenty-eight precincts were in, and Baggy was already predicting winners.

'Yep. For T. R. to run strong in a place where he has no base shows folks are fed up with Mackey Don.'

Slowly, the returns dribbled in, from places I'd never heard of: Pleasant Hill, Shady Grove, Klebie, Three Corners.

The Padgitts voted at a tiny precinct called Dancing Creek. When the clerk announced the votes from there, and Coley got 31 votes and the other three got 8 combined, there was a refreshing round of boos from the crowd. Clanton East followed, the largest precinct and the one I voted in. Coley got 285 votes, Tryce 47, and when T. R.'s total of 644 was announced, the place went wild.

Baggy grabbed me and we celebrated with the rest of the town. Coley was going down without a run-off.

At midnight, I left the office and strolled round the square, taking in the sounds and images of this wonderful tradition. I felt quite proud of the town. In the aftermath of a brutal murder and its baffling verdict, we had rallied, fought back, and spoken clearly that we would not tolerate corruption. The strong vote against Coley was our way of hitting at the Padgitts.

T. R. Meredith got 61 per cent of the vote, a stunning landslide. We printed 8,000 copies of our 'Election Special' and sold every one of them. I became a staunch believer in voting every year. Democracy at its finest.

A WEEK BEFORE THANKSGIVING in 1971, Clanton was rocked by the news that one of its sons had been killed in Vietnam. Pete Mooney, a nineteen-year-old staff sergeant, was captured in an ambush near Hué, in central Vietnam. A few hours later his body was found.

I didn't know the Mooneys, but Margaret certainly did. She called me with the news and said she needed a few days off. Her son and Pete had been close friends since childhood.

Pete Mooney had graduated from Clanton High School in 1970. He had played varsity football and baseball, and was awarded his colours in both for three years. He was an honours student who had planned to work for two years, save his money, then go to college. He was unlucky enough to have a high draft number, and in December 1970 he got his notice.

According to Margaret, and this was something I could not print, Pete had been reluctant to report for training. He and his father had fought for weeks over the war. The son wanted to go to Canada and avoid the whole mess. The father was horrified that his son would be labelled a coward, a draft dodger. Mrs Mooney tried the role of peacemaker, but in her heart, she too was reluctant to send her son to war. Pete finally relented, and now he was coming home in a box.

The funeral was at the First Baptist Church, where the Mooneys had been active for many years. I sat with Margaret and her husband. It was my first and last funeral for a nineteen-year-old soldier. By concentrating on the coffin, I could almost avoid the sobbing and, at times, wailing around me. His high-school football coach gave a eulogy that drained every eye in the church, mine included.

After an hour, we made our way to the Clanton cemetery, where Pete was laid to rest with full military pomp and ceremony. When the lone bugler played 'Tap', the gut-wrenching cry of Pete's mother made me shudder. She clung to the coffin until they began to lower it. His father collapsed and was tended to by several deacons.

What a waste, I said over and over as I walked alone back to the office. That night, still alone, I cursed myself for being so silent, so cowardly. I was the editor of the newspaper, dammit!

PETE MOONEY was preceded in death by more than 50,000 of his fellow countrymen. In 1969, President Nixon and his National Security Adviser, Henry Kissinger, made the decision that the war in Vietnam could not be won, or, rather, that the United States would no longer try to win it. They kept this to themselves. They did not stop the draft, however. Instead, they pursued the cynical strategy of appearing to be confident of a successful outcome.

From the time this decision was made until the end of the war, approximately 18,000 more men were killed, including Pete Mooney.

I ran my editorial on the front page, under a large photo of Pete in his army uniform. It read:

The death of Pete Mooney should make us ask the glaring question—What the hell are we doing in Vietnam? A gifted student, talented athlete, school leader, future community leader, one of our best and brightest, gunned down at the edge of a river we've never heard of in a country we care little about.

The official reason, one that goes back twenty years, is that we are there fighting Communism. If we see it spreading, then, in the words of ex-President Lyndon Johnson, we are to take '. . . all necessary measures to prevent further aggression.'

Vietnam was divided into two countries in 1954. North Vietnam is a poor country run by a Communist named Ho Chi Minh. South Vietnam is a poor country that was run by a brutal dictator named Ngo Dinh Diem until he was murdered in a coup in 1963. Since then the country has been run by the military.

Vietnam has been at war since 1946 when the French began their fateful attempt to keep out the Communists. Our failure has been even grander than that of the French, and we're not finished yet.

How many more Pete Mooneys will die before our government decides to leave Vietnam to its own course? Right now we're burying young soldiers while the politicians who are running the war contemplate getting out.

When I returned from Thursday lunch with Miss Callie (lamb stew indoors by the fire), Bubba Crockett was waiting in my office. He wore jeans, boots, a flannel shirt, long hair, and after he introduced himself he thanked me for the editorial. He had some things he wanted to get off his chest.

He'd grown up in Clanton, finished school here in 1966. His father owned the nursery two miles south of town; they were landscapers. He got his draft notice in 1967 and gave no thought to doing anything other than racing off to fight Communists. His unit landed in the south, just in time for the Tet Offensive. Two days on the ground, and he had lost three of his closest friends.

The horror of fighting could not accurately be described, though Bubba was descriptive enough for me. Men burning, screaming for help, tripping over body parts, dragging bodies off the battlefield, hours with no sleep, no food, running out of ammo. His battalion lost 100 men in the first five days.

He talked of the frustration of fighting a war that the government would not allow them to win. 'We were better soldiers,' he said. 'And our equipment was vastly superior. Our commanders were superb, but the fools in Washington wouldn't let them fight a war.'

Bubba knew the Mooney family and had begged Pete not to go.

'These idiots around here still support the war, can you believe that?' he said. 'More than fifty thousand dead and now we're pulling out, and these people will argue with you that it was a great cause.'

'They don't argue with you,' I said.

'They do not. I've punched a couple of them. You play poker?'

I did not, but I'd heard many colourful stories about various poker games around town. Quickly, I thought this might be interesting. 'A little,' I said, figuring I could get Baggy to teach me.

'We play on Thursday nights, in a shed at the nursery. Several guys who fought over there. You might enjoy it.'

'Tonight?'

'Yeah, around eight.'

'I'll be there,' I said, wondering where I could find Baggy.

THERE WERE FIVE OF US round the table that evening, all in our mid-twenties. Three had served in Vietnam—Bubba, Darrell Radke, whose family owned a propane company, and Cedric Young, a black guy with a severe leg injury. The fourth player was Bubba's older brother David, who had been rejected by the draft because of his eyesight, and who, I think, was there just for the marijuana.

We talked a lot about drugs. None of the three veterans had seen or heard of pot or anything else prior to joining the army. In Vietnam, though, drug use was rampant. Pot was smoked when they were bored and homesick, and it was smoked to calm their nerves in battle. No wonder we lost the war—everybody was stoned.

They expressed great admiration for my editorial and great bitterness for having been sent over there. All three had been scarred in some way; Cedric's was obvious. Bubba's and Darrell's was more of a smouldering anger, a barely contained rage and desire to lash out, but at whom?

Late in the game, they began swapping stories of gruesome battlefield scenes. I had heard that many soldiers refused to talk about their war experiences. Those three didn't mind at all. It was therapeutic.

They played poker almost every Thursday night, and I was always welcome. When I left them at midnight, having lost $100, they were still drinking, still smoking pot, still talking about Vietnam. I'd had enough of the war for one day.

THE FOLLOWING WEEK I devoted an entire page to the war controversy I had created. It was covered with letters to the editor, seventeen in all, only two of which were even somewhat supportive of my antiwar feelings. I was called a Communist, a liberal, a traitor and, the worst, a coward because I had not worn the uniform. I didn't care. I had stirred up a hornet's nest and the town was at least debating the war.

The response was astounding. A group of high-school students came to my rescue with a hand-delivered batch of letters of their own. They were passionately against the war, had no plans to go and fight in it, and, furthermore, found it odd that most of the letters the prior week were from folks too old for the forces. 'It's our blood, not yours,' was my favourite line.

The following week, I devoted a page to the letters from the students. There were also three late arrivals from the warmongering crowd, and I printed them too. The response was another flood of letters, all of which I printed.

Through the pages of the *Times*, we fought the war until Christmas when everyone suddenly called a truce and settled in for the holidays.

MR MAX HOCUTT died on New Year's Day 1972. Before the funeral Wilma and Gilma came to see me.

'We want you to buy the place,' Gilma said. She had barely finished the sentence before Wilma started another one.

'We sell it to you . . .'

'For a hundred thousand . . .'

'We take the money . . .'

'And move to Florida . . .'

They explained that they wanted to go and spend the rest of their days in Florida. Their beloved mansion was simply too much for them to maintain.

'We want you to buy the Mercedes too . . .'

'We don't drive, you know . . .'

'Max always took us . . .'

Unlike the house, Max's Mercedes was in mint condition.

The house had six bedrooms, four floors and a basement, four or five bathrooms, living and dining rooms, library, kitchen, verandahs that were falling in, and an attic that I felt certain was crammed with family treasures buried there centuries ago. It would take months just to clean it before the remodellers moved in. A hundred thousand dollars was a low price for such a mansion, but there were not enough newspapers sold in the entire state to restore the place.

I had been looking at real estate, but, frankly, I'd been so spoiled by paying them fifty dollars a month that I found it hard to leave. Why would I risk financial ruin by buying that money pit?

I bought it two days after the funeral.

ON A COLD, wet Thursday in February, I drove over to the Ruffin residence in Lowtown. Esau was waiting on the verandah. He seemed subdued, and things did not improve inside.

I hugged Miss Callie and knew something was terribly wrong. Esau picked up an envelope and said, 'This is a draft notice. For Sam.' He tossed it on the table for me to see, then left the kitchen.

Talk was slow over lunch. They were preoccupied and confused. Esau at times felt the proper thing to do was for Sam to honour any commitment his country required. Miss Callie felt like she had already lost Sam once. The thought of losing him again was unbearable.

That night I called Sam and gave him the bad news. He was in Toledo spending a few days with Max. We talked for over an hour, and I was relentless in my conviction that he had no business going to Vietnam. Fortunately, Max felt the same way.

Over the course of the next week, I spent hours on the phone with Sam, Bobby, Al, Leon, Max and Mario, as we shared our views about what Sam should do. Neither he nor any of his brothers believed the war was just, but Mario and Al felt strongly that it was wrong to break the law. Max and I were the biggest doves in the bunch, with Bobby and Leon somewhere in the middle. Sam seemed to twist in the wind and change daily, but after two weeks of soul-searching, he slipped into the underground and surfaced in Ontario.

To Esau and Miss Callie it seemed as if he had moved a million miles away. Not nearly as far as Vietnam, I told them.

NEARLY TWO YEARS after the trial, the Supreme Court of Mississippi finally affirmed the conviction of Danny Padgitt. Four months earlier it had ruled, by a majority of six to three, that the conviction would stand. Lucien Wilbanks filed a petition for rehearing, on the grounds that Ernie Gaddis had been given too much freedom in abusing Danny Padgitt on cross-examination. With his leading questions about the presence of Rhoda's children in the bedroom, watching the rape, Ernie had effectively been allowed to place before the jury highly prejudicial facts that simply were not in evidence. The vote to affirm the conviction was five to four. The case was over.

I plastered the good news across the front of the *Times* and hoped I would never again hear the name of Danny Padgitt.

PART THREE

CHAPTER 9

In April 1972 Mr Lester Klump of Shady Grove and his son, Lester Junior, began the transformation of the Hocutt House. Five years and two months later they finished the renovation. The ordeal was over, and the results were splendid.

Once I accepted the languid pace at which the contractors worked,

I settled in for the long haul and worked hard selling ad copy. After work each Friday I would sit down with Lester Senior, usually at a makeshift plywood table in a hallway, and over a cold beer we would tally up the labour and materials for the week, add 10 per cent, and I would write him a cheque. For the first two years I kept a running total of the cost of the renovation, but then I stopped. I didn't want to know what it was costing.

I was broke but I didn't care. I had something magnificent to show for the time, effort and investment. The house had been built around 1900 by Dr Miles Hocutt. It had a distinctive Victorian style, with two high gabled roofs in the front, a turret that ran up four levels, and wide covered verandahs that swept round the house on both sides.

Inside, the pine floors on all three levels had been restored to their original beauty. Walls had been removed, rooms and hallways opened up. The Klumps had removed the entire kitchen and built another from the basement up. I turned the library into a den and knocked out more walls so that upon entering the front foyer you could see through the den to the kitchen in the distance. I added windows everywhere.

Mr Klump admitted he had never tasted champagne, but he happily chugged it down as we completed our little ceremony on a side verandah. I handed him what I hoped would be his last cheque, we shook hands, posed for a photograph by Wiley Meek, then popped the cork.

Many of the rooms were bare; it would take years to properly decorate the place, and it would require the assistance of someone with far more knowledge and taste than I possessed. Half-empty, though, the house was still spectacular. It needed a party!

I borrowed $2,000 from the bank and ordered wine and champagne from Memphis. I found a suitable caterer from Tupelo. (The only one in Clanton specialised in ribs and catfish and I wanted something a bit classier.)

The official invitation list of 300 included everybody I knew in town, and a few I did not. The unofficial list was composed of those who'd heard me say, 'We'll have a huge party when it's finished.' I invited BeeBee and three of her friends from Memphis. I invited my father but he was too worried about the bond market. I invited Miss Callie and Esau, Reverend Thurston Small, three clerks from the courthouse, three schoolteachers, an assistant basketball coach, a teller at the bank, and the newest lawyer in town. That made a total of twelve blacks, and I would've invited more if I had known more. I was determined to have the first integrated party in Clanton.

Harry Rex brought moonshine and Bubba Crockett and friends arrived stoned and ready to party. Mr Mitlo wore the only tuxedo. Piston made an appearance, and was seen leaving through the back door with a carry-out bag filled with finger food. Woody Gates and the Country Boys played for hours on a side verandah. The Klumps were there with all their labourers; it was a fine moment for them and I made sure they got all the credit. Lucien Wilbanks arrived late and was soon in a heated argument about politics with Senator Theo Morton, whose wife told me it was the grandest party she'd seen in Clanton in twenty years. Our new sheriff, Tryce McNatt, dropped by with several of his uniformed deputies. (T. R. Meredith had died of colon cancer the year before.) One of my favourites, Judge Reuben V. Atlee, held court in the den with colourful stories about Dr Miles Hocutt. Baggy passed out in a first-floor bedroom, where I found him the next afternoon. The Stukes twins, who owned the hardware store, showed up in brand-new, matching overalls. They were seventy years old, lived together, never married, and wore matching overalls every day. There was no dress code; the invitation said, 'Open Attire'.

The front lawn was covered with two large white tents, and at times the crowd spilled from under them. The party began at 1 p.m., Saturday afternoon, and would've gone past midnight if the wine and food had lasted. By ten, Woody Gates and his band were exhausted, there was nothing left to eat or drink, and nothing left to see. The house had been thoroughly seen and enjoyed.

Late the next morning, I scrambled eggs for BeeBee and her friends. We sat on the verandah and drank coffee and admired the mess made just hours before. It took me a week to clean up.

THROUGH THE YEARS in Clanton I'd heard plenty of horror stories of imprisonment at the state penitentiary at Parchman. Living conditions were wretched—cramped barracks, ghastly food, scant medical care, a slave system, brutal sex. Forced labour, sadistic guards, the list was endless and pathetic.

When I thought of Danny Padgitt, which I did often, I was always comforted by the belief that he was getting what he deserved there.

My assumption was wrong.

In the late sixties, in an effort to ease the overcrowding at Parchman, the state had built two satellite prisons. The plan had been to place a thousand nonviolent offenders in more civilised confinement. They would obtain job training, even qualify for work release.

One such satellite was near the small town of Broomfield.

Judge Loopus died in 1972. During the Padgitt trial, his stenographer had been a young woman named Darla Clabo who had since left the area. When she walked into my office one afternoon in the summer of 1977, I knew I had seen her somewhere in the distant past.

Darla introduced herself and I quickly remembered where I'd seen her. For five straight days during the Padgitt trial she had sat below the bench, next to the exhibit table, taking down every word. She was now living in Alabama, she said, and had driven five hours to tell me something. First, she swore me to absolute secrecy.

Her home town was Broomfield. Two weeks earlier she had been visiting her mother when she saw a familiar face walking down the sidewalk around lunchtime. It was Danny Padgitt. She was so startled she tripped on the edge of a kerb and almost fell into the street.

Padgitt and a buddy walked into a local diner and sat down for lunch. Darla decided not to go in. There was a chance Padgitt might recognise her, though she wasn't sure why that frightened her.

The man with him wore navy slacks and a short-sleeved white shirt with the words 'Broomfield Correctional Facility' in very small letters over the pocket. Danny was wearing white dungarees and a white shirt. Danny and his personal guard enjoyed a long lunch and appeared to be good friends. From her car, Darla watched them leave the diner. She followed from a distance as they took a leisurely stroll for a few blocks until Danny entered a building that housed the regional office of the Mississippi Highway Department. The guard got into a camp vehicle and drove away.

The following morning, Darla's mother entered the building under the pretext of filing a complaint about a road in need of repair. She was rudely informed that no such procedure existed, and in the ensuing brouhaha managed to catch a glimpse of Padgitt. He was holding a clipboard and appeared to be just another useless pencil-pusher.

Darla's mother had a friend whose son worked as a clerk at the Broomfield camp. He confirmed that Danny Padgitt had been moved there in the summer of 1974. When she finished with the story, she said, 'Are you going to expose him?'

I was reeling, but I could already see the story. 'I will investigate,' I said. 'Depends on what I find.'

'Please do. It ain't right. That little punk should be on death row.'

'I agree.'

She swore me to secrecy again, and left her address. She wanted a copy of the paper if we did the story.

AT SIX THE NEXT MORNING Wiley and I drove to Broomfield in his Ford pick-up. At eleven thirty we took our positions along Main Street, near the highway department office building. Since Padgitt would certainly recognise either one of us, we faced the challenge of trying to hide on a busy street in a strange town without acting suspiciously. Wiley sat low in his truck, camera loaded and ready. I hid behind a newspaper on a bench.

At noon a prison vehicle stopped in front of the building. The guard went inside, collected his prisoner, and they walked to lunch.

ON JULY 17, 1977, our front page had four large photos—one of Danny walking along the sidewalk sharing a laugh with the guard, one of them as they entered the City Grill, one of the office building, one of the gate to the Broomfield camp. My headline howled: NO PRISON FOR PADGITT—HE'S OFF AT CAMP.

The story was as venomous and slanted as I could possibly make it. I made a dozen phone calls to the highway department until I found a supervisor who knew something about Padgitt. The supervisor refused to answer questions, and I made him sound like a criminal himself. Penetrating Broomfield camp was just as frustrating. I detailed my efforts and tilted the story so it sounded as though all the bureaucrats were covering up for Padgitt. I called the warden at Parchman, the attorney general, and finally the governor himself. They were all too busy, of course, so I chatted with their bootlickers and made them sound like morons.

Senator Theo Morton appeared to be shocked. He promised to get right to the bottom of it and call me back. At press time, I was still waiting.

The reaction in Clanton was mixed. Many of those who stopped me on the street were angry and wanted something done. They truly believed that when Padgitt had been sentenced to life he would spend the rest of his days in hell at Parchman. But among a few there was the frustrating, almost cynical lack of surprise. They figured the Padgitts had worked their magic once more, found the right pockets, pulled the right strings. Harry Rex was in this camp. 'What's the big fuss, boy? They've bought governors before.'

The photo of Danny walking down the street, free as a bird, frightened Miss Callie considerably. 'She didn't sleep last night,' Esau mumbled to me when I arrived for lunch that Thursday. 'I wish you hadn't found him.'

Fortunately, the Memphis and Jackson newspapers picked up the story, and it took on a life of its own. They turned up the heat to a point where the politicians had to get involved. The governor and Senator Morton were jockeying to lead the parade to get the boy sent back to Parchman.

Two weeks after I broke the story, Danny Padgitt was 'reassigned' to the state penitentiary. The next day, I received two phone calls, one at the office, one at home. Different voices, but with the same message. I was a dead man.

I notified the FBI in Oxford, and two agents visited me in Clanton. For a month, Sheriff McNatt kept a patrol car in front of my office around the clock. Another one sat in my driveway during the night.

After a seven-year hiatus, I was carrying a gun again.

THERE WAS NO immediate bloodshed. As time passed the threats became less ominous. I never stopped carrying a gun, but I found it hard to believe that the Padgitts would risk the severe backlash that would come if they knocked off the editor of the local paper.

They kept to themselves like never before. After the defeat of Sheriff Coley in 1971, they retrenched even deeper into Padgitt Island. They grew their crops and smuggled them off the island in planes, pick-ups and flat-bed trucks ostensibly loaded with timber.

With typical Padgitt shrewdness, and sensing that the marijuana business might become too risky, they began pumping money into legitimate enterprises. They bought a highway contracting company and quickly turned it into a reliable bidder for government projects. Highway construction was a notably corrupt business in Mississippi, and the Padgitts knew how to play the game.

I watched these activities as closely as possible. I knew the names of some of the companies the Padgitts had bought, but it was virtually impossible to keep up with them. And on the surface it all appeared legitimate.

I waited, but for what I wasn't certain. Danny Padgitt would return one day, and when he did he might simply disappear into the island and never be seen again. Or he might do otherwise.

FEW PEOPLE IN CLANTON did not attend church. Those who did seemed to know exactly which ones did not, and once it was known that the owner and editor of the *Times* did not go to church, I became the most famous dropout in town. I decided to do something about it.

Each week Margaret put together our Religion page, which included an extensive menu of churches arranged by denominations, listing reunions, pot-luck suppers, and countless other activities.

Working from this page, I made a list of all the churches in Ford County. The total was eighty-eight, and my goal was to visit each one of them, something I was sure had never been done before.

The denominations were varied and baffling—how could Protestants, all of whom claimed to follow the same basic tenets, get themselves so divided? The county was heavily Baptist, but they were a fractured bunch. The Pentecostals were in second place, and evidently they had fought with themselves as much as the Baptists. There were no Catholics, Episcopalians or Mormons.

In 1974 I'd begun my epic adventure to visit every church in the county at the Calvary Full Gospel, a rowdy Pentecostal assemblage on a gravel road two miles out of town. As advertised, the service began at ten thirty, and I found a spot on the back pew, as far away from the action as I could get. I was greeted warmly and word spread that a bona fide visitor was present. Preacher Bob wore a white suit, navy shirt, white tie, and his thick black hair plastered to his skull. His sermon lasted for fifty-five minutes, and left me exhausted. At times the building shook with folks stomping the floor. Windows rattled as they were overcome with the spirit and yelled upwards. Preacher Bob 'laid hands' on three sick folks suffering vague diseases, and they claimed to be healed.

'Repent!' Preacher Bob shouted, and heads ducked.

Things finally ran out of gas, and two hours after I sat down I bolted from the building. I needed a drink.

I wrote a pleasant little report about my visit to Calvary Full Gospel and ran it on the Religion page. I commented on the warm atmosphere of the church, the lovely solo by Miss Helen Hatcher, the powerful sermon by Preacher Bob, and so on.

Needless to say, this proved to be very popular, and after that I went to church at least twice a month.

During my tour of churches, I heard many preachers chide their followers to return in a few hours to properly complete the observance of the Sabbath. I tried a few Sunday-night services, usually in an effort to catch some colourful ritual such as snake handling or disease healing, but, for the most part, I limited my study of comparative religions to the daylight hours.

Others had different Sunday-night rituals. Harry Rex helped a Mexican named Pepe lease a building and open a restaurant near the square. Pepe's became successful during the 1970s with decent food that was always on the spicy side. Pepe couldn't resist the peppers, regardless of how they scalded the throats of his gringo customers.

On Sundays all alcohol was banned in Ford County. It could not be sold at retail or in restaurants. Pepe had a back room with a long table and a door that would lock. He allowed Harry Rex and his guests to use the room and eat and drink all we wanted. There were usually a dozen of us, all male, all young, about half currently married. Harry Rex threatened our lives if we told anyone about Pepe's back room.

The Clanton city police raided us once, but Pepe suddenly couldn't speak a word of English. The door to the back room was locked, and partially hidden too. Pepe turned off the lights, and for twenty minutes we waited in the dark listening to the cops try to communicate with Pepe. I don't know why we were worried. The city judge was at the end of the table slogging down his fourth or fifth margarita.

Those Sunday nights at Pepe's were often long and rowdy, and afterwards we were in no condition to drive. I would walk to my office and sleep on the sofa. I was there snoring off the tequila one night when the phone rang after midnight. It was a reporter I knew from the big daily in Memphis.

'Are you covering the parole hearing tomorrow?' he asked. Tomorrow? In my toxic fog I had no idea what day it was.

'What parole hearing?' I mumbled, trying desperately to wake myself up and put two thoughts together.

'Danny Padgitt's. It's scheduled for ten a.m. at Parchman.'

'You gotta be kidding!'

'Nope. I just found out. Evidently, they don't advertise these.'

I sat in the darkness for a long time, cursing once again the backwardness of a state that conducted such important matters in such ridiculous ways. How could parole even be considered for Danny Padgitt? Eight years had passed since the murder and his conviction. He had received two life sentences of at least ten years each. We assumed that meant a minimum of twenty years.

I drove home at around 3 a.m., slept fitfully, and at eight o'clock jumped in my car with a cup of cold coffee, headed for Parchman.

AN HOUR WEST of Ford County the land flattened dramatically and the Delta began. It was a region rich in farming and poor in living conditions, but I was in no mood to take in the sights. I was too nervous about crashing a clandestine parole hearing.

Before setting off I had called up Harry Rex. He told me that for an inmate with a few connections and some cash, the parole system was a marvellous labyrinth of contradictory laws that allowed the Parole Board to pass out favours. Somewhere between the judicial system, the penal system and the parole system, Danny Padgitt's two 'consecutive' life terms must have been changed to two 'concurrent' sentences, he explained.

After two hours, I saw fences next to fields, then razor wire. Soon I was turning into the main gate. I informed a guard in the booth that I was a reporter, there for a parole hearing. 'Straight ahead, left at the second building,' he said helpfully as he wrote down my name.

There was a cluster of buildings close to the highway, and a row of white-frame houses. I sprinted inside the building, looking for the first secretary. I found her, and she sent me to the first floor. It was just about ten.

There were people at the end of the hallway, loitering outside a room. One was a prison guard, one was a state trooper.

'I'm here for a parole hearing,' I announced.

'In there,' the guard said, pointing. Without knocking, I yanked open the door, as any intrepid reporter would, and stepped inside.

There were five members of the Parole Board, and they were seated behind a slightly elevated table with their name plates in front of them. Along one wall another table held the Padgitt crowd—Danny, his father, his mother, an uncle and Lucien Wilbanks. Opposite them, behind another table, were various clerks and functionaries.

Everyone stared at me as I stormed in. My eyes locked onto Danny Padgitt's, and for a second both of us managed to convey the contempt we felt for the other.

'Can I help you?' a large ole boy growled from the centre of the Board. His name was Barrett Ray Jeter, the chairman. Like the other four, he'd been appointed by the governor as a reward for vote-gathering.

'I'm here for the Padgitt hearing,' I said.

'He's a reporter!' Lucien yelled, and for a second I thought I might get arrested on the spot and carried deeper into the prison.

'Your name?' Jeter demanded.

'Willie Traynor of *The Ford County Times*,' I said, glaring at Lucien.

'This is a closed hearing, Mr Traynor,' Jeter said.

'Who has the right to attend?' I asked.

'The Parole Board, the parolee, his family, his witnesses, his lawyer, and any witnesses for the other side.' The 'other side' meant the victim's family, which in this setting sounded like the bad guys.

By process of elimination, I quickly deduced that I had to become a witness if I wanted to watch the show. 'Well, since there's no one else here from Ford County in opposition, I'm a witness.'

'You can't be a reporter and a witness,' Jeter said.

'Where is that written in the Mississippi Code?' I asked.

Jeter nodded at a young man in a dark suit. 'I'm the attorney for the Parole Board,' he said politely. 'You can testify in this hearing, Mr Traynor, but you cannot report it.'

I planned to report the hearing in full then hide behind the First Amendment. 'So be it,' I said. 'You guys make the rules.' The lines had been drawn; I was on one side, everybody else was on the other.

'Let's proceed,' Jeter said, and I took a seat.

The attorney for the Parole Board passed out a report. He recited the basics of the Padgitt sentence, and was careful not to use the words 'consecutive' or 'concurrent'. Based on the inmate's 'exemplary' record during his incarceration, he had qualified for 'good time', so after subtracting the time the inmate spent in the county jail awaiting trial, he was now eligible for parole.

Danny's caseworker ploughed through a lengthy narrative of her relationship with the inmate. She concluded with the gratuitous opinion that he was 'fully remorseful', 'fully rehabilitated', 'no threat whatsoever to society', even ready to become a 'productive citizen'.

How much did all this cost? I couldn't help but wonder. And how long had it taken for the Padgitts to find the right pockets?

Lucien went next. With no one—Gaddis, Sheriff McNatt . . . not even poor Hank Hooten—to contradict him, he launched into a fictional recounting of the facts of the crimes, and in particular the testimony of an 'airtight' alibi witness, Lydia Vince. His reconstructed version of the trial had the jury waivering on a verdict of not guilty. He carped on about how unfair the trial had been. When he finally shut up two of the board members appeared to be asleep.

Danny went last and did a good job of walking the fine line between denying his crimes and showing remorse for them.

'I have learned from my mistakes,' he said, as if rape and murder were simple indiscretions where no one really got hurt. 'I have grown from them.'

In prison he had been a veritable whirlwind of positive energy—volunteering in the library, singing in the choir, helping with the rodeo, organising teams to go into schools and scare kids away from crime. Danny closed with an impassioned plea for his release.

'How many witnesses in opposition?' Jeter announced. I stood, looked around me, then said, 'I guess it's just me.'

'Proceed, Mr Traynor.'

I had no idea what to say, nor did I know what was permissible or objectionable in such a forum. But based on what I had just sat through, I figured I could say anything I damned well pleased.

I looked up at the Board members and jumped into an extremely graphic description of the rape and the murder. I unloaded everything I could possibly remember, and I put special emphasis on the fact that the two children witnessed some or all of the attack.

I kept waiting for Lucien to object, but there was nothing but silence in their camp. I described the wounds. I painted the heart-breaking scene of Rhoda dying in the arms of Mr Deece, and saying, 'It was Danny Padgitt. It was Danny Padgitt.'

I called Lucien a liar and mocked his memory of the trial. It took the jury less than an hour to find the defendant guilty, I explained.

And with a recollection that surprised even me, I recounted Danny's pathetic performance on the witness stand: his lying to cover up his lies; his total lack of truthfulness. 'He should've been indicted for perjury,' I told the Board. 'And when he had finished testifying, instead of returning to his seat, he walked to the jury box, shook his finger in the faces of the jurors, and said, "You convict me, and I'll get every damned one of you."'

A Board member named Mr Horace Adler jerked upright in his seat and blurted towards the Padgitts, 'Is that true?'

'It's in the record,' I said quickly before Lucien had the chance to lie again. He was slowly getting to his feet.

'Is that true, Mr Wilbanks?' Adler insisted.

'I have the transcript,' I said. 'I'll be happy to send it to you.'

'Is that true?' Adler asked for the third time.

'There were three hundred people in the courtroom,' I said, staring at Lucien and saying with my eyes, Don't do it. Don't lie about it.

Lucien was standing and trying to think of a response. Everyone was waiting. Finally, 'I don't remember everything that was said,' he began, and I snorted loudly. 'Perhaps my client did say something to that effect, but it was an emotional moment, and taken in context—'

'Context my ass!' I yelled at Lucien and took a step towards him as if I might throw a punch. A guard stepped towards me and I stopped. 'It's all in the trial transcript!' I said angrily. Then I turned to the Board and said, 'How can you sit there and let them lie like this?'

'Anything else, Mr Traynor?' Jeter asked.

'Yes! I hope this Board will not make a mockery out of our system and let this man go free after eight years. He's lucky to be sitting here instead of on death row, where he belongs. And I hope that the next time you have a hearing on his parole, you will invite some of the good folks from Ford County. Perhaps the sheriff or the prosecutor. And could you notify members of the victim's family? They have the right to be here so you can see their faces when you turn this murderer loose.'

I sat down and glared at Lucien Wilbanks. I decided that I would work diligently to hate him for the rest of either his life or mine, whichever ended first. Jeter announced a brief recess, and I assumed they needed time to regroup in a back room. Perhaps Mr Padgitt could be summoned to provide some extra cash for a Board member or two.

We waited thirty minutes before they filed back in. Jeter called for a vote. Two voted in favour of parole, two against, one abstained. 'Parole is denied at this time,' Jeter announced, and Mrs Padgitt burst into tears. She hugged Danny before they took him away.

Lucien and the Padgitts walked by, very close to me as they left the room. I ignored them and just stared at the floor, exhausted, hung over, shocked at the denial.

THE PAROLE HEARING was front-page news in *The Ford County Times*. I loaded the report with every detail I could remember, and on page five let loose with a blistering editorial about the process. I sent a copy to each member of the Parole Board and to its attorney, and, because I was so worked up, every member of the state legislature. Most ignored it, but the attorney for the Parole Board did not.

He wrote me a lengthy letter in which he said he was deeply concerned about my 'wilful violation of Parole Board procedures.' My lawyer, Harry Rex, assured me the Parole Board's policy of secret meetings was patently unconstitutional, in clear violation of the First Amendment, and he would happily defend me in federal court. For a reduced hourly rate, of course. I swapped heated letters with the Board's lawyer for a month before he seemed to lose interest in pursuing me.

Rafe, Harry Rex's chief ambulance chaser, had a sidekick named Buster, a large, thick-chested cowboy with a gun in every pocket. I hired Buster for $100 a week to pretend he was my own personal legbreaker. For a few hours a day he would hang around the front of the office, or sit in my driveway so folks would know that Willie Traynor was important enough to have a bodyguard. If the Padgitts got close enough to take a shot, they would at least get something in return.

AFTER YEARS of steadily gaining weight and ignoring the warnings of her doctors, Miss Callie finally relented. After a visit to her clinic, she announced to Esau that she was going on a diet—1,500 calories a day, except, mercifully, Thursday. A month passed and I couldn't discern any loss of weight. But the day after the *Times* story on the parole hearing, she suddenly looked as though she'd lost fifty pounds.

Instead of frying a chicken, she baked one. Instead of whipping mashed potatoes with butter and cream, she boiled them. It was still delicious, but I'd become accustomed to my weekly dose of grease.

After the prayer, I handed her two letters from Sam. As always, she read them immediately while I jumped into the lunch. And as always, she smiled and wiped a tear. 'He's doing fine,' she said, and he was.

With typical Ruffin tenacity, Sam had completed his first college degree, in economics, and was saving for law school. But he was terribly homesick. He missed his momma. And her cooking.

President Carter had pardoned the draft dodgers and Sam was wrestling with the decision to stay in Canada, or come home. Many of his expatriate friends up there were vowing to stay and pursue Canadian citizenship, and he was heavily influenced by them. There was also a woman involved, though he had not told his parents.

Sometimes we began with the news, but often it was the obituaries or even the classifieds. Since she read every word, Miss Callie knew who was selling a new litter of beagles and who wanted to buy a good used riding mower.

She loved the legal notices, one of the most lucrative sections of the paper. Deeds, foreclosures, divorce filings, probate matters, bankruptcy announcements, dozens of legal notices were required by law to be published in the county paper. We got them all.

'I see Mr Everett Wainwright's estate is being probated,' she said.

'I vaguely remember his obituary,' I said with a mouthful. 'Did you know him?'

'He owned a grocery store for many years.' I could tell by the inflection in her voice that she did not care for Mr Wainwright.

'Good guy or bad buy?'

'He had two sets of prices, one for the whites, a higher one for Negroes. His goods were never marked in any way, and he was the only cashier. A white customer would call out, "Say, Mr Wainwright, how much is this can of condensed milk?" and he'd holler back, "Thirty-eight cents." A minute later I would say, "Pardon me, Mr Wainwright, but how much is this can of condensed milk?" And he'd snap, "Fifty-four cents." He was very open about it. He didn't care.'

For almost nine years I'd heard stories of the old days. At times I thought I'd heard them all, but Miss Callie's collection was endless.

'Why did you shop there?'

'It was the only store where we could shop. Is it true Mr Wainwright left all his money to the Methodist church?' she asked.

'That's the rumour.'

'Folks say he was trying to buy his way into heaven,' she said, nudging the conversation once again to the topic of the afterlife. Miss Callie was deeply concerned about my soul. She was worried that I had not properly become a Christian; that I had not been 'born again' or 'saved'. My infant baptism was insufficient in her view. Once a person reaches a certain age, the 'age of accountability', then, in order to be 'saved' from everlasting damnation, that person must walk down the aisle of a church and make a public profession of faith.

Miss Callie carried a heavy burden because I had not done this, but she was convinced that one day soon the Lord would reach down and touch my heart. I would decide to follow him, and she and I would spend eternity together. Miss Callie was truly living for the day when she 'went Home to glory'.

CHAPTER 10

Big news hit Clanton in the spring of 1978. Bargain City was coming! Bargain City was a national chain rapidly marching through the small towns of the south. Most of the town rejoiced. Some of us, though, felt it was the beginning of the end.

The company was taking over the world with its 'big box' discount warehouses that offered everything at low prices. The stores were spacious and clean and included cafés, pharmacies, banks, even travel agents. A small town without a Bargain City store was irrelevant and insignificant. They optioned fifty acres on Market Street, about a mile from the Clanton square. Some of the neighbours protested, and the city council held a public hearing on whether to allow the store to be built.

The council room was packed with people holding red and white Bargain City signs: BARGAIN CITY—A GOOD NEIGHBOUR and WE WANT JOBS. The company mouthpiece painted a rosy picture of economic growth, sales tax revenues, 150 jobs for the locals, and the best products at the lowest prices.

Mrs Dorothy Hockett spoke in opposition. Her property was adjacent to the site and she did not want the invasion of noise and lights. The city council seemed sympathetic, but the vote had long since been decided. When no one else would speak against Bargain City, I stood and walked to the podium.

I was driven by a belief that to preserve the downtown area of Clanton we had to protect the stores and shops, cafés and offices around the square. Most of the jobs they were promising would be at minimum wage. The increase in sales tax revenues to the city would be at the expense of the merchants Bargain City would quickly drive out of business. I mentioned the town of Titus, about an hour south of Clanton. Two years earlier, Bargain City opened there. Since then, fourteen retail stores and one café had closed. Main Street was almost deserted.

I handed the mayor a study by an economics professor at the University of Georgia. He had tracked Bargain City across the south for the previous six years and evaluated the financial and social impact the company had on small towns. The study concluded that Bargain City was economically devastating for most small towns. And the real damage was cultural. With boarded-up stores and empty sidewalks, the rich town life of main streets and courthouse squares was quickly dying.

A petition in support of Bargain City had 480 names. Our petition in opposition had 12. The council voted unanimously, 5–0, to approve it.

I wrote a harsh editorial and for a month read nasty letters addressed to me. For the first time, I was called a 'tree-hugger'.

Within a month, the bulldozers had completely razed fifty acres. The kerbs and gutters were in, and a grand opening was announced for December 1, just in time for Christmas. I could not deny advertising to Bargain City. So in mid-November, I met with a representative of the company and we laid out a series of ads for the opening. I charged them as much as possible; they never complained.

On December 1, Senator Morton cut the ribbon. A rowdy mob burst through the doors and began shopping as if the hungry had found food. I buried the story on page seven, and this angered Senator Morton, who expected his ribbon cutting to be front and centre.

That Christmas season was brutal for the downtown merchants. Three days after Christmas, the first casualty was reported when the old Western Auto store announced it was closing. It had occupied the same building for forty years, selling bicycles and appliances and televisions. Mr Hollis Barr, the owner, told me that a certain Zenith colour TV cost him $438, and he was trying to sell it for $510. The identical model was for sale at Bargain City for $399.

The closing of Western Auto was, of course, front-page news.

It was followed in January by the closing of Swain's pharmacy next to the Tea Shoppe, and then Maggie's Gifts. I treated each closing as if it were a death, and my stories had the air of obituaries.

I spent one afternoon with the Stukes twins in their hardware store. It was a wonderful old building, with dusty wooden floors, sagging shelves that held a million items, a wood-burning stove in the back where serious things got debated when business was slow. We had plenty of time to talk that cold winter day because there were almost no customers in the store. Business was down 70 per cent.

The following month they closed the doors to the store their father had opened in 1922. On the front page, I ran a photo of the founder sitting behind the counter. I also fired off an editorial, sort of an 'I-told-you-so' reminder to whoever was still reading my little tirades.

'You're preachin' too much,' Harry Rex warned me over and over. 'And nobody's listenin'.'

THE FRONT OFFICE of the *Times* was seldom attended. There were some tables with copies of the current edition strewn about. There was a counter that Margaret sometimes used to lay out ads. The bell on the front door rang all day long as people came and went. Occasionally a stranger would venture upstairs to my office.

I looked up one afternoon in March 1979 and there was a gentleman in a nice suit standing at my office door. His name was Gary McGrew, a consultant from Nashville, whose area of expertise was small-town newspapers. As I fixed a pot of coffee, he explained that a client of his was planning to buy several newspapers in Mississippi. Because I had 7,000 subscribers, no debt, an offset press, and because we now ran the printing for six smaller weeklies, his client was very interested in buying *The Ford County Times*.

'How interested?' I asked.

'Extremely. If we could look at the books, we could value your company.'

He left and I made a few phone calls to verify his credibility. He checked out fine, and I collected my current financials. Three days later we met again, this time at night. I did not want Wiley or Baggy or anyone else hanging around. News that the *Times* was changing hands would be hot gossip.

McGrew crunched the numbers like a seasoned analyst. I waited, oddly nervous, as if the verdict might drastically change my life.

'You're clearing a hundred grand after taxes, plus you're taking a salary of fifty grand. Depreciation is another twenty, no interest because you have no debt. That's one-seventy in cash flow, times the standard multiple of six, comes to one million twenty thousand.'

'And the building?' I asked.

He glanced around as if the ceiling might collapse any moment. 'These places typically don't sell for much.'

'A hundred thousand,' I said.

'OK. And a hundred thousand for the press. The total value is somewhere in the neighbourhood of one-point-two million.'

'Is that an offer?' I asked, even more anxious.

'It might be. I'll have to discuss it with my client.'

I had no intention of selling the *Times*. I had stumbled into the business, got a few lucky breaks, worked hard, and now, nine years later, my little company was worth over a million dollars.

I was young, still single though I was tired of being lonely and living alone. I had accepted the reality that I would not find a bride in Ford County. All the good ones were snatched up by their twentieth birthday, and I was too old to compete at that level. I dated all the young divorcées, most of whom were quick to hop in the sack and wake up in my fine home, and dream about spending all the money I was rumoured to be making.

But it's funny what a million bucks will do to you. Once it was in play, it was never far from my thoughts. The job became more tedious. I grew to resent the pressure of the deadlines. I told myself that I no longer had to hustle the street selling ads.

A week later, I told Gary McGrew that the *Times* was not for sale. He said his client had decided to buy three papers by the end of the year, so I had time to think about it.

Remarkably, word of our discussions never leaked.

ON A THURSDAY AFTERNOON in early May, I received a phone call from the attorney for the Parole Board. The next Padgitt hearing would take place the following Monday, but I would not be permitted to attend the hearing. 'You violated our rules last time by reporting on what happened,' he told me.

'I'm banned?'

'That's correct.'

'I'll be there anyway.'

I hung up and called Sheriff McNatt. He, too, had been notified of the hearing, but wasn't sure if he could attend. He was hot on the trail of a missing child (from Wisconsin), and it was obvious he had little interest in getting mixed up with the Padgitts.

Our district attorney since Ernie Gaddis's retirement was Rufus Buckley. He had an armed robbery trial scheduled for Monday in Van Buren County. Circuit Judge Omar Noose was presiding over the same trial, so he was off the hook. I began to think that no one would be there to speak in opposition to Padgitt's release.

I walked over to Harry Rex's with the news. He had an ugly divorce trial starting on Monday in Tupelo; otherwise he might have gone with me to Parchman. 'The boy's gonna be released, Willie,' he said. 'Once the parole hearings start, it's just a matter of time.'

'But somebody has to fight it.'

'Why bother? He's gettin' out eventually. Why piss off the Padgitts? You won't get any volunteers.'

Volunteers were indeed hard to find as the entire town ducked for cover. I had envisioned an angry mob packing into the parole board hearing and disrupting the meeting. My angry mob consisted of three people. Wiley Meek agreed to ride over with me, though he had no interest in speaking. If they were serious about banning me from the room, Wiley would sit through it and give me the details. Sheriff McNatt surprised us with his presence.

Security was tight in the hall outside the hearing room. When the Board attorney saw me he became angry and we exchanged words. Guards in uniform surrounded me and I was escorted from the building and placed in my car, then watched by two thick-necked ruffians.

According to Wiley, the hearing went like clockwork. Lucien was there with various Padgitts. The Board attorney read a staff report that made Danny sound like an Eagle Scout. Lucien spoke for ten minutes, the usual lawyerly bullshit. Danny's father pleaded emotionally for his son's release. He was desperately needed back home, where the family had interests in timber, gravel, asphalt, trucking, contracting and freight. He would have to work so many hours each week that he couldn't possibly get into more trouble.

Sheriff McNatt gamely stood up for the people of Ford County. He was nervous and not a good speaker, but did a credible job of replaying the crime.

By a vote of 4–1, Danny Padgitt was paroled from prison.

CLANTON WAS QUIETLY disappointed. During the trial, the town had a real thirst for blood and was bitter when the jury didn't deliver the death penalty. But nine years had passed, and since the parole hearing it had been accepted that Danny Padgitt would eventually get out. No one expected it so soon, but after the hearing we were over the shock.

His release was influenced by two unusual factors. The first was that Rhoda Kassellaw had lived a lonely life and had no family in the area. There were no grieving parents to arouse sympathy and demand justice. Her children were gone and forgotten.

The second was that the Padgitts lived in another world. They were so rarely seen in public, it was not difficult to convince ourselves that Danny would simply go to the island and never be seen again. In my editorial about his release, I said 'a cold-blooded killer is once more among us'. But that wasn't really true.

The front-page story and the editorial drew not a single letter from the public. Folks talked about the release, but not for long.

Baggy eased into my office late one morning a week after Padgitt's release, and closed the door, always a good sign. He'd picked up some gossip so juicy that it had to be delivered with the door shut.

He glanced around as if the walls were bugged, then said, 'It cost the Padgitts a hundred grand to spring the boy.'

'No,' I said. This always spurred him to tell more.

'That's what I'm tellin' you,' he said smugly.

'Who got the money?'

'That's the good part. You won't believe it.'

'Who?'

'You'll be shocked.'

'Are you gonna tell me or not?'

'Theo.'

'Senator Morton?'

'That's what I'm tellin' you.'

I was sufficiently shocked, and I had to give the impression of being so or the story would lose steam. 'Theo?' I asked.

'He's vice-chairman of the Corrections Committee in the Senate. Knows how to pull the strings. He wanted a hundred grand, the Padgitts wanted to pay it, they cut a deal, the boy walks.'

'I thought Theo was above taking bribes,' I said, and I was serious. This drew an exaggerated snort.

'Don't be so naive,' he said. Again, he knew everything.

'Where did you hear it?'

'Can't say.' There was a chance that his poker gang had cooked up the rumour to see how fast it would race around the square before it got back to them. But there was an equally good chance Baggy was onto something. It really didn't matter, though. Cash couldn't be traced.

ELEVEN YEARS after he fled Ford County, Sam Ruffin returned in much the same manner as he left—on a bus in the middle of the night. I arrived for my Thursday lunch and there sat Sam, rocking on the verandah, with a smile as wide as his mother's. Miss Callie fried a chicken and cooked every vegetable in her garden. Esau joined us and we feasted for three hours.

Sam now had one college degree under his belt and was planning on law school. He had almost married a Canadian woman but things blew up over her family's heated opposition to the union.

He planned to stay in Clanton for a few days, venturing out of Lowtown only at night. I promised to fish around and see what I could learn about Trooper Durant. From the legal notices we printed, I knew that he had remarried, then divorced a second time.

Sam wanted to see the town, so late that afternoon I picked him up in my Spitfire. Hiding under a baseball cap, he took in the sights of the town he still called home. I showed him my office, my house, Bargain City, and the sprawl west of town. We circled the courthouse and I told him the story of the sniper and Baggy's dramatic escape.

As I dropped him off, he said, 'Is Padgitt really out of prison?'

'No one's seen him,' I said. 'But I'm sure he's back home.'

'Do you expect trouble?'

'No, not really.'

'Neither do I. But I can't convince Momma.'

'Nothing will happen, Sam.'

THE SINGLE SHOT that killed Lenny Fargarson, the crippled boy, was fired from a 30.06 hunting rifle. The killer could have been as far as 200 yards away from the front porch where Lenny died. He lived with his parents on a gravel road two miles outside Dumas. Thick woods began just beyond the wide lawn round the house, and there was a good chance whoever pulled the trigger had climbed a tree and had a perfectly concealed view of poor Lenny, whose affliction had recently confined him to a wheelchair.

No one heard the shot. Lenny was sitting on the verandah, in his wheelchair, reading a book. His father, a rural mail carrier, was out delivering mail. His mother was shopping at Bargain City. In all like-lihood, Lenny felt no pain and died instantly. The bullet entered the right side of his head, just over the jaw, and created a massive exit wound above his left ear. When his mother found him, he'd been dead for some time. She somehow managed to control herself and refrain from touching his body or the scene. Blood was all over the porch, even dripping onto the front steps.

Wiley heard the report on the police scanner he had installed in his home. He called me with the chilling announcement, 'It's begun. Fargarson, the crippled boy, is dead.'

Wiley swung by the office, I jumped in his pick-up, and we were off to the crime scene. Neither of us said a word.

Lenny was still on the porch. The shot had knocked him out of his wheelchair and he lay on his side, with his face towards the house. Sheriff McNatt asked us not to take photos, and we readily complied. The paper would not have used them anyway.

When the body was finally loaded onto a gurney and placed in an ambulance, Sheriff McNatt came over and leaned on the pick-up next to me. 'Are you thinkin' what I'm thinkin'?' he said.

'Yep.'

'Can you find me a list of the jurors?'

Though we had never printed the names of the jurors, I had the information in an old file. 'Sure,' I said. 'What's your plan?'

'We gotta notify those folks.'

As we were leaving, the deputies were beginning to comb the thick woods around the Fargarson home.

I TOOK THE LIST to the sheriff's office, and we looked over it together. In 1977, I had written the obituary for Mr Fred Bilroy, a retired forest ranger who died of pneumonia. As far as I knew, the other ten were still alive.

McNatt gave the list to his deputies, who dispersed to deliver news no one wanted to hear. I volunteered to tell Callie Ruffin.

She was on the verandah watching Esau and Sam wage war over a game of checkers. They were delighted to see me, but the mood quickly changed. 'I have some disturbing news, Miss Callie,' I said sombrely. 'Lenny Fargarson, that crippled boy on the jury with you, was murdered this afternoon.'

She covered her mouth and fell into her rocker. Sam steadied her, then patted her shoulder. I gave a brief description of what happened.

'He was such a good Christian boy,' Miss Callie said. She wasn't crying, but she was on the verge. Esau went to fetch her a blood pressure pill. He and Sam sat beside her rocker while I sat in the swing. For a long time little was said. Miss Callie lapsed into a long, brooding spell. Fargarson's death truly saddened her, but it was also terrifying.

Esau fixed sweet tea with lemon, and when he returned from the inside of the house he quietly slid a double-barrelled shotgun behind the rocker, within his reach but out of her sight.

It was a warm spring night, under a half-moon, and Lowtown was busy with kids on bikes, neighbours talking across fences, a rowdy basketball game under way down the street.

As the hours passed, the foot traffic thinned and the neighbours withdrew. I decided that if Miss Callie stayed at home she would be a very difficult target. I didn't mention this, but I'm sure Sam and Esau were having the same thoughts. When she was ready for bed, I said my good nights and drove back to the jail. It was crawling with deputies, and had the carnival-like atmosphere that only a good murder could bring.

Just two of the jurors had not been found. Both had moved, and Sheriff McNatt was trying to track them down. He asked about Miss Callie and I said she was safe. I did not tell him Sam was home.

He closed the door to his office and said he had a favour to ask. 'Tomorrow, can you go talk to Lucien Wilbanks? Take Harry Rex with you, seeing as he's the only one round here that still talks to Lucien. See if he will act as go-between to the Padgitts. Feel him out. If it goes well, then maybe I'll talk to him. It's different if the sheriff goes bargin' in at first.'

'I'd rather be lashed with a bullwhip,' I said, and I wasn't joking.

'But you'll do it?'

'I'll sleep on it.'

HARRY REX wasn't too thrilled with the idea either, but nevertheless at around eight thirty the next morning we walked into the Wilbanks Building, two doors down from the coffee shop.

Ethel Twitty, the long-time secretary, greeted us rudely, almost sneering at Harry Rex, who mumbled under his breath, 'Meanest bitch in town.' I think she heard him. It was obvious they had been catfighting for many years. Her boss was in. What did we want?

'We want to see Lucien,' Harry Rex said.'Why else would we be here?' She rang him up as we waited. 'I don't have all day!' Harry Rex snapped at her at one point.

'Go ahead,' she said, more to get rid of us than anything else. We climbed the steps. Lucien's office was huge, with ten-foot ceilings and a row of French doors overlooking the square, directly across from the *Times*, although thankfully I couldn't see Lucien's balcony from my verandah.

He greeted us indifferently, as if we had interrupted a long serious meditation. Though it was early, his cluttered desk gave the impression of a man who'd worked all night. He had long greyish hair that ran down his neck, and an unfashionable goatee, and the tired red eyes of a serious drinker. 'What's the occasion?' he asked. We glared at each other, both conveying as much contempt as possible.

'Had a murder yesterday, Lucien,' Harry Rex said. 'Lenny Fargarson, that crippled boy on the jury.'

'I'm assuming this is off the record,' he said in my direction.

'It is,' I said. 'Completely. Sheriff McNatt asked me to stop by and say hello. I invited Harry Rex.'

'So we're just socialising?'

'Have you talked to Danny Padgitt lately?' Harry Rex asked.

'Not since he was paroled.'

'Is he in the county?'

'He's in the state, I'm not sure exactly where. If he crosses the state line without permission he violates the conditions of his parole.'

'Sheriff McNatt would like to talk to him,' I said.

'Oh would he? Why should that concern you and me? Tell the sheriff to go talk to him.'

'It's not that simple, Lucien, and you know it,' Harry Rex said.

'Does the sheriff have any proof against my client? Any evidence? You can't just round up the usual suspects, you know.'

'There was a direct threat against the jurors,' I said.

'Nine years ago.'

'It was still a threat, and we all remember it. Now, two weeks after he's paroled, one of his jurors is dead.'

'That's not enough, fellas. Show me more and I might consult with my client. Right now there's nothing but naked speculation.'

'You don't know where he is, do you, Lucien?' Harry Rex said.

'I assume he's on the island, with the rest of them.' He used the word 'them' as if they were a bunch of rats.

'What happens if another juror gets shot?' Harry Rex pressed on.

Lucien dropped a legal pad on his desk and rested there on his elbows. 'What am I supposed to do, Harry Rex? Call the boy up, say "Hey, Danny, I'm sure you're not killin' your jurors, but, if by chance you are, then be a good boy and stop it." You think he'll listen to me?'

'What happens if another juror gets shot?' Harry Rex repeated.

'Then I guess another juror will die.'

· I jumped to my feet and headed for the door. 'You're a sick bastard,' I said.

'Not a word of this in print,' he snarled behind me.

'Go to hell,' I yelled as I slammed his door.

AFTER WORK that evening I stopped by Pepe's and bought an array of Mexican carry-out, then drove to Lowtown, where I found Sam playing basketball, Miss Callie asleep inside, and Esau guarding the house with his shotgun. Eventually, we ate on the verandah, though she only nibbled at the foreign food. She wasn't hungry. Esau said she'd eaten little during the day.

I brought my backgammon board and taught Sam the game. Esau preferred checkers. Miss Callie was certain any activity that involved the rolling of dice was patently sinful, but she wasn't up to a lecture.

Buster, my part-time pit bull, drove by every half-hour. He would slow in front of the Ruffins', I'd wave as if things were fine, he'd return to the Hocutt House. A patrol car was parked two doors down from the Ruffin house. Sheriff McNatt had hired three black deputies, and two of them had been assigned to keep an eye on the home.

Others were watching as well. After Miss Callie went to bed, Esau pointed across the street to the darkened screened verandah where the Braxtons lived. 'Tully's over there,' he said. 'Watchin' everythin'.'

I left after eleven, crossed the tracks, and drove the empty streets of Clanton. The town pulsed with tension, with anticipation, because whatever had been started was far from over.

MISS CALLIE insisted on attending the funeral of Lenny Fargarson. Sam and Esau objected strenuously, but, as always, once she made up her mind, then all conversations were over.

I called Pastor Cooper of the Maranatha Primitive Baptist Church, where the funeral was to be held, to forewarn him. His response was, 'She will be very welcome in our little church. But get here early.'

With rare exceptions blacks and whites did not worship together in Ford County. They fervently believed in the same Lord, but chose very different styles of worshipping him. The majority of whites expected to be outside the church building at five past noon on Sunday, and seated for lunch by twelve thirty. Blacks really didn't care what time the service broke up, or what time it began for that matter. Several congregations simply went on all day, with a short break for lunch in the fellowship hall, then back to the sanctuary for another round. Such zealotry would have killed a white Christian.

But funerals were different. When Miss Callie, along with Sam and Esau, walked into the Maranatha Primitive Baptist Church, there were a few quick stares but nothing more. Had they walked in on a Sunday morning for regular worship, there would have been resentment.

We arrived forty-five minutes early, and the little church was almost filled. I watched through the tall open windows as the cars kept coming. A loudspeaker had been hung from one of the ancient oaks and a large crowd gathered round it after the building was full. The choir started with 'The Old Rugged Cross', and the tears began flowing. Pastor Cooper's soothing message was a gentle warning for us not to question why bad things happen to good people. God is always in control, and though we are too small to understand His infinite wisdom and majesty, He will one day reveal Himself to us. Lenny was with Him now, and that was where Lenny longed to be.

They buried him behind the church, in an immaculate little cemetery inside a wrought-iron fence. Miss Callie clutched my hand and prayed fervently when the casket was lowered into the ground. There was punch and cookies in the fellowship hall and most of the crowd hung around to have one last word with Mr and Mrs Fargarson. The horror of finding her son with half his head blown off had reduced Mrs Fargarson to a shuddering ghost.

Sheriff McNatt caught my attention and nodded as if he wanted to talk. We walked to the front of the church where no one could hear us. 'Any luck with Wilbanks?' he asked.

'No,' I said. 'Harry Rex went back yesterday and got nowhere.'

'I guess I'll talk to him,' he said.

'You can, but you won't get anywhere.'

'We got nothin' else. We've combed the woods around the house, not a track or a trace of anything.'

'So your only evidence is a single bullet.'

'That and a dead body.'

'Has anybody seen Danny Padgitt?'

'Not yet. I keep two cars up on 401, where it turns onto the island. They can't see everything, but at least the Padgitts know we're there.'

The Ruffins were slowly moving towards us, talking to one of the black deputies.

'She's probably the safest one,' McNatt said.

'Is anybody safe?'

'We'll find out. He'll try again, Willie, you mark my word. I'm convinced of it.'

'Me too.'

NED RAY ZOOK owned 4,000 acres in the eastern part of the county. He farmed cotton and soya beans, and his operations were large enough to maintain sufficient profits. Sometime during the early hours of June 14, a vandal entered Zook's equipment shed and partially drained the oil from the engines of two of his tractors. The oil was collected in cans and hidden among the supplies, so when the operators arrived at around 6 a.m. for the day's work there was no sign of foul play. One operator checked the oil as he was supposed to do, saw the shortage and added four quarts. The other operator had checked his the afternoon before, as was his habit, so when his tractor ground to a sudden halt an hour later, its operator had to hike back to the shed and report the breakdown to the farm manager.

Two hours later, a service truck bounced along the field road and manoeuvred itself close to the disabled tractor. Two servicemen got out, walked round the tractor for an initial look, then began removing tools and wrenches from the truck. The sun baked them and they were soon sweating. To make their day somewhat more pleasant, they turned on the radio in their truck and cranked up the volume.

The music muffled the crack of a distant rifle shot. It hit Mo Teale directly in the upper back, ripped through his lungs, and tore a hole in his chest as it exited. Teale's partner, Red, said over and over that the only thing he heard was a fierce grunt just a second or two before Mo fell under the front axle. He thought at first that something from the tractor had snapped loose and injured Mo. Red dragged him to the truck and raced away, much more concerned about his buddy than what might have injured him. At the equipment shed, the farm manager called an ambulance, but it was too late. Mo Teale died there, on the concrete floor of a small, dusty office. 'Mr John Deere' we'd called him during the trial.

McNatt's men found the cans of oil that had been drained by the vandal, and they found a window that had been prised open for entry into the shed. They would dust for fingerprints and find none. They would look for footprints on the gravel flooring, and find none. In the dirt beside the tractor they did find the 30.06 shell, and it was quickly matched with the one that killed Lenny Fargarson.

I HUNG AROUND the sheriff's office until well after dark. Deputies and constables loitered about, comparing stories, creating new details. The phones rang nonstop. McNatt barricaded himself in his office with his top boys and tried to decide what to do next. His priority was the protection of the surviving eight jurors. Three were already dead—Mr Fred Bilroy (of pneumonia), and now Lenny Fargarson and Mo Teale. One juror had moved to Florida. At that moment, each of the eight had a patrol car parked very near their front doors.

I left and went to the office to work on the story about the murder of Mo Teale, but I was sidetracked by the lights at Harry Rex's. He was in his conference room, knee-deep in depositions. We grabbed two beers out of his small office refrigerator and went for a drive.

In a working-class section of town known as Coventry we drove along a narrow street and passed a house with cars parked like fallen dominoes in the front yard. 'That's where Maxine Root lives,' he said. 'She was on the jury.'

I vaguely remembered Mrs Root. Her neighbours were scattered around the carport in folding lawn chairs. Rifles were visible. Every light in the house was on. A patrol car was parked by the mailbox, two deputies leaning on its hood, watching us very closely as we drove by. Harry Rex stopped and said, 'Evenin', Troy,' to one of the deputies.

'Hey, Harry Rex,' Troy said, taking a step towards us.

'Quite a party they got goin', huh?'

'Better keep movin',' Troy said. 'They got itchy fingers.'

'Take care.' We eased away and swung over to Lowtown, where Miss Callie was no less defended. The street in front of her house was packed with cars and barely passable. Groups of men sat on the cars, some smoking, some holding rifles. Across the street the verandahs and gardens were filled with people. Half of Lowtown had gathered there to make sure she felt secure. There was a festival atmosphere, the feeling of a unique event.

With our white faces, Harry Rex and I received closer scrutiny. We didn't stop until he could speak with the deputies, and once they approved our presence the pack relaxed. We parked and I walked to the house, where Sam met me at the front steps. Harry Rex stayed behind, chatting with the deputies.

She was inside, in her bedroom, reading her Bible with a friend from church. Several deacons were on the porch with Sam and Esau, and they were anxious for details of the Teale murder. I filled them in with as much as I could tell, which wasn't much at all.

Around midnight, the crowd began to break up. Sam and the deputies had organised a rotation of all-night sentries, armed guards on the verandah and back porch. There was no shortage of volunteers.

We drove the streets to the Hocutt House, where we found Buster asleep in his car in the driveway. We found some bourbon and sat on a verandah, trying to appreciate the situation.

'He's very patient,' Harry Rex said. 'Wait a few days when all these neighbours get tired of house sittin', when everybody relaxes a little. The jurors can't live locked inside their homes. He's not finished.'

One murder might be considered a random act. Two meant there was a pattern. The third would send a small army of cops and vigilantes onto Padgitt Island for an all-out war.

'He'll wait,' Harry Rex said. 'Probably for a long time.' It was clear that Danny Padgitt had advanced from a brutal crime of passion to cold-blooded executions.

'I'm thinking about selling the paper, Harry Rex,' I said.

He took a long drink of bourbon. 'Why would you do that?'

'Money. This company in Georgia is making a serious offer.'

'How much?'

'A lot. More than I ever dreamed of. I wouldn't work for a long time. Maybe never.'

The idea of not working hit him hard. His daily routine was ten hours of nonstop chaos with some very emotional divorce clients. He made a comfortable living, but he certainly scraped for every penny. 'How long have you had the paper?' he asked.

'Nine years.'

'Kinda hard to imagine the paper without you. What will you do?'

'Take a break, travel, see the world, find a nice lady, marry her, get her pregnant, have some kids. This is a big house.'

'So you wouldn't move away?'

'To where? This is home.'

Another long sip, then, 'I don't know. Let me sleep on it.' With that, he walked off the verandah and drove away.

WITH THE BODIES piling up, it was inevitable the story would attract more attention than the *Times* could give it. The next morning, a reporter I knew from the Memphis paper arrived in my office, and about twenty minutes later one from the Jackson paper joined us.

I gave them the background on both murders, the Padgitt parole, and the fear that had gripped the county. We were not competitors—most of my subscribers also took either the Memphis or Jackson dailies. And, frankly, I was losing interest; not in the current crisis, but in journalism as a vocation. The world was calling me, and I found it increasingly difficult to stay focused.

The two reporters eventually left to pursue their own angles. A few minutes later Sam called with a rather urgent, 'You need to come over.'

A ragtag little unit was still guarding the Ruffin porch. All four were bleary-eyed and in need of sleep. Sam took me through to the kitchen where Miss Callie was shelling butter beans. She gave me a warm smile and the standard bear hug, but she was a troubled woman. 'In here,' she said. Sam nodded and we followed her into her small bedroom. She closed the door behind us as if intruders were lurking, then she disappeared into a walk-in cupboard.

She emerged with an old spiral notebook that had obviously been well hidden. 'Something doesn't make sense,' she said as she sat on the edge of the bed. Sam sat beside her and I backed into an old rocker. She was flipping through the handwritten notes she had kept during the trial. 'Here it is,' she said.

'We gave our solemn promises that we would never talk about what happened in the jury room,' she said, 'but this is too important not to tell. When we found Mr Padgitt guilty, the vote was quick and unanimous. But when we came to the issue of the death penalty, things got very heated, there were sharp words, even some accusations and threats. Not a pleasant thing to sit through. When the battle lines became clear, there were three people opposed to the death penalty, and they were not about to change their minds.'

She showed me a page in her notebook. In her clear and distinctive handwriting there were two columns—one had nine names, the other had only three—L. Fargarson, Mo Teal and Maxine Root. I gawked at the names, thinking that maybe I was looking at the killer's list.

Why would Danny Padgitt be killing the jurors who refused to give him the death penalty? The ones who had effectively saved his life?

'He's killing the wrong ones, isn't he?' Sam asked. 'I mean, if you're out for revenge why go after the folks who tried to save you?'

'As I said, it doesn't make sense,' Miss Callie said.

'You're assuming he knows how each juror voted. As far as I know, the jurors never told anyone how the vote went. There's a good chance he's picking off the easy ones first, and Mr Fargarson and Mr Teale just happened to be more accessible.'

'That's very coincidental,' Sam said.

We pondered that for a long time. Maybe we were trying to make sense of something that was completely incomprehensible.

'I need to give this information to the sheriff,' I said.

'We promised we'd never tell.'

'That was nine years ago, Mother,' Sam said. 'No one could have predicted then what's happening now.'

'It's especially important for Maxine Root,' I said.

There was a commotion at the front door. Bobby, Leon and Al had arrived. They had met in St Louis, then driven all night to Clanton. We had coffee round the kitchen table, and I filled them in on recent developments. Miss Callie suddenly sprang to life and was pondering meals and making a list of vegetables for Esau to pick.

SHERIFF MCNATT was out making the rounds, visiting each juror. I had to unload on someone, so I barged into Harry Rex's office and waited impatiently while he finished a deposition. When we were alone, I told him about Miss Callie's list and the division of the jurors. As usual, he had a different, far more cynical theory.

'Those three were supposed to hang the jury on guilt,' he said after a quick analysis. 'They caved for some reason, probably thought they were doin' the right thing by keepin' him out of the gas chamber, but of course Padgitt ain't thinkin' that way. He figures he'll get his three stooges first, then go after the rest.'

'Lenny Fargarson was no stooge for Danny Padgitt,' I argued.

'Just because he's crippled?'

'Just because he was a very devout Christian.'

'He was unemployed, Willie. He was once able to work, but he knew his condition would only deteriorate over the years. Maybe he needed money. Hell, everybody needs money. The Padgitts have trucks full of cash.'

'I don't buy it.'

'It makes more sense than any of your screwball theories. What are you sayin'—somebody else is pickin' off the jurors?'

'I didn't say that. Look, Padgitt doesn't know how the vote went. He was in Parchman twelve hours after the verdict. He's made his list. Fargarson was first because he was such an easy target. Teale was second because Padgitt could choose the setting.'

'Who's third?'

'I don't know, but these folks won't stay locked in their homes for ever. He'll bide his time, let things die down, then start again.'

Harry Rex's phone had never stopped ringing. He glared at it during a pause, then said, 'I got work to do.'

'I guess I'll go see the sheriff. See you later.' I was out of his office when he yelled, 'Say, Willie. One other thing.'

I turned to face him.

'Sell it, take the money, go play for a while. You've earned it.'

'Thanks.'

'But don't leave Clanton, you hear?'

'I won't.'

WHEN I WALKED into the sheriff's office, he looked puzzled. He had just finished a conversation with Mr Earl Youry, one of the jurors, who had called to say that he remembered that the crippled boy and Mo Teale had been adamant in their refusal to impose the death penalty.

I closed the door and relayed my conversation with Miss Callie. 'I saw her notes, Sheriff,' I said. 'The third vote was Maxine Root.'

For an hour we rehashed the same arguments I'd had with Sam and Harry Rex, and again it made no sense. He did not believe that the Padgitts had bought or intimidated either Lenny or Mo Teale. But, both of us conceded, with Lucien Wilbanks involved it was entirely possible Padgitt knew more about the deliberations than we did.

While I was in his office, he called Maxine Root. She worked as a bookkeeper at a factory north of town, and had insisted on going to work. Two of McNatt's deputies were outside the building, watching for trouble and waiting to haul Maxine back home at quitting time.

They chatted on the phone like old friends for a few minutes, then McNatt said, 'Say, Maxine, I know that you and Mo Teale and the Fargarson boy were the only three who voted against the death penalty for Danny Padgitt—' He paused as she interrupted.

'Well, it's not important how I found out. What's important here is that makes me real nervous about your safety. Extra nervous.'

He listened to her for a few minutes. As she rambled on he interrupted occasionally with such things as: 'Well, Maxine, I can't just charge out there and arrest the boy.'

And, 'You tell your brothers to keep those guns in their trucks.'

And, 'It's too late to give him the death penalty, Maxine. You did what you thought was right at the time.'

She was crying when the conversation ended. 'Poor thing,' McNatt said, 'her nerves are shot to hell.'

'Can't blame her,' I said. 'I'm ducking under windows myself.'

CHAPTER 11

The funeral for Mo Teale was held at the Willow Road Methodist Church, number thirty-six on my list and one of my favourites. Because I had never met Mr Teale, I did not go to his funeral. However, there were many in attendance who had never met him. The funeral procession stretched for blocks and, for good measure, swung by the square and proceeded down Jackson Avenue, just outside the *Times* offices. It did not disrupt traffic at all—everyone was at the funeral.

LATER THAT DAY, using Harry Rex as an intermediary, Lucien Wilbanks called a meeting with Sheriff McNatt. I was specifically mentioned by Lucien, and specifically not invited. Didn't matter; Harry Rex took notes and told me everything, with the understanding that nothing would get printed.

Also present in Lucien's office was Rufus Buckley, the district attorney who had succeeded Ernie Gaddis on his retirement. Buckley was a publicity hog who, though reluctant to meddle in Padgitt's parole, was now anxious to lead the mob to lynch him.

Lucien began by saying that he had talked with both Danny Padgitt and his father, Gill. They had met somewhere outside of Clanton and away from the island. Danny was doing fine, working each day in the office of the family's highway contracting firm.

Not surprisingly, Danny denied any involvement in the murders of Lenny Fargarson and Mo Teale. He was shocked by what was happening and angry that he was widely considered to be the chief suspect. At the time of Lenny Fargarson's death, on the afternoon of May 23, Danny was in his office, and there were four people who could vouch for his presence there. The Fargarson home was at least a thirty-minute drive from Padgitt Island, and the four witnesses were certain that Danny was either in his office or very close to it throughout the afternoon.

'How many of these witnesses are named Padgitt?' McNatt asked.

'We're not giving names, yet,' Lucien said.

On June 3, Mo Teale was shot at approximately nine fifteen in the morning. At that precise moment, Danny was standing beside a newly surfaced highway in Tippah County, getting documents signed by one of the Padgitt construction foremen. The foreman, along with two labourers, was willing to testify Danny was there at that moment. The job was at least two hours away from Ned Ray Zook's farm.

Lucien presented airtight alibis for both murders, though his small audience was very sceptical. Given the Padgitts' capacity to lie, break legs and bribe, they could find witnesses for anything.

Sheriff McNatt voiced his scepticism. He explained to Lucien that his investigation was continuing, and if and when he had probable cause, he would get his arrest warrant and descend upon the island. If a hundred troopers were necessary to flush out Danny, then so be it.

Lucien said that would not be necessary. If a valid arrest warrant was obtained, he would do his best to bring the boy in himself.

'And if there's another killing,' McNatt said, 'this place will erupt. You'll have a thousand rednecks crossin' the bridge and shootin' every Padgitt they can find.'

Buckley said that he and Judge Omar Noose had spoken twice about the killings, and he was reasonably confident that Noose was 'almost ready' to issue a warrant for Danny's arrest. Lucien attacked him with a barrage of questions about probable cause and sufficient evidence, and the meeting deteriorated into nit-picking legalities.

The sheriff finally broke it up by announcing he'd heard enough and walked out of Lucien's office.

IN THE NINE YEARS since I'd bought the *Times*, I had never left it for more than four days. It went to press every Tuesday, was published every Wednesday, and by every Thursday of my life I was facing a formidable deadline.

One reason for the newspaper's success was the fact that I wrote so much about so many in a town where so little happened. Each edition had thirty-six pages. Subtracting five for classifieds, three for legals and about six for advertisements, I was faced each week with the task of filling approximately twenty-two pages with local news.

Margaret put together one page for religion and one page for weddings. Davey Bigmouth Bass took two pages for sports. Baggy, whose production nine years earlier had been feeble at best, had succumbed almost completely to booze and was now good for only one story each week. Staff reporters came and went with frustrating regularity. We usually had one on board, sometimes two, and they were often more trouble than they were worth. I had to proofread and edit their work to the point of wishing I had simply done it myself.

And so I wrote. Twenty pages or more a week, fifty-two weeks of the year.

I woke up each morning thinking of either a new story or a new angle for an old one. Any bit of news or any unusual event was inspiration to puff up a piece and stick it somewhere in the paper. I wrote about dogs, antique trucks, a legendary tornado, a haunted house, a missing pony, Civil War treasure, a rabid skunk. And all the usual stuff—court proceedings, elections, crime, new businesses, bankrupt businesses, new characters in town. I was tired of writing.

And I was tired of Clanton. With some reluctance the town had come to accept me. But it was a very small place, and at times I felt suffocated. I spent so many weekends at home, with little to do but read and write, that I became accustomed to it. And that frustrated me. I tried the poker nights with Bubba Crockett and the redneck cookouts with Harry Rex. But I never felt as though I belonged.

I suspected the town was weary of me, too. Because of my preachy opposition to the war in Vietnam, I would always be considered a radical liberal. And I did little to diminish this reputation. Throughout the seventies, I was always on a soapbox. And while this made for interesting reading and sold papers, it also transformed me into something of an oddity. I was viewed as a malcontent, one with a pulpit.

As I grew older, I wanted to be a regular citizen. I would always be an outsider, but that didn't bother me any more. I wanted to come and go, to live in Clanton as I saw fit, then leave for long periods of time when I got bored. And it was amazing how the prospect of money can change your future. I became consumed with the dream of walking away, of taking a sabbatical to some place I'd never been, of seeing the world.

The next meeting with Gary McGrew was at a restaurant in Tupelo. Over lunch we again looked at my books, negotiated this point and that one. If I sold, I wanted the owner to honour the new five-year contracts I'd given to Davey Bigmouth Bass, Hardy and Margaret. Baggy would either retire soon or die of liver poisoning. Wiley had always been a part-timer, and his interest in chasing subjects for photos was waning. He was the only employee I'd told about the negotiations, and he had encouraged me to take the money and run.

The offer was at $1.3 million. A consultant I'd hired in Knoxville had valued the *Times* at $1.35 million.

'Confidentially, we've bought the papers in Tyler and Van Buren counties,' McGrew said. 'Things are falling into place. But there's a new wrinkle. The paper in Polk County might be for sale. Frankly, we're taking a look at it if you pass.'

The *Polk County Herald* had 4,000 readers and lousy management. I saw it every week.

'I really want a million and a half bucks,' I said.

'I'm not sure we can go that high, Willie.'

'You'll have to if you want the paper.'

A sense of urgency had arisen. McGrew hinted at a deadline, then finally said, 'My client is anxious to reach a conclusion. He wants to close the deal by the 1st of next month, or he'll go elsewhere.'

The tactic didn't bother me. I was tired of talking too. Either I sold, or I didn't. It was time to make a decision.

'That's twenty-three days from now,' I said.

'It is.'

'Fair enough.'

THE LONG DAYS of summer arrived, and the insufferable heat and humidity settled in for their annual stay. I made my usual rounds—to the churches on my list, to the softball fields, to the local golf tournament. But Clanton was waiting, and the wait was all we talked about.

Inevitably, the noose around the neck of each remaining juror was loosened somewhat. They naturally got tired of being prisoners in their homes, of altering their lifelong routines, of having packs of neighbours guard their homes at night. They began to resume normal lives.

The patience of the killer was unnerving. He knew his victims would grow weary of all that protection. He knew they would drop their guard, make a mistake. We knew it too.

Bobby, Al, Max and Leon had, at various times, argued strenuously for Miss Callie to go and stay with any of them for a month or so. Sam and I, and even Esau, had joined in these rather vigorous requests, but she would not budge. God would protect her.

In nine years, the only time I lost my temper with Miss Callie was during an argument about spending a month in Milwaukee with Bobby. 'Those big cities are dangerous,' she had said.

'No place is as dangerous as Clanton right now,' I had replied.

Later, when I raised my voice, she told me she did not appreciate my lack of respect, and I quickly shut up.

NINETEEN SEVENTY-NINE was a year for local elections in Mississippi, my third as a registered voter. The sheriff's race was uncontested, something that was unheard of. Senator Theo Morton drew an opponent who brought me an ad that screamed the question—WHY DID SENATOR MORTON GET DANNY PADGITT PAROLED? CASH! THAT'S WHY! As much as I wanted to run the ad, I did not have the energy for a libel suit.

The county was still fixated on the murders of Fargarson and Teale, and, more important, on who might be next. Sheriff McNatt and the investigators from the state police had exhausted every possible lead. All we could do was wait.

As the Fourth of July approached, there was a noticeable lack of excitement about the annual celebration. Though almost everyone felt safe, there was a dark cloud hanging over the county. Oddly, rumours persisted that something bad would happen when we all gathered round the courthouse on the Fourth. Rumours, though, had never been born with such creativity, nor spread as rapidly, as in the month of June.

ON JUNE 25, in a fancy law office in Tupelo, I signed a pile of documents that transferred ownership of the *Times* to a media company owned in part by Mr Ray Noble of Atlanta. Mr Noble handed me a cheque for $1.5 million, and I quickly walked it down the street, where my newest friend, Stu Holland, was waiting in his office in the Merchants Bank. News of such a deposit in Clanton would leak overnight, so I buried the money with Stu, then drove home.

It was the longest one-hour drive of my life. It was exhilarating because adventure was calling me, and I now had the means to answer.

And it was a sad drive because I was giving up such a large and rewarding part of my life. The paper and I had grown and matured together; me as an adult, it as a prosperous entity. It had become what any small-town paper should be—a lively observer of current events, a recorder of history, a commentator on politics and social issues. As for me, I was a young man who had blindly and doggedly built something from scratch. Now all I wanted to do was find a beach. Then a girl.

When I returned to Clanton, I walked into Margaret's office, closed the door, and told her about the sale. She burst into tears, and before long my eyes were moist as well. Her fierce loyalty had always amazed me, and though she, like Miss Callie, worried way too much about my soul, she had grown to love me nonetheless. I explained that the new owners were wonderful people, planned no drastic changes, and had approved her new five-year contract at an increased salary. This made her cry even more.

Hardy did not cry. He was moody, cantankerous, drank too much like most pressmen, and if the new owners didn't like him then he'd simply quit and go fishing. He did appreciate the new contract though. As did Davey Bigmouth Bass. He was shocked at the news, but rallied nicely at the idea of earning more money.

Baggy was on vacation somewhere out west, with his brother, not his wife. I could not, in good conscience, make him a part of the deal. Baggy was on his own.

We had five other employees, and I personally broke the news to each of them. When it was finally over I was drained. I met Harry Rex in the back room at Pepe's and we celebrated with margaritas.

I was anxious to leave town and go somewhere, but it would be impossible until the killings stopped.

FOR MOST OF JUNE, the Ruffin professors scrambled back and forth to Clanton. They juggled assignments and vacations, trying their best to make sure at least one of them was always with Miss Callie. Sam stayed in Lowtown to protect his mother, but also to keep his own profile low. Trooper Durant was still around, though he was married again and his two renegade sons had left the area.

A hasty reunion was put together for the week before the Fourth of July. Because my house had five empty bedrooms, I insisted that it be filled with Ruffins. The family had grown considerably since I first met them in 1970. All but Sam were married, and there were twenty-one grandchildren. The total came to thirty-five Ruffins, not counting Sam, Callie and Esau, and thirty-four made it to Clanton. Leon's wife had a sick father in Chicago.

Of the thirty-four, twenty-three moved into the Hocutt House for a few days. Bobby's wife, Bonnie, took over my kitchen, and three times a day I was sent to the grocery store with a list of things she urgently needed. I bought ice cream by the ton and the kids soon learned I would fetch it for them at any hour of the day.

Since my verandahs were long and wide and seldom used, the Ruffins gravitated towards them. Sam brought Miss Callie and Esau over late in the afternoons for serious visiting. She was desperate to get out of Lowtown. Her warm little house had become a prison.

At various times, I heard her children talk with great concern about their mother. The threat of somehow getting shot was discussed less than her health. Over the years she had managed to lose somewhere around eighty pounds. Now it was back, and her blood pressure had the doctors concerned. The stress was taking its toll. She was not as spry, didn't smile as much, and had noticeably less energy.

It was all blamed on the 'Padgitt mess'. As soon as he got caught and the killings stopped, then Miss Callie would bounce back.

That was the optimistic view, the one shared by most of her children.

On July 2, a Monday, Bonnie prepared a light lunch of salads and pizzas. We ate on a side verandah under slow-moving and practically useless wicker fans. There was a slight breeze, however, and with the temperature in the nineties we were able to enjoy a long lazy meal.

I had yet to find the right moment to tell Miss Callie that I was leaving the paper. I knew she would be shocked, and disappointed. But I could think of no reason why we couldn't continue our Thursday lunches. In nine years we had missed only seven, all due to illness.

The lazy post-meal chatter suddenly came to a halt. There were sirens in the distance, somewhere across town.

THE BOX was twelve inches square, five inches deep, white in colour with red and blue stars and stripes. It was a gift package from the Bolan Pecan Farm in Hazelhurst, Mississippi, sent to Mrs Maxine Root by her sister in Concord, California.

It had been almost a month since Maxine had reluctantly admitted to Sheriff McNatt that she had not been in favour of the death penalty for Danny Padgitt. Since the two men who stuck with her were now dead, she recognised that she might be the next victim.

For years after the trial, Maxine had wrestled with the verdict. The town was bitter over it and she felt the hostility. Thankfully, the jurors kept their vows of silence, and she and Lenny and Mo avoided any additional abuse. Now the world knew how she'd voted, and a crazy man was stalking her. Her nerves were shot; she couldn't sleep; she was sick of hiding in her own home. She was taking so many different pills that they were all counteracting each other to the point that nothing worked.

She started crying when she saw the box of pecans. Someone out there loved her. Her precious sister Jane was thinking about her. She went to the phone and dialled Jane's number. They had not talked in a week.

Jane was thrilled to hear from her and they chatted about the situation in Clanton. 'You're a dear to send the pecans,' Maxine said.

'What pecans?' Jane asked.

A pause. 'The gift box from Bolan Pecans. A big one.'

Another pause. 'Not me, sis. Must've been someone else.'

Maxine hung up moments later and examined the box. A sticker on the front said—A Gift from Jane Parham. She knew no other Jane Parham besides her sister. Very gently, she picked it up.

Travis, the part-time deputy, happened by the house. He was accompanied by one Teddy Ray, a pimple-faced boy with an oversized uniform. Maxine hustled them into the kitchen where the box sat benignly on the counter. The lone sentry, a neighbour who was usually stationed in the front garden, was also tagging along, and the four of them just stared at the package while Maxine recounted her conversation with Jane.

With great hesitation, Travis picked up the box and shook it slightly. 'Seems a mite heavy for pecans,' he observed. He looked at the neighbour with a rifle, who seemed ready to duck at anything.

'You think it's a bomb?' the neighbour asked.

'Oh my God,' Maxine mumbled and appeared ready to collapse.

'Could be,' Travis said, gawking in horror at what he was holding.

'Get it outside,' Maxine said.

'Shouldn't we call the sheriff?' Teddy Ray managed to ask.

'I guess so,' Travis said.

'What if it's got a timer or something?' asked the neighbour.

Travis hesitated for a moment, then with the voice of absolutely no experience, said, 'I know what to do.'

They stepped through the kitchen door onto a narrow porch. Travis carefully placed the box at the very edge. When he removed his .44 magnum, Maxine said, 'What are you doing?'

'We're gonna see if it's a bomb,' Travis said. Teddy Ray and the neighbour scurried off to the safety of the grass, fifty feet away.

'You're gonna shoot my pecans?' Maxine asked.

'You got a better idea?' Travis snapped back.

'I guess not.'

Travis leaned out through the screen door, took aim and fired.

The explosion ripped the porch completely from the house, tore a gaping hole in the back wall, and sprayed shrapnel for 100 yards. It shattered windows, peeled up planks, and it wounded the four observers. Teddy Ray and the neighbour both took bits of metal in their chests and legs. Travis's firing hand was mangled. A small nail penetrated Maxine's right jaw.

For a moment, they were all unconscious, knocked silly by three pounds of plastic explosives packed with nails, glass and ball bearings.

JUDGE OMAR NOOSE was holding court in Clanton that afternoon. In fact, he later said that he heard the explosion. Rufus Buckley and Sheriff McNatt met with him for over an hour in chambers, and he finally issued a warrant for Danny Padgitt's arrest.

Lucien was notified, and he took the news without objection. At that moment, not even Padgitt's lawyer could argue with the strategy of bringing him in for processing. He could always be released later.

A few minutes after 5 p.m., a convoy of police cars headed for Padgitt Island. Harry Rex now owned a police scanner and we sat in his office, sipping beer, listening to it squawk with unchecked fury. It had to be the most exciting arrest in the history of our county. Would the Padgitts thwart the arrest? Would there be gunfire? A small war?

From the chatter, we were able to follow most of what was happening. At Highway 42, McNatt and his men were met by ten 'units' of the state highway patrol. We assumed a 'unit' meant nothing more than a car, but it sounded far more serious. They proceeded to Highway 401, turned onto the county road that led to the island, and at the bridge where everyone expected some dramatic showdown, there sat Danny Padgitt in the car with Lucien Wilbanks.

The voices on the scanner were quick and anxious:

'They're gettin' out of the car.'

'Let's shoot both of them.'

'Wilbanks is holdin' up his hands. Smart-ass!'

'It's Danny Padgitt, all right. Hands held high.'

'I'd like to knock that smile off his face.'

'They got the cuffs on him.'

'Dammit!' Harry Rex yelled across his desk. 'I wanted some gun-fire. Just like in the old days.'

That evening, when I returned to the Hocutt House the Ruffin clan was in a festive mood. News that Padgitt was in custody had brought a great sense of relief. Miss Callie was as relaxed as I'd seen her in a long time. We sat on the verandah for a long time, telling stories, laughing, listening to Aretha Franklin and the Temptations, even listening to an occasional burst of fireworks.

UNKNOWN TO ANYONE, Lucien Wilbanks and Judge Noose had struck a deal in the hectic hours before the arrest. The judge was worried about what might happen if Danny Padgitt chose to retreat into the safety of the island, or, worse, resist the arrest with force. The county was a powder keg waiting for a match. The cops were ready for blood because of Teddy Ray and Travis, whose gunslinging stupidity was being temporarily ignored while they recovered from their wounds.

Lucien appreciated the situation. He agreed to deliver his client on one condition—he wanted an immediate bail hearing. He had at least a dozen witnesses who were willing to provide 'airtight' alibis for Danny, and truly believed that someone else was behind the killings.

Lucien was also one month away from being disbarred in an unrelated mess. He knew the end was coming, and the bail hearing would be his last performance.

Judge Noose agreed to a hearing and set it for 10 a.m. the next day, July 3. In a scene eerily reminiscent of one nine years earlier, Danny Padgitt once again packed the Ford County courthouse. It was a hostile crowd, anxious to get a look at him, hopeful that he might be strung up on the spot. Maxine Root's family, a notoriously rough bunch of loggers, arrived early and sat near the front. They frightened me, and we were ostensibly on the same side. Maxine was reported to be resting well and expected home in a few days.

Miss Callie had insisted on arriving early and getting a good seat.

She wore a Sunday dress and delighted in sitting in such a public gathering surrounded by her family. Mr and Mrs Fargarson were sitting at the rear, two rows from the back, and I couldn't begin to comprehend what they were thinking.

There were no Padgitts present; they had enough sense to stay clear of the courtroom. The sight of one of them would've touched off a riot. Harry Rex whispered that they were huddled together upstairs in the jury room, with the door locked. We never saw them.

Rufus Buckley arrived with his entourage to represent the State of Mississippi. One advantage in selling the *Times* was that I would never be forced to spend time with him. He was arrogant and pompous, and everything he did was designed to get him to the governor's office.

As I watched the courtroom fill up, I realised it was the last time I would cover such a proceeding for the *Times*. I found no sadness in that. I had mentally checked out, and now that Danny was in custody, I was even more anxious to escape Clanton and go see the world.

At just after 10 a.m., all seats were filled and Lucien Wilbanks emerged from a door behind the bench. It had the feel of a sporting event; he was a player; we all wanted to boo. Two bailiffs quickly followed him, and one announced, 'All rise for the Court!'

Judge Noose ambled forth in his black robe and sat on his throne. 'Please be seated,' he said into the microphone.

He nodded, a side door opened, and Danny Padgitt, handcuffed and shackled at the ankles, was led in by three deputies.

'This is a bail hearing,' Noose announced to the courtroom. 'There's no reason why it cannot be handled judiciously and briefly.'

It would be much briefer than anyone anticipated.

A cannon exploded somewhere above us, and for a split second I thought we'd all been shot. Something cracked sharply through the heavy air of the courtroom, and for a town so jittery to begin with we all froze in one horrible snapshot of disbelief.

Then Danny Padgitt grunted in a delayed reaction, and all hell broke loose. Women screamed. Men screamed. Someone shouted, 'He's been shot!'

I lowered my head a few inches, but I didn't want to miss anything. Every deputy yanked out a revolver and looked for someone to shoot, up and down, front and back, here and there.

The second shot hit Danny in the ribs, but it had not been necessary. The first had gone through his head. The second shot drew the attention of a deputy in the front, who was pointing to the balcony.

The double doors to the courtroom flew open, and the stampede was on. In the hysteria that followed, I stayed in my seat and tried to take in everything. Lucien Wilbanks was hovering over his client. Rufus Buckley was on his hands and knees, scurrying in front of the jury box in an effort to escape. And I'll never forget Judge Noose, sitting calmly at the bench, reading glasses perched on the tip of his nose, watching the chaos as if he saw it every week.

Each second seemed to last a minute.

The shots that hit Danny had been fired from the ceiling above the balcony. And, though the balcony had been filled with people, no one had seen the rifle drop down a few inches ten feet above their heads. Like the rest of us, they had been preoccupied with getting a first glance at Danny Padgitt.

Back in the late sixties, in an effort to improve the courthouse lighting, a dropped ceiling had been installed. The sniper found the perfect spot on a heating duct just above a panel in the ceiling. There, in the dark crawl space, he watched the courtroom below through a five-inch slit he'd created by lifting one of the water-stained panels.

When I thought the shooting was over, I crept closer to the bar. The cops were yelling for everybody to get out of the courtroom. Danny was under the table, attended to by Lucien and several deputies. I could see his feet, and they were not moving.

A minute or two passed, and the confusion was subsiding. Suddenly, there was more gunfire; thankfully, now it was outside. I looked out of a courtroom window and saw people scampering into the stores round the square.

Sheriff McNatt had just found the crawl space when he heard shots above him. He and two deputies climbed the stairs to the second floor, then slowly took the cramped circular stairway through the dome. The door to the cupola was jammed shut, but just above it they could hear the anxious footsteps of the sniper. And they could hear shell casings hit the floor.

His only target was the law offices of Lucien Wilbanks. With great deliberation he was blowing the upstairs windows out, one by one. Downstairs, Ethel Twitty was under her desk, screaming.

I finally left the courtroom and hustled downstairs to the main floor, where the crowd was waiting, uncertain what to do. Each one of us was thinking, 'How long will this go on?'

I huddled with the Ruffin family. Miss Callie had fainted when the first shot jolted the courtroom. Max and Bobby were clutching her, anxious to get her home.

AFTER HOLDING the town hostage for an hour, the sniper ran out of ammunition. He saved the last bullet for himself. Sheriff McNatt waited a few minutes, then entered the cupola. The body of Hank Hooten was naked again. And as dead as fresh roadkill.

A deputy ran down the stairs and yelled, 'It's over! He's dead! It's Hank Hooten!'

The bewildered expressions were almost amusing. Hank Hooten? Everyone said the name but no words came out. Hank Hooten?

We spilled outside under the trees and lingered for a while, not certain whether we should stay in case there was another incredible event, or go home and try to comprehend the one we'd just lived through. The Ruffin clan left quickly; Miss Callie was not feeling well.

Eventually, an ambulance carried away the two corpses and I walked back to my office, stunned. The entire town was muted.

I eventually made some phone calls, found who I wanted, and around noon left the office and headed south to Whitfield.

What madness, I thought. How did such a pleasant little town end up in such a nightmare? I just wanted out.

THE STATE MENTAL HOSPITAL was twenty miles east of Jackson on an interstate highway. I bluffed my way through the guardhouse, using the name of a doctor I'd located fishing around with the phone.

Dr Vero was very busy, but when I informed the girl at the desk that I was not leaving, and that I would follow him home if necessary, he somehow found the time to squeeze me in.

Vero had long hair and a greyish beard. Two diplomas on his wall tracked him through Northwestern and Johns Hopkins.

I told him what had happened that morning in Clanton. After my narrative he said, 'I can't talk about Mr Hooten. As I explained on the phone, we have a doctor–patient privilege.'

'Had. Not have.'

'It survives, Mr Traynor. I'm afraid I can't discuss this patient.'

I launched into a long and detailed account of the Padgitt case, from the trial to the parole to the last month and the tension in Clanton. My angle was that the town needed to know what made Hank Hooten snap. How sick was he? Why was he released? There were many questions, and before 'we' could put the tragic episode behind 'us', then 'we' needed the truth.

'How much will you print?' he asked.

'I'll print only what you tell me to print.'

'Let's take a walk.'

On a bench, in a small shaded courtyard, we sipped coffee from paper cups. 'This is what you can print,' Vero began. 'Mr Hooten was admitted here in January 1971. He was diagnosed as schizophrenic, confined here, treated here, and released in October 1976.'

'Who diagnosed him?' I asked.

'We now go off the record. I must have your word on that.'

'I swear on the Bible that this will not be printed,' I said.

He hesitated for a long time, then he relaxed a little, and said, 'I treated Mr Hooten initially. His family had a history of schizophrenia. Quite often genetics play a role in the disease. He was institutionalised while he was in college, and remarkably, managed to finish law school. After his second divorce, he moved to Clanton in the mid-sixties, looking for a place to start over. Another divorce followed. He adored women, but could not survive in a relationship. He was quite enamoured with Rhoda Kassellaw and claimed he asked her to marry him. Her murder was very traumatic. And when the jury refused to send her killer to death, he, shall I say, slipped over the edge.'

'Thank you for using layman's terms,' I said. I remembered the diagnosis around town—'slap-ass crazy'.

'He heard voices, the principal one being that of Miss Kassellaw. Her two small children also talked to him. They described the horror of watching their mother get raped and murdered in her own bed, and they blamed Mr Hooten for not saving her. Her killer, Mr Padgitt, also tormented him with taunts from prison.'

'Did he mention the jurors?'

'Oh, yes, all the time. He knew that three of them—Mr Fargarson, Mr Teale and Mrs Root—had refused to bring back a death penalty. He would scream their names in the middle of the night.'

'That's amazing. The jurors vowed to never discuss their deliberations. We didn't know how they voted until a month ago.'

'Well, he was the assistant prosecutor.'

'Yes, he was.' I vividly remembered Hank Hooten sitting beside Ernie Gaddis at the trial, never saying a word, looking bored and detached from the proceedings. 'Did he express a desire to seek revenge?'

A sip of coffee, another pause as he debated whether to answer. 'Yes. He hated them. He wanted them dead, along with Mr Padgitt.'

'Then why was he released?'

'I can't talk about his release, Mr Traynor. I wasn't here at the time, and there might be some liability on the part of this institution.'

'You weren't here?'

'I left for two years to teach in Chicago. When I returned eighteen months ago, Mr Hooten was gone.'

'But you've reviewed his file.'

'Yes, and his condition improved dramatically while I was away. He was released to a community treatment programme in Tupelo, and from there he sort of fell off our radar. Needless to say, Mr Traynor, the treatment of the mentally ill is not a priority in this state, nor in many others.'

'Would you have released him?'

'I cannot answer that, Mr Traynor. I think I've said enough.'

I thanked him for his time, for his candour, and once again promised to protect his confidence. He asked for a copy of whatever I printed.

I stopped at a fast-food place in Jackson for a cheeseburger. At a payphone I called the office, half wondering if I'd missed more shootings. Margaret was relieved to hear my voice.

'You must come home, Willie, and quickly,' she said. 'Callie Ruffin has had a stroke.'

'Is it serious?'

'I'm afraid so.'

CHAPTER 12

At one end of the hospital there was a modern chapel where I found the Ruffins, all eight children, all twenty-one grandchildren, and every spouse but Leon's wife. Reverend Thurston Small was there, along with a sizable contingent from the church. Esau was upstairs in the intensive-care unit, waiting outside Miss Callie's room.

Sam told me that she had woken from a nap with a sharp pain in her left arm, then numbness in her leg, and before long she was mumbling incoherently. An ambulance rushed her to the hospital. The doctor was certain it was initially a stroke, one that precipitated a mild heart attack. Her condition was described as 'serious but stable'.

Visitors were not allowed, so there was little to do but wait and pray. After an hour in the chapel, I was ready for bed. Max, third in the birth order but the undeniable leader, organised a schedule for the night. At least two of Miss Callie's children would be somewhere in the hospital at all times.

We checked with the doctor again at around eleven, and he sounded reasonably optimistic that she was still stable, so we left Mario and Gloria in the chapel, and moved en masse to the Hocutt House where we ate ice cream on a side verandah. Sam had taken Esau home to Lowtown. I was delighted that the rest of the family preferred staying at my place.

Everyone was exhausted, especially the children. Around midnight, Al gathered the family together in my den for one last word of prayer. Sitting there on my sofa, fervently holding hands with Bonnie and with Mario's wife, I felt the presence of the Lord. I knew my beloved friend, their mother and grandmother, would be fine.

Two hours later I was lying in bed, wide awake, still hearing the sharp crack of the rifle in the courtroom, the thud of the bullet as it hit Danny, the panic that followed. I rewound and replayed every word of Dr Vero's, and wondered in what manner of hell poor Hank Hooten had been living for the past few years. Why had he been set loose on society again?

And I worried about Miss Callie, though her condition seemed to be under control and she was in good hands. Eventually I fell asleep.

Bobby Ruffin called at nine thirty. Miss Callie was awake, sitting up, sipping some tea, and they were allowing visitors for a few minutes. I hurried to the hospital. Sam met me in the hall. 'Don't talk about anything that happened yesterday, OK?' he said as we walked to the ICU. 'They won't even allow the grandkids in; afraid that would make her heart rate go crazy. Everything is real quiet.'

She was awake, but barely. I had expected to see the bright eyes and brilliant smile, but Miss Callie was barely conscious. She recognised me, we hugged, I patted her right hand. The left one had an IV. Sam, Esau and Gloria were in the room.

I wanted a few minutes alone so I could finally tell her I was selling the paper, but she was in no condition for such news. Perhaps in a day or so we could have a lively chat about it.

After fifteen minutes, the doctor showed up and asked us to leave. We left, we came back, and the vigil continued throughout the Fourth of July, though we were not allowed inside the ICU again.

THE MAYOR DECIDED there would be no fireworks for the Fourth. We'd heard enough explosions, suffered enough from gunpowder. Given the town's lingering jumpiness, there was no organised objection. The bands marched, the parade went on, the political speeches were the same as before, though with fewer candidates. There was ice cream, lemonade, barbecue, cotton candy—the usual food and snacks on the courthouse lawn.

But the town was subdued. Or maybe it was just me. Maybe I was just so tired of the place that nothing seemed right about it.

After the speeches, I left the square and drove back to the hospital. In the waiting room on the first floor I found Bobby with Al's wife; they were watching television like two zombies. I had just opened a magazine when Sam came running in.

'She's had another heart attack!' he said.

The three of us jumped to our feet as if we had somewhere to go.

'It just happened! They got the red team in there!'

'I'll call the house,' I said, and stepped to the payphone in the hall. Max answered the phone, and fifteen minutes later the Ruffins were streaming into the chapel.

Just after 8 p.m. her treating physician entered the chapel. His heavy eyes and wrinkled brow conveyed an unmistakable message. As he described a 'significant cardiac arrest' the eight children of Miss Callie deflated as a group. She was on a respirator, no longer able to breathe by herself.

Within an hour, the chapel was full of her friends. Reverend Thurston Small led a nonstop prayer group near the altar, and people joined it and left it as they wished. Poor Esau sat on the back row, slumped over, thoroughly drained.

For hours, we waited. And though we tried to be optimistic, there was a feeling of doom. By midnight we were numb and rapidly losing track of time. I wanted to leave, if only to walk outside and breathe fresh air. The doctor, however, had warned us to stay close.

The horror of the ordeal hit when he gathered us around and gravely said it was time for a 'final moment with the family'. There were gasps, then tears. I'll never forget hearing Sam say out loud, 'A final moment?'

'This is it?' Gloria asked in absolute terror.

Frightened and bewildered, we followed the doctor out of the chapel, down the hall, up a flight of stairs, all of us moving with the heavy feet of someone marching to his own execution.

As the family filed into the cramped little room, the doctor touched my arm and said, 'This should be just for the family.'

'Right,' I said, stopping.

'It's OK,' Sam said. 'He's with us.'

We packed around Miss Callie and her machines, most of which had been disconnected. The two smallest grandchildren were placed at the foot of her bed. Esau stood closest to her, gently patting her face. Her eyes were closed; she did not appear to be breathing.

She was very much at peace. Her husband and children touched some part of her, and the crying was heartbreaking.

When Max got his emotions under control, he touched Miss Callie's arm and said, 'Let us pray.' We bowed our heads and most of the crying stopped, for a moment anyway. 'Dear Lord, not our will but yours. Into thine hands we commend the spirit of this faithful child of God. Prepare a place for her now in your heavenly kingdom. Amen.'

AT SUNRISE, I was sitting on the verandah outside my office. I wanted to be alone, to have a good cry in private. The crying around my house was more than I could bear.

As I had dreamed of travelling the world, I had the recurring vision of returning to Clanton with gifts for Miss Callie. I'd bring her a silver vase from England, linens from the Italy she would never see, perfumes from Paris, chocolates from Belgium. Through me, she would vicariously see the world. She would always be there, waiting eagerly for my return, anxious to see what I'd brought her.

I ached with the loss of my dear friend. Its suddenness was cruel, as it always is. Its depth was so immense that I could not, at that time, imagine a recovery.

As the town slowly came to life below me, I walked to my desk and sat down. I took my pen, and for a long time stared at a blank notepad. Eventually, slowly, with great agony, I began the last obituary.

JOHN GRISHAM

The Last Juror, has been something of a labour of love for John Grisham—apart from anything else, it has been fifteen years in the writing. He intended it to be a follow-up title to *A Time to Kill*—his first novel and the book in which he originated the fictional Ford County setting, but work on the book was delayed when sales of *A Time to Kill* were overshadowed by the phenomenal success of *The Firm*, Grisham's first legal thriller. Suddenly, his original plan of alternating the Ford County books with legal thrillers had to be shelved. 'I was content to concentrate on the legal thrillers and take readers around the world. The Ford County books could wait, and have waited, until now. But,' he says, 'the story was always there, slowly taking shape, waiting to be completed.'

John Grisham was brought up in the southern states of America and moved to Mississippi with his parents when he was twelve. As a child he dreamed of becoming a professional baseball player but, as he grew up, he acknowledged that he didn't have the 'right stuff' to go professional, and instead decided to become a lawyer. He ran his own legal practice in Southaven for nearly a decade, squeezing his writing into the early mornings before work, until the success of *The Firm* enabled him to give up the real-life legal battles and write full-time.

Although many of his novels have been adapted for the big screen Grisham has usually kept his distance from Hollywood, leaving the scriptwriting to others. Recently, however, he has been working on a film of his own called *Mickey*, about fathers, sons and baseball. Drawing on his own experiences of coaching his son Ty and other local youngsters, *Mickey* actually started out as a book. When the story drew no interest from Hollywood, the author and a friend, director Hugh Wilson, decided to finance, produce and market the film themselves.

John Grisham is married to his college sweetheart, Renee, and as well as Ty they have a daughter, Shea. The family divide their time between their farm in Mississippi and a plantation near Charlottesville, Virginia.

The Various Haunts of Men

SUSAN HILL

Lafferton is a peaceful English cathedral city, a place where people go quietly about their lives, sheltered from the kind of unrest and chaos that so often breeds in large cities.

However, even in the midst of this ordinary, everyday world, there is no refuge, ultimately, from the darkest impulses of the human mind . . .

The Tape

Last week I found a letter from you. I didn't think I had kept any of them. I thought I had destroyed everything from you. But this one had somehow been overlooked. I found it among some old tax returns. I wasn't going to read it. As soon as I saw your handwriting, I felt revulsion. I threw it in the bin. But later I retrieved it and read it. You complained several times in it that I never told you anything. 'You haven't told me anything at all since you were a little boy,' you wrote.

If only you knew how little I had told you even then.

Once I had read your letter, I began to realise that now I can tell you things. I need to tell you. I have held on to some secrets for far too long. After all, you cannot do anything about them now.

The first thing I must tell you is that very early on I learned how to lie. I lied about the pier. I went there, when I told you that I had not, and not just once, I went often. I saved the money, or found it lying about. A few times, if there was no other way, I stole the money. I am still ashamed of doing that.

But I had to keep going back to watch the Execution. You remember that peep show, don't you? The coin went into the slot, the light went on, then three little figures came jerking into the execution chamber: the parson, the hangman and the condemned man. They stopped. The parson's head nodded and the noose dropped down; the executioner's arms went up and put the noose round the man's neck. Then the trap door opened beneath his feet and he dropped and swung there for a few seconds, before the light snapped off and it was over.

One day I went down to the pier and they'd taken the machine away. I felt angry, but also a sort of desperate frustration, which went

*on boiling inside me for a long time. I didn't know how to get rid of it.
It has taken me all these years to find out.*

*Perhaps you knew all along that I disobeyed and went down to the
pier, because you once said, 'I know everything.' I hated that. I
needed secrets, things that were mine only and never yours.*

*But now I want you to know things, and if I still have secrets—and
I do—I want to share them, just with you. And now I can choose to
tell you and how much and when. Now, I am the one who decides.*

One

A Thursday morning in December. Six thirty. Still dark. Foggy.
Angela Randall was not afraid of the dark, but driving home at
this hour and at the end of a difficult shift, she found the ectoplasmic
fog unnerving. What lights there were seemed distant, small furred
islands of amber that gave neither illumination nor comfort.

She drove slowly. It was the cyclists she feared most, appearing
suddenly in front of her, out of the darkness and fog, usually without
reflective strips, quite often even without lights. She was not a confident driver. The dread of running over a cyclist or a pedestrian was
always with her. She knew what horror and grief death in a road accident brought. She could still hear the knock on the front door, still
see the outline of police helmets through the frosted glass.

She had been fifteen. Now, she was fifty-three. She found it hard to
remember her mother alive; those images had been blotted out by that
other—the face bruised and stitched, the small body beneath the sheet
in the cold mortuary light. There had been no one else to identify Elsa
Randall. Angela was the next of kin. Her father had died before she
was a year old, and there were no siblings, aunts or cousins.

At fifteen, she had been left entirely, devastatingly alone, but
through the following forty years she had come to make the best of it.
Until the last couple of years, she had not wanted anything else. She
had a few friends, she enjoyed her job, she had embarked on an Open
University degree. Above all, she blessed the day, twelve years ago,
when she had at last saved enough to sell her flat in Bevham and buy
the small house some twenty miles away in Lafferton.

Lafferton suited her perfectly, with its wide, leafy avenues and fine
Georgian houses. The cathedral was magnificent, and there were

quality shops, pleasant cafés. She felt comfortable in Lafferton.

It had shocked her, though, when she arrived at an age her mother had never been. Anxiety about future illness, infirmity, old age, crept up to the edges of her consciousness. Her life began to seem hollow.

But in April, when Angela Randall had fallen in love, the hollowness had been replaced by a passionate certainty, a conviction of destiny. She had at first been bewildered, a stranger to this all-consuming emotion, but had quickly come to believe that her move to Lafferton had been part of a plan leading to this culmination. She no longer gave loneliness and old age a thought. She had been rescued. Angela Randall loved with a dedication that had taken over her life. Before long, she knew, it would also take over the life of another.

As she left the protecting walls of the town centre, the fog and darkness closed in around the car. She turned left into Devonshire Drive and slowed down to fifteen miles an hour. Her eyes were sore, with tiredness and the strain of peering into the fog. It had been a difficult night at the care home. Sometimes the old people were settled and peaceful and there was rarely a call. But tonight five of the residents had gone down with an acute sickness virus, and at two o'clock they had had to call out Dr Deerbon. Miss Parkinson had walked in her sleep again and managed to reach the front door, unlock and unbolt it and get halfway down the path before any of them realised. Dementia was not pretty. The best anyone could do was damage limitation and safe confinement in a clean, friendly environment. 'You'll take me in, won't you,' she had more than once joked to Carol Ashton, who ran the Four Ways Home, 'if I ever get that way?' Well, she had no need to worry about any of that now. She knew she would not grow old alone, whatever her condition.

As she turned into Barn Close, she could make out her own white gate through the thinning fog. She let out a long sigh, releasing the tension in her neck and shoulders. She was home and she had a long sleep and a four-day break ahead.

Outside the car, the fog was like damp cobwebs across her skin, but from the Hill a slight breeze was blowing. Perhaps by the time she was ready to go out again, it would have dispersed the last of the fog. It would not have occurred to Angela Randall to change her routine. She was a woman of regular habit, and if she missed her run even for a day she noticed the difference the next time she went out.

She went into her tidy, spotless house. The carpets, an indulgence for which she had saved carefully, were thick. When she shut the front door, there was a soft, deep silence, padded, comforting.

During the next hour, she ate a small bowl of muesli and drank a single cup of tea. An egg on toast, with a rasher of lean bacon, tomatoes and more tea would come later, after her run.

She went upstairs to her bedroom, changed out of her uniform and dropped it into the laundry basket. She put on a clean white T-shirt and grey track suit and running shoes, and slipped the front-door key on a ribbon round her neck underneath her track-suit top.

As she closed the front door behind her, a thin, sour dawn was breaking over the Hill. The fog still hung about, wreathing among the trees and bushes on the slopes. Lights were coming on in the houses, but curtains were not yet drawn. No one looked out, keen to begin the day. It was not that sort of morning. At the far end of Barn Close, where the path to the field began, Angela Randall broke into a jog. A few minutes later, she was running, steadily and purposefully, across the open green and onto the Hill and, after only a few yards, into a sudden bolster of muffling, dense, clammy fog.

SUNDAY MORNING at a quarter past five and a gale blowing. Cat Deerbon lifted the phone on the second ring.

'Dr Deerbon here.'

'Oh dear . . .' an elderly woman's voice faltered. 'I'm sorry, I don't like disturbing you in the middle of the night, Doctor. I am sorry . . .'

'It's what I'm here for. Who is it?'

'Iris Chater, Doctor. It's Harry . . . I heard him. I came down and he was making a funny noise with his breathing. He isn't right, Doctor.'

'I'll come.'

The call was not unexpected. Harry Chater was eighty, a diabetic, had had two severe strokes, and recently Cat had diagnosed a slow-growing carcinoma in the bowel. His wife had insisted that he would be better at home than in hospital. Which, Cat thought, letting herself quietly out of the house, he almost certainly was.

She reversed the car out into the lane. It was pitch-dark and raining and the trees around the paddock were tossing wildly, caught for a moment in her headlights. It was eight miles from the village of Atch Sedby into Lafferton, and there was no one else on the road.

The moon came out from behind the fast-scudding clouds just as she reached Lafferton and saw the cathedral rising up ahead. Nelson Street was one of a grid of twelve terraces known as The Apostles. At 37, two-thirds of the way down, the lights were on.

Harry Chater was going to die, probably within the next hour. Cat knew that as she walked into the stuffy, crowded little front room. He was a man who had been heavy but was now shrunken into himself.

Iris Chater went back to the chair beside his bed and took his hand. 'Come on, perk up, Harry. Here's Dr Deerbon to see you. Dr Cat . . . you'll be pleased it's her.'

Cat knelt beside the low bed and felt the heat from the gas fire burning into her back. There was not a great deal she could do for Harry Chater, but what she would not do was call an ambulance and send him off to die, probably on a hard trolley in a corridor at Bevham General. She could make him as comfortable as possible, bringing in the oxygen cylinder from her car to ease his breathing, and she could stay with them both, unless she was called elsewhere. Cat Deerbon was thirty-four, a young GP, but one who, from a family of doctors going back three generations, had inherited the conviction that some old ways were still the best.

When Cat came back with the oxygen, Iris Chater was stroking her husband's hollow cheek. His pulse was weak, his breathing uneven, his hands cold. 'You can do something for him, can't you, Doctor?'

'I can make him more comfortable. Just help me lift him up on the pillows, Mrs Chater.'

Outside, the gale hurled itself at the windows. The gas fire sputtered.

'He isn't suffering, is he?' Iris Chater still held her husband's hand. 'It isn't very nice, is it, that mask over his poor face?'

'It eases things for him. I think he's quite comfortable, you know.'

The woman looked at Cat. Her own face was grey too, and creased with strain. She was nine years her husband's junior, a neat, energetic woman, but now she looked almost as old and ill as he did.

'It's been no life for him, not since the spring. He's hated this . . . being dependent, being weak.'

Cat adjusted the oxygen mask on Harry's face and got up. 'I think we could both do with some tea,' she said.

Iris Chater started from the chair. 'I'll get it, Doctor.'

'No,' Cat said gently, 'stay with Harry. He knows you're there, you know. He'll want you beside him.'

She went out to the small kitchen and filled the kettle. Outside, the wind slammed a gate. She prayed that her phone would not ring. A lot of Cat and Chris Deerbon's colleagues had become demoralised by the increasing administrative burden of general practice. It would be easy to give in, to palm the out-of-hours stuff onto locums. Cat was having none of it. Helping Harry Chater through his dying, and looking after his wife as best she could, were the jobs that mattered.

She filled the teapot and picked up the tray.

HALF AN HOUR LATER, Harry took a last, uncertain breath, and died.

The silence in the stifling room was immense, a silence that had the particular quality Cat always noticed at a death, as though the earth had momentarily stopped turning.

'Thank you for staying, Doctor. I'm glad you were here.'

'So am I.'

'There's everything to do now, isn't there? Where should I start?'

Cat took the woman's hand. 'There's no hurry. Sit with him for as long as you need to. Say goodbye in your own way. The rest can wait.'

When she left, the gale had died down and light was breaking. Cat stood by the car cooling her face after the heat of the Chaters' sitting room. The undertaker was on his way now and Iris Chater's neighbour was with her. All the dreary, necessary business that attends on death was under way. Her own job was done.

From Nelson Street at this hour on a Sunday it was a two-minute drive to Cathedral Close. There was a seven o'clock Communion service that Cat decided to slip into, after checking home.

'Hi. You're awake.'

'Ha ha.' Chris Deerbon held the receiver away from him so that Cat could hear the familiar sound of her children fighting. 'You?'

'OK. Harry Chater died. I stayed with them. If it's all right with you, I'll go to the seven o'clock, then take a coffee off my brother.'

'Simon's back?'

'He should have flown in last night.'

'You go. I'll take these two out on the ponies. You need to catch up with Si. I'm sorry about Harry Chater. Salt of the earth, he was.'

'Yes, but he'd had enough. I'm just glad I was there.'

THE SIDE DOOR of the Cathedral Church of St Michael and All Angels closed almost soundlessly. Much of the building was in shadow, but the lights were on, and candles lit, in the side chapel. Cat looked up into the space that seemed to billow out up to the fan-vaulted roof, then took her place among the couple of dozen kneeling people.

As she went up to the Communion rail, there came vividly into her mind the last time she and her brother had been here side by side. It had been at the funeral of three young brothers murdered by their uncle. Simon had been in the cathedral officially, as the officer in charge of the police investigation, Cat as the family GP. On her other side had been Paula Osgood, the forensic pathologist on the case. Paula had later confided to Cat that she was pregnant with her second child. How had she coped when examining those three small bodies?

The short service ended and she stood. A woman already making her way down the aisle caught Cat's eye and smiled.

Cat let her get ahead, then made quickly for the door on the other side of the centre aisle. From here, she could make a getaway across Cathedral Green and down the path that led to the close before anyone waylaid her for an apologetic, unofficial consultation.

FEW PEOPLE, apart from some cathedral clergy, now lived in the fine Georgian houses of the small close, most of which had long ago become offices for solicitors and chartered accountants.

Simon Serrailler's building was at the far end, with windows both onto the close and, at the back, overlooking a quiet stretch of the River Gleen. The entrance to 6 St Michael's was here beside a curved iron bridge leading to the opposite towpath. A posse of mallards was swirling about beneath it. In the spring it was possible to sit at Simon's window and watch kingfishers flash between the banks.

Cat pressed the bell at the top of the stepping stones of brass plates, beside a narrow strip of wood elegantly lettered: *Serrailler*. She had never been surprised at her brother's choosing to live alone at the top of a building surrounded by offices, which were empty for most of the time he was at home, and with only the ducks for company. Si was different from either of his triplet siblings, Cat and Ivo, even more different from their parents. He had never fitted easily into a family of loudly argumentative medics. How such a self-contained, quiet man fitted, and fitted well, into the police force was a mystery.

The building was dim and silent. Cat's footsteps echoed on the wooden stairs, up and up four narrow flights. *Serrailler*. The same lettering on the plate beside the bell.

'Cat! Hi!' Her brother bent from his six feet four to envelop her in a bear hug.

'I had an early call and then went to the seven o'clock service.'

'So you're here for breakfast?'

'Coffee anyway. Shouldn't think you've got food in. How was Italy?'

Simon went into the kitchen but Cat did not follow; she wanted to luxuriate in this room. It ran the length of the house and had long windows. Light poured in, onto Simon's pictures and his few carefully chosen pieces of furniture. Everything centred here, in this one calm room, where Cat came, she thought, for almost the same reasons she went to church—peace, quiet, beauty and recharging of spiritual batteries. Her brother's flat bore no relation to her own hugger-mugger farmhouse, always noisy and untidy, spilling over with children and animals. She loved it, but a small, vital nugget of herself belonged here, in this sanctuary of light and tranquillity.

Simon brought in a tray with the cafetière of coffee and took it over to the table in the window that overlooked the close and the back of the cathedral. Cat sat cupping her hands round a warm pottery mug, listening to her brother describe Siena, Verona and Florence, in each of which he had just spent four days.

'Was it still warmish?'

'Golden days, chilly nights. Perfect for working outside every day.'

'Can I see anything?'

'Still packed.'

'OK.' She knew better than to push Simon into showing her any of his drawings before he had selected what he considered the best.

When he had finished school, Simon had gone to art college, against the wishes, advice and ambitions of their parents. He had never shown the slightest interest in medicine, and couldn't be persuaded even to continue sciences beyond O level. He had drawn. He had always drawn. He had gone to art school to draw—not to take photographs, design clothes or to study conceptual art. He drew beautifully: people, animals, plants, buildings, odd corners of everyday life.

But he had not completed the course. He had been disappointed and disillusioned. No one, he said, was interested in teaching drawing. Instead he had read law at King's College, London, got a first and joined the police force. He had been fast-tracked into the CID and up the ranks to become detective chief inspector at thirty-two.

Twice a year and for snatched weekends in between, he went to Italy, Spain, France, Greece or further afield to draw. In the force, the artist who signed his work Simon Osler—Osler was his middle name—was unknown, as was DCI Simon Serrailler to those who went to his sell-out exhibitions in places far from Lafferton.

Cat refilled her mug. They had caught up with Simon's holiday, her family and local gossip. The next bit would be more difficult.

'Si—there is one thing.'

He glanced up, his face wary. How strange it is, Cat thought, that he and Ivo are two men of triplets and yet so unlike they might not even be brothers. Simon was the only one for generations to have fair hair, though his eyes were the Serrailler eyes, dark as sloes. She herself was recognisably Ivo's sister, though none of them saw much of him now. Ivo had worked as a flying doctor in the Australian outback for the past six years.

'It's Dad's seventieth birthday next Sunday.'

Simon looked out at the cathedral. He said nothing.

'Mum's doing lunch. You will come, won't you?'

'Yes.' His voice gave away nothing.

'It'll mean a lot to him.'

'I doubt it.'

'Don't be childish. Let it go. You know you can get lost in the throng—God knows there'll be enough of us.' She went to rinse her coffee mug in the sink. 'I must get back. Work tomorrow, then?'

Simon's face relaxed. They were on safe ground again. Her brother lived for his work and his drawing. Cat only occasionally wished that there was more. She knew of one thing, but it was a subject they only discussed if he raised it. He rarely did.

She gave him another hug and left quickly. 'See you next Sunday.'

'You will.'

WHEN CAT HAD GONE, Simon Serrailler made a second pot of coffee. In a moment he would unpack, but first he put in a call to Bevham CID. Work might not begin again officially until the following day but he could not wait until then to catch up, check on his cases, and more importantly find out what was new.

Two and a half weeks was a long time.

The Tape

I wonder if you ever realised how much I hated the dog. I hated it because it was your pet and you loved it but I also hated it just for itself. The dog slept on your bed. The dog licked your face. It hated me as much as I hated it. I knew that.

But strangely enough, if it had not been for the dog, I might never have discovered what I wanted to become, what my destiny was.

I know you remember the day. I was lying on the hearth rug teasing the dog by waving my fingers under its nose until it snapped, then whipping them away. I timed it to the split second and would never have been caught if I had continued in the same way. But I made a mistake. I leaned over it and growled to frighten it. Instead, it sprang up and bit my face, tearing a piece of flesh out of my upper lip.

I was sure you would take the dog to be destroyed for doing that to me, but you told me that it was my own fault.

'Perhaps that will teach you not to tease her,' you said. Can you understand how hurt I was by that? Can you?

I had never been to a hospital. You took me there on the bus, with a clean handkerchief pressed to my lip. I did not know what a hospital would be like, that it would be an exciting and dangerous place, and yet also a place of comfort and safety. I wanted to stay for ever.

What they did to me hurt. They bathed my lip in antiseptic. I loved its smell. Then they stitched my upper lip. The pain was indescribable yet I loved the doctor who did it, and the nurse in the shining white cap who held my hand. You had stayed outside.

So, you see, the fact that you loved the dog more than you loved me did not matter in the end because I had found my way.

Two

Thursday morning and the dawn just coming up through a dove-grey mist. On the Hill, a green island emerging out of a vaporous sea, the trees are all but bare, but the scrub and bramble are still berried and have the last of their leaves. Halfway up the Hill are the Wern Stones, ancient standing stones like three witches squatting round an invisible cauldron. At midsummer, robed figures gather to dance and chant. But they are laughed at and known to be harmless.

At this hour, a few runners are pounding their way up and down and round the Hill, always alone, noticing nothing. After a time, as the light strengthens and the mist rolls back, three young men on mountain bikes race up the sandy track to the summit.

A woman walks two Dobermanns, round the Wern Stones and briskly back down to the path.

Later the sun rises, blood red over the Hill. No one sees anything unusual. The Hill is the same as always, with its standing stones and crown of trees, yielding no secrets. Vehicles keep to the paved paths, and in any case it has rained; any tyre marks have been washed away.

DEBBIE PARKER LAY in bed, curled tight, knees drawn up. Outside her window the sun shone, but her curtains were dark blue and closed.

She heard Sandy's alarm, Sandy's shower water, Sandy's Radio BEV, but none of it meant anything to her. When Sandy had gone to work Debbie could sleep again, shutting out the sun, the day, life.

There was always a split second when she woke and felt OK, before the blackening misery crawled across her brain, like a stain seeping across absorbent paper. Mornings were bad. She woke to headaches that fogged her mind. If she made a mighty effort, went out and walked around town, the pain got slowly better. Midafternoon and she felt she could cope. Evenings were often quite good. Nights were not, even if she had had a few drinks. She woke around three with a start, heart beating too hard, sweating with fear.

'Debbie . . .'

Go away. Don't come in here.

'Ten to eight.'

The door opened, shooting light across the wall. Debbie did not move, did not speak.

'Come on.' The curtains were rasped open. The noise was like having her teeth pulled. Sandy Marsh, bouncy, bubbly, bright—and concerned. 'I've brought you some tea.'

'I'm OK.'

'You're not OK . . . I think you need to go and see the doctor.'

'I'm not ill,' Debbie mumbled into the yeasty hollow of bedclothes.

'You're not well either. Look at you. Maybe you've got that thing called SAD . . . it is December. It's a fact that more people top themselves in December and February than the rest of the year.'

Debbie sat up. 'Oh great. Thanks.'

Sandy's face was creased with concern. 'I'm sorry. I can't believe I said that. Oh God.' She reached out to hug her.

'You'll be late,' Debbie said.

'Stuff late. You're more important. Come on.'

In the end, Debbie got up and trailed to the shower. But before the shower came the mirror.

The acne was worse. Her whole face was blemished by the angry rash. She had been to the doctor about it once. He had given her foul-smelling ointment that had done no good at all. She hadn't bothered to finish the pot. 'I hate doctors,' she said to Sandy, sitting in their kitchen. Sandy had made toast and more tea.

They had known each other since primary school, and rented the flat together eight months ago when Sandy's mother had remarried. But what should have been good fun somehow never had been. Debbie had lost her job when the building society closed its Lafferton branch. Then the blackness had started creeping up on her.

'All the doctor will give me is a load of pills that'll space me out.'

Sandy stirred her tea. 'Maybe there's someone else you could see.'

'Like who?'

'Those sort of people who advertise in the health shop.'

'What? Like that creepy acupuncturist? Healers and herbal people? Bit cranky.'

'A lot of people swear by all that. Just take down some names.'

DOING SOMETHING made her feel better. There was a flicker of cheerfulness as she walked down to the health shop in Alms Street, near the cathedral. I might be OK, Debbie thought. I could get fit, lose two stone, find something to clear my skin. A new life.

The cards were crammed together on the cork board; she had to unpin several to get at the names and numbers. In the end she took down the details of three—aromatherapist, reflexologist and herbalist—and, after dithering a moment, one other . . . someone called Dava. She felt drawn to the card, a deep, intense blue dusted with a swirl of tiny stars. DAVA. SPIRITUAL HEALING. INNER HARMONY.

She stared at it, felt herself being pulled into the depths of the blue card. When she came out of the health shop, she felt better. And now and then, when she thought of the blue card during the day, she seemed to be able to draw something from it. At any rate, the blackness shrank back to the far edges of her mind, and stayed there.

'I WOULD LIKE to see someone in higher authority, please.'

Running a care home for fifteen elderly people in all stages of dementia had trained Carol Ashton to be patient and firm. She was also skilled in getting even the most recalcitrant to do as she asked eventually. All of which the desk sergeant recognised.

'You mustn't think we take reports of missing persons lightly, Mrs Ashton. But a surprisingly large number of people go missing.'

'I know. I also know that many of them turn up safe and well. All the same, I'd like to see someone who will take the matter further.'

Carol Ashton turned away from the desk and sat down on the bench seat against the wall. She had brought a book, knowing that she might have to wait for some time, but in fact she had barely time to read one paragraph. The desk sergeant had recognised a woman who would get out of his hair only when she had what she came for.

'Mrs Ashton? I'm DS Graffham. Will you come through?'

Daft, Carol thought, to be surprised that it was a woman, but somehow in her mind, detectives were always men.

The room she was ushered into was a dingy little featureless box with a metal table and two chairs, beige paint.

'I understand you are very concerned about an employee who has not been into work for a few days?'

She was pretty—elfin haircut, sharp features, big eyes.

'Angela—Angela Randall.'

'OK, tell me about Angela Randall . . . but before you do, can I get you a hot drink? I'm afraid it will have to come out of the machine.'

She will go far, Carol Ashton thought, stirring the tea. At least I hope she will. I hope someone doesn't see her as too relaxed. DS Graffham leaned back in her chair, looking straight at her, waiting.

'I run a care home for the elderly demented. The Four Ways.'

'And Mrs Randall works there with you?'

'Miss Randall. Angela. Yes. She's been with us for nearly six years. She's hard-working, caring, reliable, and being single without dependants she's happy to do night duty all the time. That's rare.'

'When did you last see her?'

'The last time she was at work, actually. She'd rung me in the middle of the night. I only live four doors down. Some of the patients got a nasty bug and I was needed. Angela was there then.'

'How did she seem?'

'Rushed off her feet of course, we all were. We didn't have much time to chat. But she was the same as ever—calm and dependable.'

'And she didn't come in the next night?'

'No, she wasn't due. She had a weekend and then four days off. Then I was off for a few days. When I got back there was a report that she hadn't been into work for four nights and hadn't rung in sick. That's out of character. Angela Randall would never just not turn up.'

'So what did you do?'

'Rang her—several times. There was never a reply.'

'Did you go round to her house?'

'No. No, I didn't.'

'Why ever not?' DS Graffham looked at her sharply.

Carol Ashton felt uneasy. She stirred the tea dregs. 'Angela is a very private person. It may sound strange but I have no idea, after six years, if she is divorced—or just single. She's perfectly friendly but she doesn't give anything away and you can easily overstep the mark with her. She can just . . . close up, you know? I've never been to her house, and I just wouldn't call on her. That must sound ridiculous.'

'It doesn't actually. There are people like that. Do you know of any family she may have?'

'No. She's never mentioned any at all.'

'Had she a history of depression . . . or anything that would cause her to be taken ill suddenly—diabetes or a heart condition?'

'No. She's never been ill—maybe a bad cold a couple of times.

I encourage staff to stay at home then. Our residents are vulnerable.'

'How old is she?'

'Fifty-three.'

'Is there anything you can think of that was different or strange about Miss Randall in the last few weeks . . . couple of months, say?'

Carol hesitated. There was something. 'It's hard to explain . . . Nothing was ever said. But once or twice I've thought she seemed a bit . . . distracted . . . miles away. I'd never noticed it in the past.'

'You think something was worrying her?'

'No . . . Oh, I don't know. Forget I said it. What will happen now?'

'We'll get someone round to her house to check.' She stood up. 'But don't worry, missing people have usually gone somewhere of their own free will. They either turn up again or get in touch. Very few come to any harm. Especially not sensible middle-aged ladies.'

'Thank you for that.'

'It's the truth.' The young woman smiled suddenly, so that Carol Ashton saw that she was not merely pretty, she was striking—and beautiful. 'And you came here. You did the right thing.'

'YOU HAVE SIXTY SECONDS to explain why we should take this one beyond the routine, Freya.'

DI Billy Cameron splayed himself back in his chair, hands held behind his head, a hairy, overweight, sweating bear of a man.

Freya Graffham recognised the DI for the sort of policeman the Met had once had in abundance—large and tough-talking with soft centres. She knew she would not find it easy to get round DI Cameron.

'Angela Randall, aged fifty-three, a woman who lives an orderly and predictable life. No family, no close friends, has never let her employer down. Not ill or depressed, as far as we know. Uniform went round today and found the house neat as a pin, car in the garage, table laid for breakfast, eggs in the saucepan, bread in the toaster.'

Cameron looked at her. 'Ninety-nine out of a hundred missing persons are a waste of police time, Freya. There'll be a secret lover somewhere . . . or she's topped herself. Bear that in mind before you go getting carried away.'

'Thanks, guv. I'll keep it simple.'

FREYA DROVE straight to Barn Close, taking young DC Nathan Coates with her and, when they arrived, sending him round to check with the neighbours. Freya wanted Angela Randall's house to herself.

'Weird,' one of the uniform patrol who had first been there had said, and as Freya closed the front door behind her she sensed at once what he meant. It was extraordinarily silent, almost like a heavy, dense textile surrounding her, impenetrable and tightly packed.

What kind of woman lived—or perhaps had lived—here? Freya went from room to room, trying to build up a picture. Clearly she was clean and tidy. The house was almost anonymous, like an out-of-date show home in which no one had ever lived. Freya opened drawers and cupboards: crockery, cutlery, linen; the bureau contained some papers—bank statements, pay slips, a building society book in which £1,236.98 was deposited, utility bills, paid and ticked off. On the shelves in the front room were a few unrevealing books—an atlas, a dictionary, a Delia Smith cookery course, a wild-flower guide.

'Come on, come on,' Freya muttered, 'give.'

It was what was not here that seemed significant; there was nothing personal—no photographs, letters, postcards from friends. Her handbag, which had been found on a chair in the kitchen, yielded nothing beyond a wallet with two credit cards, twenty pounds and some change, spectacles and tissues. The address book beside the telephone listed plumber, electrician, doctor, dentist, a hairdresser, an acupuncturist, the Four Ways Nursing Home, with Carol Ashton's private line listed separately. Angela Randall had apparently no relative, friend or godchild. How could anyone live such a barren life?

Freya went upstairs. The bathroom yielded plain, basic toiletries from Boots. No pampering went on here. The spare bedroom was clearly never used—the bed was stripped bare and the wardrobe contained a few blankets and pillows, plus two empty suitcases. So Angela Randall had not taken off on holiday.

In the main bedroom, the clothes in the wardrobe were scarcely more personal than everything else—beige coat, brown skirt, navy jumper, black suit, camel suit, white, blue and grey cotton shirts. But there were two track suits of good quality from a sports shop, and a pair of brand-new running shoes, still boxed—expensive.

So far, DS Graffham's mental picture of Angela Randall had been blank, like a jigsaw to which she had not been given any pieces. Now she had found the first to be fitted in. A single woman in her fifties had become a serious runner who spent £150 on one pair of shoes.

Freya was about to close the doors of the wardrobe and go downstairs to meet DC Coates when something caught her eye, a faint gleam at the very back of the cupboard. She reached in.

It was a small box wrapped in gold paper, tied with a gold ribbon. A small gold envelope was attached. Freya opened it.

To You, with all possible love from your devoted, Me.

She weighed the package in her hand. It was not heavy, did not smell or rattle. Was Angela Randall the 'You' or the 'Me'?

Freya went downstairs and let herself out of the front door as the DC was coming up the path. 'Any joy?' she asked.

'Not much. Neighbours that were in said she was always pleasant, kept herself to herself, no visitors. Only thing was, Mrs Savage on the corner said she'd taken up running in the last six months or so. She went out of the house every morning at the same time, regardless of whether she had just come in from night duty or just got up.' .

'Where did she go?'

'Up on the Hill, unless it was wet; then she went down the road.'

'And when did Mrs Savage last see her?'

'She is pretty sure she saw her going out for her run on the morning after Mrs Ashton reported her as last having been to work . . . Mrs Savage hasn't seen her since then. Thought she'd gone away.'

'Anything else?'

'Nope.'

'OK, let's get back. I've got a present to open.'

AN HOUR LATER, the golden gift stood on Freya Graffham's desk, shining like a prop for one of the three kings in a nativity play.

To You, with all possible love from your devoted, Me.

Freya hesitated. Going into Angela Randall's house, even searching through her drawers and cupboards, had seemed a job, routine. But opening this parcel felt like an invasion of privacy.

Freya smoothed her thumb over the gold paper, then took a paper knife to the neatly taped edges. The paper sprang open, revealing a gold box. Inside it, deep in a nest of blue velvet, was a pair of gold cuff links, set with deep blue lapis lazuli.

Not *for* Angela Randall then, but *from* her.

Freya looked at the cuff links . . . an intimate secret exposed on her desk. An extravagant gift from a lonely woman in late-middle age . . . to whom? A lover? Obviously. Yet if so, why had there been no other indication of a man in Angela Randall's life?

She went to fetch coffee from the machine. Without any clue to the woman's whereabouts or movements, with no suicide note and no body, she knew perfectly well she could not justify spending any more time on the case. Angela Randall had disappeared, and until she turned up again in some form, she was merely the number she had had assigned to her . . . Missing Person BH140076/CT.

CAT DEERBON STOOD at the window of her consulting room, looking out at the surgery car park. Rain streamed down the glass. It was almost nine o'clock and still not fully light.

Monday morning—a full list of appointments, two drugs reps, calls, an afternoon antenatal clinic, and Hannah to be taken to the dentist after school . . . But none of this troubled her very much, set beside the fact that Karin McCafferty had an appointment.

I can't do it, she thought—and it was a feeling so rare that it alone worried her.

Karin McCafferty was forty-four, a patient who had become a friend when Cat's mother, Dr Meriel Serrailler, had engaged her to redesign the garden at Hallam House. Cat saw her now—tall, with red hair that sprang from her head, and a long, oval, creamy-skinned face. Karin had given up a high-powered career in banking to become a garden designer and plantswoman, a change that had transformed her, she said.

Karin was great company, interested in a multitude of things as well as gardens. She and Mike McCafferty—a dull man, Cat thought—had been married for twenty-two years. No children.

The X-rays and report from the oncologist at Bevham General were on Cat's desk.

Her telephone rang. 'It's nearly quarter past.' Jean in reception.

'Sorry, sorry . . . wheel them in.'

She pushed Karin's results to one side. Fourteen other people needed her attention. She turned to smile at the first of them.

IRIS CHATER HAD AGED since her husband's death. But Cat knew, watching her walk disconsolately into the room, that the process was reversible. The shock and stress of bereavement, the tears, lack of sleep and loneliness had drained her. But she was not too old for time and rest to heal and restore her. Now, she sighed as she sat down.

'How are you coping?'

'I'm managing, Doctor, I'm not too bad. And I know Harry is best off now. I do know that.' Her sad eyes filled with tears.

Cat pushed the box of tissues across her desk.

'I hear him in the night . . . I wake up and I can still hear him breathing. I feel him with me in the room. I suppose that sounds daft.'

'No, it sounds normal.'

'I'm not going mad then?'

'Definitely not.'

Iris Chater relaxed, and her face took on a little more colour.

'Apart from missing Harry, how's your own health?'

'I'm just tired really. I can't eat much either.' She shifted in her chair, picked up her bag and put it down again.

'Just eat when you feel like it. Eat what you fancy . . . Your appetite will get back to normal when it's ready.'

'I see.'

Iris Chater was not ill; she needed reassurance and a listening ear. Nevertheless, Cat sensed that she was holding something back. She waited a moment, but nothing came.

'What you're going through is normal, Mrs Chater. You won't feel yourself again for a while yet, you know. Pop in and see me again in a month. In the meantime, if there's anything at all . . .'

The rest of the surgery took its course, through sore throats and period pains to ear infections and arthritic joints.

At twenty to twelve, Jean brought in a mug of coffee.

'There's just Mrs McCafferty.'

'Give me a couple of minutes.'

Jean smiled sympathetically as she went out.

HOW OFTEN, Cat wondered later, have I been helped through a difficult consultation by the patient? Been comforted myself by people who have just been told that their illness is terminal?

Karin McCafferty had been calm, controlled—and sympathetic. 'It's rotten for you too . . . probably worse with a patient you know as well as you know me.' She had given Cat a hug. 'But I'm OK . . . and I liked Dr Monk very much.'

It had been three weeks since Karin had first come to the surgery about the lump in her breast. Cat had suspected at once that it was malignant, but had been shocked at the results of the X-rays, which had shown extensive involvement of the lymph glands. The biopsy had revealed a particularly aggressive type of cancer. Now, Karin had had her first consultation with the consultant oncologist, Jill Monk.

'You can't begin to know how sorry I am.'

'Yes I can. And look what you've done . . . got me an appointment lightning fast and I know what a difference that can make.'

Karin looked bright—too bright, Cat thought. 'It's early days,' she said carefully, 'it takes time for all the implications to sink in.'

'Oh, it's sunk, don't you worry.'

'Sorry, I don't mean to patronise you.'

'You're not. People are meant to ask "Why me?" But why not me? It's random. After I saw Dr Monk, I got home, had a huge Scotch and howled my eyes out. But that's that. So let's talk about what's next.'

Cat glanced down at the oncologist's letter. It did not make cheerful reading. 'Surgery is the immediate way forward, as she told you. In this instance, she won't want to be too . . . conservative.'

'Full mastectomy, including the glands, yes, she said.'

'She might want to do a double mastectomy. Then chemo, certainly, and radiotherapy, possibly. Bevham General is a centre of excellence for oncology and I wouldn't recommend you go privately . . . though if you want an amenity bed, by all means pay for that.'

I'm babbling, Cat thought. Karin was unnerving her. She sat without fidgeting, apparently relaxed, and kept her eyes on Cat's face.

'Cat, I have thought about it . . . I have thought hard and carefully. And I've talked to Mike. And I don't want any of this. The only suggestion of Dr Monk's I did consider was the surgery. But chemo and radiotherapy I won't go near.'

'I'm not sure I understand you.'

'I want to go down the other route . . . alternative, complementary, whatever you call it. I'm sure it's a better way, Cat. I won't destroy my immune system with toxins and I won't be subjected to overdoses of radiation. You're my doctor and of course I will listen to what you have to say. But it is my body, my decision, and I live with it. Or not, I suppose. But whatever, it isn't yours so don't worry."

'Of course I worry . . . all my training and experience and instinct tell me to worry because you are wrong. Just plain wrong.' Cat got up and walked to the window. It was still raining.

'Are you washing your hands of me?'

'Look, Karin, it is my job to give you my professional advice. It's also my job to support you in any medical decisions you make. And you are a good friend. And the more certain I am that you are making the wrong decision, the greater my support has to be. OK?'

'Sorry. I'll need you.'

'You will.'

'I didn't think that you'd be so against the alternative way.'

'I'm not—in some circumstances, quite the contrary. I send patients to Nick Haydn for osteopathy, and to Aidan Sharpe who does acupuncture. But they don't cure cancer, Karin. The *most* complementary therapies could do is help get you through the proper treatment, make you less sick maybe and relax you generally.'

'So why don't I just get a facial and have my nails done?'

Karin stood up. Cat knew that she had put her back up and she was furious with herself. She walked with Karin towards the door.

'Promise me that at least you'll think hard about it.'
'I'll think. But I won't be changing my mind.'
'Don't burn your boats. It's your life we're talking about here.'
'Exactly.'

But then Karin had turned and given Cat another warm and accepting hug, before walking, calm and confident, out of the surgery.

'YOU CAN'T GO along with it, for God's sake.' Chris Deerbon faced Cat across the kitchen table, as they sat drinking mugs of tea late that night. He had just come in from a call. 'It's not an option, you know that . . . She hasn't the luxury of choice.'

'It worries me, of course it does, but Karin was very adamant.'

'She probably hasn't taken it in properly yet.'

'I think she has. If I'm going to support her I'm going to have to do some research . . . at least steer her clear of the real cranks.'

'I don't think you should encourage her even that far. She has to have surgery and chemo.' Chris got up and put the kettle back on the hob. He was totally opposed to all alternative treatments. 'There's too much of it about. Let Karin McCafferty loose among those loonies up at Starly Tor and she'll be dancing round Stonehenge at dawn.'

When Chris had left on the next night call, Cat had a bath, and then got into bed, propping her laptop on her knees. 'Cancer,' she typed into Google. 'Therapies. Alternative. Complementary.'

An hour and a half later, when Chris came in from dispatching a teenager with acute appendicitis to hospital, she was deep into a research article discussing the effects of a sustained programme of meditation and visualisation on cancer patients in New Jersey.

She had filled several pages of a notebook beside her. The least she knew she could do for Karin McCafferty was take her seriously.

IRIS CHATER lay on the sofa in the front room. The tiredness was worse, even though she had just slept for over two hours. The curtains were half drawn and she could see that it had turned dark outside. That was one of the harder things about being alone at this back end of the year: the short days and never-ending nights.

But for the moment, warm under a rug, she felt comfortable, and oddly happy. The room seemed to hold her in a glowing embrace and the warmth eased the arthritis in her knees. Best of all, she had the feeling that Harry was in the room with her. She spoke his name aloud, quietly, tentatively, startled by the sound of her own voice.

'Harry?'

She heard nothing but she knew he had answered her.

'Oh, Harry love, it's very hard. You won't go right away from me, will you? So long as I know you're here with me, I can manage.'

She willed him to be sitting in the chair opposite, to be able to see him, to have him show her he was all right, and not changed.

'I want to see you, Harry.'

The gas fire flared suddenly, and the flame went blue for a second. She held her breath, willing and praying.

'I want to see you,' she wailed aloud, and the sudden cold certainty that she would not was as bitter and sharp as at the beginning.

The tap on the back door made her start, until she heard Pauline Moss calling and struggled to get up from the sofa.

'I'm all right, I'm in here.'

Pauline was a good friend, but there were days when Iris thought she would prefer never to see or speak to another living soul again.

'I've made some drop scones. Shall I put the kettle on?'

Iris Chater wiped her eyes and replaced her spectacles.

'Hello, my dear—oh, did I wake you? I'm sorry.'

'No, no, I was just lying having a think. Time I pulled myself out of it.' She followed Pauline back into the kitchen. 'You are good.'

'I'm not, I'm selfish. I wanted drop scones and you gave me the excuse. I'll never get that weight off now with Christmas coming up.'

Christmas. Iris couldn't imagine it, didn't want to try.

They went into the front room and sat beside the fire. When the drop scones had been eaten and they were on their second cups of tea, Iris Chater looked affectionately across at her friend. 'I don't know what I'd have done without you these past few weeks. And all the time Harry was ill.' She reached forward to pour a last half-cup of tea from the pot. 'Harry's still here, you know.'

Pauline smiled. 'Well, of course he is . . . He's looking after you.'

'I mean here, in this room. It startles me sometimes. Only . . . I want to see him, to hear him . . . not just feel it. It's such a comfort, Pauline. I don't want it to fade away.'

The room was warm. The lamplight caught a row of brass monkeys on the shelf and made them glow.

'Have you ever, you know, thought of going to see someone? One of those spiritualists? A medium.'

Hearing Pauline speak aloud the idea that had been in her own mind made her flush and her heart jump.

'A lot of people do. A lot say that they do have a gift.'

'I'd be afraid.'

'What of?'

'Just . . . it would upset me.' She looked down at her cup. 'Besides, how would I go about finding one? I'd want to be careful.'

'The spiritualist church in Passage Street might have a notice board.'

'I never like the look of that place, it's a bit of a Nissen hut.'

'Well, I'll ask about a bit. I suppose you need someone to recommend you, don't you? Now, do you want to come in later and watch *The Weakest Link*?'

'I won't tonight, Pauline, I've a few bits to do.'

'Well, if you change your mind.'

'I know. You're a good friend.'

For a long time after Pauline had gone, Iris sat turning the idea of going to a medium over in her mind. In the end, she went next door to watch television with Pauline after all.

But no quiz programme could keep her from missing Harry or from thinking about having the chance to be in touch with him, if only she could summon up the courage. She worried about it all evening, and woke twice in the night, to worry again.

DS FREYA GRAFFHAM stood in the entrance hall of the Four Ways Nursing Home, waiting to be directed to Carol Ashton's office. The smell—polish and chrysanthemums to the fore, but with heavy notes of stewing meat—took her back to the corridors of her convent school.

Carol Ashton's office was bright and pleasant with pictures, plants and a comfortable chair.

'Have you found Angela? Do please sit down . . .'

'I'm sorry, I'm afraid we haven't.'

'It seems so long. I'm certain something has happened to her.'

'Mrs Ashton, I'm trying to build up a picture of Angela Randall. I wonder if you'd mind going back over a couple of things again?'

'I'll do anything, of course I will.'

'Do you know if she had any close relationships?'

'You mean a man? A love relationship?' The suggestion seemed to take Carol Ashton aback. 'I think I told you she isn't the sort who talks about her private life. But she's never mentioned anyone.'

'No one she might have bought expensive presents for?'

'I doubt it. What kind of presents do you mean?'

'We found a pair of gold cuff links in the house, gift-wrapped and with a note indicating some sort of affectionate relationship.'

'Goodness.'

'You can't think of anyone?'

'I can't. There just isn't anything like that about Angela.' She was thoughtful for a moment. 'If I had to choose a single word to describe her, I'm afraid it would be "chilly". That doesn't mean I don't like her because I do, and I respect her for her conscientiousness and loyalty.'

'I understand what you mean, don't worry.' Freya got up. 'There really is every possibility that she'll simply return home. The more private she is, perhaps the less likely she would be to confide in anyone if there was some problem in her life.'

For the rest of the afternoon Freya was at Bevham attending a seminar on Internet crime, with special reference to paedophiles. Regional HQ were setting up a special unit and keen to attract recruits. Freya Graffham was not in the least tempted to put her name forward for what she saw as a grubby, upsetting area of police work, but it paid to show keenness by signing up for a seminar. She had thought when she left the Met that she would be glad to leave ambition behind, together with the stress of a London that was becoming increasingly dangerous and depressing, and a short, unhappy marriage. Now she could feel the change beginning to heal and refresh her already. Lafferton had far more to offer than she had anticipated; she was happy sorting out her new house, and above all she was enjoying her job again. Enthusiasm filled her, as well as a confidence she thought she had lost during her last miserable year in London.

The seminar was followed by questions. Most went into Internet technicalities, and she found herself thinking yet again about Angela Randall, but the final question caught her attention, not because of what was asked but because of the questioner, DCI Simon Serrailler. He had interviewed her, but since her arrival at Lafferton had been on leave. She was reminded at once of how young he seemed for his rank.

At the end of the seminar he made his way across. 'I'm glad you could make it. Not very pretty, is it?'

'Grim. A couple of times I had to switch off, I'm afraid.'

'So we won't be losing you to the new unit?'

'Er . . . no.'

'Good. Perhaps you'll come and see me tomorrow, let me know how you're settling in?'

'I will, sir, thank you. I'm enjoying it very much.'

DCI Serrailler smiled, then turned away as someone tapped his arm.

THE STREETS OF BEVHAM were bright and crowded with late-night shoppers, and the Salvation Army band was playing carols. 'While Shepherds watched' came faintly through Freya's car window.

The previous Christmas had been the last she and Don had spent together, almost in silence, hostility and misery like a stormy sea between them. This year, having gently rejected pleas for joining the family Christmas at her sister's Cumbrian farm, she was looking forward to shutting her new front door and being by herself.

At the three slow sets of traffic lights down the high street, she thought again of Angela Randall. Where was she now, at this minute, at this bright, busy, happy season? Whatever DI Cameron might say, Freya Graffham knew she could not leave this one. She wanted to make her mark, that much she recognised. But that was the least of it.

She drove out of the city through the dark lanes, towards Lafferton and home, her mind full of the missing woman and a deep unease.

Three

'Starly . . . Starly . . . all change, please.'

Debbie Parker started, and for a second couldn't remember why she was sitting with cramped legs and stiff neck on an emptying bus.

'Late night, was it?' The driver muttered as she shuffled out.

She stood on the pavement watching the bus turn round and pull up at the stop on the other side of the street. The engine died and the driver climbed out. Everything went quiet. Tuesday afternoon in January was not a time when a place like Starly bustled with people.

She had over an hour to kill before her appointment with Dava. She would get a coffee somewhere and browse the shops.

The little town was set on two steep slopes that formed a T, with the main shopping street on the long side. Starly Primary School was opposite her, next to a Baptist chapel. Bank. Post office. At the junction of the T, the road went even more steeply downhill, and she saw that everything that made Starly the centre of New Age interests was clustered here. Every building had either a shop or some sort of centre . . . Feng shui. Crystals. Vegetarian and wholefoods. Herbalist. The New Age Book Centre. And in between the shops were doors with signs to the consulting rooms of healers and psychics.

The street was quiet, the shops mainly empty. Everything had a dispirited air. She found a small wholefood café and had a decaffeinated coffee and a piece of hard flapjack. The girl who served her had a cold.

'Could you tell me where Pilgrim Street is, please?' she asked.

'Oh, yeah, it's the alley behind here. Turn up by the candle shop.'

'Thanks. It's difficult in a place you don't know.'

'Yeah, right.'

She walked up the dim lane and caught sight of the blue—her blue, as she thought of it now—a patch of it that seemed to glow on the wall of a cottage. *Dava*. There was the same dusting of gold stars as she knew was on the card in her pocket.

It was still too early. She walked twice round the grid of sloping streets. There were very few people about. It was cold. At five to twelve, she rang the bell under the blue sign.

The door opened and a woman in a long skirt and a scarf tied round her head showed Debbie into a hall. Coloured light came in dimly through a stained-glass panel. She opened a second door and held it open for Debbie to go inside. There was a round table and two chairs, and the walls were hung with some sort of softly draped fabric. Candles were burning, giving off a sweet smell.

'Please come in, Debbie.'

He was sitting at the table, wearing a collarless velvet coat, like a clergyman's cassock. He had long brown hair and there was a chain with a plain silver Celtic cross round his neck.

Debbie's heart thudded.

'Don't be nervous. Please—come and sit down.'

He waited in silence for Debbie to unbutton her jacket and put her rucksack down. She fidgeted, nervous and uncertain. But then she looked up and into his eyes. They were steady on her face, large eyes with thick lashes, and they were blue, a blue as deep and magnetic as the blue of the card. Debbie gave a great, shuddering sigh of relaxation. She was no longer anxious, no longer afraid.

'Good,' Dava said. His voice was rather ordinary. 'Welcome to the Sanctuary, Debbie. Whatever troubles and fears you have brought to me today, we will look at them carefully and I will begin to heal you. Whatever pain—mental, physical or spiritual—is dragging you down, we will deal with. Not all at once. But gradually you will begin to feel renewed, in harmony with yourself and the world.'

Listening to Dava was like listening to running water or breezes riffling softly through leaves. As he spoke, he looked at her steadily and the power of his eyes was so great that she was forced to look away. It was like not being able to stare into the sun.

'First, I will take you through a simple meditation to relax you and free any tensions. I will tune into your energies and sense the strength or weaknesses of your chakra. Then I can discover what your problems are. But you can also tell me what in particular you have come to consult me about. Have you any questions or worries, Debbie, before we begin? Please feel free to ask anything at all.'

He sat with his hands folded in front of him on the table. She had never known anyone sit so still. He seemed scarcely to be breathing.

'No.' Her mouth was dry and her voice sounded unfamiliar. 'No, thank you. I'm . . . I'm very happy with everything.'

'Good. Good, Debbie. Then close your eyes and let me begin.'

SHE WAS FLOATING somewhere above the ground surrounded by a soft violet-blue haze. She was listening to birdsong and running streams, waves hushing over sand and wind in trees . . .

She had been talking about her childhood, when her mother had been alive. She had talked about walking with her through leaves in a golden wood, laughing as they threw snowballs. She had talked about her mother lying in bed pale and hideously thin, about the death and the funeral, and how she had gone out and sat in the garden rather than listen to her father's weeping. She talked about her new step-mother and how she had hated her in those early weeks.

Now, she found herself floating upwards, like a deep-sea diver coming gently to the surface of the water.

'Good, Debbie . . . Rest there. Rest quietly.'

Tears were streaming down her face. She was lying on a couch and the ceiling above her was blue and dusted with tiny gold stars.

Dava sat on a stool beside her. 'When you're ready, sit up.'

'Have I been asleep? Was I dreaming?' she asked.

'We call it a trance sleep . . . a waking sleep. It is deeply healing and tonight you will sleep better than you have for months. But you were safe. Quite safe.' Dava got up with a swish of his long coat, and went back to his seat. 'When you feel ready, come over here again and sit down. You have a bright shining path ahead of you, Debbie, but there are obstacles in the way. Tell me about them. Tell me what is it about yourself that you want to change?'

'I'm fat. I hate my spots. I hate the blackness that comes down.' She had never imagined being able to speak so easily, listing the things she was ashamed of as if they were items on a shopping list.

'After this consultation, I will be sending you written instructions and some prescriptions. A diet sheet—but that is so simple. Eat only organic vegetables, fruit and wholefoods. Drink only water or herbal teas. Eat no animal products, no dairy, no bread, no sugars. Drink no alcohol, no coffee, tea or chocolate. I will also make up some herbs, and an ointment for your skin. The black moods and the headaches will lift, slowly. At first they may become worse. Just rest. And walk as much as you can in the fresh air. Walk and dance and run, and let your soul sing. The process of healing and harmony has begun. I see love and light surrounding you and a joyful future, once we have cleared the darkness and the obstacles from your path.'

There was a silence. Dava had closed his eyes. One of the incense sticks burning in a jar on the table flaked into a pile of soft grey ash.

Dava opened his eyes and got up in one, brisk movement. 'I will send you another appointment for a time that is auspicious.'

She looked directly into his eyes but they now had an opaque, veiled look. His face was expressionless.

'Thank you . . . yes. Thanks.' She stumbled out of the door, flushing with embarrassment. The woman in the long skirt was standing there. She said nothing. The front door swung silently open, and Debbie found herself in the lane alone.

She half ran down the steep slope and round the corner to the wholefood café. It was only when she was halfway through her mug of coffee and slice of carrot cake that Debbie remembered she was forbidden to have either. But she needed them. She stayed in the café until it was time to walk up the hill to catch her bus home.

SHE WOKE A LITTLE after eight o'clock the following morning. The first thing she realised was that she had indeed slept deeply, peacefully and without dreaming. Fifteen minutes later, she was still lying in her cocoon, wide awake and blissful in the realisation that the black fog had not crept over her to blot out the rest of the day.

She got up tentatively, as if movement might trigger the descent of the blackness. But she showered and dressed and it did not happen.

Sandy was in the kitchen, loading the washing machine.

'You look different,' she said at once. 'You all right?'

Debbie put the kettle on and reached for mugs and milk. She was not yet sure how much she wanted to talk about Dava. 'A bit blotto. I slept too long. Come on, tell me about your holiday.'

For ten minutes or so, Sandy did. The winter sun shone through the kitchen window. Debbie kept testing herself to see how she felt, as if she were touching a tooth to see if it were still sore. When Sandy had finished speaking they sipped their tea in silence at the wobbly Formica-topped table.

'Well, something has happened to me,' Debbie said eventually.

The first few sentences came slowly as she tried to convey the power and the impact and the beauty of Dava, but then the words poured out, rushing together, describing everything he had told her. Sandy listened intently, without interrupting.

The sun moved up the wall behind them. Debbie's words dried up and the kitchen was quiet. She felt drained by the effort.

'Are you going again?' Sandy asked.

'He'll send me an appointment . . . when it's auspicious.'

'Right.' Sandy's voice conveyed nothing, neither approval and enthusiasm nor suspicion.

'He's sending me some tablets . . . herbal things for the headaches and some skin ointment.'

'Is it expensive?'

'I don't think it can be. He isn't someone who would take a lot of money off you, you can tell. He knows I'm on benefit anyway.'

'Right.'

Debbie looked at her sharply. 'Listen, it's all OK, Sand. It's fantastic. I mean, I feel really, really better just since yesterday.'

'Great.' Sandy got up and took the mugs to the sink. She rinsed and drained them, then she glanced round. 'You do look better.'

'I feel like I'm reborn.' Debbie straightened her back and felt herself to be floating above the ground as she went out of the kitchen.

The sun slid off the wall, leaving the room in shadow.

JAKE SPURRIER took a long time to put on his shoes and zip up his jacket, partly because everything took ages these days because he felt tired, partly because he was hating the idea of a visit to Mr Sharpe.

'Jake, it doesn't hurt.'

'It did hurt. When I went for my sore throats and he stuck the needles into my neck, it mega hurt.'

'You didn't have another sore throat afterwards though, did you?'

'I've got one now.'

As he turned away, Jenny Spurrier looked anxiously at her ten-year-old son. He had never been especially robust, but lately he had been complaining of tiredness, and he was paler than normal. The acupuncture had cured Jake's sore throats before and generally given him more energy and stamina. He had played football for the school team for a whole season, only missing one game because of a cold. In the last month or so, though, he had become run-down again, and he had been put on the bench by the football coach.

'You want to get back on the team, don't you, Jake?'

Jake grumbled, but his mother knew how to get to him. 'OK, OK.'
He stood up from finishing his shoelaces and fell towards Jenny.

'Jake, what's the matter? It's all right . . . Sit down here. Bend forwards and put your head on your knees.'

'Everything went all wobbly . . . The floor wasn't there.'

'You felt faint. It happens sometimes when you stand up quickly.
Just sit there for a minute. We won't go until you feel all right.'

Ten minutes later, Jenny Spurrier put a protesting Jake into the
front seat of the car.

'I can put the belt on myself. I'm OK, Mum, don't fuss . . .'

'Sorry.'

But he was too pale, Jenny thought, far too pale.

AS THEY WALKED into the bright reception area of Aidan Sharpe's
surgery, Jenny felt herself relax for the first time in days. Jake was
going to be looked after. Jake was going to be all right.

There was a water cooler, there were comfortable chairs and a sofa,
and a bowl of sweet-smelling hyacinths on the receptionist's desk.
Aidan Sharpe's professional qualification and membership certifi-
cates were framed on the wall beside the reception desk.

'Mum, have I got to have it done?'

But Jenny had no time to answer.

'Good morning, Mrs Spurrier . . . Jake.' Aidan Sharpe was crossing
the room from his surgery, his white coat crisp, his brown brogues
shining, his small goatee beard neatly cut.

The surgery was more businesslike than the outer room, with a
desk and chair, the treatment couch and the tray with needles and
steriliser. But the sun was on this side, filling the room with light.

'How long is it since I saw you, Jake?' Aidan Sharpe looked down
at his notes. 'Eighteen months. And the sore throats cleared up?'

'It only took the two treatments,' Jenny said. 'He's been so well.'

'But they're back now, and you said there was something else
worrying you about Jake, Mrs Spurrier?'

He wrote carefully as Jenny Spurrier took him through Jake's tiredness, aching legs, loss of appetite, and that morning's near-faint.

'OK, Jake, would you swap places with Mum please? I want to
have a look at you in a good light. Great. Let's look at the throat first.'

He took a sterile spatula from its packet and pressed the back of
Jake's tongue down, then examined his eyes and ears.

'Right, Jake, take off your outer clothes and T-shirt, just keep on
your pants. Then lie on the couch. I'll have a look at the rest of you.'

Jake lay, watching the sun make bright discs on the white ceiling as it reflected against the metal rim of the lamp.

The acupuncturist was touching Jake's calf gently. 'Rough game?'

'No, they just came.'

'I see. Any more bruises like that?'

'I had one on my arm but I think it's gone.' He looked, but saw that another bruise had formed, larger than the first.

'Right. Have you had any nosebleeds recently?'

'No.'

'You did, don't you remember?' his mother said. 'A week ago.'

'Any more since then, Jake? At school?'

'No.'

There had been, but Jake had had enough of being interrogated.

'OK, Jake, you can get dressed now and then would you just wait outside for a few moments while I go through the boring bits with your mum. Mrs Cooper has some orange squash if you're thirsty.'

'Aren't you going to stick the needles in me?'

'Not today.'

'Yessss.' Jake pulled on his clothes, and vanished before the acupuncturist could change his mind.

'Mrs Spurrier, I'd like you to make an appointment with Dr Deerbon for Jake as soon as possible.'

'Why?'

Aidan Sharpe was looking at her steadily. 'I don't want to make any diagnosis. I'm not a doctor, you know.'

'As good as. Better than some I've known.'

'Thank you.' A smile of pride and pleasure lit up his face. 'All the same, I need a report from the GP before I can consider giving him any treatment. There may be nothing wrong, but some of his symptoms need to be investigated. I'll drop Dr Deerbon a note.' He stood up. 'When I've heard from her and if she's happy, we'll make another appointment. There'll be no charge for this consultation.'

'Oh, I must pay you. We've taken up your professional time.'

'No, Mrs Spurrier. I don't charge when I don't treat. Now, let's go and release young Jake from the acupuncturist's prison.'

AIDAN SHARPE saw Jenny Spurrier and her son cheerfully off the premises, but when he returned to the receptionist his face was grave.

'Julie, I've got ten minutes before Mr Cromer. Would you try and get me Dr Deerbon—Dr Cat?'

Cat's voice came through straight away.

'Aidan? Good morning. What can I do for you?'

'Jake Spurrier . . . aged ten. Felstead Road.'

'I know. Mother is Jenny. Nice family.'

'Yes. I'm afraid I'm rather concerned. She brought the boy in to me this morning. I saw him about eighteen months ago for sore throats. Gave him a couple of treatments and they cleared up.'

'I remember.'

'Well, I didn't treat Jake today and I've suggested his mother bring him to you. He reports fatigue, nosebleeds, aching limbs, occasional faintness, and has a nasty strep throat. He also has some bruising on his arms and legs. Alarm bells rang pretty quickly.'

'Pallor?'

'Yes.'

'All the signs then. Thanks very much, Aidan, I'm glad you picked up on it. I'll get them to put him in as an emergency appointment. A blood test will tell us what we want to know pretty smartly.'

'Let me know, will you?'

Aidan Sharpe put down the phone and swung his chair round to look out of the window onto the garden. Two squirrels were leaping from tree to tree at the far end, then racing across the grass. If Jake Spurrier had one of the aggressive forms of childhood leukaemia, as he suspected, it would be a long time before he'd be racing about, playing with such abandon—if he ever did.

THE SENSATION of well-being and tranquillity that Dava had created did not fade or weaken during the next few days. Debbie Parker slept wonderfully well each night and woke calmly, happy to face the day.

She threw out every tin, packet and jar of food from the cupboard and her section of the fridge, and spent almost a week's benefit money on organic fruit, vegetables and cereals. She went out every day and walked, around parts of Lafferton she had never been near before, in the park, along the towpath and on the Hill.

Sandy watched her, and said nothing. She was concerned, but it was a relief not to see her flatmate grey and crushed under her misery, not to have to coax her out of bed in the mornings.

Almost a week after Debbie had gone to Starly, a package arrived.

The tablets smelt like compost and the plastic pot of ointment was of a repellent texture. They were packed with a list of instructions and a bill for seventy-five pounds.

She had not asked how much it would all cost and now, defiantly, she told herself that she did not care. Dava was making her better.

She'd write to her father and ask if he could send her a hundred pounds for some treatment for her skin.

That night she undressed, washed her face and patted it dry, as directed, on a clean towel. The ointment had to be applied only at night, before going to bed. It made her skin tingle slightly.

Something about the ritual made her feel in contact with Dava, and the calm feeling, as if she were drifting out to sea, lulled her into one of the new, dream-free sleeps.

SOMETHING WAS WRONG. She was dreaming again, but the dream was part of a struggle to come awake. She could not make out whether she was in pain or could not breathe, and in the half-waking dream someone had glued her eyelids together and, even when she prised them apart, there was darkness and a burning sensation. Then, through it, there was a sudden, painful flash and Sandy's voice.

'Debs . . . wake up, you were screaming, you were having a nightmare. Oh my God, what's happened to your face?'

Debbie sat up. She could see a little now, through the slits that were her eyes. Her face felt strange. Her skin was burning.

'It's that bloody ointment. It's made your whole face swell up.'

Debbie's breathing hurt too. She felt as if she were pushing against a door when she breathed out, only someone was pushing it back.

'I'm going to ring the doctors. They'll come, it'll be OK.'

She heard Sandy leave the room but still there was only a slit of light. If she lay down it was harder still to breathe. Her chest creaked.

'The doctor's coming and she said to turn on all the taps and get the bathroom steamy, and take you in there. Oh, Debbie, promise me you won't go to any more cranks.'

The steam was good. Debbie felt her chest loosening slightly, but her eyes remained almost closed and her skin felt as if she had scalded herself. She thought she was going to be sick.

Half an hour later, she was sitting on the couch, breathing easily through a nebuliser as the injection of antihistamine Dr Deerbon had given her took effect. Her eyelids were still swollen but she could see the doctor in a blurred outline against the light of the lamp.

'What should I do?' Sandy said anxiously to Cat Deerbon, as she showed her into the bathroom to wash her hands.

'She'll be sleepy soon, and her breathing is almost back to normal. Keep the nebuliser by her, though, and if she gets worse again call an ambulance. I've left some antihistamine tablets for her. Could you show me these herbal potions she got hold of?'

Sandy fetched the bottle and the ointment. 'Makes you wonder what's in them to do that to her.'

'People do get allergic reactions to all sorts of medicines, even the usual stuff you get at the chemist. It's a very individual thing. But I'll take these for now; I want to try to find out what's in them.' Cat picked up her bag. 'I'll ring in the morning to find out how Debbie is. Call me if you're worried; I'm on duty all weekend. And would you tell her I'd like to see her in the surgery on Monday?'

As she drove home Cat made a mental note to talk to one or two colleagues about the person calling himself Dava.

ON ONE OF HER FIRST free evenings in Lafferton, Freya Graffham had gone to the cathedral for a performance of Handel's *Messiah*. She had sung alto in it more times than she could remember, as she had sung in many other things before Don had objected and, in an attempt to placate him, she had resigned from her choir. Don had resented anything that took Freya out of the house without him.

As she sat revelling in Handel's mighty choruses, she had wondered briefly again how she could have married Don Ballinger. Her tastes and pleasures had been crushed under his disapproval, her personality barely allowed to express itself. Sitting in that glorious building listening to music she knew so well, she had realised again that she was free, answerable only to herself.

'*Every valley shall be exalted.*'

She wanted to join in. She knew every alto line, every biblical word.

In the programme she had found details of the St Michael's Singers, who had backed the professional soloists, and the address of the auditions secretary. When she got home, she had written to ask for details of the next audition.

THE AUDITION was in the church hall the following week. Four others were there, and she and two of them, a man and an older woman, were accepted. The audition was not an easy one—the standard of the St Michael's Singers was high—but from the moment she took her note from the piano, she felt as if she were soaring as joyfully as a bird. She had missed singing more than she had realised.

The choirmaster filled them in on the coming season, and asked if anyone could give a hand with the choir's social evening in a week's time. Freya volunteered, work permitting, and later that evening she tried the number that the choirmaster had given her for the member arranging the catering.

'Hello, my name is Freya Graffham, I've been given this number by the choirmaster at the St Michael's—'

An irritable male voice interrupted. 'You want my wife.'

Another husband who sounded as if the less he had to do with his wife's activities the better.

'Meriel speaking.'

Freya began to explain why she was phoning but was cut short, this time by a cry of delight.

'You don't mean you're offering to help? You saint!'

'I could make some puddings for you. How many will be coming?'

'Anywhere between twenty and a hundred and fifty, my dear— they're all hopeless at replying. If it is a hundred and fifty, God help us as we're having the party here. My husband will explode.'

'I'll do half a dozen or so different things then. Shall I bring them on the day?'

'Please. And I hope you'll be coming to the party. It's so good to have new faces—and voices of course. Do you live in Lafferton? I don't recognise your name.'

'I only moved here a month or so ago. But I'm so pleased I managed to get into the choir. I belonged to a choral society in London.'

'Wonderful. Well, here's the address.'

Freya took down the address and directions, then the woman rang off briskly. The warmth in her voice and her welcome had made Freya feel good. She smiled to herself. She had her music back, and now her social life looked like getting established.

THE NEXT TIME Freya was off duty, she spent the afternoon buying clothes in Bevham. As she came out of a boutique, she glanced up and noticed the name E J. DUCKHAM & SON over the window of a smart jeweller's next door. The box containing the gold and lapis lazuli cuff links had had this name printed on the inside of the lid.

Uniform had done the usual checks and reported nothing. She made a mental note to recheck the report before visiting the shop herself. Someone in a small, expensive jeweller's would surely remember something about the purchase of such a pair of cuff links.

THE FOLLOWING SATURDAY, Freya spent the morning putting the finishing touches to a dozen pies, gateaux and puddings before packing them into bakers' trays borrowed from the station canteen.

Finding the house was easy. There were stone pillars and a drive that wound between beech trees, under which spread a mass of snowdrops.

The house was Edwardian, red brick with tall chimneys. On the wide lawn were more snowdrops, and the first few ice-blue crocuses.

'You're Freya? Welcome, welcome. This is so good of you.'

She was tall and thin, with a shrewd, intelligent face. She wore jeans and a T-shirt, her hair was grey and pinned up on top of her head and she might be anywhere between fifty-five and seventy-five.

She held out her hand. 'Meriel Serrailler.'

'Goodness, surely you must be . . .'

'Who?' And as her hostess turned, Freya saw the resemblance immediately. It was the nose.

'Serrailler. My DCI is called Simon Serrailler.'

'My son. Heavens above, you're a policewoman!'

'DS Freya Graffham, Lafferton CID.'

They made three journeys to bring every tray into the kitchen, after which Meriel Serrailler took off the cloths and gazed admiringly at the chocolate torte, grapefruit and mint mousse, rhubarb and honey crumble, hazelnut and coffee pavlova, and soft-berry charlotte.

'My dear, what a feast! Why on earth are you a policewoman? Why aren't you running your own pudding empire?'

Half an hour later, they were sitting at the scrubbed wooden table with mugs of Earl Grey and pieces of shortbread, and Freya knew a great deal more about Lafferton, the cathedral, the St Michael's Singers, Bevham General Hospital, and the various medical Serraillers. She felt as if she had known this woman half her life.

Meriel Serrailler had been a beauty, but age had made her lined and bony. And, Freya thought, it didn't matter a jot. Beauty may have gone, but intelligence, charm, and a lively interest in people shone out.

'Now it's your turn. I want to know where you've come from and why and who you've met in Lafferton and what you've joined.'

Freya was about to launch into an account of herself when a car drew up outside and someone came straight into the house.

The door opened on Freya's DCI.

Freya started to get up. 'Good afternoon, sir.'

'Oh, don't start all that for heaven's sake, you're not on duty now,' Meriel said. 'Hello, darling, I hope you haven't come to stay, you know it's the St Michael's supper tonight. Look at all this, isn't it wonderful? I've just told Freya she's wasted as a detective.'

'She's nothing of the kind.' Simon Serrailler sat down next to his mother and reached for the teapot. Then he glanced at Freya, smiled, and started dunking shortbread in his tea.

Afterwards, Freya decided that it was not one thing that she remembered, it was everything—the winter light through the leaded windows, the warmth of the kitchen, the sight of a pot of purple crocuses on the window ledge; her delight in this new friendship with Meriel Serrailler. Everything came together, in a moment of extraordinary assurance and clarity.

For a few seconds she dared not look up.

When, eventually, she raised her head she saw he was not looking at her, but at his mother. She saw the similarity of their bone structure and the complete dissimilarity of their colouring. She looked at the fingers of his right hand, curled round the handle of the mug, those of his left spread out flat on the table. He was saying, 'I promise I'll go next week.'

It is called a *coup de foudre*, she thought. It is falling in love terrifyingly and completely in an instant. It is this.

SHE DRANK THE LAST of her tea and stood up. She had to get out quickly, be alone in her car. I do not want this, she said impatiently to herself, I am not ready and it is not right. I do not want any of this.

Meriel Serrailler came with her to the door. 'You are so, so kind! I can't tell you what a difference you've made. Now, we'll see you later.'

Damn, Freya thought, damn, damn, damn.

He called goodbye to her from the kitchen, but she was going, out of the door and almost running to the car. Her fingers getting into a tangle with the key and the lock.

Damn.

She heard the gravel flying up under her wheels and the screech of her skidding tyres.

For a few miles, she drove fast, before coming to a village with a small bridge that curved over the river. Freya stopped and got out, then stood at the foot of the bridge looking down into the water.

She was shocked by what had just happened. When she had seen the DCI at the seminar in Bevham, she had thought him pleasant, young for his rank, and with unusual looks. Today, when he had sat down at the kitchen table, she had looked at him and fallen in love.

Simon Serrailler's face looked up at her from the cold water. The shape of his hands, the strands of his fair hair, the movement of his head as he turned it towards her were bitten into her memory.

She shivered.

To You, with all possible love from your devoted, Me.

In that split second, Freya knew what Angela Randall's note meant. She understood her. A lonely, middle-aged woman had fallen in love;

the love was probably unrequited, possibly unsuitable, and Angela Randall was in thrall to it. Women in such situations recklessly buy the object of their love expensive presents, regardless of whether they can afford it, even careless as to whether they will be welcomed.

Freya felt a vivid moment of empathy with the woman, and a certainty that she was right.

The Tape

You once told me that you came to the hospital and waited for the chance of seeing me, as you said, 'looking like a doctor'. You waited almost three hours but mine was not one of the white-coated figures who went past, and in the end you gave up and went home. You had no idea that the students were in a different building, and during the first year rarely wore white coats. But you wanted to see me because you knew that when you did you would believe that I was actually there, a real medical student. You were so proud of me then.

During those first few months, I did not really believe that I had achieved the thing I had longed for and worked towards since the day I had had my lip stitched at the hospital. The medical lectures were interesting enough but I wanted the real medical training to begin. I wanted to dissect the human body.

The first time we went into the dissecting lab and I saw the corpses on the slabs, I felt faint, not from shock or distaste but with excitement. This was where I had wanted to be for so long. But after a couple of weeks, it all seemed pedestrian. It was not enough.

I struggled through much of the learning. The chemical formulae, the physiology, the lists of diseases had to be committed to memory, and I found it hard. But I would never have given up. You had sacrificed everything for me to be there and I have never forgotten that.

What spurred me on was the prospect of going into the operating theatre and watching real surgical work on bodies that were alive, with hearts that throbbed and blood pumping through their veins.

Then one day I asked a question about post-mortem examinations and, for an answer, I was sent to observe one.

I wish you could understand what I felt when I first walked through the swinging plastic doors leading to that brightly lit, white-tiled room. Perhaps everyone who studies medicine has a defining moment that shows them the pattern of their future.

For me, the defining moment came in the mortuary.

Four

The doctor's surgery was a couple of miles away on the other side of the town and normally she would have caught a bus. But this morning Debbie walked. And every step she took made her feel more in tune with the universe. She remembered everything Dava had said to her about expanding her mind and spirit and she felt intensely conscious of the expanse of blue sky above her and the earth deep below her, to which she was attached by powerful natural forces.

She knew that she did not really need to visit Dr Deerbon this morning. Dava would guide her through the changes that would take place on her way to a new life. She would be slim, with a clear skin; she would make more friends. Her whole being would expand.

She reached Manor House Surgery damp with sweat and with a blister forming on her left heel, but happy. The room was full of young women with coughing toddlers and old men complaining about the delay, and the magazines were dogeared, but to Debbie everything was beautiful and part of the one harmonious whole.

'Debbie Parker, please.'

Dr Deerbon looked pale and had a cold. It seemed to have put her in a bad mood. 'For goodness sake, what were you thinking of, Debbie? Had you any idea what you were taking or what the stuff you put on your face had got in it?'

Debbie felt crushed.

'Let me have a look at your skin. Come over to the light.'

'I didn't know it would do any harm, did I? You said yourself people can have reactions to all sorts of ordinary things.'

'Yes, I did. I'm sorry, Debbie. Blame a bad night but I shouldn't take it out on you. Now, let's sort out this acne. I'm giving you an antibiotic, which you'll take for six weeks. Make sure you finish the course. The acne will gradually improve and it won't come back.'

'And is that it? No creams and stuff?'

'No. You don't need to put anything on your skin; the antibiotics will do the job.' She looked down at Debbie's notes. 'You haven't had asthma before, have you?'

'No. I don't think so, anyway.'

'Probably a one-off reaction then, but I'm going to prescribe you an inhaler. You may well never have another attack for the rest of your life, but even one has to be taken as a warning. The nurse will take you through how to use it.'

'Right. Thanks.' Debbie stood up.

'Don't go. I want to talk to you about this person you saw at Starly.'

'Oh.'

'I keep an open mind about complementary therapies, but there are a lot of cranks about. They can do harm. You've been depressed and that can make you vulnerable. So, who did you see?'

Debbie trusted Dava—he spoke to her as no one else ever had—but she felt foolish in the face of Dr Deerbon's questioning.

'He's . . . he was really good, Doctor. It was just talk, really.'

'Talk isn't always harmless. Besides, he prescribed the pills and the ointment. I took them away the other night, did your flatmate tell you? I'm having them analysed. So what did he do?'

'It was just talking, like I said.'

Debbie was not going to tell her about the couch and the floating feeling, the strange sense of having been out of herself.

'Would you be willing to give me a name?'

'He's called Dava.'

'Dava what?'

Debbie shrugged.

'Did he give you any medical advice?'

'No. He talked a lot about spiritual things. He said I should . . . be in tune with the universe. I should take walks in the fresh air. He gave me a diet. I have to eat everything organic and wholefoods . . . wholegrains and fruit and vegetables, no meat, no dairy stuff.'

'Plenty of soya? Most of them seem to be keen on that.'

'Is it bad?'

Dr. Deerbon smiled. 'No. But some people are allergic to it.'

'So can I do it? The diet?'

'Yes. Make sure you have enough protein . . . some fish or eggs. The fruit and vegetables and wholegrain are good, but give yourself a treat from time to time. Have a glass of wine or a bar of chocolate.'

'OK. Thanks, then. Is that it?'

'That's it, end of lecture.'

Debbie turned with her hand on the doorknob. 'He made me feel wonderful. Do you see? He made me see everything differently.'

DEBBIE DID NOT WALK home. It had started to drizzle and her blister was painful, so she caught a bus. She felt confused. Dr Deerbon did not seem to have disapproved of the diet or the exercise. But there had been something about her expression and tone of voice that had made Debbie feel uneasy.

Dava had done her more good than anyone, hadn't he? She felt positive and happy for the first time in months. It had not been Dava's fault that she had reacted badly to the medicine; that could happen any time, to anyone. Dr Deerbon had said as much.

She got off the bus in the centre of Lafferton and bought herself a bar of organic chocolate to munch on the way home. That ought to please both of them, she thought, as she stripped off the wrapper.

There was a letter for her on the doormat. When she slit open the envelope in the kitchen, she saw the blue of the card immediately.

DAVA
Please attend for your next appointment promptly at 2.15 on Tuesday, January 30. This time has been carefully selected as being the most auspicious for your therapy.

The kitchen seemed to glow all day with the emanation of spiritual light from the card. Later, Debbie realised that she wanted to do everything Dava had told her over and over again, so that when she went for the next appointment he would be proud of her. So, after putting an Elastoplast on her blister she went out to walk.

The afternoon was dank and it was drizzling as she made her way to the Hill. She felt drawn to this ancient green heart of Lafferton; she knew that the Wern Stones were supposed to have special powers. It was said that if they were ever split open, all the secrets of Lafferton over generations would be found engraved within.

It was almost dark now. A couple walked a dog along the path ahead of her but they turned off, back onto the road. Debbie walked briskly along the track that led towards the Wern Stones. After a short time it became quite steep. Debbie stopped and leant against a tree, out of breath. Below, she saw a few dim orange lights from the town. The night smelt of damp grass. She tried to think of the spinning earth beneath and the heavens over her head and, for a moment, she was able to conjure up a sense of being in harmony with them.

She was brought up by a slight sound, a step, or a rustle of wind in the undergrowth. She turned her head, trying to make it out. There was no wind; the air was still. It came again, a few yards below her.

Debbie was numbed by fear. Her heart pounded in her ears. She could not see and dared not move. She was disorientated and did not know which way would lead her back to the road. How stupid was she to come up here alone after dark, without having told anyone where she was going? The dark and the silence were pressing in on her. She gripped the cold trunk of the tree for support and comfort.

Somewhere not far away in the darkness something made a slight sound, not a rustle or a whisper this time but a faint, thin scratching.

The drizzle began again, chill on her face and hands. Then, below on the path, she saw the lights of a vehicle and heard the engine. If she could keep her footing on the grass and get safely to the path, she might get to the car, which would have a driver, another human being, then everything would be normal again.

Taking a deep breath and leaving hold of the tree, Debbie began to stumble down the grassy track. It was raining heavily now, and when she came onto the lower slopes, half running, she slithered and fell. As she struggled to her feet, a light glared into her face momentarily. She was nearer to the road than she had realised and the light was from the headlights of a van.

Debbie watched, unable to move, as the van turned and headed back the way it had come. The driver obviously hadn't seen her. Her chest was hurting with the strain of running but slowly she began walking the mile or so back to her flat. From now on she would only go walking on the Hill when it was light, especially early in the morning. Dawn was a propitious time, Debbie knew.

THERE WERE PLENTY of cars lined up in the drive of Hallam House when Freya arrived for the choir party, and lights were shining in welcome in all the ground-floor windows. She heard a sudden burst of laughter and a spurt of shyness flared through her, but she ignored it, got out of her car and went into the house to join the party.

Freya's puddings were praised and demolished, and she promised recipes to several people. She enjoyed herself and picked up her new friendship with Meriel at once, but took a dislike to her husband, a man with a sarcastic tongue and a disapproving expression.

The evening was a good one, but she did nothing but glance towards the door, hoping that Simon Serrailler would arrive. When she looked at her watch and saw that it was after ten, she realised he would not be coming at all, and she felt a disappointment so acute that she could take no pleasure in anything, and so she left.

That night she slept on and off for no more than an hour, and otherwise tossed about in bed until her covers were a scramble. When the luminous hands on her bedside clock showed four fifteen, she switched on the lamp. The only thing she knew that might keep her mind occupied, and stop it from turning back to Simon Serrailler, was work, and the only case that presented both a puzzle and challenge in her present load was that of the missing woman, Angela Randall. She took the pad she kept on her bedside table and started to make notes. She had built up a picture of the woman from the search of her house, and from what her employer at the nursing home had told her. After ten minutes, Freya suddenly felt exhausted. She was not going into the station early, because she had to do some checks at the new business park on the edge of town relating to a dull embezzlement case. After that, though, and without the DI's knowledge, she would spend some more time, preferably with the help of young DC Nathan Coates, on Angela Randall.

She turned out the lamp and fell heavily to sleep.

DETECTIVE CONSTABLE Nathan Coates had been going through the computer data base of convicted drug offenders since just after eight thirty. It was now eleven and he was on his third plastic cup of coffee.

'Morning, Nathan.'

He looked up and saw Freya. A grin lit up his eyes.

Freya liked Nathan, almost because rather than in spite of his face, which was a caricature of a villain's mugshot, looking as if it had been flattened by a door, the nose squashed, the cheekbones dented and covered with livid bumps, the mouth large. He also had a grin that lit up his eyes and, together with his cheerful willingness to shoulder the dreariest of jobs, helped endear this young officer not only to the rest of CID but to the entire station.

'I've come to take you away from all that,' she said.

'Oh, it's not so bad, Sarge. At least I get to be in the warm with caffeine on tap. Besides, I hate these druggies, honest to God.'

Freya knew that Nathan came from a Bevham council estate that had been governed by drug dealers for much of his growing up. He had watched schoolfriends succumb and become addicts, several had died, others were now caught up in a life of petty crime, or worse.

'You're a star,' said Freya, 'but I need you for something else, just for an hour or so.'

'OK, Sarge.' Nathan shut down the data base and followed Freya to her desk, where she filled him in on Angela Randall.

'Weird. She don't sound like the sort who'd just take off.'

'I'm glad you agree. I'm concerned about this one, but as far as the DI is concerned, it's just another missing person.'

'I get the picture, Sarge. What do you want me to do?'

'Go back over the missing persons file for the last year, eighteen months, see if any other case has a look of this one . . . you know the sort of thing. I can't be specific but if it's there it'll ring bells. Read up the notes on Randall first. Pull out anything and leave it on my desk.'

'Are you off again?'

'Officially, I'm back at the business park among the embezzlers.'

'And?'

'I'm nipping into Bevham to visit a very expensive jeweller's.'

'Sugar Daddy lent you his credit card for the day then?'

Freya took her jacket off the back of her chair. 'Certainly.'

E. J. DUCKHAM & SON had an entry bell and a CCTV that scrutinised potential shoppers before they were allowed in. Freya cast a lingering look in the windows at diamond necklaces and earrings without any visible price, sapphire, emerald, ruby and diamond rings, Rolex and Patek Phillipe watches, and pressed the bell for entry. As the door swung soundlessly back, she flipped open her warrant card.

The place had that velvet hush special to jewellers and designer dress salons; the woman behind the counter was impeccably groomed and coiffed, and the man who came to greet Freya had the smooth charm she associated with Jermyn Street, from where his pinstripe suit and lavender tie must surely have come.

'I do hope you've come bearing good news about Miss Randall, Sergeant. One of your officers was in here a week or so ago, asking about her. I gather she has gone away unexpectedly?'

'We're pursuing several lines of inquiry as to exactly what has happened, Mr Duckham. Do you know her well?'

'Not at all, but she has been a very good customer of ours over the past few months, and we pride ourselves here on personal service.'

'The uniformed officer will have questioned you about the cuff links Miss Randall purchased in early December.'

'Indeed. Extremely nice ones. Lapis lazuli. Beautifully made.'

'Could you tell me how much they were?'

He looked disapproving.

'I understand that is not the sort of information you would normally give out but this might be important.'

After another hesitation, the man sighed, then went into a glass-panelled office at the back of the shop, where Freya could see him tapping a keyboard. Behind the counter on the opposite side of the shop the woman with the coiffed hair was polishing a crystal rose bowl. She glanced up, did not meet Freya's smile, and carried on polishing.

'The cuff links were two hundred and seventy-five pounds.'

'A present for someone Miss Randall knew well, clearly.'

'I really couldn't say.'

'But you do say that she was a regular customer . . . How often had she been in during the past year?'

'Half a dozen times, at least.'

'Did she just browse?'

'No. She always bought something, I think . . . There was one occasion when we hadn't exactly what she was looking for—a particular watch—but we managed to obtain one eventually.'

'What kind of watch?'

'Showing the phases of the moon. It was an Omega, from the 1950s.'

'Expensive, then?'

'It depends what you call expensive. We have watches costing twenty-five thousand pounds.'

'But this one?'

'Less than two thousand.'

Freya got up. 'Would you have a photograph of the watch?'

'No. But we bought it at auction from Goldstein and Crow in Birmingham. You might try them.'

'I'd like you to give me a list of every item Angela Randall bought from you, Mr Duckham, with descriptions, cost and date purchased.'

'We regard our customers' purchases as confidential. But . . . I suppose I can do this, if you really think it is going to be of use.'

'It is. How long will it take you?'

'So long as we don't have a rush of customers . . . an hour, perhaps?'

'Make it forty minutes.'

AN HOUR LATER Freya headed back to Lafferton and the Four Ways Nursing Home, Mr Duckham's list in her bag.

Carol Ashton was with the undertaker, the girl said. There had been a death in the night and she would not be free for another ten minutes. Freya waited in the office, and went through the list again.

1 gold tiepin. April 14, 2000. £145
1 gentleman's Omega watch. June 5, 2000. £1,350
1 silver business-card holder. August 16, 2000. £240
1 signet ring, gold, single diamond. October 4, 2000. £1,225
1 silver letter opener. October 27, 2000. £150
1 pair of gold and lapis lazuli cuff links. December 4, 2000. £275

Nothing for herself, nothing for another woman, everything for a man at a total cost of over £3,000 in a single year.

When Carol Ashton came in, apologising for the delay, Freya said at once, 'No news, I'm afraid, but we're following up a couple of leads.' She handed over the list. 'I'd like you to look at this list, please. They are items purchased by Miss Randall from Duckham's, the jeweller in Bevham, during last year.'

'What?' Carol Ashton ran her eyes down it quickly and looked at Freya in bewilderment. 'Are you sure?'

'May I ask you how much she earned with you, Mrs Ashton?'

'Angela was on thirteen and a half thousand a year,' she said.

'Not a fortune.'

'Wages in the care industry are low. I pay the standard rate.'

'I'm not criticising you. Do you know of any other income Angela Randall might have had?'

'I'm sure she didn't have another job . . . She wouldn't have had the energy. It's demanding, working nights in a home like this.'

'Private income?'

'I wouldn't have thought so, but I don't actually know.'

'Have you any idea who she might have bought all these expensive things for?'

'I'm afraid I haven't a clue.'

'Are you surprised by this?'

Carol Ashton considered for a moment. 'Yes, I am, very. I mean, it looks as if these items were bought for . . . well . . .'

'A lover?'

Carol Ashton shook her head. 'I can't believe that. It wouldn't surprise me if Angela had never had any serious relationship. She was always clean and well groomed but she didn't put herself out to look fashionable. At least, not that I ever saw.'

'Spinsterish?'

'It sounds awful, doesn't it? Patronising, somehow. But yes.'

Freya got up and took the list back. 'If you remember something she mentioned, some remark she might have dropped, anything that rings a bell, especially in connection with this, would you phone me?'

'Of course, but I doubt you'll hear from me. I'm astonished. It just shows, though, how little you know about people you see every day.'

AT THE STATION, Freya found Nathan Coates back at his computer working on the drug data base.

'Have you been through missing persons?'

'Yes, Sarge, back for two years. I've left a couple of them on your desk. A teenage girl reported missing eighteen months ago, who was last sighted near the railway station. The other one's a bloke.'

'Oh well. Thanks anyway.'

'No prob. Made a change.' His grin cheered her up as usual.

The two missing persons he had pulled out of the list seemed at first sight to have nothing in common with Angela Randall, as Nathan had supposed, and certainly the teenage girl looked like the typical runaway from unhappy home circumstances.

Freya glanced at the details of the missing man and almost dismissed it, until she noticed a line Nathan had highlighted in red pen.

Last sighting, 6.30 a.m. Tuesday March 7, 2000, riding mountain bike on the Hill, reported by Alan John Turner, 57, of Flat 6, Mead House, Brewer Street, Lafferton, when walking dog.

Was it worth sending Nathan out to check Mr Turner's story? Probably not, but Brewer Street was only two minutes from her own house, so there was nothing to stop her taking a short detour on her way home. She slipped Nathan's notes into her bag and turned wearily back to the embezzlement case.

After a long, dull afternoon on the computer she drove to Brewer Street and parked in front of Mead House.

A small Oriental woman answered the doorbell of Flat 6 and told Freya with smiles and great charm that Mr Turner had left there a few months ago for retirement on the Costa del Sol.

IT WAS HALF PAST THREE. The house was quiet. Into the quietness pulsed the sound of waves unfolding silkily up a sandy beach. Winter sunlight filtered through the cream linen curtains.

Karin McCafferty lay on the small chaise longue in her bedroom, her feet on the raised end, head and shoulders flat, arms embracing her upper body. In her mind's eye, she pictured a field of green spring grass dotted with clumps of ugly black weeds. She breathed deeply, then pictured a gate on the far side of the meadow. She walked across the springy turf and unlatched it. Sheep came pouring through the open gate, and spread out across the field. At Karin's silent signal, each sheep went towards one of the ugly weeds and began to eat it, slowly and systematically—roots, leaves, stem, the entire plant. When it had finished, the hole out of which the weed had grown had disappeared, was healed over with newly sprung, fresh young grass.

Karin watched the picture with absolute concentration, astonished at its vividness. The meadow represented her body, the grass the healthy tissue, the weeds her cancer, which the sheep had just consumed. The places where the weed-cancer had grown from were healthy, every cell renewed and replenished. She lay, looking intently as the sheep trotted away, through the gate and out of sight behind a nearby hill. She was whole and healed, the cancer cells obliterated.

She was brought back to herself by the ringing doorbell and went down to find Cat Deerbon on the step. 'Say if this is a bad moment. I've got an afternoon off, Sam and Hannah are out to tea.'

Karin smiled. 'It's great! Come in.'

'You have the look of someone who was asleep.'

'Do I?' Karin glanced in the mirror on the way through to the kitchen. Her eyes looked slightly bleary. 'I wasn't sleeping, I'd just finished doing an hour of visualisation.'

'So I see.' Cat was reading the book left open on the table.

'Tea?'

'Love some.'

Cat went over to the bookshelves and picked out title after title on alternative cancer therapies . . . *Eating Your Way Out of Cancer. The Kid Glove War: Fighting Cancer the Gentle Way. Cancer Therapies: the Complementary Approach. Self-Help, Self-Healing.*

'You must have spent a fortune.'

'One way of putting it. China or Indian?'

'Whatever you're having.'

'I'm having peppermint. I don't take caffeine.'

'Right.'

'I can hear what you're thinking. What's caffeine got to do with cancer? How is peppermint tea going to beat a malignant tumour?'

'Wrong. I was thinking we could all do with a bit less caffeine injected into our day. I'll have peppermint as well, please . . . I like it. So stop being so paranoid, Karin.'

'Anyway, this is your afternoon off. Let's talk about gardening or the Lafferton gossip; you didn't come to discuss my treatment.'

'It's exactly what I did come to discuss. You promised to keep me up to speed with what you're doing and you haven't. So I'm here.'

Karin smiled again. 'I'm glad you're not going to give me an easy ride, Cat. I need to be able to defend myself every step of the way. God, there's a lot of bunkum out there. I'm appalled. How can people peddle some of the stuff they do? How can they take money for it from desperately ill people, who'll try anything? I went up to Starly . . . yes, you might well groan. That place is a shrine to quackery.'

'I know.'

'OK, here's where it's at. I'm on an organic, wholefood diet, lots of fresh raw vegetables and fruits, wholegrains. I've cut out caffeine and dairy produce and sugar, I have soya milk. I blend my own juices. I take vitamin supplements. I do meditation and a visualisation programme. I walk two miles a day.'

Cat looked closely at her friend. She was looking well. Her skin was beautiful, hair glossy, her eyes shone with health; she had a radiance Cat had not seen in her before and she told her as much.

'I feel fantastic, Cat. I can't believe there's anything wrong with me.'

'I'm sorry to sound brutal, but you know that there is.'

'It's your job to remind me. Thanks.'

'Have you been to see any alternative therapists?'

'A spiritual healer. She gives me a marvellous sense of peace, and I seem to be handing myself over to something else, trusting in something else . . . not the healer. I suppose people would call it God.'

'I would.'

'I've seen a homeopath.'

Cat snorted. 'That's useless, Karin. If it seems to work, either the problem would have got better by itself anyway, or it's placebo.'

'We'll have to differ then. She isn't trying to cure the cancer; she's treating me as a whole person. And please don't look like that and don't say "Right" in that tone of voice you have when you do.'

'I'll try not. Anything else?'

'I'm spending two days at the Bristol Cancer Help Centre. Otherwise I'm reading. Thinking. Changing my life around. Still working on your mother's garden. I've cut out the others, but I love going up to Hallam House. Your ma is a tonic.' She paused. 'There is one thing you ought to know about. There's a new therapist in Starly who calls himself a psychic surgeon.'

'A what?'

'I looked it up on the Internet. It's pretty spooky. There are a lot of them in the Philippines apparently. A psychic surgeon claims to be possessed by someone who was a doctor in another century.'

'It can't mean surgery as in "surgery"?'

'I'm not sure. It's all magic circle stuff so far as I can make out, but it deceives a lot of vulnerable people. Two women in the café in Starly were talking about someone who'd had a throat tumour removed by this guy.'

'Oh my God. What exactly is supposed to happen?'

'It's got to be sleight of hand . . . but as far as I can make out, there are instruments and there's blood.'

'This has got to be stopped.'

'How? Is it illegal?'

'I'm bloody well going to find out.' Cat looked straight at her friend. 'You're not thinking of going?'

'I might. I'm quite interested in sorting the sheep from the goats.'

'Listen, you know my take on all this. It's certainly true that a good diet, exercise, a positive attitude are beneficial. Beneficial but incidental, Karin. The rest is crap, not all of it harmless.'

'I don't buy this psychic surgery stuff, Cat. Give me some credit.'

Cat frowned. 'I'm torn,' she said. 'I'd like to find out about this psychic surgeon but I don't want you to put yourself at risk.'

'Come on, Cat, I'm tough, I can look after myself. Now—has your mother told you about the new hothouse she's planning?'

Cat knew better than to try and turn the conversation back to Karin's health. Besides, she quite wanted to know about her mother's latest garden extravagance, mainly so that she would be prepared when her father flew into a rage about it.

Five

Iris Chater wanted to look her best for Harry. He had always noticed when she'd bought a new frock or had her hair done and now she wanted to show him she still cared what he thought. She had chosen her clothes as carefully as ever, every day picking out a necklace and polishing her shoes. She only ever wore a bit of lipstick and a dab from a compact, but she kept her skin nice with a cream every night.

But today was different. This was special. She glanced down at the piece of paper Pauline had given her.

She decided on the camel two-piece she'd bought for one of their anniversaries but hardly worn since, with her brown court shoes and a caramel silk scarf with a diamond pattern.

She had sat, evening after evening, trying to decide whether to visit the medium whose name and address Pauline had written out for her. She had not spoken to anyone else about it, not even to Pauline. It was just between her and Harry. One evening, she had been lying on the couch, a magazine on her lap, and she had missed Harry, missed his face, his voice, his jokes, more than she had missed him since the day he died. She had cried then, desperate, desolate tears, and in the middle of them had said aloud, 'Harry, what shall I do?'

'Come and talk to me.'

It was Harry's voice, clear and strong in her inner ear. 'Come and talk to me.' She had held her breath and waited, urging him to go on.

'Should I go to the medium, Harry? Is that what you want me to do? Why can't you just talk to me now?'

The gas fire flickered its blue flame.

'Harry?'

But that was all. 'Come and talk to me.'

The next morning, she had gathered all her courage and telephoned the number on Pauline's piece of paper. She heard a recorded message on an answerphone.

'Hello. This is Sheila Innis. I am so sorry I am not able to answer your call personally, but I am sure you understand that when I am working I can't be disturbed. If you wish to book an appointment please call back between five and seven o'clock. Otherwise, please leave a message after the beep. Thank you.'

Her voice was reassuring, clear, pleasant, with a certain warmth but no false intimacy. Iris rang off and made a note to call that evening.

She thought she was much calmer now that she had come to a decision, and had heard the medium's voice. There was nothing spooky or unusual about her. But at ten past five her hand was shaking as she reached for the receiver.

'Sheila Innis, can I help you?'

'I'd . . . I'd like to make an appointment please.'

'Of course. Would you give me your name?'

'Chater. Mrs Iris Chater.'

She gave her address and telephone number and her date of birth. Nothing else was required.

'I see people individually every afternoon between two and five, Mrs Chater, and there are group sessions in the evenings.'

'Oh, no, I want to see you by myself.'

'I understand. I've just had a cancellation for three o'clock on the 6th of February. Would that suit you?'

'Oh, yes, I can come then. It'll be quite suitable.'

'Do you have the address?'

'Yes. I know the road. Thank you very much.'

'And Mrs Chater? Please don't worry. Everyone's uncertain at first, but I think you'll feel quite at ease when we've met and you're sitting comfortably in my sitting room. I'll look forward to seeing you.'

Iris Chater sat by the telephone, weak with relief. She had done the right thing. Sheila Innis had reassured her.

'I'm coming to talk to you, Harry,' she said, 'just like you wanted.'

FEBRUARY 6 WAS LIKE a spring day, balmy and with a blue sky and watery sun. The crocuses had come up, egg yellow and Maundy purple, in rings beneath the trees. Harry had never been a real gardener, any more than she was, but they had both loved spring flowers, so that she felt they were together as she walked to Priam Crescent.

The house was a small detached one, with bay windows on either side of the front door. The front garden had a magnolia tree, beneath which were white and gold crocuses. Iris Chater felt her heart lift. She wasn't apprehensive or worried as she rang the doorbell.

If she had had any shreds of uncertainty left, the sight of Sheila Innis would have dispelled them.

'Mrs Chater? Do come inside. I must ask you first, do you object to cats because if so, I'll go ahead and move Otto to another room?'

'Oh, don't do that. I like cats.'

'He's very old now and just sleeps but there's a patch of sunshine in my working room that he finds very attractive.'

She was perhaps fifty, no more, plump, with hair that had been fair and was greying a little, short and well cut. She wore a tweed skirt and a yellow blouse, flat shoes. She smiled warmly, a smile Iris Chater felt reached into her, to put her at her ease . . . and something more. It was the smile of someone she felt knew her.

The cat, Otto, was lying on the pale green carpet near some French windows, taking advantage of every centimetre of sunshine.

It was a pleasant room. A three-piece suite was upholstered in a damask fabric and a green slightly darker than the carpet, a polished table held a vase of yellow tulips, a bureau had framed photographs.

'Please, sit down.'

Sheila Innis took the opposite chair, her back to the French windows and the light. There was a grandmother clock set against the wall beside her. It was a lovely room, Iris Chater thought, a peaceful room. She felt more relaxed than she had done for weeks.

'Mrs Chater, have you ever visited a medium before?'

'Oh, no. No, never.'

'I don't want you to tell me anything else about yourself. I wanted to know that because past experiences do affect people. Now, I'll just tell you briefly what to expect. First of all, we will continue to sit here like this. I don't go into a trance at individual sessions, but I close my eyes to allow me to concentrate better. The other important thing is that nothing may happen. There may be no one from the other side who comes forward. Although it's disappointing, there is nothing I can do. I won't make things up. If someone tries to make contact, and if they have messages for you, I hear them, and I usually see them . . . it's like a picture coming into my mind. Am I making sense?'

Iris Chater looked across and saw the woman smile again, that warm, attractive, lovely smile. It was a smile she trusted.

'Yes,' she said, 'I think so.'

'Do you have anything else to ask?'

'No, thank you.'

'Fine. Just relax then, Mrs Chater.'

For several minutes, Sheila Innis sat, her hands folded in her lap, her eyes closed. Iris waited, pleasantly at ease. Perhaps Harry would not come. She wondered how much she would mind.

'Nina,' Sheila Innis said. 'I have someone here called Nina . . . She's holding something up . . . It's a comb. A blue comb . . . She's asking if you remember the blue comb.'

Iris tried to picture a blue comb but it meant nothing at all.

'I'm sure it's Nina . . . no, is it Nita? Yes, I'm sorry, it's Nita.'

'Nita Ramsden? Goodness, I'd forgotten her; it's donkey's years ago.' Why would Nita Ramsden want to talk to her?

'She's laughing now. She's about . . . eighteen or nineteen with short curly hair and she's wearing an apron . . .'

'An overall . . . it's an overall. Dear God, it must be Nita. We worked together . . . more than fifty years ago. What does she say?'

'She's not speaking, she's just laughing. She's pretty, isn't she?'

'Nita was ever so pretty.'

'A nice-looking young man is standing behind her. He says . . . I can't get his name, but he says you were all friends in a gang together.'

'Donald?'

'Is that it? He's wagging his finger. He's quite a cheeky young man.'

'He was Nita's fiancé.'

For several moments, then, Sheila Innis was silent. Her eyes were tightly closed and she seemed to be listening intently. Nita Ramsden and Donald. How strange. Why them? It wasn't what she wanted. But then Sheila Innis began to talk again rapidly.

'She's come closer now. She's saying she's sorry you had to wait such a long time in the cold. Now she's showing me a bicycle . . . She's riding it over a bridge . . . Is that a bridge?'

Iris Chater felt her neck prickle. Her hands were very cold. The room seemed cold, so that she pulled her silk scarf back up round her.

'She says it was all over in a minute but there was a second when everything seemed to go still. She knew she couldn't do anything and then it was over. She's showing me the bicycle again . . . the wheel's completely buckled and the handlebars are forced round.'

'She was killed on her bicycle. We used to meet on the corner and that day I waited twenty minutes for her but she didn't come so I went on to work . . . and she'd been killed, she'd swerved under a tram. Oh, Nita . . . Poor little Nita. Is it really you?'

'She's saying you had good times. Didn't we have good times, Iris, you and me and Donald and Norman. Didn't we have good times?'

'Yes,' Iris whispered, her mouth dry, 'yes, Nita, we had good times.'

Sheila Innis was silent again now, her hands still resting together in her lap. The sun had moved round and the cat had moved with it.

'Is . . . is there someone who says he's Harry?'

The medium did not reply. Iris waited, wondering about Nita, from fifty years ago, pretty little Nita killed on her bicycle. Why should Nita have come through when Harry hadn't?

After a few more minutes, the medium opened her eyes, and then quickly made a gesture with her hands, running them down her body from the top of her head as if she was brushing something away.

She smiled across at Iris. 'I'm sorry,' she said, 'there's no one else this afternoon. I sense I've disappointed you. You wanted someone to come through. Was it your husband? Did he pass over recently?'

'Harry. My Harry died just before Christmas.'

'That's very soon, Mrs Chater. It might be too soon. Sometimes when people first pass over . . . they find it difficult to come through. Perhaps leave it a month? I'm glad to keep on trying. It's entirely up to you.' She stood. 'Please don't be too downhearted. I sense Harry is very close to you and looking after you and that he's happy.'

For the first time, Iris Chater felt suspicious. Easy words, she thought.

At the door, Sheila Innis put her hand on her arm. 'I think you might benefit from one of my evening groups. Sometimes there's an atmosphere that encourages those in the spirit world who haven't been able to come through. We get some remarkable results.'

Iris wanted to escape. There was something intense about the way Sheila Innis was looking at her, something about her eyes.

'I'd . . . I'd have to think about it. I'm not sure.'

'Of course. Just telephone me.'

'Thank you. Yes.' When she reached the top of the path, Iris glanced back and saw that the medium was watching her leave.

'ALL RIGHT, NATHAN, tell me what your thinking is.'

DC Nathan Coates had a notepad open in front of him. It was after eight o'clock and he and Freya were the only people in the CID room. She had filled him in on Angela Randall, and told him that the DI wouldn't countenance any more official time being spent on what he regarded as just another missing-person case.

'I can't get you any overtime on this, Nathan, and I can't even justify your spending ordinary time on it.'

'That's OK, Sarge. If you think there's something, I'm up for it.'

'Thanks, but keep shtum, right?'

Apart from Angela Randall and the missing mountain biker, a nineteen-year-old called Tim Galloway, Nathan had pulled out one more name that looked as if it might have a connection.

Carrie del Santo. Aged nineteen. Known prostitute. Last seen running through the Cathedral Close in the early hours of Good Friday, 1997. On bail for soliciting. Not reported missing for several weeks.

'What struck you about her in relation to Angela Randall?'

'I pulled her out because of the early-morning sighting. But she's got form, so had good reason to scarper. Got to be foreign with a name like that. She's probably hopped it overseas.'

'Keep her in. Check her nationality and maybe a place name but don't spend too much time on it. Then it's back to the mountain biker.'

'Tim Galloway. Last seen early one morning, and on the Hill.'

'And male.'

'Yeah. I'm sorry, Sarge, but that's it. Load of teenagers fallen out with new stepfathers or bullied at school. Couple of blokes obviously walked out on their wives, one or two under suspicion of fraud. And that's going back five years. I'm sorry I haven't done any better for you.' His young, squashed-up face looked downcast.

'You've done fine, Nathan. Come on, I'll buy you a drink.'

The Cross Keys was a few yards from the station. As they stepped out into the night, DCI Simon Serrailler's black police Rover pulled up into its parking space. Freya felt her stomach clench.

Serrailler took the steps two at a time, giving them a brief nod of recognition. Freya looked back and caught a glimpse of his blond head going out of sight fast up the inside staircase.

Seconds later, two other senior officers' cars, one with a police driver, swung into the forecourt.

'Something's up,' Freya said.

Nathan nodded. 'Operation Merlin. Big drug round-up . . . uniform and drug squad.'

'How come you get to know everything I don't, Nathan?'

He tapped the side of his nose and grinned.

Not, she thought as they pushed into the busy pub, that she wanted to know anything about a drug op. There had been enough of them in the Met to last her a lifetime.

'What'll you have? This is your overtime pay, Nathan, so make the most of it.'

'Thanks, Sarge, I'll have a lemonade.'

'Oh, please.'

'With a whisky chaser.'

Nathan commandeered a corner table while Freya got the drinks.

'I suppose we'll hear about the drugs op in the morning.'

Nathan shook his head. 'It's only just started.' He took a gulp of lemonade, swallowed it, and then downed his whisky in one.

'How do you like Serrailler?' he asked, so unexpectedly that Freya was caught before she could prevent herself from flushing. She bent down quickly and ferreted in her bag, but when she sat upright again Nathan Coates was looking at her over his glass.

She said, 'Sorry. The DCI? Seems fine. Hardly talked to him. Now, Cameron . . . God, there were still a lot of Billy Camerons left in the Met—tough as they come, all overweight, all smoked like chimneys, but if they were on your side, you couldn't do better.'

Nathan shrugged. 'I think Cameron's just coasting till he gets his pension. He's dead straight, though.'

'Which is always saying a lot.'

'Serrailler's different.'

'You're not suggesting he isn't straight . . . ?'

'Christ, no. I mean he's different. Not your average copper.'

Freya stood up. 'A chaser and more of that fizzy gut rot?'

'Nah, Em will have dinner on; it's her turn. I'll have to move. Thanks anyway.' He drained his glass. 'But don't let me stop you.'

'Somehow, I don't fancy drinking on my own in the Cross Keys. People might start to wonder.'

'Course they might, good looker like you, Sarge.' Nathan swung the pub door open and held it for her with his grin and a bow.

Across at the station, Freya went to her car, Nathan to the cycle racks. He and his girlfriend Emma, a midwife at Bevham General, lived in a flat only a few streets away.

'Thanks for the drink, Sarge. See you tomorrow.'

'Good night, Nathan.'

Freya glanced at Simon Serrailler's Rover. The lights were still on in his office on the second floor. She wanted to wait, hoping that he would emerge again on his way home, that they might exchange a word, that he might . . .

Damn. Damn, Damn, Bugger, Bugger, Sod it, Damn.

Nathan glided by on his cycle, looking at her. Then he stopped, and put one foot to the ground. Freya turned.

'OK?'

He said nothing until she went back a few steps closer to him. He had his cycle helmet on, a gleaming electric-blue shell under which his lumpy face looked even odder. His expression was concerned.

'Serrailler,' he said.

She took a half-step back, further into the shadow.

'It's a hiding to nothing, Sarge. Know what I mean?'

Then he pushed off and sped away.

DEBBIE PARKER lay in bed propped up on three pillows, with a small sheaf of cards in front of her. Dava had given them to her the previous afternoon. The session with him had been even more affecting than the first; she had lain on his couch and been taken on a journey through what he called the Five Portals, gateways to her spiritual self. She had seen beautiful gardens with magical flowers, crystal caves filled with feathery angels and other beings of light. She had felt wonderful, floating on a cloud of peace and harmony.

'The negative forces that were causing you so much distress are weakening,' he said softly. 'Eventually, they will cease to exist. Now, breathe deeply and slowly. I want you to focus your mind on your own individual colour, which is blue. Look into the heart and centre of your blue, Debbie. I am going to give you some words and phrases, and some cards to prompt you. Read them over and over.'

Three cards were printed with Dava's phrases.

BLUE—Peaceful. Spiritually healing. Sensitive. Sincere.

BLUE—Brings peace, tranquillity, faith, trust.

BLUE—Is your note of harmony with the universe.

The other cards were printed with diagrams of the chakras, and drawings of her own healing flowers and herbs, her own special dates highlighted on a calendar, and her auspicious times of day. The first of these was 7.35 p.m., a strange time, with which Debbie found it hard to identify. The second, though, she related to immediately.

Dawn, the hour between the first lightening of the morning sky and sunrise, is your most auspicious time. It is now that you are most in tune with the universe and at your most vibrant. This is the hour that is most propitious for you to take new decisions, your most creative hour. Rise early and celebrate your dawn hours and sleep when your energies begin to fade, after sunset.

She read until she was too tired to read more and then she put out her light and lay on her back, marvelling at the fact that she felt totally different since seeing Dava—happier, more confident. She knew that before long she would feel well enough to look for a job.

She let herself relax, felt her breaths come more slowly and deeply, and then began to focus on the circle of vibrant blue she conjured up in her mind, with its heart of deepest violet.

The healing power of it flowed into her mind and her veins.

She fell asleep.

HER ALARM BUZZED on low vibration at six the next morning. She was anxious not to wake Sandy. Through the kitchen window she saw only darkness, but it was not raining. She had a glass of orange juice, ate a soya yogurt and put two Penguin biscuits in the pocket of her fleece. She clicked off the light and softly closed the back door.

Away on the main road, there was the noise of light traffic, but she saw no one else walking or riding a bike. Two of Dava's cards were in her fleece pocket and she carried a small torch. She was determined not to be caught out and frightened half to death by a rabbit or a stray dog like the last time she went walking on the Hill.

Once she was on the track, the feel of the ground beneath her feet steadied her and she climbed easily. As her torch beam picked out the Wern Stones she went happily towards them and, when she reached one, put out her hand and touched its cold, damp surface. She felt its heaviness pressed into the earth and the strength of ages coming to her through it. She turned and looked up at the sky. There was a thin line of light at the horizon.

She climbed on, past the undergrowth where she had been so terrified before, but this time pointing her torch beam right into it and seeing nothing but innocent branches, brambles and rabbit holes. On and up. She was getting out of breath now. She had already lost a few pounds, though she had not been able to give up the chocolate bars or biscuits, and felt for one now in her pocket, stripped down the metallic wrap and bit deep into it.

The light was strengthening steadily. At the top of the Hill, where the great circle of ancient oaks stood, she sat on a stone bench and turned towards the east. The sky was now tinted rose red in a thin line where it joined the dark earth. She was acutely, thrillingly conscious that this was her own special time, when she was most keenly in tune with the universe. She held her breath. Just ahead of her in the trees a bird began to sing. She could make out the cathedral clearly now, the stone tower touched by the rising sun. The world was being re-created before her eyes, like a picture painted by some invisible hand.

'My time,' she said joyfully, 'this is my time.'

Suddenly, she had a strange sense that she was in some way different to all those people in their ordinary little houses and flats and bungalows below her in Lafferton, that she had been picked out for special knowledge. She was Dava's chosen one.

She was also hungry and needed to go to the loo. The dawn was up, her special time was over. She slipped the torch in her pocket and headed joyfully back down the track.

At the bottom, she recognised the white van, parked at an angle across the path. She was sure it was the van that had been parked here last time. She stopped.

Someone seemed to be half slumped on the front seat, almost hanging out of the open van door. There was no movement at all. Either the van had broken down and the man was leaning in to fiddle with something down near the foot pedals, or he was hurt or ill.

She went nearer and pushed herself between the open van door and the bushes, thinking quickly, wondering if she should run for help.

The branches of the hedge fell back and she was beside his legs as he lay across the front seat, but then he moved, pulling himself quickly backwards with a single strong movement. She felt relieved, realising that she had been dreading what she might have found— blood, or him dead of a heart attack.

He stood upright and looked straight at her, smiling.

'Hello, Debbie,' he said.

THE CALDEN BUSINESS PARK on the outskirts of Lafferton had been built just over a year previously and contained various well-designed units, including two-storey office blocks, smaller storage units and lock-up garages. The whole was pleasantly landscaped, with sloping lawns and newly established rowan trees.

The white van drove down the service road and turned right at the far end, to where the block of cabin units gave out onto the perimeter fence. The last unit was the largest and had its entrance at the side. There was a small office in front and a large area behind, to which the van backed up. The doors were opened, then those of the unit, revealing steel runners onto which the refrigerated box containing Debbie Parker's body was rolled straight to the back. Then the doors were closed and double-locked again, and the van driven into the garage.

From there an inner door led through to the unit. In the office, with its door marked FLETCHER EUROPEAN AGENCIES, he switched on the fluorescent overhead lights and then the percolator.

While the coffee was brewing, he slipped off his jacket and shoes, opened a metal locker and took out a set of green overalls and a pair of rubber overshoes. The cream slatted blind was permanently pulled down, hiding any view of the office from passers-by.

He sat at the desk drinking the hot coffee, calming himself after the dangerous few moments on the path at the bottom of the Hill. Here he felt safe, he was on his own territory; there, anything might go wrong. Nothing much ever had, though the young mountain biker had been difficult, strong and agile. That one had made him sweat.

The fat girl had been easy, trusting and friendly, caught off guard. He had planned it well this time, left nothing to chance, and it had worked like a dream. But he had not finished, not by any means.

He unlocked a side drawer of the metal desk and took out a folder. Inside was a typewritten list. He read it now, for pleasure.

Young man, 18–30	Young woman, 18–30
Mature man, 40–70	Mature woman, 40–60
Elderly man, 70 plus	Elderly woman, 65 plus

Two entries on the typed list had ticks in red pen beside them and now he took the same pen out of the drawer and formed a red tick mark beside the entry: 'Young woman, 18–30'.

Three ticks. Six entries.

The clock on the desk read 7.20 a.m. He placed the paper back in the file and locked the drawer, then went across the room and through a door to the store. He switched on the overhead lights and at once the place was lit in exactly the way all pathology rooms were lit. There was a steel sink in one corner and a channel in the rubber floor leading into a central drain. Against the wall were what looked like the doors of large grey filing cabinets. Propped up beside them was the metal table. He wheeled it to the centre under the main light and over the drain. A metal trolley with a sliding drawer was set up in the same way. The drawer swung out to reveal the instruments. He crossed to where the rectangular box stood on its metal runners and swung it round until it was level with the table.

Debbie Parker's body was already cool to the touch. Sharp surgical scissors slit her fleece jacket, trousers, jumper and underclothes, all of which were dropped into a black bin bag, to be disposed of later. Her wristwatch, house keys and torch went into a separate box. There were three cards in one of her pockets. He studied them for a second or two, then dropped them into the bag on top of the clothes.

He walked slowly round the metal table, looking down at the girl's flabby naked body, with its pitted facial skin and acned shoulders. He felt nothing. That was correct. At post-mortems the pathologist felt nothing, only curiosity and intellectual and professional interest. As he went he dictated, as the pathologist did, noting everything about the body under his scrutiny, quietly and professionally.

When he was ready, he took up the scalpel. He had too little time now but he wasn't able to wait and tonight he could come back and spend as long as he liked taking Young Woman, 18–30, expertly apart. Debbie Parker had ceased to exist as a human being. She was now a sample, a specimen of her sex and age, no more.

He bent forward and made the first precise incision.

CAT DEERBON kept one room in their farmhouse out of bounds to children and dogs. It had become known mockingly as the Smart Sitting Room and it was in there that they had now gathered. Supper had been eaten, and they had brought glasses of wine in with them. A cafetière and a pot of tea were on the low table. It was rare for Cat to be able to hold a meeting at home, but it was half-term and her mother had taken Sam and Hannah to London for assorted treats, including the London Eye.

The others, sitting back comfortably with their wine and coffee, were her husband Chris, the osteopath Nick Haydn, the acupuncturist Aidan Sharpe, and Gerald Tait, senior partner at a GP practice on the other side of Lafferton. He represented the older generation but his outlook was up-to-date and his sympathies were broad.

Over supper, the talk had been general. Now they were to focus.

Cat set down her glass. 'OK. Chris and I have become concerned over the last few months about some of the alternative therapists working in our area. At best they take a lot of money from gullible people. But a number of these so-called therapists are not harmless. As you know, neither Chris nor I are against properly qualified complementary practitioners working in proven disciplines. That's why we asked you, Aidan and Nick. You know what you're doing and you follow the first principle of all orthodox doctors: Do no harm.'

Aidan Sharpe cleared his throat. 'Thank you, Cat. I am grateful for that and I'm sure Nick is. Nevertheless, I'm afraid we still come in for a good deal of hostile criticism for what we do.'

He had a strangely precise and formal way of speaking. It probably went with the exactness and precision of his skills, Cat thought. She did not pretend to understand or accept the theory behind traditional Chinese acupuncture, but she respected that it had a long and honourable history—and that it often worked.

Nick Haydn sprawled at one end of a sofa, a big, broad Rugby player with huge hands, a therapist who could manipulate people's bodies with energy and strength when necessary, his way of working in contrast to that of Sharpe—for whom, Cat noted, he seemed to have a certain antipathy.

'What has brought all this up now?' Nick asked. 'Starly's been the haunt of hippies and New Agers for years. They don't take any business away from me—my appointment book is always full.'

Aidan Sharpe nodded across at him in agreement.

'Two things really,' Cat said. 'First, I had an emergency call recently to a young girl who had consulted a practitioner up there about her acne. She got some herbal capsules and an ointment from this guy. She had a serious allergic reaction to one or both and her flatmate had to call me out. She was fine but I had the stuff analysed by a mate at BG. The tablets were rubbish—dried parsley mainly—but the ointment contained several things I wouldn't allow near anyone's skin.'

'Who in God's name gave her the stuff?' Gerald Tait looked angry.

'A man who rejoices in the name of Dava.'

'Dava what?' Nick asked.

'Oh, he has nothing so orthodox as a surname. Just Dava.'

Nick snorted in derision.

'There's worse.' Cat looked down at the notes she had made. 'A psychic surgeon has started practising up there.'

Gerald Tait looked round at the others. 'This is a new one to me. What in heaven's name is a "psychic surgeon"?'

'May I interpose here?' Aidan straightened his bow tie. 'I happen to know a bit about psychic surgery. Anyone who knows about conjuring can tell you how it works. They prey upon the gullible. But of course there has to be a success rate of sorts, otherwise they'd quickly run out of clients, so they have accomplices.'

'Like all the best magicians,' Chris said. 'The girl who helps with the sawing in half, the plant in the audience who volunteers.'

'Exactly. The accomplices pose as patients with anything from an apparent broken leg to an intestinal tumour. They come along with case notes, letters from bogus consultants and so on, and, of course, they are cured and proclaim that a miracle has been performed on them, so lo and behold, the queues form.'

'What about the "surgery"?' Gerald Tait asked.

Aidan Sharpe gave them a lecture on the practice. The 'surgeon' actually touched and manipulated the bodies of his clients, scoring their flesh with his thumbnail or a stick that he had palmed, and then he pretended to remove tissue from inside the body.

'And you're telling us this is what is going on ten miles from here, Cat? Dear God. Something has to be done.'

'That's why I wanted us to meet, Gerald.'

'Can't the police do anything? Can't you ask your brother?'

'He's up to his neck in a drug operation and I haven't managed to speak to him yet. But I do plan to talk to him about it.'

'Meanwhile, I think it's very good that we're meeting like this and I do want to thank you for your gesture of faith in Nick and myself,' Aidan said in his precise way. 'We must all start to keep notes of any alternative therapists we come across.'

'Maybe a colour-coding system,' Nick suggested. 'Red for danger, blue for OK, green for thoroughly recommended. Bags I be green.'

'It's the reds that are important,' Aidan Sharpe said.

The Tape

Of course I didn't tell you. How could I have told you? I concealed it from you for all those years, because if you had found out you would have blamed me as you always blamed me for everything.

I had worked incredibly hard, staying up night after night learning the grind of chemical formulae, pharmacology, tropical diseases—everything I found uninteresting but had to know. They were a means to an end and it was only the thought of the end that got me through.

When I entered the pathology room for the first time, I knew that I had found it. The place became a second home. Towards the end I was observing a post-mortem just about every day. The senior staff admired my ambition and seriousness, I know that, and were privately marking me out as one of their own, a future colleague.

After a time, of course, watching did not satisfy me. Then one night I looked up from Congenital Diseases of the Eye *and knew what I was going to do. I set aside the textbook and began to think, and the excitement that welled up in me was like none I had experienced before.*

Six

As Sandy walked from the shower into her bedroom wrapped in a towelling dressing gown, the pips sounded for the eleven o'clock news on her bedside radio. She felt a flicker of anxiety. Debbie had not said that she would be out or left a note and that was unusual, but she had been going to the occasional meeting of one of the weirdo groups she had joined at Starly. The meetings did not usually go on late, though; until tonight, Debbie had been back by ten, drinking herbal tea and telling Sandy all about chakras and auras. Sandy had to admit that Debbie was looking better—her skin was clearing up, though that was almost certainly because of Dr Deerbon's antibiotics, and she had definitely lost weight. You couldn't knock something that was so clearly doing her good.

Sandy got out her manicure set and went into the sitting room, where she painted her fingernails while watching an old episode of *Friends*. When it was over, she wandered about the flat, putting on the kettle for tea, switching on the radio and turning it off again. At half past twelve she went into Debbie's room to look for her address book. There might be a note of a meeting. Then she saw Debbie's handbag hanging over the back of a chair. Sandy stared at it, hesitating, then unzipped it and looked inside. Wallet, comb, tissues, notebook . . . all the usual rubble. But her house keys had gone.

Sandy was puzzled. There was no way Debbie would have gone out to a meeting or an evening with one of her new friends without her bag. She went to the telephone and phoned the police.

WHEN FREYA ARRIVED at Lafferton Police Station the next morning, a copy of a routine report about a missing girl was on her desk. DC Nathan Coates had picked up on it.

'What do you think, Sarge?' he asked.

She scanned the details. 'Hospitals?'

'Nothing.'

'Hm.' Freya went to get herself the first coffee of the day. The phrase 'psychiatric history' had jumped out, making it likely this was a depressed girl who would turn up, hopefully alive but possibly dead if she had been suicidal. She stood on the landing, sipping from the plastic cup. That was the most likely scenario, and yet . . .

221

Nathan came through the swing doors behind her. 'Sarge, the flat-mate is downstairs. Come in just now to report still no sign.'

Freya threw her empty cup in the bin and headed for the stairs.

Sandy Marsh was white-faced with anxiety and it took all Freya's skill to soothe her and extract the detail. The first thing she asked about was Debbie Parker's mental state and the girl had leapt to her defence angrily. 'Look, she was depressed for a bit. She lost her job and she . . . she had really low self-esteem . . . she's a bit overweight and . . . don't want to be disloyal, I'm not criticising her, you do understand that. She's my best friend and I feel responsible for her.'

'That's why you need to tell me everything, Sandy. You want her found fast. You mustn't hold anything back out of loyalty.'

'OK, well, she's more than a bit, she's quite a lot overweight. That got worse after she lost her job and got depressed and she's had bad acne. But she was just coming out of all that, you see. She went to see a therapist up at Starly and he gave her a really good diet—not a slimming diet, not dangerous, just really sensible eating.'

'Have you the name and address of the therapist?'

'Well . . . just a name. He calls himself Dava. I think he was harmless . . . well, apart from the stuff he gave her to take.'

Freya looked up sharply. 'Stuff?'

Sandy told her about Debbie's allergic reaction.

'Is it in the flat still?'

'No, Dr Deerbon took it away. She said she wanted to find out from someone at the hospital what was in it.'

'Do you think Debbie could have gone to see this man last night?'

'I doubt it. Besides, she'd never go far without taking her bag.'

The bag. Freya had flagged that mentally as soon as she had read the first report. No female went out for an evening, or even for an hour, without taking her bag, and according to Sandy it was the only one Debbie Parker owned and everything had been in it.

'Only she took her house keys,' the girl said now.

'You might do that if you slipped out to the corner shop.'

'We don't have a corner shop and she didn't take her purse.'

'Now, you're quite sure that she hadn't had any bad news, or had a sudden really low patch? Depression's a treacherous thing; it can strike again even when people feel they've turned a corner.'

'I know she was better. She was feeling good about herself. She talked about looking for a job. She was taking exercise, long walks.'

Oh God, Freya thought. 'If she went out for a walk she wouldn't have taken her handbag, would she?'

'No, it would just get in the way. It's a big bag.'

'But she would take her house keys.'

'Yes. So that's what I thought she was doing. At first. But she wouldn't have been walking until after midnight.'

'Did she walk anywhere in particular, take a regular route?'

'In the daytime she might walk all the way into town, perhaps go to a shop or have a coffee there. But mostly she went onto the Hill.'

Freya's heart sank at the same time as she felt a surge of excitement. That made three. The mountain biker, Angela Randall and now Debbie Parker. Three people who had gone walking or running or riding alone on the Hill. Three people who had disappeared without trace.

'I think you'd better go home now,' Freya said, 'in case Debbie comes back.'

'I ought to ring her dad and stepmum, oughtn't I?'

'Hold on till lunchtime. Then if she hasn't come back, yes, but try not to panic them. I'd like to put out a message on Radio BEV, asking if anyone has seen Debbie. Here's a card with the station number, and my extension. If I'm out and you need to leave a message or just talk to someone, speak to DC Nathan Coates.'

She watched the girl walk slowly away across the station forecourt, her head bent, slight, pretty, desperately worried. As well she might be, Freya thought, heading up the stairs to the DI's office.

He wasn't there. Freya went back to the CID room to where Nathan was entering data on to the computer. When he heard her brief report on the missing girl his face lit up. 'We go for it, right?'

'Yes, except that Cameron isn't in his office.'

'Cameron's off,' someone shouted from another desk. 'Got a hospital appointment.'

Freya tapped her pen on the side of her desk for a few seconds then made for the swing doors.

'COME IN.'

Because it was work, and she was keyed up about it, Freya was able to control that trembling sense of anticipation at seeing and talking to Simon Serrailler. Angela Randall and Debbie Parker were at the front of her mind and she wanted to get the wheels turning.

'Freya . . .' He shoved the fair hair back from where it flopped over his forehead. He looked tired. 'Sit down, sit down.'

She outlined the facts about Debbie Parker, then quickly related her case to that of Angela Randall, with the relevant links to the mountain biker neatly placed at the end.

'You're right,' he said when she had finished. 'The three together—and certainly the two missing women—look like more than coincidence. We've got to find Debbie Parker . . . What do you propose?'

'Local radio appeal; piece in the evening paper with her photograph; posters, but on hold for say forty-eight hours. And a full search of the Hill. Interview the therapist at Starly Tor.'

'Good. What about the father and stepmother?'

'I told the flatmate to hold off a bit longer in case Debbie turned up.'

He looked at his watch. 'No, they need to be told now. Get them down here. I want every blade of grass on the Hill looked under. I want the reports on Angela Randall and the biker on my desk and I'd like you to go up to Starly and take this hippie practitioner apart.'

She got up. 'I'll get on with it.'

'Who do you want with you?'

'Nathan Coates. He's already doing some checking for me.'

Serrailler nodded. 'Good work, Freya.'

She made for the door and went back downstairs. She crossed the CID room almost at a run, signalling thumbs up to Nathan on her way.

'We're on. The DCI is going for it. Uniform will be combing the Hill and there's a local radio appeal going out. I need to have the flatmate in here again—can you get a car to pick her up, Nathan?—then ring Radio BEV newsdesk and alert them. I'm going to write the appeal for info and we're passing that to the *Echo* for this evening as well. Oh, and can you ask Sandy Marsh to bring in a photo of Debbie if she can find one, the more recent the better?'

Nathan jumped for his phone. 'What's for me after that, Sarge?'

'You and I are having a drive out to Starly. We can have a dandelion sandwich at the wholefood café.'

THAT AFTERNOON, having spoken again to Sandy Marsh, Freya drove up to the Hill to find a full search under way. Police were spread out in a line moving slowly up the steep paths combing the ground, others were beating the scrub and undergrowth. The whole area had been sealed off. As she got out of her car, she saw Simon Serrailler talking to the uniformed inspector in charge of the search, and went across. All her energies and attention were focused now on the hunt for Debbie Parker; she had put her feelings about him into a locked area of herself, to be ignored while the investigation was going on.

'Freya?' He turned to her at once. 'Anything?'

'Not sure.' She nodded to the inspector, who detached himself and went back to the police van that was the search team's meeting point.

'I've just spoken to Sandy Marsh, Debbie's flatmate. It's suddenly occurred to her that she didn't actually see Debbie yesterday morning. She was certainly there the previous night. But Sandy wonders if Debbie might have got up before she did the next morning and gone for one of her long walks.'

Serrailler frowned. 'Any response from the radio appeal?'

'The usual time-wasters, nothing concrete. I think we ought to put out another appeal and mention Angela Randall's disappearance as well. I'm sure the two are linked. Someone's memory might be jogged by this into remembering the other woman.'

'It might, but I'd rather we held off until Debbie's parents are here and we've had a chance to fill them in. And I don't want the press having any excuse to start howling "SERIAL KILLER".'

'Right.'

He smiled briefly at her, before turning back to the police van.

Freya walked back to her car, carrying his smile with her.

'COLIN . . .'

He had never before heard Annie shout and this wasn't a shout you ignored. The place could have been on fire.

'Colin . . .' She came in without knocking. 'I've just heard the news on Radio BEV. One of them has gone missing.'

Colin Davison, aka Dava, had hung his robe up and was shrugging on his denim jacket. He had had clients wall-to-wall since nine o'clock, with only time for a mug of coffee, and he was hungry. But what his secretary had just said was alarming.

'Who are we talking about, Annie? Calm down.'

'She came earlier in the week and once before, I've looked her up. Debbie. Debbie Parker. Plump girl with spots.'

He remembered her perfectly well. She had been one of the instantly trusting ones, drinking everything in and determined to turn her life around. The second time she had been, the change had been noticeable. It took so little, he had thought, nothing they couldn't have done for themselves, yet they came to him, and came back for more, needing to be led by the hand. He felt sorry for them really.

'So what's happened to her?'

'The police are appealing for anyone who's seen her. She hasn't been home. Do you think you ought to ring them?'

'What for? I shouldn't think I was the last person to set eyes on her. There's no information we can give them.'

He looked down at the appointment book. Just one and not until three o'clock, and tomorrow just one in the morning. Not good.

'Time to do a spot more advertising,' he said to Annie. 'I'll give it some thought over my sarnie.'

Colin Davison looked ordinary, walking down the hill towards the wholefood café, an insignificant man anywhere between forty and fifty with nothing of the charismatic Dava about him. Something happened when he dimmed the lights and put on his robe, something gave him power and presence whenever a client walked in. He felt it and he knew it worked. Colin was no cynic. In his own way he believed in what he did, though by no means in everything he said. If he tarted it up a bit, that was harmless enough and it all helped—the music he played, the appointment at the time 'most propitious for you', the cards he gave them. They needed him.

The café was quite full, and as he went in Stephen Garlick saw him and indicated a spare seat next to him. Colin got a plate of quiche and salad and a cinnamon muffin and took them over. He liked Stephen, who kept the shop that did next-to-no business selling candles and wind chimes. He was a bit of a dreamer, but honest and incorruptible. Sometimes, when he was with Steve, Colin felt slightly ashamed.

'Hi.'

'I was hoping to catch you,' Steve said. 'Have you heard about the person who's taken 12 Hen Lane?'

Colin shook his head, his mouth full of quiche.

'His name is Anthony Orford. He calls himself a psychic surgeon.'

Colin put down his fork. 'Oh my God. I've heard of him. He claims to be taken over by the spirit of some doctor who lived like a hundred years ago and performs operations . . . only they're not. I'm not sure how he does it, but he's cured people of tumours, ulcers, MS . . . Once people discover where he is, the queues will form and the rest of us will be empty.'

'I shouldn't think you need to worry. It's different from what you do.' Stephen drained his mug and got up.

'Do you know when he's opening up?'

'No idea. The decorators are there now, though. Can't be long.'

Colin groaned. He had read enough about Anthony Orford to know he was a serious threat to his own business. And pretending to perform operations on people was way out of line. People like that gave decent therapists like him a seriously bad name.

He finished his lunch and walked back to his consulting room.

'There you are.' Annie said dramatically when he walked in the door. 'The police are here.'

Annie had put them in his room, a man and a woman. The man was examining the wall charts of the chakras and the woman was sitting with one leg over the other—good legs, he noted—writing.

'Sorry, I was out on my lunch break. I'm Colin Davison.'

He had always believed in being charming to the police. It was surprising how often it paid off.

'Detective Sergeant Freya Graffham, and this is DC Nathan Coates.'

Colin shook hands with them both and sat down at his desk. No point, he thought, in pretending he didn't know what this was about.

'I take it you must be here because of Debbie Parker?'

If the policewoman was surprised by his directness she did not acknowledge it by a flicker. 'That's right. How did you hear about her?'

'Annie, my assistant—she heard the news bulletin on Radio BEV.'

'Debbie was a patient of yours?'

'I call them clients, Sergeant. I'm not a doctor. Yes, she came to see me twice. The second time was only this week. Nice girl.'

'Can you tell me why she saw you? Was she ill?'

'Well, as I said, I'm not a doctor. If someone's physically ill and hasn't consulted their GP, I send them straight there. If they've already been and they just need some spiritual uplift and aid with the deepest part of their psyche to help in their healing, we work on that.'

'And did Debbie say she'd been to her doctor?'

'Yes.' It seemed better to lie. They weren't going to know. 'Her real problem was her lack of self-esteem. I was beginning to get her to look deeply into herself and discover her true path.'

Gobbledegook, the sergeant was thinking. It might as well have been written across her forehead.

'How'd she seem when she last came here?' The young man had one of the ugliest faces he'd ever seen. 'Did she seem dead unhappy? You know what I'm saying—as if she might try and run away?'

'If you mean do I think she was suicidal, then no. Nothing like.'

'Do you take any details of your client's personal lives, Mr Davison?'

He quite liked the woman. She was straight, not asking one thing and getting at another. He gave her a smile. 'Not really. I discover a great deal as I get to know them. I have names and addresses obviously. But details of parents, siblings, all that, I don't put down.'

'Did Debbie say anything in the course of her sessions that you think might give us any lead as to where she might have gone?'

He sat looking at his desk for a long time, then he shook his head. 'No. Debbie wasn't happy about herself but she was getting more positive. She was moving forward.'

'So not as likely to run away as she had been?'

'Her way of running was down into herself, into the darkness.'

'What kind of treatment did you give her?' The man again.

Colin sighed. 'I suggested she change her diet. Wholefoods, fruit and vegetables and wholegrains. No dairy fats, sugars or caffeine.'

'Anything else?'

'Exercise. I suggested she start by walking, brisk walks, a bit further each day. She needed to be in the fresh air as much as possible.'

'Do you know where she went to walk?'

'She mentioned the towpath by the river at Lafferton. And, of course, the Hill. The Wern Stones have ancient origins; it's a place of very positive energies. As well as a good healthy climb.'

'So you suggested she go on the Hill?'

'I can't remember if I actually suggested it—that might have come from her. She lives near it, doesn't she?'

The woman leaned forward slightly, holding his glance. 'This is very important, Mr Davidson. We have a major police search covering the Hill at the moment.'

The atmosphere in the room had changed. Suddenly, they were talking life or death. He could picture the line of uniformed men beating with sticks to and fro, to and fro, creeping slowly forwards.

'I do understand,' he said quietly. 'I know that the Hill was mentioned as a place she might go but I honestly can't remember if I suggested it or she did. Is that where she was last seen?'

'We're gathering information all the time, Mr Davison.' The sergeant stood up and handed him her card. 'If anything, the smallest thing, occurs to you, please phone us as a matter of urgency.'

'Of course. I'll meditate about it tonight.'

'We'd really appreciate that.' The young man's tone was ironic but when Colin looked at him, his face was blank.

Seven

Freya walked out of the cathedral into the cool, starry night, joyful at being in the fresh air again. She had come to the St Michael's Singers rehearsal in spite of feeling more like a hot bath and early bed, because she knew she needed not only the distraction of the music, but the balm it poured into her and the uplift the singing provided. It hadn't failed. Now she felt more at peace within herself.

Her car was on the other side of the cathedral as there had been no place left when she had arrived, and as she turned the corner, away from the main west door, everything went wonderfully quiet. The houses around her were dark, but the old-fashioned street lamps shed pools of topaz light onto the cobbles.

On such a night it was a joy to be walking slowly through these ancient spaces, but Freya's mind was filled with the two missing women. They had been walking or running alone—but then what had happened and where were they now, safe or in danger, alive or dead? Thinking deeply about the case, she took a step off the path as a car swung round the corner, picking her up in its headlights. Freya turned as the driver braked and hooted.

'Freya?'

She was blinded by the glare. The window of the silver BMW slid down as the headlights dipped.

'Who is this?' But as she took a couple of steps nearer she saw him with a shock of pleasure. 'Sir?'

'What are you doing walking in the close alone?'

'Coming from a choir practice in the cathedral. I was so late I couldn't get a space so I had to park my car down here.'

'Was my mother singing?'

'Not half. She's gone to the Cross Keys with the others but I didn't feel like it tonight.'

'Hang on.'

He swung his car into a space beside one of the darkened houses, switched off the engine and got out.

'Are you here to look for Meriel?'

He laughed. 'No, to come home. I live here.'

'Good heavens. I thought this end of the close was just offices.'

'Pretty much. There are offices and there's me. The clergy are all at the top end near the cathedral.'

'Well, well.'

'Come up and see. Come and have a drink at the end of a bad day.'

How easy momentous words often sounded, she thought, how casually spoken. *Come up and see. Come and have a drink.* She followed him into the dark, silent building and up the stairs, looking at his back, his head, the white-blond hair, his long legs, the shoes he wore, the colour of his socks. She could scarcely believe it was happening.

He walked in ahead of her. Lights went on. Freya stood in the doorway of a room that took her breath away.

He glanced at her and smiled. 'Drink? Coffee?'

'It had better be coffee,' she said. Her voice sounded odd.

'Sit down. Do you mind if I have a whisky?'

'Of course I don't.'

He went through a door on the left. More lights, brighter lights on pale walls. The kitchen.

Freya looked again at the room. It was perfect. It had everything she might have chosen, but designed and arranged better than she could have done it—furniture, rugs, pictures, books, the lighting exactly right. She walked across to look at a set of four framed drawings in a group above the brown leather sofa. They were of Venice— the domes of Santa Maria della Salute, San Giorgio Maggiore and two churches she did not know, the line vibrant and clear, the detail minute and yet beautifully economical. The initials SO were just visible in each lower right-hand corner.

'Here we are.' He came out of the kitchen with a tray and set down cafetière, milk and sugar and small pottery mug on the low table.

'Who did these? I love them.'

'I did. O is my middle initial.'

'Simon, they're beautiful. What are you doing in the police force?'

'Ah, but would I enjoy art so much if I did it twenty-four/seven? Drawing keeps me sane.' He went to a white-painted cube on the wall, opened the front and took out a whisky bottle and glass.

'How long have you been drawing?'

'Always. I went to art school but I left because no one was interested in drawing. Everyone wanted conceptual stuff.'

'But then'—Freya sat down on the sofa—'the police force?'

'I went to university to read law so that I could come in on fast track as a graduate. It was always either drawing or policing.'

'But your parents are doctors.'

'My entire family going back three generations have been medics. I'm the black sheep.'

'I'd have thought you were a refreshing change.'

'My mother has come round to seeing it a bit like that now.'

'Your father?'

'No.'

He said it in a way that defied her to ask more. She did not, but pressed the plunger on her cafetière and watched it sink slowly down, crushing the layer of coffee grains to the bottom.

Simon took the deep easy chair opposite her, crossed his long legs easily, and leaned back, whisky in hand. 'I didn't get back to the Hill before the search was called off but I presume nothing was found?'

'Nothing at all.' She found it impossible to look at him. She poured her coffee to keep her head down. Her hand was shaking.

She wanted him to talk, to get to know the sound of his voice so well that when she left here she would be able to carry it with her.

'But we're off duty. How long have you been a choral singer?'

AN HOUR AND A HALF later, Freya had talked about herself and her past life more intimately than she had ever talked to anyone. Simon was a listener, prompting only occasionally, looking at her all the time as she spoke. She found herself talking about her family, her training, the Met, her marriage and its breakdown, and wanting to go on and on, wanting him to know everything about her.

She was in love with him, she knew that now, but tonight had changed things. She no longer wanted to reject the acute awareness of her reaction. She had never known a man who had given her such full and concentrated attention, who had listened to her as if she were important, as if there was no one else of interest to him in the world.

The cathedral bells chimed midnight, making her aware of how long she had talked, how much of herself she had yielded up.

'Goodness,' she said. 'I have to go. Thank you for this. I went to choir so that my mind would stop spinning the case round and round. Singing and then coming here really have given me what I needed.'

'It's important to get as far away as possible from this sort of case, if not physically then mentally. It can drain you otherwise.' He got up and strolled across to the door with her. 'I'll come down,' he said.

'No, I'm fine.'

'It's late, it's dark, there's no one about and you're on your own.'

She laughed. 'Simon, I'm a police officer.'

He put the flat door on the latch and looked at her, his handsome face stern. 'And two women are missing.'

She looked at him for a long minute. 'Yes,' she said quietly.

'I wish I was not thinking about them the way I am,' Simon said, touching a hand to her back to guide her as she began to descend the stairs. The touch burned into her.

At her car, he held the driver's door for her. She hesitated a fraction of a second. He did not move.

'Thank you again.'

'My pleasure. Good night, Freya.'

He lifted a hand and stood watching until she had driven down the close to the arch at the far end and away.

CAROL ASHTON was in a greater state of anxiety than usual when she got home late from the Four Ways Nursing Home. One of the patients had disappeared some time after four o'clock in the afternoon, and it was not until twenty past six that the police patrol car brought him back, having found him sitting on a bench beside the river wearing nothing but pyjamas and slippers.

Now she picked up the *Echo* to read over a much needed gin, only to find that the disappearance of Debbie Parker was the main front-page story. Carol read the report quickly, looking for some mention of Angela Randall. There was none.

The two cases seemed to have plenty of similarities, so why was there no reference to Angela? What were the police doing? Had her case simply been filed away and forgotten? Carol felt upset. She owed it to her missing colleague to remind the police of her name.

She finished her gin and tonic and went to the telephone.

'I'm sorry, DS Graffham isn't in,' the voice answered. 'Can anyone else help you?'

Carol hesitated. She didn't want to have to tell the whole story from scratch to someone who knew nothing about it. 'Can I leave her a message?'

She gave her name and number and asked for the sergeant to call her urgently.

But she won't, she thought, going into the kitchen. In her experience, people seldom rang back. She started to beat two eggs for an omelette, but she felt too restless to leave things until the next morning. She went back to the phone.

'Bevham and District Newspapers, good evening.'

A few minutes later, she was speaking to someone called Rachel Carr. Forty minutes later, Rachel Carr was ringing her doorbell.

'MRS ASHTON, tell me about this lady who you say is missing— Angela Randall. I gather she works for you?'

Rachel Carr was a tall, sharp-faced young woman with oval designer spectacles and an expensive-looking pale suede jacket. She had put a small recording machine on the coffee table between them. Carol watched the little spools go round as she talked, about herself and the Four Ways, about Angela, about her disappearance, about speaking to the police twice, and finally, about the shock of reading that another single woman had gone missing.

'So of course I looked at the report expecting there to be something about Angela . . . well, it was obvious. Only there just wasn't.'

'Have you contacted the police this evening?'

'Yes, but the person I saw wasn't there. They just suggested I ring tomorrow morning.'

'So you feel the police are being rather lax?'

'Not exactly . . . I mean, we don't know what's going on, do we? I want to find out, that's all. I'm puzzled. I owe it to Angela. She hasn't got anyone else to fight for her.'

'I know this is a difficult question to answer, but—what do you think has happened to Angela Randall?'

Carol looked at her hands. She was reluctant to say what she thought out loud. She swallowed. 'As time has gone on, I can't see what innocent explanation there can be.'

The reporter's expression was both grave and expectant. 'I don't want to distress you, Mrs Ashton, but do you think it likely that by now Miss Randall may be dead?'

'It's what I'm afraid of.'

Rachel Carr raised her eyebrows slightly. 'Do you think this other young woman might be dead too?'

'Dear God, I hope not. It isn't long, is it? She might have been found by now . . . it's only a couple of days, not like Angela.'

'Do you blame the police for the delay in finding anything out about Miss Randall?'

Did she? She wondered if she had already said too much, implied things she was not really sure about. All the same . . .

'I'm angry,' she said, 'and I'm upset. It's too long. And now this new case. If there were a connection . . . I'm quite frightened. I think anyone might be, don't you?'

'You think other Lafferton women have good reason to be frightened at the moment then?'

Did she? If it came to the worst . . .

After a moment, Carol Ashton nodded.

RACHEL CARR raced back to the office, in her red Mazda MX5. She had been waiting for a story like this for a long time. Don Pilkington, the *Echo*'s editor, had already gone, but the news editor, Graham Gant, was still at his desk. Rachel pulled up a chair and began to talk excitedly, not pausing until she had filled him in on everything.

'I want us to go big on this one, Graham. Two women are missing so why have the police only told us about one? What are they trying to cover up? Why isn't the Hill policed properly? Why—?'

Graham Gant held up his hand wearily. 'OK, Rachel, get on to

Lafferton and ask them about this other missing woman. Anything else, and certainly anything in the nature of an anti-police campaign, you have to run past the editor.'

'I'll ring him at home.'

'You won't get him, he's at a big Masonic dinner in Bevham.'

Rachel snorted.

'Let's get the details about this other woman and we'll headline it tomorrow if there's still no news on either of them. But wait till you can talk to Don before you start whipping up public anxiety.'

Rachel stormed across the room to her own desk in frustration. It was always the same, the big boys in league with each other. She picked up the phone and put in a call to the police station, but by now it was nearly ten and no one was in CID.

The duty sergeant said there was no recent news on the missing girl and would not comment on any other missing persons. 'I suggest you ring back in the morning and speak to DS Graffham.'

'What time does he wander in?'

'She. DS Freya Graffham. Any time after nine. If she isn't available, you could ask to speak to DC Coates. Sorry I can't be of more help to you tonight, madam.'

Rachel slammed the receiver down. She didn't relish having to wait until the morning to get permission from the editor, then speak to some poxy woman detective, who would probably make her hang about until there was another press briefing.

An hour later, she had written a story that was, she thought, too high-profile to be confined to the *Lafferton Echo*. And it was hardly her fault if the editor was at a dinner. She called up her email address book and clicked on an entry for the editor of the *Bevham Post*.

DCI Simon Serrailler was not given to shouting. He preferred to make his anger known by speaking softly and icily. He had called Freya and Nathan to his office and was pointing to the newspaper on his desk. 'I take it you have both seen this morning's *Post*?'

'Yes, sir.'

'Gawd knows where it came from, guv. Not out of here.'

'Freya?'

'Categorically not, sir.'

'So how does this reporter—Rachel Carr—know about the other missing woman? How has she found out her name, her address, where she works? Someone must have talked to her.'

'No one in the station. Nathan and I have been the only ones looking into the case in detail and neither of us briefed this reporter.' There was a sliver of ice in Freya's own voice.

'OK, I take your word for it. But these are exactly the sort of head-lines I wanted to avoid . . . Serial killer, for God's sake. There isn't even a body. Right, I want a press briefing called for noon. I want local radio, television, news agencies, the lot—and get onto it now before they get onto us. I've put the search team out onto the Hill again but they'll have finished by this afternoon. Any joy at Starly?'

'Debbie Parker had two appointments with the therapist that calls himself Dava,' Freya said. 'He gave us the New Age psychobabble, but I didn't get the impression he had anything to hide.'

'All the same, we'll keep him in the frame for the time being. I want this press briefing to be organised and professional. We're in control and we have to get that message across. Public confidence is going to take a knock from this rubbish. Oh, and if national press get wind of the story and call up, put them on to me. Say nothing.'

'Sir.'

Freya hesitated for a second, letting Nathan go first out of the door. The telephone rang.

'Serrailler. Good morning, sir. I have read it, yes.'

Freya fled.

'WE ARE BECOMING increasingly concerned for Debbie Parker's safety and have had search teams out on the Hill and its surrounding area, where it is thought she may have been out walking.'

More press had come into the conference room for the noon brief-ing than had attended for a long time. They smelt blood. Freya and Nathan were sitting on the rostrum with the inspector in charge of searching the Hill. DCI Serrailler was speaking.

'Another Lafferton woman, Angela Randall of 4 Barn Close, was reported missing on December 18 last year, but although we made an investigation at the time, we had no reason to see her disappearance as suspicious. However, in the light of the disappearance of Debbie Parker, we are looking at that of Miss Randall again, and will be making a broadcast appeal to the public about it. We'll naturally keep you all informed of developments. Meanwhile, I would be grateful if the press would refrain from wild and lurid speculation, which is not only distressing for the families and friends of the missing women but causes general public alarm.'

Rachel Carr stood up. 'Chief Inspector, why did you conceal the disappearance of Angela Randall?'

'No one has concealed anything, Miss . . .'

'Sorry, Rachel Carr, Bevham Newspapers . . .'

'Well, Miss Carr, we cannot put out a public appeal for every person who goes missing, even in a place the size of Lafferton.'

'But you're taking her case seriously now?'

'As I said, Miss Carr, we made initial investigations when her disappearance was first reported. We take every case of a missing person seriously. Are there any more questions?'

'Jason Fox, County News Agency. Chief Inspector, are you worried for the safety of one or both of the missing women?'

'Yes, there is cause for concern. But I would stress that we have no evidence that any harm has come to either woman.'

'Is this a murder inquiry?'

'Has the search of the Hill yielded any trace of either woman?'

'Why has no search been made of other parts of the town?'

'Are people advised to stay away from the Hill?'

And, from Rachel Carr again, 'Are you looking for anyone in connection with these missing women? Do you think they have been abducted or murdered?' And yet again, 'Is there a serial killer preying upon the women of Lafferton?'

AS FREYA WALKED across the CID room after the briefing, Simon Serrailler caught her attention and said, 'Freya, would you come and see me for a minute, please?'

'That woman from the *Echo* is out for blood,' she said as she followed him into his room.

Simon made a dismissive gesture. 'She's just a local terrier. Now, Debbie Parker. I have a feeling that if there are going to be any clues as to why she went off and where she is now, we'll find them in Starly. You saw that one therapist, but I want the picture of Debbie on Have You Seen leaflets. Spray them around every shop, consulting room, café . . . We want anyone who recognises her or knows her.'

'Sir. What about Angela Randall?'

'What about her?'

'Well, so far as we know she had nothing to do with Starly.'

'No. The only lead for her is the very tenuous one of the Hill. Until anything new comes up about her, we concentrate on Debbie Parker.'

'Right.'

She might have fallen in love with Simon Serrailler but professionally she disagreed with his dismissal of the Angela Randall case. A picture of her sterile, lonely little house came to Freya's mind, then the expensive cuff links with their note—a note that revealed an obsessive passion. Freya knew, walking back to her CID room, why she was not prepared to let the case slip out of sight. She understood Angela Randall, and what motivated her, only too well.

'IS THIS A GOOD moment, or are you feeding children, giving hay to horses . . . ?'

'Hi, Karin. I'm catching up on GP paperwork so all interruptions welcome. How are things? What have you been up to?'

'Well, reflexology, for one. It's utter bliss. I nearly went to sleep. They burn lovely scented candles. Sweet girl, too. I didn't tell her anything and after a bit she asked if I had problems in my breasts.'

'Good guess. Women of your age often have.'

'Cynic. I felt terrific afterwards.'

'Can I make a suggestion here?'

'That's what you're for, you're my doctor.'

'I think you should go for another scan. I want to see what is actually happening . . . as against what you feel.'

'Not yet. I just need a bit longer.'

Cat sighed, then decided not to push her for the time being. 'OK, so where next? Feng shui?'

'The psychic surgeon.'

'No, Karin, absolutely not.'

'Listen, this one isn't about me. I don't believe in it, I think it's trickery and I think it probably ought to be stopped, but at the moment all we have is rumour. Someone has to go and find out and then bring back a proper account. I'm doing everyone a favour here.'

'Then I'm coming with you. I want to know what's going on as well. Maybe you can be a guinea pig. But you're vulnerable.'

'It's Thursday morning at ten fifteen. You'll be in surgery.'

'Yes. Damn. Look, if anything worries you, come straight out. We're not talking scented candles here.'

'I know.'

'And, Karin? The scan. This is your doctor speaking.'

'Goodbye, Cat.'

KARIN PULLED into the car park behind the market square in Starly at ten on Thursday morning. It was quiet, and the sun caught the tree trunks with lemon-coloured light as she walked down the hill. She had been determined and positive about taking charge of her own health. Nevertheless, in the dark watches of the night she did have misgivings about rejecting proven medical treatment, and was gripped by fear that her delay might mean she would be beyond help. In the day, when she read the books so full of miracles and success stories, everything changed and she felt fit and sure of herself again.

At ten past ten she walked through the freshly painted door of a house at the bottom of the hill, her right hand curled round the mobile phone in her pocket for reassurance. Reflexologists and aromatherapists were one thing, a psychic surgeon quite another.

'Good morning. Have you an appointment?'

The middle-aged woman in the camel jumper could have been the receptionist for a Harley Street consultant. Karin gave her name.

'Yes, thank you, Mrs McCafferty. Would you take a seat? Dr Groatman will be with you shortly.'

'I'm sorry?'

The woman smiled. 'Dr Groatman. That is the name of the consultant who treats patients through Anthony.'

'I see. And I take it this doctor—'

'Lived in the 1830s in London.'

'Right.'

The woman smiled before turning back to her computer.

As Karin picked up a copy of *World Healing*, the inner door opened and an elderly woman came out looking confused and pale.

'Mrs Cornwell? Please come and sit down for a moment. I'll get you some water.' The receptionist went to a cooler at the far end of the room. 'Drink this, Mrs Cornwell. How are you feeling?'

The woman took out a handkerchief and wiped her face. 'A bit faint.'

'That's quite usual. Just drink the water slowly and don't get up. Have you any discomfort?'

The woman looked up in surprise. 'No, none at all. Isn't that odd?'

The receptionist smiled. 'It's usual.'

Then the door opened again and a slight, sandy-haired man came through and went straight across to the desk without looking at either woman. He looked briefly at a folder on the desk before walking back across the room and closing the inner door behind him. There was silence. Mrs Cornwell sipped her water and continued to look bemused; the receptionist returned to her work.

A buzzer sounded.

'Would you go through please, Mrs McCafferty?' The receptionist was smiling. 'Straight through the door. Dr Groatman is waiting.'

Karin's legs felt weak and her throat dry. I must be mad, she thought. Wishing Cat had come with her, she went slowly across the room.

THE MAN WAS VERY BENT and walked with a limp. He wore a caliper and one shoulder was higher than the other. His hair was the same sandy colour as the man who had walked through the reception room, but tousled and sticking up from his head. He wore a white coat and stood by an examination couch. The room was lit dimly, with slatted blinds shielding the window. There was a sink with a tap. A bare vinyl floor. Nothing else.

'On the couch, please. What is the name you use?' His voice was gruff with a slight accent she could not place.

'Karin.'

'Lie down, please.'

Karin lay. He stood above her and passed his hands rapidly over her body without touching it.

'You have cancer. I feel your cancer in the breast and the glands and spread to the stomach. Please unbutton your shirt but do not remove it and do not remove the underclothing.'

Now the accent was definitely foreign, perhaps German or Dutch. While she unbuttoned her shirt he looked away.

'I should remove this growth here in the neck gland. This is the core tumour. We get rid of this, others will shrink and disappear. They feed off the parent tumour.'

Everything in her wanted to shut out the sight of him. He reached under the couch and swung out a tray of instruments. Karin heard the sound of a bucket being moved. She forced herself to watch, to observe closely. He took an instrument from the tray and seemed to fold his hand over it. Then he reached towards her neck.

'You need not be afraid, nothing to fear. Look at your heart rate, far too quick, ridiculous. Calm down. I am making you well. The tumour will go, you will be well. What is there to be afraid of?'

She felt him take a fold of the flesh in her neck, low down, then a curious sensation, as if something were being drawn across her skin, and the hand twisting and moving within her neck. His eyes were half closed, but she knew he was aware that she was looking at him. The twisting movement sharpened, she felt a stinging pain and a wrench.

'Ah. There. Good.'

His hand moved swiftly away from her and down. Something dropped into the bucket. When his hand came up the fingers were bloody. Now his hands were hovering above her again.

'You are in God's hands, Karin. Safe now. You will be fully well. You need to rest and you should eat well. Do not deny your body. Give it what it asks for. Drink plenty of water. Rest. Goodbye.'

He stood motionless. After a few seconds, Karin swung her legs off the couch and got up unsteadily. Dr Groatman neither helped her nor spoke and his facial expression did not flicker.

As she put her hand on the door leading back into the reception office, he said softly, 'Mistrust and suspicion are dangerous companions. Keep an open mind and a generous heart, Karin, or you will negate my healing work.' His voice was unpleasant and whatever accent there had been was quite gone.

Karin almost fell into the outer room.

Two people were waiting.

'Please sit down and drink a glass of water, Mrs McCafferty.'

'No, I have to go, sorry . . .'

'You really must. You need to centre yourself. Please.'

Trembling, she sat and sipped the paper tumbler of water. The woman was right: she needed it. She was thirsty and unsteady. The buzzer sounded for the next patient.

'Do I pay you now?'

'Yes, please. Take your time; wait until you feel quite calm again.'

'I'm fine. Thanks.'

Karin stood. She did not faint. The room remained still. She crossed to the desk and the smiling woman handed her a small card. *Mrs K. McCafferty. For treatment: £100. Please make cheques payable to SUDBURY & CO.*

She came out into the fresh air, doing sums furiously. She had been in the consulting room perhaps ten minutes, no more. But say one patient every half hour, from nine till five, with an hour for lunch— fourteen patients a day, fourteen at £100 = £1,400.

Back in the car, she rang Cat.

'Dr Deerbon is out on an emergency call. May I take a message?'

Karin left her name, and asked Cat to ring her that evening at home.

She drove back slowly to Lafferton, trying to put the morning's experience out of her mind. She went into the house, made a cup of tea and took it over to the sofa with her mail. Five minutes later she was asleep.

When she woke, over two hours later, she felt an extraordinary sense of peace and refreshment. She remembered the morning— Starly, the strange consulting room, the man with the bent back and lame leg, his odd accent, his brusque remarks. She had been nervous and suspicious, relieved to get away. Yet now she felt full of strength and well-being, as if something within her had indeed changed. She wondered what she could say to Cat Deerbon now.

Eight

He thought he knew everything about himself. He had never had any real interest in the chase and the capture. They were means to an end. He had to find the people, to select them carefully, track them down, and then of necessity still them. But none of that gave him pleasure. Sadists and psychopaths, evil people, obtained gratification from the act of murder. He was not like that.

What he did was altogether different.

So he was shocked to realise that he longed to return to the Hill, now that temporarily he could not do so. He wanted to retrace his steps, to stand where he had stood with each of them, to recall everything.

He dared not take the van and he could not go in his car. Too many people knew it, knew him and might wave to him. He would have to walk and it must be after dark. People avoided the Hill now. He knew he ought to avoid it too. So why was he so desperate that he was prepared to take a risk now? He felt the need building up inside him and he understood that he must control it.

To calm himself, he drove down to the business park. It was after seven o'clock and the units were locked and in darkness. He let himself in, clicked on the fluorescent lighting, then walked to the door at the back and into the heart of his kingdom. Everything that mattered was here. He checked the thermometers and dials, as he did every day. His hand hovered first over one drawer handle, then reached out for the second on the right.

The drawer came forward silently on its runners. He stared down at the white marble face. Angela Randall. Her obsession with him had been flattering at first. But after a time, the letters, the gifts, the pleas, had become irksome. In the end he had despised her. Not that she was here for that reason; emotion had never been allowed to influence his work in any way. She was here because she had been the right age and sex, and had been easy to track down on the Hill.

Before he switched off the lights and padlocked the doors, he spent some time looking at them all. He was a little dissatisfied with his work on the young man, who had been so fit, so lean and well muscled, and he wondered if it ought to be repeated. But the capture had been the most difficult, the boy had struggled, he had been strong. Not like poor fat Debbie.

Three drawers remained empty. If things continued as they were on the Hill, it would be some time before he would be able to fill them. The delay was frustrating, not part of the plan. Yet surely it was a weakness in him not to have allowed for the unpredictable.

He paced around the room until he had his impatience under control, then left, to return home and revise his plans.

'OK, SPILL THE BEANS.'

Cat poured out their mugs of tea. Her daughter Hannah had gone to watch children's television with her tea on a plate, leaving Cat and Karin in the kitchen to talk.

Karin was quiet for a moment, assembling her thoughts. The cat jumped on to the sofa and curled up beside her.

'It's worrying. I think he ought to be stopped, I really do.' Karin told her about her visit to the psychic surgeon, in as much detail as she could. Cat listened, sipping her tea, occasionally frowning. From the television next door came the sound of a recorder band playing 'Morning has Broken'. When Karin had finished, Cat said nothing, only got up to refill the kettle, before going to check on Hannah.

She returned, and dumped Hannah's plate and mug on the draining board. 'OK, I've taken it in. I'm horrified. This man is dangerous, you're right, though it sounds as if he was careful not to touch you in any way that could lay him open to a charge of assault.'

Karin nodded. 'It was uppermost in my mind from the minute I walked into the room. He was very, very careful.'

'Of course he would be with a woman who was obviously watchful and intelligent. Would he behave so impeccably with a young girl, or even a child . . . Does he see children?'

'I don't know. The people waiting were all older.'

'The wickedness is that he gives people false hope with this pantomime. That some of them will be convinced they are cured.'

'I found it quite frightening.'

'I bet you did. Dear God, imagine if you were old and frail and you actually believed he was cutting you open and taking bits out of you. I wonder if anyone has ever died of shock.'

'To find that out you'd need to discover where he came from, where he's worked before. I think I'll do some research, trawl the Internet.'

'Good idea.'

From the television room the hornpipe marked the end of *Blue Peter*.

Karin stood up. 'Thanks for the tea. I'll leave you to enjoy some quality time with your daughter.'

Cat made a face.

Outside, the wind cut across the garden, slamming the car door out of Karin's hand. She looked back at the lighted kitchen window, watching Cat lift Hannah up onto the worktop beside the sink. Both of them were laughing, and not for the first time Karin envied Cat not only for her children but the warm and happy atmosphere she always found in her house.

IT WAS ALMOST MIDNIGHT when Cat telephoned her brother.

'I didn't think you'd be tucked up,' she said.

'I've only been in half an hour.'

'And I'm on call so there's never any point in going to bed early. Si, have you anything doing up at Starly . . . officially?'

'Sort of. We did a house-to-house the other day, trying for info on the missing girl Debbie Parker. Drew a blank though.'

'Yes, I knew she'd seen a therapist up there. She was my patient.'

'Is . . . I like to remain optimistic.'

'Did you encounter a chap calling himself a psychic surgeon?'

'A what?'

She repeated Karin's story.

'He's new to me. I can check whether our people saw him. I think Debbie Parker favoured a chap who calls himself Dava.'

'She told me about Dava. Listen, Si, this Dr Groatman, or Anthony Orford, or whatever his real name is—he's dangerous. For all sorts of reasons. He ought to be put out of business.'

'From what you've told me, it doesn't sound as if he's laid himself open to a charge of assault. And as you know yourself, anyone can set up as an alternative practitioner, no training, no qualifications. If we could prove he had actually taken an instrument and opened someone up, we could certainly arrest him. Has he?'

'It's all sleight of hand.'

'How does he get patients?'

'Word of mouth. People tell of his miracles.'

'How long has he been in Starly?'

'Not long. Karin is going to try and find out where he was before.'

'And why he left. I'll get some checks run tomorrow, but right now we've no reason even to question him.'

'Shit. I'm really wound up about this one. Think of the serious ill-nesses people might be taking to him instead of coming to us.'

'There is one thing you might do . . . What is the next best thing to setting the police on to him? Possibly even better?'

'Not a clue.'

'The press. Get a reporter to pose as a patient and then nosy around Starly. If there is any dirty linen, it'll be hung out all over the district.'

'Can you think of anyone who'd be interested?'

'Oh, indeed,' Cat heard the smile in her brother's voice, 'I know just the person. Got a pen?'

RACHEL CARR was in the office by eight every morning. She had found out that the early news reporter caught whatever worms had been turned up overnight, and she was never going to let a colleague beat her to them. So when Cat Deerbon rang she took the call and within a few seconds of listening the adrenaline was pumping.

By midmorning, Rachel had the go-ahead from her editor, put in a couple of calls to people who might come up with something about the psychic surgeon and made an appointment to see him herself. Having been told that he was fully booked for six weeks, she pleaded acute pain and distress and said that he was her only hope.

'Hold on one moment, please.'

The receptionist was back within twenty seconds to say she could fit Rachel in on Friday afternoon. 'Dr Groatman does try to keep some spaces for people who are in great pain. There may be a small further charge to cover the extra administration.'

'It doesn't matter what it costs. Thank you so much.'

Rachel put the phone down, went straight on to the Internet and keyed Dr+Charles+Groatman+psychic+surgeon into Google.

The website it gave her was out of date. Dr Charles Groatman, aka Brian Urchmont, advertised himself as practising at a clinic in Brighton. Beside his photograph were extracts from letters of thanks, praise and recommendation from grateful patients and details of surgery hours. Rachel thought for a moment, then remembered Duggie Hotten, who had been a senior reporter when she was starting out and had gone on to the *Brighton Argus*.

She was put straight through.

'Rachel Carr, of course I remember. What are you doing now?'

'Chief reporter at Lafferton.' She hoped no one was listening.

'Great stuff. What can I do?'

She began to tell him but he was there before her.

'God, just start me on the subject of our psychic surgeon. We've a mountain of stuff on him but he's always come out of it smelling of roses—sort of. So he's in your neck of the woods. Good luck.'

'I'm doing an investigative. Can you let me have any clippings?'

'Sure. He's a tricky one, Rache. Watch your back. He's got a nose for a journalist and he screams "Libel" like a stuck pig. He also turns up all sorts of people to defend him, grateful patients whose lives he saved, you know the stuff. We had a mountain of letters.'

'What happened?'

'We dropped it. Too much flak. Besides, he isn't doing anything illegal. He's very, very careful.'

'Great stuff, Duggie, I owe you.'

FREYA NEEDED ANSWERS to some of the questions that preoccupied her about Simon Serrailler whenever her mind was not focused on work. She wanted to find out more about his life.

There was no choir practice that week, the choirmaster having sent a message that he had a bad cold. At half past eight, Freya went out anyway. She had no plan; she simply went, parking by the side of the cathedral as usual.

It was dark. The streets were quiet. The Close was empty apart from a woman on a bicycle. Freya lingered until she had gone, then she walked, keeping to the shadows, towards the end houses.

If the lights were on, meaning he was there, she would be happy. She could stand and look up, picture him in the room, stay as long as she needed.

As she stepped across the grass at the side of the path, she heard a car. Simon Serrailler drove past her. Freya stopped dead. If he turned, he would see her. She stepped back into the shadows.

A couple of other cars were parked outside his house. Simon drew up beside them and doused the headlights. In the light of the street lamp Freya saw both car doors open. He got out first, and then a woman. She was slim and wore a pale trench coat.

Freya felt suddenly, horribly sick.

They walked towards his building, but instead of going in, stopped at one of the other parked cars. Simon had his arm round the woman's shoulders and was bending to say something. At the car, she turned to him and he held his arms out to her.

Freya turned away. She could not run; she was paralysed, frozen as a wild creature in headlights. She did not want to see any more, she wanted not to be here, enduring all this. She was furious with herself.

She heard the car door slam, the engine start. She turned back quickly. Simon was standing in his doorway, his hand raised. Then, as the car drove away, past Freya, he turned, pushed open the front door and went inside.

Freya waited. It had begun to rain. In a couple of minutes the lights went on at the top of the dark building. She pictured the flat, the lamps, the pictures. Simon. Then, she walked away.

WHEN IRIS CHATER left the house, the biting wind had dropped so that although it was cold, it was pleasant to walk. She got off the bus a stop early, to calm her nerves.

It had taken her a long time to decide. After she had visited Sheila Innis the first time, she was upset about Harry not having come to speak to her, but somehow she had known she would go to the group séance eventually. It had just been a case of waiting until what seemed like the right moment. In the end it was curiosity that had decided her.

When she had told Pauline about the visit to the medium she had been interested and sympathetic about Harry's silence. All the same, something held Iris back from saying that she was going to a séance. Maybe she would talk about it eventually, maybe she wouldn't.

Mrs Innis had said to be there at seven. 'There'll be six others, Mrs Chater, and you'll find everyone very friendly and the whole meeting quite informal and relaxed.'

As she turned into the avenue, all the stories her mother used to tell about table-turning and Ouija boards revolved round her head. She tried to keep the pleasant room in Sheila Innis's house in mind, the flowers and nice curtains, the fat cat Otto. A couple of minutes later she was standing on the doorstep. Sheila Innis opened the door.

This time it was a different room with a long table and chairs. The curtains were drawn and the lamps lit, so that Iris Chater felt quite comfortable when she walked in, almost at home. There were six others: one elderly man, four women all middle-aged to elderly and a younger man. He looked unhappy, Iris thought, and ill at ease.

Sheila Innis came in. 'Good evening, everyone.'

They all murmured except the young man.

The medium took her place at the top of the table. 'We have to welcome just one new guest this evening. Iris, if I may introduce you in that way. We don't like to be too formal.'

They all looked at her and smiled, and Iris felt as if she belonged with them. She wondered why she had been so nervous.

The lights dimmed, though no one had got up to touch a switch. One standard lamp set behind Sheila Innis remained a little brighter, although it left her face shadowed. Everyone had gone very still.

'Let us ask for a blessing on our circle tonight. Let us invite our spirit guides to join us and our loved ones on the other side to come near. Let us at the same time warn any malicious or mischievous spirits to leave us and to seek guidance and peace in other realms.'

It was like praying, but not quite. Iris closed her eyes and folded her hands and imagined herself in church.

'I have someone with me . . . a young woman. She has an unusual bangle on her wrist . . . I can't see it closely . . . Come nearer, dear, show me the bangle . . . Thank you, now she's holding it up. It's silver, and in the shape of a snake . . . the head and tip of the tail come together at her wrist but don't quite meet. Does anyone . . . ?'

'It's Carol. My Carol had a bangle like that. She went on holiday to Bali and brought it back, not long before she was killed.'

'Can you speak louder . . . ? Is it Carol? She's nodding now and laughing. Now she's drawing something in the air . . . She's drawing big circles with her arm. She's saying you . . . yes, that you took her to the fair. She went with Kerry—'

'Kenny . . . her brother Kenny, my son. Oh, they did, we did, we all went to the fair and she went on the big wheel. It *is* Carol!'

Iris looked at the woman opposite. She was smiling and crying at the same time, and wiping her eyes on a tissue someone had handed her, so that her mascara smudged and smeared her cheeks.

Iris wondered when Harry would come—if he would, among so many other people. He had been shy, he hadn't liked groups of strangers. Maybe he would rather not get in touch here.

The person to Iris's right clutched her hand suddenly, making her start. The woman was staring huge-eyed at Sheila Innis. Something Iris would never have imagined or believed was happening, something she did not understand and could never have explained.

Sheila Innis was not Sheila Innis any more. Her face was changing as they watched. It was ageing and caving in at the mouth, the nose seemed larger and the cheeks more sunken, the chin more prominent. The face was that of a very old woman, scowling and with a malevolent stare. Iris gripped her neighbour's hand in return.

'Someone did away with me. I was put away. I was locked up. I know which one of you it was and you know, don't you? You thought you could get rid of me and take the money when I was dead. Well, you took the money and much good it did you. You know who you are and I know who you are. Look at me, look, look . . .'

There was a slight movement. The younger man had bent his head, but his face was a terrible yellow colour, waxen and sick.

They went on staring, speechless and horrified, at Sheila Innis who was no longer Sheila Innis. Iris thought she might faint, her heart seemed to leap painfully in her chest; she could not breathe easily.

The lights went up abruptly. Sheila Innis was sitting with her eyes open, looking as if she had been woken out of a deep sleep.

A minute later the door opened and a man with a moustache came in carrying a large tray of cups and saucers, which he set on the table, smiling round as if, Iris thought, he'd happened into a meeting of the WI instead of a séance that had become sinister and frightening.

People began to move and take the cups. The man left the room and then reappeared, with a second tray, of teapot, milk and sugar.

Sheila Innis smiled. 'Thank you, dear,' she said.

She stood beside the others, holding her teacup, chatting. As if nothing had happened, and her face had never turned into that of an evil old woman. Iris had given up hope of hearing from Harry now. He wouldn't come with all of this going on.

'How are you, Mrs Chater? I do hope we hear from your loved one in the second part of the evening. I'm sure several will be waiting to come through. I'll use the board this time. I get very good results.'

Iris stood up. 'I'm afraid I have to go, I have to be back for . . . my neighbour. She isn't well. I promised I wouldn't be out for long.'

Sheila Innis placed her hand on Iris's arm. 'Don't worry, Mrs Chater. Sometimes things seem a bit strange when you're new . . . Of course, I'm in trance, I don't know what happens.'

But Iris had her handbag over her arm. The room felt hot and something in it smelt sickly sweet. 'I'm sorry.'

No one took any notice of her going except the young man, who looked up and stared, out of pale, vacant eyes.

Outside, the air was mild and cool and smelt of hedgerows and car exhaust. It smelt wonderful, Iris thought, trembling with relief.

As she turned into the road she realised that, in leaving the house so hastily, she had not phoned for a taxi. However, the evening was pleasant and she didn't mind the thought of walking into town.

She began by walking fast, but after a few yards she was so breathless she was forced to stop. When she began to walk again, her legs felt watery and the breathlessness was worse. Iris sat down on the low stone wall of a house. There were lights on. If she felt no better, she would ring the bell and ask them if they would phone a taxi for her. People never minded being helpful in that way.

Yes. That was what she would do. As she stood up, a pain in her chest gripped her in metal pincers and crushed the breath from her. A second surge of pain. Iris struggled to stand, tried to call out, but then she was safe, a car was coming. She managed to stand, even lifted her right arm a little to wave. The car was slowing down. She felt the brightness of the headlights envelop her in warmth and light and safety. The light was beautiful.

'Harry,' she said. But no more.

Nine

Detective Sergeant Freya Graffham had spent most of a long cold day with Nathan Coates hanging about an underpass near the Sir Eric Anderson High School. For the rest of the time, they had sat in parked cars, watching, waiting, and drinking paper cups of coffee. The drugs operation was in its fourth week and it was known that suppliers were using the underpass to target the high-school pupils.

Freya was cold and full of the pent-up irritation that a pointless day without anything to show for it always brought on. The kids had long gone, the cleaners were in the school and the underpass was deserted.

'OK, that's it. Operation home time.'

Nathan gave a thumbs up and started the car happily.

'Thought for a moment you was going to offer overtime, Sarge.'

'Waste of police resources, Constable.'

'Yeah, like the rest of the day. You going out anywhere tonight?'

'No. Choir tomorrow.'

'Night in with the telly, then. You should live a bit more, Sarge. Come clubbing with me and Em one Friday.'

'Sure, gooseberry really suits me.'

'Nah, we'll fix you up first. Some really nice young doctors at Bevham General.' Nathan gave her a quick sideways glance. 'Blonds, isn't it?' he said.

'That will do, DC Coates.'

'Sorry, that was out of order. Only I don't want you pining away.'

'I am not pining away. Now, let's hear about you, Constable.'

'Me, well, you know. Very happily shacked up with my Em.'

'Exactly. And how long have you been shacked up?'

'Be two years.'

'Time you did the decent thing, then.'

'What decent thing would that be, Sarge?'

'Marry the girl, Constable Coates. She deserves more than

"shacked up". If she'd be mad enough to say yes, of course.'

'Yeah, yeah.'

'Don't you *want* to settle down?'

'I *am* settled.'

Freya shook her head. 'It's different, being married.' She meant it. Her own mistake had not made her disapprove of marriage in general.

Nathan slewed the car neatly into a space in front of the station, and they went inside.

Freya entered the emptying CID room and looked round. It had the usual seedy, end-of-the-day air. She spent five minutes tidying her desk so that she would not feel too depressed at the sight of it in the morning, took her suede jacket off the back of the chair, and went back out into the corridor.

A light was on in Simon Serrailler's office and the door was ajar. Freya hesitated. Don't do it, leave it. If Nathan had noticed, how many others might have done so? Don't do it. Where's your pride?

She tapped on the door.

'Come in.'

He had his jacket off, tie loosened, blond hair all over the place. The files on his desk were a foot thick.

'Freya—thank God, an excuse to stop. Come in, please come in.'

'Don't tell me this is all drug stuff.'

'A ton of it. Any joy today?'

She shook her head. 'There was never going to be.'

'Grin and bear it, Freya. We might well get somewhere. The minnows can and do lead us to the sharks, you know.' He looked at her for a second. 'But that isn't why you're here, is it?'

Freya went still. What did he mean? What had he noticed?

Then the DCI stood up and pushed his chair back. 'I've had enough. I'm absolutely bushed. So are you. We both need a decent dinner. Do you know the Italian place in Brethren Lane?'

The floor lurched beneath Freya's feet.

'If we go in my car, we can leave it in the close and walk to Giovanni's, it's five minutes. You can keep yours here and get a taxi home. That way we can enjoy a bottle of wine.' Simon was at the door, jacket over his shoulder. He glanced round. 'Or—not?'

These are the times you remember until you die, these ordinary, unplanned, astonishingly joyful things.

'God, sorry . . . I was miles away. Thanks—sounds good.'

'Low blood sugar. Makes you tired and faint and cross. Giovanni's fegato alla Veneziana will sort it. Come on.'

THE RESTAURANT was a glowing oasis, one of the small, old-fashioned Italian places that made no concessions to fashion. They were greeted effusively by the proprietor and given a cosy table near the window.

'I love it because it's straight out of the sixties,' Simon said. 'Look, the candles really do come in Chianti bottles with straw waistcoats.'

The menus arrived, the specials of the day were described lovingly by a waiter with the sort of Italian accent people used to joke about.

'The difference is that the food is fantastic. There may be prawn cocktail but it contains huge, salty fresh prawns in the most wonderful creamy homemade mayonnaise and the veal is thin as tissue paper and the liver melts in your mouth.'

'The best sort of comfort food.'

A bottle of Chianti arrived and was poured into huge glasses.

'Comfort drink.' Simon lifted his to her and smiled, that devastating smile. The restaurant was full but there was no one else at all in the room, in the world. This is happiness, Freya thought, this, now.

And then they talked, as they had talked on the evening in his flat, filling in more of the spaces they had left then, discovering more about each other's lives. The food was exactly as he had said, wonderfully cooked, wonderfully fresh.

The restaurant began to empty. Rain battered against the windows.

Simon Serrailler caught her glance and held it. 'Thanks for this,' he said, and smiled again.

Freya heard Nathan's voice in her head, his face worried for her. *Barking up the wrong tree there, Sarge.*

She looked across the table. Oh, no. Absolutely the right tree.

Simon stirred his coffee. 'You like it in Lafferton, don't you?'

'Love it. I should have moved long before I did. I've been lucky to find friends so quickly, too, lucky with people at work. Lucky.' Then, as she said it, she remembered the others, remembering what she owed them.

'Just one thing, sir—it's work though, so if you'd prefer not . . .'

'No, fine. And it's Simon in here.'

She felt herself flush. Focus, she said, focus. 'I'm unhappy that the missing persons case has been downgraded.'

Serrailler sighed. 'I know, but the Super had a good look at the files and said enough. I couldn't justify putting up a fight. The public appeals drew precious little and we've no evidence of foul play. We simply can't give it high priority any longer. You know that.'

'But those women didn't go off voluntarily. Nor did the mountain biker. There's something . . . I know there's something.' She crushed a sugar cube into fragments on the tablecloth with the back of her spoon. 'Come on, you agree with me, don't you?'

'Probably. But whatever gut feeling you and I have won't—'

'—justify any more resources. God, I hate that word.'

'What—resources?'

'Why don't we all just say what we mean, which is money? It all boils down to money. People's lives boil down to money.'

'No. The first tiny scrap of evidence that any of these missing people has come to harm and we upgrade the whole thing.'

The waiter was ostentatiously brushing non-existent crumbs off the table next to them.

'God, we're the last. What time is it?'

Simon laughed. 'Twenty past twelve.'

Freya reached for her bag, but he was already on his feet and Giovanni was coming over to him, handing him the bill. The whole thing was accomplished swiftly and smoothly.

'I'll walk you up to the taxi rank in the square.'

'No, it's not far. You're almost on your own doorstep. I'm fine on my own.'

'Not at this time of night, even in Lafferton.'

'I've been on the beat in some shady bits of London.'

'Forget you're a copper. Think of yourself as a young, attractive and therefore vulnerable female.'

This is now. This is the beginning. This is all.

They reached the town square. At the rank on the far side, a couple of cabs waited, both empty, but as they neared them, a driver appeared.

'In a puff of smoke,' Simon said. 'They go into holes in the ground for warmth.'

And then it was over, the engine had started, Simon opened the cab door and closed it after her so quickly she was mumbling her thanks as they were moving off. She looked back to see him raise a hand briefly, and then go off in the direction of the cathedral and his flat.

THE FOLLOWING MORNING she walked the whole way to work. It took forty minutes and the wind was so bitter Freya could hardly feel her face as she went in through the doors. DC Nathan Coates came fast down the room as soon as he saw her.

'Thought you were never coming, Sarge.'

Freya flung her coat and scarf onto her chair. 'What's up?'

'Elderly woman gone missing. Neighbour reported her going out at about half past six yesterday evening, on foot. Hasn't come home all night. Neighbour has key. Went in last night. Everything normal, but coat and handbag gone. She hadn't just slipped to the postbox.'

'Relatives?'

'No. Widow. No children.'

'I need some coffee.'

In the canteen there was the usual morning smell of frying bacon, the usual hubbub. Freya bought two coffees and they sat by the window. 'Right. Similarities with our other missing women?'

Nathan stirred three packets of sugar into his cup. 'Woman out on her own. No apparent reason to disappear. No messages. No note. No traces. Though it's early—we haven't done the full checks yet.'

'Uniform will have to go to the railway station, bus terminal, hospital and so on. Differences?'

'She was nowhere near the Hill.'

'That is significant. Still, let's go and see this neighbour—and then I hope we can get the DCI to take it seriously, upgrade the whole inquiry again, before someone else goes missing.'

She drained her cup and tidied up Nathan's sugar bags.

'Gawd, Sarge, it's worse than having a wife. Is this what it's going to be like, I ask myself?'

'Do I hear right?'

She glanced at Nathan as they swung through the doors out of the canteen. His pockmarked, lovely-ugly face was beetroot red.

'Hey!'

'No, no, listen, I haven't said anything, hold on . . . only you made me think, that's all.'

'Well, don't think too long. *Do.*'

PAULINE MOSS was looking out for them from the window and came to the door as the car drew up. She looked distraught.

'She isn't back, there's been no call, nothing . . .' she said, leading Freya and Nathan into her living room. 'I've been up all the night worrying about her. She never goes off like that, she hasn't spent a night away from home for years—not since before Harry was ill.'

'I take it you know Mrs Chater well?'

'Ever so well, we've been neighbours nearly thirty years. We don't live in each other's pockets you know, but we see each other most days, we have coffee or tea.'

'When did you last see her?'

'Yesterday morning. She was pegging out and I called her over for a cup of coffee. We talked about going on an outing next month.

A coach outing to Chatsworth. They've got beautiful grounds.'

'Did she seem to like the idea?'

'Yes, she did, she said it was time to look forward a bit.'

'So there was nothing to suggest she was going away somewhere else on her own?'

'She'd never do that. Besides, you don't go off without telling anyone, and in the evening, do you? And she'd only her handbag.'

'I gather Mrs Chater had no relatives?'

'No. They'd no children. It was always a sadness, that. Harry had a sister but she died, oh, five years back.'

'Did you see her go out?'

'No. I heard her front door go and her footsteps pass . . . that was all. I didn't think much of it, only that she hadn't mentioned going out, but then, as I say, we don't live in each other's pockets.'

'So you've no idea where she was going?'

Pauline shook her head. She had an idea but she didn't want to mention it. Had Iris gone back to the medium? She'd been so disappointed that Harry hadn't 'come through'. Had she given it another try? Well, she'd clearly not wanted to talk about it. It didn't seem right to mention it to two strangers, even if they were police.

'How has she seemed recently? Was she still depressed after her husband's death?'

Pauline looked hard at the young man. He had a face only a mother could love. 'I don't think that's the right word, you know,' she said. 'Her husband of forty-one years had passed on. She wasn't depressed; you aren't, you're grieving, sad. But not depressed.'

'Sorry, love.' He may have that face, but he had a winning smile.

Pauline got up. 'I'll make us a pot of tea?'

'Thought you'd never ask. Let's give you a hand.'

Freya smiled, and stayed behind in the sitting room. Nathan could charm the birds off the trees, and it invariably helped him find out little things that had been 'forgotten'.

The pot of tea was accompanied by homemade scones.

'We've been lucky, Iris and me,' Pauline Moss said, after tea had been poured and scones buttered. 'We've had the same houses, same streets, same shops, and each other. It helps, when you're left on your own, that some things stay the same. You rely on that. I did, Iris has. I feel for them on their own without knowing who's next door.'

She chattered on easily. A contented life, Freya thought, the old-fashioned life still lived by so many people up and down the length of the country . . . home cooking, gardening, neighbourliness.

At last Nathan picked a couple of crumbs off his plate and turned a beam of appreciation onto Pauline Moss.

'You've been really helpful, Mrs Moss,' Freya said. 'Now, do you have a key to Mrs Chater's house? I'd like to take a quick look.'

Pauline nodded and stood up. 'I'll let you in.'

'Thank you.'

They followed Pauline Moss into 39 Nelson Street. Another house belonging to a woman who had disappeared, another set of rooms full of another person's life and private affairs. But there was a warmth and a comfort here that had been absent from Angela Randall's little house. Iris Chater's rooms were crammed full of furniture, ornaments, rugs, pictures, knick-knacks, clocks, photographs.

Iris Chater had meant to come back. The whole place gave out that message. It was as clear to Freya as was her certainty that this missing woman was linked to the others. She didn't need to probe further. 'Thank you, Mrs Moss,' she said. 'If you remember anything you think might be relevant, please ring. Here's the station number.'

They went out into the sunshine. Pauline Moss closed the door of 39, and turned to face them. It was Nathan she spoke to. 'I don't like to ask this, only I can't help it, it's been in my mind all night.'

Nathan put a hand on her arm. 'What is it, love?'

'That missing girl there was a search for on the Hill . . .'

'There's nothing to say your neighbour has been up there, so don't you worry.' Nathan's voice was soothing.

'Thank you,' she said. Nathan patted her arm again.

Freya pulled out into the road. 'You missed your vocation, DC Coates. You'd make a lovely vicar. Such a way with the ladies.'

'Comes in handy. There's something Mrs Moss hasn't told us yet.'

'Yet?'

'Oh, she'll come out with it. I'll pop back later.'

'Time it right, she'll have made a fresh tray of scones.'

SIMON SERRAILLER listened as attentively as he always did to any of his team—it was one of the best things about him that he was never dismissive, never poured scorn, even if in the end he came down on the other side. He leaned back in his chair while Freya filled him in.

'No obvious links, I recognise that, but this is just one too many.'

'I agree. Mrs Chater had been bereaved and that is sometimes a reason why people go missing . . . But I'm not arguing with you. High priority then, please . . . house-to-house, hospitals and stations, radio appeals, get the press onto it.'

HE HAD ALWAYS DISLIKED acting on impulse. That was the way mistakes were made. But the police had cordoned off the Hill and crawled over it, and now the public were too afraid to go there. It had spoilt his plans and so he had done what he had sworn he would never do and acted on impulse, without preparation.

It seemed to have been successful but he was not settled, not satisfied. He felt on edge, he needed to go over and over it all trying to spot the flaw, the tiny mistake that might prove his undoing.

To begin with, he had not planned to go out that night. But he had been paying bills, doing accounts, going over his VAT returns, and the room had been stuffy. He had walked down to the postbox and the fresh air had cleared his head. Something smelt new, smelt of spring. When he had reached home again, he had been filled with a restless need to do something else, go somewhere else.

The van, of course, was at the unit. He had locked his front door and taken the car, and driven slowly, aimlessly, about the streets.

When he saw her, everything clicked into place. He knew at once. *Elderly woman.*

She was leaning against a wall, as if to get her breath. Any conscientious passer-by might have been concerned for her, and stopped. As he got out of the car, she began to slump and slide sideways, down onto the pavement beside the wall. The street was empty. No one walking, no car. Every house had curtains drawn.

He bent over her. She seemed to have suffered either a stroke or a heart attack. He knew the signs. But when he raised her up, she was still alive—barely breathing, her colour bad, but alive.

He lifted her and opened the back door of the car and watched her fall heavily sideways onto the seat. He drove fast, but by the time he reached the unit she was dead. Then he had to work quickly, because of the security patrol that came round intermittently.

He carried her round to the side of the unit and unlocked it, swung up the door. It was a struggle to keep hold of her and switch on the light. But then she was undressed, bagged and put away, the drawer slid out and back and it was done. The clothes and the handbag went into the usual heavy-duty black bin liner. The dustmen came on Thursday, when the black bin liner would be put out along with several others. The more normal things were, the better.

He left the unit and got into his car more tense and anxious than he had been for years. As he drove away, his heart pounded and his hands were slippery on the wheel. But he saw no one. The security patrol did not come. He was out onto the main road and speeding home.

FREYA PICKED UP the evening paper on her way home. An article by Rachel Carr was spread across the middle pages of the *Lafferton Echo*, under the headline MIRACLE WORKER OR CLEVER CONMAN? There were photographs of the outside of the psychic surgeon's consulting rooms, as well as a photograph of Rachel Carr in a neat box beside her name. Smug, Freya thought, smug and arrogant.

For now, she had other things on her mind, as she bathed, washed and blow-dried her hair carefully, chose a dress, changed her mind, chose another, and finally rejected that one too in favour of her black silk trousers, black satin jacket and pink silk shirt. Meriel Serrailler had invited her to dinner and Simon was almost certain to be there.

But when Meriel led her into the drawing room where people were having drinks, Simon was not the first person she saw. That was the slim, slight, woman with whom Simon had driven up to his building on the night Freya had been hanging about outside it in the dark.

Her stomach plummeted as though in a fast-descending lift. Simon was here, then, in some other room. She wondered how she could leave, now, whether she could plead sudden sickness.

Meriel had hold of her arm. 'Freya, I don't think you've met Cat?'

The woman smiled. It was an open, warm, welcoming, friendly smile. Freya hated her. The woman held out her hand.

'Hello. I've heard a lot about you from Simon. You work with him, don't you?'

Freya could not speak; she smiled and shook the woman's hand. Then, somehow, words miraculously came out of her mouth. 'How do you know?'

'God, this family is hopeless . . . Mother didn't even introduce you properly. I'm Cat Deerbon. Formerly Serrailler. Simon's my brother.'

The room settled back into place.

Freya was introduced to Cat's husband, to a large osteopath with a thick neck, and to a tall and rather beautiful woman in a long coat of printed velvet. The group, Cat Deerbon said, had been in the middle of discussing an article in that evening's paper.

'Not the psychic surgeon, by any chance?'

'Yes. Does this mean the police are interested?'

'No, no . . . or not officially anyway. I clocked it all the same.'

They went into dinner, and it was clear that the party was complete. Simon was not there and she felt bitterly disappointed. But tonight, she thought, taking a forkful of fish terrine, is for making new friends. She glanced at Cat across the table. Yes, definitely Cat and not only because she was Simon's sister. Cat because she was warm and engaging, intelligent and quick, the sort of person Freya responded to immediately. For the moment, though, she had to attend to those on either side of her. She had been put on the right hand of her host, but at the moment Richard Serrailler was going round the table pouring wine. Freya turned to her right.

'We haven't been properly introduced,' she said.

He was probably in his fifties, with an immaculately cut dark grey suit, a bow tie in a paisley pattern and, she noted, elegant, well-manicured hands. Surgeon, she decided, and real not psychic.

'Aidan Sharpe. How do you do? I take it you sing in the choir with Meriel?'

'I do. She took me under her wing . . .'

'Meriel has a way of scooping people up and wrapping them in the wonderfully rich blanket of her world, and before they know it they're manning a stall at the hospice bazaar.'

'Funny you should say that.'

Freya finished her terrine. Her neighbour had cut his into the finest slivers, before picking each one up carefully on his fork.

'Are you a doctor?' he asked.

'No,' she said. 'I'm a detective sergeant.'

Aidan Sharpe's expression did not change. He was a good-looking man—would have been better without the goatee, Freya decided. 'May I guess at your profession?'

He smiled. 'I always enjoy this.'

'Oh?'

'Do you remember . . .? No, of course not, you're far too young. There was a television programme called *What's My Line?* People with unusual jobs were quizzed by a panel—I think they were only allowed to answer yes or no—and the panel was supposed to work its way towards discovering their job. They performed a mime at the beginning but that was the only clue.'

'OK. Do your mime.'

'Lord . . . I'm not sure I can.' He sat silent for a moment, then put his thumb and forefinger carefully together and made a single, care-ful, almost delicate forward movement with them.

It meant nothing to Freya and she said so. 'In fact, I had you down as a surgeon. But if you are, I don't know what you were doing then.'

He smiled again. A girl in a white apron removed their plates.

'Are you a surgeon?'

'No.'

'Damn.'

258

Meriel brought in a huge casserole dish and set it down on the table. After their plates were heaped with duck in a rich apricot gravy, Freya said, 'OK, I give up.'

'Sure?'

'I shall probably kick myself for not getting it.'

'Somehow I don't think you will.' Aidan Sharpe gave her an almost flirtatious look. 'I am an acupuncturist.'

They both laughed, Freya with astonishment, Sharpe with delight.

'I didn't think much of the mime.'

'No, I'm afraid it's almost impossible to do one.'

'Well, well. In that case, tell me what you think about this man Orford . . . the psychic surgeon—if you've heard about him.'

Aidan laid down his knife and fork. 'Oh, I've heard about him all right,' he said, 'and it makes me very angry.'

The conversation got no further for the moment. The vegetables came round and Freya turned to hand a dish to Richard Serrailler.

'Thank you, Sergeant.' He turned away abruptly to pass the vegetables on, then picked up his knife and fork.

'I'm not on duty,' Freya said lightly. 'Freya is fine.'

Richard Serrailler merely grunted. He was as handsome as his son, with the same nose and brow, the same straight forward-flopping hair, only grey. But his lean face seemed set in a permanent sneer.

'I work with Simon,' she said.

'I could wish you didn't, of course. He may have told you.'

Deciding to play dumb, Freya looked at him with widened eyes. 'You mean you disapprove of me? But please explain why. You must have heard something derogatory.'

'Nothing to do with you.'

'Now I'm very confused. Do sort this out for me, Dr Serrailler.'

He did not offer the use of his Christian name, merely said, 'My son should have been a doctor. He would have made a decent one.'

'He makes a more than decent DCI.'

'Strange choice of job.'

'No. Exciting, challenging. Dangerous. Important.'

'You have a high opinion of yourself.'

If the man had not been Simon's father she would have asked if he enjoyed being offensive, whether or not she was a guest at his table. Instead, she ate a mouthful of duck very slowly before saying, 'How many doctors are there in your family exactly?'

'Seven living—four of us are now retired.'

'In that case, you can afford to spare one son.'

'That is for me to decide.'

'Not for him?'

But Richard Serrailler had already turned pointedly to the man on his other side, the osteopath Nick Haydn. Freya let her rage subside.

'Difficult,' she heard Aidan say quietly. 'Don't worry, my dear. It's not you; it's everyone. Forget it.'

'Thank you for that.'

He smiled and reached out to pour her more wine but she put her hand over her glass.

'Water?'

'I can—'

But he was on his feet, and bringing the bottle to her from the other side of the table. The acupuncturist might not be immediately attractive, but his manners and kindness were appealing after her brush with Serrailler. At the end of dinner, she made her way to the drawing room behind him, and went straight to where he had made a group with Nick Haydn and Cat Deerbon.

'I wanted to ask you more about the psychic surgeon,' Freya said. 'Partly out of curiosity, though there is a police angle, I'd better say.'

'The person you should talk to is Karin,' Cat said, nodding to the beautiful woman sitting next to Meriel Serrailler on the window seat. 'She's actually been to him.'

'What?' Aidan looked horrified.

'Ask her. But it sounds very much like an extremely clever magic trick . . . the sort that makes you blink, it's so effective. I don't think this man is actually doing anything other than conning people.'

'That's more than enough, isn't it?'

'I couldn't agree more.'

Cat looked at Freya. 'Has it anything to do with my missing patient?'

'Which one?' Freya asked levelly.

IT WAS TEN MINUTES to one before the party broke up. Meriel kissed her on both cheeks and gave her a warm hug. Richard Serrailler shook hands and said nothing at all.

Cat came out to her car. 'Freya, here's my home number. Maybe you could come to lunch one Sunday?'

Freya took the card with delight. It was something else, someone else, that drew her closer to Simon.

Back at home, there was a message on her machine from Nathan.

'Evening, Sarge . . . message from the DCI. Case conference about the missing women. High priority. Nine sharp. Cheers.'

'GOOD MORNING, EVERYONE. I'll get straight into it. As you know, we now have three women reported as missing in Lafferton, and we must regard these disappearances as highly suspicious. I want to know what we've got so far in the way of links. Are there any links? Did these women have anything in common?'

'Well . . . the fact that they are women obviously,' Freya said. 'But they differ in age—one twenty, one fifty-three, one seventy-one.'

'The Hill links two of them.'

'Two of them live alone.'

Serrailler nodded. 'Angela Randall is single and it appears has no close relatives. Iris Chater is widowed and lives alone. She has no children.'

'Yeah, but Debbie Parker has a dad and stepmum. I know they don't live here but it breaks the pattern,' Nathan Coates said.

'OK, any other contributions? Anything at all.'

'Angela Randall,' Freya said thoughtfully. 'I found an expensive pair of cuff links, gift-wrapped and with a cryptic message on the card, in her wardrobe. Turns out she'd bought a number of expensive gifts—things for men—from the same jeweller in the course of eight months or so. Now, we know from her employer at the nursing home that she apparently had no close relationships, and from her neighbours that she never had visitors. So who were the presents for? The card said, "To You, with all possible love from your devoted, Me."'

'If there was a man in Angela Randall's life he's the only one in the case. Debbie Parker didn't have a boyfriend, Mrs Chater lost her husband just before Christmas.' Serrailler thought for a moment. 'Let's get another radio appeal out, another press conference. I'm going to get uniform to extend the house-to-house to the whole of central Lafferton. We'll get the divers into the river, and we'll cover every area of waste ground, every playing field, the lot. I don't want anyone in Lafferton to be left in ignorance of the fact that these women are missing.'

'National press, sir?'

'Yes. National press, television and radio as of this evening. Unfortunately, all this coincides with the drugs op moving up a gear. We've had some excellent new information, as some of you will know. So we're stretched. I'm heading up the drugs op, but I want to be kept informed about everything, absolutely everything, to do with these women. Freya, you're in charge for the moment. Everyone reports to you. We've got to find these women.'

The Tape

It was over six months before I could bring myself to tell you that I was no longer a medical student, and then I lied. I wrote and said that I had been advised not to continue with my studies on medical grounds. I had always had mild asthma but it had become much worse and a serious attack might weaken my heart.

After that you had no idea where I was for almost two years. I simply slipped out of your life. I did not know whether you made attempts to find me. It was not you I worried about.

I spent some years trying to work out a future for myself. I took temporary jobs so that I could live, clerical jobs mainly. I was reliable, hard-working, methodical. But throughout that time, I was planning, scheming. I could not be a doctor but I had never given up the desire to work in some area of medical treatment.

I toyed with the idea of becoming an assistant in a hospital pathology lab, probably abroad. But I could never have played second fiddle to some 'qualified' pathologist, and every other medical career I considered I rejected because it was inferior.

In the end, it happened by chance. I took on a job some distance away from the room I had rented. I had to take a train and then walk for ten minutes, a dull walk but one I could vary each day, taking a short cut down one of several residential avenues. I remember clearly the morning I walked down Spencer Avenue. The houses were mainly gabled and mock Tudor, the sort of road you had always aspired to.

The house was two-thirds of the way down the street and had black and white half-timbering and a lilac tree in full bloom to the right of the house. But it was the plate attached to the gatepost that drew my attention. A dentist? A gynaecologist? A psychiatrist?

I was startled when I read what was actually there, under the name, John F. L. Shinner.

I had never considered it, did not even know a great deal of what it involved. But I stared at the plate with a sense of revelation.

I began to walk quickly, not because I was late but because I was excited. I saw my life opening up in front of me. I would train, and I would practise. It would be very like practising medicine and I would be answerable to myself only.

I do not know why the attraction to my future career was so strong, so compulsive, for I knew little about it or how long it would take me to qualify. But I knew that I would tell you nothing until I had

*achieved it all. And I have never regretted anything for one instant.
I knew that I was right and so it proved.*

*As for the other matters—I believe they were always there, lying
below the surface of my mind. I was to be fulfilled and satisfied in a
career I was good at, but the old needs had not been defeated. There
would have to be another way of accomplishing what I wanted to do.
But it could wait. And although it had to wait for years, I have succeeded in the end, haven't I? I have done everything.*

Ten

'Sarge?'
'Hi, Nathan, what did Pauline Moss give you?'
'Chocolate cake to die for.'
'And?'
'And the old girl was going to a medium. Trying to get in touch
with her Harry.'
'Why didn't she tell us that before?'
'Said she felt it was a sort of betrayal, like, didn't think Mrs Chater
wanted anyone knowing. Apparently, Mrs Chater told her she'd gone
there once, then went quiet about it.'
'Did you get the name?'
'On my way.'
'Good boy. By the way, the DCI's going for a reconstruction—
Debbie Parker walking round the perimeter road of the Hill in the
early morning. It's on Thursday.'
'What about you?'
'I'm off to the jeweller in Bevham . . . And I want you to go up to
Starly later, interview our friend Dava again, give him a real grilling.'
'Hold on, Sarge, when do I get my lunch?'
'You don't need lunch, you've had half a chocolate cake.'
'Sarge! Have a heart.'
'OK, you can have a cup of dandelion tea in that green café.'
Nathan made a retching noise and rang off.

FREYA'S FAVOURITE CAFÉ was just emptying after the lunchtime
crowds. She found a table in the window, ordered a brie and salad
ciabatta and a large cappuccino, and got out her notebook. It always

helped if she could think quietly for half an hour after an interview, jotting as she went along if anything came to her. But nothing did. The visit to Duckham's had been a waste of time. The jeweller was polite, cool and willing to be helpful, but could tell her nothing more.

Freya bit into her ciabatta and the salad dressing dribbled out of the bread and down her chin. As she started to wipe it with the paper napkin, she glanced up and saw someone on the other side of the café window, trying to attract her attention. It was Simon Serrailler's sister.

Any interruption was welcome, but Cat Deerbon was more welcome than anyone else Freya could think of, save her brother.

'Isn't it typical? Someone always catches you dribbling salad dressing down yourself. There's no way of eating this thing politely.'

'Like éclairs.'

'Join me—have a coffee? Or one of these?'

Cat Deerbon sat down, and dumped a couple of carrier bags on the floor. 'I'd love a large espresso and . . . what?' She looked at the menu. 'A toasted teacake. How nice to see you again. Aren't you on duty?'

'Yes, I've just interviewed someone, but we're allowed to eat. You?'

'Half day. And the children look like waifs their clothes are so outgrown. I had to do something about it.'

Freya looked more closely at her. When you knew that she and Simon were brother and sister, you could see a resemblance, about the eyes and mouth, but their colouring was different. It would never have seemed likely that they were two of triplets.

Cat bit into her teacake and the hot butter ran down her chin. They giggled. Freya wanted to ask Cat about Simon, to hear about him, everything, how he behaved as a child, his relationship with his father, who his friends are . . . but it seemed impossible to begin.

Cat stirred her espresso a couple of times and said, 'There's something I need to clear up. Was my father rude to you the other evening?'

Freya made a face. 'Ish.'

Cat's face coloured quickly. 'God, he makes me so furious. He does it to wreck anything Mother does, anything to stop other people having a good time, anything to put a curse on the event.'

'He seems rather bitter. Has he had disappointments?'

'No. Well—Si not going into medicine was a blow. And he hated retiring, hated it. He wallowed in self-pity for a couple of years and then took to being rude. I'm sorry you copped it and I apologise.'

'Don't think about it. I was more puzzled than anything else.'

Cat sipped her coffee. 'There's Martha too, of course. Has Si mentioned her?'

'No.'

'I suppose he wouldn't tell people at work. He finds it difficult.'

'I have seen Simon outside work.'

'Oh?' Cat looked at her sharply.

'We had dinner.'

'Right.' Cat took another sip of her coffee, then said, 'Martha is our younger sister . . . ten years younger than us. You know we're triplets? There's Ivo as well, in Australia.'

'Yes, Simon told me.'

'Martha is seriously handicapped, mentally and physically. She lives in a special home at Chanvy Wood. It has eaten my father's life away and he barely mentions her—I don't think he and I have had more than two or three conversations about Martha in my life. If anything made him bitter and angry and resentful it was that.'

'Hard for Meriel.'

'Very. But then, a lot of things have been hard for her and she has simply shouldered them and batted on. Ma drives me nuts sometimes, but I admire her more than I can express.'

'Does your father blame anyone for Martha's condition?'

'Oh, himself, probably, deep down in a place no one would ever be able to get to. Of course, it was simply a chromosomal accident. There's no history of it in either family. But it's hard to be rational about something like that when it happens to you.'

'I wonder why Simon didn't mention it.'

'Simon has a lot of my father in him, but in a more positive way. There are places just as deep in him. You just don't go there.'

'No one?'

Cat gave her a long look. 'No one. It's none of my business, Freya, but . . . just don't try. I love my brother dearly but I'm probably the only woman in the world apart from Mother who can do so.'

She drained her coffee and reached down to get her carrier bags together. 'I must get off home with my vests and knickers.' She started to get out her purse but Freya put out her hand.

'No, these are on me.'

'Come and see us at home then, will you? If you could bear the chaos of Sunday lunch?'

'I'd love to.'

'I'll ring.' Cat bent down suddenly and touched Freya's cheek with her own. 'I'm really glad I looked in through the window.'

Freya watched her leave, bundling with her bags through the door, and felt elated. She liked Cat for herself. She also thought that, in spite of the warning about Simon, Cat liked her and might even see her as good for her brother. Please, she thought, putting her notebook away, yes, please.

CAT HAD ENJOYED her chance meeting with Freya Graffham. She liked her. But as she drove home, she wished that Simon did not have a place in the picture. She had recognised the signs given out by Freya only too well. Si attracted women, unsurprisingly. Si liked women, took them out, talked to them and, more important, listened to them. After which, he panicked. Besides, there was presumably still Diana.

Cat was the only member of the family who knew about Diana Mason. They had met five years ago in Florence, where Simon had gone to draw. They had struck up a conversation, discovered their hotels were in the same street. That might have been that, except that when they returned to England, Si had telephoned her.

Diana Mason lived in London and had been widowed twenty years before and never wanted to remarry. She owned a chain of restaurants, all called Mason, in London, and in smart places like Bath, Winchester, Cambridge and Brighton. The relationship between Diana and Simon was unorthodox, and it suited them both. Cat had long ago decided that they were not in love with one another, and that for this very reason it worked well. They enjoyed one another's company, saw one another for a weekend several times a year. But they were independent people who preferred not to have permanent ties. They both liked their own space, their own friends, their own lives.

Added to which, Diana Mason was ten years older.

Simon almost never mentioned her, even to Cat, who had sometimes wondered how much either of them would mind if the other fell seriously in love with someone else. Probably not much.

Still, women like Freya Graffham, nice women, worried her. Si was either obtuse or chose not to notice the broken hearts that regularly lay about him. In a way, he was indifferent, even callous, and Freya, for one, deserved better. But how to warn her, how to broach the subject at all was a problem. And if Freya was as in love with her brother as Cat suspected, she would be beyond the stage of taking kindly to any warnings whatsoever.

HE HAD GONE to the unit at half past five that morning to look at the real Debbie so that he had her clearly in mind. When he arrived on the perimeter of the Hill, crowds of them were already there for the police reconstruction, police vans, reporters, television crews. Plenty of people had heard about it and come to stare, women mainly, and a few teenagers before they went to catch the school buses.

He had been determined to stay away, knowing perfectly well what all the profilers said about people like him always returning to the scene. But he wanted to see how the police managed things, what mistakes they made. There could be no outcome, of course, because he was the only one who knew what had happened.

He hesitated. In the group of uniformed police around one of the vans, he saw the young woman he had met at the dinner party, Freya Graffham. If she saw him, he would have to speak to her, and have a reason for being here. He moved out of her line of sight a little and began to think. But it came to him quickly. He knew what he was going to say and rather looked forward to saying it. But the scene was set, the actors were waiting, the curtain was about to rise. He went to the left a little along the path, to get a clear view.

He could see at once that they had got it wrong. The girl was not fat enough and her hair was too fair. But the fleece jacket was right, and the acne. Another young woman was talking to her, head close, gesturing with her hands. The flatmate.

Someone called for quiet. There was a moment of stillness. Then the girl began walking and the cameras started to roll.

She was crossing the road now. He wanted to tell her to move faster, to look up at the Hill, not ahead. The girl was too conscious of the camera, her walk was too hesitant.

Everyone else watched intently, some of them, including Freya Graffham, following in a group behind the girl. He was certain Freya had not seen him. Better that way. His story would be of more use later.

The girl was on the Hill now and the others were staying back. The weather was not right but as he watched her, apparently alone, going towards the point at which they had met, he realised that excitement was rising in him. He knew what was going to happen, it was running in his head, reeling out like a film he had already seen. For a few seconds, she veered in the wrong direction and he wanted to call out to her, but then she turned again and then everything was right, as though she were obeying his silent orders. Every footstep was as he directed. He had to stop himself from running to meet her. She was almost there, poor, fat, badly dressed, spotty girl. How could there be two of them in the world? He had no need of two but if he had been on his own, he would have taken her all the same.

She was a few yards away. He held his breath until his chest was strained. Someone shouted. The woman. Freya Graffham.

'OK, Caroline, OK, you can stop there.'

Freya came running up and the pack of them followed. Everything was ruined. The film had broken down.

He watched Graffham, her hand on the girl's shoulder. He could no longer hear her. The girl had taken him to the edge and then the policewoman had pulled him back.

He wanted to kill her.

THE DESK OFFICER was about to ring up when Freya Graffham came through the door into the lobby, on her way out. She stopped.

'Mr Sharpe? Hello. Is there anything I can help with?'

'Aidan, please,' he said. 'It's about the missing girl, Debbie Parker.'

'Right, we'll go in here.'

He followed her into a small interview room.

'Do sit down. Can I get you a coffee?'

He shook his head. 'Remind me to tell you one day what frightful things coffee does to your entire system, mental and physical.'

He sat down. She was prettier than he remembered, with a shining cap of hair. He had been right to come down and not to telephone, and to arrive as she was leaving the building. She would listen, too; what he had to say would not be dismissed, if only because they had met socially, and she had good manners. Aidan smiled.

'Now, Debbie Parker. We did a reconstruction of her last known movements early this morning.'

'Really? So it is known where she was last seen?'

Freya made a face. 'Not exactly. We are pretty sure she went for a walk in the area of the Hill, and from what we can piece together it was likely to have been early in the morning. We hoped someone might just have seen her . . . memories can be jogged surprisingly long after the event if we get it right.'

'Have you had a lot of response?'

Freya shrugged. 'This and that. There are always a fair few cranks, of course . . . people who would have seen the moon turn pink if we put it about that we wanted them to contact us about it.'

She seemed so relaxed, so friendly, but she was giving nothing away, throwing up the usual smokescreen. He was not deceived for a moment. The reconstruction had brought in no useful response from the general public. But then, that was always going to be the case.

'I'm DS in charge at the moment, so if you do think you have anything that might help us, I'm the person to tell.'

He leaned back in the chair and sighed. 'I don't know, I just don't know. All I know is that I've been worrying about it. It is going to sound very feeble and pathetic if I tell you that I haven't been here before simply because I forgot. No excuse. I forgot.'

'What did you forget?'

'That Debbie Parker had been to see me.'

'You mean as a patient?'

'Yes. She came just once. She had rather bad acne, poor thing. Acupuncture does have a proven effect on skin conditions.'

'When did Debbie Parker come to see you?'

'I looked it up. It was October. She had an initial consultation and one treatment. I wasn't surprised she didn't come back. She'd seemed nervous, couldn't take the needles. They don't hurt, but some people are afraid of them. They can't relax. Debbie was an unhappy girl.'

'Did she mention having suicidal feelings?'

'Oh, no. Nothing like that. So far as I remember, she said she sometimes felt "a bit down"—but then, so do many patients.'

'You didn't think there was an immediate risk of suicide?'

He sighed and shook his head. 'But you can see why I now blame myself, can't you?'

'We have no reason at all to suppose Debbie has taken her own life—that she is dead at all.'

'Off the record, isn't it the most likely explanation?' Tell me, he thought, urging her, what the official police verdict is going to be.

Freya Graffham merely shook her head slightly. 'I'm grateful to you for coming in. It slots another piece into the puzzle. So thank you. And don't worry about not remembering earlier.'

Efficient. Cool. Professional. But not tough, he thought.

She walked out of the station and down the steps with him. 'I don't suppose you would remember if either of the other two missing women had consulted you?'

It was a typical ploy, to leave one last question and then spring it, as an afterthought. He did not stumble, did not hesitate.

'I read about one other woman. I can't remember the name.'

'Angela Randall.'

He stood, thinking for a moment, then shook his head. 'I'll check, but I don't think so. You said there were two others besides Debbie?'

'The third hasn't been seen for a couple of days.'

'Oh, in that case . . .'

'Yes?'

She is watching me. She is trying to discover something. 'How long is it before you panic?' he asked, smiling.

But she did not smile back. 'We don't. We take everything more or less seriously according to individual circumstances.'

'And what were these?'

'Different from the other two.'

Yes. Different. Unplanned. A mistake.

'I doubt if I'll uncover any more patients among your missing persons but give me a name.'

'Chater. Mrs Iris Chater. Aged seventy-one.'

'I'll go over my records . . . for how far back, do you suggest?'

'Try a couple of years initially. Do you keep full records for longer?'

He pressed the remote control and his car headlights flashed in response. He walked over to the driver's door, opened it, and only then turned back to her with a smile. 'I never destroy any records. I'll check and telephone you. May I have a number?'

'If I'm not here at the station, a message will always reach me.'

She stood on the bottom step and watched his car move off. As it turned out into the main road, Aidan Sharpe waved.

'CAN YOU LOOK UP a man called Aidan Sharpe?'

'Hang on, Sarge . . . Let me grab a pen.'

'S-h-a-r-p-e . . . he's an acupuncturist here in Lafferton. Look up the national register, double-check his qualifications. I'm sure he won't have form, but run it through.'

'What am I looking for?'

'I don't know. Anything. Nothing probably.'

'Thanks a bunch. What is it about this guy?'

'He wears a bow tie.'

Five minutes later, Nathan swivelled his chair round to face her. 'Sarge? Your bow tie.'

'Anything?'

'Nope. Fully qualified, got his letters and all that."

'Where did he train?'

'London and China. He got a pigtail and all?'

THE PHONE DRILLED into Cat Deerbon's strange dream about a white pony. It was half past three. She answered automatically, before remembering that she was not on call.

'Cat? It's Karin . . . listen, I'm so sorry to wake you . . .'

Cat sat up. Chris stirred, mumbled, and slept on.

'It's OK, don't worry, but just hold on a few seconds. I'll put this phone down and pick up the other.'

She slipped out of bed and went quietly down to the kitchen. 'OK, I'm here. What's wrong?'

There was a silence. Cat waited. She knew that Karin would respond better if she was not pumped with questions.

'I'm scared. I've been awake for a long time. I couldn't not ring you.'

'I'm glad you did. Is Mike there?'

'No, he's in New York. Anyway, I can't talk to him. I know I'm doing the right thing. There's no way I can go down the other road.'

'This isn't just pride talking, is it? If so, forget it. Doesn't matter.'

'It isn't pride.'

'Has something happened?'

'No . . . not really.'

'I'll take that as a yes, then.'

'I've had awful backache. In the middle and a bit lower down.'

'All the time?'

'On and off. But more on. Just for a few days.'

'Do you want me to come over now?'

'Christ, no, please. I'm just scared, Cat. I haven't been scared before. I've had it all under control.'

'Part of the problem?'

'I don't know. But tonight . . . everything . . . death . . . tombs . . . oxygen masks . . . pain. Awful pain they can't do anything about.'

'Give me half an hour.'

'No, listen—'

'And I shall need a double espresso.'

Cat clicked off the phone.

KARIN OPENED the front door. She was wearing a long white waffle dressing gown, and her hair was tied up. There was never anything unkempt or dishevelled about her, Cat thought, even in the early hours of the morning. But she had lost weight, too much weight too quickly, and her face had a new look—something about the eyes, something about the prominence of the bones.

Cat kissed her on both cheeks and gave her a long hug. Her body felt slight.

'You're a saint,' Karin said.

'Nope, just a doc.'

'And a friend.'

'That first.'

'Did you really mean double espresso?'

'Maybe tea would be better.'

'Definitely better.' Karin filled the kettle. 'I was in such a state tonight I didn't know what to do. I haven't looked death in the face like that until now. I didn't care for its expression.'

'Apart from the frights, how have you been?'

'OK, until I got backache.'

'I'll have a look at you in a minute, if you like. Have you been working in the garden?'

Karin shook her head and set two full mugs in front of them. Cat noticed that, for once, Karin's was plain Indian tea too, not herbal.

'Anything else?'

Karin shrugged. 'Tired. That's nothing.' Her skin, always beautiful, had a transparent sheen.

'Will you go for a scan?'

'Oh, Cat, what's the point? We both know what it is, what's happening to me. Why have it underlined? I'd rather not know.'

'That isn't like you.'

'It's like this me.' She lifted her mug, took a sip of tea, set it down again, and looked across at Cat, her eyes brimming with tears. 'What's going to happen?' she asked.

'I honestly don't know. I need something to go on, Karin.'

'OK, then, I'll do it for you. Secondaries. Probably in the spine. But I'm *not* going to go to hospital, I'm *not* seeing an oncologist. When I need a doctor I'll have you, if that's OK. I'm going on with my healer. It really helps.'

'What are you eating?'

'Raw organic vegetables, a bit of fruit. Water.'

'What? Listen, Karin, it isn't what you are eating that's worrying me so much as what you are not—you need good nourishment. Of course you need fresh fruit and veg, but you also need milk, eggs, a bit of cheese, lots of fish, a bit of yeast to give you extra vitamin B, wholegrains—oats are best. A glass of good red wine every evening.'

'You've just crammed a dozen toxic substances into one sentence.'

Cat snorted and poured herself a second mug of tea.

'What can you do about my back? And my general mopes? Do I live with those while I get better?' Karin's eyes were huge and anxious on Cat's face.

'Depends. If you had a scan so that I could pinpoint what was wrong with your back I'd possibly send you to see Aidan Sharpe. I have a lot of faith in him; he wouldn't treat you if he didn't think it was right. It might well help the back pain.'

'OK.'

'But he would want you to get a scan too.'

'OK.' Karin sounded suddenly exhausted and defeated. She sat, staring down into her empty mug.

'And I think you should start on a course of antidepressants . . . one of the newer kind, the SSRI group. They'll work quickly . . . a week and you'll start feeling better. If you're still serious about tackling this your way—or my way, come to that—you need to be on top and you're not. Let's get your mood up and your fighting spirit will come back. Deal?'

Karin was silent for a moment. 'Go over it all again.'

'Right. See me later this morning. I'll get them to put you in at half eight, before my surgery. I'll have a look at you, prescribe your tablets. And book an MRI scan at BG. For a time when I can come with you. Meanwhile, come to lunch and I'll put some decent food inside you. Let's go from there. And don't let things get like this again. Talk to me, talk to Chris, ring us whenever. Don't ever sit here brooding, especially when Mike's away. Things grow.'

'God, they did.'

Cat wound her scarf round her neck and picked up her car keys. 'I'll see you in the morning.'

Eleven

The weather had jerked forwards into warm spring. In CID, the sun came pouring through the large windows and made the room hot and stuffy. Freya Graffham was sitting at her desk, her sense of frustration almost at boiling point. The investigation into the missing women had not moved an inch forward since the reconstruction of Debbie Parker's early-morning walk. Nathan had drawn a blank on the medium visited by Iris Chater. All Sheila Innis had told him was that Mrs Chater had left a séance at her house at around 9 p.m. alone. The rest of them had remained inside. Mrs Chater had not been seen by anyone since. Like Angela Randall and Debbie Parker, she had vanished into thin air. And any day now, Freya knew, the inquiry would be downgraded and she would be put on another case.

The ringing of the phone at her elbow made her jump.

'DS Graffham.'

'Freya? Good afternoon, how nice to have got straight through to you.' The rather prissy and cultivated voice identified itself.

'Aidan . . . how are you?'

'Isn't this miraculous weather? Doesn't it make your heart lift?'

'It does. The whole of CID is plotting a daring breakout.'

'I can't offer an escape to the sun, I'm afraid, but I did wonder if you would have a drink with me this evening?'

She hesitated. This was a social invitation, and any reason she had to meet Aidan Sharpe was professional. She had no interest in forming a closer relationship. On the other hand, there was no reason why she shouldn't combine work and relaxation in some small measure.

'That would be very nice. Thank you. Where shall we meet?'

'There is a very pleasant new bar in the Ross Hotel.'

'The Embassy Room? I've heard about it . . . not been though.'

'Good. Shall we meet there at six forty-five?'

Nathan was looking at her with interest as she put down the phone. Freya shook her head. 'Uh-huh. It's sort of work.'

'Yeah, right.'

'Right—it's Mr Bow Tie, Nathan.'

'Got you. Still, swish place.'

'So I'm told.'

'Sting him for one of them cocktails with little brollies.'

'OK. Right now I'm going for a cuppa.'

'Thought you'd never ask.'

Nathan jumped up onto his desk and off the other side.

THE WAITING ROOM was empty, the magazines tidied up in neat piles, the receptionist had left for the day. Karin sat down, feeling tense.

Because she was Cat's patient, and because he had met Karin socially, Aidan Sharpe had given her an immediate appointment at the end of his working day, and she was grateful. But now that she was here, she felt uneasy. She had been sailing along in such a blithe way, refusing to acknowledge the existence of any shadows, let alone peer into them. Now it was all catching up with her.

'Mrs McCafferty, I'm so sorry to keep you.'

She stood up. 'Karin,' she said, though they had not managed to speak much at the Serraillers' dinner party.

'Do come through.'

Aidan Sharpe's surgery discomfited her. Though there was nothing particularly unusual about its pastel blandness, it did not feel relaxing, calming at all. She sat down uncertainly.

He wore a white coat, high at the neck.

'Cat gave me your scan results. I gather you are having back pain?'

'Yes.' No, Karin wanted to say. Her throat tightened.

'Is it painful intermittently or most of the time?'

He had a folder in his hand and glanced down at a sheet he had slipped out of it. Her scan results, presumably.

After Cat's visit in the early hours of the morning, Karin had lost confidence in the road she had chosen and agreed to the scan and blood tests. The results had been worrying.

'I don't get a lot of respite from it. It varies in intensity though, depending on what I'm doing. I can distract myself by moving about.'

'I see. Right. If you'd like to go behind that screen, take off your things down to your underwear and slip on the robe hanging up there?'

The room had seemed to be silent, but when Karin lay down on the high couch she heard the faintest humming sound, as if the floor beneath her were charged with some high-pitched electricity.

Aidan Sharpe sat on a high stool beside her and took her hand to feel her pulse. Karin looked up. His eyes were staring not at her but into her. They were extraordinary eyes, cold, small, like little hard stones, and the lids veiled them slightly. He scarcely blinked.

'Your pulse is very unsteady.'

She moved her head slightly. In the ceiling above, the fluorescent light was white-blue and pulsating gently.

She heard the sound of metal on metal. Aidan Sharpe had let her wrist go and was reaching for the tray of needles. He selected one and, turning back, looked down at her again. The eyes were so odd, narrowed yet staring and strangely expressionless.

'Relax, please.'

The needle touched her temple and hot pain shot through her back.

'Good.'

Another needle, beside her left nostril and the same back pain, lower down. Jesus, God, help me—Karin thought.

There were more needles, carefully positioned. After a few moments, she began to feel drowsy and light-headed. The pain in her back had gone but her legs felt heavy and numb.

Aidan Sharpe continued to stare at her as he worked but he did not speak. The needles seemed to be pinning her to the couch, so that she was afraid to attempt the slightest movement, afraid that her flesh would be torn and the hair ripped from her scalp.

She looked up. His eyes were more needles, penetrating her skull. She was hot and thirsty, and had lost all sense of time. Hours might have passed or only a few moments.

She wondered if anyone knew where she was. Mike was away again, and she was not expected anywhere that evening. Why am I thinking like this? she thought, and made a tremendous effort not to sink down and down but to struggle up, towards the surface of consciousness and control. Aidan Sharpe was very still.

'You may feel a little light-headed.' His voice was soft.

Karin tried to speak.

'Don't move, please.' Something in his voice warned her to do as he asked, some cold, dry thing lacking emotion, but infinitely powerful.

Now, her chest seemed to be cracking open as she tried to get her breath. Her head was swimming and her limbs were losing sensation, except for her fingers, which were tingling. She became aware of Aidan Sharpe reaching down to her. She saw the pattern of small jazzy yellow commas on the navy surface of his bow tie.

'Don't try to sit up.'

His hands were on her arms and seemed to be pressing against her so that she could not move. She struggled slightly.

The navy-and-yellow pattern danced electrically in her brain. It was the last thing she was conscious of before she dropped down into swirling darkness.

THE EMBASSY ROOM was not chrome and neon, as Freya had expected, but pale curved wood and bright pink tweed. When she walked in, just before six forty-five, it was packed, the young after-work crowd jostling with couples starting on an evening out.

Aidan Sharpe had not arrived. Freya found a corner table for two, with some difficulty, and ordered a non-alcoholic cocktail that came with a parasol and strawberries on sticks.

She sat back in the curved chair, suddenly overcome with an intense desire to be sitting here with Simon, talking, laughing, taking time before going on somewhere for dinner. Instead, she was about to spend an hour with a prim alternative therapist in his fifties who wore a bow tie.

Whichever direction he had come from she had not seen him, so that he startled her by materialising at her side and kissing her hand.

'I'm so sorry . . . my last patient felt faint and I had to take her home. Do you like it here? It's rather interesting.'

Freya could have applied several adjectives to the Embassy Room but 'interesting' was not one of them. She took a silent bet that he would order gin and tonic, and won. 'I suppose you're pretty booked up,' she said. 'Acupuncture seems so fashionable.'

'Oh dear, I hope not. Fashionable today, out of fashion tomorrow.'

'Like this place.'

'No, my dear, I rather think the Embassy Room is here to stay, and so is my profession.'

His drink arrived. As Aidan Sharpe bent down to reach for his glass, the cuff of his jacket shot up. Freya's stomach clenched. The watch on his wrist was gold, with Roman numerals and a separate midnight-blue dial in one corner showing the phases of the moon.

She looked up and straight into Aidan Sharpe's odd, expressionless, intensely staring eyes.

A couple getting up to leave the adjacent table knocked over a chair, which fell against Freya's, and in the apologies and fuss the moment was fractured, but she was in no doubt that he had seen her looking at the watch, and noticed her split second of awareness.

'This place could be in London,' Freya said. 'Lafferton is definitely coming on line.' She relaxed back and looked around, apparently at ease, thinking hard. The jeweller had said that phases-of-the-moon watches were hard to find these days—hard but not impossible, and certainly the one Angela Randall had bought was not unique. It could be a coincidence. But Freya had learned to listen to her instincts. Since the Serraillers' party, her instincts about Aidan Sharpe had been uneasy ones.

She turned back to him. He was sitting upright, very still, holding his drink and looking at her, with a smile on his mouth but not in his eyes. 'Why did you come to Lafferton?' He sounded amused.

'Personal reasons . . . and I'd had enough of London. The Met's tough and it can be shitty.'

'You may not find Lafferton a country retreat.'

'I don't want one. Yes, it has the usual problems . . . petty criminals, drugs. But the whole atmosphere is a relief after London.'

'You seem to have found things to do.' Again the sliver of a smile.

'I've made some friends. Joined things.'

'I imagine house prices were a pleasant surprise.'

'Lord, yes. I bought my house for a good bit less than I got for my Ealing one. Nice to have money in the bank for once.'

'I imagine you've bought somewhere outside Lafferton. There are so many nice villages within easy reach.'

'No, the Old Town. I wanted to be in the middle of things.'

'You couldn't have done better . . . that grid of streets around the cathedral is perfect. The Apostles?'

'Sanctuary Street.'

'One of the nicest. Will you stay in Lafferton?'

Freya shrugged noncommittally. Aidan's eyes had not left her face throughout the light, easy conversation.

'Let me order you another drink.'

'No, thank you. I'm afraid I have to go.'

'Really?'

She could not read his tone. Disbelieving?

'Paperwork.'

'How many more patients I would treat, how many more crimes you would solve, if it were not for paperwork.' He picked up the bill and they made their way through the crowd to the cash desk.

Freya turned as she waited for him to pay, and over the top of a group of heads saw that of Simon Serrailler, taller than most, fairer than any. He had almost certainly not noticed her.

Aidan Sharpe put his hand on her elbow and guided her to the door. His grip was strong. 'Thank you so much,' she said. 'Now I know what the Embassy Room is really like.'

'Fun?' But there was no trace of fun in his voice.

'Great fun.'

She flicked the switch to unlock the doors of her car and got in quickly. It was growing dark but the lights outside the bar were brilliant, attracting the crowds to them like moths.

Freya glanced in her mirror and saw Aidan Sharpe standing beside his own dark blue BMW, staring at her, a stare she could feel long after she could see it.

She reached her house, switched on all the lamps and drew the curtains. The living room was warm. She took her post and briefcase to the table and poured herself a glass of wine. There were two messages on her machine. The first was from Cat inviting her to Sunday lunch. She took the number down and clicked onto the next message.

'Freya, it's Simon Serrailler. Twenty past six. I thought we might have gone for a drink but you're not there. We'll catch up another time.'

Damn. Damn, damn, damn. She had wasted an hour in the creepy company of Bow Tie when she could have been, as she had so wanted to be, in the Embassy with Simon.

'Damn.' This time she said it aloud into the silent room.

THERE WERE GREY FRONDS twining about in front of Karin and she was trying to weave her way through them but they clung to her face and hands and pulled her back. They smelt sulphurous and foul and the water she was swimming in was murky.

Then suddenly she was clear and free. She sat up.

Her bedroom was lit by a low lamp on the dressing table and for a second she was confused by the soft glow after the slimy dimness of her dream. She leaned forward, knees hunched in front of her. There was a jug and glass on the bedside table but she had no recollection at all of having put it there. She poured out some water. Drinking it helped not only to ease her dry throat but somehow to clear her senses, until she realised with a shock that her last memory was of being on the couch in Aidan Sharpe's consulting rooms. His hands had been on her arms and he had been staring at her intently. Everything else was a blank. He must have driven her back and carried her up here. She was fully clothed and lying under the coverlet. The curtains had been drawn and the lamp switched on. Presumably he had also fetched the water.

Her next feeling was one of anger. She had been to the acupuncturist as a patient in good faith and the treatment had possibly caused her to feel faint and giddy. But she might have been at risk and should not have been brought home, semiconscious, dumped on her bed and left alone. His behaviour had been strange throughout the treatment, she remembered now; she had felt uneasy and threatened, had wanted to leave. He had neither explained anything to her nor seemed concerned about her reaction.

She drank another glass of water, got up cautiously and went to the bathroom. She felt tired, but not unsteady and when she had washed her hands and face and tied her hair back, she came back to her room, picked up the telephone and dialled Cat, who answered at once.

'Have you got a minute? Something's happened.'

'Sure. What's wrong?'

Karin took a breath and began to tell her carefully and as calmly as she could manage. Cat listened without interruption.

'So I'm here, I'm OK, but I'm still a bit fazed.'

'I don't understand. Aidan's always been totally reliable. I'd come over but I'm here alone with the children until Chris gets back and my car is in for service . . . Do you want to come here? You can stay the night.'

'I don't think I'm up to driving.'

'No, probably not. Acupuncture can wipe you out a bit . . . that's normal by the way, don't worry about feeling tired and light-headed.'

Karin looked round the bedroom. She didn't want to be alone here.

'I could get a taxi. If you wouldn't mind . . .'

'Come when you like.'

BY NINE, the taxi had dropped Karin at the Deerbons' door. She had shovelled her night things into a holdall, locked the house and fled. Cat put her on the sofa with her legs up and took her blood pressure.

'It's fine . . . a bit low but that's the treatment. I prescribe peppermint tea—you'd better stay off booze tonight.'

'Am I being hysterical?'

'No, but I'm concerned. It isn't like you . . . You faced our friend the psychic surgeon and came out of it OK.'

'How well do you know him?'

'Aidan? Not very. I refer patients to him sometimes. He's been here to dinner and we have this informal group, which he comes to . . . and talks a lot of sense. But it's really a professional acquaintance.'

'Do you find him sinister?'

Cat looked at her sharply. 'Not especially. Buttoned up. I should think he's got some repressions; he isn't married—isn't anything at all, so far as I know. What do you mean by sinister?'

Karin shrugged. 'Take no notice. I just got thoroughly wound up.'

'I think you did. It was probably a slight panic attack and when you're in the middle of one of those you can lose all sense of proportion. Ordinary things and people seem sinister and threatening. It's a phase. You've never been like it before. It's related to everything else.'

Karin sipped her tea and listened to Cat in cool, reassuring GP mode and felt infinitely better for being here, more in control, quite calm. But the anger at what had happened was still there. That and the sensation of unease when she remembered Aidan Sharpe.

'What should I do?'

Cat shook her head. 'Nothing. I'll give Aidan a ring tomorrow. You're my patient and this wasn't on. I'm sure he checked that you were OK before leaving you, but the fact that you don't remember anything means you were at some risk. He should have rung me.'

'Thanks. You don't think I should . . .?'

Cat stood up. 'I think you should have a bath. Use my bathroom, the children aren't allowed in there. You can have a slug of the lovely smelly stuff Mum gave me for my birthday. Then you're going to the spare room with a soothing book, a hot-water bottle and a pill.'

THE COMBINATION of them all, plus the very fact of being here in the house she always thought of as being the happiest she knew, sent Karin into a dreamless sleep that lasted until after eight the next morning. Whatever unease she had felt about her visit to Aidan Sharpe had been soothed away, so that all she felt now was rather foolish. She had been faint, which Cat said could be a normal reaction to the treatment. She had been slightly disorientated and had panicked as a result. That was all. Aidan Sharpe had driven her home and seen that she was safely in bed. She remembered none of it but that did not mean she had been unconscious. Probably he ought to have contacted Cat but by then it had been out of hours and clearly he had not been too worried about leaving her alone. He was conscientious, he had a good reputation, Cat thought well of him.

A slant of sunlight filtered through the pretty spare-room curtains, and she heard Sam and Hannah laughing downstairs.

Life seemed very good. Life was what she wanted desperately, more of this unremarkable, miraculous life, any amount more.

'WHERE ARE YOU?'

'Hi, Sarge. We're hanging around at the Meadow Field estate.'

'Nothing gone up yet?'

'Naah. I reckon somebody's got wind of us. Word is uniform are doing a bust on the Calden Business Park later. I'm going to see if I can get to go; my brain cells are dying off here.'

'Your what?'

'Ha ha. You sound as if you survived your drink with Bow Tie, Sarge.'

'The Embassy Room is something else.'

'Maybe I'll take Em there when she gets back from staying at her gran's. I been thinking, Sarge . . . what you said the other day.'

'About getting married?'

'Yeah. I quite fancy it now, you know.'

'Then do it. Don't mess about . . . Nathan, listen—Bow Tie. He was wearing a phases-of-the-moon watch.'

'Right. Angela Randall. Might be coincidence.'

'It might. Anything else?'

'No. Nothing concrete.'

'Yeah, well, that's the whole problem about these missing women, ain't it? Got to go, Sarge, something's happening. Cheers.'

The phone cut off.

Freya went down to the canteen. The place was nearly empty. She got coffee and a banana and took them over to a window table.

Aidan Sharpe had come to the station, out of the blue, to report that Debbie Parker had been a patient of his, though the fact had at first slipped his mind. Why had it? And if the watch had been a gift from Angela Randall, how had he known her? As a patient? If so, why had he not said so? Why had her name rung no bells with him?

She would send Nathan to interview him. If there was anything there, he would get at it. His instincts were sound. But frankly, she thought, throwing her banana skin into the bin, it was clutching at straws.

HE SCARCELY SLEPT and at six he was driving towards the business park. He had looked at himself in the mirror that morning and for the first time seen fear and uncertainty on his face. He had been careless, impetuous. He had been almost uncontrollably tempted to kill Karin McCafferty. The urge had never come over him like that, unbidden and at random, and he was terrified at how powerful and irrational it had been. He did not need Karin McCafferty, though her condition might have been marginally interesting.

But he had not known if anyone was aware of her appointment with him; he had not made careful checks and planned ahead. One impulse had been enough. He did not want to become a risk taker.

Karin McCafferty had panicked and reacted badly to the treatment. It happened occasionally. He had driven her home, taken her key from her bag, helped her upstairs and onto her bed and stayed with her for fifteen minutes, to see that she was safe to be left. That had been another risk, taken because he was in a hurry to meet Freya Graffham.

Then, recalling the policewoman, he smiled. She found him of interest, he could tell. She would not have met him otherwise. It had been the right move to make, and he had redeemed himself in his own eyes after the mistake. There would not be any more of those.

He turned into the business park. The first avenue was empty but as he reached the second, leading towards the side road in which his own unit was situated, he saw four police cars and three others, unmarked, together with a white police van whose back doors were open. Dog handlers and their dogs were gathering on the pathway.

He turned hard left onto the south avenue. As he reached the main road, another two police cars came screeching in.

The fact that there was clearly some kind of raid ought not to have unnerved him. They would scarcely be interested in his own unit, but he needed to find out exactly what was going on. He sat in the lay-by thinking carefully, not allowing himself to panic.

He could return to the business park and simply ask one of the policemen, although he doubted if he would be given any information. He could telephone Freya Graffham, but that would give rise to inevitable questions. Or he could do nothing.

He started the car and drove towards home.

AT ONE O'CLOCK, the CID room was half empty. At ten past, the doors blew open and a dozen or so people came banging in, including DC Coates, looking mutinous.

'Honest, Sarge, I'm thinking of putting in for dog-handling.' He crashed into his chair and hitched one leg up over the side. 'They've had a fantastic time this morning sniffing all over the business park and what have we been doing?'

'Sitting in a car on the Meadow Field estate.'

'Right. Now it's all called off again. You got anything for me, Sarge, only I could do with a bit of action.'

'Go and find DC Hardy, will you, Nathan? I want you to go and talk to Aidan Sharpe.'

NATHAN COATES parked outside Aidan Sharpe's house and consulting room in Wellow Wood Drive. This was the bit of Lafferton he knew little of and liked less. The detached houses with mock-Tudor gables and wrought-iron gates seemed stand-offish and unneighbourly. If he and Emma got married he would like a cottage in one of the villages outside Lafferton. He would never want to cut himself off in a place like this, however big the bay windows, however flashy the blue BMWs parked in the driveways—like the one outside Aidan Sharpe's house.

He peered into it as he and DC Will Hardy walked up to the surgery door and rang the bell. He pushed open the front door and stepped inside. The receptionist wore fashionable oval spectacles and one of those professional smiles. 'Can I help you?'

Nathan flipped open his ID wallet. 'DC Coates, Lafferton CID. I'd like a word with Mr Sharpe.'

She looked startled, but did not lose her poise. 'Mr Sharpe has a patient with him at the moment. I'm afraid I can't interrupt.'

'That's fine. We'll hang on.'

'Yes, of course. Please take a seat and I'll tell him as soon as he's free. Can I get you a cup of tea or coffee? A glass of mineral water?'

Nathan and Will shook their heads. 'No, thanks.'

They sat down and glanced at the magazines . . . posh magazines, *Vogue*, *Tatler*, *Country Life*, the *Spectator*, all up-to-date. The room smelt of flowers and polish and something faintly antiseptic.

The door opened, and an elegant middle-aged woman came through.

'Please sit down, Mrs Savage. I'll make up your account in a moment.' She glanced across at Nathan. 'I'll have a word with Mr Sharpe.' She walked out, high heels clicking smartly.

Nathan grinned at the woman. 'Painful, is it?'

She gave him an unsmiling glance. 'No.'

'Never fancied it myself. Still, if you think it does you good . . .'

She leaned forward, picked up the shiny new copy of *Country Life*.

The high heels came clicking back. 'Mr Sharpe asks if you could come back at five thirty. He'll be glad to see you then.'

WHEN NATHAN and DC Hardy returned they found the door slightly ajar and the reception room empty.

'DC Coates?'

He seemed to have materialised silently, oozing out of the walls. The bow tie was red with thin navy stripes.

'I do apologise for asking you to come back, but I was in the middle of my surgery,' he said. 'And this is?'

'DC Hardy.'

Aidan Sharpe nodded. 'Please come through.'

They were led through a door marked PRIVATE and along a short passage into a sitting room.

'How can I help you? I imagine this is about that poor girl Debbie Parker. Have you news of her?'

'Afraid not, sir, though we're following some leads.'

'Ah, yes. Leads.'

The room was oppressive, with a huge desk and bookcases of heavy dark oak and a sofa and armchairs covered in brown leather.

Opposite him, Aidan Sharpe sat very still in an armchair, hands together, finger to finger. His eyes stared. Surprise him, Nathan decided, no lead-up, no charm, straight in.

'Do you own a watch showing moon phases?'

Not a flicker. The eyes did not leave Nathan's face, the fingers were motionless. 'I do.'

'Are you wearing it now, sir?'

'I am.'

'I'd like to see it, please.'

'May I ask why?'

'Just take it off, Mr Sharpe.'

A thin smile, like the flick of a lizard's tongue. Gone.

'I'd like to know why you want me to do that.'

'Where did you get the watch?'

'If you mean where was it bought, I have no idea. It was a gift.'

'Who from, sir?'

'That is my business.'

'We're investigating the disappearance of three women.'

Sharpe did not react.

'One was a Miss Angela Randall. Was she a patient of yours?'

'I have a large number of patients. I would have to check.'

'You came to tell us Debbie Parker was your patient.'

Silence. The eyes stared.

'So you'd know if Angela Randall was a patient too, wouldn't you?'

'As I say, I would have to check. I'll ask my secretary to do it tomorrow. If she finds that this . . . Miss Randall has been treated here, I will contact Sergeant Graffham.'

'Can I see your watch, Mr Sharpe?'

He smiled, shot his cuff, slipped off the wristwatch and held it out. It was nice, thin as a wafer. The moon had little stars beside it on dark blue enamel. It was a half-moon.

Nathan handed it back. 'Thanks. That will be all for the time being. But if you could check your records in the morning like you agreed?'

'By all means.'

On the way to the front door Aidan Sharpe said, 'There seemed to be something important going on early this morning . . . I happened to drive by the business park. There were police everywhere—vans, tracker dogs . . . What on earth was that all about?'

'Sorry, sir, not my department.'

'A drug raid, do you suppose?'

'For all I know, Mr Sharpe. Thanks for your help.'

NATHAN STOPPED the car round the next corner and took out his mobile phone. 'Sarge?'

'What did he say?'

'Not a lot. I asked who'd given him the watch . . . got nowhere. He claims not to remember if Randall was a patient; said he'd ring you if he found her name in his records.'

'Me?'

'Yeah. Sergeant Graffham, he said. Don't want to chat with the low life. He's creepy, ain't he? Spooky.'

'But that was it?'

'One thing . . . just when I was leaving he asked what had been going on at the business park earlier. Said he'd driven by and seen all the vans and tracker dogs and that. Asked if it was a drugs raid. Only, what was he doing up there so early in the morning? It was all done and dusted before eight. And another thing was, they were up the far end; if he was just passing he couldn't have seen nothing from the end of the road.'

Twelve

Angela Randall. Silly bitch. She had caused trouble from the beginning. There had been the difficult telephone calls. Letters. Cards. Twice she had appeared on his doorstep at night, her face full of mooning self-pity, longing to be invited in. She had repelled him. Eventually, he had refused to treat her, and in any case she had no physical problems; her problems were the distorted emotional ones of a menopausal spinster.

When the first two gifts had arrived he had sent them back. Then there were others, always sent anonymously, always with the same ludicrous notes. After a while, he had decided to ignore them but the gifts had continued, expensive, unsuitable gifts, humiliating her. He had not cared in the slightest.

But now she was the one causing trouble. He thought of her lying in the unit, scrawny and pitiful, though he never felt pity.

Freya Graffham had noticed the watch, but how had she come to know about it in the first place? Angela Randall must have left a receipt or something lying around in her house.

He buttered bread and cut the plastic wrapping from round a pack of smoked mackerel. He was tired, on edge. He sighed now as he mixed a salad. His hand had been forced again and there was not enough time. He knew what he must do next.

He sat down, and began to eat and think methodically.

THE CATHEDRAL WAS FULL. Sitting in the middle of the rows of altos, listening to the mighty waves of sound coming from the orchestra below, Freya Graffham felt exhilarated. The cathedral acoustics were not easy, and the pianissimo sections had a tendency to vanish like fine coils of candlesmoke up into the roof, but the fact that the building was so full helped and the crescendos were magnificent.

The high of the performance carried them all on, long after it was over, after they had finally left the cathedral to a silence that was somehow still full of music, after the post-performance drinks and sandwiches and mutual congratulations in St Michael's Hall. It carried each of them out into the streets, into their cars, laughing and calling, and floated them home.

Freya had walked from home tonight and only parted from half a dozen of the others on the corner of her own street. It was a mild, soft night, full of stars. She was tired, but before she slept she would have a bath, watch a late-night film and gradually unwind.

She closed the front door and went into the kitchen, humming quietly and feeling the comfortable atmosphere settle around her.

At first, she was uncertain if there had been a sound at the front door or not. She stood still. The soft knock came again.

It was twenty minutes to midnight and all the upstairs lights in the houses of her neighbours were out. Then she remembered Simon's telephone message and her heart missed a beat. She ran a comb through her short hair before going quickly to open the door.

Before she had time to take in what was happening, Aidan Sharpe had stepped quickly inside and shut and locked the door in one movement. He put the key in his pocket.

'I want to talk to you,' he said.

Freya turned back into the living room and went rapidly across to the table. Usually her mobile phone was in her bag or her jacket pocket but tonight, because of the concert, she had left it behind here.

'We won't want to be disturbed.' He was at her elbow and his gloved hand flashed in front of her to take the handset.

'Give that back, please.'

'Sit down, Miss Graffham. You're not on duty now.'

'Give—'

From the left pocket of his jacket he pulled a syringe. It was full of a clear liquid. Freya swallowed, her mouth suddenly dry.

'I said sit down.'

His voice was very soft and held the note of manic calm and sweet reason she had heard before in dangerous men. She did as he asked. Aidan Sharpe sat in the armchair opposite her and leaned back, the faintest of smiles on his mouth. Freya began to think rapidly about her means of escape. One door in the room led to the hall, the other to the kitchen and from there the back door led to the passageway that ran between her house and the neighbouring one.

'I want to talk to you,' Aidan Sharpe said again.

'About Angela Randall? Or Debbie . . . or perhaps both of them?'

'Shut up. Angela Randall was a stupid bitch.'

'You said "was" . . . Does—?'

'I told you to shut up.'

She had to remain rational and calm and not give off the smell of fear, nor betray what she was planning by the slightest flicker.

'She had no pride, you see; she lay at my feet like a bitch on heat,

287

she sent me fawning messages. Where was the pride in that? She sent me gifts. This . . .' He shot his cuff and displayed the watch. 'And so many other things. I sold off most of them, I didn't want them round me, but I kept the watch. A relative used to have one like it when I was a boy. I was fond of him. I haven't seen a watch like it since.'

His voice had changed again, become casual in tone, as if he wanted to lull her, to make this seem like a chat between friends. Freya was calculating how many strides she needed to make to reach the kitchen and the outside door, how easy it would be to get to the end of the passageway.

'I like my work, you know, I find it satisfying. I'm good at it. And I sacrificed a lot to qualify. But it was never going to be enough, not when you consider how near I was to being a doctor. I was unjustly treated, victimised and betrayed. I had everything mapped out and they ruined it all. I discovered I didn't need them at all. The joke has been mine for years. The study of the human body, the detailed comparison between one and another. I have come to know more about it than anyone in the world because I have had the luxury of time and been able to set up my own private place for research.'

He fell silent for a moment, hands behind his head and absolutely still, looking across the room at her. Staring. Staring

Freya had been confronted before by angry and violent men, by the deranged and dangerous, but Aidan Sharpe was mad in the most dangerous way of all, controlledly, quietly, rationally mad. This was a smiling psychopath, with all the strength and cunning of one who thinks himself untouchable. Faced with him holding that potentially deadly syringe, listening to his monotonous, gloating voice, she understood the paralysis of every hunted and cornered creature.

'Wouldn't you like to hear more? I've teased you, haven't I?'

'If you feel the need to tell me, please do.'

Aidan Sharpe laughed, almost a natural-sounding laugh. 'My dear Freya, how charming! Up pops the well-trained detective sergeant who passed her practical psychology course . . . "Humour him, win him over by listening to him patiently. He will feel the need to confess, so let him." I have no need to confess, I assure you. I enjoy my work and I will do so for many years to come. Confession is not on the agenda. What is to say that these three women won't reappear?'

'But I think you want to tell me the reason why they won't.'

'Do I? How concerned are you? How curious are you?'

'Very.'

'The knowledge will be of no use to you, of course.'

Freya felt her stomach clench. She thought she might be sick.

'You understand what I am saying.'

The walls of the room seemed very near, the air felt as if it was giving out. Her chest hurt her as she tried to breathe normally. Wait. Remain calm and think. You have to get out of here and there are only two exits. He has the front-door key in his pocket so you have to get out through the kitchen. Keep him talking. Hold his attention and then think, one move at a time. When you do move, move fast, into the kitchen, out of the door, up the passageway and scream as you go and keep on screaming, 'Police! Police!' Never mind if no one is likely to hear, it will throw him. Think. Is the back door bolted? Yes. Is the key in it? No, it's on the shelf which means another move. As you go, reach for the key, unlock, unbolt . . . No, he will be right behind you, trying to stop you. When you reach the kitchen door, swing round on him and catch him off guard. You can bring him down. He is not large or very heavy. If necessary, chop him across the neck and wind him, then knock him out. It won't be easy. You will have to fight.

She sat without moving. 'Are you going to tell me?' she asked.

'I should like a drink. Shall we be companionable and have a drink?'

Don't make your move while you are getting the bottle and glasses from the cupboard. He is expecting you to, so don't.

She set a bottle of whisky down on the low table between them. 'If you want water, I'll have to go into the kitchen.'

'I would like water.'

She hesitated, then got up. So did he. He followed close behind her and stood watching her take the jug and fill it from the cold tap. She did not glance at the door leading to the passage, merely turned and went back into the living room. She felt his warmth behind her.

'Thank you,' he said as she added water to his drink. 'Please join me.'

Freya shook her head.

'Something else then? I don't like drinking alone.'

She poured herself a glass of water.

Aidan Sharpe smiled. 'That's right. Humour him, don't make him angry. But, my dear, I am not in the least angry.' He sipped his whisky, looking at her across the top of the glass.

She was glad of the water.

'Tell me,' he said, in a voice so pleasant and reasonable she was taken aback. 'What do you think motivates a serial killer? I imagine you must have come across one or two during your time in the Met?'

She opened her mouth and her tongue felt sticky. 'They . . . they are less common than people imagine. But, yes.'

'And?'

She knew what to answer but could not say it. It seemed ludicrous to engage in a discussion with this man on the motives of murderers.

'Has it ever occurred to you that there may be good motives?'

She shook her head. Speech was beyond her now.

'I kill in the course of my work.' He stared at her and paused.

Don't react, don't move a muscle, don't give anything away.

'The benefits will be immense. The study of the human body in its many stages will lead eventually to more knowledge about the process of ageing and disease than has ever been gained before. Those I kill die to benefit mankind and, as you have discovered, they leave scarcely any behind to mourn them.'

Freya wondered what his motive could be in telling her that he had killed. Pride? Boastfulness? She glanced at him. He looked such a neat, trimmed, contained little man. But he was right about one thing. She did want to know. Before escaping, she needed him to tell her what he had done with the missing women and how, and whether there had been others before now, others nobody knew about.

She drank more water.

'They are perfectly safe, you know,' he said, smiling again. 'I take very good care of them.'

Then she saw in his eyes not only that he was mad but the extent of his madness and the intensity of its focus.

'I plan. I go to a lot of trouble. Sometimes I wait for months. I waited a long time for poor Debbie Parker.'

'Iris Chater?' She heard her own voice, odd, distorted in her ears.

Aidan Sharpe inclined his head. 'You're right,' he said, as if in real regret. 'There was no plan. I went against my instincts. It was foolish. But I didn't kill her. She died of a heart attack and I kept the body. I took a risk and as it happens it paid off, but it might not have done.'

'You mean . . . you are sorry?'

'Oh, no, not that. I regret taking a chance. But if it had not been Mrs Chater it would have had to be someone like her. An elderly woman was next on the list. How could I be sorry?'

Freya was dazed, with fear and with a wild sense that she herself was becoming deranged, locked with a madman in his own claustrophobic mental world.

'You're very quiet, Freya. I expected a torrent of questions. Has nothing I have said interested you? You seem detached.'

The questions were there, like bats fluttering round inside the walls of her skull, but she could not open her mouth. She was simply clinging on to the awareness of what she must do and how.

'Perhaps I might have a little more of your excellent whisky?' Aidan Sharpe bent slightly forward and reached out his hand.

A light went on inside Freya's brain. Now, she said. Go. Go. Go.

'YES!' NATHAN SHOUTED. 'Yessss!' and jumped onto the dining table.

'Get down, you idiot.' But Emma was laughing.

'Naw, I might pull you up here and we'll have a dance. I want to dance, Em. Where can we go to dance?'

'Get down—and there isn't anywhere at this time of night.'

He began a mock tap routine, waving his arms in the air.

Emma had said yes. He knew she would and had been terrified she wouldn't. He would wait, he thought, he wouldn't ask her now, she'd just had a long journey, she was tired, he'd wait till the weekend.

She'd dropped her bag and gone straight to the shower. Ten minutes later, as she had walked into the kitchen with her damp hair tied up and wearing her old velour track suit, he had turned round from the sink where he was washing his hands and said, 'Em, I really, really want to marry you. Will you marry me?'

'Yes,' Em had said and gone to the fridge to get a bottle of water.

'You what?'

She had glanced up. 'Can you open this top? I never can. I said yes.'

That had been a couple of hours ago and Nathan had still not come down from his high of excitement, delight and disbelief. 'Yessss,' he shouted again.

'*Get down!*'

He jumped lightly onto the floor.

'Let's go out and find somewhere, Em . . . You're going to marry me. We can't just leave it there. Let's knock someone up. Haven't you got any mates just coming off duty?'

'No. They're either in bed asleep or they're working. Same as yours.'

'Let's just go for a drink, then.'

'Where?'

'We'll find somewhere.'

'Not anywhere legal we won't.'

'Hey—there's that bottle of champagne you won in the raffle. 'I'll tell you where we're going. Do you know who pushed me into this "Will you marry me" thingy?'

'You mean it wasn't your own idea?'

'Yeah, well, I just hadn't got round to it.'

'I'd noticed.'

'It was something Sergeant Graffham said made me think about it. Honestly, you owe her, Em.'

'I'll remember to thank her.'

'You can do it now. We're going round there. We're going to dance outside her house and we're taking this bottle. Come on.'

'Nathan, don't be stupid. You can't just barge round to your sergeant's house and wake her up.'

'Oh, she won't have gone to bed, she never does till two in the morning, she told me, and anyway, she was singing in some concert tonight in the cathedral so she'll definitely be up for a drink. Come on, I'll push your bike.'

'I don't need pushing. Are you sure, Nath? I don't know . . .'

But Nathan had grabbed her hand and the bottle of champagne and propelled her out of the door.

The streets were empty and peaceful. Their bikes made a silky swishing sound on the dry tarmac.

'Tell you what, why don't we go the long way round, on the road past the Hill?' Emma whisked off ahead, giggling, catching him out, so that he had to pedal furiously to reach her.

FREYA GOT into the kitchen, unlocked the back door and hurtled down the narrow passageway. She had managed to surprise him after all.

He did not catch her until she had her hand on the bolt of the side door into the street, but then she felt a pain in the middle of her back as he put his fist into it, taking her breath away, and another as he wrenched her wrist from the door. He had not looked as strong as this.

Freya began to scream. She screamed until he put his arm across her mouth and throat, at the same time pushing her hard, back into the kitchen, back into the sitting room. She tripped and fell, hitting her face on the floor.

Her arm almost came out of its socket in a wrenching pain, as he yanked her to her feet. She saw his face, intensely white with two scarlet patches on the cheekbones, a grim and dreadful concentration on his features, the syringe held aloft. Freya lashed out with her foot and raised her knee at the same time, trying to get to his groin, but he had her arm again and twisted it so hard behind her back she felt the bone crack. Sickness surged up.

Don't let, don't let him, don't let . . .

A split second of pain so intense that it did not feel like pain at all but was like a brilliant light boring through her skull.

Don't . . . Then nothing.

THEY RACED ONE ANOTHER all the way, sweeping past the Hill road in the darkness, their laughter floating up towards the Wern Stones.

'Hey, hey, hey . . . !' Nathan shouted, and stuck both legs out at the sides of his bike as they swerved round the narrow corners.

Emma was still ahead of him as they reached Freya's street.

'There you are, told you, her light's on,' Nathan shouted.

They pedalled the last few yards alongside the parked cars, past all the darkened houses to the one with a dim light still showing. Nathan skidded off his bike and propped it up against the low wall. 'What shall we do, sing? Let's give her a song.'

'Shut up, you'll wake the street. Just tap on the door and if she doesn't answer—'

'Course she'll answer.' Nathan opened the gate and marched up the path, waving the bottle of champagne and laughing, dragging Emma by the hand behind him.

SHE LAY ON THE FLOOR, a few feet away from him, one leg bent awkwardly back, her head face down on the carpet. The blood had begun to seep out from under her. He was angry with himself for his carelessness. But she had forced his hand. It was her fault.

He did not touch her. In a few minutes, when he was calm, he would walk to his car, which was parked at the far end of the quiet, dark street. He knew there would be a few moments when danger would be acute, as he carried her out of the house, but people were asleep, no cars had come down the road for over an hour and it was too late for people walking home from the pub.

Then he heard the noise outside. Voices. Voices and suppressed laughter. What was happening? He waited, even his breathing held in suspense. People drunk, banging on doors at random? Kids?

There was a short silence. He thought they had moved on. Then someone knocked, softly at first, then more loudly. After a moment, the letterbox flap went up and a voice came in a stage whisper into the hall. 'Sarge? Oy . . . Sarge . . . it's Nathan.'

The bloody little constable with the ugly face. His heart began to pound fast. He needed to think, to plan, and he had no time. He went to the back door that led from the kitchen into the passageway. It opened without any sound and he slipped into the garden. He could hear their voices again at the front.

He stopped, waited. He felt grass under his feet. He could see a little now. It was quite a long garden and there were shrubs at the bottom and then a shed. He moved on. At the very end of the garden, he came up against a low brick wall with a tree beside it. From the street, he heard voices again and knocking.

Aidan Sharpe put one foot on the low wall, hauled himself up easily with the aid of a branch and slithered down into soil at the end of the garden of the house behind. Then he walked up a long stretch of grass and slipped between two houses and into the street. It was dark here too. No lights in any of the houses. Nothing. He removed his gloves and made sure they were tucked well into his pocket.

It was so easy that he smiled to himself. He had been meant to get away. Of course, he could not collect his car now, so he walked the two and a half miles back to his own house.

His only regret was that although Freya Graffham's death had been necessary she would now be wasted. Such a pity, he thought. She could have been of further use.

Thirteen

The room was full. CID and uniform sat and stood three-deep. There was a murmur but none of the usual uproar, chair-scraping, joking and laughter. As they had come in that morning they had heard that Freya had been taken to BG in an ambulance, but as yet there was no further news.

The room went still as DCI Simon Serrailler walked in. DC Nathan Coates, looking shattered, followed him.

'Good morning, everyone. Most of you will know what this is about, but I want to fill you all in. Last night, DC Nathan Coates went to DS Graffham's house at approximately twelve twenty, accompanied by Nurse Emma Steele. They had become engaged earlier in the evening and wanted to share the good news. They cycled round to Sergeant Graffham's house on the offchance of her still being up. They found the lights on and Sergeant Graffham's car parked outside. When there was no answer to the front door or to either the house phone or Sergeant Graffham's mobile, which they could hear ringing inside, they broke in and found her lying on the floor of her living room. She was unconscious and had serious injuries. There was no sign of forced entry or of any damage in the house. The kitchen door, which leads to a passageway at the side of the house, was unlocked.

'Sergeant Graffham has been leading investigations into the disappearance of three Lafferton women, Angela Randall, Debbie Parker and Iris Chater, and I am concentrating on matters surrounding this in the search for . . .'

The door opened quietly. Everyone looked at Inspector Jenny Leadbetter, who inclined her head to Serrailler.

'Excuse me a moment.'

He went out and closed the door. People looked at one another, shuffled their feet, shifted in their chairs. Someone opened a window.

The DCI came back. They looked at him and knew. The skin seemed to have tightened over his face.

He cleared his throat and looked down.

No one seemed to be breathing.

'I have just had a message from the hospital. I'm sorry . . . Freya Graffham died fifteen minutes ago from her injuries. She hadn't regained consciousness. This is therefore now a murder inquiry. I'll call another conference later today. Thanks, everyone.'

He strode very fast out of the room, only pausing fractionally to beckon Nathan Coates to follow.

IN HIS OWN ROOM, the DCI poured a cup of coffee from his percolator and sat down. Nathan was clutching a polystyrene beaker of cold tea as if it were a lifeline. Neither wanted to speak. Nathan swirled the dregs of his tea round. Outside in the corridor people came and went.

Simon Serrailler leaned forward. 'I'm taking charge of this, Nathan. Do you feel up to being part of the team? If not, you can go on to something routine . . . no one's going to blame you.'

'Do I hell, guv! I want me own hands round the bugger's throat.'

'Well, don't let either your anger or your distress get the better of your judgment. I know it's difficult.'

'I owe her.'

'I know.'

'I want to arrest him.'

'Sharpe? Not enough evidence, Nathan.'

'The watch.'

'We can ask him to hand it over and the jeweller will tell us one way or the other. But even if he wears a watch given to him by Angela Randall, it doesn't mean he had anything to do with her disappearance or with that of the other women, and it certainly doesn't mean he attacked . . . murdered Sergeant Graffham last night.'

'She was on to him, guv, and he knew it. When I went to his place yesterday he knew it. He's clever but he ain't as clever as he thinks.'

'Yes, and I'll want him taken apart and his premises too. Forensic are all over Sergeant Graffham's house now and if there's anything from him or anyone else they'll find it. Let's pray they do and we can pick him up with something solid.'

'What should I do now, guv?'

'Go back to the sergeant's house. See where they're at. I want this fast-tracking. I'm going to interview Sharpe. Is there anything in particular you think I should press him about?'

Nathan swigged the cold tea. 'There's what he said about the business park.' He looked across the desk and Simon Serrailler saw that his eyes were full of tears. 'We just wasn't there soon enough. We mucked about, rode round by the Hill for a lark . . . if we hadn't done that we'd have got there in time.'

'You don't know that.'

'I bloody do know that,' Nathan shouted, and then wiped his sleeve across his eyes. 'Sorry, guv, sorry.'

'All right, Nathan. Take it easy this morning. You're in shock.' He stood up and looked vaguely out of the window. 'We all are.'

HE HAD SLEPT at once and easily, and neither dreamed nor stirred, but just after five he woke, surfacing instantly, remembering everything, and then he broke into the sweat of panic, knowing that they either knew or must soon know. He had been careless at the house, getting away in a hurry, leaving her body on the floor. His car was parked in the street. Soon enough they would find it.

He got up and stood at the window. There would be no need for questioning, no need for them to use their wits. He had handed it all to them, made it all so easy. He felt afraid. But he could still think clearly. His mind never let him down.

He knew exactly where to go and what to do.

Fifteen minutes later he was carrying a nylon holdall along Wellow Wood Drive, heading towards the main road to Bevham.

The business park worried him. The police had been there early yesterday. But his luck held. The avenues were deserted. No police. No cars. No one opening up his unit early. He saw his own unit at the end of the side road with a huge relief of tension. It was all he could do to stop himself breaking into a run.

Inside he stood shaking, sweat breaking out over his body. He went into the front office and checked that the slatted blinds were down. It was light enough for him not to need the fluorescent tubes.

He put his bag down and unzipped it, took out food, milk, a book, toothbrush and disposable razor. He could stay here a day or two and then leave at the right moment, after dark. They would be watching his house. He could not go back there so he had brought money, cards, passport, everything he could think of to give him a start.

They might track him down here eventually, but for now this was his refuge, the place where he felt most himself, most alive.

JUST AFTER NINE THIRTY, DCI Simon Serrailler's car turned into the drive of Aidan Sharpe's house. As he got out, the front door opened and a middle-aged woman came quickly towards him.

'Have you come to tell me bad news?'

Serrailler flicked his ID card. 'I'm sorry, you are . . . ?'

'Julie Cooper, Mr Sharpe's practice manager . . . Please tell me what has happened.'

'Can we go inside, Mrs Cooper?'

She hesitated, then turned and led him into the reception area.

'I've come to see Mr Aidan Sharpe. I gather he isn't here?'

'Well, no, of course, that's what I mean. When I got here, everything was normal . . . only he's always in first, getting ready, and he wasn't. His car isn't here either. He has never done anything like this.'

'When did you last see Mr Sharpe?'

'Yesterday afternoon. I left at five as usual. He was here then.'

'Did he say he was going anywhere?'

'No. Of course he didn't. I'd have remembered, wouldn't I?'

'Did you notice anything unusual about his behaviour?'

'No. Nothing at all. Nothing . . . I hope you're going to find out what's happened, where Mr Sharpe is, I—'

'I'd like you to stay here please, in case Mr Sharpe comes back.'

'I have to let his patients for the day know . . .'

'Fine, if you could get on with that. There'll be an officer here, in case Mr Sharpe returns. Don't worry about that.'

'What do you mean?'

'We need to interview him, Mrs Cooper.'

BY THE TIME Simon arrived, the teams who had been crawling over every inch of Freya Graffham's house were still working—invading, scouring, prying, fingerprinting, photographing.

He walked slowly into the house, and at once her image was there in front of him. The house was her, exactly her, he saw it at once. Welcoming and agreeable, quite informal, very distinctive.

'Morning, sir.'

The white-overalled officer glanced up from a section of carpet from which he was extracting small tufts with tweezers.

'Anything yet?'

'Lots of prints. Not necessarily his, though. Some dark hairs on the back of that chair, shoe print out in the garden . . . You should have enough to go on. As long as there's a comparison, of course.'

'I want it yesterday.'

'I know, sir. I didn't know the sergeant myself but it's always the worst, one of your own.'

Simon went out of the kitchen door and into the narrow garden. Two white suits were working on their hands and knees in the soil at the far end. He left them to do their stuff. They would get Sharpe, it wouldn't be hard. Tie it up. Then he could go home, close the door of his flat and try to work out what he felt about Freya Graffham.

By FIVE, the reports had come through.

'Nathan?'

'Sir?'

'Sharpe left his car in Freya's street. He won't get far; we've got his description out. You'd better try his house. I've put a couple of uniform up there in case he turns up.'

'Which he won't.'

'Probably not. But get a photo of him, will you? Put a picture out to the press with a description. Then you might as well go home.'

'No chance. I'm here until we get him.'

'Don't be ridiculous, it might be days.'

'I'm not budging, guv. I mean, are you off home to put your feet up?'

No one else but Nathan, Simon Serrailler thought as he put his phone away, could have got a smile out of him just now.

AIDAN SHARPE had apparently been camera shy. They turned his house upside-down, to the distress of Julie Cooper, and found nothing.

'There ain't no pictures of anyone,' Nathan said as they trawled through. 'You'd think the bleedin' camera hadn't been invented.'

'I know there was one in the paper,' the receptionist said suddenly. 'It was a while ago, at a professional dinner. If it would help you find him . . .' No one had told her why her employer was wanted. 'I hope it hasn't anything to do with those others,' she had said when Nathan had arrived. 'Those missing women. Do you think it has?'

Nathan felt sorry for her. 'Which paper was it?' he asked.

'The *Echo*, but as I said, it was a while ago.'

'Shouldn't think he's changed much.'

Nor had he. The paper scanned the image and emailed it through to the station. Aidan Sharpe stood, wearing a dinner jacket and holding a glass, looking faintly supercilious in a small group of men.

Simon Serrailler stared down at the face, the small beard, the carefully combed-back hair, the odd eyes. He had rarely felt like this. He couldn't afford to. His job was detection, not vengeance, not judgment, not even punishment, but looking at the smug image of Aidan Sharpe he felt a desire for them all which was biblical in its intensity.

He picked up the phone and called Nathan in.

'Get this copied, get them to separate him out and make the image clearer. I want it in tomorrow morning's papers and you can go up to the business park first thing and hawk it about.'

'Right. I suppose it's something to get on with.' He glanced up at Simon, his monkey face bruised-looking, his eyes red.

'You can start as early as you want, but when you've sorted out the pictures, go home, eat and get some sleep. Understood?'

'Guv.' Nathan took the print-out and left.

Half an hour later, Simon drove his own car out of the station and headed for his sister's farmhouse.

HE WAITED UNTIL just after midnight when he heard the security patrol go round, before clearing the instrument table and folding it back against the wall. Then he stood in the centre of the main room.

They were all here, all around him, on trolleys. They were no longer just the things he worked with; now they had a value to him far beyond the original. Earlier, he had read over the details of the way each of them had died, from their file.

> Angela Randall—stab wounds causing fatal haemorrhage
> Debbie Parker—strangulation
> Tim Galloway—blunt trauma to the left temple
> Iris Chater—cardiac arrest

When his notes were found and his discoveries made public, his contribution would be recognised. People would understand.

Then he said goodbye. He spent a few moments with each of them, touching their faces, speaking to them quietly, saying their names.

He glanced round once more, hitched on his jacket and stowed all he needed for the journey in one of the pockets. Then, for the last time, he went outside and locked the door behind him.

It was a cool night and there was a half-moon. He felt quite calm, confident even, because matters had not been taken out of his hands. He was still his own master.

He walked to the perimeter road and, for a moment, had to press himself quickly against the trunk of a tree as a car flashed by, but then there was nothing but quietness and stillness.

He stepped onto the grass and began to climb, steadily and with a calm purpose, up the Hill.

A LITTLE AFTER SIX THIRTY, Netty Salmon, large and stout and dressed in her usual old sheepskin, marched her Dobermanns up the Hill. It was drizzling slightly and there was a crown of low, misty cloud around the trees at the summit. But Ms Salmon strode on, calf muscles flexing rhythmically, up the steep path behind the dogs.

She paused at the usual spot to get her breath and, as she did so, the dogs began to bark. Netty Salmon looked up. The dogs had raced to the top of the Hill and were standing at the foot of one of the trees.

She clambered nearer, peering into the drizzle. Something was swinging from a high branch of the tree—some sort of effigy. Puzzled, she climbed the last stretch until she was beside the now hysterical dogs, immediately beneath the oak tree, then looked up again.

She was not a nervous woman. She did not scream when she recognised a man's body hanging from a rope. She merely turned and began to march back down the Hill, dragging the dogs, until she saw a pair of young men on mountain bikes riding towards her and held her arms out wide to stop them.

THREE POLICE CARS, including that of DCI Simon Serrailler, swept up the avenue of the business park and turned left. Nathan Coates was waiting with two men outside a small green-painted unit at the far end.

'Nathan.'

'Morning, guv. This is Mr Connolly, the site manager, and Terry Putterby, the security guard. Mr Connolly here recognised the press photo, like I said, only he called himself Dr Fentiman. But it's him.'

'Right.' Serrailler looked at the site manager. 'Do you have keys?'

'I do, but these units are rented in good faith. I should—'

'No one's blaming you for anything. I do have a warrant.'

'It was only I—'

'Right. Now, I've no idea if he's in here, but if he is he'll be dangerous. I'm going in first, uniform back-up is behind. Nathan—'

'I'm in there with you.'

Simon knew better than to argue. 'Just be careful. If he's cornered he'll think he's got nothing to lose. He'll have heard us.' He spoke briefly, bringing the others up behind him to surround the unit. 'May I have the keys, please? Then you gentlemen stay right over there.'

Serrailler turned the key in the lock and stepped quickly inside, Nathan at his heels. There was silence. Simon put his hand on the inner door that led to the office, then opened it quickly.

'Sharpe?' He looked round quickly. No one. 'Doesn't look as if he did much business. We'll get forensics in here later.'

'Here, sir.' Nathan took a small package from the shelf.

'Addressed to Dr Cat Deerbon, sir.'

Simon looked round sharply. The brown envelope was unsealed and Nathan tipped it up. Three tapes slid out onto the shelf.

'OK, bag them up. Now, there's the big storage area at the back and some sort of inner room. He could be in either. The side entrance is covered, he can't get past anyone this way but watch it.'

They moved forward.

The DCI rapped on the metal door. 'Sharpe?'

The silence was so dense they could have heard the dust settle.

Serrailler slid the bolt, put the key in the lock and turned it. Then he waited a full minute. He could feel Nathan's breath on his neck.

'We're coming in.'

He flung open the door wide and the two of them went through it into what, for a split second, they thought was an empty space.

'Oh dear God.' Simon Serrailler spoke in a voice so low Nathan Coates did not catch the words but had to follow the DCI's glance across to the far end of the unit.

'Jesus Christ,' Nathan would have said, only when he opened his mouth, nothing but an odd little mewling cry came out of it.

The Tape

I have told you now. I have talked to you. I have made up for the lies and the silences. Now more than ever, when perhaps we are about to come face to face, I must tell you the truth, mustn't I?

I used to hate talking to you. I hated it when you tried to make me tell you things, tried to get under my skin.

But I have come to like laying everything bare at last. I like it that you know me—what I choose to let you know. Because, in the end, I do have the choice and the power. The last word. Not you. I.

Fourteen

Freya Graffham's light oak coffin lay on its rests at the chancel steps. The cathedral was full. Police from Freya's old teams in the Met sat with those from Lafferton. Gold braid gleamed. DCI Simon Serrailler sat at the aisle end of a pew, from which he had got up and walked to the lectern to read the Old Testament lesson. Nathan Coates sat with his fiancée in the second row, among Freya's other colleagues. In her place among the altos, Meriel Serrailler sat listening to the familiar words from the old Prayer Book and felt not only sadness, not only the loss of a new friend whom she had liked so much, but a regret for something more. She made the best of things; it was how she had sustained a long marriage to an angry and bitter man. But for some reason Freya's death brought it into clear focus. The waste of time, the waste of life, the sense of things left undone.

Nathan Coates got up and walked to the lectern. His face was tight with the effort of control and in his light grey suit and black tie he looked like a schoolboy. He put both hands on the lectern and cleared his throat. Emma clenched her hands in feeling for him. At first he had said he couldn't do this, that he would be afraid of weeping. Then, abruptly, he had changed his mind. 'Pulled myself together,' he'd said to her. She knew how hard this was going to be.

'The lesson is from the Gospel of St Luke Chapter Ten. "A certain man went down from Jerusalem to Jericho, and fell among thieves . . ."'

His voice became stronger as he read on through the parable of the Good Samaritan, so that at the end it sounded clear and proud and vibrant through the building. As he went back to his pew he paused beside the coffin and bowed his head.

'Let us pray.'

Emma took Nathan's hand and held it pressed between both of her own to still the shaking.

KARIN McCAFFERTY felt tired. She had almost stayed at home, urged by Mike not to push herself to come. Mike, who was terrified for her, terrified for himself, helpless in the face of what he now saw as her death sentence. He had not believed in the way she had taken, nor understood her reasons. Now, when he seemed to be right—when everyone seemed to be right but her—he found excuses to go away so that he did not have to watch her worsen and become weaker.

But I am not worse, she said now, as they stood for the last hymn, I know. I know. For weeks past she had felt herself shielded, cocooned within the circle of some strong protective force. Slowly, she was being healed and strengthened. She was not in the least afraid.

The moment she had heard what had happened, Karin had closed the door in her mind that led to the room in which she had lain on a couch with Aidan Sharpe leaning over her, closed it, locked it. She could not begin to understand. Better simply to leave it alone.

SIMON SERRAILLER stood in the pulpit. He had a sheet of notes on the lectern in front of him and did not refer to it once.

'We are here to say goodbye to Freya Graffham, daughter, sister and aunt, colleague and friend, and to honour her, and I know this is one of the hardest things any of us will ever have to do. Freya was with us in Lafferton CID for a short time but few people have made such an impressive mark or endeared themselves to us so strongly.'

Cat's eyes did not leave her brother's face. He brought Freya to life again, captured something of her vibrancy. He spoke bitterly about the circumstances of her death, regretted the waste and the evil, praised the bravery of his colleagues, reminded them of the risks run by police officers every day, asked them for their support and prayers for the living, even as they honoured one who was dead. It was a passionate address and it moved the congregation once more to tears.

Then the commendation and the blessing. Suddenly, Cat's mind went to Aidan Sharpe; he was vivid before her, smug, unrepentant, smiling. It seemed that she looked evil full in the face.

The six police bearers, including Simon and Nathan Coates, stepped forward and shouldered Freya's coffin.

God help us, Cat thought, looking intently at the pale wood, at the single wreath of white roses and freesias lying on top, and the solemn faces of the bearers. She bent her head as they went past.

THE POLICE GUARD of honour lined the cathedral path as the coffin was carried down to the hearse, and as the car moved off Nathan Coates wept without restraint in Emma's arms.

Gradually the area cleared. The senior officers had left first. Lafferton Police Station was open for anyone from the congregation to sign a book of condolence in Freya Graffham's memory.

'Sir.'

Simon looked round. 'Nathan.'

'That was everything . . . what you said.'

'Thank you.'

'I don't believe it, though. I don't believe that was her we just carried. I can't get my head round it.'

'No.'

'Nathan . . .' Emma prompted gently.

Nathan wiped his eyes. 'Yeah, I know. It's only that we're getting married, guv. We was going to wait, have a proper do, but we can't. Not now. We're going to the registry office Thursday morning, early. Just us and one of my brothers and Emma's mum and dad. Only . . .'

'Would you be one of our witnesses?' Emma finished for him.

'I'd be absolutely delighted.'

'Thanks. Thanks a lot. See you back at the station then.'

They went off, getting a lift with another of the CID.

But Simon had told his driver not to wait. As the last few people left and he heard the choirboys coming out of the side door of the cathedral, he turned and went back into the great building.

The air was still vibrant with the service, the notes of the organ, the voices, the prayers still hung suspended there. He walked slowly up the side aisle and looked at the space at the foot of the chancel where Freya's coffin had stood. Freya. He could not picture her and he did not know for now what he felt or thought. It would come. He was a man who let such things fall as they would.

There was an abrupt squeak from the organ. Simon glanced up. The organist closed the cover and switched off the light above.

Outside, the sun had almost slipped off the great west door.

Simon walked quickly out into the close towards his own building. He would not go back to the station. Let them think what they would. For the rest of the day he could face no one at all.

In his flat, he threw his jacket onto the sofa, then went into the kitchen and poured himself a whisky and water. It was cool here, cool and peaceful. The cathedral clock struck four.

After a moment, seeing the light blinking on his answerphone, he leaned over and clicked it on.

The voice was both warm and businesslike. 'It's Diana. Haven't spoken for a bit. Miss you. Give me a call back?'

It was the only message.

Simon paused for a second, before pressing the button to erase it.

SUSAN HILL

It is impossible to pigeonhole Susan Hill's writings within a particular genre. During her career, she has successfully tackled literary fiction, a memoir, children's books, nonfiction, plays and even a short stint writing for the BBC radio series, *The Archers*. Asked if there is any genre she wouldn't attempt the author says, 'Science fiction. Intergalactic things do not interest me.'

Hill wrote her first novel while still at school. Called *The Enclosure*, it was about a middle-aged couple—an unusual subject for one so young. She explains: 'When you're young, the world of adults is intriguing and I was trying to work out what it was all about.' Published when she was nineteen, and studying English at King's College, London, the novel marked the start of a career that has brought her numerous literary prizes, including the Whitbread and the Somerset Maugham awards. She has also had the accolade of having some of her books, including *I'm The King of the Castle* and *Strange Meeting*, used as set texts in schools.

Susan Hill's gothic ghost story, *The Woman in Black,* has been adapted for the theatre by playwright Stephen Mallatratt and the play has kept London theatre audiences spellbound since it opened in 1989. She is pleased with the adaptation and says, 'I have seen it times without number and it never fails to chill me.'

The Various Haunts of Men is the author's first crime novel and the first of a trilogy featuring the enigmatic Detective Chief Inspector Simon Serrailler. 'They are crime novels rather than detective stories because simple puzzles and whodunnits don't interest me,' she says. 'I want to dissect what makes people commit evil deeds, what the difference is between madness and badness, how good versus evil—the old battle—plays itself out in one person, in a community, and in modern policing and law.' She is already at work on the second book and says, 'I am loving writing these. I write them fast.'

Married to the Shakespearean scholar Stanley Wells, Susan Hill has two daughters and lives in a Gloucestershire farmhouse, from where she runs her own small publishing company, Long Barn Books.

1

Tom Broadbent turned the last corner of the winding drive and found his two brothers already waiting at the great iron gates of the Broadbent compound. Philip, irritated, was knocking the dottle out of his pipe on one of the gateposts while Vernon gave the buzzer a couple of vigorous presses. The house stood beyond them, silent and dark, rising from the top of the hill like some pasha's palace, its clerestories, chimneys and towers gilded in the rich afternoon light of Santa Fe, New Mexico.

'It's not like Father to be late,' said Philip. He looked pretty much the same, Tom thought: briar pipe, sardonic eye, cheeks well shaved and aftershaved, hair brushed straight back from a tall brow, gold watch winking at the wrist, dressed in grey worsted slacks and navy jacket. His English accent seemed to have got a shade plummier.

Vernon, on the other hand, in his gaucho pants, sandals, long hair and beard, looked like Jesus Christ. 'He's playing another one of his games with us,' he said, pressing the buzzer again.

The smell of Philip's tobacco drifted on the air. He turned to Tom. 'And how are things, Tom, out there among the Indians?'

'Fine. And with you?'

'Terrific. Couldn't be better.'

'Vernon?' Tom asked.

'Everything's fine. Just great.'

The conversation faltered. Tom never had much to say to his brothers. After a long moment Philip gave the buzzer a fresh series of jabs and scowled through the wrought iron, grasping the bars. There was a creaking sound as the gate opened slightly under his weight.

'The gate's unlocked,' Philip said in surprise. 'He *never* leaves the gate unlocked.'

They put their shoulders to the heavy gate and swung it open. Vernon and Philip went back to get their cars and park them inside, while Tom walked in. He came face-to-face with the house—his childhood home. How many years since his last visit? Three? It filled him with conflicting sensations, the adult coming back to the scene of his childhood. It was a Santa Fe compound in the grandest sense. The gravelled driveway swept in a semicircle past a massive pair of seventeenth-century wooden doors. The house itself was a low adobe structure with curving walls, sculpted buttresses, real chimney pots— a work of sculptural art in itself. It was surrounded by cottonwood trees and an emerald lawn. Situated at the top of a hill, it had sweeping views of the mountains and high desert, the lights of town, and the summer thunderclouds rearing over the Jemez Mountains.

One of the garage doors was open and Tom saw his father's green Mercedes parked in the bay. He heard his brother's cars come crunching round the driveway, stopping by the portal. The doors slammed and they joined Tom in front of the house.

'What are we waiting for?' asked Philip, mounting the portal and striding up to the doors, giving the doorbell a firm series of presses.

There was nothing but silence.

Philip, always impatient, gave the bell a final stab. Tom could hear the deep chimes going off inside the house.

'Halloo!' Philip called through cupped hands.

Still nothing.

'Do you think he's all right?' Tom asked.

'Of course he's all right,' said Philip crossly. He pounded on the great Mexican door with a closed fist, booming and rattling it.

As Tom looked about, he saw that the garden had an unkempt look, the grass unmowed, new weeds sprouting in the tulip beds. 'I'm going to take a look in a window,' he said.

He forced his way through a hedge of trimmed chamisa, tiptoed through a flowerbed and peered in at the living-room window. Something was wrong, but it took him a moment to realise just what. The room seemed normal: same leather sofas and wing chairs, same coffee table. But above the stone fireplace there had been a painting and now it was gone. He racked his brains. Was it the Braque or the Monet? Then he noticed that the Roman bronze statue of a boy to the left of the fireplace was also gone. The bookshelves revealed holes where books had been taken out. Beyond the doorway to the hall he could see trash lying on the floor: crumpled paper, bubble wrap and a roll of packing tape.

'What's up, Doc?' Philip's voice came floating round the corner.

'You'd better have a look.'

Philip picked his way through the bushes, a look of annoyance screwed into his face. Vernon followed.

Philip peeked through the window and gasped. 'The Lippi,' he said. 'Over the sofa. The Lippi's gone! And the Braque over the fireplace! He's taken it all away! He's sold it!'

Vernon spoke. 'Philip, don't get excited. He probably just packed the stuff up. Maybe he's moving. You've been telling him for years this house was too big and isolated.'

Philip's face relaxed abruptly. 'Yes. Of course.'

'That must be what this mysterious meeting's about,' Vernon said.

Philip nodded. 'You're right. Of course they've been packing. But what a mess they've made. When Father sees this he'll have a fit.'

A troubled feeling began to gather in the pit of Tom's stomach. If their father was moving, it was a strange way to go about it.

'I'm going to break in,' he said.

Philip took his pipe out of his mouth. 'The alarm.'

'The hell with the alarm.'

Tom went round to the back of the house, his brothers following. He climbed over a wall into a small enclosed garden. There was a bedroom window at eye level. Tom wrestled a stone out of the raised flowerbed wall. He took it to the window, lifted it to his shoulder and sent it crashing through the window. As the tinkling of glass subsided they all waited, listening.

Silence.

'No alarm,' said Philip. He stared through the broken window and Tom could see a sudden thought blooming on his face. Philip cursed, and in a flash had vaulted through the window frame—pipe and all.

Vernon looked at Tom. 'What's with him?'

Without answering, Tom climbed through the window frame. Vernon followed.

The bedroom was like the rest of the house—stripped of all art. It was a mess: dirty footprints on the carpet, trash, strips of packing tape, bubble wrap and packing popcorn. Tom went to the hall. The view disclosed more bare walls where he remembered a Picasso, another Braque and a pair of Mayan stelae. Gone, all gone.

He ventured down the hall to the living room. Philip was standing in the middle of the room, his face absolutely white.

'I told him this would happen. He was so bloody careless, keeping all this stuff here. So damn bloody careless.'

'What?' Vernon cried, alarmed. 'What's happened, Philip?'

Philip's voice was barely above a whisper. 'We've been robbed!'

DETECTIVE LIEUTENANT Hutch Barnaby of the Santa Fe Police Department kicked back in his chair and raised a fresh cup of Starbucks to his lips. The aroma of the bitter roast filled his nose as he looked out of the window at the beautiful spring day. Except for the faint ringing of a phone in the outer office, life was good.

He heard, at the edges of consciousness, the competent voice of Doreen answering the phone. Her crisp vowels floated in through the open door: 'Hold on, excuse me, could you speak a little slower? I'll get you the sergeant—'

Barnaby drowned out the conversation with a noisy sip of coffee and extended his foot to his office door, giving it a little nudge shut. Blessed silence returned. He waited. And then it came: the knock.

Damn that phone call.

Barnaby rose slightly from his slouched position. 'Yes?'

Sergeant Harry Fenton opened the door, a keen look on his face. 'Hutch? The Broadbent place was robbed. I got one of the sons on the phone.'

Hutch Barnaby didn't move a muscle. 'Robbed of what?'

'Everything.' Fenton's black eyes glittered with relish.

Barnaby lowered his chair to the floor with a small clunk. *Damn.*

As Barnaby and Fenton drove out on the Old Santa Fe Trail, Fenton talked about the robbery. The collection, he'd heard, was worth half a billion. If the truth were anything close to that, Fenton said, it would be on the front page of the *New York Times*.

Barnaby stopped at the end of the winding driveway that led up to the Broadbent eyrie. As they walked up the road, he scanned the ground. He could see the blurred tracks of a truck, coming and going. They had come in bold as brass. So either Broadbent was away or they had killed him—more likely the latter.

The road went round a corner and levelled out, and a pair of open gates came into view. He paused to examine them. They were mechanical gates powered by two motors. The electrical box was open and inside he could see a key.

He turned to Fenton. 'What do you make of that?'

'Drove a truck up here, had a key to the gate—these guys were professional. We'll probably find Broadbent's cadaver in the house.'

'That's why I like you, Fenton. You're my second brain.'

He heard a shout and glanced up to see three men crossing the lawn, coming towards him. The sons, walking right across the lawn.

Barnaby scowled. 'Jesus! Don't you know this is a crime scene!'

The others halted, but the lead character, a tall man in a suit, kept coming. 'And who might you be?' His voice was cool, supercilious.

'I'm Detective Lieutenant Hutchinson Barnaby,' he said, 'and this is Sergeant Fenton. Santa Fe Police Department. You the sons?'

'We are,' said the suit.

Barnaby took a moment to look them over as potential suspects. The hippie had an honest, open face; maybe not the brightest bulb in the store but no robber. The one in cowboy boots had real horse shit on the boots, Barnaby noted with respect. And then there was the guy in the suit, who looked like he was from New York. As far as Barnaby was concerned, anyone from New York was a potential murderer.

'This is a crime scene, so I'm going to have to ask you gentlemen to leave the premises. Go out through the gate and wait for me. I'll be out in about twenty minutes to talk to you. OK?'

As Barnaby walked towards the house he told himself that he had better be careful—there was going to be a lot of second-guessing on this one. The Feds, Interpol, God knows who else would be involved. He figured a quick look round before the crime-lab people arrived would be in order. He looked at the broken window, the confusion of footsteps on the gravel, the trampled shrubbery. The fresh tracks were the sons', but there were a lot of older traces here as well. He could see where the moving van had parked, where it had backed round. It looked as if a week or two had passed since the robbery.

He stepped inside the house. He looked at the packing tape, bubble wrap, nails, discarded pieces of wood. There was sawdust on the rug and faint depressions. They had actually set up a table saw. It had been an exceptionally competent piece of work. Noisy, too. He sniffed the air. No sweet-and-sour-pork smell of a stiff.

Inside, the robbery felt as old as it did outside. Clots of mud tracked in by a boot were dry. Barnaby thought back: last rainfall was two weeks ago today. That's when it had happened; within twenty-four hours of the rain, when the ground was still muddy.

He wandered down the hall. There were pedestals with bronze labels where statues had once stood. There were faint rectangles with hooks on the walls where paintings had once been. There were straw rings and iron stands where antique pots had once sat, and empty shelves with dust holes where treasures had once stood. There were dark slots on the bookshelves where books had been removed.

He reached the bedroom door and looked at the parade of dirty footprints coming and going. More dried mud. Christ, there must have been half a dozen of them. This was a big moving job, and it would have taken a day at least, maybe two. Someone must have seen the activity up here, the house ablaze all night long, the truck headlights winding down the hill. The house, sitting on its mountaintop, was visible to all Santa Fe.

A shrink-wrapping machine sat inside the bedroom. He found stacks of timber, rolls of felt, metal strapping tape, bolts and wing nuts, and a couple of power saws. Couple of thousand dollars' worth of abandoned equipment. In the living room they'd left a $10,000 television, along with a VCR, DVD and two computers. Barnaby carefully stepped over a videotape cassette lying on the floor.

He moved swiftly and methodically through the rooms. Every one had been hit. In one room a bunch of boxes had been unpacked and paper lay scattered on the floor. He picked up a piece: some kind of bill of lading, dated a month ago, for $24,000 worth of French pots and pans, Japanese knives. Was the guy starting a restaurant?

Back in the bedroom, in a walk-in closet, he found a huge steel door, partway open. Without touching the door he slipped inside. The vault was empty, save some scattered trash and a bunch of wooden map cases. Slipping out his handkerchief, he used it to open a drawer. The velvet bore indentations where objects had once nested. He slid it shut and turned to the door itself. As with the locked cases he'd seen in the other rooms, there were no signs of a forced entry.

'The perps had all the codes and keys,' said Fenton.

Barnaby nodded. This was no robbery.

HE FOUND THE SONS standing in the shade of a piñon tree. As Barnaby approached, the guy in the suit asked, 'Did you find anything?'

'Like what?'

The man scowled. 'Do you have any idea what's been stolen here? We're talking hundreds of millions. Good God, how could anyone expect to get away with this? Some of these are *world-famous* works of art. There's a Filippo Lippi worth forty million dollars alone. You've got to call the FBI, contact Interpol, shut down the airports—'

'Lieutenant Barnaby has some questions,' said Fenton, in a voice with an undercurrent of menace. 'State your names, please.'

The one with the cowboy boots stepped forward. 'I'm Tom Broadbent and these are my brothers, Vernon and Philip.'

'Look, officer,' the one named Philip said, 'no offence, but I *really* don't think the Santa Fe Police Department is equipped to handle this.'

Barnaby checked his watch. He still had thirty minutes before the crime-lab truck arrived from Albuquerque. 'May I ask a few questions, Philip? OK if I use first names here?'

'Fine, fine, just get on with it.'

'Ages?'

'I'm thirty-three,' Tom said.

'Thirty-five,' said Vernon.

'Thirty-seven,' said Philip.

'Tell me, how is it that all three of you just happened to be here at once?' He directed his gaze towards the New Age type, Vernon, the one who looked like the least competent liar.

'Our father sent us a letter.'

'What about?'

'Well . . .' Vernon glanced at his brothers nervously. 'He didn't say.'

'Any guesses?'

'Not really.'

Barnaby switched his gaze to Tom. He found he liked Tom's face. It was a no-bullshit face. 'So, Tom, you want to help me out here?'

'I think it was to talk to us about our inheritance.'

'Inheritance? How old was your father?'

'Sixty.'

Fenton leaned forward to interrupt, his voice harsh. 'Was he *sick*?'

'He was dying of cancer,' said Tom coldly.

'I'm sorry,' said Barnaby. 'Any of you got your copy of the letter?'

All three produced the same letter, handwritten, on ivory laid paper. Barnaby took one and read:

Dear Tom,

I want you to come to my house in Santa Fe, on April 15, at exactly 1.00 p.m. regarding a very important matter affecting your future. I've asked Philip and Vernon as well. Do your old man this one last courtesy.

Father

'Any chance of a recovery from the cancer?' Fenton asked.

'None, as I understand it,' Philip said. 'He had gone through radiation treatment and chemotherapy, but the cancer had metastasised and there was no getting rid of it. He declined further treatment.'

Fenton thrust his head forward. 'How long did he have to live?'

'About six months.'

'So he invited you here for what? To do a little eeny meeny miny mo with his stuff?'

Philip said icily, 'I suppose that's possible.'

Barnaby broke in smoothly. 'But with a collection like this, Philip, wouldn't he have made arrangements to leave it to a museum?'

'Maxwell Broadbent *loathed* museums.'

'Why?'

'Museums had taken the lead in criticising our father's somewhat unorthodox collecting practices.'

'Which were?'

'Buying artwork of dubious provenance, dealing with tomb robbers and looters, smuggling antiquities across borders. He even robbed tombs himself.'

'So he planned to leave it all to you three?'

There was an awkward silence. 'That,' said Philip finally, 'was the assumption.'

Fenton broke in. 'Church? Wife? Girlfriend?'

Philip removed the pipe from between his teeth and answered in imitation of Fenton's clipped style: 'Atheist. Divorced. Misogynist.'

Barnaby held out the bill of lading for the shipment of cookware. 'Any idea what this is all about or where the stuff might have gone?'

They examined it, shook their heads and handed it back. 'He didn't even like to cook,' said Tom.

Barnaby shoved the document into his pocket. 'Tell me about your father. Looks, personality, character . . .'

It was Tom who spoke. 'He's one of a kind . . . a giant of a man, six foot five, fit, handsome, broad shoulders, white hair and beard. People say he looks like Hemingway. He's the kind of man who's never wrong, who rides roughshod over everyone and gets everything he wants.'

'You say he was divorced from your mother?'

'You mean our *mothers*? He was divorced from two of them, widowed by the third. There were also two other wives he didn't breed with and any number of girlfriends.'

'Any fights over alimony?' Fenton asked.

'Naturally,' said Philip. 'Alimony, palimony, it never ended.'

'But he raised you kids himself?'

Philip paused, then said, 'In his own unique way, yes.'

'Any woman in his life now?'

'Only for purposes of mild physical activity in the evening,' said Philip. 'She will get nothing, I assure you.'

Tom broke in. 'Do you think our father is OK?'

'To be honest, I haven't seen any evidence of a murder here.'

'Could they have kidnapped him?'

Barnaby shook his head. 'Not likely. Why deal with a hostage?' He glanced at his watch. Five, maybe seven minutes left before the scene-of-crime boys would be here. Time to ask the question. 'Insured?' He made it sound as casual as possible.

A dark look passed over Philip's face. 'No.'

Even Barnaby couldn't hide his surprise. '*No?*'

'Last year I tried to arrange for insurance. No one would cover the collection as long as it was kept in this house with this security environment. You can see for yourself how vulnerable the place is.'

'Why didn't your father upgrade his security?'

'Our father was a very difficult man. No one could tell him what to do. He had a lot of guns in the house. I guess he thought he could fight 'em off, Wild West style.'

Barnaby was disturbed. He was sure it wasn't a simple robbery, but without insurance, why rob yourself?

'What was in the vault?' he asked.

Philip dabbed at his sweating face with a trembling hand. 'It held gemstones, jewellery, South and Central American gold, rare coins and stamps, all extremely valuable.'

'The burglars seem to have had the combination to the vault as well as keys to everything. Did your father have anyone he trusted— a lawyer, for example—who might have kept a second set of keys or had the combination to the vault?'

'He trusted nobody.'

'Did he have a maid?'

'He had a woman who came daily.'

'Gardener?'

'A full-time man.'

'Any others?'

'He employed a full-time cook and a nurse who looked in three days a week.'

Barnaby asked, 'Where are they now? This robbery took place two weeks ago. Somebody dismissed the help.'

Tom said, 'The robbery occurred *two weeks ago*?'

'That's right.'

'But I only got my letter by Federal Express three days ago.'

This was interesting. 'Did you notice the sender's address?'

'It was some kind of drop-shipping place, like Mail Boxes Etc.'

Barnaby looked at Tom for a long time, and then he looked at the other two brothers. If it wasn't insurance fraud, then what was it? This was no damn robbery. A crazy idea began to form, still vague. A truly nutty idea. But it was starting to take shape almost against his will, assembling itself into something like a theory.

Barnaby then remembered the big-screen television, the VCR, and the videotape lying on the floor. No, not lying: *placed* on the floor, next to the remote. What was the hand-lettered title? WATCH ME.

That was it! Like water freezing, it all locked into place. He knew what had happened. Barnaby cleared his throat. 'Come with me.'

The sons followed him back into the house, into the living room.

'What's this all about?' Philip was getting agitated.

Barnaby picked up the tape and the remote. 'We're going to watch a video.' He flicked on the TV set and slid the tape into the VCR.

'Is this some kind of joke?' Philip asked, his face flushed.

A burst of sound from the video silenced Philip, and then the face of Maxwell Broadbent, larger than life, materialised on the screen.

His voice, deep and booming, reverberated in the empty room.

'Greetings from the dead.'

TOM BROADBENT STARED at the life-size image of his father on the screen. The camera panned back, revealing Maxwell Broadbent standing in front of the giant desk in his study. The room had not yet been stripped; the Lippi painting of the Madonna was still on the wall behind him, the bookshelves were still filled with books, and the other paintings and statues were all in their places.

His father's enormous presence filled the screen and, by extension, the room where they were sitting. He paced in front of the camera, agitated, stroking his close-cropped beard. 'When I was young, I had nothing. I came to New York from Erie, Pennsylvania, with just thirty-five dollars and my father's old suit. Dad was a good man, but he was a bricklayer. Mom was dead. I was pretty much alone in the world.'

'Not *this* story again,' moaned Philip.

'It was the fall of 1963. I pounded the streets until I found a job washing dishes at Mama Gina's on East 88th and Lex. Gina's wasn't far from the Metropolitan Museum of Art. I went in there one day on a whim, and it changed my life. I began going to that museum every day. I fell in love with the place. I'd never seen such beauty'—he waved his large hand—'Christ, but you know all this.'

'We certainly do,' said Philip dryly.

'The point is, I started with nothing. I worked hard. I had a vision for my life, a goal. I dreamed of finding a lost city, of digging up treasures, owning them. I saved until I had enough to go to Central America. I went there not because I wanted to make money—though that was part of it, I'll admit—but because I had a passion. And I found my lost city. That got me started. I dealt in art and antiquities only as a way to finance my collecting. And look'—he gestured open-palmed to the unseen collection in the house around him—'here's the result. One of the greatest private collections of art and antiquities in the world. These aren't just things. Every piece in here has a story, a memory for me. How I first saw it, how I fell in love with it, how I acquired it. Each piece is part of me.'

He seized a jade object on his desk and held it towards the camera. 'Like this Olmec head, which I found in a tomb in Piedra Lumbre. I remember the day . . . the heat, the snakes . . . and I remember seeing it for the first time, lying there in the dust of the tomb, where it had been for two thousand years.' He put the piece back down. 'For two thousand years it had rested there—an object of such exquisite beauty it makes you want to cry. It wasn't created to vegetate in the darkness. I rescued it and brought it back to life.'

His voice cracked with emotion, then he leaned forward. 'As I've watched you three grow up, I've been dismayed to see in you a feeling of entitlement. Privilege. A rich-kid's syndrome. A feeling that you don't have to work too hard, study too hard, exert yourselves—because you're the sons of Maxwell Broadbent. Because someday, without lifting a goddamn finger, you'll be rich.'

'Bullshit,' said Vernon angrily.

'Philip, you're an assistant professor of art history at a junior college on Long Island. Tom, a horse vet in Utah. And Vernon . . . I don't know what you're doing now, probably living in some ashram giving your money to a fraudulent guru.'

'Not true!' said Vernon. 'Go to hell!'

'And on top of that,' their father went on, 'you three don't get along. You never learned to cooperate, to be brothers. I started to think: What kind of father have I been? Have I taught my sons independence? Have I taught them the value of work? Have I taught them self-reliance? Have I taught them to take care of each other?' He paused and fairly shouted out, 'No! After everything—the schools, Europe, the camping trips—I've raised three quasi-failures. It's my fault it ended up this way, but there it is. And then I found out I was dying, and that put me in a panic. How was I going to fix things?'

He paused again. He was breathing hard and his face was flushed. 'I had to figure out what to do with my collection. I wasn't going to give it to a museum or university. And I wasn't going to let some auction house or dealer get rich from all my hard work. I had always planned to leave it to you. But when it came down to it, I realised it would be the very worst thing I could do to you. No way was I going to hand over to you half a billion dollars that you hadn't earned. And then it came to me. It was brilliant! All my life I'd been excavating tombs and dealing in grave goods. I knew all the tricks for hiding tombs, every booby trap, everything. I suddenly realised that I, too, could take it with me. And then I could do something for you that would really be a legacy.'

He leaned forward again. 'You're going to earn this money. I've arranged to bury myself and my collection in a tomb somewhere in the world. I challenge you to find me. If you do, you can rob my tomb and have it all. That's my challenge to you, my three sons.'

He walked over to the camera. His arm reached out to turn it off, and then, as an afterthought, he paused, his blurry face looming gigantically on the screen: 'I've never been much on sentiment, so I'll just say to you, goodbye. Goodbye, Philip, Vernon and Tom. Goodbye and good luck. I love you.'

The screen went dead.

HUTCH BARNABY ROSE and coughed by way of breaking the shocked silence. 'Fenton? Seems we're not needed here any longer.'

Fenton nodded, rising awkwardly, actually blushing.

Barnaby turned to the brothers. 'As you can see, this isn't a police matter. We'll leave you to, ah, sort things out on your own.' They began edging towards the door archway that led to the hall.

Philip rose. 'Officer Barnaby?' His voice was half choked. 'I trust you won't mention this to anybody. It wouldn't be helpful if . . . if the whole world started looking for the tomb.'

'Good point. No reason to mention it to anyone. I'll call off the SOC boys.' He backed out and disappeared. A moment later they heard the great front door of the house clanking shut.

'The son of a bitch,' Philip said quietly. 'I can't believe it.'

Tom glanced at his brother's white face. He knew he'd been living rather well on his assistant professor's salary. He needed the money.

'What now?' Vernon asked.

Philip stared at him. 'We go and find the tomb, of course.'

'How?'

'A man can't bury himself with half a billion dollars of art without help. We find out who helped him.'

'I don't believe it,' Tom said. 'He never trusted anybody in his life.'

Philip slipped his pipe out of his trouser pocket and lit it with a shaking hand. 'I say we go talk to Marcus Hauser. He's the key.'

Vernon looked up. 'Hauser? Father hasn't been in contact with him in forty years.'

'He's the only one who really knew Father. They spent two years in Central America together. If anyone knows where Father went, it's him.'

'Father *hates* Hauser.'

'I expect they had a reconciliation, with Father sick and all. I'm telling you, Hauser's involved. We've got to move fast. I've got debts—I've got obligations.'

'Been spending your inheritance already?' Vernon muttered.

Philip turned to Vernon coolly. 'Who was it took twenty grand from Father just last year?'

'That was a loan. I'll pay it back.'

'Of course you will,' said Philip sarcastically.

Vernon coloured. 'What about the forty thousand that Father spent on sending you to graduate school? Have you paid that back yet?'

'That was a gift. He paid for Tom's vet school, too—right, Tom? And if *you* had gone to graduate school, Vernon, he would have paid for yours. Instead, you went and lived with that swami in India.'

'Go to hell,' said Vernon.

Tom looked from one brother to the other. It was happening, just as it had happened a thousand times before. Usually he stepped in and tried to be peacemaker. Just as often it did no good.

'The hell with you, too,' Philip said. He put the pipe between his teeth with a click, turned on his heels and left.

2

The building wasn't an old brownstone as it would have been in a Bogart film, but a glass and steel monstrosity that teetered into the sky above West Fifty-seventh Street: an ugly eighties skyscraper. At least, thought Philip, the rent would be high. And that meant Marcus Aurelius Hauser was a successful private investigator.

An elevator whisked him up to the thirtieth floor, and he was soon at the cherry doors leading into the offices of Marcus Hauser, PI.

Philip paused inside the doorway. The room appeared empty.

'Yeah?' came a voice from behind a half-moon wall of glass bricks.

Philip walked round and found himself staring at the back of a man sitting at a vast kidney-shaped desk, which instead of facing the door to his office faced a wall of windows that looked over the Hudson River. Without turning, the man gestured towards an armchair. Philip crossed the floor, seated himself and settled in to study Marcus Hauser: ex-Vietnam Green Beret; ex-tomb robber; ex-lieutenant, Bureau of Alcohol, Tobacco and Firearms, Manhattan field office.

In his father's photo albums Philip had seen pictures of Hauser as a young man, dressed in jungle khakis, packing some kind of firearm on his hip. He felt disconcerted finally seeing him in the flesh. He looked smaller than Philip had imagined and he was overdressed in a brown suit with collar pin, waistcoat, gold chain and watch fob. There was the scent of cologne about him, and what little hair he had was excessively pomaded and curled. Gold rings winked on no fewer than four of his fingers. His hands had been manicured, his nails cleaned and polished. Philip found himself wondering if this was the same Marcus Hauser who had tramped through the jungles with his father in search of lost cities and ancient tombs.

He cleared his throat. 'Mr Hauser?'

'Marcus,' came the rapid reply, like a cracking good tennis volley. His voice was equally disconcerting: high, nasal, working-class accent. His eyes, however, were as green and cool as a crocodile's.

Philip recrossed his legs and, without asking permission, took out his pipe and began to fill it. Hauser smiled, slid open his desk drawer, pulled out a humidor and removed an enormous Churchill. 'So glad you smoke,' he said, rolling the cigar between his fingers, sliding a gold monogrammed clipper out of his pocket and giving the end a snip. When he had lit up, he leaned back in his chair and said, 'What can I do for the son of my old partner, Maxwell Broadbent?'

'May we speak in confidentiality?'

'Naturally.'

'Six months ago my father was diagnosed with cancer.' Philip observed Hauser's face to see if he had already known. But Hauser's face was as opaque as his mahogany desk. 'Lung cancer,' Philip continued. 'They gave him six months to live, and that was three months ago.' Philip paused. 'Has he been in touch with you?'

Hauser shook his head, took another puff. 'Not for forty years.'

'Last month,' Philip said, 'my father disappeared, along with his collection. He left us a video. It was a last will and testament of sorts. In it, he said he was taking his collection with him to the grave.'

'He did *what*?' Hauser leaned forward, suddenly interested. The mask had fallen for a moment: he was genuinely astonished.

'He took it with him. Everything. Just like a pharaoh. He has buried himself in a tomb somewhere in the world and has issued us with a challenge. If we find the tomb, we can rob it. That, you see, is his idea of making us earn our inheritance.'

Hauser leaned back and laughed long and loud. 'Only Max could come up with a scheme like that.'

'So you don't know anything about this?' Philip asked.

'Nothing.' Hauser seemed to be telling the truth.

'You grew up with Max. You spent a year with him in the jungle. You know him and how he worked better than anyone. I wondered if you'd be willing, as a PI, to help me find his tomb?'

'Are you working with your brothers?'

'Half-brothers. No. I've decided to find this tomb on my own. I'll share what I find with them, of course.'

'Tell me about them.'

'Tom's the youngest. When we were children, he was the kid who'd be the first to jump off the cliff into the water, the first to throw the rock at the wasp's nest. Got kicked out of a couple of schools but cleaned up his act in college and has been on the straight and narrow ever since.'

'And the other one?'

'Vernon. Right now he's in some cult. He was always the lost one. He's tried it all: drugs, gurus, encounter groups. He flunked out of college and hasn't been able to hold down a steady job. He was a sweet kid, but he's . . . *incompetent* at adulthood.'

'What are they doing now?'

'Tom went home to his ranch in Utah. The last I heard he had given up on searching for the tomb. Vernon says he's going to find the tomb on his own, doesn't want me to be part of it.'

'Anyone else know about this besides your two brothers?'

'There were two cops in Santa Fe who saw the videotape and know the whole story.'

'Names?'

'Barnaby and Fenton.'

Hauser made a note. A light on the phone blinked once and he picked up the receiver. He listened for a long time, spoke softly and rapidly, made a call and then another. Philip felt annoyed that Hauser was doing other business in front of him, wasting his time.

Hauser hung up. 'Well now, Philip, what do you know about me?'

'Only that you were my father's partner in exploration. And that you two had a falling-out.'

'That's right. We spent almost two years in Central America together, looking for Mayan tombs to excavate. This was back in the early sixties when it was more or less legal. We found a few things, but it was only after I left that Max made his big strike and became rich. I went on to Vietnam.'

'And the falling-out? Father never talked about it.'

There was a faint pause. 'I can hardly remember it now. You know how it is when two people are thrown together for a long stretch of time, they get on each other's nerves.'

The phone blinked and Hauser picked it up. Philip rose. 'I'll come back when you're less busy,' he said curtly.

Hauser wagged a gold-ringed finger at Philip to wait, listened for a minute, and then hung up. 'So tell me, Philip. What's so special about Honduras?'

'Honduras? What's that got to do with anything?'

'Because that's where Max went.'

Philip stared at him. 'So you *were* in on it!'

Hauser smiled. 'Not at all. That was the substance of the phone call I just received. Almost four weeks ago today his pilot flew him and a planeload of cargo to a city in Honduras called San Pedro Sula. From there he took a military helicopter to a place called Brus Lagoon. And then he vanished.'

'You found all this out just now?'

'As soon as I talk to the pilot, I'll know a lot more. Like what kind of cargo the plane was carrying and how much it weighed. Your father didn't make any effort to cover his tracks going down to Honduras. Did you know he and I were there together? I'm not surprised that's where he went. It's a big country with the most inaccessible interior in the world—thick jungle, uninhabited, mountainous, cut by deep gorges and sealed off by the Mosquito Coast. That's where I expect he went—into the interior.' Hauser paused, then added: 'I'm taking the case.'

Philip didn't recall having offered Hauser the job yet. But the guy had already demonstrated his competence, and since he now knew the story, he would probably do. 'We haven't talked about a fee.'

'I'll need a retainer. I expect the expenses in this case are going to run high. Anytime you do business in a shitcan Third World country you have to pay off every Tomás, Rico and Orlando.'

'A retainer? Like how much?'

'Two hundred and fifty thousand dollars.'

'What makes you think I've got that kind of money?'

'I never *think* anything, Mr Broadbent. I know. Sell the Klee watercolour you own. I should be able to get you four hundred for it.'

Philip exploded. 'Sell it? Never. My father gave me that painting. And how did you know about it, anyway?'

Hauser smiled and opened the soft white palms of his hand. 'You do want to hire the best, don't you, Mr Broadbent?'

'Yes, but this is blackmail.'

'Let me explain how I work.' Hauser leaned forward. 'My first loyalty is to the case, not the client. When I take a case, I solve it, regardless of the consequences to the client. I keep the retainer. If I succeed, I get an additional fixed fee.'

'You can't expect me to sell that painting, Mr Hauser. It's the only thing I have of any value from my father. I love that painting.'

Philip found Hauser gazing at him in a way that made him feel odd. The man's eyes were vacant, his face emotionless. 'The painting is the sacrifice you need to make to recover your inheritance.'

Philip hesitated. 'You think we'll succeed?'

'I do.'

Philip gazed at him. He could always buy the painting back. 'All right, I'll sell the Klee.'

Hauser's eyes narrowed. 'If successful, my fee will be one million dollars.' Then he added, 'We don't have much time, Mr Broadbent. I've already booked us tickets to San Pedro Sula, leaving first thing next week.'

WHEN VERNON BROADBENT finished chanting, he opened his eyes, took a few deep breaths and rose, still cradling the fragile feeling of peace and serenity that the hour of meditation had given him. He went to the door and paused, looking out over the hills of Big Sur to the wide blue Pacific beyond. The wind off the ocean caught his robes and filled them with cool air.

He had been living at the Ashram for more than a year, and now, in his thirty-sixth year, he finally believed he had found the place he wanted to be. He had rejected the materialism of his childhood and for years had tried to find some deeper truth to his life. What else was the point of life, if not to find out *why*?

Now he had the chance, with this inheritance, to do some real good for the world. But how? Should he try to find the tomb on his own? Should he call Tom? He had to make a decision, and quickly.

He tucked up his linen robes and made his way down the path to the Teacher's hut—a sprawling redwood structure nestling among a stand of oaks. He knocked on the door. After a moment, a low, resonant voice called out from the depths of the compound: 'Come in.'

He removed his sandals on the verandah and stepped inside. The house was Japanese in style, simple and ascetic, with sliding screens of rice paper, floors covered with beige mats, and expanses of polished wood planking. The interior smelt of incense.

Vernon found the Teacher in his meditation room, sitting cross-legged on a mat, his eyes closed. He opened them but did not rise. Vernon stood, waiting respectfully. The Teacher's fit, handsome figure was draped in a simple robe of undyed linen. He was about sixty, with long grey hair, astute blue eyes and a trimmed salt-and-pepper beard. When he spoke his voice was soft and resonant, with a faint Brooklyn accent. Formerly a professor of philosophy at Berkeley, here at the Ashram he had founded a community devoted to prayer, meditation and spiritual growth. It was pleasantly nondenominational, loosely based on Buddhism. Under the Teacher's gentle guidance, each worshipped in his own way, at a cost of $700 per week, room and board included.

'Sit down,' the Teacher said.

Vernon sat.

'How can I help you?'

Vernon collected his thoughts and took a breath. He told the Teacher about his father's cancer, the inheritance, the challenge to find his tomb. When he had finished, there was silence. Vernon remembered the Teacher's many negative comments about the evil effects of money and wondered if he would tell him to forgo the inheritance.

'Let's have tea,' said the Teacher, his voice exceptionally tender, placing his hand on Vernon's elbow. They sat and he called for tea. When it arrived, they sipped in silence. Then the Teacher asked, 'How much is this inheritance worth?'

'After taxes, my share would probably be worth a hundred million.'

If this sum surprised the Teacher, he didn't show it, though his blue eyes were unusually bright. 'Few are given the opportunity that you have been given, Vernon. You must not let it pass you by.' He stood up and spoke with power and resonance. 'We need to recover that inheritance. We need to recover it now.'

BY THE TIME Tom had finished treating the sick horse, the sun was setting over Toh Atin Mesa, casting long golden shadows across the sagebrush and chamisa. Beyond rose up a 1,000-foot wall of sculpted sandstone, glowing red in the dying light. Tom gave the animal another quick lookover and turned to the Navajo girl—the horse's owner. 'He's going to make it. Just a touch of sand colic.'

She broke into a relieved smile.

'He's hungry. Lead him round the corral a few times and then give him a scoop of psyllium mixed in with his oats. Let him water afterwards. Wait half an hour, then give him some hay. He'll be fine.'

The Navajo grandmother—who had ridden five miles to the vet clinic to get him—took his hand. 'Thank you, Doctor.'

Tom gave a little bow. 'At your service.' He thought ahead to the ride back to Bluff with anticipation. The trail had taken him through some of the most beautiful red-rock country in the Southwest, through the Jurassic sandstone beds known as the Morrison Formation, rich with dinosaur fossils. There were a lot of remote canyons running up into Toh Atin Mesa. Someday, he thought, he'd take a little side trip up one of those canyons.

'What do we owe you, Doctor?' the grandmother asked.

Tom glanced around at the shabby tar-paper hogan, the broken-down car half sunk in tumbleweeds, the skinny sheep. 'Five dollars.'

The woman fished into her velveteen blouse and removed some soiled dollar bills, counting out five for him.

Tom had touched his hat and just turned to get his horse when he noticed a tiny cloud of dust on the horizon. A horse and rider were approaching fast from the direction he had come, the dark speck getting bigger in the great golden bowl of the desert. He wondered if it was Shane, his vet partner. It alarmed him. It would have to be one hell of an emergency for Shane to ride out there to get him.

As the figure materialised, he realised it wasn't Shane but a woman. And she was riding his horse Knock.

The woman trotted into the settlement, covered with dust from her journey, the horse lathered up and blowing. She stopped and swung down. She had been riding bareback across eight miles of desert. Totally crazy. And what was she doing with his best horse?

She strode towards him. 'I'm Sally Colorado,' she said. 'I tried to find you at your clinic, but your partner said you'd ridden out here.' She held out her hand. Tom, caught off-guard, took it. Her honey-coloured hair spilled down her shoulders over a white cotton shirt, now powdered with dust. The shirt was tucked into a pair of jeans at a slender waist. When she smiled it seemed her eyes changed colour from green to blue, so bright was the effect. She wore a pair of turquoise earrings, but the colour in her eyes was richer than the colour of the stone.

Tom realised he was still holding her hand, and released it.

'I just had to find you,' she said. 'I couldn't wait.'

'An emergency?'

'It's not a vet emergency, if that's what you mean.'

'Then what kind of emergency is it?'

'I'll tell you on the ride back.'

'I can't believe Shane let you take my best horse and ride it like that, without a saddle or bridle. You could have been killed!'

'Shane didn't give him to me.' The woman smiled.

'How did you get him, then?'

'I stole him.'

It took a moment of consternation before Tom could bring himself to laugh.

The sun had set by the time they headed north, riding together, back to Bluff. Tom finally said, 'All right. Let's hear what was so important that you had to steal a horse for it and risk your neck. I'm all ears, Miss . . . Colorado.'

'Call me Sally.'

'All right, Sally. Let's hear your story.' Tom found himself watching her ride with a feeling of pleasure. She looked like she'd been born on a horse.

'I'm an anthropologist,' Sally began. 'More specifically, I'm an ethnopharmacologist. I study indigenous medicine with Professor Julian Clyve at Yale. He's the man who cracked Mayan hieroglyphics a few years ago. A brilliant piece of work. It was in all the papers.'

'No doubt.' She had a sharp, clean profile, a small nose, and a funny way of sticking out her lower lip. She had a little dimple when she smiled, but only on one side of her mouth. She was an amazingly beautiful woman.

'Professor Clyve has assembled the largest collection of Mayan writing in existence, a library of every inscription known in ancient Mayan. It consists of rubbings from stone inscriptions, pages from Mayan codices and copies of inscriptions on pots and tablets.'

Tom could just see the doddering old pedagogue shuffling among his heaps of dusty manuscripts.

'The greatest of the Mayan inscriptions were contained in what we call codices. They were the original books of the Maya, written in glyphs on bark paper. The Spanish burned most of them as books of the devil, but a couple of incomplete codices managed to survive here and there. A complete Mayan codex has never been found. Last year, Professor Clyve found *this* in the back of a filing cabinet that belonged to one of his deceased colleagues.'

She drew a folded sheet of paper out of her breast pocket and handed it to him. Tom took it. It was an old, yellowing photocopy of a page of a manuscript written in hieroglyphics, with some drawings of leaves and flowers in the margins. It looked vaguely familiar.

'My Mayan reading skills are a little rusty. What does it say?'

'It describes the medicinal qualities of a certain plant found in the Central American rain forest.'

'What does it do? Cure cancer?'

Sally smiled. 'If only. The plant is called the *K'ik'-te*, or blood tree. This page describes how you boil the bark, add ashes as an alkali, and apply the paste as a poultice to a wound.'

'Interesting.' Tom handed the sheet back to her.

'It's more than interesting; it's medically correct. There's a mild antibiotic in the bark. That page comes from a Mayan codex of medicine written around AD 800. It contains two *thousand* medical prescriptions and preparations, not just from plants but from everything in the rain forest—insects, animals, even minerals. There may in fact be a cure for cancer in there, or at least some types of cancer. Professor Clyve asked me to locate the owner and see if I couldn't arrange for him to translate and publish the Codex. It's the only complete Mayan codex known. It would be a stunning cap to his already distinguished career.'

'And for yours, too, I imagine.'

'Yes. Here's a book that contains all the medicinal secrets of the rain forest, accumulated over centuries. We're talking about the richest rain forest in the world, with hundreds of thousands of species of plants and animals—many still unknown to science. The Maya knew every plant, every animal, everything in that rain forest. *And everything they knew went into this book*. Do you realise what this means?'

'Surely,' said Tom, 'medicine has advanced a long way from the ancient Maya.'

Sally Colorado snorted. 'Twenty-five percent of all our drugs originally came from plants. And yet, only one-half of one per cent of the world's two hundred and sixty-five thousand plant species have been evaluated for their medicinal properties. Think of the potential! Tom, this codex could be the greatest medical discovery ever.'

'I see your point.'

'When Professor Clyve and I translate and publish this codex, it will *revolutionise* medicine. And if that doesn't convince you, here's something else. The Central American rain forest is disappearing under the loggers' saw. This book will save it. The rain forest will suddenly be worth a lot more standing up than cut down. Drug companies will pay those countries billions in royalties.'

'No doubt keeping a tidy profit themselves. So what's this book got to do with me?'

A full moon was now rising over the Hobgoblin Rocks, painting them with silver. It was a lovely evening.

'The Codex belongs to your father.'

Tom stopped his horse and looked at her.

'Maxwell Broadbent stole it from a Mayan tomb almost forty years ago. He wrote to Yale asking for help in translating it. But Mayan script hadn't been cracked then. The man who got the letter assumed it was a fake and shoved it in a file without answering. Professor Clyve found it forty years later. He knew instantly that it was real. No one could fake Mayan script forty years ago for the simple reason that no one could read it. But Professor Clyve could read it. He's the only man on earth who can read Mayan script fluently. I've been trying to reach your father for weeks, but he seems to have dropped off the face of the earth. So finally, in desperation, I tracked you down.'

Tom stared at her in the gathering twilight, then he began to laugh.

'What's so funny?' she asked hotly.

Tom took a deep breath. 'Sally, I've got some bad news for you.'

WHEN HE HAD FINISHED telling her everything, there was a long silence.

At last Sally said, 'So what are you going to do about it?'

Tom sighed. 'Nothing.'

'Nothing? What do you mean, *nothing*? You're not giving up your inheritance, are you?'

Tom didn't answer at once. They had reached the top of the plateau, and they paused to look at the view. He could see the yellow cluster of lights of the town of Bluff and, at the edge of town, the buildings that made up his modest veterinary practice. To the left, the immense stone vertebrae of Comb Ridge rose up, ghostly bones in the moonlight. It reminded him all over again of why he had originally come to Bluff. Life with Maxwell Broadbent as a father had been impossible: a never-ending drama of exhortation, challenge, competition, criticism and instruction. He had come here to escape, to find peace, to leave all that behind. That, and of course Sarah.

'Yes,' he responded at last. 'I'm giving it up.'

'Why?'

'I'm not sure I can explain it. You'd have to understand my father. All my life, he tried to control everything my two brothers and I did. He had big plans for us. But no matter what I did, what any of us did, it was never good enough. We were never good enough for him. And now this. I'm not going to play his game any longer. Enough is enough.' He paused, wondering why he was telling her so much.

'Go on,' she said.

'He wanted me to become a doctor. I wanted to be a palaeontologist, to hunt for dinosaur fossils. Father thought that was ridiculous; "infantile" he called it. We compromised on vet school. Naturally, he expected me to go to Kentucky and look after million-dollar racehorses and maybe become an equine medical researcher, making great discoveries and putting the Broadbent name in the history books. Instead I came out here to the Navajo reservation. This is what I want to do; this is what I love doing. These horses need me and these people need me. And this landscape, southern Utah, is the most beautiful in the world, with some of the greatest Jurassic and Cretaceous fossil beds anywhere. But my father thought that I'd taken his money to go to vet school and cheated him by coming out here. To him it was a huge failure and disappointment.'

'And so that's it? You're just going to let the whole inheritance go, Codex and all?'

'That's right.'

He found Sally looking at him, her hair faintly luminous in the silvery light of the moon. 'How much are you giving up, if I may ask?'

He felt a twinge, not for the first time, at the sheer size of it. 'A hundred million, give or take.'

Sally whistled. 'You've got guts.'

He shrugged.

'And your brothers?'

'Philip's joined with my father's former partner to go and find the hidden tomb. Vernon's going it alone, I hear. Why don't you team up with one of them?'

'I already tried. Vernon left the country a week ago and Philip's also disappeared. They went to Honduras. You were my last choice.'

Tom shook his head. 'Honduras? That was fast. When they return with the loot, you can get the Codex from them.'

'I can't risk it. They have no idea what it is, what it's worth.

Anything could happen. At least give me a little help here, Tom. Come to Santa Fe with me. Perhaps you could introduce me to your father's friends, take me to see the police? Tell me about his travels, his habits? Give me two days. Help me do this. Just two days.'

'No.'

'Ever had a horse die on you?'

'All the time.'

'A horse you loved?'

Tom immediately thought of his own horse, Pedernal, who had died from an antibiotic-resistant strain of strangles. He would never again own a horse as beautiful.

'Would better drugs have saved it?' Sally asked.

Tom looked towards the distant lights of Bluff. Two days wasn't much and she did have a point. 'All right. You win. Two days.'

JIMMY MARTINEZ felt drained. The funeral had been long, the interment longer. He could still feel the grit of the dirt on his right hand. It was always hell when one of their own had to be buried, let alone two.

The buzzer rang and Doreen said, 'Two people to see, ah, Barnaby and Fenton.'

He sighed heavily. This was all he needed. 'Send them in.'

His partner, Willson, was looking up. 'You want me—?'

'You stay.'

They appeared in the doorway, a stunning blonde and a tall guy in cowboy boots. Martinez sat up, smoothed a hand over his head. 'Please sit down,' he said.

'We're here to see Lieutenant Barnaby, not—'

'I know who you're here to see. Please take a seat.'

They sat down, reluctantly.

'I'm Officer Martinez,' he said, addressing the blonde. 'May I ask what your business with Officer Barnaby is?'

'We'd prefer to deal directly with Officer Barnaby,' said the man.

'You can't.'

'Why not?' He flared up.

'He's dead.'

They stared back at him. 'How?'

'Automobile accident.' Martinez sighed. 'Perhaps if you told me who you were and how I could help you?'

The man spoke. 'I'm Tom Broadbent. About ten days ago Lieutenant Barnaby investigated a possible break-in at our house off the Old Santa Fe Trail. I wondered if he had filed a report?'

Martinez glanced over at Willson.

'He didn't file a report,' Willson said.

'Did he say anything?'

'He said it had been some kind of misunderstanding. That Mr Broadbent had moved some artworks and his sons had mistakenly assumed they had been stolen. As a crime hadn't been committed, there was no reason to open a file.'

'Can we talk to his partner, Fenton?'

'He also passed away in the accident.'

'What happened?'

'Car went off the Ski Basin Road at Nun's Corner.'

'I'm sorry.'

'So are we.'

'So there's no paperwork, nothing on the investigation up at the Broadbent house?'

'Nothing.'

There was a silence, then Martinez said, 'Is there anything else we can do for you folks?'

THE CAR HUMMED NORTH towards the Utah border, along a vast and lonely highway between endless prairies of sagebrush and chamisa. Shiprock towered in the distance, a dark thrust of stone in the blue sky. Tom, driving, felt relief that it was over. He had done what he promised: he had helped Sally find out where his father had gone. What she did next was up to her. He was now out of it.

He cast a surreptitious glance at her sitting in the passenger seat. She had been silent for the past hour. She hadn't said what her plans were and Tom wasn't sure he wanted to know.

'So he went to Honduras,' Sally said. 'But you still have no idea as to where?'

'I've told you all I know, Sally. Forty years ago he spent some time in Honduras with Marcus Hauser, looking for tombs. They got swindled, so I heard, buying a fake treasure map of some kind, and they spent months tramping through the jungle and nearly died. They had some kind of falling out and that was that.'

'Are you sure he didn't find anything?'

'That's what he always said. The mountains of southern Honduras were uninhabited.'

She nodded, eyes looking ahead at the empty desert.

'So what are you going to do?' Tom finally asked.

'I'm going to Honduras.'

'All by yourself?'

'Why not?'

Tom said nothing. He didn't need a complication like Sally Colorado in his life.What she did was her business.

Sally shook her heavy gold hair back from her head, unleashing a faint scent of shampoo. 'There's something bothering me. I just can't get it out of my head.'

'What's that?'

'Barnaby and Fenton. Doesn't it seem strange that right after they investigate your father's so-called robbery they come up dead? There's something about the timing of their "accident" I don't like.'

'I know the Ski Basin Road, Sally. Nun's Corner is a hellacious curve. They aren't the first ones to get killed there.'

'What were they doing on the Ski Basin Road? Ski season's over.'

Tom sighed. 'If you're so worried, why don't you call that policeman, Martinez, and find out?'

'I will.' Sally slipped her cellphone out of her bag and dialled. Tom listened while she was transferred to Martinez.

'This is Sally Colorado,' she said. 'Remember us?' Pause. 'I wanted to ask you a question about Barnaby and Fenton. Why did they go up to the ski basin?' A very long wait. 'Yes, it was tragic,' Sally said. 'And where were they about to go on this fishing trip?' A final silence. 'Thanks.'

Sally slowly shut the phone and looked at Tom. He felt a knot in his stomach; her face had gone pale.

'They went up to the ski basin to check on a report of vandalism. Turned out to be phoney. Their brakes failed on the way down. It was especially tragic, coming as it did the day before Barnaby and Fenton were about to go on the tarpon-fishing trip of a lifetime.'

Tom asked the question he didn't want to ask. 'Where?'

'Honduras. A place called Laguna de Brus.'

Tom slowed, checked his rearview mirror, and with a screech of tyres, manipulating both the brakes and the gas, pulled a one-eighty.

'Are you crazy? What are you doing?'

'Going to the nearest airport.'

'Why?'

'Because someone who would kill police officers could sure as hell kill my two brothers.'

'You think someone found out about the hidden inheritance?'

'Absolutely.' He accelerated towards the vanishing point on the horizon. 'Looks like we're going to Honduras. Together.'

3

In the 'executive suite' of the Sheraton Royale de San Pedro Sula, Tom wallowed on an overstuffed sofa, examining a map of southern Honduras. Maxwell had flown with all his cargo to the town of Brus Laguna on the Mosquito Coast at the mouth of the Río Patuca. And then he had disappeared. The locals said he had gone upriver, which was the only route into the vast, mountainous and wild interior. Tom had also discovered that they were now at least a week behind Philip and almost two weeks behind Vernon.

He followed the wandering blue line of the river on the map with his finger, through swamps and hills and high plateaus, until it vanished in a web of tributaries pouring out of a rugged line of parallel mountain ranges. The map showed no roads or towns; it was truly a lost world.

Sally, wrapped in a towel, came out of the bathroom humming to herself, then crossed their sitting room, her wet hair spilling down her back. Tom followed her with his eyes as she disappeared into her bedroom. Ten minutes later, she re-emerged, dressed in lightweight khakis and a long-sleeved shirt, bought during a shopping expedition that morning.

'We need to find a guide to take us up the Patuca River, and I have no idea where to start.' She picked up the phone book and began leafing through it. 'I wonder if there's a listing in here for "Adventure Travel" or something.'

'I've got a better idea. We need to find the local watering hole for foreign journalists. They're the savviest travellers in the world.'

'Chalk one up to you.'

She bent over and pulled a pair of trousers from a bag and tossed them at him, followed by a shirt, a pair of socks and some lightweight hiking shoes. They all landed in a pile in front of him. 'Now you can take off those macho cowboy boots.'

Tom scooped up his clothes and went into his room to put them on. They seemed to be mostly pockets.

When he came out, Sally eyed him sideways and said, 'After a few days in the jungle, maybe you won't look quite so silly.'

'Thanks.' Tom went to the phone and called the front desk. The journalists, it seemed, hung out in a bar called Los Charcos.

Los Charcos was an elegant, wood-panelled affair off the lobby of a fine old hotel. It was air-conditioned to Arctic conditions.

'Let me do the talking,' Sally said. 'My Spanish is better than yours.'

They took seats at the bar.

'*Hola*,' said Sally cheerfully to the bartender, a man with a heavy-lidded face. 'I'm looking for the man from the *New York Times*.'

'Mr Sewell? I haven't seen him since the hurricane, *señorita*.'

'Well, what reporters do you have? I'm looking for an American, someone who knows the country.'

'Would an Englishman suffice?'

'Fine.'

'Over there,' he murmured, pointing with his lips, 'is Derek Dunn. He is writing a book.'

'What about?'

'Travel and adventure.'

'Has he written any other books? Give me a title.'

'*Slow Water* was his last book.'

Sally dropped a twenty-dollar bill on the bar and headed towards Dunn. Tom followed. Dunn was sitting by himself in a snug, working on a drink, a man with a shock of blond hair over a beefy red face. Sally halted, then exclaimed, 'Say, you're Derek Dunn, aren't you?'

'I have been known to answer by that name, yes,' he said.

'Oh, how exciting! *Slow Water* is one of my *favourite* books!'

Dunn rose, exposing a robust frame, trim and fit, dressed in worn khaki trousers and a simple short-sleeved cotton shirt.

'Thank you very much indeed,' he said. 'And you are?'

'Sally Colorado.' She pumped his hand.

She's already got him grinning like an idiot, thought Tom. He felt foolish in his new clothes that smelt of a menswear shop. Dunn, in contrast, looked like he had been to the ends of the earth and back.

'Won't you join me for a drink?'

'It would be an honour,' cried Sally.

Dunn guided her into the banquette next to him.

'I'll have what you're having,' she said.

'Gin and tonic.' Dunn waved at the bartender and then glanced up at Tom. 'You're welcome to sit too, you know.'

Tom took a seat, saying nothing. He was starting to lose his enthusiasm for this idea. He did not like the red-faced Mr Dunn, who was looking very intently at Sally—and not just at her face.

The bartender came over. Dunn spoke in Spanish. 'Gin and tonic for me and the lady. And—?' He glanced at Tom.

'Lemonade,' said Tom sourly.

'*Y una limonada,*' added Dunn, his tone conveying what he thought of Tom's choice of beverage. He turned in his chair, placing his back to Tom, devoting his attention to Sally. 'You might be interested to know I'm working on a new book. It's about the Mosquito Coast.'

'Oh, that's just where we're going!' Sally clapped her hands in excitement, like a girl.

Tom regretted his choice of drink. He was going to need something a little stronger to get through this. He looked round for the waiter.

'My book chronicles a journey I took along the length of the Mosquito Coast, through the maze of lagoons that mark where the jungle meets the sea. I was the first white man to make the trip.'

'Incredible. How on earth did you do it?'

'Motorised dugout. The only mode of transportation in those parts besides foot travel. It's tough country down there.'

'Really?'

Dunn seemed to take this as his cue. He leaned back. 'For starters, there are the usual mosquitoes, chiggers, ticks, blackfly and botfly.'

'Lovely,' said Tom. He had finally got the waiter's attention. 'Whisky. Make it a double.'

Dunn looked at Tom, a smile playing about his lips. 'Are you familiar with the toothpick fish? This isn't a story for the ladies.'

'Do tell,' said Tom. 'Sally's no stranger to crudity.'

Sally flashed him a look.

'Lives in the rivers around here. Let's say you go for a nice morning dip. The toothpick fish swims right up your johnson, then flares out a set of spines and anchors itself in your urethra.'

Tom's drink paused halfway to his mouth.

'Blocks the urethra. If you don't find a surgeon damn quick, your bladder bursts.'

'Surgeon?' Tom said weakly.

Dunn leaned back. 'That's right.'

Tom's throat had gone dry. 'What kind of surgery?'

'Amputation.'

The drink finally made it to Tom's mouth, where he took a slug, and then another.

Dunn laughed loudly. 'I'm sure you've heard all about the piranhas, electric eels, anacondas, that sort of thing.' He waved his hand disparagingly. 'The dangers of those are greatly exaggerated. Watch out for the monkey spiders, though—'

'So sorry, but we'll have to leave the monkey spiders for another day,' said Tom, looking at his watch. He realised that Mr Derek Dunn had his hand under the table, resting on Sally's knee.

'Not having second thoughts are you, old chap?'

'Not at all,' said Tom.

'Well!' said Sally brightly. 'We've been looking for a guide and wondered if you could recommend someone.'

'Where are you chaps headed?'

'Brus Laguna.'

'You *are* getting off the tourist trail.' Suddenly his eyes narrowed. 'You're not a writer, are you?'

Sally laughed. 'Oh, no, I'm an archaeologist, and he's a horse vet. But we're just here as tourists. We like to have adventures.'

'An archaeologist? There aren't many ruins around here. You can't build in a swamp, and no civilised people would ever live in those interior mountains. If it's ruins you're after, Sally, why don't you head over to Copán? Perhaps I could tell you more about it over dinner.'

The hand was still on her knee, squeezing and rubbing.

'Right,' said Sally. 'Maybe. Getting back to the guide. Do you have any recommendations?'

'Guide? Oh, yes. The man for you is Don Orlando Ocotal. A Tawahka Indian. Absolutely reliable. Knows the country like the back of his hand. He was with me on my last trip.'

'How do we find him?'

'He lives up the Patuca River, a place called Pito Solo, the last settlement on the river before the interior swamps begin. That's forty, fifty miles upriver from Brus. Don Orlando. He's your man.' Derek Dunn revolved in his seat and faced Tom with his big sweaty face. 'Say, I'm a bit short of funds—royalty check in the mail and all that. Perhaps you could spot us another round, what say?'

THEY FLEW TO BRUS, left their luggage at a cinderblock barracks that called itself a hotel, then went down to the river to rent a boat. It was afternoon, and the heat had rendered the air dead and listless.

They found the river at the far end of town. It lay between steep banks, about 200 yards across, and curved away between thick walls of jungle. The thick brown water moved sluggishly, and smelt of mud. A trail made of logs descended the embankment, ending at a platform of bamboo sticks that formed a rickety dock. Four dugout canoes were tied up. They were each about thirty feet long and four feet across, hewn from a single gigantic tree and tapering to a spearlike prow in front. The stern had been cut off flat and had a mounted board designed to accommodate a small outboard engine. Planks were laid fore and aft for seats.

They scrambled down the embankment to take a closer look. Sally noted that three of the dugouts had six-horsepower engines bolted to the sterns. The fourth, longer and heavier, sported an eighteen-horse.

'There's the local hot rod,' said Sally, pointing. 'That's the one for us.'

Tom looked around. The place seemed deserted.

'There's somebody.' Sally pointed to an open-sided bamboo shed fifty yards down the river bank. A small fire smoked next to a pile of empty tin cans. A hammock had been strung between two trees in a spot of shade and inside the hammock a man slept.

Sally advanced. '*Hola*,' she said.

After a moment the man opened one eye. '*Sí?*'

'We want to rent a boat.' She spoke in Spanish.

He sat up in the hammock, scratched his head and grinned. 'I speak good American. We talk American. Someday I go to America.'

'That's good. We're going to Pito Solo,' said Tom.

He nodded, yawned, scratched. 'OK. I take you.'

'We'd like to rent the big boat. The one with the eighteen-horse-power engine.'

He shook his head. 'That stupid boat belong to army mans.'

'We'd like to leave tomorrow morning,' Tom said. 'How long is the journey?'

'Three days.'

'Three *days*? I thought it was forty or fifty miles.'

'Water going down. Maybe get stuck. Have to pole. Much wading. Cannot use engine.'

'Wading?' Tom asked. 'What about that toothpick fish?'

The man looked at him blankly.

'Don't worry, Tom,' Sally said, 'you can wear tight underwear.'

'Ah, *sí!* The candiru!' The man laughed. 'That favourite gringo story. Candiru. I swim in river every day and I still got my *chuc-chuc*. You got *piss* in river first. Candiru smell piss in river, swim up, and chop! If you no piss when you swim, you got no problem!'

'Anyone else come through here lately? Any gringos, I mean.'

'*Sí*. We very busy. Last month, white man come with many boxes and Indians from the mountains.'

'What Indians?' Tom asked excitedly.

'Naked mountain Indians.' He spat.

'Where did he get his boats?'

'He bring many new dugouts from La Ceiba.'

'And did the boats return?'

'Boats not return. Mans go upriver, never come back.'

'Anyone else come through?'

'*Sí*. Last week Jesus Christ came through with drunken guides.'

'Jesus Christ?' Sally asked.

'Yes, Jesus Christ with long hair, beard, robes and sandals.'

'That's got to be Vernon,' said Tom. 'Was he with anyone?'

'Yes. He with St Peter.'

Tom rolled his eyes. 'Any others?'

'*Sí*. Then come two gringos with twelve soldiers in two dugouts also from La Ceiba.'

'What did the gringos look like?'

'One tall, smoke pipe, angry. Other shorter with gold rings.'

'Philip,' said Tom.

They quickly made a deal for a boat to Pito Solo and Tom gave him a ten-dollar advance. 'We leave at first light tomorrow.'

'*Bueno!* I be ready!'

When they got back to the cinderblock barracks hotel, they were surprised to see a Jeep parked there with an army officer and two soldiers inside. The landlady stood to one side, her hands clasped, her face pale with fright.

'I don't like the look of this,' said Sally.

The officer stepped forward, a man with a straight back, a spotless uniform and polished boots. He gave a bow. 'Do I have the honour of greeting Señor Tom Broadbent and Señorita Sally Colorado? I am Lieutenant Vespán.' He took their hands, one at a time.

'What's the problem?' asked Sally.

The man smiled broadly, exposing a row of silver teeth. 'I am devastated to inform you that you are under arrest.'

Tom stared at the diminutive officer. 'On what charge?' he asked.

'We will discuss that in San Pedro Sula. Please come with me.'

There was an awkward silence. Sally said, 'No.'

'Señorita, let us not make difficulty.'

'I'm not creating difficulties. I'm just not going.'

'Sally,' Tom said, 'may I point out these men have guns?'

'Good. Let them shoot me and then explain it to the US government.' She spread her arms out to make a target.

The officer nodded at his two men, who set their guns down, briskly stepped forward and seized Sally. She yelled and struggled.

Tom took a step forward. 'Get your hands off her.'

The two men hoisted her up and began carrying her, struggling, to the Jeep. Tom took a swing at the first man and sent him flying.

The next thing he knew he was lying on his back, looking up into the hot blue sky. The officer stood over him, red-faced and angry. Tom could feel a throbbing sensation at the base of his skull where the man had struck him with the butt of his gun.

The soldiers pulled him roughly to his feet. Sally had stopped struggling and looked pale.

They allowed themselves to be taken to the Jeep. The lieutenant shoved Tom onto the back seat and pushed Sally in next to him. Their backpacks and bags had already been collected from the hotel and were piled in the back. The Jeep started down the road to the airstrip. There, a shabby military helicopter was sitting on the grass. A metal panel on the side of the helicopter was off, and a man with a wrench was fiddling with the engine. The Jeep came sliding to a stop.

'What are you doing?' the lieutenant asked sharply in Spanish.

'I am sorry, *teniente*, but there is a small problem. We need a part.'

'Can you fly without it?'

'No, *teniente*. Shall I radio for them to send a plane with the part?'

'Yes, you deficient! Radio for the part!'

The pilot climbed into the chopper, radioed, and then came out. 'It will be coming tomorrow morning, *teniente*. That is the earliest.'

The lieutenant locked them in a wooden shed at the airstrip with their sleeping-bags and a flashlight, and put the two soldiers outside to guard them. Gradually, the aching in Tom's head subsided, and as it did he began to get angry. He felt that their arrest had probably been engineered by the nameless enemy who had killed Barnaby and Fenton. His brothers were in even more danger than he thought.

'Give me the flashlight,' Tom said.

He shone it around. The shed couldn't have been more shoddily built, just a post-and-beam frame with boards nailed over it and a tin roof. An idea began to take shape—a plan of escape.

AT THREE O'CLOCK that morning they took their places, Sally by the door and Tom braced at the back wall. He whispered a three-count and they both kicked simultaneously, Sally's assault on the door masking the sound of Tom's kick to the boards on the back wall. The shabby board popped off, just as Tom hoped.

One of the soldiers cursed. 'What are you doing?'

'I have to go to the bathroom!' Sally cried.

'No, no, you must go in there.'

Tom whispered the countdown again, *one, two, three, kick*. Sally gave the door another blow while he kicked out a second board.

'Stop!' said the soldier.

'But I have to go, *cabrón!*'

'*Señorita*, I am sorry, but you must take care of it in there. I am under orders not to open the door.'

One, two, three, kick! The third board popped off. The opening was now big enough to squeeze through. Dogs in town began to bark.

'One more kick and I call the *teniente!*'

'Sally, let's go,' hissed Tom, gesturing to her in the dark.

He pushed her through the hole and handed out their sleeping-bags and the flashlight. They ran at a crouch down the jungle track to the river. In five minutes they were down by the boats. Tom flashed the light over the army dugout with the eighteen-horse engine. It had two large plastic tanks full of gasoline. He began untying the prow. Suddenly he heard a voice, speaking low, from the darkness.

'You no want that boat.'

It was the man they had hired earlier that day.

'Let stupid army mans take that boat. Water going down. At every bend in river they get stuck. You take my boat. You no get stuck. That way you escape.' He leapt like a cat onto the dock and untied a slender dugout with a six-horsepower engine. 'Get in.'

'Are you coming with us?' Sally asked.

'No. I tell stupid army mans you rob me.' He started unhooking the tanks from the army boat and loading them into the back of their dugout canoe. Tom and Sally climbed in. Tom fished in his pocket and offered the man some money.

'Not now. If they search me and find money, I get shot.'

'How can we pay you?' Tom asked.

'You pay me later. I always here. My name Manuel Waono. You go now. Fast.'

'How do we find Pito Solo?'

'Last village on river.' He pushed them off with a big, bare foot.

Tom lowered the engine into the water, primed it, choked it, gave it a pull. It roared into life. He turned the throttle as far as it would go, and the tinny engine whined and shuddered. The long wooden canoe began to move through the water. Tom steered while Sally stood in the bow, probing the river ahead with the flashlight.

Not a minute later, back at the dock, Manuel began shouting in Spanish: 'Help! I am robbed! My boat, they stole my boat!'

'Christ, he didn't wait long,' Tom muttered.

Soon a cacophony of excited voices came drifting towards them over the dark river. Then the bright light of a gas lantern came bobbing down the embankment, along with flashlights, illuminating a knot of people gathering on the dock. There was a sudden hush and then a voice rang out in English: the voice of Lieutenant Vespán. 'Turn round or I order my men to shoot, please!'

'He's bullshitting,' said Sally. 'He'll never shoot.'

There was a sudden burst of automatic-weapons fire coming across the water, shockingly loud and close.

'Shit!' Tom yelled, throwing himself down. The boat began to yaw. He reached up with one hand and steadied the engine handle.

Sally was still standing in the prow. 'Tom, they're shooting into the air. They're not going to risk hitting us. We're Americans.'

There was a second burst of gunfire. This time Tom distinctly heard the slap of bullets hitting the water around them. Instantly Sally landed on the floor of the dugout next to him.

Tom shoved the tiller sideways, sending the dugout into a sharp evasive manoeuvre. There were two more short bursts of gunfire. He steered the boat on a zigzag course, trying to throw the marksmen off their aim. At each lull, Sally raised her head and shone the light ahead so they could see where they were going. They would be safe, at least for the moment, once they got round the bend in the river.

Several rounds nicked the gunwale, showering them with splinters, but slowly the boat came round the bend, out of the line of fire, and the river fell silent. They had made it.

Tom helped Sally up and found her hand was shaking. Then he realised his own hand was shaking, too. He flicked on the flashlight to see what lay ahead. Darkness suffocated the river and a growing cloud of mosquitoes whined around them.

'I don't suppose you have a can of bug repellent in one of those pockets of yours?' Tom asked.

'As a matter of fact, I did manage to grab my waist pack in the Jeep.' She fished the small pack out of an enormous pocket on her thigh and unzipped it. She began rummaging through, pulling out waterproof matches, a map and a chocolate bar.

'I'm not even sure what's in here.'

She began sorting through the jumble of items while Tom held the flashlight. There was no bug stuff. She swore and put everything back. As she did, a photograph fell out. Tom shone the light on it. It showed a strikingly handsome young man with dark eyebrows and a chiselled chin. The grave expression that furrowed his eyebrows, the firm full set of his lips, the tweed jacket, and the way he tilted his head all showed him to be a man who took himself very seriously.

'Who's that?' Tom asked.

'Oh,' said Sally. 'That's Professor Julian Clyve.'

'That's Clyve? Why, he's so young! I imagined him to be some dotty old man in a cardigan puffing on a pipe.'

'He wouldn't be happy to hear you say that! He's the youngest full professor in the history of the department. He entered Stanford at sixteen, graduated at nineteen, and had his PhD by the time he was twenty-two. He's a true genius.'

'Why are you carrying around a photo of your professor?'

'Why,' said Sally lightly, 'we're engaged. Didn't I tell you?'

'No.'

'You seem surprised.'

'Well, I am. After all, you're not wearing an engagement ring.'

'Julian doesn't believe in those bourgeois conventions.'

Tom busied himself driving the boat and the swampy night heat flowed past them. A bird cried in the darkness. In the silence that followed, Tom heard a noise. He switched off the engine immediately, his heart pounding. The sound came again: the sputter of an outboard starter being pulled.

'They found some gasoline. They're coming after us.'

The boat was starting to drift back down with the current. Tom unshipped a pole from the bottom of the boat and stuck it in the water. The boat swung a little to the current and steadied. There was another sputter and then a roar. The roar subsided into a hum. There could be no doubt: it was the sound of an outboard.

Tom went to restart their engine.

'Don't,' said Sally. 'They'll hear it. And we can't outrace them.' She flashed the light along the wall of jungle on either side of the water. The water extended into the trees and spread out, drowning the jungle. 'We can hide instead.'

Tom poled the dugout towards the edge of the flooded forest. There was a small opening—a narrow lane of water that looked like it might have been a stream in drier times. He poled up it, and the boat promptly bumped into something: a sunken log.

'Out,' Tom said.

The water was only a foot deep, but underneath it was another two feet of mud, which they sank into with a flurry of bubbles. A stench of marsh gas rose up. They struggled to get the nose of the boat onto the log, then heaved the boat across it. As they scrambled over it themselves and climbed back in, the sound of the outboard grew louder.

Sally picked up the second pole and they both poled forward into the flooded forest. Tom switched off the flashlight, and a moment later a powerful spotlight came blinking through the trees.

'We're still too close,' said Tom. 'They'll see us.' He grabbed some hanging vines and used them to pull the boat into a thicket of ferns and bushes just before the spotlight flashed through the forest again. Tom reached out and pulled Sally down to the bottom of the dugout.

The sound of the motorboat grew very loud. The boat had slowed down and the spotlight was probing the forest where they were hidden. Tom could hear the crackle of a walkie-talkie and the murmur of voices. The beam lit up the jungle around them like a movie set—and then slowly moved on. Blessed darkness returned and the sound of the outboard grew fainter.

Tom sat up in time to see the flash of the spotlight in the forest up ahead as the boat went round a bend. 'They're gone,' he said.

Sally sat up, brushing her tangled hair out of her face. The mosquitoes had gathered round them in a thick, whining cloud. Tom could feel them everywhere, in his hair, crawling into his ears, trying to get up his nose, crawling down his neck. Each blow killed a dozen, instantly replaced. When he tried to breathe, he breathed mosquitoes.

'We've got to get out of here,' Sally said, slapping.

Tom began pulling dry twigs off the bushes around them.

'What are you doing?'

'Building a fire.'

'Where?'

'You'll see.' When he'd collected a pile of twigs, he leaned over the side and scooped up some mud from the swamp. He patted it into a pancake on the bottom of the dugout, covered it with leaves, and then built a small tepee of sticks and dry leaves on top. 'Match?'

Sally handed him a match, and he lit the fire. As soon as it was going well, he added some green leaves and twigs. A curl of smoke drifted up and gathered in the still air. Tom plucked a large leaf from a nearby bush and used it as a fan to wave the smoke over Sally. The furious cloud of mosquitoes was driven back.

'There's a nice trick,' said Sally.

'My father showed it to me on a canoe trip in northern Maine.'

Sally took out the map and began examining it by flashlight. 'It looks like there are a lot of side channels to the river. I think we should stick to those until we reach Pito Solo.'

'Good idea. And I think we'll have to pole from now on. We can't risk using the engine.'

Sally nodded.

'You tend the fire,' said Tom. 'I'll pole, and then we'll switch. We won't stop until we reach Pito Solo.'

'Right.'

Tom pushed the boat back into the river and poled close to the flooded forest. Soon they came to a small side channel winding away from the main one, and took it.

Tom said, 'I don't think Lieutenant Vespán had any intention of taking us back to San Pedro Sula. I think he planned to have us fall out of his helicopter. If it weren't for that missing part, we'd be dead.'

4

For two days, Tom and Sally poled upstream, following winding side channels and keeping a strict policy of silence. They travelled by day and night, taking turns to sleep. They had little to eat except Sally's chocolate bars and some fruit she collected along the way. They saw no sign of the soldiers.

The morning of the third day, they spied a house on stilts built over the water. It had wattle-and-daub walls and a thatched roof. Beyond that was a river bank, with granite boulders and a steep embankment—the first dry land they had seen in days. As they approached, a rickety bamboo dock came into view at the water's edge.

'What do you think?' Tom asked. 'Should we stop?'

Sally stood up. A boy was fishing from the dock.

'Pito Solo?'

But the boy was already running away.

'Let's give it a try,' said Tom. 'If we don't get something to eat, we're finished.' He poled into the dock.

Sally and Tom jumped out and the dock swayed and creaked alarmingly. They scrambled up the slippery embankment.

'There's a track,' Sally said, pointing into the mist.

At the end of the track a village sat on a rise above the flooded rain forest, a motley collection of wattle-and-daub huts with roofs of tin or thatch. As Tom and Sally wandered through it, chickens strutted away from them, and skinny dogs slunk along the hut walls, eyeing them sideways. The village seemed deserted. It ended as quickly as it began, in a solid wall of jungle.

Suddenly Tom heard a rustle. He looked around. At first he saw nothing, and then he realised that a hundred dark eyes were peering at him from the jungle foliage. They were the eyes of children.

'I wish I had my chocolate bars,' Sally said. She hunted in her pockets and found a dollar.

'Hello? Who wants an American dollar?'

A shout went up, and a large number of children burst from the foliage, shouting and jostling, their hands extended.

'Who speaks Spanish?' asked Sally, holding up the dollar.

Everyone shouted at once in Spanish. Out of the hubbub an older girl stepped forward. 'Can I help you?' she said, with great poise and dignity. She looked about thirteen and was pretty, wearing a tie-dyed T-shirt, a pair of shorts and two gold earrings. Thick brown braids went down her back.

Sally gave her the dollar. 'What is your name?'

'Marisol.'

'That's a nice name. We are looking for Don Orlando Ocotal. Can you take us to him?'

'He went away with the *yanquis* more than a week ago.'

'Which *yanquis*?'

'The tall angry gringo with the bites all over his face and the smiling one with the gold rings on his fingers.'

Tom looked at Sally. 'Sounds like Philip got our guide first.' He turned back to the girl. 'We're going upriver and we need a guide.'

The girl said, 'I will take you to my grandfather, Don Alfonso Boswas, who is the head of the village. He knows everything.'

The girl led them to what looked like the worst hut in the village, a leaning pile of sticks with almost no mud remaining in the cracks. She stood aside at the door and they stepped inside.

An old man sat in the centre of the hut, on a stool, his bony knees sticking out of the great holes in his trousers, a few wisps of white hair on his balding skull. He was smoking a corncob pipe. A machete lay on the ground next to him. He was small and wore glasses that magnified his eyes, giving him a wide-eyed look of surprise. It was impossible to imagine he was the chief of the village; he looked, instead, the village's poorest man.

'Come in, come in. I am Don Alfonso Boswas. Sit down.' He spoke a curiously formal, old-fashioned Spanish.

Tom and Sally took two rickety stools. 'I'm Tom Broadbent,' Tom said, 'and this is Sally Colorado.'

The old man stood, bowed formally, and reseated himself.

'We're looking for a guide to go upriver.'

'Humph,' he said. 'All of a sudden these *yanquis* are all crazy to go upriver and get lost in the Meambar Swamp. Why?'

Tom hesitated, nonplussed by the unexpected question.

'We're trying to find Tom's father,' said Sally. 'Maxwell Broadbent. He came through here about a month ago with a group of Indians in dugout canoes. They probably had a lot of crates with them.'

The old man looked at Tom, squinting. 'I see that you and your wife are hungry. Marisol!' He spoke to her in an Indian language and the girl left. Then he turned back to Tom. 'So that was your father who came through here, eh? You don't look crazy to me. A boy with a crazy father is usually crazy too.'

'My mother was normal,' said Tom.

Don Alfonso laughed uproariously and slapped his knee. 'That is good. Yes, they stopped here to buy food. The white man was like a bear and his voice carried half a mile. I told him he was crazy to go on into the Meambar Swamp, but he did not listen. He must be a great chief from America. We had a good evening together with many laughs. He gave me *this*.'

He reached over to where some burlap sacks were folded up, fumbled about with his hands, then held something towards them in the palm of his hand. As the sun struck it, the object glinted the colour of pigeon's blood. He placed it in Tom's hand.

'A star ruby,' breathed Tom. It was one of the gems in his father's collection, worth a small, perhaps even a large, fortune. He felt a sudden rush of emotion. It was so like his father to make an extravagant gift to someone he liked.

'Yes. A ruby. With it my grandchildren will go to America.' He squirrelled it away again among the sacks. 'Why is your father doing this? He was as evasive as a coati when I tried to find out.'

Tom glanced at Sally. She nodded. 'My father is dying,' he said. 'He went upriver with all his possessions . . . to be buried. He has issued a challenge to us that if we want our inheritance, we will have to find his tomb.'

Don Alfonso nodded. 'Yes, this is something we Tawahka Indians once did. We buried ourselves with our property and it always made our sons angry. But then the missionaries came and explained that Jesus would give us new things in heaven so we didn't need to bury anything with the dead. So we stopped doing it. But I prefer the old way. It is better to bury yourself with your possessions than let the sons fight over them. Even before you are dead they are fighting.

That is why I already gave everything I owned to my sons and daughters and live like a wretch. Now my sons have nothing to fight over, and, what is more important, they do not wish me dead.'

'Did any other white people come by?' Sally asked.

'Ten days ago two dugouts with four men—two mountain Indians and two white men—stopped. I thought the younger one might be Jesus Christ, but at the missionary school they said he was only a type of person called a *hippie*. They stayed a day, then they went on. A week ago four dugouts with twelve army soldiers and two gringos arrived. They hired Don Orlando to guide them and left. Are they all looking for your father's tomb?'

'Yes. They're my two brothers.'

'Why are you not cooperating?'

Tom didn't answer.

Sally spoke. 'You mentioned mountain Indians with the first white man. Do you know where they come from?'

'They are naked savage Indians from the highlands who paint themselves red and black. They are not Christians. We are a little bit Christian here in Pito Solo. Not much, just enough to get by when the missionaries come with North American food and medicine. Then we sing and clap for Jesus. That is how I got my new glasses.'

Tom said, 'Don Alfonso, we need a guide to take us upriver, and we need supplies and equipment. Can you help us?'

Don Alfonso puffed his pipe, then nodded. 'I will take you.'

'Oh, no,' Tom said, looking at the feeble old man with alarm. 'That isn't what I was asking. We couldn't take you away from the village where you're needed.'

'Me? Needed? The village would like nothing more than to get rid of old Don Alfonso!'

'It'll be a long, hard journey, not suitable for a man of your age.'

'I am still as strong as a tapir! I'm young enough to marry again. I, Don Alfonso Boswas, will take you through the Meambar Swamp.'

'No,' said Tom. 'You will not. We need a younger guide.'

'You cannot avoid it. I dreamed you would come and that I would go with you. So it is decided. I speak English and Spanish, but I prefer Spanish. English sounds like one is being choked.'

Tom glanced at Sally, exasperated. The old man was impossible.

At that moment Marisol returned with an older woman. They were carrying wooden trenchers laid with palm leaves, on which were piled hot tortillas, fried plantains, roasted meats and nuts, and fruit.

Tom had never been so hungry in his life. He and Sally tucked into the feast, joined by Don Alfonso, while Marisol and the woman watched in satisfied silence.

When the meal was over, Don Alfonso leaned back.

'Now look,' said Tom as firmly as he could. 'Dream or no dream, you're not coming with us. We need a younger man.'

'I will bring two young men with me, Chori and Pingo. I'm the only one besides Don Orlando who knows the way through the Meambar Swamp. Without a guide you will die.'

'I must decline your offer, Don Alfonso.'

'You don't have much time. The soldiers are after you.'

'They were here?' Tom asked, alarmed.

'They came this morning. They will be back.'

Tom glanced at Sally again, and then back to Don Alfonso. 'We haven't done anything wrong. I'll explain—'

'You do not need to explain. The soldiers are evil men. We must start provisioning immediately. Marisol!'

'Yes, grandfather?'

'We will need tarpaulins, matches, gasoline, two-cycle engine oil, tools, a camping stove, frying pan, cooking pot, cutlery and water canteens.' He continued to reel off the list of supplies and food.

'Do you have medicine?' Tom asked.

'We have much North American medicine, thanks to the missionaries. We did a lot of clapping for Jesus to get those medicines. Marisol, tell the people to come with the items for sale at fair prices.'

Marisol ran off, and in less than ten minutes returned, leading a file of old men, women and children, each carrying something.

'Buy what you want and tell the others to go away,' Marisol said. 'They will tell you the price. Do not bargain; it is not our way. Just say yes or no. The prices are fair.' She gestured at the first man in line. He stepped forward and held out five old burlap sacks.

'Four hundred lempiras,' said the girl.

'What's that in dollars?' said Tom.

'Two.'

'We'll take them.'

The next person stepped forward with a sack of beans, a sack of loose dry corn and an aluminium pot and lid. 'One dollar.'

The procession of goods continued: plastic tarps, sacks of beans and rice, dried and smoked meats, bananas, a fifty-five-gallon drum of petrol, a box of salt.

Suddenly a hush fell over the crowd. Tom could hear the faint buzz of an outboard motor.

Marisol spoke rapidly to the villagers, then turned to Sally and Tom. 'You must follow me into the forest. Quickly.'

The crowd had dispersed and the village fell silent, seemingly empty again. Marisol calmly led the way into the forest, following an almost invisible trail. After ten minutes of walking, she stopped. 'We wait here until the soldiers leave.'

'What about our boat?' Sally asked. 'Won't they recognise it?'

'We already hid your boat.' Marisol turned her dark eyes back down the trail and waited, as still and quiet as a deer.

A distant shot echoed through the forest, then another.

Sally grabbed Tom's arm. 'They might be shooting people on account of us. We've got to go give ourselves up.'

'No,' said Marisol, sharply. 'Maybe they're shooting into the air. We can do nothing except wait.' A tear made a track down her face.

'We never should have stopped here,' said Sally, switching into English. 'We had no right to put these people in danger. Tom, we've *got* to go back to the village and face those soldiers.'

'You're right.' Tom turned to go.

'They *will* shoot us if you go back,' Marisol said.

THIRTY MINUTES LATER, Tom saw movement in the forest, and an old, shawled woman came tramping down the trail. Marisol rushed forward with a sob, and they spoke rapidly in their own language.

Marisol turned to Tom and Sally with a look of huge relief. 'It is as I said. The soldiers just shot into the air to frighten us. Then they went away. We convinced them that you had not come to the village, that you had not passed by. They have gone back downriver.'

As they approached the hut, Tom could see Don Alfonso standing outside, smoking his pipe, looking unconcerned. His face broke into a big smile as they approached.

'Chori! Pingo! Get out here! Come out and meet your new *yanqui* bosses! Chori and Pingo do not speak Spanish, they speak only Tawahka, but I yell at them in Spanish to show them my superiority.'

Two magnificent specimens of manhood bowed out of the door of the hut, naked from the waist up, their muscled bodies gleaming with oil. The one named Pingo had Western-style tattoos on his arms, Indian tattoos on his face, and held a three-foot machete in his fist. Chori had an old Springfield rifle and a bow slung over his shoulder. A leather bag was strung round his waist and he carried a Pulaski—a firefighter's axe—in one hand.

'We will load the boat. We leave the village as soon as possible.'

Sally looked at Tom. 'Seems Don Alfonso's going to be our guide.'

Chori and Pingo carried the supplies down to the river's edge. Their dugout was back. In half an hour the supplies were loaded in a heap in the middle of the dugout and tied down with a plastic tarp.

The river bank was now crowded with people. When it seemed that the whole village was assembled, Don Alfonso moved through the crowd. He was wearing a brand-new pair of shorts and a T-shirt that said NO FEAR. His face was wreathed in smiles as he joined Tom and Sally on the bamboo dock.

'Everyone has come to say goodbye. We get into the boat now.'

Chori and Pingo, still stripped to the waist, had already taken their places, one in the bow and the other the stern. Don Alfonso helped Tom and Sally in while two boys stood at either end of the boat, holding the lines, ready to cast off. Then the old man got in himself. He turned and faced the crowd. A hush fell. When the silence was absolute, Don Alfonso started speaking in the most formal Spanish.

'My friends and countrymen, many years ago it was prophesied that white men would come and I would take them on a long journey. And now they are here. We are setting off on a perilous voyage across the Meambar Swamp.

'You may ask why we make this great journey! I will tell you. This American has come here to rescue his father, who lost his mind and abandoned his family, taking with him all their possessions, leaving them destitute. His poor wife has been weeping for him every day and she cannot feed her family or protect them from wild animals. Their house is falling down and the thatch has rotted, letting in the rain. No one will marry his sisters and they will soon be forced into whoredom. His nephews have taken to drink. This young man, this good son, has come to cure his father from his madness and take him back to America, where he can live to a respectable old age and die in his hammock and not bring further dishonour and starvation to his family. Then his sisters will find husbands and he will be able to play dominoes in the hot afternoon instead of working.

'Long ago, my friends, I dreamed that I would leave you in this way, that I would go away on a great journey to the end of the earth. I am now one hundred and twenty-one years of age and finally this dream has come to pass. There are not many men who could do this thing at my age. I still have much blood in my veins, and if my Rosita were still alive she would be smiling every day.

'Goodbye, my friends, your beloved Don Alfonso Boswas is departing the village with tears of sadness in his eyes. Remember me always and tell my story to your children and tell them to tell their children, to the end of time.'

A great cheer went up. Firecrackers went off and all the dogs started barking. Some of the old men began beating sticks together in a complex rhythm. The laden boat was pushed out into the current, and Chori started the engine. The craft nosed forward in the water. Don Alfonso continued standing, waving and blowing kisses to the wildly cheering crowd until long after the boat had rounded the bend. Then he finally sat down, dug into the heap of supplies, extracted his pipe, packed it full of tobacco and began to smoke.

Tom took out their map of Honduras and examined it.

Don Alfonso snatched it out of his hand. He examined it first one way, then another. 'What is this? North America?'

'No, it's southeastern Honduras. That's the Patuca River and there's Brus. The village of Pito Solo should be here, but it's not marked. Neither, it seems, is the Meambar Swamp.'

'So, according to this map, we do not exist and the Meambar Swamp does not exist. Take care to keep this very important map dry. We may need it to start a fire someday.'

5

The camp had been set up with the usual military precision on an island of high ground surrounded by swamp. Philip sat by the fire, smoking his pipe and listening to the evening sounds of the rain forest.

Don Orlando Ocotal, the guide they had picked up at that sorry village on the river, was sitting by himself, tending the fire and cooking. He was a strange fellow, this Ocotal—small, silent, utterly dignified, a man who seemed to have an unshakable conviction of his own worth. He certainly knew his stuff, guiding them through an incredible maze of channels, day after day, without the slightest hesitation.

There were shouts, and Philip turned to see Marcus Hauser coming back from the hunt, alongside four soldiers carrying a dead tapir slung on a pole. They hoisted the animal up with a block and tackle from a tree branch. Hauser left the men and came to sit down next to Philip. There was a faint smell of aftershave, tobacco smoke and blood. Hauser took out a cigar, clipped it and lit it. Then he took in a lungful of smoke and let it trickle back out of his nose, like a dragon.

'We're making excellent progress, Philip, don't you think?'

'Admirable.' Philip slapped at a mosquito. He couldn't understand how Hauser managed to avoid getting bitten, despite the fact that he never seemed to use insect repellent.

Hauser exhaled a cloud of smoke. 'But I have a question for you, Philip. My question is, who was the one person your father trusted?'

It was a good question. One that Philip had been considering for some time. 'It wasn't a girlfriend or an ex-wife. He constantly complained about his doctors and lawyers. He had no real friends. The only man he trusted was his pilot.'

'And I've already determined he wasn't in on the deal,' Hauser said. 'Did your father have some kind of secret life? A secret affair? A son born out of wedlock who he favoured above you three?'

Philip felt himself go cold at this suggestion. 'I have no idea.'

Hauser waved his cigar. 'Something to think about, eh, Philip?'

He fell silent. The intimacy encouraged Philip to ask a question he had been wanting to ask for some time. 'What happened between you and father?'

'Did you know we were childhood friends?'

'Yes.'

'We grew up together in Erie. We played ball together on the block where we lived, we went to school together, we went to our first whorehouse together. We knew each other pretty well. But when you go into the jungle, when you're shoved up against the wall of survival, things come out. You discover things in yourself that you never knew were there. That's what happened to us. We got out there in the middle of the jungle, lost, bitten, starving, half dead with fever, and we found out who we really were. You know what I discovered? I discovered that I despised your father.'

Philip looked at Hauser. The man returned the look, his face as calm and smooth and opaque as always. He felt his flesh creep. He asked, 'So what did you discover in yourself, Hauser?'

He could see that the question took Hauser by surprise. The man laughed it off, threw the cigar butt into the fire, and rose. 'You'll find out soon enough.'

THE DUGOUT PUSHED through the thick black water, the engine whining with the effort. The river had divided and divided until it had become a labyrinth of channels and stagnant pools. Everywhere Tom could see whirling clouds of insects. Pingo stayed in the bow, wielding a huge machete with which he took an occasional swipe at a vine hanging in the water. The channels were often too shallow to use the engine and Chori would lift the outboard out of the muddy water and pole. Don Alfonso sat cross-legged atop the tarp-covered heap of supplies, puffing on his pipe and peering ahead.

'What are these hellish insects?' Sally cried, slapping furiously.

'Tapir-fly,' said Don Alfonso. He reached into his pocket and extended a blackened corncob pipe towards her. '*Señorita*, you should take up smoking, which discourages the insects.'

'No, thank you. Smoking causes cancer.'

'On the contrary, smoking leads to good digestion and a long life.'

'Right.'

As they proceeded deeper into the swamp, the vegetation seemed to press in from all sides, forming layered walls of glossy leaves, ferns and vines. The air was dead and thick and smelt of methane. The boat pushed through it as if it were hot soup.

'How do you know this is the way my father went?' Tom asked.

'There are many pathways in the Meambar Swamp,' Don Alfonso said, 'but there is only one way through. I, Don Alfonso, know that way, and so did your father. I can read the signs.'

'What do you read?'

'There have been three groups of voyagers before us. The first group came through a month ago. The second and third groups were only a few days apart, and they came through about a week ago.'

'How can you tell all this?' Sally asked.

'I see a notch chopped in a sunken log. I see a cut vine. I see a pole mark on a sunken sandbar or a groove made in the muddy shallows by a keel. Those marks, in this dead water, last for weeks.'

Sally pointed to a tree. 'Look, over there is a gumbo-limbo tree, *Bursera simaruba*. The Maya use the sap for bug bites.' She turned to Don Alfonso. 'Let's head over there and collect some.'

Don Alfonso took his pipe out of his mouth. 'My grandfather used to collect this plant. We call it *lucawa*.' He gazed at Sally with a new-found respect. 'I did not know you were a *curandera*.'

'I'm not really,' said Sally. 'I spent some time in the north living with the Maya while I was in college. I was studying their medicine.'

Chori brought the boat up alongside the tree. Sally gave the bark a chop with her machete and then peeled off a vertical strip of bark. The sap immediately began oozing out in reddish droplets. She scraped some off, rolled up her trousers and smeared it on her bug bites, then rubbed it into her neck, wrists and the backs of her hands. She scraped some more of the gooey sap off the bark with the machete and held it out to Tom. He took a step over and she rubbed it into the back of his badly bitten neck. The itching, burning sensation ebbed away.

'How does it feel?'

Tom moved his neck. 'Sticky, but good.' He liked the feeling of her hands on his neck.

Sally handed him the machete with its dollop of sap. 'You can do your own legs and arms.'

'Thanks.' He smeared it on, surprised at how effective it was.

That afternoon they passed the first rock Tom had seen in days. Beyond, sunlight filtered down into an overgrown clearing made in an island of high ground.

'Here is where we will camp,' announced Don Alfonso.

They brought the dugout alongside the rock and tied it up. Pingo and Chori leapt out with their machetes and began mowing down the new growth. Don Alfonso strolled around and examined the ground, scuffing it with a foot, picking up a vine or a leaf.

'It looks like someone's camped here,' Tom said to Don Alfonso.

'Yes. This area was cleared about a month ago. I see a fire ring and the remains of a hut. The last people were here perhaps a week ago.'

'All this grew up in a week?'

Don Alfonso nodded. 'The forest does not like a hole.' He poked around the remains of the fire and then picked up something. It was a cigar ring from a Cuba Libre, mouldy and half dissolved.

'My father's brand,' said Tom, looking at it. It gave him a strange feeling. His father had camped in this very spot and left this tiny clue. He put it in his pocket and began collecting wood for the fire.

Chori and Pingo set about building a hut, while Don Alfonso shouted directions. They started by driving six stout poles into the earth, making a framework of flexible sticks, over which they tied plastic tarps. The hammocks were strung between the poles, each with its own mosquito netting, and a final piece of tarp was hung vertically, making a private room for Sally.

When they were done, Don Alfonso examined the hut with a squinty eye, then nodded and turned. 'The *curandera* has her own private sleeping quarters, which can be enlarged for an additional guest, should she need company.' The old man gave Tom another exaggerated wink. He found himself reddening.

'I am quite content to sleep alone,' said Sally coldly.

Don Alfonso looked disappointed. He leaned towards Tom as if to speak to him in private. His voice, however, was perfectly audible to everyone. 'She is a very beautiful woman, Tomás, even if she is old.'

'Excuse me, I'm twenty-nine.'

'*Ehi, señorita*, you are even older than I thought. Tomás, you must hurry. She is almost too old to marry now.'

'In our culture,' Sally said, 'twenty-nine is considered young.'

Don Alfonso shook his head sadly. Tom couldn't suppress a laugh. Sally rounded on him. 'What's so funny?'

'The little culture clash here,' he said, catching his breath.

Sally switched to English. 'I don't appreciate this sexist little tête-à-tête between you and that dirty old man.' She turned to Don Alfonso. 'For a supposedly one-hundred-and-twenty-one-year-old man, you certainly spend a lot of your time thinking about sex.'

'A man never stops thinking about love, *señorita*. Even when he grows old and his member shrivels like a yucca fruit left to dry in the sun. I may be one hundred and twenty-one, but I have as much blood as a teenager.'

'Stop it!' Sally cried, clapping her hands over her ears. 'No more!' She walked off and flipped back the door to the hut, flashing Tom an angry glance just before she disappeared.

Don Alfonso continued speaking in a loud voice. 'I do not understand. Here she is twenty-nine and unmarried. Her father will have to pay an enormous dowry to get rid of her. And here you are, almost an old man, and you do not have a wife either. Why do you two not marry? Perhaps you are homosexual? It is all right if you are, Tomás. Chori will accommodate you. He is not particular.'

'No, thank you, Don Alfonso.'

'Then I do not understand, Tomás.'

'Sally,' said Tom, 'is engaged to marry another man.'

Don Alfonso's eyebrows shot up. 'And where is this man now?'

'Back in America.'

'He cannot love her!'

Sally's voice came from the hut. 'He loves me and I love him, and I'll thank you both to shut up.'

'*BUENAS TARDES*,' murmured Don Orlando Ocotal, taking a seat next to Philip at the fire.

'*Buenas tardes*,' Philip said, taking the pipe out of his mouth, surprised. It was the first time Ocotal had spoken to him the entire trip.

They had reached a large lake at the edge of the swamp and were camped on a sandy island that actually had a beach. The bugs were gone, the air was fresh, and for the first time in a week Philip could see more than twenty feet in one direction. The only thing that spoilt it was that the water lapping on the sand was the colour of black coffee. As usual, Hauser was out hunting with a couple of soldiers while the others were at their own fire, playing cards. The air was drowsy with heat and the green-gold light of late afternoon.

Ocotal abruptly leaned forward and said, 'I overheard the soldiers talking last night.'

Philip raised his eyebrows. 'And?'

'Do not react to what I say. They are going to kill you.' He said it so low and rapidly that Philip almost thought he hadn't heard properly. He sat there dumbfounded as the words sank in.

Ocotal went on. 'They are going to kill me, too.'

'Are you sure?'

Ocotal nodded.

In a panic, Philip considered this. Could Ocotal be trusted? Why would Hauser kill him? To steal the inheritance? It seemed impossible. Like something out of a movie. 'What do you plan to do?'

'Steal a boat and run. Hide in the swamp.'

'You mean *now?*'

'You want to wait?'

'But the soldiers are right over there. We'll never get away. What did you hear the soldiers say? Perhaps it was just a misunderstanding.'

'Listen to me, you deficient,' Ocotal hissed. 'There is no time! I go now. If you come, come now. If not, *adiós.*'

He rose easily, lazily, and began strolling towards where the dugouts were beached. In a panic Philip turned his eyes from him to the soldiers. They were still playing cards, oblivious. From where they were sitting, at the base of a tree, they could not see the boats.

What should he do? He felt paralysed. A monumental decision had been thrust on him. Could Hauser really be that cold-blooded?

Ocotal was now sauntering along the beach, casually looking up into the trees. He stood by a boat and with his knee, slowly and without seeming to do so, began edging it into the water.

It was happening too fast. Really, it hinged on what kind of man Hauser was. Was he really capable of murder?

Ocotal now had the boat in the water and with a smooth motion stepped into it, picking up the pole and getting ready to shove off.

Philip stood up and walked quickly down to the beach. Ocotal was already offshore, pole planted, ready to shove the boat into the channel. He paused long enough for Philip to wade out and climb in, then he planted the pole and silently propelled them out into the swamp.

THE FOLLOWING MORNING, the fine weather had come to an end. Clouds gathered, thunder shook the treetops and the rain came pouring down. By the time Tom and the rest had set off, the surface of the river was grey and frothing under the force of a violent downpour, the sound of rain deafening among the vegetation. The maze of channels they were following seemed to get ever narrower and more convoluted. Tom had never seen a swamp so thick, so labyrinthine, so impenetrable. He could scarcely believe that Don Alfonso knew which way to go.

By noon, the rain ended suddenly, as if a spigot had been turned off. For another few minutes the water continued running down the tree trunks, with a noise like a waterfall, leaving the jungle misty, dripping and hushed.

At times their way was blocked with hanging vines and aerial roots that grew down from above. Pingo remained in front, hacking them down with his machete, while Chori poled from the back. Every blow of the machete dislodged tree frogs, insects and other creatures that dropped into the water, providing a feast for the piranhas below.

Then a strange sound developed in the canopy above them. It sounded like a thousand smacking, gurgling noises, accompanied by a rustling in the branches that grew in volume. There followed the flashing of black shapes, just visible through the leaves.

Chori shipped his paddle, and instantly a bow and arrow was in his hands and pointed skywards. He loosed his arrow. There was a sudden commotion above and a monkey came falling out of the branches, landing in the water five feet from the dugout.

Chori snatched the bundle of black fur out of the water. '*Ehi! Ehi!*' he said with a vast grin. '*Uakaris! Mmmm.*'

'There are two!' said Don Alfonso, in a high state of excitement. 'This was a very lucky strike, Tomasito. It is a mother and her baby.'

The baby was still clinging to the mother, squealing in terror.

'You shot a monkey?' Sally said, her voice high. 'That's *awful*!'

Don Alfonso's face fell. 'You do not like monkey? The brains of this monkey are truly a delicacy when roasted lightly in the skull.'

'We can't eat a monkey! It's . . . it's practically *cannibalism*.'

The baby leapt off the dead body of its mother and crouched in terror, hands over its head, making a high-pitched scream.

'*Ehi!*' Chori said, reaching to grab the baby monkey while raising the machete with the other hand, ready to deliver the *coup de grâce*.

'No!' Tom snatched the little monkey up into his arms. It nestled down and stopped screaming. Chori stared in surprise.

Don Alfonso leaned forward. 'I do not understand. What is this about cannibalism?'

'We consider monkeys to be almost human,' Tom said.

Don Alfonso said something sharply to Chori, whose grin vanished in a look of disappointment. Don Alfonso turned back to them. 'I did not know monkeys were sacred to North Americans. I am sorry.' He picked up the mother's body and tossed it into the water; there was a swirl and it was gone.

Tom felt the monkey nestling more vigorously into the crook of his arm, whimpering and trying to burrow into the warmth. He looked down. A little black face peeped up at him, eyes wide, and a tiny hand reached out. The monkey was no more than eight inches long and weighed no more than three or four pounds. His hair was soft and short, and he had large brown eyes, a tiny pink nose, little human ears, and four miniature hands with delicate fingers.

Tom found Sally looking at him with a smile on her face. 'What?'

'Looks like you've made a new friend.'

'Oh no.'

'Oh yes.'

The little monkey had recovered from his terror. He crawled out on Tom's arm and began poking around his chest. His little black hands went scurrying and plucking into the folds of Tom's clothing and he made a smacking sound with his lips. Then he lifted up the flap of Tom's giant, explorer-style pocket, climbed in it and wriggled himself into place. He sat there, arms folded, peering around.

Sally laughed. 'Oh, Tom, he *really* likes you now.'

'What do they eat?' Tom asked Don Alfonso.

'Everything. Insects, leaves, grubs. You will not have any trouble feeding your new friend.'

'Who says he's my responsibility?'

'Because he chose you, Tomasito. You belong to him now.'

'He's a hairy little bugger,' said Sally in English.

'Hairy Bugger. That's what we'll call him.'

THAT AFTERNOON, at one particularly convoluted maze of channels, Don Alfonso stopped the boat and spent more than ten minutes examining the water, tasting it, dropping spitballs into it and watching them drift to the bottom. Finally he sat up. 'There is a problem.'

'Are we lost?' Tom asked.

'No. *They* are lost.'

'Who?'

'One of your brothers. They took that channel to the left, which leads to the Plaza Negra, the Black Place, the rotten heart of the swamp where the demons live.'

'How long ago?'

'At least a week.'

'Is there a place to camp near here?'

'There is a small island a quarter of a mile further.'

'We'll stop there and unload,' said Tom. 'We'll leave Pingo and Sally in camp, while you and I and Chori take the dugout on a search for my brother. We've no time to lose.'

They landed on a sodden mud-island while rain poured down on them like a waterfall. Don Alfonso supervised the unloading and then reprovisioning of the boat, holding back the supplies they would need for their journey.

'We may be gone for two or three days,' Don Alfonso said. 'We must prepare to spend several nights in the dugout.'

Tom handed Sally the monkey. 'Take care of him, OK?'

'Of course.'

The boat pulled away and Tom watched her, a dim figure growing dimmer in the pouring rain.

Chori poled down the channel. Five minutes later Tom heard a screeching in the branches above the boat, and a little black ball came bouncing from branch to branch and finally shot out of an overhead tree and landed on his head, shrieking. It was Hairy Bugger.

THE STORM REACHED a climax as their dugout arrived at the channel to the Black Place. Lightning flashed and thunder echoed through the forest, sometimes only seconds apart, like an artillery barrage. The tops of the trees, 200 feet above their heads, shook and thrashed.

The channel soon divided into a maze of shallow waterways winding amid expanses of stinking mud. Don Alfonso stopped from time to time to check for pole marks in the bottom. Night came so imperceptibly that Tom was startled when Don Alfonso called a halt.

'We will sleep in the dugout like savages,' Don Alfonso said.

Tom bundled himself in his mosquito netting, found a place in their heap of gear and tried to sleep. The rain finally ceased, but he was still soaked to the skin. Tom thought of his brothers, especially Vernon. Could he be lost in the swamp, sick perhaps, maybe even dying? He subsided into a troubled night of dreams.

They found the dead body the next day. It was floating in the water. Chori brought the dugout alongside. A dozen dead piranhas floated round the corpse, their goggle eyes filmed over, their mouths open.

The hair was short and black. It was not Vernon.

'It is one of those boys from Puerto Lempira,' said Don Alfonso. 'He was bitten by a poisonous snake.'

'How do you know he was killed by a snake?' Tom asked.

'You see the dead piranhas? Those are the ones who ate the flesh in the area of the snakebite. They were poisoned.'

Chori pushed the body away with the pole and they paddled on, making slow work of it. The swamp was endless, the boat grazing the muddy bottom and frequently getting stuck, forcing them to get out and push. Often they had to double back, following tortuous channels. Towards noon, Don Alfonso held up his hand, Chori stopped paddling, and they listened. Tom could hear a distant voice, distraught— someone crying hysterically for help. It sounded like Vernon.

Tom cupped his hands. 'Vernon! It's me, Tom!'

There was a burst of desperate shouting that echoed through the trees, distorted and unintelligible.

'It's him,' said Tom. 'Hurry.'

Chori paddled forward, and soon Tom could see the vague outlines of a dugout canoe in the twilight of the swamp. A person was in the bow, screaming and gesturing. It was Vernon.

They reached the boat, and Tom pulled Vernon into their own.

Vernon collapsed into his brother's arms. 'Tell me I'm not dead,' he cried.

'You're OK, you're not dead. We're here now. You're safe.'

'Thank God. Thank God. I was sure the end had come . . .' His voice trailed away.

Tom helped Vernon sit. He was shocked at his brother's appearance. His face and neck were swollen with bites and smeared with blood from scratching. His clothes were filthy, his hair was tangled and foul, and he was even skinnier than usual. As soon as they got back to camp, he would send Vernon back to civilisation with Pingo.

'Don Alfonso,' Tom said, 'let's get out of here.'

'But the Teacher . . .' Vernon said.

Tom stopped. 'The Teacher?'

Vernon nodded towards the dugout. 'Sick.'

Tom leaned over and peered down. There, in a sodden sleeping-bag, almost hidden among the mess of equipment and soggy supplies in the bottom of the canoe, was the swollen face of a man surrounded by a wild head of white hair and a beard. He stared back up at Tom with baleful blue eyes, saying nothing.

'Who's this?'

'My teacher from the Ashram.'

'What's wrong with him?'

'He's got a fever. He stopped speaking two days ago.'

Tom pulled the medicine chest out of their supplies and stepped into the other dugout. The Teacher followed his every movement with his eyes. Tom bent over and felt the man's forehead. It was burning hot. The pulse was thready and fast. Tom injected him with a broad-spectrum antibiotic and an antimalarial.

'Don Alfonso, do you have any idea what disease this man has?'

Don Alfonso climbed into the boat and bent over the man. He tapped his chest, looked into his eyes, felt his pulse, examined his hands, then looked up. 'Yes, I know well this disease.'

'What is it?'

'It's called death.'

'No,' said Vernon, agitated. 'Don't say that. He's not dying.'

Tom was sorry he had asked for Don Alfonso's opinion. 'We'll bring him back to camp in the dugout. Chori can pole that dugout, and I'll pole ours.' He turned to Vernon. 'We found one dead guide back there. Where's the other?'

'A jaguar dropped down on him at night and dragged him into a tree. We could hear his screams . . . It was . . .' The sentence finished in a choking sound. 'Tom, get me out of here.'

THEY ARRIVED BACK at the camp just after nightfall. Vernon put up one of their tents, and they carried the Teacher up from the boat and put him inside.

Vernon insisted on spending the night with him in the tent. The next morning, Vernon roused them all with a call for help. Tom was the first to arrive. The Teacher was sitting up in his sleeping-bag, highly agitated. His face was pale and dry and his eyes glittered like chips of blue porcelain, darting about wildly, focusing on nothing.

All at once he spoke. 'Vernon!' he cried, groping about with his hands. 'Oh my God, where are you, Vernon? Where am I?'

Vernon grasped his hands and knelt. 'I'm here, Teacher. We're in the tent. We're taking you back to America. You're going to be fine.'

'What a fool I was!' the Teacher shouted. 'I had everything! Money. A house by the sea. I was surrounded by people who revered me. So what did I do? Ha! It wasn't enough! I wanted more! A hundred million dollars more! *And look what happened to me!*' He roared out these last words and then fell back heavily. He lay there, his eyes staring wide open, but the glitter was gone. He was dead.

Vernon stared in horror, unable to speak. Tom put his hand on his shoulder and found him shaking.

'Prepare one of the boats to return,' Tom said to Don Alfonso. 'Pingo can take Vernon back to Brus while we go on—if you don't have any objections.'

Don Alfonso began shouting orders to Chori and Pingo.

Vernon went to dig a grave, and Tom and Sally joined in. They chopped through roots with Chori's axe and dug into the soil underneath. In twenty minutes a shallow grave had been hollowed out of the hard clay soil. They dragged the Teacher's body to the hole, laid him in, packed a layer of clay on top of him, then filled the grave with smooth boulders from the river bank. Don Alfonso, Chori and Pingo were already in the boats, fretting, waiting to go.

'Are you all right?' Tom asked, putting his arm round his brother.

'I've made a decision,' Vernon said. 'I'm going on with you.'

'Vernon, it's all arranged.'

'What have I got to go back to? I can't go back to the Ashram. Please, Tom.'

There was such a depth of pleading in Vernon's voice that Tom was surprised—and, despite himself, a little glad. He grasped Vernon's shoulder. 'All right. We'll do this together, just as Father wanted.'

6

Marcus Hauser examined his white shirt front, and, finding a small beetle making its laborious way up it, he plucked it off, crushed it between thumb and forefinger with a satisfying crackle and tossed it away. He turned his attention back to Philip Broadbent, who was squatting on the ground, shackled, filthy, bug-bitten, unshaven.

Hauser glanced over to where the guide, Don Orlando Ocotal, was being held by three of his soldiers. Ocotal had almost made good his escape, which Hauser had only prevented by the most dogged pursuit. A whole day had been wasted. Ocotal's fatal flaw had been to assume a gringo, a *yanqui*, would not be able to track him in the swamp. He evidently hadn't heard of a place called Vietnam.

So much the better. Now it was out in the open. They were almost through the swamp anyway, and Ocotal had outlived his usefulness.

The lesson he would teach Ocotal would be good for Philip, too.

Hauser inhaled the fecund jungle air. 'Do you remember, Philip, when we were packing the boats? You wanted to know what we were going to do with these manacles and chains?'

Philip did not answer.

Hauser remembered explaining that the manacles were an important psychological tool to manage the soldiers, a sort of portable brig. Of course, he would never actually use them. 'Now you know,' Hauser said. 'They were for you.'

'You're a psychopath.'

'I am a rational human addressing a great wrong.'

'What wrong is this?'

'Your father and I were partners. He deprived me of my share of the loot from his first big discovery.'

'That was forty years ago.'

'Which only compounds the crime. He cheated me out of a fortune. I went on to a lovely place called Vietnam, while he went on to riches. Now I stand to gain it all back and more. The irony of it is delicious. And to think, Philip, you brought me this on a silver platter.'

Philip said nothing.

Hauser inhaled again. He loved the heat and he loved the air. He never felt so healthy and alive as in the jungle. He turned to one of the soldiers. 'Now we will do Ocotal. Come, Philip, you won't want to miss this.'

The two dugouts were already packed, and the soldiers shoved Ocotal and Philip into one. They fired up the engines and headed into the maze of pools and channels at the far end of the lake.

Hauser stood in the bow keeping an eye out. 'That way.'

The boats motored on until they came to a stagnant pool, cut off from the main channel by the lowering water. The piranhas, Hauser knew, had been concentrated in the pool by the subsiding water and had eaten all the available food. Woe to any animal that blundered into one of those stagnant pools.

'Cut the engine. Drop anchor.'

The engines sputtered off and the ensuing silence was broken only by the two soft splashes of the rock anchors.

Hauser turned and looked at Ocotal. 'Stand him up.'

The soldiers pulled Ocotal to his feet. Hauser took a step forward and gazed on his face. The Indian, dressed in a Western shirt and shorts, was straight and cool. His eyes showed neither fear nor hatred. This Tawahka Indian, Hauser thought, had proven to be one of those people motivated by notions of honour and loyalty. Hauser disliked such people. They were inflexible.

'Well, *Don* Orlando,' Hauser said, giving the honorific an ironic emphasis. 'Have you anything to say for yourself?'

The Indian gazed at him unblinkingly.

Hauser removed his pocketknife. 'Hold him tight.'

The soldiers grasped him. His hands were tied behind his back, and his feet were loosely tied together.

Hauser opened the little knife, reached out and scored a long cut across Ocotal's chest, cutting through the fabric of his shirt to his skin below. It wasn't a deep cut, but the blood began to run.

The Indian did not even flinch.

Hauser made a second shallow cut on the shoulders, and two more cuts on the arms and back. Still the Indian showed nothing.

'Throw him in.'

The solders gave him a shove and he went over the side. After the splash there was a moment of calm, and then the water began to swirl, slowly at first, and then with more agitation, until the pool seethed. There were flashes of silver in the brown water like fluttering coins, until a red cloud billowed up, turning the water opaque.

FOR THREE DAYS, Tom and his group continued travelling through the heart of the swamp along an interconnecting web of channels, camping on mud-islands scarcely higher than the water line, cooking beans and rice with wet wood over smoking fires because Chori could find no fresh game. They carried along with them a permanent, malevolent humming cloud of blackflies.

'I'll think I'll take that pipe now,' said Sally. 'I'd rather die of cancer than endure this.'

With a smile of triumph Don Alfonso removed it from his pocket. 'You will see—smoking will lead to a long and happy life.'

Tom could see a patch of sunlight up ahead, and as they moved forward he saw that a giant tree had recently fallen, leaving a hole in the canopy. The trunk lay across the channel, blocking their path.

Chori picked up his Pulaski and hopped out of the bow and onto the log. Gripping the slippery surface with his bare feet, he began to chop, the chips flying. In half an hour he had notched the log deep enough to slide the boats through.

They all climbed out and began to push. Beyond the log the water suddenly became deep. Tom waded through it, up to his waist, trying not to think of the toothpick fish and the piranhas.

Vernon was ahead of him, pushing the dugout forward, when Tom saw a slow undulation in the water to their right. Simultaneously he heard Don Alfonso's piercing cry. 'Anaconda!' Tom scrambled in but Vernon was too slow. There was a swirl of water, a sudden humplike rise, and with a scream—cut short—Vernon disappeared beneath the brown water. The snake's glossy back slid past, exposing briefly a body as thick as a small tree trunk, before it disappeared.

Tom pulled his machete out of his belt and dived into the water. He kicked, swimming down as deep as he could. He couldn't see more than a foot into the murky, brown glow. He scissor-kicked towards the middle, feeling ahead with his free hand, trying to find the snake among the slimy sunken logs.

One of the logs suddenly flexed under his touch. It was a muscled tube, as hard as mahogany, but he could feel the skin moving, the waves of contracting muscles. He shoved the machete into its soft underbelly. The snake exploded into a whiplike motion, which slammed him back in the water, knocking out his air. He clawed his way to the surface, then realised he no longer had the machete. Now roiling coils of the snake flew out of the water in a glossy arc, and for a moment Vernon's hand appeared, clutched into a fist, followed by his head. A gasp and he was gone.

'Another machete!'

Pingo tossed him one, handle first. He grabbed at it and began slashing at the coils lashing about on the surface.

'The head!' Don Alfonso cried from the boat. 'Go for the head!'

Where was the head in this mass of snake? Tom had a sudden idea and jabbed the snake with the machete, prodding him into a fury— and then, rearing out of the water, came the brute's head, ugly and small, with two slitty eyes searching for the source of its torment. It lunged at him, mouth open, and Tom shoved the machete right into the pink cavity and straight down the monster's gullet. The snake jerked and twisted and bit down, but Tom, clutching the handle, held on even as his arm was being bitten, giving the machete one hard twist after another. He could feel the flesh yielding inside, the sudden gush of cold reptilian blood; the head began thrashing back and forth, almost jerking his arm out of its socket. With all his remaining strength he gave the machete a final massive twist, and the blade came out behind the snake's head. He rotated it and felt a spasmodic tremble in the jaws as the snake was decapitated from the inside. He prised open the mouth with his other hand and pulled his arm out, searching frantically for his brother amid the still-churning water.

Vernon suddenly rose to the surface of the pond, face down. Tom grabbed him and dragged him through the water to the boat, where Pingo and Sally hauled him in. Tom fell in after him and passed out.

Sally was leaning over him when he came to, her blonde hair like a waterfall swaying above him, cleaning the teeth marks in his arm.

'Vernon—?'

'He's OK,' Sally said. 'Don Alfonso's helping him. He just swallowed some water and got a nasty bite on his thigh.'

Tom tried to sit up. The blackflies were swirling about him worse than ever, and he breathed them in with each breath. She pushed him back down with a gentle hand on his chest. 'Don't move.' She sucked in smoke from her pipe and blew it round him, chasing the flies away.

TOM LAY IN HIS HAMMOCK that evening, nursing his arm. Vernon had recovered well and was cheerfully helping Don Alfonso boil some unknown bird that Chori had shot for dinner.

Only thirty days had passed since Tom left Bluff, but it seemed an eternity. His horses, the red sandstone hills etched against the blue skies, the drenching sunlight and the eagles . . . It all seemed to have happened to someone else. It was strange . . . He had moved to Bluff with Sarah, his fiancée. She loved horses and the outdoors as much as he did, but Bluff turned out to be too quiet for her, and one day she'd packed and left. He had just established his vet practice, and there was no way he could pull out. Not that he wanted to. That was two years ago, and he hadn't had a relationship since.

He turned in his hammock, his arm throbbing, and glanced over at Sally. The partition was rolled up for ventilation and she was lying in her hammock reading a thriller Vernon had brought. He watched her turn the page, brush back her hair, sigh, turn another page. She was beautiful, even if she was a bit of a pain in the neck.

Sally laid down the book and smiled at him. 'How are you feeling?'

'Fine.'

'That was a real Indiana Jones rescue back there.'

Tom shrugged. 'I wasn't going to stand around while a snake ate my brother.' This wasn't really what he wanted to talk about. He asked, 'Tell me about this fiancé of yours, this Professor Clyve.'

'Well.' Sally smiled at the memory. 'I went to Yale to study with him. He's brilliant, a genius in the real sense of the word. I'll never forget when we first met. I thought he was just going to be another academic type, but—wow! He looked like Tom Cruise.'

'Do you have a wedding date?'

'Julian doesn't believe in weddings. We'll just go to a justice of the peace.'

'What about your parents? Won't they be disappointed?'

'I don't have any parents.'

Tom felt his face flush. 'I'm sorry.'

'Don't be,' Sally said. 'My father died when I was eleven, and my mother passed away ten years ago. I've got used to it.'

'Tell me about your father.'

'He was a cowboy. The foreman of a corporate-owned cattle ranch in southern Arizona. He fell off a windmill he was trying to fix and broke his neck. They shouldn't have asked him to go up there, but the judge decided the accident was his fault, because he'd been drinking.'

'I'm sorry, I don't mean to pry.'

'It's good to talk about it.'

'I figured your father would have owned the ranch.'

'You thought I was a little rich girl?'

'Well, yes, I did assume something like that. After all, here you are a Yalie, and with your riding ability . . .' He thought of Sarah. He'd had enough of rich girls to last him the rest of his life.

Sally laughed, but it was a bitter laugh. 'I've had to fight for every little thing I have. And that includes Yale.'

Tom felt his colour deepening. He had been reckless in his assumptions. She wasn't like Sarah at all.

'Despite his shortcomings,' Sally continued, 'my father was a wonderful dad. He taught me how to ride and shoot. What about your childhood? What was it like?'

Tom sighed. 'Where should I begin? We were to the manor born, so to speak. Giant house, pool, cook, housekeeper, stables, a thousand acres of land. Father lavished everything on us. He had big plans for us. At seven we each had to choose a musical instrument. We were sent to the best schools. Every minute of the day was scheduled: riding lessons, tutors, private sports coaches. We each had to choose a sport. Not for the fun or exercise, but to *excel* in.'

'How awful. And your mother, what was she like?'

'Our three mothers. We're half-brothers. Father was unlucky in love, you might say.'

'He got custody of all three of you?'

'What Max wanted, Max got. Our mothers weren't a big part of our lives, and mine died when I was young anyway. Father wanted to raise us by himself, without interference. He was going to create three geniuses who would change the world. He tried to choose our careers for us. Even our girlfriends. We got something out of it in the end, I suppose. I learned to love horses. Philip fell in love with Renaissance painting. And Vernon—well, he just fell in love with wandering.'

'So he chose your girlfriends?'

Tom wished he hadn't mentioned that detail. 'He tried.'

'And?'

Tom felt his face flushing. The thought of Sarah—perfect, beautiful, brilliant, talented, wealthy Sarah—came flooding in.

'Who was she?' Sally asked.

Women always seemed to know. 'Just some girl my father introduced me to. Daughter of a friend of his. It was, ironically, the one time I really wanted to do what my father wanted me to do.'

'What happened?'

'Didn't work out.' He didn't add the part about him finding her riding some other guy in their own bed. What Sarah wanted, Sarah got, too. She could deny herself nothing.

Sally shook her head. 'Your father was really a piece of work. He could have written a book on how *not* to raise children.'

Tom knew he shouldn't say it, he knew it would cause trouble, but he couldn't stop himself. He said, 'Father would've *loved* Julian.'

There was a sudden silence. He could feel Sally staring at him. 'Excuse me?'

'All I meant is that Julian's just the kind of person Father wanted us to be. Stanford at sixteen, famous professor at Yale, "a genius in the real sense of the word", as you put it.'

'I won't dignify that comment with an answer,' she said stiffly, her face colouring with anger as she picked up her novel and began to read.

TWO DAYS AFTER the snake attack, as they were poling along another endless water channel, Tom noticed a brightening of the swamp, sunlight through the trees—and then with astonishing suddenness the two dugouts broke free of the Meambar Swamp. It was like entering a new world. They were on the edge of a huge lake, the water as black as ink. The late-afternoon sun was breaking through the clouds and Tom felt a surge of relief at finally being released from the green prison of the swamp. A fresh breeze swept away the blackflies. Tom could see blue hills on the far shore, and beyond them a faint line of mountains.

'The Laguna Negra!' Don Alfonso cried.

Chori and Pingo lowered the outboards and fired them up. The boats set off for the far end of the lake. Tom enjoyed the delicious flow of air on his skin.

They camped on a sandy beach. Chori and Pingo went hunting and returned an hour later with a gutted and quartered deer, the bloody chunks wrapped in palm fronds.

'Splendid!' cried Don Alfonso. 'Tomás, we will eat deer chops tonight and smoke the rest for our overland journey.'

Don Alfonso roasted the loin chops over the fire while Pingo and Chori built a smoking rack over a second fire. They sliced off pieces of meat with their machetes and flipped them over the rack, then piled wet wood on the fire, generating fragrant clouds of smoke.

Tom asked. 'Don Alfonso, where do we go from here?'

'Five rivers flow into the Laguna Negra. We must find out which river your father went up.'

'Are they navigable by boat?'

'The lower parts are said to be.'

'"Said to be"?' Tom asked. 'You haven't been up them?'

'None of my people have been up them. The country back there is very dangerous. The animals are not afraid of people, and there is a city of demons from which no one ever returns.'

'A city of demons?' Vernon asked, suddenly interested.

'Yes. La Ciudad Blanca. The White City. It lies in ruins.'

'That's where Father went,' Vernon said matter-of-factly.

Tom stared at him. 'How can you know?'

'I don't *know*. But Father would love a story like that. He'd check it out for sure. And stories like that are often based in reality. I bet he did find a lost city there, some big old ruin.'

'But there aren't supposed to be any ruins in those mountains.' Tom turned to Don Alfonso. 'Is this White City common knowledge?'

Don Alfonso nodded slowly. 'It is talked about.'

'Where is it?'

Don Alfonso shook his head. 'It has no fixed location but moves about the highest peaks of the Sierra Azul, always shifting and hiding in the mists of the mountain.'

'So it's a myth?' Tom glanced at Vernon.

'Oh, no, Tomás, it's real. They say it can only be reached by crossing a bottomless gorge.'

'Father hung out in bars,' Vernon said, 'buying rounds for Indians, loggers and gold prospectors, listening for gossip about ruins and lost cities. Think about it. Father wouldn't build a tomb to bury himself in. He'd simply reuse one of the tombs he robbed long ago.'

After a moment, Tom said, 'Vernon, that's brilliant.'

'And he'd get the Indians to help him.

The fire crackled. There was a dead silence.

'But Father never mentioned anything about a White City.'

Vernon smiled. 'Exactly. You know why? Because *that's* where he made his big discovery, the one that got him started. He arrived down here dead broke and he came back with a boatload of treasure.'

'I'm convinced,' said Sally.

'I even know how Father bought the Indians' help,' Vernon said. 'How?'

'Remember those receipts the Santa Fe policeman found in Father's house for all that cookware? That's how he paid them: cooking pots for the natives.' Vernon turned to Don Alfonso. 'Which river do you take to get there?'

The old man sighed. 'The Macaturi will take you partway, but you cannot go farther than the Falls. The Sierra Azul lies many days beyond them, beyond the mountains and valleys and more mountains. It is an impossible journey. Your father could not have done it.'

'Don Alfonso, you don't know our father. Are you coming with us?'

'It is my fate to come with you,' he said softly. 'Of course, we will all die before we reach the Sierra Azul. I am old and ready to die. But it will be sad for me to see Chori and Pingo die, and Vernon die, and to see the *curandera* die. And it will be very sad for me to see you die, Tomás, because you are now my friend.'

7

The Macaturi was more navigable than the Patuca, deep and clean, without sandbars or hidden snags. As they motored up the river, the sun broke over the distant hills, tingeing them a greenish gold. The two boats continued in silence for several hours. As they rounded a bend, a large tree appeared, lying across the river, blocking their way. It had recently fallen, and the leaves were still green.

'This is strange,' muttered Don Alfonso. Suddenly he dived for the tiller and shoved it to the right. 'Get down!' he screamed.

At the same instant a burst of automatic-weapons fire rang out.

Tom threw himself on Sally, slamming her to the bottom of the boat as a line of bullets ripped through the side of the dugout, showering them with splinters. He could hear the shouts of the attackers. Don Alfonso crouched in the stern, one hand still on the tiller, steering them towards the shelter of an overhanging embankment.

An unearthly scream rose up from the boat behind them.

Tom lay on top of Sally. He could see nothing but her blonde hair and the scarred wooden hull beneath them. The firing continued, but the bullets seemed to be passing above their heads. The boat scraped the bottom, the propeller grinding on rocks in the shallows.

The firing and the screaming stopped at the same time. They had reached the cover of the embankment. Don Alfonso scrambled back to his feet and looked behind. Tom could hear him shouting in Tawahka, but there was no answer.

Tom rose cautiously, lifting Sally. There were flecks of blood on her cheek where splinters of wood had cut her.

'Are you all right?'

She nodded mutely.

He turned to the dugout behind, calling to his brother. 'Vernon! Vernon! Are you hurt?'

Vernon rose shakily from the centre of the boat. 'No, but Pingo's hurt real bad.'

The cough and roar of a boat engine sounded upriver, and then a second one. Tom could hear distant shouts.

Sally turned to Chori. 'Give me your gun.'

Chori looked at her, uncomprehending.

Without waiting, Sally grabbed the gun, checked to see it was loaded, slammed the bolt back and crouched in the stern.

Tom could see two boats coming round the bend in the river, the soldiers aiming their automatic weapons. He heard a single shot from Sally's gun just as a burst of gunfire raked the vegetation hanging over them. The shot had the desired effect: the two boats veered off for the cover of the river bank.

Don Alfonso was steering their boat under the embankment, the propeller striking rocks and whining as it was forced out of the water. Vernon had taken the tiller of the other boat and was following. More bullets whizzed overhead, and there was a dull metallic clank as one of the rounds struck the engine.

The engine spluttered, then there was a *whoosh* as it caught fire, the boat turning broadside to the sluggish current. The fire spread with incredible speed, the flames leaping up from the melting rubber fuel lines. The prow of Vernon's boat bumped into their hull from behind, jamming up against it as burning oil began to spread on the bottom of their boat, licking up around the fuel tanks.

'Out!' said Tom. 'They're going to blow. Grab what you can!'

They threw themselves into the shallows along the river bank. Vernon and Chori carried Pingo up the embankment. The others scrambled up and they all took cover. Tom looked back to see their boats drifting downstream, flames leaping. Beyond, the boats with the soldiers were cautiously angling in towards shore. Sally, still carrying Chori's rifle, fired a second shot through the screen of vegetation.

They retreated deeper into the jungle, taking turns to carry Pingo. From behind Tom could hear more shouting, followed by some random shooting through the forest. The men had evidently landed their boats and were halfheartedly chasing them. But as the fugitives pushed deeper into the forest, the sporadic gunfire grew fainter until the sounds disappeared altogether.

They halted in a grassy clearing. Tom and Vernon laid Pingo down, and Tom bent over him, desperately feeling for a pulse. There was none. He glanced up at Chori. 'I'm sorry.'

Don Alfonso said, 'There is no time to be sorry. We must go.'

'And leave the body here?'

'Chori will stay with it.'

'But the soldiers are surely coming—'

Don Alfonso cut him off. 'Yes. And Chori must do what he must do.' He turned to Sally. 'You keep his gun and ammunition. We will not see Chori again. Let us go.'

'We can't leave him here!' Tom protested.

Don Alfonso grabbed Tom's shoulders. His hands were surprisingly strong, like steel clamps. He spoke quietly but with intensity. 'Chori has unfinished business with Pingo's killers.'

'Without a gun?' Sally asked as Chori took a tattered box of ammunition out of his leather bag and handed it to her.

'Silent arrows are more effective in the jungle. He will kill enough of them to die with honour. This is our way. Do not interfere.'

Without a backwards glance, Don Alfonso turned, swiped his machete across a wall of vegetation and plunged through the opening. They followed, struggling to keep up with the old man. They walked for hours up and down ravines, wading through swift streams, at times hacking their way through dense stands of bamboo or ferns.

When the light began to die in the treetops, Don Alfonso halted. Without a word he sat on a fallen tree trunk, fished out his pipe and lit it. Tom watched the match flare up and wondered how many more they had. They had lost almost everything with the boats.

'What now?' Vernon asked.

'We camp,' said Don Alfonso. He pointed. 'Make a fire. There.'

Vernon got to work and Tom helped.

Don Alfonso pointed at Sally. 'You. Go hunting. You may be a woman, but you shoot like a man and have the courage of a man.'

Tom looked at Sally. Her face was smudged, her long blonde hair in tangles, the gun slung over her shoulder. He could see in her face everything he was feeling: the shock and surprise of the attack, horror at the death of Pingo, dread at the loss of all their supplies, determination to survive. She nodded and went off into the forest.

Don Alfonso looked at Tom. 'You and I will build a hut.'

AN HOUR LATER, night had fallen. They were sitting round the fire, eating the last of a stew made from a large rodent Sally had shot. A small thatched hut stood nearby, and Don Alfonso sat beside a pile of palm leaves, stripping them and weaving them into hammocks.

'Who were those soldiers?' Tom asked Don Alfonso.

'The soldiers who came upriver with your other brother Philip.'

'Philip would never permit an attack on us,' said Vernon.

'No,' said Tom. He felt his heart sink. There must have been a mutiny on Philip's expedition, or something else had happened. At any rate, Philip must be in grave danger—if not already dead. The unknown enemy, therefore, had to be Hauser. He was the one who had killed the two policemen in Santa Fe, who had arranged for their capture in Brus, who was behind this most recent attack on them.

'The question,' Sally said, 'is whether we go on or go back.'

'It'd be suicide to go on,' Vernon said. 'We've got nothing—no food, no clothes, no tents, sleeping-bags or food.'

'Philip's up ahead,' said Tom. 'And he's in trouble. It's obvious Hauser's the one behind the killing of the two policemen in Santa Fe.'

There was a silence, then Sally spoke. 'Maybe we should go back, resupply and return. We won't be able to help him like this, Tom.'

Tom glanced at Don Alfonso. There was a studiously neutral expression on the old man's face. 'Don Alfonso, do you have an opinion?'

Don Alfonso laid the hammock down. He looked Tom in the eye. 'I do not have an opinion. I have instead a statement of fact.'

'Which is?'

'Behind us is a deadly swamp in which the water is lowering every day. We have no dugout. It will take a week at least to make another. But we cannot stay in one place for a week, because the soldiers will find us, and the manufacture of a dugout creates clouds of smoke. So we must keep moving, on foot, through the jungle, towards the Sierra Azul. To go back is to die. That is my statement of fact.'

THEY SPENT the following day in camp. Don Alfonso cut a stack of palm fronds and sat cross-legged, pulling them into fibrous strips and weaving palm-leaf backpacks and more hammocks. Sally hunted and brought back a small antelope, which Tom dressed and smoked over the fire. Vernon collected fruits and manioc root. By the end of the day they had a small supply of food for their journey.

They inventoried their supplies. Between them they had several boxes of waterproof matches and a box of ammunition with thirty rounds. Tom's daypack containing a tiny camping stove with aluminium pots and pans, and two bottles of white gas. Vernon had escaped with a pair of binoculars. Don Alfonso had three pipes, some chocolate bars, two packs of pipe tobacco, a small whetstone and a roll of fishing line with hooks, all of which had been in his greasy leather bag. They all had their machetes.

The next morning they set off. Tom cleared the trail wielding a freshly sharpened machete, while Don Alfonso went behind, murmuring which way to go. After a few miles they came out on what appeared to be an old animal trail running through a cool forest.

By the early afternoon the trail had reached the base of a mountain range. The terrain pitched up from the forest floor, becoming a tangled slope of moss-covered boulders. The trail went almost straight up. As they gained altitude the air became fresher. The stately trees of the jungle gave way to their dwarfish, twisted cousins of the mountains, their branches hung with moss. In the late afternoon they came out on a flat ridge, which ended in an outcropping of rocks.

Don Alfonso set down his palm-leaf backpack. 'This is a good place to camp. Sally, you and Tom go hunting. Vernon, you build the fire and then the hut. I will rest.'

Sally slung the gun over her shoulder and they set off, following an animal trail. The forest was cool and deep. Through gaps in the trees, Tom could see the Macaturi River glinting in scimitar-like curves through the rain forest far below.

A cough echoed from the forested slopes above them. It sounded like a human cough, only deeper, throatier.

'That,' said Sally, 'sounds feline.'

'Feline, as in jaguar?'

'Yes.'

They moved side by side through the foliage, palming the leaves and ferns out of the way. The mountain slopes were curiously silent.

'It feels strange up here,' said Tom. 'Unreal.'

'It's a cloud forest,' said Sally. 'A high-altitude rain forest.'

She moved ahead, the rifle at the ready. Tom fell behind her. There was another cough, deep and booming.

'That sounded closer,' said Tom.

They clambered across a slope covered with giant boulders, squeezing through moss-covered faces of rock, and came out facing a thick stand of bamboo. Sally moved round it. Clouds were already pressing down on them and tendrils of mist drifted through the trees. The view below them had vanished into whiteness.

They crept forward. In front of them was a second cluster of giant mossy boulders, rolled and piled together, forming a honeycomb of dark holes and crawlspaces.

'There's something moving in those rocks,' Sally whispered.

They waited, crouching. Tom could feel the mists collecting round him, soaking his clothes.

After about ten long minutes, a head appeared at an opening in the rocks, with two bright black eyes. Then an animal looking like a giant guinea pig came sniffing out.

The shot rang out instantly and the animal squealed loudly and rolled belly up. Sally stood up.

'Nice shooting,' Tom said.

'Thanks.' Sally stood up. 'I'll go on ahead.'

Tom nodded and watched her move silently into the mist below, then he unsheathed his machete and went to examine the animal. It was some kind of rodent. He sliced it open, pulled out the guts, cut off the paws and head and skinned it. As hungry as he was, he began to lose his appetite. He wasn't squeamish, but he didn't like being part of the killing as opposed to the healing.

He quartered the animal and wrapped the meat up in palm leaves. As he finished, he heard a soft purr, so close that he flinched. He waited, listening, his whole body tense. Suddenly a bloodcurdling scream split the forest, trailing off into a hungry growl. He jumped up, machete in his hand, left the chopped-up rodent and headed towards where Sally had disappeared. 'Sally!' he called. 'Are you all right?'

Silence.

He began to run down the slope, his heart in a panic. 'Sally!'

Sally emerged from the mists, carrying the gun, with a scowl on her face. 'Your shouting caused me to miss a shot.'

'I was worried, that's all. That jaguar's hunting us.'

'Jaguars don't hunt people.'

They climbed back to where the body of the rodent had been. There were only a few torn and bloody palm leaves on the ground.

Sally laughed. 'That's all it was doing—chasing you away so it could eat our dinner!'

'I wasn't chased away—I came looking for you.'

'Don't worry about it. I probably would have run, too.'

Tom suppressed a tart reply, and they started back towards camp. As they approached the first rock pile, the jaguar screamed again.

'He's ahead of us, Sally. Let's play it safe and skirt those rocks.'

They climbed uphill into the thickening mists. There were trees all around them, crooked trees with low branches hung with moss. Tom realised they were now upwind of the animal. It had moved round them so that it could scent them.

'Sally, I can *feel* it hunting us.'

'It's just curious.'

Tom froze. There, about ten yards ahead, was the jaguar. It was standing on a branch above their path, calmly looking at them, twitching its tail. Its magnificence took Tom's breath away.

Sally did not raise her gun to shoot, and Tom understood why. It was impossible to contemplate destroying such a beautiful animal.

After a moment's hesitation the jaguar leapt effortlessly to another tree branch and walked along it, eyeing them the whole time, its muscles rippling under its golden pelt, moving like flowing honey. Then it stopped, slowly sinking down onto its haunches. It looked at them boldly, utterly unafraid, making no effort to hide, motionless except for the faintest twitching of the tip of its tail.

Tom backed up slowly, and Sally followed suit. The jaguar remained on its perch watching them as they disappeared from view into the shifting mists.

When they got back to camp, Don Alfonso listened to their story about the jaguar. 'We must be very careful,' he said. 'We must not talk about this animal any more. Otherwise, it will follow us to hear what we say. He is proud and does not like to be spoken ill of. Next time you have the opportunity, kill it.'

THAT NIGHT THE FOREST was so quiet that Tom had trouble sleeping. Sometime after midnight, he crept out of his hammock and ducked out of the hut. He was astonished at the sight that greeted him. The forest was aglow with phosphorescence, as if glowing powder had been dusted over everything, outlining rotting logs and stumps, dead leaves and mushrooms. It was as if the heavens had fallen to earth.

He crept back into the makeshift hut and gave Sally a little shake. She rolled over, her hair a tangle of heavy gold. Like all of them, she was sleeping in her clothes. 'What is it?' she said in a sleepy voice.

'There's something you have to see.'

'I'm sleeping.'

'You've got to see this. Trust me.'

Grumbling, she got out of her hammock and stepped outside. She halted and stood there in silence, staring. Minutes passed. 'My God,' she breathed. 'I've never seen anything so beautiful.'

The glow cast a faint illumination on Sally's face, barely outlining it against the darkness.

On an impulse, he took her hand. She didn't withdraw it.

'Tom?'

'Yes?'

'Why did you want me to see this?'

'Well, I . . .'He hesitated. 'I wanted to share it with you, that's all.'

'That's all?' She looked at him for a long time. Her eyes seemed unusually luminescent—or maybe it was just a trick of the light. Finally she said, 'Thank you, Tom.'

WHEN THEY SET OFF the next morning, the mists were so thick they couldn't see more than ten feet in any direction. They climbed farther up the mountain, following the faint animal trail through a forest of gnarled trees that seemed to get denser as they gained altitude. And then, quite suddenly, they walked out of the mist and into the sunlight. Tom paused, astonished. Hairy Bugger, who had been sleeping in Tom's pocket, took the opportunity to poke his head out and look around. They were now looking out over a sea of white. On the puffy horizon the sun was sinking into an orange sea of fire and the forest was draped with brilliant flowers.

'We're above the clouds,' cried Sally.

'We will camp at the top,' said Don Alfonso, striking off with a newly invigorated step.

The trail crested the ridge and all of a sudden they were at the summit. Fifty miles distant Tom could see a line of sharp blue peaks breaking through the clouds, like a chain of islands in the sky.

'The Sierra Azul,' said Don Alfonso, in a small, queer voice.

AS THEY CAME DOWN from the mountains, the rain forest changed. The terrain was rough: a landscape cut by ravines and torrential rivers, with high ridges in between. They continued to follow the animal trail, but it was so overgrown that they had to take turns hacking their way forward. They slipped and fell going up the steep muddy trails and slid and fell going down. In a hard day's travel they might make five miles and by the end of each day they were all exhausted.

The days began to run together. Not once did the rain stop or the mists lift. Their hammocks rotted and had to be rewoven, their clothes began to fall apart. Their bodies were covered with stings, bites, scrapes, cuts, scabs and sores. The hunting was almost non-existent. They never had enough to eat.

And always, at night and even during the day, they could hear the coughing of the jaguar. No one spoke about it—Don Alfonso had forbidden it—but it was never far from Tom's mind.

On the fourth or fifth night—Tom had begun to lose count—they camped atop a ridge, wedged among massive rotting tree trunks. It had rained, and steam rose from the ground. They ate early—a boiled lizard with matta root. After eating, Sally stood up with the gun.

'Jaguar or no jaguar, I'm going hunting.'

'I'm coming,' Tom said.

They picked their way down a ravine, over mossy boulders and tree trunks, until they reached a stream. They moved along it, Indian file, through the curling mists.

Sally paused, held up her hand. Slowly she raised the gun, aimed and fired. An animal thrashed and squealed in the undergrowth.

'I don't know what it was, except that it was stout and furry.'

In the bushes they found the animal.

'Some kind of peccary,' said Tom.

He pulled out his machete, gutted the animal, cut a pole, and tied the legs together. They slid the body on the pole and hefted it over their shoulders. It would make a fine meal, with meat left over for smoking. They began heading back.

They hadn't gone more than twenty yards when they were stopped by the jaguar, standing in the middle of the trail. It stared at them.

'Back up,' said Tom. 'Nice and easy.' But as they backed up, the jaguar took a step forward, and another, pacing them on padded paws.

'Remember what Don Alfonso said?'

'I can't do it,' Sally whispered.

'Shoot over its head.'

Sally raised the muzzle of the gun and squeezed off a round.

The jaguar gave a small shiver but otherwise made no sign it had heard, just continued to stare at them with green eyes, the tip of the tail twitching as rhythmically as a metronome.

'We'll go round it,' Sally said.

They edged off the trail into the forest. The animal made no move to follow them and soon it was lost to sight. After a few hundred yards Tom began to cut back towards the ridge line. They heard the cat cough twice off to their left, so they moved further down from the ridge. The forest became darker, the trees smaller and closer together.

A low, booming cough came from directly behind them.

Sally turned angrily. 'Get out of here!' she yelled. 'Scat!'

They went on, redoubling their pace, Tom in the lead, slashing a path through the undergrowth.

And then, with a sudden flash of gold, the jaguar seemed to congeal out of the mist ahead of them. It stood on a low branch, tensed.

They stopped, then backed up slowly while the animal watched. With a liquid movement, it leapt to one side of them, and in three bounds it had positioned itself on a branch behind them, blocking their retreat.

Sally kept her gun aimed at the jaguar, but she didn't shoot. They stared at the animal and the animal stared at them.

'I think maybe the time has come to kill it,' Tom whispered.

'I can't.'

Somehow, that was the answer Tom wanted to hear. Never had he seen an animal so vital, so supple or so magnificent.

Then, all of a sudden, the jaguar turned and took itself away, jumping lightly from branch to branch, until it had disappeared.

Sally smiled. 'I told you it was just curious.'

'That's some curiosity, following us for fifty miles.' Tom looked around. Finally he tucked his machete back into his belt and picked up the pole holding the dead peccary.

They had gone just five paces when the jaguar dropped down on them with a piercing shriek, landing on Sally's back. The gun went off uselessly. They hit the ground together, and the force of the blow knocked the jaguar off.

Tom threw himself on the animal's back, squeezing it between his legs like a bronco, clawing for its eyes with both thumbs. He felt the massive body flex and snap like a steel spring under him. The jaguar screamed again, leaping and twisting its body round in midair as Tom drew his machete. Then the animal was on him, a smothering of rank fur bearing down on him and the pointed machete. Tom could feel the blade slide up into the jaguar, and there was a powerful rush of hot blood in his face. The machete must have penetrated the animals' lungs, because its screams turned into a suffocated gurgle and the creature went limp. Tom pushed it off him and removed the machete.

He rushed over to Sally, who was struggling to get up. She

screamed when she saw him. 'My God, Tom, are you all right?'

'Are *you* all right?'

'What did it do to you!' She tried to reach for his face.

He suddenly understood. 'It's not my blood,' he said weakly, bending over her. 'Let me look at your back.'

She rolled onto her stomach. The shirt was in tatters. Four scores ran across one shoulder. He pulled away what remained of her shirt, then stripped off his own shirt and soaked one end in a puddle of water. Sally grunted slightly as he cleaned the wounds. Then he took some moss and made a pad and tied it onto the wounds with her shirt. He wrapped his shirt round her and helped her to sit up.

'Can you stand up?'

'Sure.'

He helped her up; she staggered, then recovered. 'Give me my gun.' Tom fetched it. 'I'll carry it.'

'No, I'll carry it over the other shoulder. You carry the peccary.'

Tom didn't argue. He slung the peccary over his shoulder and paused to take one last look at the jaguar stretched out on its side.

Back at the camp, Vernon and Don Alfonso listened to their story. When Tom was finished Don Alfonso laid a hand on his arm and said, 'You are one crazy *yanqui*, Tomasito, you know that?'

Tom and Sally retreated into the privacy of the hut, and he redressed her wound while she sat cross-legged on the ground with her shirt off, mending it with bark thread Don Alfonso had made. She kept looking at him out of the corner of her eye, trying to suppress a smile. Finally she said, 'Have I thanked you for saving my life yet?'

'I don't need thanks.'

'Yes, you do.' She put down the shirt, turned round, put her arms round his neck and kissed him softly on the lips.

IT RAINED for a week solid, without letup. Every day they pushed forward, up and down canyons, along precarious cliffs, across roaring streams, all of it buried in the thickest jungle Tom thought possible. If they made four miles it was a good day. After seven days of this, Tom woke one morning to find the rain had finally ceased.

That day was worse than before, for when the rains ceased the insects appeared. Towards afternoon they climbed down into a ravine echoing with the sound of roaring water. As they descended, the roar became louder, and Tom realised a major river lay at the bottom. When the foliage broke at the banks of the river, Don Alfonso, who was in front, retreated in confusion, motioning them to stay back.

'What's wrong?' Tom asked.

'There is a dead man across the river, under a tree.'

Tom followed Don Alfonso to the river bank. On the other side of the river there was a clearing with a large tree in the middle. Tom could just see a bit of colour behind the tree. He borrowed Vernon's binoculars to examine it more closely. A bare foot, horribly swollen, was visible; the rest of him was hidden behind the trunk. As Tom looked he saw a bluish puff of smoke drift from behind the tree.

'Unless a dead man can smoke, that man's alive,' said Tom.

They felled a tree, the sound of the axe echoing through the forest, but the smoker did not move. After the tree had come crashing down, forming a wobbly bridge across the river, Tom and Vernon crossed over, and picked their way along the river bank to the clearing.

They stepped round the tree and found a wreck of a human being. He sat with his back against the trunk, smoking a briar pipe. He did not seem to be an Indian, although his skin was almost black. His clothing was in tatters and his face was scratched raw and bleeding from insect bites. His feet were cut and swollen. He was so thin, the bones of his body stuck out grotesquely, and he stared at them out of hollow eyes. He looked more dead than alive.

And then he gave a start, like a little shiver. The pipe came out of his mouth and he spoke, his voice little more than a whisper. 'How are you, brothers of mine?'

Tom jumped, he was so startled by hearing his brother Philip's voice coming from this living corpse.

'*Philip?*' Vernon whispered.

The voice croaked an affirmative.

'What are you doing here?'

'Dying.' He spoke matter-of-factly.

Tom turned to Vernon. 'Go and get Don Alfonso and Sally. Tell them we found Philip and that we're making camp here.'

Tom continued to look at his eldest brother, too shocked to speak.

Don Alfonso arrived, glanced at Philip appraisingly, then began clearing an area to set up camp.

When Philip saw Sally he removed the pipe and blinked.

'I'm Sally Colorado,' she said, taking his hand in hers. 'We need to clean you up.'

Philip managed a nod.

They carried him to the river, laid him on some banana leaves and stripped him. Philip's body was covered with sores, many of which were infected. They carefully washed him and then carried him back to the clearing and laid him on some palm leaves near the fire.

Sally began sorting the herbs and roots she had collected. After Tom had cleaned the sores, she dusted the wounds with a herbal antibiotic and bandaged Philip up with strips of pounded bark that had been sterilised in boiling water and then smoke-dried in the fire. They washed and dried his tattered clothes and re-dressed him in them, having no others. They propped him up and Sally gave him a mug of herbal tea.

Philip took a sip of tea and then another. Don Alfonso, meanwhile, had pulled half a dozen fish out of the stream and was grilling them on skewers at the fire. The smell of roasting fish came wafting over.

'Strange how I have no appetite,' said Philip.

'That's not uncommon when you're starving,' said Tom.

Don Alfonso served out the fish on leaves. They ate in silence.

Then Philip spoke. 'Well, here we are. A little family reunion in the Honduran jungle.' He looked round, his eyes sparkling.

'Glad to see you feeling better,' said Tom. 'You feel like telling us what happened?'

Philip carefully filled his pipe and lit it. 'The one thing they didn't take from me was my tobacco and pipe, thank God.' He puffed slowly, his eyes half closed, gathering his thoughts.

'After I left you two, I flew back to New York and looked up Father's old partner, Marcus Aurelius Hauser. He's a private eye, of all things. With two phone calls he was able to learn that Father had gone to Honduras, so I figured he was competent and hired him. We flew to Honduras; he organised an expedition and hired twelve soldiers. We flew to Brus and piled into dugout canoes. We picked up a guide and proceeded across the Meambar Swamp. Then Hauser staged a coup. He'd been planning it all along. He chained me up like a dog and fed our guide to the piranhas . . .'

Philip's voice faltered and he sucked on his pipe, his bony hand trembling. 'Hauser left five GI Josés behind to ambush you all and took me and the other seven up the Macaturi. When the soldiers returned there were only three of them, and one had an arrow sticking through his thigh. I heard them say they'd killed two people. We left the boats at the Falls and followed Father's trail on foot. Hauser kept me around to use as a bargaining chip with you. He ran into a group of mountain Indians, killed several, and chased the rest back to the village. He then attacked the village and managed to capture the chief. Once he had the chief as a hostage, we made our way up into the mountains towards the White City.'

'Hauser knows it's the White City?'

'He learned it from an Indian prisoner. But he doesn't know where the tomb is in the White City. Apparently only the chief and a few elders know the exact location of Father's tomb.'

'How did you escape?' Tom asked.

Philip closed his eyes. 'Kidnapping the chief stirred up the Indians. They attacked Hauser while he was en route to the White City. He'd taken the chains off me to use them on the chief. I managed to get away. I spent the last ten days walking—crawling, actually—back here, surviving on insects and lizards. Three days ago I reached this river. There was no way to cross. I was starving and I couldn't walk any more. So I sat down under a tree to wait for the end.'

'My God, Philip, how awful.'

'On the contrary. I didn't care any more. About anything. I'd never felt so free in my life as while I was sitting under that tree. I believe I might have actually been happy for a moment or two.'

8

The temple lay buried in lianas, the front colonnade supported by square pillars of limestone streaked with green moss.

'Stay outside,' Hauser said to his men, and slashed a hole in the screen of vegetation. He shone a flashlight around the interior. It was dry and sheltered—a good place to establish his headquarters.

He strolled deeper into the temple. At the back stood another row of square stone pillars framing a ruined doorway leading out to a gloomy courtyard. He stepped through. On the far side of the courtyard a second doorway led into a small chamber.

Hauser came back out to his waiting soldiers. Two of them held between them the captured chief, a bowed old man, almost naked except for a loincloth and a piece of leather tied over his shoulder.

Hauser gestured to the *teniente*. 'We'll stay here. Have the soldiers clean this room out for my bed and table.' He nodded to the old man. 'Chain him in the room across the courtyard and put a guard on him.'

The soldiers hustled the old Indian chief into the temple. Hauser settled down on a block of stone and lit a fresh cigar.

As he smoked, he looked at the ruins of a pyramid in front of him. Important burials were often found in Mayan pyramids. Hauser was convinced old Max had reburied himself in a tomb he once robbed. If so, it had to be an important tomb, to hold all of Max's stuff.

The stairway going up the pyramid had been heaved apart by tree roots, which had levered out many blocks and sent them tumbling to the bottom. At the top was the small room, with a shallow stone altar where the Maya sacrificed their victims. That would have been something to see.

Hauser smoked with pleasure. The White City was impressive, even covered as it was by vegetation. In his day, Max had hardly scratched the surface. There was a great deal more worth taking here. Even a simple block with, say, a jaguar head carved on it could fetch a hundred grand. He'd have to be careful to keep the location secret.

The *teniente* appeared and saluted. 'Ready, sir. He speaks no Spanish.'

'Thank you. I'll make myself understood.'

Hauser walked through the ruined temple and ducked through the low stone doorway into the inner courtyard. He went into the small room at the back. The Indian was chained to one of the pillars. Hauser shone the flashlight in his face and saw no trace of fear.

'My name's Marcus,' he said with a smile. 'Here's the situation, Chief. I want you to tell me where you buried Maxwell Broadbent. If you don't, bad things will happen to you and your people.'

The Indian returned his gaze. Not defiant, just observing.

'Max-well Broad-bent?' Hauser repeated slowly, enunciating every syllable. He made a universal gesture indicating a question—a shrug with hands turned up.

The Indian said nothing. Hauser puffed vigorously on the cigar, getting a good long glow to the tip. Then he stopped, removed it from his mouth and held it up in front of the man's face. 'Care for a cigar?'

SALLY SPOKE FIRST. 'We've got to do *something*.'

'Like what?' Vernon asked. His voice sounded tired. The sun had set long ago and the fire had fallen to a heap of coals.

'We go to the mountain Indians, offer our services. In partnership with them, we can defeat Hauser.'

Don Alfonso spread his hands. '*Curandera*, they will kill us before we can speak. And what can we do? We have one rifle against professional soldiers with automatic weapons. We are weak—and we have a man who cannot walk. We must go back.'

'You said we'd never get across the swamp.'

'They left their boats at the Macaturi Falls. We go and steal them.'

'And then?' Sally asked.

'I go back to Pito Solo and you go home.'

Sally was furious. 'I, personally, can't just walk away.'

Don Alfonso laid a hand on hers. '*Curandera*, do not underestimate the mountain Indians. I would not want to be one of these soldiers in their hands.'

No one spoke for a few minutes. Tom felt very, very tired. 'It's our fault, Don Alfonso, or rather, our father's fault. We're responsible.'

'Tomás, none of this means anything, this business of your fault, his fault, my fault. We can do nothing. We are powerless.'

Philip nodded in agreement. 'I've had it with this crazy journey. We can't save the world.'

'I agree,' said Vernon.

Tom found them all looking at him. A vote of sorts was being taken. He just couldn't see himself giving up. He had come too far. 'I'll never be able to live with myself if we just go back. I'm with Sally.'

But it was still three against two.

EVEN BEFORE THE SUN ROSE, Don Alfonso was up and breaking camp. Tom watched him flinging together their meagre belongings. He felt sick. It was over. Hauser had won.

Sally said, 'Wherever Hauser goes with that Codex, whatever he does, I'm going to be on his trail. We may be returning to civilisation, but this isn't over by any means.'

Philip's feet were still infected, leaving him unable to walk. Don Alfonso wove a carrying hammock, like a stretcher with two poles. When the time came to leave, Tom and Vernon hoisted him onto their shoulders. They set off through the narrow corridor of vegetation, Sally in front wielding a machete, Don Alfonso taking up the rear.

It began to rain. Carrying Philip proved to be more difficult than Tom anticipated. It was almost impossible to haul him up the slippery trails. Carrying him along wobbly logs laid across roaring rivers was an exercise in terror. Utterly exhausted, they camped that afternoon on the only level piece of ground they could find—a wallow of mud. Their dinner that night was a raw root and some rotten fruit.

The rain continued to pour, turning the streams into torrents. The next day and the next were more of the same. By the fourth day they had managed to travel less than ten miles. Philip, in his already half-starved condition, was weakening rapidly. On the fifth day, around noon, Don Alfonso called a halt. He reached down to pluck a feather from the trail. It had a piece of plaited twine attached to it.

'Mountain Indians,' he whispered 'We must get off the trail now.'

Following the trail had been bad enough. Now walking became almost impossible. They pushed into a wall of ferns and lianas so thick it seemed to push back. They took turns hacking a path a few hundred yards long through the undergrowth; then two of them would carry Philip in his hammock along the path. There they would stop and take turns cutting another hundred yards through the forest. They proceeded this way for two more days, without seeing a letup in the downpour. After that, the days and nights just blended into one another. They waded through knee-deep mud, sliding and crawling uphill and falling and sliding back down again. It now took all four of them to lift Philip.

Tom began to lose all track of time. He felt strange, light-headed. The end was soon coming, he realised: the moment when they could go no further. Arriving in an open area, where a giant tree had fallen in such a way that it was possible to shelter under its enormous trunk, by silent, mutual consent they all stopped to camp. With the last of their strength the group cut poles and laid them against the trunk, thatching them with ferns. It seemed to be around noon. They crawled underneath and huddled together on the muddy ground.

The rain lifted during the night, and when dawn came the sunlight broke over the treetops. For the first time in weeks they could see blue sky through the opening left in the canopy by the fallen tree.

Tom felt a hand on his shoulder. It was Sally's.

'Come over here.' She spoke in a grave voice.

Tom was suddenly afraid. 'It's not Philip?'

'No. It's Don Alfonso.'

Tom got up and knelt beside Don Alfonso lay in his hammock. He took his withered old hand. It was hot.

'I am sorry, Tomasito, but I am a useless old man and I am dying.'

'Don't talk like that, Don Alfonso.' He put his hand on Don Alfonso's forehead and was shocked by the heat.

'Death has come calling, and one cannot say to Death, "Come back next week, I'm busy."'

Tom stood up, fighting a wave of faintness. He went to check on Philip. Like Don Alfonso he had a high fever.

Vernon got a fire going despite Don Alfonso's muttered entreaties not to light one, and Sally brewed a medicinal tea. When she took a mug to the old man, his whole face had sagged, collapsing inwards, the skin losing its colour and taking on a waxy hue. His breathing was laboured, but he was still conscious. 'I will drink your tea,

Curandera,' he said, 'but not even your medicine will save me.'

She knelt. 'Don Alfonso, you've talked yourself into dying. You can talk yourself out of it.'

He took her hand. 'No, *Curandera*. When I was a little boy, I had a bad fever, and my mother took me to a *bruja*, a witch. The *bruja* told me that my time of dying was not then, but that I would die far from home, among strangers, within sight of blue mountains.' His eyes glanced up at the Sierra Azul, framed in the gap in the treetops.

'She could have been talking about any blue mountains.'

'*Curandera*, she was talking about those mountains, which are as blue as the great ocean itself.'

Sally blinked away a tear. 'Don Alfonso, quit talking nonsense.'

At this, Don Alfonso smiled. 'It is a wonderful thing when an old man has a beautiful girl weeping at his deathbed.'

'This isn't your deathbed, and I'm not crying.'

'Do not worry, *Curandera*. I came on this journey knowing it would be my last. I did not want to die in my hut a weak, foolish old person. I wanted to die as a *man*.' He shuddered. 'Only I did not think I would die under a tree in the stinking mud, leaving you alone.'

'Then don't. We love you, Don Alfonso. The hell with that *bruja*.'

Don Alfonso took her hand and smiled. '*Curandera*, there is one thing the *bruja* got wrong. She said I was going to die among strangers. This is not true. I die among friends.'

THEY DUG A GRAVE. It was a slow, exhausting process, and they were so weak they could barely lift the shovel. When they'd finished, they wrapped Don Alfonso's body in his hammock, lifted him into the waterlogged hole and filled it in. Tom fashioned a rough cross and planted it at the head of the grave.

Dark clouds rolled in, ending their sunny respite. There was a crack of thunder and a scattered sound of drops in the canopy.

Sally came to Tom. 'I'm going hunting.'

Tom nodded. He took the fishing line to try his luck in the river they had crossed a mile back. Vernon stayed to take care of Philip.

Sally caught nothing; Tom returned with a fish that weighed no more than six ounces. While they'd been gone, Philip had developed a high fever and delirium. His eyes were glittering with heat and he was mumbling disconnected phrases. They boiled the fish in a pot with some manioc root and then spoonfed some stew to him, then divided the rest among themselves. After eating, they remained under the tree as the rain poured down, waiting for darkness.

Tom was the first to wake, just before dawn. Philip's fever had worsened overnight. He tossed and mumbled, his fingers plucking uselessly at his collar. Tom felt desperate. Sally's herbal medicines were ineffectual in the face of this raging fever. Finally, he spoke.

'We're going to have to stay here until Philip recovers. We'll make an all-out effort to hunt, fish and gather edible plants. We'll use this time to build up our strength and get ready for the long trip home.'

Sally and Vernon nodded, although they all knew that Philip was not going to recover.

'All right,' said Tom, rising. 'To work. Sally will go hunting. I'm going to take the fishing line. Vernon, you stay here and take care of Philip.' He collected the line and hooks and pushed off in a straight line away from the Sierra Azul, tearing notches in the sides of ferns as he passed to mark his trail.

Two hours later he arrived, exhausted, at a muddy cascade of water, having caught a small lizard to use as bait. He attached the struggling reptile onto the hook and tossed it into the torrent. Five hours later, with just enough light to get back to camp, he quit. He had lost three of six hooks and a good portion of fishing line and caught nothing.

Tom returned to camp to find Philip tossing in a restless sleep and Sally still out. He sat down next to Vernon at the fire. His brother handed him a mug of tea. 'He's been like that all day.'

Tom nodded, took the mug and drank. His stomach felt hollow, but he was not hungry.

'Sally hasn't been back?'

'No, but I heard a couple of shots.'

As if on cue, they heard the rustle of vegetation and Sally appeared. She said nothing, just slung her rifle down and sat by the fire.

'No luck?' Tom asked.

'Bagged a couple of stumps.' She wiped the mud off her face.

Tom smiled and took her hand. 'None of the stumps in the forest will be safe as long as the great hunter Sally stalks her prey.'

TOM WOKE UP before dawn with a feeling of pressure at the base of his skull. He turned on the damp ground, and the pressure became a headache. Then he swung his feet round and sat up, only to find that he could barely keep upright. He sank back, his head reeling, staring up into the darkness, which seemed to fill with confused swirls of red and brown and the whispering of voices. The soft, worried chatter of Hairy Bugger came from close by. Tom looked round and finally, in the darkness, made out the little monkey, sitting on the ground. He seemed to know that something was wrong with Tom.

It was more than just the effects of hunger. Tom realised he was sick. Oh God, he thought, not now. He tried to seek out Sally or Vernon in the swirling darkness, but he could see nothing. The sound of the rain drumming on the forest leaves all around him was drilling into his skull. He felt himself drift off to sleep.

When he woke, it was brighter but still raining. Sally was crouching over him. She saw his eyes open and tried to smile.

Tom looked at Sally and felt alarmed. Her face looked flushed. 'You're not getting sick, too?'

Sally laid a hand on his cheek. 'Yes, I'm getting sick, too.'

'I'll get better,' Tom said. 'And then I'll take care of you. We'll get out of this mess.'

She shook her head. 'No, Tom, we won't. And we don't have much time.' She paused, looking at him steadily. 'I need to tell you something, Tom. It seems I've fallen in love with you.'

Tom could barely speak. 'But what about—?'

'Julian? He's the perfect dream guy, handsome, brilliant . . . but the feeling I had for him isn't at all like what I feel for you.'

He tried to speak, finally managing to croak out: 'I love you, too.'

She smiled sadly and laid her head on his chest. 'I know that . . . and I'm glad. I'm just sorry we've both run out of time.'

He put his hand on her hair. 'This is a hell of a place to fall in love.'

'You're not kidding.'

'Maybe in another life . . .' Tom struggled to maintain his hold on reality. 'We'll have another chance, somehow . . . somewhere . . .' His mind began to whirl. What was he trying to say? He closed his eyes, trying to steady the vertigo, but that only made it worse. He tried opening his eyes, but there was nothing but a swirl of green and brown, and he drifted into oblivion.

DEATH CAME FOR TOM, but not cloaked in black carrying a scythe. It came in the form of a savage, striped in red and yellow, bristling with green feathers, with green eyes and black hair, peering down at him. But the death that Tom expected did not come. Instead, the terrifying figure forced some hot liquid down his throat, then forced it again. Tom struggled feebly and then accepted it and fell asleep.

He woke with a dry feeling in his throat and a throbbing headache. He was in a thatched hut in a dry hammock, dressed in clean clothes. The sun was shining outside the hut. He lifted his head, raising it as much as his hammering headache would allow. The hammock next to his was empty. His heart lurched. Who had been in that hammock? Sally? Vernon? Who had died?

'Hello?' he asked feebly, trying to sit up. 'Anybody here?'

He heard a sound outside, then Sally came in, lifting up the flap. She was like a sudden eruption of gold. 'Tom! I'm so glad you're better.'

'Oh, Sally, I saw that empty hammock and I thought . . .'

Sally came over and took his hand. 'We're all still here. Philip's still sick, but much better. Vernon should be better tomorrow. They are both in their hammocks.'

'What happened? Where are we?'

'We're still in the same place. You can thank Borabay when he comes back. He went out hunting.'

'Borabay?'

'A mountain Indian. He found us and nursed us back to health.'

'Why?'

'I don't know. He's a *curandero*. Not like me, but a real *curandero*. He gave us medicine, fed us, saved our lives. He even speaks a funny kind of English. We've had a fever he calls *bisi*.'

She handed him a cup filled with a sweet beverage. He drank it down and felt his hunger intensify. 'I smell something cooking.'

'Turtle stew à la Borabay. I'll bring you some.' She laid her hand on his cheek, then leaned over and gave him a kiss.

Tom ate the stew she gave him, then fell soundly asleep. When he woke, his headache was gone and he was able to get out of his hammock and walk out of the hut. His legs felt like rubber. They were in the same clearing with the same fallen tree, but it had been transformed from a dank thicket into a cheerful, open camp. The ferns had been cut and used to pave the muddy ground, forming a pleasant, springy carpet. There were two palm-thatch huts and a fire ring with logs for seats. The sun was streaming through the hole in the treetops. The Sierra Azul loomed in the gap, purple against the blue sky. Sally was sitting next to the fire, and when he came over she leapt to her feet and took his arm, helping him sit down.

'Eat some more stew. Borabay has been lecturing us that we have to eat as much as we can.'

'Where is this mysterious Borabay?'

'Hunting.'

Tom took some stew from the pot bubbling on the fire, then heard a shout. He looked up to see the most amazing little Indian walking across the meadow. His upper body and face were painted red, with a circle of black round the eyes and yellow stripes painted diagonally across his chest. Feathers bristled from bands on his upper arms and two enormous plugs were inserted into stretched ear lobes, which waggled with each step. He had black hair, cut off straight, and his eyes were a hazel colour, almost green. The face was handsome.

Borabay stepped up to the fire, holding a blowpipe in one hand and a dead animal—species unknown—in the other.

'Brother, I bring meat,' he said in English, and grinned. Then he chucked the animal to the ground and strode over. He embraced Tom twice, with a kiss on each side of the neck. Then he stepped back and placed a hand on his chest. 'My name Borabay, brother.'

'I'm Tom.'

'You, me, him, we brothers.'

'Thank you for saving our lives,' Tom said.

'Thankee. Thankee. You eat more!'

'Where did you learn English?'

'My mother teach me.'

'You speak well.'

'Thankee. I go to America someday with you, brother.' Borabay glanced at Hairy Bugger, who was in his usual place in Tom's pocket.

The monkey looked at him, then ducked deeper into the pocket.

Borabay laughed. 'He think I want eat him. He know we Tara like monkey. Now I make food.' He went back to where he had dropped his game and collected it, along with a pot. He withdrew from the camp, squatted down and began skinning the animal.

Tom turned to Sally. 'What happened? Where did Borabay come from?'

'Borabay found us sick and dying. He cleared the area, built the huts, moved us in, fed us, treated us. He collected herbs and insects and he used those to make medicines. I was the first person to get well. That was two days ago. The fever we've had, this *bisi*, seems to be short but intense. If you don't die in the first two days it's over. It seems that *bisi* is what killed Don Alfonso.'

VERNON'S FEVER BROKE that night. He woke up the next morning, lucid but weak. They spent the day resting again, while Borabay went out collecting food. The Indian returned in the afternoon with roots, fruits, nuts and fresh fish. He spent the rest of the day roasting, smoking and salting the food, then bundling it in dry grass and leaves.

'Are we going somewhere?' Tom asked him.

'Yes.'

'Where?'

Borabay said, 'We talk later.'

Philip came limping out of his hut, his feet still bandaged, briar pipe in his mouth. He came over to the fire and sat down.

Vernon joined them, shakily settling down on a log.

'Welcome back to the land of the living,' said Philip. 'What now, brothers of mine? Do we scurry back, tails between our legs? And let Hauser help himself to the Lippi, the Braques, the Monet and all the rest?' He paused. 'Or do we head on up into the Sierra Azul and maybe end up with our entrails hanging in the bushes?'

Vernon looked up, his face still haggard. 'Answer the question yourself. You're the one who brought Hauser up here.'

'This isn't the time or the place for recriminations,' said Tom.

Vernon turned to Tom. 'Philip brought that psychopath up here, and he needs to answer for it.'

'I acted in good faith. I had no idea Hauser would turn out to be a monster. The real culprit here, since no one else seems inclined to admit it, is Father.' Philip looked around. 'Isn't anyone here just a *wee bit angry* at what Father's done to us? He nearly killed us.'

Borabay rose to his feet. 'This not good talk.'

'This doesn't involve you, Borabay,' said Philip.

'No more bad talk, brother.'

Philip turned on him. 'I don't care if you did save our lives, *stay out of our family business.*' A vein pulsed in Philip's forehead.

'You listen me, little brother, or I wimp your ass,' Borabay said defiantly, standing up to his full height, his fists balled.

There was a beat, then Philip began to laugh and shake his head. His body relaxed. 'Christ, is this guy for real?'

'We're all a little stressed,' said Tom. 'But Borabay's right. This is no place to argue.'

'Tonight,' Borabay said, 'we talk, very important.'

'About what?' Philip demanded.

Borabay turned away. 'You see.'

BORABAY SERVED THEM a three-course dinner: fish soup and vegetables, steaks, and a gruel of cooked fruit. When the last dish was consumed, the pipes came out against the insects of dusk. It was a clear evening, and a gibbous moon was rising behind the outline of the Sierra Azul. They sat round the fire, waiting for Borabay to speak.

The Indian puffed for a while, then laid down his pipe and looked around. 'Here we are, brothers.' He paused. 'I start story at beginning, forty years ago, in year before I was born. In that year white man come up river and over mountains all alone. Arrive at Tara village almost dead. He first white man anyone see. They take him in hut, feed him, bring him back to life. This man live with Tara people, learn to speak our language. They ask why he come. He say to find White City, which we call Sukia Tara. It is city of our ancestors. Now we go there only to bury dead. They take him to Sukia Tara. They not know then that he want to steal from Sukia Tara. This man, he soon take Tara woman to be wife.'

'Figures,' said Philip with a sarcastic laugh. 'Father was never one to pass up a little action on the side.'

Borabay stared at him. 'That woman is my mother.'

'He *married* your mother?' Tom said.

'Of course he marry my mother,' Borabay said. 'How else we be brother, brother?'

Tom stared at Borabay, the painted face, the tattoos, the disks in his ears—as well as the green eyes, the tall brow, the stubborn set of the lips, the finely cut cheekbones. 'Oh my God,' he breathed.

'What?' Vernon asked. 'Tom, what is it?'

Tom glanced at Philip and found his older brother equally thunderstruck. Philip was slowly rising to his feet, staring at Borabay.

Borabay spoke, 'Then after father marry mother, mother born me. I name Borabay, after Father.'

'Borabay,' murmured Philip, 'Broadbent—they're the same name.'

'You mean he's our *brother*?' Vernon asked wildly, finally getting it.

No one answered. Philip, now on his feet, took a step towards Borabay and leaned over to gaze into his face from close range. Borabay gave a nervous laugh. 'What you see, brother? Ghost?'

'In a way, yes.' He reached out and touched his face. 'My God,' he whispered. 'You *are* our brother. You're the oldest brother. Good lord, I wasn't the first born. I'm the second son and I never knew it.'

'Why you think I save your lives? We all brother. We all have same father, Masseral Borabay. We all Borabay.'

Sally's laugh suddenly rose into the sky. 'As if we didn't already have enough Broadbents around here! Now there's another one! Four of them! Is the world ready?'

Vernon, the last to understand, was the first to recover his presence of mind. He went over to Borabay. 'I'm very glad to welcome you as my brother,' he said, and gave Borabay a hug. Borabay looked a little surprised and then gave Vernon another pair of embraces, Indian style.

Then Vernon stood aside while Tom stepped forward. With a grin he hugged Borabay and the Indian responded with his ritual embraces.

Philip followed. He held out his hand. 'Borabay, I'm not one for hugging and kissing. What we gringos do is shake hands. I'll teach you. Hold out your hand.'

Borabay held out his hand. Philip seized it and gave it a good shake.

'What a family reunion,' said Philip, shaking his head with wonder. 'Dear old Father, full of surprises, even after death.'

'But that what I want to tell you,' said Borabay. 'Father *not* dead.'

'Father's still *alive*?' Philip cried out. 'You mean he hasn't been buried yet?'

'I finish story, please. After Father stay with Tara for year, my mother born me. But Father, he talk about White City, go up there for days, maybe weeks at a time. Chief say it is forbidden, but Father not listen. He search and dig for gold. Then he find place of tombs, open tomb of ancient Tara king and rob it. With help of bad Tara mans he escape down river with treasure and disappear.'

'Leaving your mother barefoot with a baby,' Philip said sarcastically, 'just like he did his other wives.'

Borabay turned. '*I telling story, brother. You and flapper take five!*'

Tom felt the shock of déjà vu. 'You and your flapper take five' was a pure Maxwellism, one of his father's favourite expressions.

'I never see Father again—until now. Mother die two years ago. Then little while ago, Father come back. Big surprise. I very glad to meet him. He say he dying. He say he sorry. He say he bring back treasure he stole from Tara people. In return, he want to be buried in tomb of Tara king along with treasure of white man. He talk to Cah, chief of Tara people. Cah say OK, you come back with treasure and we bury you in tomb. So Father go away and come back with many boxes. Cah send men to coast to bring up treasure.'

'Did Father remember you?' Tom asked.

'Oh, yes. He very happy. We go fishing.'

'Really, now?' said Philip, irritated. 'Fishing?'

'Philip—' Tom began.

Borabay said, 'I continue story now. Cah arrange everything for Father's funeral. When day come, there is big funeral feast for Father. All Tara people come. Father give everyone cooking pots and pans.'

'He would love that,' said Philip. 'I can just see the old bastard lording it over his own funeral.'

'You right, Philip. Father love it. He eat, drink too much, laugh, sing. Father open boxes so everyone can look at white man's sacred treasures. Everyone love sacred Mother Mary holding baby Jesus.'

'The Lippi!' cried Philip. To think of it stuck in a damp tomb!'

Borabay went on: 'But Cah trick Father. At end of funeral, he sup-posed to give Father special poison drink to make him die painless death. But Cah give Father drink to make him *sleep*. So sleeping Father is carried into tomb with treasure. They shut door, lock him in tomb. Only Cah know he only sleeping. So he later wake up in tomb.'

Philip said, 'With no food and water . . . *My God, how horrible.*'

'Brothers,' said Borabay, 'in Tara tradition, much food and water put in tomb for afterlife.'

Tom felt a crawling sensation in his spine as the implications of this sank in. 'How long has he been sealed in the tomb?'

'Thirty-two days.'

'Why in hell did Cah do this?' Vernon asked.

'Cah was boy when Father rob tomb, son of chief. Father humiliate father of Cah by robbing tomb. This Cah's revenge.'

'Couldn't you stop it?'

'I not know Cah's plan until later. Then I try to save Father. At tomb entrance is giant stone door. I cannot move. Cah find out I go to Sukia Tara to save Father. He take me prisoner. He say I dirty man, half Tara, half white. He going to kill me. Then crazy white man and soldiers come and capture Cah, take him to White City. I escape. I hear soldiers talk about you, so I come back for you.'

'What can we do?' Philip asked.

Borabay's eyes travelled round the fire, looking at each one of them in turn. Then he spoke, his voice low and resonant: 'We rescue him.'

9

Hauser pored over the crude diagram of the White City that he had drawn over the past two days. The city was so overgrown that making a accurate map was impossible. There were several pyramids, dozens of temples and other structures, hundreds of places where a tomb could be hidden. Unless they got lucky, it could take weeks.

A soldier came to the doorway and saluted.

'Report.'

'The sons are twenty miles back, sir, beyond the Ocata River cross-ing. They are recovering from sickness. There is a Tara Indian taking care of them.'

'Weapons?'

'One useless old hunting rifle belonging to the woman. A bow and arrow and a blowpipe, of course—'

'Yes, yes.' Hauser, despite himself, felt a twinge of respect for the three sons. By all rights they should be dead. Max had been like that, too: stubborn and lucky. A brief image of Max, stripped to the waist, slashing his way through the jungle, came into his mind. But then Max had ditched him and . . . Hauser shook his head. That was the past. The future—and Broadbent's fortune—belonged to him.

The *teniente* spoke. 'Shall I send back a detail of soldiers to kill them? This time we will be sure to finish them, sir, I promise you.'

'No,' Hauser said. 'Leave them alone. Let them come.'

AFTER THREE MORE DAYS of Borabay's ministrations, Philip was able to walk. One sunny morning they broke camp and set off for the Tara village in the foothills of the Sierra Azul. By noon they had reached the river where they had first discovered Philip, covering in five hours the distance that had taken them five days to travel on their desperate retreat. Beyond the river, as they got closer to the Sierra Azul, Borabay began to move more cautiously. They entered the foothills and began to gain altitude.

They stopped for the night in an old Tara encampment. Borabay waded through waist-high vegetation, his machete singing, clearing a path to the best-preserved cluster of huts. 'You go in, set up hammocks, get rest. I make dinner.'

Tom looked at Sally. He felt his heart beat so strongly in his chest that it was almost audible. Without exchanging a word, they entered the smaller of the huts. It was warm inside and smelt of dry grass. Rays of sunlight pierced little holes in the palm thatch, dappling the interior with flecks of afternoon light. Tom hung up his hammock and then watched Sally set up hers. The spots of light were like a handful of gold coins flung into her hair. When she was done, Tom stepped towards her and took her hand. It was trembling slightly. He drew her to him and kissed her. She moved closer.

They undressed each other and lay down together in the warm darkness, and they made love while the sun set, the little coins of light turning red and then fading as the sun sank behind the trees.

THE FOLLOWING MORNING, they left the abandoned Tara settlement and entered the foothills of the Sierra Azul, where the trail began to ascend through forests and meadows. Here and there, Tom caught a glimpse of an abandoned thatched hut, sinking into ruin.

They entered a deep, cool forest. Borabay suddenly insisted on going ahead and, in a change from his usual silent pace, proceeded noisily, singing, whacking unnecessarily at vegetation and stopping frequently to 'rest'. Something was making him nervous.

When they came to a small clearing, Borabay halted. 'Lunch!' he cried and began to sing loudly while unpacking.

'We had lunch two hours ago,' said Vernon.

'We have lunch again!' The Indian unshouldered his bow and arrows, and Tom noticed he laid them down some distance away.

Borabay helped the others out of their backpacks and put them with the bow and arrows, on the far side of the clearing. Then he came over to Sally and put an arm round her, drawing her close. 'Give me gun, Sally,' he said in a low voice.

She unshouldered her gun. Borabay then took away their machetes.

'What's going on?' Vernon asked.

'Nothing, nothing, we rest here.' He began passing round some dried plantains. 'You hungry, brothers? Very good banana!'

'I don't like this,' said Philip.

Vernon tucked into the plaintains. 'Delicious,' he said. 'We should eat two lunches every day.'

'Very good! Two lunches!' said Borabay, laughing uproariously.

And then it happened. Without noise or apparent movement, Tom suddenly realised they were surrounded by men with bows drawn to the limit, a hundred stone-tipped arrows pointing at them.

Vernon let out a scream and fell to the ground and was instantly surrounded by bristling, tense men, with fifty arrows drawn and poised inches from his throat and chest.

'No move!' Borabay cried. He turned and spoke rapidly to the men. Slowly, the bows began to relax and the men stepped back. He continued talking, less rapidly and at a lower pitch, but just as urgently. Finally the men lowered their arrows completely.

'You move now,' said Borabay. 'Stand up. No smile. No shake hand. Look everyone in eye. No *smile*.'

They did as they were told, rising.

'Go get packs and weapons and knifes. Do not show you afraid. Make angry face but say nothing. Smile and you die.'

They followed Borabay's orders. There was a flurry of raised bows as Tom picked up his machete, but when he sheathed it in his belt the bows went back down. Following Borabay's instructions, Tom raked the warriors with a baleful stare. They stared back ferociously.

Borabay was now talking in a lower voice, but sounded angry. He was directing his comments to one man, taller than the others, with a brilliant set of feathers bristling from rings on his upper arms.

The man looked at Tom and stepped forward. Halted.

'Brother, take step towards man, tell him in angry voice he must apologise.'

Tom scowled and stepped towards the warrior. 'How dare you draw your bows at us?' he demanded.

Borabay translated. The man answered angrily, gesturing with a spear close to Tom's face.

Borabay spoke. 'He say, "Who are you? Why you come into Tara land without invitation?" You tell him in angry voice you come to save your father. Shout at him.'

Tom obeyed, raising his voice, taking another step towards the warrior and shouting at him inches from his face. The man answered in an even angrier voice, shaking his spear in front of Tom's nose. At this, many of the warriors put up their bows again.

'He say Father cause big trouble for Tara and he very angry. Brother, you must be very angry now. You tell them to put down bows. Say you no talk unless they put arrows away. Make big insult.'

Tom, sweating, now feigned anger. 'How dare you threaten us?' he cried. 'We have come to your land in peace and you offer us war! Is this how the Tara treat their guests? Are you animals or people?'

Tom caught a flash of approval from Borabay as he translated—no doubt adding his own nuances.

The bows came down, and this time the men unnocked their arrows and put them back into their quivers.

'Now you smile. Short smile, not big smile.'

Tom flashed a smile, then let his face settle back into sternness.

Borabay spoke at length, then turned to Tom. 'You must hug and kiss that warrior in Tara way.'

Tom gave the man an awkward hug and a pair of kisses on the neck, just as Borabay had done to him so many times.

'Good,' said Borabay, almost giddy with relief. 'Everything fine now! We go to Tara village.'

THE VILLAGE CONSISTED of an open plaza of packed earth surrounded by two rings of thatched huts with no windows, just a hole in the peak. Cooking fires were burning in front of many of the huts, tended by women who, Tom noticed, were cooking with the French cooking pots that Maxwell Broadbent had brought them. As he followed the group of warriors into the centre of the plaza, various people came out of their huts. The small children were completely naked; the older ones wore dirty shorts. The women wore a piece of cloth tied round their waists, and their breasts were smeared with red. Many had disks in their lips and ears. Only the men wore feathers.

There was no formal greeting. The warriors who had brought them in wandered off, while the women and children gaped.

'What do we do now?' Tom asked, looking around.

'Wait,' said Borabay.

A toothless old woman soon emerged from one of the huts, bent double from age, leaning on a stick. She made her way towards them with excruciating slowness, her beady eyes never leaving their faces. She finally arrived in front of Tom and peered up at him.

Borabay said quietly, 'Do nothing.'

She raised a withered hand and gave Tom a blow across the knees, then whacked him across the thighs, three times—all the while muttering to herself. She then raised her stick and struck him across the shins and again on the buttocks. She dropped the stick and reached up and groped him between his legs. Tom swallowed and tried not to flinch. Then she reached up towards Tom's head, making a motion with her fingers. Tom bent slightly and she grabbed his hair and gave such a yank that tears sprang to his eyes. She stepped back, gave him a toothless smile and spoke at length.

Borabay translated. 'She say contrary to appearance you are definitely a man. She invite you and your brothers stay in village as guest of the Tara people. She accept your help for fight against bad men in White City. She say now you in charge.'

'Who is she?'

'She is wife of Cah. You now war chief.'

Tom was stunned. 'How can that be? I've been here ten minutes.'

'She say Tara warriors fail against white man and many killed. You white man, too, maybe you understand enemy better. Tomorrow, you lead fight against bad men.'

'Tomorrow?' Tom said. 'Thanks, but I decline the responsibility.'

'You not have choice,' said Borabay. 'She say if you do not, Tara warriors kill us all.'

THAT NIGHT THE VILLAGERS lit a bonfire, and a party of sorts got under way, starting with a multicourse feast. Everyone went to bed late. Borabay roused them a few hours later. It was still dark.

'We go now. You speak to people.'

Tom stared at him. 'I have to give a *speech*?'

'I help you.'

The bonfire had been heaped with fresh logs, and Tom could see the whole village standing respectfully, waiting for his speech.

Borabay whispered, 'Tom, you tell me to get ten best warriors.'

Tom gave the order and Borabay then went through the crowd, clapping his hands, slapping the shoulders of various men, and in five minutes had ten warriors lined up with them.

'Now you give speech. Talk big. How you going to rescue Father, kill bad mans. Don't worry, whatever you say, I fix up good.'

Tom stepped forward and looked round at all the faces. The hubbub of talk died quickly. Now they were looking at him with hope. He suddenly remembered Don Alfonso's speech to his people before they left Pito Solo. He had to give a speech like that, even if it was all lies and empty promises.

He took a deep breath. 'My friends! We have come to the Tara lands from a distant place called America!'

At the word America, even before Borabay could translate, there was a rustle of excitement.

'We have come many thousands of miles, by plane, by dugout and on foot. For forty days and nights we have travelled.'

Borabay declaimed this. Tom now had their undivided attention.

'A great evil has befallen the Tara people. A barbarian named Hauser has come from the other side of the world with mercenary soldiers to kill the Tara people and rob their tombs. They have kidnapped your chief and killed your warriors. As I speak, they are in the White City, defiling it with their presence.'

Borabay translated, and there was a loud murmur of agreement.

'We are here, the four sons of Maxwell Broadbent, to rid the Tara people of this man. We have come to save our own father, Maxwell Broadbent, from the darkness of his tomb.'

He paused for Borabay's translation. A sea of faces, lit by the firelight, gazed at him with rapt attention.

'My brother here, Borabay, will lead us up to the mountains, where we will make plans for an attack. Tomorrow, we will fight.'

At this there was an eruption of an odd sound like rapid grunting or laughing—the Tara equivalent, it seemed, of cheering and clapping. Tom could feel his monkey, Hairy Bugger, scrunching himself down into the bottom of his pocket, trying to hide.

Borabay spoke softly to Tom. 'Ask them to pray and make offering.'

Tom cleared his throat. 'The Tara people, all of you, have a very important role to play in the coming struggle. I ask you to pray for us.

I ask you to make offerings for us. I ask you to do this every day until we return victorious.'

Borabay's voice rang out with these declarations, and it had an electric effect. People surged forward, murmuring in excitement. Tom felt they believed in him far more than he believed in himself.

A cracked voice rang out, and the people instantly fell back, leaving the old woman, Cah's wife, standing alone, leaning on her stick. She looked up and fixed her eyes on Tom. There was a long silence as she raised her stick, drew it back and gave him a tremendous blow across the thighs. Tom tried not to flinch or grimace.

Then the old woman cried out something in a wizened voice.

'What'd she say?'

Borabay turned. 'She speak a strong Tara expression. It mean something like: "You kill or you die."'

PROFESSOR JULIAN CLYVE propped up his feet and creaked back in his old chair with his hands behind his head. It was a blustery May day, the wind twisting and torturing the leaves of the sycamore tree outside his window. Sally had been gone for over a month now. There had been no word. He hadn't expected to hear anything, but Clyve still found the long silence perturbing. When Sally had left, they had both expected that the retrieval of the Codex would usher in one more academic triumph in Professor's Clyve's life. But while Sally had been gone, Clyve had changed his mind. He was a Rhodes scholar, a full professor at Yale, with a string of prizes and academic honours. The fact was, he hardly needed another honour. What he needed—let's face it—was money. Here he was, at the top of his profession, earning less than the average plumber. It was unfair.

Now, finally, he would have the means to do something about it. He glanced at the calendar. Tomorrow the first instalment of the $2 million from the giant Swiss drug company, Hartz, was to arrive. The coded email confirmation should be coming soon from the Cayman Islands. He would have to spend the money outside the United States, of course. A snug villa on the Costiera Amalfitana would be a nice place to park it. A million for the villa and the second million for expenses. Ravello was supposed to be nice. He and Sally could take their honeymoon there.

He thought back to his meeting with the CEO and the Hartz board. They had been sceptical, of course, but when they saw the page Julian had already translated their mouths were almost watering. The Codex would bring them many billions. Most drug companies had research departments that evaluated indigenous medicines, but here was the ultimate cookbook, and Julian was about the only person in the world, apart from Sally, who could translate it accurately. Hartz would have to strike a deal with the Broadbents over it, but as the largest pharmaceutical company in the world it was in the best position to pay. And without his translation skills, what use would the Codex be to the Broadbents, anyway? Everything would be done correctly: the company had, of course, insisted. The Swiss were like that.

He wondered how Sally would react when she learned that the Codex was going to disappear into the maw of some multinational corporation. Knowing her, she would not take it well. But once they started to enjoy the $2 million Hartz had agreed to pay him as a finder's fee— not to mention the generous remuneration he expected to receive for doing the translation—she'd get over it. And he would show her that this was the right thing to do. It took money to develop new drugs. Nobody was going to do it for free. Profit made the world go round.

As for himself, poverty had been fine for a few years, while he was young and idealistic, but it would become unendurable over thirty. And Professor Julian Clyve was fast approaching thirty.

AFTER TEN HOURS of hiking into the mountains, Tom and his brothers topped a bare, windswept ridge. A stupendous view of mountains greeted their eyes, a violent sea of peaks and valleys, layered towards the horizon in deepening shades of purple.

Borabay pointed. 'Sukia Tara, the White City,' he said.

Tom squinted in the bright afternoon sun. About five miles away, across a chasm, rose two pinnacles of white rock. Nestled between them was a flat, isolated saddle of land, cut off on both sides by chasms and surrounded by jagged peaks. It was a lone patch of green, a lush piece of cloud forest that looked as if it had broken off from somewhere else to lodge between the two fangs of white rock.

Vernon raised his binoculars, examined the White City, then passed them to Tom.

The green plateau leapt into magnification. Tom scanned it, slowly. It was heavily covered in trees and what appeared to be impenetrable mats of vines and creepers. Whatever ruined city lay in that strange hanging valley was well covered by jungle. But as Tom scrutinised it, here and there, rising from the verdure, he could make out whitish outcrops that began to take on faint patterns: a corner, a broken stretch of wall. And as he looked further at what he thought was a steep hill, he realised it was a ruined pyramid, heavily overgrown.

The mesa the city had been constructed on was, truly, an island in the sky. It hung between the two peaks, separated from the rest of the Sierra Azul by sheer cliffs. It looked cut off until he saw a thread of yellow curving across one of the chasms—a crude suspension bridge. As he focused on the bridge, he could see it was well guarded by soldiers. They were using a ruined stone fortress evidently built to protect the original inhabitants of the White City. Hauser and his men had cut down a large swath of forest at the foot of the bridge.

A river ran down from the mountains and poured into the chasm, turning into a graceful filament of white and disappearing into the mists below. As Tom watched, mists billowed up from the chasm, obscuring the bridge and blocking their view of the White City itself.

Tom shivered. Their father had probably stood in the same place forty years ago. No doubt he had been able to pick out the faint outlines of the city amid the chaos of vegetation. Here was where he made his first discovery, and this was where he had ended up, shut up alive in a dark tomb.

He passed the binoculars to Sally. She examined the White City for a long time. Then she lowered the glasses and turned to Tom, her face flushed with excitement. 'It's Maya,' she said. 'There's a central ball court, a pyramid and some multistoreyed pavilions.'

Philip took the binoculars next and scanned the city. Tom heard an intake of breath. 'There are men down there,' he said. 'Cutting trees at the base of the pyramid.'

There was a faint *crump* of dynamite, and a puff of dust rose up from the city like a small white flower.

Tom said, 'We're going to have to find Father's tomb before they do. Or . . .' He left the sentence unfinished.

THEY SPENT THE REST of the afternoon in the cover of the trees, observing Hauser and his men. The wind brought them the sounds of chain saws and the distant rumble of explosives.

'Where is Father's tomb?' Tom asked Borabay.

'In cliffs below city on far side. Place of dead.'

'Will Hauser find it?'

'Yes. Trail down is hidden, but he find it in end. Maybe tomorrow. Maybe two weeks.'

As night fell, lights illuminated the suspension bridge and the area around it. Hauser was taking no chances. He had come well equipped with everything, including a generator.

They ate dinner in silence. At the conclusion of the meal, Philip spoke what was on everyone's mind. 'I think we better get the hell out of here and come back with help. We can't do this on our own.'

'Philip,' said Tom, 'when they find the tomb and open it, what do you think's going to happen?'

'They'll rob it.'

'No, the first thing Hauser will do is murder Father. If we're going to save him, we've got to act *now*.'

'I don't want to be the one to say no to rescuing Father, but Tom, for God's sake, we have an old rifle, maybe ten rounds, and some painted warriors with bows and arrows. Those soldiers have automatic weapons, grenade launchers and dynamite. And they've got the advantage of defending an incredibly secure position.'

'Maybe we can offer Hauser a deal: let Father out and Hauser can keep the tomb's riches,' said Vernon. 'We'll sign it all over to him.'

'Don't even *think* of trusting Hauser or making a deal with him.'

'All right, we've eliminated getting into the White City by a frontal attack. That leaves only one course of action.' Vernon smoothed the sand near the fire and drew a map while he explained his plan.

When he was finished, Philip shook his head. 'This is a crazy plan. I say we go back, get help and return. It may take them months to find Father's tomb.'

Borabay interrupted. 'Philip, if we run away now, Tara people kill us. We make promise. Cannot break promise.'

'I didn't make any promise; that was Tom. Anyway, we can slip past the Tara village and be gone before they even know we're missing.'

'That coward way, brother. That leave Father die in tomb. There not enough food and water in tomb to last much longer.'

Tom glanced through the trees. Almost five miles distant, he could see lights clustered in the White City. There was another explosion. Hauser and his men were working round the clock.

'Enough talk,' said Tom. 'We have a plan. Who's in?'

'I'm in,' said Vernon.

Borabay nodded. 'I'm in.'

'I'm in,' said Sally.

Now all eyes were on Philip. He made an angry gesture. 'For heaven's sake, you already know what my answer's going to be!'

'Which is?' Vernon asked.

'It's *no*! This is a James Bond plan. It'll never succeed in real life. Don't do it. For God's sake, I don't want to lose my brothers, too.'

'We have to, Philip,' said Tom.

'No one *has* to do anything! Maybe this is blasphemy, but isn't it just a little bit true that Father brought this down on himself?'

'So we just let him die?'

'I'm just asking you, please, not to throw your lives away.' He threw up his hands and stomped off in the darkness.

Vernon was about to shout a reply, but Tom touched his arm and shook his head. Perhaps Philip was right and it *was* a suicide mission. But Tom personally had no choice. If he didn't do something now, he wouldn't be able to live with himself later. It was as simple as that.

'There's no reason to wait,' said Tom. 'We leave tonight at two a.m. It should take us a couple of hours to get down there. Everyone knows what they have to do. Borabay, you can explain the plan to your warriors.' Tom glanced over at Vernon. The idea had been his, Vernon's, the brother who never took the lead. He reached out and grasped his brother's shoulder. 'Good going,' he said.

TOM ROSE from his hammock at one o'clock. The night was black. Clouds had blotted out the stars and a restless wind rustled and murmured through the trees. He found most of the others up. Borabay unbanked the fire, piled in fresh sticks and put a pot on to boil.

Sally joined them and began checking her Springfield by the fire. Her faced looked drawn and tired. 'Do you remember what General Patton said was always the first casualty of a battle?' she asked Tom.

'No.'

'The battle plan.'

'So you don't think our plan is going to work?' Tom asked.

She shook her head. 'Probably not.' She looked back down at the rifle, giving it an unnecessary polish with the cleaning rag.

Vernon joined them, and the four of them drank their tea in silence. Tom looked round for Philip, but his brother had not even come out of the hut. He nodded to Borabay and they all rose. Sally threw the gun over her shoulder, and they all picked up palm-leaf backpacks containing food, water, matches, camping stove and other essentials. They set off, Borabay in the lead, the warriors bringing up the rear, moving down through the grove of trees and out into the open.

Ten minutes from the camp, Tom heard running from behind, and they all stopped, the warriors with their arrows nocked and drawn. In a moment Philip appeared, breathing hard.

'Here to wish us luck?' Vernon asked, sarcasm in his voice.

Philip took a moment to catch his breath. 'I don't know why I would even think of joining this harebrained scheme. But, damn it, I'm not going to let you go off to your deaths alone.'

10

Hauser lit another Churchill. The aroma of fine Cuban long leaf surrounded him like a cocoon of elegance and satisfaction. He was well hidden at a strategic point above the suspension bridge, where he had a good view of the bridge and the soldiers in their stone fort on the far side. He pushed aside some ferns and raised a pair of binoculars to his eyes. He had a strong feeling that the three Broadbent brothers were going to make their break to cross the bridge that night. They wouldn't wait; they couldn't wait. They had to get to the tomb before he did, if they wanted any chance of saving some of the masterpieces for themselves.

He puffed contentedly, thinking of Maxwell Broadbent. He had lugged half a billion dollars' worth of fine art and antiquities up here, all on a whim. As outrageous as it was, it was perfectly in character. Max was the man of the big gesture, the spectacle, the show. Hauser remembered back to that defining fifty-day trek in the jungle. They they had heard there was a Mayan temple somewhere in the Guatemalan lowlands. Fifty harrowing days and nights, hacking their way along overgrown trails, stung and bitten and scratched, starving and sick. They had eventually stumbled into a Lacandon village, but the villagers wouldn't talk. The temple was there somewhere, all right. No doubt about it. But the villagers were silent. Hauser had just about got a girl to the point of talking when Max had thwarted him. Pointed a gun at his head, the bastard, disarmed him. That was the final straw. Max had ordered Hauser away like he was some dog. Hauser had no choice but to give up the search. But Max had gone on to find the White City. He'd looted a rich tomb up here, and now that tomb, all these years later, had become his own.

Hauser enjoyed another long suck on the cigar. In his years in combat, he had learned something important about people: when things got tough, you could never tell who was going to make it and who was going to fold. The three Broadbent sons had done well. He had to hand it to them. They would perform this final service and then their road would come to an end.

A faint sound of ululating, whooping and yelling broke the silence. He raised the binoculars. Far to the left of the stone fort, he could see a shower of arrows come sailing out of the jungle. The Indians were attacking. Hauser smiled. It was a diversion, of course, designed to draw the attention of his soldiers away from the bridge. He could see his own men huddling behind the stone walls, guns at the ready, loading their grenade launchers. At least they had an assignment to fake what they were already good at: failure.

More arrows came sailing out of the forest, followed by another eruption of bloodcurdling yells. The soldiers answered with a panicky burst of gunfire. A grenade went sailing into the forest, and there was a flash and a bang. For once the soldiers were getting it right. Now that the Broadbents had made their move, Hauser knew exactly how it was going to unfold.

SALLY HAD CRAWLED to within 200 yards of the soldiers guarding the bridge. She lay behind a fallen tree trunk, her Springfield resting on the smooth wood. She hadn't said goodbye to Tom; they had simply kissed and he'd gone. She tried not to think about what was going to happen. It was a crazy plan. She doubted if they'd ever get across the bridge, but even if they did, and were able to rescue their father, they'd never get back.

The Springfield dated back to before World War I, but the optics were excellent. Chori had taken good care of it. Sally had already calculated the distance from her hiding place to where the soldiers were hunkered down inside the ruined stone fort, and had adjusted the scope accordingly. The fact was, 200 yards wasn't much of a challenge for her, especially with a stationary target as large as a man.

Since she had arrived at the tree trunk she had been thinking about what it would mean to kill another person and whether she could do it. She knew she could. To save Tom's life she would do it.

Hairy Bugger was sitting in a little cage made of woven vines. Sally was glad he was there to keep her company, although he'd been fretting and grumping at Tom's absence and his own imprisonment. She took a handful of nuts from her pocket and gave him a few.

Right on schedule, she heard a yell from the forest on the far side of the soldiers, followed by whoops, shrieks and ululations that sounded more like a hundred warriors than ten. A shower of arrows flashed out of the woods. The soldiers began firing back, but it was an unusually incompetent display of military prowess.

To her left Sally saw a flash of movement. The four Broadbents were running at a crouch across the open area towards the bridgehead. They had 200 yards of brush and fallen tree trunks to negotiate but they were making good time. The soldiers seemed fully occupied with the feint attack on their flank. Sally watched through the scope, ready to provide covering fire.

The Broadbents reached the bridge. It spanned a gap of 600 feet, and had been well engineered, with four cables of twisted fibre, two above and two below, carrying the load. Vertical cords between the upper and lower sets of cables supported the surface of the bridge itself, which was formed from pieces of bamboo lashed midway between the two sets of cables. One by one the Broadbents swung underneath it, climbing out over the chasm on one of the lower cables, sidestepping their way and using the upright cords as hand-holds. The timing was right: the mists were rising heavily and within fifty yards the four brothers had disappeared.

As soon as they reached the far side of the bridge, they plunged into the cloud forest, running as fast as they could, with Borabay in the lead. After twenty minutes a broken stone wall loomed ahead.

Borabay stopped and crouched down, taking one of a number of reed bundles from his pack. There was a flare of light and he stood up holding a burning bundle of reeds. The wall leapt into view: it was made with giant limestone blocks, almost obscured by a heavy mat of vines. They walked along it and soon came to a small doorway with vines hanging down across it like a beaded curtain. Pushing the vines aside, they ducked through the doorway into a ruined court-yard. Borabay led them across the courtyard and up a staircase. He walked along the top of the wall and descended some steps on the other side, then passed through a jumble of toppled columns into an inner courtyard full of fallen blocks of stone. They climbed over the blocks, passed through a doorway framed by stone jaguars, and entered an underground passageway. The torch revealed stone walls crusted with lime, a ceiling bristling with stalactites. They went past a stone altar littered with bones, and came out of the tunnel and across a platform dotted with broken statues.

Suddenly they came to the edge of a vast precipice on the far side of the plateau. Borabay paused to light a fresh brand, and tossed the spent one over the cliff. He led them along a trail skirting the edge, then through a cleverly hidden gap in the rock that seemed to lead over the cliff. But as they came through the gap a trail appeared, chis-elled into the edge, which soon became a steep staircase cut into the mountain. It switchbacked down the cliff and ended at a concealed terrace paved with smoothly fitted stones. On one side were the jagged cliffs of the White City mesa. On the other was a sheer drop of thousands of feet. Hundreds of black doors riddled the cliffs above, with precipitous trails and staircases connecting them.

'Place of tombs,' said Borabay.

My God, thought Tom. To think that Father is up there somewhere.

Borabay led them through a dark doorway in the cliff and they now ascended a spiral staircase cut into the rock. The cliff face was honeycombed with tombs, and the stairs passed open niches with bones inside them, a skull with a bit of hair, mummified bodies rustling with insects, mice and small snakes, disturbed by the light and retreating back into darkness. Some of the tomb doors were smashed, as if broken into by grave robbers or shaken loose by earthquakes.

The stairs turned and ended on a ledge, ten feet wide, halfway up the cliff face. Borabay held the brand up to a massive stone door. Other tomb doors they had passed had been unadorned; this one, however, had a relief carved into its face: a Mayan glyph. Borabay paused, then took a step back, saying something in his own language, like a prayer. Then he turned and whispered, 'Father's tomb.'

Seven weeks had passed since Tom and his two brothers had gathered at the gates to their father's estate—but it felt like a lifetime. They had finally made it. They had reached the tomb.

'Do you know how to open it?' asked Philip.

'No.'

Borabay lit more of the reed bundles and set the burning torches in niches in the rock walls. Together they made a minute inspection of the door. It was set into a doorway squared out of the white limestone of the cliffs and there were a number of holes drilled into the rock on either side of the door. Tom held his hand over one and felt a cool flow of air—evidently air holes to the tomb.

The eastern sky brightened with a predawn light as they rapped on the door, called, hammered, pressed and tried everything to open it. Nothing worked.

Finally Tom said, 'If we go back and take a look at one of those broken tomb doors, maybe we can figure out how it works.'

They retraced their steps and, four or five tombs back, came to a broken door. It had cracked down the middle and one part had fallen outwards. Borabay lit another brand, then hesitated.

He turned to Philip. 'I coward,' he said, handing him the brand. 'You braver than me, little brother. You go.'

Philip gave Borabay a squeeze on the shoulder and took the brand. He went into the tomb and Tom and Vernon followed him.

It was not a large space, perhaps eight feet by ten. In the centre was a raised stone platform, and on it sat a mummy bundle. Its long black hair was braided down its back, and the dried lips were drawn back from its teeth. One hand of the mummy held a polished cylinder of wood about eighteen inches long, decorated with glyphs.

Tom knelt down to see how the door worked. There was a groove in the stone floor and set into it were polished stone rollers on which the door rested.

'It's a simple mechanism,' he said. 'You get the door rolling and it opens by itself. The trick is, how do you start the door rolling?'

They examined it all around, but there was no obvious answer.

When they emerged from the tomb Borabay was waiting for them, an anxious expression on his face. 'What find?'

'Nothing,' said Philip.

Vernon emerged from the tomb holding the cylinder of wood that the mummy had been clutching. 'What's this, Borabay?'

'Key to underworld.'

Vernon smiled. 'Interesting.' He carried it back to their father's tomb. 'Funny the stick should fit so perfectly into these air holes. See?' He shoved the stick into one of the holes, then went from hole to hole, testing with his hand the flow of air from each. Finally he stopped. 'Here's one with no breeze coming out of it.' He inserted the stick. It went in about fourteen inches and stopped, leaving four inches exposed. Vernon picked up a heavy, smooth stone and handed it to Philip. 'You do the honours. Whack the end of the stick.'

Philip took the stone and brought it down hard against the end of the stick. There was a *chunk* as the stick entered the hole, then silence. Nothing happened. Philip examined the hole. The wooden dowel had gone all the way in and stuck.

'Damn it!' Philip cried, losing his temper. He rushed at the tomb door and gave it a savage kick. 'Open up, damn you!'

A sudden grinding noise filled the air, the ground vibrated and the stone door began to slide open. A dark crack appeared and gradually widened as the door moved in the groove along its stone rollers. In a moment, with a clunk, it came to a halt.

The tomb was open.

HAUSER WAITED in the dawn light, his finger stroking the blunt trigger of his Steyr AUG. The metal barrel, warmed from constant contact, felt almost alive. He had tucked himself into a comfortable niche along the trail that led down the cliff. He knew the Broadbents were below and would have to come back the same way. They had done exactly what he had hoped. They had led him to old Max's tomb.

Now they had served their purpose. There was no rush; the light was not bright enough and he wanted to give them time to relax, to assume they were safe.

THE FOUR BROTHERS stared into the rectangle of darkness. They could not move, they could not speak. The seconds ticked on as the flow of foul air ebbed. No one wanted to see what horror lay within.

And then there was a sound: a cough. And another: the shuffle of a foot. Another shuffle.

Tom knew it then: their father was alive! He was coming out of the tomb! Still Tom could not move and neither could the others. Just as the tension became unbearable, in the centre of the black rectangle, a ghostly face began to materialise. Another shambling step brought the figure into reality.

He was almost more horrifying than a corpse: stark naked, shrunken, stooped, filthy, cadaverous, smelling like death itself. His mouth hung open like a madman's. He blinked in the dawn light, his colourless eyes vacant, uncomprehending.

Maxwell Broadbent.

The hollow eyes, sunk in dark pools of flesh, were darting from each of their faces to the next. He took a long, noisy breath and finally a cracked sound came from his lips. They leaned forward, straining to understand.

'*What the hell took you so long?*'

The spell was broken. Tom and the others rushed forward and embraced the old man. He gripped them fiercely, all at once and then each one in turn, his arms surprisingly strong.

After a long moment Maxwell Broadbent stepped back. He seemed to have expanded to his usual size.

'Jesus Christ,' he said, wiping his face. 'Christ almighty, I'm glad you're here.' He shook his great grey head. 'God, I must stink. Look at me. I'm a mess. Naked, filthy, revolting!'

Philip pulled off his shirt. 'Here, let me give you this.'

'Thank you, Philip.' Maxwell put on the shirt and buttoned it up, his fingers fumbling clumsily.

When Philip began taking off his trousers, Broadbent held up a bony hand. 'I'm not going to strip my own sons.'

Borabay reached into his palm-leaf pack and pulled out a long piece of decorated cloth. 'You wear this.'

'Going native, am I?'

Broadbent fitted it round his waist and Borabay helped him tie it with a knotted hemp cord.

'Thank God you're alive,' said Vernon.

'At first I wasn't so sure myself,' Broadbent said. 'For a while there I thought I'd died and gone to hell.'

'What, you? The old atheist now believing in hell?' said Philip.

He looked up at Philip and smiled. 'So much has changed.'

'Don't tell me you found God.'

Broadbent wagged his head and clapped a hand on Philip's shoulder. He gave it an affectionate shake. 'Good to see you, son.'

He turned to Vernon. 'And you, too, Vernon.' He looked around, turning his crinkly blue eyes on each of them. 'Tom, Vernon, Philip, Borabay—I'm overwhelmed.' He placed a hand on each of their heads in turn. 'You made it. You found me. My food and water were almost gone. I could only have lasted a day or two more. You've given me a second chance. I don't deserve it but I'm going to take it. I did a lot of thinking in that dark tomb . . .'

'Are you OK?' Vernon asked.

'If it's the cancer you're talking about, I'm sure it's still there—just hasn't kicked in yet. I've still got a couple of months. But so far, so good: I feel great.' He looked round. 'Let's get the hell out of here.'

Tom said, 'Unfortunately, it's not going to be that simple.'

'How so?'

'We've got a problem, and his name is Hauser.'

'Hauser!' Broadbent was astonished.

Tom nodded and told their father the details of their journeys.

'Hauser!' Broadbent repeated, looking at Philip. 'You teamed up with that bastard?'

'I'm sorry,' said Philip. 'I figured—'

'You figured he'd know where I went. My fault: I should have seen that was a possibility. Hauser's a ruthless sadist, almost killed a girl once. The biggest mistake in my life was partnering with him.' Broadbent eased himself down on a shelf of rock and shook his shaggy head. 'I can't believe the risks you took getting here. God, what a mistake I made. The last one of many, in fact.'

'You our father,' said Borabay.

Broadbent snorted. 'Some father. Putting you to a ridiculous test like this. It seemed a good idea at the time. I can't understand what got into me. What a stupid, foolish old bastard I've been.'

Tom turned to Borabay. 'We need to plan our escape.'

'Yes, brother. I think of this. We wait here until dark. Then we go

back.' He glanced up at the clear sky. 'It rain tonight, give us cover.'
He began to unpack some food from his palm-leaf backpack.

Broadbent shuffled over. 'Ah, fresh fruit.' He picked up a mango
and bit into it, the juice running out of his mouth. 'This is heaven.'
He crammed the rest of the mango into his mouth and then polished
off a couple of *curwa* fruits and some smoked lizard fillets. Then he
leaned back against the stone wall, gazing out over the mountains.

'Father,' Philip asked, 'if you don't mind telling us, what happened
to you in that tomb?'

'Philip, I'll tell you how it was. We had a big funeral—no doubt
Borabay told you about it. I drank Cah's infernal drink. The next
thing I knew, I was waking up. It was pitch-black. I've never been so
frightened in my life. I thought: "Not only am I dead, but I've gone to
hell!" And then I began to recover a bit of my sanity. That's when I
crawled around and realised I was in the tomb—and it dawned on me
that Cah had buried me alive. When I found the food and water I
knew I was in for a long ordeal. I had planned this whole thing to be
a light-hearted challenge for the three of you. And then suddenly my
life depended on your success.'

'A light-hearted challenge?' Philip repeated sceptically.

'I wanted to shock you into doing something more important with
your lives. What I didn't realise before is that each of you *is* doing
something important—that is, living the life *you* want to live. Who
am I to judge?' He shook his head. 'Here I was locked up with what I
thought was my treasure, my life's work—and suddenly it meant
nothing. I couldn't even see it. I found myself looking back on my
whole life with a kind of loathing. I had been a bad father to you; a
bad husband, greedy, selfish.'

He lapsed into silence, looking out over the vast landscape, the
endless mountains and jungles. He shifted, coughed. 'Funny, I feel
like I've died and been reborn.'

The four brothers and their father rested in the shade along a shelf
of rock to the side of the tomb door. After they had eaten most of
their food, Tom passed round a canteen of water. There was so much
he had wanted to say to his father, and he had no doubt his brothers
felt the same way—and yet, after the initial outburst of talk, they had
fallen silent. Somehow it was enough to be together.

Finally Maxwell Broadbent spoke again. 'So Marcus Hauser is out
there, looking to rob *my* tomb.' He shook his head. 'What a world.'

'I'm sorry,' said Philip again.

'It was my fault,' said Broadbent. 'No more apologies.'

This was something new, Tom thought: Maxwell Broadbent admitting he was wrong. He seemed to be the same gruff old man, but he had changed. Definitely, he had changed.

Philip cleared his throat. 'Father?'

'Yes, son?'

'I don't mean to bring up an unwelcome subject, but what are we going to do about the stuff in your tomb?'

Tom thought immediately of the Codex. He had to bring it out—not only for himself, but for Sally and for the world.

Broadbent gazed at the ground for a moment before speaking. 'It doesn't seem important to me any more. But I suppose we should take the Lippi and anything else that's easy to carry. At least we can keep a few things out of Hauser's hands. It kills me to think he's going to get most of the stuff, but I guess it can't be helped.'

'When we get out, we'll report it to the FBI, Interpol—'

'Hauser's going to get away with it, Philip, and you know it. Which reminds me. There was something odd about the boxes in the tomb, something that I've been wondering about. As much as I hate to go back in there, there's something I've got to check out.'

'I'll help you,' Philip said, springing to his feet.

'No. I need to go in there alone. Borabay, give me a light.'

Borabay lit a bundle of reeds and handed it to his father.

The old man disappeared through the doorway. The light moved deeper into the darkness and vanished.

Philip stood up and stretched his legs. He lit his pipe. 'I hate to think of Hauser getting his hands on the Lippi.'

A voice, cool and amused, came floating towards them: 'I say, did someone mention my name?'

HAUSER SPOKE SOFTLY, his weapon levelled and ready to go at the slightest movement. The three brothers and the Indian, sitting on the far side of the open tomb door, turned their heads towards him.

'Do not discommode yourselves by rising. Do not move at all, except to blink.' He paused. 'Philip, so good to see you recovered.' He took a step forward, braced, ready to mow them down at the slightest movement. 'And how kind of you to guide me to the tomb. You've even opened the door for me! Very considerate. Now, listen carefully. If you follow my directions no one will be hurt.'

Hauser paused to examine the four faces in front of him. No one was gearing up to play the hero. These were sensible people. He said: 'Someone tell the Indian that he needs to put his bow and arrows down. Slowly and smoothly—no sudden movements, please.'

Borabay took off his quiver and bow and let them fall.

'So the Indian understands English. Good. And now I will ask each of you fellows to unsheath and drop your machetes one at a time. You first, Philip. Remain seated.'

Philip unsheathed his machete and dropped it.

'Vernon?'

Vernon did the same and then Tom.

'Now, Philip, I want you to go over to where you have piled your packs, get them, and bring them to me. Easy does it.'

Philip collected the packs and placed them at Hauser's feet.

'Excellent! Return to your place. Good. Now let's empty our pockets. Turn the pockets inside out and drop everything on the ground.'

They complied. Hauser was surprised to see that they had not, as he supposed, been loading up with treasures from the tomb.

'And now you'll stand up in unison. In *slow* motion. Good! Now, just moving your legs from the knees down, taking small steps, keeping your arms *very* still, you will move back. One step at a time.'

As they shuffled back, Hauser stepped forward. They had bunched up instinctively; it made everything so much easier.

'Everything's just fine,' he said softly. 'I don't want to hurt anybody—all I want is Max's grave goods.' His finger caressed the smooth plastic curve of the trigger, found its place, began to tighten it back to full auto position. They were in place. There was nothing they could do now. They were as good as dead.

He squeezed for real now, felt that imperceptible *give* in the trigger, that millisecond release after the feeling of resistance, and simultaneously saw a swift movement in his peripheral field of vision. There was an explosion of sparks and flame and he fell, firing wildly as he went, the bullets ricocheting off the stone walls, and before he hit the ground he had a terrifying glimpse of what had struck him.

The thing had come out of the tomb, face white as a vampire, sunken-eyed, stinking of decomposition, its bony limbs holding aloft a burning brand that it had just struck him with, and it was still coming at him with a shrieking mouth full of brown teeth.

Hauser rolled when he hit the ground. He twisted, trying to get back into firing position, but the ragged spectre fell on him, roaring and stabbing and slashing him across the face with the burning brand; there were showers of sparks, and he smelt burning hair as he tried to ward off the blows with one hand, clutching his gun with the other. It was impossible to get off a shot while the attacker was trying to gouge out his eyes with the torch. He managed to wrench free and then fired blindly, hoping to hit something, anything. But the spectre seemed to have vanished.

He stopped firing and sat up gingerly. He yanked the canteen out of his pack and doused his face. Hot coals and sparks from the brand had lodged inside his nose, under one eyelid, in his hair and on his cheek. He opened, painfully, his right eye. As he gently probed around it with his fingertip, he realised the damage was all to the eyebrow and lid; he hadn't lost his vision. He poured some water into his handkerchief, wrung it out, and blotted his face.

What the hell happened? Hauser *knew* that face, even after forty years; he knew every detail of it. There was no doubt: it was Max Broadbent himself who had come shrieking out of that tomb like a banshee—Broadbent, who was supposed to be dead and buried.

Hauser swore. Broadbent was alive and at this very moment escaping. Sitting here, he'd given them at least a three-minute start.

He got to his feet, reshouldered his Steyr, took a step forward and stopped. There was blood on the ground—a half-dollar-sized splotch. And further along another generous splash. Broadbent was bleeding. He had managed to hit him and perhaps some of the others after all. The advantage was still his.

He looked up the stone staircase and began to run.

THEY REACHED THE TRAIL at the top of the cliffs and sprinted for the green walls of lianas and creepers that covered the ruined ramparts of the White City. As they reached the covering shade, Tom saw his father stumble. Streaks of blood were running down one of his legs.

'Wait! Father's hit!'

'It's nothing.' The old man stumbled again and grunted.

Tom examined the wound, wiping away the blood, locating the entrance and exit wounds. The bullet had passed through the right lower abdomen, coming out in the back, where it seemed to have avoided the kidney. It was a serious wound and his father was losing blood, but at least no arteries or major veins had been cut.

Tom took off his own shirt and with one savage pull tore a strip of cloth away, then another. He bound these as best he could round his father's midriff, trying to stem the loss of blood.

'Put your arm round my shoulder,' Tom said.

'I'll take the other,' Vernon said.

Tom felt the arm go round him—it was skinny and hard, like a cable of steel. He took some of his father's weight. 'Let's go.'

They jogged along the base of the wall, looking for an opening. Borabay plunged through a doorway and they scrambled across a courtyard, through another doorway and along a collapsed gallery. Tom and Vernon took turns to support their father as they moved on, passing through a series of dim tunnels, Borabay leading them in sharp turns and doubling back in an effort to throw off their pursuer. They came out into a grove of giant trees, then travelled for another twenty minutes. The jungle became riotously luxuriant and thick.

Borabay paused, peering around. 'This way,' he said, pointing to the thickest part.

'How?' Philip said, looking at the impenetrable wall of growth.

Borabay dropped to his knees and crawled ahead into a small opening. They did likewise, Max grunting with pain. Tom saw that hidden under the matted vines was a network of animal trails. They crawled into the thickest of the vegetation, squeezing along the trails. It was dark and rank. They crawled for what seemed like an eternity, but was probably no more than twenty minutes, until they came to an open area underneath a vine-choked tree, whose lower branches created a tentlike space, impenetrable on all sides.

'We stay here,' Borabay said. 'We wait until night.'

Broadbent sagged back against the tree trunk with a groan. Tom knelt over his father, stripped off the blood-soaked strips of material and examined the wound. It was bad. Borabay knelt next to him and carefully examined it himself. Then he took some leaves he had plucked from somewhere during their flight, crushed and rubbed them between his palms and made two poultices. Vernon volunteered his shirt and Tom tore it into strips, using them to tie the poultices into place.

Philip said, 'Father, you saved our lives back there. We'd be dead if you hadn't jumped on Hauser.'

'The sins of my youth, come back to haunt me.' The old man winced.

Borabay squatted on his heels and looked around at all of them. 'I go now. I come back in half-hour. If I no come back, when night come you wait till rain start and cross bridge without me. OK?'

'Where are you going?' Vernon asked.

'To get Hauser.' He sprang up and was gone.

Tom hesitated for a moment and then stood up. If he was going to go back for the Codex, it was now or never.

'There's something I have to do, too.'

'What?' Philip and Vernon looked at him incredulously.

Tom couldn't find the words or the time to defend his decision. 'I'll meet up with you at the bridge tonight, after the storm hits.'

'Tom, have you gone crazy?' Max rumbled.

Tom didn't answer. He turned and slipped off into the jungle.

In twenty minutes he had crawled back out of the vine maze. The necropolis of tombs was to the east: that much he knew. He didn't want to think about the decision he had just made: whether it was right or wrong to leave his father and brothers, whether it was crazy, whether it was too dangerous. It was all beside the point. Getting the Codex was something he just had to do.

He went east.

HAUSER'S EYES SCANNED the ground ahead, reading it like a book: a seedpod pressed into the earth, a creased blade of grass. Every detail told him where the Broadbents had gone as clearly as if they had left a trail of breadcrumbs. He followed their route rapidly, Steyr AUG at the ready. He felt relaxed now. He knew the Broadbents were unarmed, and he knew they would have to cross the bridge. It was only a matter of time before he caught up with them.

He followed the traces—dew swiped from a leaf, a spot of blood on the soil—into a ruined gallery and turned on his flashlight. Moss scraped from a stone, an imprint in the soft ground—any idiot could follow these tracks. As he emerged into a broad forest, he saw one particularly clear trace.

Too clear. He froze, listened, and then crouched and minutely examined the ground ahead. Amateurish. The Vietcong would laugh at this one: a bent sapling, a loop of vine hidden under leaves—an almost invisible tripwire. He took one careful step back, picked up a stick and lobbed it at the tripwire.

There was a snap, the sapling shot up, the loop jerked. And then Hauser felt a sudden breath of air and a tug on his trouserleg. He looked down. Embedded in the loose crease of his khakis was a small dart, its fire-hardened tip dribbling a dark liquid.

The poisoned dart had missed him by less than an inch.

For several minutes he remained frozen. He examined every square inch of ground around him, every tree, every limb. Satisfied there was no other trap, he leaned over and was about to pluck the dart out when he stopped again—and just in time. The sides of the dart had imbedded in them two nearly invisible spines, also wet with poison, ready to prick the finger of whoever tried to grasp it.

He took a twig and flicked the dart off his trousers.

Very clever. This was the Indian's work, no doubt about it.

Hauser moved forward more slowly now, with newfound respect.

TOM RAN THROUGH THE FOREST, swinging wide of their earlier trail to avoid running into Hauser. His path took him through a maze of ruined temples, buried under thick mats of vines. He had no light and sometimes he had to feel his way down dark passageways.

He soon arrived at the eastern edge of the plateau. He paused, catching his breath, and then crept to the cliff and looked down, trying to orientate himself. It seemed to him that the necropolis should lie somewhere to the south, so he went to the right, following the trail that skirted the cliffs. In another ten minutes he recognised the terrace and walls above the necropolis and found the hidden trail. He scurried down, listening at each switchback in case Hauser was still there, but he had long gone. A moment later he came to the dark opening to his father's tomb.

Their backpacks lay on the ground where they had dropped them. Tom picked up his machete and resheathed it and then rifled through the packs, taking out some reed bundles and a box of matches. He lit one of the bundles and stepped into the tomb.

The flickering light illuminated a raised funeral slab of dark stone, carved stone, surrounded by boxes and crates banded with stainless steel and bolted shut. The boxes were stencilled and labelled, and it took Tom only a few minutes to find the crate containing the Codex.

He dragged the heavy crate outside into the light. The box itself weighed eighty pounds, and it contained other books besides the Codex. Tom examined the quarter-inch bolts and wing nuts holding together the steel bands that clamped down the fibreglass-wrapped wooden sides of the box. The wing nuts were tight and hard.

He found a stone and gave one of the nuts a sharp blow, loosening it. He repeated the process and in a few minutes had removed all the wing nuts. He pulled off the steel bands. A few more massive blows cracked the fibreglass covering and Tom was able to wrench it free. Half a dozen precious books spilled out, all carefully wrapped in acid-free paper—a Mazarin Bible, illuminated manuscripts, a book of hours. Tom shoved aside the books and reached in, grasped the buckskin-covered Codex, and pulled it out.

For a moment, he stared at it. He remembered so clearly how it had sat in a little glass case in the living room. His father used to unlock the case every month or so and turn a page. The pages had drawings of plants, flowers and insects, surrounded by glyphs. He remembered staring at those strange Mayan glyphs, the dots and thick lines and grinning faces, all wrapped and tangled round each other. He hadn't even realised it was a kind of writing.

Tom emptied one of their abandoned backpacks and shoved the book inside it, then shouldered the pack and started back up the trail. He decided to head southwest, keeping an eye out for Hauser.

He entered the ruined city.

11

Hauser followed the trail more carefully now; he took every precaution against ambush, walking to one side and pausing every few minutes to examine the ground and undergrowth ahead, even smelling the air for human scent. He saw that the Broadbents were headed towards the centre of the plateau, where the jungle was thickest.

Soon the rain forest ahead became choked by a wild overgrowth of creepers and lianas. At first glance it looked impenetrable. He approached cautiously and peered down. There were animal tracks running every which way. Drops of water hung from every leaf, vine and flower, waiting for the slightest vibration to fall. No one could walk through such a minefield without leaving evidence of his passage in the form of leaves brushed free of their dew. Hauser could see exactly where they had gone. He followed their trail into the dense overgrowth, where it seemed to vanish.

Hauser scrutinised the ground. There, in the damp litter of the forest floor, were two almost invisible indentations, formed by a pair of human knees. Interesting. He squatted and peered into the green darkness. There, three feet in, was a tiny crushed mushroom, no bigger than a dime, and a scraped leaf. They had gone to earth in this mass of vegetation. Without a doubt, Hauser thought, the Indian would be hiding somewhere on a branch above the warren of tracks, poison dart at the ready, waiting for him to crawl past below.

What he had to do was to ambush the ambusher.

Hauser thought for a moment. The Indian was smart. He would already have anticipated this. The Indian was not waiting in ambush on *this* track. No. Rather, he expected Hauser to circle and come round from the other side. Therefore, the Indian was waiting on the *other side* of the gigantic mass of growth.

Hauser began circling the edge of the creeper colony, moving silently and smoothly, stopping every few moments to scan the middle storey of the jungle. Now he paused, moved a little, looked again. There was something in a tree. Just the corner of the Indian's red shirt was visible, on a branch about fifty yards to his right, and there—he could just see it—was the tip of a little reed blowpipe.

Hauser moved sideways until he had more of the Indian's shirt in sight to make a target. He raised his rifle, took careful aim, and fired.

Nothing. And yet he knew he had hit it. A sudden panic seized him: It was another trap. He flung himself sideways at the very moment the Indian came dropping down on him like a cat, sharpened stick in hand. Using a jujitsu move, Hauser threw himself forward and to the side, turning the Indian's own momentum against him, neatly throwing him off—and then he was up and placing an arc of automatic-weapon fire across where the Indian had been.

The Indian was gone, vanished.

Hauser glanced up and saw the tree with the little bit of red cloth, the tip of the blowpipe, all still in place exactly where the Indian had put them. He swallowed. Now was not the time for fear or anger. He had a job to do. He would no longer play the Indian's cat-and-mouse game, which Hauser now suspected he would lose. The time had come to flush out the Broadbents with brute force.

He turned and walked along the edge of the creeper colony, planted his feet and took aim with the Steyr AUG. First one burst, then a second, and then he walked on, pouring fire into the thick vegetation. It had the effect he had anticipated: it flushed out the Broadbents. He could hear their panicked flight, noisy, like partridges. Now he knew where they were. He sprinted along the mass of growth to cut them off as they emerged and herd them towards the bridge.

There was a sudden sound behind him and he spun towards the greater danger, squeezing the trigger and pouring firepower into the dense cover where the sound had come from. He heard a squeal and some thrashing. Coatimundi, damn it! He had shot a coatimundi!

He turned now, lowered his gun and fired in the direction of the fleeing Broadbents. He heard the coati squealing in pain behind him, the crackling of twigs, and then he realised, just in time, that this was no wounded coati—it was the Indian again.

He dropped, rolled, fired—not to kill, for the Indian had vanished into the vines, but to drive him in the same direction as the Broadbents, towards the bridge. The trick was to keep them moving, firing steadily, preventing them from peeling off and coming back round behind him. He ran, crouching and firing short bursts, left and right, cutting off any possibility of escape back to the ruined city.

He had them now.

DURING THE TWELVE HOURS Sally had waited behind the tree trunk, her thoughts had turned to her father. It was in the last summer of his life that he had taught her how to shoot. After he died, she had continued to go down to the bluffs to practise shooting apples and oranges, and later pennies and dimes. She had become an excellent shot, but she had no interest in competition or hunting.

She shifted her cramped thighs and wiggled her toes, trying to limber up the stiffened muscles. She gave another handful of nuts to Hairy Bugger, who was still sitting grumpily in his vine cage. She was glad he had been there to keep her company these past hours, even if he was in a foul mood. The poor thing loved his freedom.

Suddenly, he gave a squeak of alarm and Sally was instantly alert. Then she heard it: distant shots from the White City. With the binoculars she scanned the forest on the far side of the gorge. There were more shots and still more, growing louder. Then she saw movement.

It was Tom. He had appeared at the edge of the cliffs, running. Philip and Vernon emerged out of the jungle ahead of him, supporting a old and wounded man between them. Borabay was the last to appear, closest to the bridge.

Now she spied Hauser and his gun coming out of the trees from behind, driving them like game towards the bridge.

She lowered the binoculars and raised the Springfield, watching through the scope. The Broadbents and Borabay were about to be trapped on the bridge. But they had no other choice, with Hauser behind them and the chasm to the side. They hesitated at the bridgehead, then ran out onto the span. Hauser was shouting to the soldiers on the far side, who knelt and fired warning shots.

In a moment all five of the Broadbents, including Borabay, were trapped in the middle of the bridge, with Hauser and four soldiers at one end and four soldiers at the other. The firing died down and all was silent. Hauser, with a grin on his face, now began walking along the precarious bridge towards them, his weapon levelled.

Sally felt her heart hammering. Her moment had come. She aimed at Hauser as he strolled along the bridge. The bridge was swaying, but she felt her chances of scoring a hit were better than fifty-fifty. They would be even better once he stopped walking.

Hauser advanced to within 100 feet of the Broadbents and paused. She could kill him—she *would* kill him. She centred his torso in her cross hairs, but she did not squeeze the trigger. Instead, she asked herself: What will happen after I kill Hauser?

The answer wasn't hard to figure out. The Honduran soldiers on each side of the bridge were brutal mercenaries and would almost certainly open fire and massacre everyone on the bridge. There were ten soldiers—four at her end and now six at the other—and she couldn't hope to pick them all off, especially the six at the far end, who were virtually out of range. The chamber of her rifle held five shots, and when those were done she would have to reload five more manually, a long process. And she only had ten rounds anyway.

Whatever she did had to be done in five shots.

'WELL, WELL,' said Hauser. 'Max. We meet again.'

The old man, grasping his sons to help him stand, raised his head and spoke. 'Your quarrel is with me. Let my sons go.'

The smile on Hauser's face took on a frostier look. 'On the contrary, you're going to have the pleasure of seeing them die first.'

Borabay took a step forward, but was stayed by Philip.

'Well, then, who's first? The Indian? No, let's do him later. We'll go by age. Philip? Step away from the others.'

After a brief hesitation Philip stepped to one side. Vernon reached out to him, grasped his arm and tried to pull him back. He shook it off and took another step.

'You'll burn in hell, Hauser,' roared Broadbent.

Hauser smiled pleasantly and raised the muzzle of his rifle. Tom looked away. But the shot didn't come. Tom looked back. Hauser's attention had been diverted to something behind them. Tom turned round and saw, bounding along one of the cables of the bridge towards them, Hairy Bugger.

With a screech of joy the monkey leapt into Tom's arms, and Tom saw that he had a canister almost as large as himself tied to his midriff. It was the aluminium bottle of white gas from their camping stove. There was something scrawled on it.

I CAN HIT THIS. S

Tom wondered what the hell it meant, what Sally had in mind.

Hauser raised his gun. 'OK, everybody keep still. Now, show me what the monkey just brought you. *Slowly.*'

All at once, Sally's plan came to Tom. He untied the canister.

'Hold it out at arm's length. Let me see it.'

Tom held the canister out. 'It's a litre of white gas.'

'Toss it over the side.'

'There's a sharpshooter on our side who's got a bead on this bottle. As you know, white gas is explosively flammable.'

Hauser's face showed no reaction. He merely raised his gun.

'Hauser, if she hits this can, the bridge burns. You'll be cut off. You'll be trapped in the White City for ever.'

'If the bridge burns, you'll die, too.'

'You're going to kill us anyway.'

Hauser said, 'It's a bluff.'

Tom did not respond. Seconds ticked by. Hauser's face betrayed nothing.

Tom said, 'Hauser, she might just put a bullet through *you*.'

Hauser raised his gun, and in that moment a bullet struck the bamboo bridge surface two feet in front of Hauser's boots with a *snick*, sending a spray of bamboo splinters into his face. The report came a moment later. Hauser hastily lowered his gun.

'Now that we've established this is not bullshit, tell your soldiers to let us pass.'

'And?' said Hauser.

'You can have the bridge and the tomb. All we want is our lives.'

Now Hauser shouldered his weapon. 'My compliments,' he said.

Tom took the canister with slow movements and, using a loose piece of twine from the bridge, tied it round one of the main cables.

'Tell your men to let us pass. You stay where you are. If anything bad happens to us, our sharpshooter shoots the canister and your precious bridge burns with you on it. Understand?'

Hauser nodded.

'I didn't hear the order, Hauser.'

'Men!' Hauser called in Spanish. 'Let them leave! Do not molest them as they go! I am releasing them!'

'*Sí, señor*,' came the reply.

The Broadbents began to walk off the bridge.

HAUSER STOOD in the middle of the bridge, his mind having accepted the fact that a sharpshooter—no doubt that blonde who had come with Tom Broadbent—had him in her cross hairs. 'A useless old hunting rifle', the soldier had told him. *Right.* She had placed a bullet at his feet at over 300 yards. To think that she now had him in her sights was an unpleasant and yet oddly thrilling feeling.

He looked at the bottle tied to the cable. The distance from where he was standing to the bottle was less than 100 feet. The bridge was swaying in the updrafts from the canyon. It would be a difficult shot, hitting a target moving through three dimensions. An almost impossible shot, in fact. In ten seconds he could reach the bottle, tear it off the cable and drop it into the abyss. If he then turned and ran back towards the far end of the bridge, he would be a moving target rapidly going out of range. How likely would it be that she could hit him? He would be running fast along a *swaying* bridge—again moving in three dimensions relative to her firing point. She would not be able to draw a bead on him. On top of that she was a woman. Obviously she could shoot, but no woman could shoot that well.

It could all be done quickly, before the Broadbents escaped.

He crouched and sprang towards the can of white gas.

Almost instantly he heard the *snick* of a bullet in front of him and then the report. He kept going and got to the can just as the second report reached his ears. Another miss. This was too easy. He had just put his hand on the can when he heard a *pop* and saw a brilliant blossoming of light erupt in front of him with a *whoosh*, followed by a searing heat. He staggered back, waving his arm, surprised to see blue flames crawling all over him. He fell and rolled, thrashing around, beating at himself, but he was like a blazing Midas and everything he touched turned to fire. He kicked, shrieked, rolled—and then suddenly he was like an angel, soaring on wings of air, and he closed his eyes and allowed the long, cool, delicious fall to happen.

TOM SAW THE FIERY HUMAN meteor that was Hauser streaking into the bottomless chasm, flickering dimly and silently as it hurtled down through layers of mist before disappearing, leaving nothing behind but a faint trail of smoke.

The entire midsection of the bridge where Hauser had been standing was on fire.

'Get off the bridge!' Tom cried. 'Run!'

They ran as best they could, supporting their father, advancing towards the four soldiers, who remained blocking the far end of the bridge. The soldiers looked confused, uncertain, guns raised, liable to do anything.

The leader of the group, a lieutenant, cried, 'Halt!'

'Let us pass!' Tom cried in Spanish. They kept coming.

'No. Get back.'

'Hauser ordered you to let us pass!' Tom could feel the bridge trembling. The burning cable was going to go at any second.

'Hauser is dead,' said the lieutenant. 'I am now in charge.'

'The bridge is burning, for God's sake!'

A smile crept up on the *teniente*'s face. 'Yes.'

As if on cue the whole bridge jerked, and Tom and his father and brothers were thrown to their knees. One of the cables had parted, sending a shower of sparks into the abyss, while the bridge whipped back and forth under the sudden release of tension.

Tom struggled to his feet, helping his brothers raise their father.

'You must let us pass!'

The soldier answered with a burst of fire just above their heads. 'You die with the bridge. The White City is ours now!'

Tom turned; smoke and flames streamed from the bridge's midsection. He saw a second cable start to unravel, spilling burning bits of fibre into the air. Then it parted with a violent lashing and the entire deck of the bridge fell away. They clung to the two remaining cables, struggling to hold on to their weakened father.

'Soldiers or no soldiers,' said Tom, 'let's get the hell off this bridge.'

They began edging along the two remaining cables, their feet on the lower one, their hands on the upper, helping Broadbent along.

The *teniente* and his three soldiers advanced two steps. 'Get ready to fire!' They dropped to a stable firing position and took aim.

Tom and the others were now only twenty-five feet from land. Then the third cable parted like a spring, sending a recoil through the bridge that almost knocked them all off. The wreckage of the bridge hung from the single remaining cable, swinging back and forth.

The *teniente* pointed his gun at them. 'You die now,' he said in English.

There was a hollow thud, but it was not from his gun. A surprised look came into the *teniente*'s face, and it was as if he were bowing down before them, a long arrow sticking out of the back of his head. In that moment a bloodcurdling yell went up from the edge of the forest, followed by a shower of arrows. Tara warriors poured out of the jungle and raced across the flat area, leaping and shrieking, firing arrows on the fly. The remaining soldiers were transformed into human pincushions, struck with dozens of arrows simultaneously; they staggered about wildly before falling to the ground.

A moment later Tom and his brothers reached land—just as the final cable parted. The two blazing ends of the bridge swung lazily towards the canyon walls and crashed into them with a shudder and a cascade of burning debris.

It was over. The bridge was gone.

Tom looked ahead and saw Sally stand up out of the brush. She ran towards them as they helped their father along, aided by Tara warriors. In a few moments she had reached them. Tom folded her in his arms and they hugged, while Hairy Bugger, now safe in Tom's pocket again, squeaked his displeasure at being squeezed in the middle.

THE HUT WAS WARM and faintly perfumed with smoke and medicinal herbs. Tom entered, followed by Vernon, Philip and Sally. Maxwell Broadbent was lying in a hammock with his eyes closed. A young Tara medicine man was grinding herbs in one corner of the hut, under the watchful eye of Borabay.

Tom laid a hand on his father's forehead. His temperature was climbing. The gesture caused his father to open his eyes. His face was drawn, his eyes glittering with fever and the light of the fire.

The old man mustered a smile. 'As soon as I get better, Borabay's going to show me how to go spearfishing the Tara way.'

Tom tried to say something but couldn't get the sounds out. He swallowed. His father, sensing his discomfort, turned to him.

'Well, Tom? You're the only real doctor around here. What's the prognosis?'

Tom tried to smile. His father looked at him for a long time.

'Tom? I'm already dying of cancer. You can't tell me anything worse than that.'

'Well,' Tom began, 'the bullet perforated your peritoneal cavity. You've got an infection, and that's why you have a fever.'

'And the prognosis?'

Tom swallowed again. He knew his father would settle for nothing less than the plain, unadorned truth. 'Not good.'

'Go on.'

Tom couldn't quite bring himself to say it.

'That bad?' said his father.

Tom nodded.

'But what about these antibiotics this medicine man's giving me? And what about all those remedies in that codex you just rescued?'

'Father, the kind of infection you have, sepsis, can't be reached by any antibiotic. Nothing short of major surgery will fix it and now it's probably too late even for that. Drugs can't do everything.'

There was a silence. Broadbent turned and looked up. 'Damn,' he said at last, to the ceiling.

Tom laid his hand on his father's arm. 'I'm sorry.'

'So how long do I have?'

'Two or three days.'

Maxwell Broadbent lay back with a sigh. 'The cancer would have got me in a few months anyway. Although it would have been damned nice having those months with my sons. Or even a week.'

Borabay came over and gently laid his hand on his father's chest. 'I sorry, Father.'

Broadbent covered the hand with his. 'I sorry, too.' He turned and looked at his sons. 'And I can't even look on the Lippi Madonna one more time. When I was in that tomb, I kept thinking if I could only look on that Madonna again, everything would be all right.'

THEY SPENT THE NIGHT in the hut watching over their dying father. He was restless, but herbal antibiotics were, at least for now, holding the infection at bay. When dawn broke the old man was still lucid.

'I need some water,' he said, his voice hoarse.

Tom left the hut with a jug, heading for the nearby stream. As he walked back carrying the water, he heard a sharp voice. The old crone, the wife of Cah, had come out of her hut and was gesturing towards him with a crooked hand. '*Wakha!*' she said, beckoning.

Tom paused warily, then reluctantly followed her bent form into the smoky hut. There, in the dim light, propped up against a post, stood the *Madonna of the Grapes* by Fra Filippo Lippi. Tom stared at the Renaissance masterpiece, transfixed, hardly believing it could be real. Even in the dark it fairly glowed with internal light, the golden-haired Madonna, barely a teenager, holding her baby, who was stuffing a grape into his mouth with two pink fingers.

He turned to the old lady in astonishment. She was looking at him with a huge grin on her wrinkled face, her pink gums gleaming. She went over to the painting, picked it up and thrust it in his arms.

'*Wakha!*' She gestured for him to take it to his father's hut. She went behind, giving him little pushes with her hands. '*Teh! Teh!*'

Tom walked into the damp clearing with the Lippi cradled in his arms. Cah must have kept it back for himself. He stepped into the hut and held the painting out. Philip glanced over and let out a cry. Broadbent stared at it, his eyes widening. At first he said nothing, and then he lay back in his hammock, a look of fright on his face.

'Damn it, Tom! The hallucinations are starting.'

'No, Father.' He brought the painting close. 'It's real. Touch it.'

'No, don't touch it!' cried Philip.

Broadbent reached out a trembling hand and touched the painted surface anyway. 'Hello,' he murmured. 'I'm not dreaming. Where in the world did you get this?'

'She had it.' Tom turned to the old woman, who stood in the door-way, a toothless grin on her face.

Borabay began asking her questions and she spoke at length. Then Borabay turned to his father.

'She say her husband greedy, keep back many things from tomb.

Hide them in cave behind village. She say Cah steal almost all treasure for tomb. He fill boxes with stones instead. He say he not want to put white man treasure in Tara tomb.'

'Wouldn't you know it,' said Broadbent. 'When I was in the tomb, there were some crates that seemed hollower than they should have been. I couldn't get them open in the dark. That's what I was trying to do in the tomb just before Hauser showed up, to see if I could solve the mystery. That damned Cah. He was just as greedy as I was!'

Broadbent closed his eyes and said, 'Bring me a pen and paper. Now that I have something to leave you, I'm going to make a new will.'

They brought him a pen and a roll of bark paper.

'Shall we leave you?' asked Vernon.

'No. I need you here. You too, Sally. Come. Gather around.'

They came and stood around his hammock. Then he cleared his throat. 'Well, my sons. And'—he looked at Sally—'my future daughter-in-law. Here we are.' He paused. 'And what fine sons I have. Pity it took me so long to realise it.' His eyes, still clear, travelled around the room. 'Congratulations. You did it. You earned your inheritance, and you saved my life. You showed me what a goddamn fool of a father I've been—'

'Father—'

'No interruptions! I have some parting advice.' He wheezed. 'Here I am on my deathbed; how can I resist?' He took a deep breath. 'Philip, of all my sons, you're the one most like me. I've seen, in these past years, how the expectation of a large inheritance has cast a shadow over your life. You're not naturally greedy, but when you're waiting for a hundred million dollars, it has a corrosive effect. I've seen you living beyond your means, trying to play the rich, sophisticated connoisseur in your New York circle. You've got the same disease I had: needing to own beauty. Forget it. That's what museums are for. Live a simpler life. You have a deep appreciation for art and that should be its own reward, not the recognition and fame. And I've heard you're one hell of a teacher.'

Philip nodded curtly, not altogether pleased.

Broadbent took a ragged breath. Then he turned to Vernon. 'Vernon. You're a seeker, and I finally see just how important that choice is for you. Your problem is, you get taken in. You're an innocent. There's a rule of thumb here, Vernon: if they want money, the religion's bullshit. It doesn't cost anything to pray in a church.'

Vernon nodded.

'And now Tom. Of all my sons you're the most different from me. I

431

never really understood you. You're the least materialistic of my sons. You rejected me a long time ago, perhaps for good reasons.'

'Father—'

'Quiet! Unlike me, you're disciplined in the way you live your life. I know what you really wanted to do was become a palaeontologist and hunt dinosaur fossils. Like a fool, I pushed you into medicine. I know you're a good vet, although I've never understood why you're wasting your tremendous talents treating horses on the Navajo Indian reservation. What I've finally understood is that I must respect and honour your choices in life. Dinosaurs, horses, whatever. You do what you want with my blessing. What I have also come to see is your *integrity*. Integrity was something I never really had, and it upset me to see it so strongly in one of my sons. I don't know what you would have done with a big inheritance, and I expect you don't know, either. You don't need the money and you don't really want it.'

'Yes, Father.'

'And now, Borabay . . . you are my oldest and yet most recent son. I've only known you briefly, but in a strange way I feel I know you best of all. I've scoped you out and I realise you're a little greedy like me. You can't wait to cut out of here and go to America and enjoy the good life. You don't really fit in with the Tara. Well, that's fine. You'll learn fast. You have an advantage here because you had a good mother and you didn't have me for a father, messing you up.'

Borabay was about to say something, but Broadbent raised his hand. 'Can't a man give a deathbed speech around here without being interrupted? Borabay, your brothers will help you get to America and get citizenship. Once there you'll become more American than the natives, I have no doubt.'

'Yes, Father.'

Broadbent sighed and cast an eye on Sally. 'Tom, this is the woman I never met but wished I had. You'd be a fool to let her slip away.'

'I'm not a fish,' said Sally sharply.

'Ah! That's just what I mean! A little prickly, perhaps, but an amazing woman.'

'You're right, Father.'

Broadbent paused, breathing heavily. It was an effort now to talk; the sweat stood out on his brow.

'I am about to write my last will and testament. I want each of you to choose one thing from the collection in that cave. The rest, if you can get it out of the country, I'd like to donate to whatever museums you choose. We'll go from oldest to youngest. Borabay, you start.'

Borabay said, 'I choose last. What I want is not in cave.'

Broadbent nodded. 'All right. Philip? As if I couldn't guess.' His eyes strayed to the Madonna. 'The Lippi is yours.'

Philip tried to say something but could not.

'And now: Vernon?'

There was a silence, and then Vernon said, 'I'd like the Monet.'

'I thought that's what you'd say. I imagine you could get fifty million or more for it. And I hope you do sell it. But Vernon, please, *no* foundations. Don't give any money away. When you finally find what you're looking for, maybe then you'll have the wisdom to give a little bit of your money away, a *little* bit.'

'Thank you, Father.'

'And now, Tom, it's your turn. What's your pick?'

Tom glanced at Sally. 'We'd like the Codex.'

Broadbent nodded. 'Interesting choice. It's yours. And now, Borabay, what is this mysterious thing you want that isn't in the cave?'

Borabay came over to the bed and whispered in Broadbent's ear.

The old man nodded. 'Excellent. Consider it done.' He flourished his pen. His face was beaded with sweat, his breathing rapid and shallow. 'Now give me ten minutes by myself to make out my last will and testament, and then we will gather witnesses and execute it.'

TOM STOOD with his brothers and Sally in a cathedral-like grove of trees, watching the funeral procession winding up the trail towards the tomb, which had been freshly chiselled in the limestone cliffs above the village. Maxwell Broadbent's body came at the head of the procession, borne upon a litter by four warriors. It had been embalmed using an ancient Mayan process. During the funeral ceremony the new chief of the village had transformed the corpse into El Dorado, the Gilded One of Indian legend—the way the Maya had once buried their emperors. They had smeared the body with honey and then sprinkled it with gold dust, coating it completely, to metamorphose it into the immortal form it would take in the afterlife.

Behind their father's litter came a long procession of Indians carrying grave goods for the tomb—baskets of dried fruits and vegetables, nuts, ollas of oil and water, then a slew of traditional Mayan artefacts such as jade statues, painted pots, beaten gold dishes and jugs, weapons, quivers full of arrows, nets, spears, everything that Maxwell Broadbent might need in the afterlife.

After that, hobbling round the bend, came an Indian carrying a painting by Picasso of a naked woman with three eyes, a square head,

433

and horns, followed by the massive Pontormo scene of the Annunciation, carried by two sweating Indians, then the Bronzino portrait of Bia de' Medici, a pair of Roman statues, a Braque, two Modiglianis, a Cezanne—twentieth-century grave goods. The bizarre procession wound its way up the hillside and into the grove.

And finally came the band, if that's what you could call it: a group of men playing gourd flutes, blowing long wooden trumpets, and beating sticks—with one young boy bringing up the rear, banging with all his might a shabby, Western-style bass drum.

Tom felt a great mixture of sadness and catharsis. It was the end of an era. His father was dead, and passing before his eyes were the things he knew and loved, the things he had grown up with. They were the things his father loved, too. As the procession went into the tomb, darkness swallowed it all, men and grave goods alike—and then the men emerged, blinking and empty-handed. There his father's collection would be shut up, safe, dry, guarded and protected until the day when he and his brothers could return and claim what was theirs. The Mayan treasures, of course, would stay in the tomb for ever, to ensure that Maxwell Broadbent lived a fine and happy life in the afterworld. But the Western treasures belonged to them, held in safekeeping by the Tara tribe. It was a funeral to end all funerals. Only the Mayan emperors had been buried like this.

Maxwell Broadbent had passed away three days after signing his last will and testament. He had had only one more day of lucidity before he sank into delirium, coma and death.

It wasn't the death so much as the last lucid day of his father's life that Tom would never forget. The four sons had stayed with him. They hadn't talked much, and when they did it was of minor things— little memories, stories, forgotten places, people long gone. And yet that day of small talk had been more valuable than all the decades of important talk about the big things, the lectures, father-to-son exhortations, the advice and philosophising and dinner-time discussions. After a lifetime at cross-purposes, Maxwell finally understood them and they understood him. And they could merely chat for the pleasure of it. It was as simple, and as profound, as that.

Tom smiled. His father would have loved his funeral. A great tomb had been freshly cut out of the rock, inaugurating a new necropolis for the Tara tribe. The White City had been cut off by the burning of the bridge, leaving six of Hauser's mercenaries behind. During the six weeks the new tomb was being built, the village buzzed daily with news of the trapped soldiers. They came down to the bridgehead from time to time, firing their guns, shouting, pleading, threatening. As the weeks passed the six had dwindled to four, three and two. Now there was one, and he didn't shout or wave or fire his gun any more. He just stood there, a small, gaunt figure, saying nothing, waiting for death. Tom had tried to convince the Tara to rescue him, but the Tara were adamant: only the gods could rebuild the bridge. If the gods wanted to save him, they would.

But of course they didn't.

Now all the grave goods had been heaped in the tomb, and it was time to close it up. The men and women stood in the forest, singing a forlorn, haunting tune while a priest waved a bundle of sacred herbs, the fragrant smoke drifting past them. The ceremony went on until the sun touched the western horizon, and then it stopped. The chief struck the end of the wooden key, and the great stone door of the tomb slid shut with a sonorous boom, just as the last rays vanished.

THREE MONTHS LATER the *New York Times* announced the creation of the Alfonso Boswas Foundation, a nonprofit organisation devoted to translating and publishing a certain ninth-century Mayan codex found in the collections of the late Maxwell Broadbent. According to the foundation's president, Dr Sally Colorado, the Codex was a Mayan book of healing that would prove tremendously useful in the search for new drugs. The foundation had been established and funded by the four sons of the late Maxwell Broadbent. The article noted that he had passed away unexpectedly while on a family holiday in Central America.

Epilogue

Officer Jimmy Martinez of the Santa Fe Police Department settled back in his chair. He had just laid down the telephone. The leaves on the cottonwood tree outside the window had turned a rich, golden yellow and a cold wind swept down from the mountains. He glanced at his partner, Willson.

'The Broadbent place again?' Willson asked.

Martinez nodded. 'Yeah. You'd think those neighbours would've gotten used to it by now.'

'These rich people—who can figure 'em out?'

Martinez snorted his agreement.

'Who do you think that character up there really is? Have you ever seen anything like it? A tattooed Indian from Central America, going around in the old man's suits, smoking his pipe, riding his horses around that thousand-acre ranch, bossing the servants, playing the country gentleman, insisting everyone call him *sir*?'

'He owns the place,' said Martinez. 'It checks out, all legal.'

'Sure he owns the place! But my question is: how the hell did he get his hands on it? That estate's worth twenty, thirty million. And then to run it, shit, must be a couple of mil a year. Do you really think a guy like that has money?'

Martinez smiled. 'Yeah.'

'Whaddya mean, "Yeah"?'

'The guy's a Broadbent.'

'Are you nuts? You think that Indian with ear lobes dragging on the ground is a Broadbent? Get out, Jimmy, what've you been smoking?'

'He looks just like them.'

'You ever met them?'

'I met two of the sons. I'm telling you, he's another one of the old man's sons.'

Willson stared at him, astonished.

'The man had a reputation in that way. The other sons got the art; he got the house and a shitload of money. Simple.'

'An *Indian* son of Broadbent?'

'Sure. I bet the old man boned some woman in Central America on one of his expeditions.'

Willson sat back in his chair, deeply impressed. 'You're gonna make detective lieutenant some day, you know that, Jimmy?'

Martinez nodded modestly. 'I know.'

DOUGLAS PRESTON

Douglas Preston's most vivid childhood memories are: 'the loss of a fingertip at age three to a bicycle; the loss of two front teeth to my brother Richard's fist, and various broken bones also incurred in dust-ups with Richard.' Experimenting with home-made rockets and 'other incendiary devices', the pair often featured in the 'police notes' section of the local paper.

While Richard Preston went on to study medicine and to write *The Hot Zone*, a book about deadly viruses, Douglas took a more circuitous route to a novel-writing career. He studied science before graduating in English, and then did an eight-year stint in the publications department of the American Museum of Natural History in New York where, inspired by the fantastic collections, he wrote *Dinosaurs in the Attic* in 1985. He took his editor, Lincoln Child on a tour of the Hall of the Dinosaurs one night and, under a looming T-Rex, Child remarked that it would make the perfect setting for a thriller. So it was that *The Relic* was born—it became a film in 1997—and the two men have since collaborated on several more novels.

Preston says that inspiration for *The Codex* came from an article on archaeology that he wrote for the *New Yorker* magazine: 'Since at least the 1950s rumours had circulated among archaeologists that a large ruined city existed in the mountains of the Honduran interior. In the late nineties, I learned of a secret effort by NASA to locate the site, using foliage-penetrating radar. They did actually identify a one-mile-square feature that had all the attributes of a ruined city thickly covered by trees. However, the Honduran government refused permission to go to the site, because it lay in an area that could only be reached by passing through off-limits military airspace. My article generated so much interest in this story that I decided to work it into a novel.'

The adventure-loving Preston admits that quite a bit of his own personality went into the Indiana-Jones-like Tom Broadbent. 'I love horses and I've written several books about my adventures on horseback, retracing thousands of miles of ancient trails. Basically, unlike most children, I've never outgrown my fascination with dinosaurs and paleontology in general.'

Life & Limb

JAMIE ANDREW

A true story of tragedy and
survival against the odds

'We're not going to
make it, I know now that
we're going to die. Ever since
our hands froze I've known
that we're not going to make
it through the night . . .'

Part one: The Edge of the Knife

It was Saturday, January 23, 1999, and as our bus pulled into the bustling French resort of Chamonix all eyes turned to the mountains. High above us, far above the wooded walls of the Arve Valley, rose the lofty spikes of the Chamonix Aiguilles, glowing white, each one a diamond, shining in an infinite blue sky. The others talked excitedly about snow conditions and off-piste possibilities, but I stared up at the mountains with a different thought in mind.

We were a group of over twenty friends, mainly from Edinburgh, who had taken advantage of a budget airline's last-minute deal to snatch a week's snowboarding and skiing in the French Alps. The seven of us arriving now were the vanguard of the group. We were supposed to be eight: myself, my girlfriend Anna Wyatt, Jamie Fisher, and five others, but Jamie had been left behind at Liverpool Airport, having left it too late to get a seat on the 6 a.m. flight. He had to book the 6 p.m. flight and was condemned to spend the day at the airport, but with typical stoicism graciously waved the rest of us goodbye as we filed through to the departure lounge.

That afternoon, the seven of us checked into our chalet in nearby Argentière, hired snowboards, bought food and met up with later arrivals from our group, including Stu Fisher, Jamie's dad. We rounded off the day by cooking a big meal and cracking open more than a few bottles of wine to celebrate the beginning of the holiday.

Sunday the 24th dawned clear and sparkling. A buzz of excitement charged round the chalet, ensuring that nobody lay in bed too long, and soon we were all munching baguettes and slurping coffee.

Suddenly there was a crash from the vestibule, the inner door banged open and there stood Jamie Fisher, rucksack on his back, a trademark grin splitting his face from ear to ear.

As usual with Jamie there was some story of misadventure and unlikely fortune to tell since we'd left him, the details of which I don't recall. He told his tale with relish, taking his time for effect, but each time he glanced out of the window I could see a light in his eyes that betrayed his impatience to get up into the mountains. While the others prepared for the slopes, Jamie and I talked about going climbing.

'It's too good a chance to miss!' he urged. 'The conditions look perfect and this high pressure is settled in for at least three more days.'

I didn't need much persuading. 'What if we do something that's quite quick?' I said. 'A day or two. Then we can spend the rest of the week boarding.'

'OK. What about the Droites North Face?'

Perhaps a little more than I'd intended, but attractive nevertheless. I knew that it was high on Jamie's hit list and I had certainly wanted to do it for ages.

'How long will it take?' I asked.

'If we take the last *'frique* up to the Grands Montets this afternoon we can bivvy in the *'frique* station. It's less than a two-hour walk to the foot of the Droites and we should manage the route in a day and a half. The descent down the south side is quite easy. We'll get back to the valley by Wednesday lunchtime. Thursday at the latest.'

The *'frique*, short for *téléférique*, was the mountain cable car.

'OK, let's do it,' I said. 'That gives us all day to get ready.'

Jamie volunteered to sort out the climbing gear, buy food from town and get a final weather forecast. I wanted to spend the morning snowboarding with Anna, knowing that she would be worried about us going up into the mountains.

I gave Jamie my gear, then Anna and I grabbed our snowboards and, with a few of the others, headed for the pistes.

Argentière bustled with brightly coloured people, clumping up and down the snowy streets with skis or a snowboard slung over their shoulder. Against the picturesque backdrop of snow-laden chalets and icy peaks, tanned faces smiled. I couldn't imagine a place more the antithesis of Edinburgh in dreary January. This kind of winter break was just what I needed.

I was unable to relax that morning, however, and as we caught a cable car high up into the fields of snow at the head of the valley, a knot of tension grew in my stomach. I wasn't particularly worried about the difficulty of the route; it was a general feeling of unease that I suffered before every major climb, and I knew it wouldn't go away until the moment I first swung my ice axe. Then all that nervous energy would flow out and drive me up the mountain.

I hoped to point out the peak of Les Droites to Anna from the cable car, but it remained hidden behind the bulk of L'Aiguille Verte. However, we could see the top of the Grands Montets Téléférique, where Jamie and I planned to spend the coming night.

Anna turned away from this panorama, not relishing the prospect of my imminent departure. The cable car pulled into the station and we stepped out onto the sunlit piste.

We spent the next couple of hours enjoying some excellent snowboarding. Neither of us was particularly experienced but nor were most of our friends, and we all had great fun racing down the slopes, sometimes in control, often not, wiping out regularly in the soft snow.

Not for the first time in my life, I found myself wishing that I didn't feel so driven to climb mountains. It would be very pleasant to forget about the climb and spend the week swooping through the snow and partying with my friends. However, there was a hunger inside me that wouldn't be satisfied by such sanitised entertainment. I felt I had to experience the raw grandeur of the mountains close up. They seemed to be throwing down a gauntlet, and in taking up the challenge I somehow found fulfilment. I felt more real. More alive.

The time came to go. In front of the cable-car station, Anna and I made our goodbyes.

'Will you be careful?' she pleaded.

'Don't you worry,' I reassured her, 'I'll be back before you know it.'

'Do you promise?'

'I promise. I'll see you soon, OK?'

'OK. See you soon. Love you.'

'I love you too.'

Back in the valley I found Jamie at the chalet, busying himself with the lightweight petrol stove, sending jets of sooty yellow flame licking towards the kitchen ceiling.

'Are you sure it's a good idea, playing with that in here?'

'I'm just making sure it works all right,' he protested.

Jamie put the stove away, then we had a hurried lunch before packing. We agreed that it would be wise to go on the heavy side. By sacrificing items like sleeping-bags, spare clothes and stove, Alpine climbers can climb super-fast, accomplishing their objective in a day and avoiding a night on the mountain. This is all very well in the summer but we estimated that, with the short amount of daylight available, we would be unlikely to complete the climb and make the descent in a day. We would therefore need gear to survive the night. You don't take chances in the Alps in winter.

Apart from all our climbing equipment, we each packed a sleeping-bag, a bivvy bag, a sleeping-mat, a mug, a water bottle, a spoon and plenty of clothes. We also took the stove, one pan, Jamie's penknife and food for three days. No chances.

Soon we were rushing madly to get everything together before the last *téléférique* at a quarter past four. Hastily I scribbled a note to Anna. I drew a smiling stick man brandishing axes and crampons and below it wrote, *See you soon. xxxx.* I left the note on her pillow.

AT EXACTLY 4,000 metres, Les Droites is not one of the highest mountains in the Haute Savoie. Nor, when viewed from the south, is it one of the more impressive. On its north side, however, the mountain comes into its own. A great chain of mountains—L'Aiguille Verte, L'Aiguille du Jardin, Les Droites, Les Courtes, L'Aiguille du Triolet and Mont Dolent—forms a vast barrier of rock and ice, ten kilometres long and 1,000 metres high, which walls in the enormous snaking Argentière Glacier on its south side. Each mountain has an impressive north face, dropping sheer from the airy ridge to the edge of the glacier, but none is more impressive or more difficult than the North Face of Les Droites.

The face was conquered in 1955 by Philippe Corneau and Maurice Davaille, who took six days to produce one of the best and most difficult mixed routes in the Alps. Modern techniques and improved equipment have reduced the normal time for an ascent to two days. The first true winter ascent of the climb was made in January 1975 by a British pair, and this was the feat we hoped to emulate.

JAGGED ROCKY RIDGES and icy gullies swept by beneath us. My ears were popping as we gained altitude, and I swallowed several times to clear them. We slowed down as we approached the large tunnel in a rock buttress ahead—the site of the top station. The cabin swung gently as it eased into the station and came to a halt.

The top station of the Grands Montets Téléférique, at an altitude of 3,250 metres, is almost entirely built into the mountain. The doors slid open and we stepped out onto a large steel terrace. All around us the most magnificent peaks of the French Alps glittered and shone in the lazy afternoon sunlight.

A few skiers lingered on the terrace before making the last run of the day. We watched them as, one by one, they clicked on their skis, adjusted their goggles and schussed off. I imagined the wonderful, rushing pleasure of that descent, arcing down the wide Argentière Glacier, then through pine and fir trees, eventually to arrive breathless back at the village. Back to a warm chalet, friendly faces, a cosy bar. The knot of anxiety in my stomach tightened.

Jamie seemed immune from such thoughts and I said nothing. Les Droites and our route to it across the glacier were still hidden, so Jamie suggested climbing up the ridge above us to a spot that looked like it might offer a sneaky view.

As we left the terrace we met two men from the ski patrol, who were setting off on a final sweep down the hill. They stopped to ask us of our plans. In broken French we replied that we intended to climb '*le face nord des Droites*'.

'You know there is forecast some snow on Tuesday?'

'Yes, we know.'

'*Bonne chance!*' They skied off, and we plodded up the broad ridge.

Unaccustomed to the thin air, I found myself panting heavily as I toiled up the slope on Jamie's heels. Fortunately we had to climb only a couple of hundred metres before we arrived at a large platform on the ridge. From its edge we could peer out across the cheerless north face of the Aiguille Verte and get a sidelong glimpse of Les Droites. The lower ice field was hidden by a projecting buttress of the Verte, but we could see a series of icy grooves higher up that looked fairly continuous and reassured us that the route was probably in condition.

Below us, we could see most of tomorrow's approach route. We took note of the position of some possible false trails in the descent to the Argentière Glacier, then watched the sun sink behind the Aiguilles Rouges before stomping back down the ridge to get some dinner and make preparations for the morning.

While Jamie prepared a meal of pasta, vegetables, tinned fish and tomato sauce, I sharpened up the ice gear. I suspected we would be encountering some pretty hard ice and wanted all the equipment to be in top order. Besides, I always found there was something therapeutic in engrossing myself in a task that required close focus.

By now the darkness was total, save for the beams of our head torches and the soft twinkle of lights in the valley far below. The temperature was dropping sharply and we wolfed down the meal, probably our last hot food for a while.

I discovered that the main door into the station was still unlocked, so we moved inside to avoid a night out in the open. While laying out our mats we heard the faint sound of a television. On investigation, we found we were sharing our home for the night with two *téléférique* engineers. The guys were friendly and didn't mind us sleeping in their building. We chatted to them for a bit and they gave us some water to fill our bottles, saving us from having to melt snow. Then they wished us well with our climb and Jamie and I turned in for the night.

I SLEPT BADLY that night, the contemplation of the next day's trials preying heavily on my mind. I also thought about Anna and our parting earlier in the day. These partings were becoming more difficult. We'd been seeing each other for nearly three years now and our commitment to one another was growing.

We had met through mutual friends in Edinburgh, where Anna was working at a restaurant just up the street from where I lived. Eventually, with a bit of a prod from the mutual friends, we got together. Before we knew it, Anna and I had fallen head over heels in love, and a little over a year after we started going out we moved in together.

Anna wasn't a mountaineer, although she had done a bit of rock climbing and hillwalking. A few years before I met her, she'd taken a nasty tumble on an exposed mountain ridge in the Scottish Highlands and had been lucky to escape with only bad bruising. Perhaps that partly explained why she felt so nervous about me going up into the mountains. I knew that she wanted me to follow my heart, but also I knew she suffered every minute I was away.

I never managed to reconcile the mixed emotions I felt about leaving Anna to worry while I went climbing. Pig-headed, I left them unresolved and went anyway, although each time I felt worse about going. This was what I turned over in my head as I lay on the floor of the *'frique* station that night, trying to sleep.

Jamie, too, slept little. When I opened an eye in the small hours, I saw his dark form pacing about. Perhaps he was also feeling the tension, or perhaps he was just anxious to get going. I didn't ask him, but turned over and finally went to sleep.

I woke at 5 a.m. to the soft roar of the petrol stove.

'Time to go,' said Jamie.

This was always the worst bit for me. Getting out of a warm sleeping-bag into the freezing morning to face the previous night's dread. It was enough to make me hope for bad weather.

The weather was fine, however, so with one final groan I heaved myself upright and began to get ready.

With a grin, Jamie handed me a steaming brew and a couple of biscuits. 'Come on, you'll feel better once we get moving.'

We quickly ate our frugal breakfast and packed up. Then it was out into the crisp early morning air. We stopped on the snowy platform to put on crampons and tie into one of the ropes in preparation for the glacier, then set off down the slope.

The route started well, the first few hundred metres being through pleasantly soft snow. We soon came down onto the Argentière Glacier and bore right towards the foot of the mighty Aiguille Verte. Darkness yawned around us, cold and vast. Our route was now gently uphill and we sank to our knees in the snow with each step, puffing heavily with frosty breath. I was soon sweating like a pig and cursing my folly for torturing myself like this.

God, I hate this. I can't even remember why I'm doing it.

I felt physically sick with pent-up tension and my body screamed in complaint at such activity at this unaccustomed hour.

As we marched, the beams of our head torches occasionally picked out an unstable ice pinnacle, or *sérac*, looming up ahead, or a faint shadow in the snow warning of a possible crevasse. We picked our way round these obstacles carefully, but on the whole our way was hazard-free and we made good progress.

Daylight was creeping up on us. As the stars winked out one by one, the dark wall of mountain above us slowly began to reveal itself. Monstrous black buttresses emerged from the gloom, silver ribbons of ice and snow hanging like sheets between them. Far above, the jagged crest of the mountain ridge showed its outline against the lightening sky. A chill of apprehension ran down my spine.

We could see the shape of our objective, Les Droites, rising before us now, and it wasn't long before we could make out the details of our planned route. The great ice field was unmistakable—a vast white curtain, draped over the bottom half of the mountain. Above it reared the headwall, which defended it from the summit ridge.

We stopped to eat some chocolate and discuss our line of attack. Jamie, who had climbed Les Droites by its northeast spur a year and a half earlier, pointed out many of the possible routes: the Ginat, the Courneau-Davaille, the Colton-Brooks. We intended to begin up the original Courneau-Davaille route, but higher up we might link sections of different routes, depending on conditions.

We set off again up the steepening slope, and half an hour of hard toil brought us to the first obstacle of our climb, the *bergshrund*, a wide crevasse separating the approach slope from the main face. We stamped out a small ledge in the snow just below the *bergshrund* and geared up. By now it was broad daylight. I gazed up at the mountain, to which the harsh light had lent an unreal, intangible quality.

Jamie volunteered to lead off first, and I was happy to let him. We traversed upwards and leftwards, following the lip of the *bergshrund*, its dark chasm gaping like a hungry mouth. When we came to a point where the gap narrowed, I settled down in the snow to belay Jamie's ropes and he set off, striding confidently over the crevasse. On the far side, the ice wall was almost vertical and Jamie had to hold himself in a difficult position as he swung each axe in turn, usually several times before feeling the satisfying thunk of solid ice beneath the crumbly surface. I held my breath as I watched him kick in his crampons and progress slowly up the steep wall. He stopped to place an ice screw, holding on to one axe while fumbling with the screw in his other mittened hand. Once the screw was in and he was clipped to the rope, Jamie continued, disappearing over the top of this first wall and leaving me alone to pay out the ropes.

When there was about five metres of rope left I shouted up a warning. After a short while there was a muffled reply from Jamie.

'OK, climb when you're ready.'

'Climbing,' I yelled back. I strode across the gap and found myself suddenly on steep ice. I moved clumsily at first, kicking my feet and swinging my axes harder than necessary. My heavy sack tugged at my shoulders and I had to work hard to keep my balance. Fortunately, the ice underneath the rotten crust was good and I was able to get good solid placements. I hurried upwards and it wasn't long before I reached Jamie's ice screw. Holding tightly to my left axe, I let go of the one in my right hand, unclipped the karabiner from the rope and unscrewed the small titanium tube from the ice. With the screw safely clipped back onto my harness, I drew breath and carried on. Jamie came into view, waving to me from the ice slope above.

When I reached him we grinned at each other. I realised then that the knot in my stomach had dissolved and I suddenly felt a lot better. Now I remembered why I forced myself out into the mountains. The extraordinary sense of freedom, of independence from the everyday world, of sheer purity, made it all worth while. Exhilarated, I breathed the crisp morning air deep into my lungs.

Jamie tied off the belay and passed me the leading gear. There was no time for dawdling so I set off immediately. We were now in a wide open couloir or gully, which led up to a steeper wall guarding the entrance to the great ice field.

The ice was good now, firm but yielding to axe picks and crampon points. I began to find my rhythm. Right axe up, left axe up, right foot up, left foot up, trusting each kick of the crampon to give a good foothold, keeping the movement smooth to conserve energy. There was going to be a hell of a lot more of this to come.

After twenty metres or so I felt a need for some security. I sank my right axe into the ice so that I could free up my right hand. Fumbling with my large mitten, I managed to remove an ice screw from my harness. The air temperature was around −10°C, and when I held the karabiner in my teeth for a moment I instantly felt it freezing to my lips. I pushed the threaded end of the screw into my prepared notch in the ice, and turned. After a couple of false starts it began to bite. Soon it was in to the hilt. Bomb proof. I clipped one of the ropes into the karabiner, retrieved the right axe, and carried on climbing.

'Runner on!' I shouted to Jamie.

Even with practice, placing an ice screw takes some time, as does the second man's job of removing it. If we were to make quick progress we would have to use the screws sparingly. I climbed on until I heard Jamie shout that the rope was running out. I cut myself a ledge and placed two ice screws. In the event of one of us falling, these were the only pieces of equipment that secured us to the mountain.

I put Jamie on belay and he was soon climbing up to join me.

As he climbed, I gazed out at our surroundings. The glacier already looked a long way below us, a motionless river of whiteness, its smooth surface untouched save for our tiny trail of footprints. Ahead stood the majestic peaks of L'Aiguille du Chardonnet and L'Aiguille d'Argentière, bathed in golden morning sunlight. To both sides, sombre north faces sulked in cold shadow.

Jamie arrived at the belay, took the leading gear from me and carried on up. In this way, taking it in turn to lead a pitch, we would continue all day. It was good to be climbing with Jamie again. I had the utmost confidence in him as a partner in the mountains.

JAMIE'S FATHER had introduced him to climbing when he was a child growing up on the family farm in Zambia, and he and his two brothers were always encouraged in the spirit of adventure. By the time he got to university, Jamie was pursuing a career as a climber with almost religious passion. It began with rock climbing in Scotland, Wales and northern England, and snow and ice climbing in the north of Scotland, but he soon progressed to Alpine mountaineering, at which he excelled. In the past few years he had been on a couple of audacious expeditions to the Himalayas, and had gained a lot of valuable experience. There was no doubt that he was destined to be a very successful mountaineer.

I was less ambitious. In a few months I would be thirty. As the years passed I was gradually becoming settled and no longer felt a need to push life to the extremes. Like Jamie, I had begun my climbing as a teenager. I wasn't a strong climber to begin with, but I knew how to use my body to its best advantage and I learned to read the patterns in the rock and quickly figure out and execute sequences of moves. Of course I often found the climbing frightening, but by assessing and managing the risks I was able to push myself to the limit of my capabilities. This exploration of my own boundaries was one of the chief attractions of climbing for me. Before long, my strength and my confidence improved, and I was managing harder and harder climbs.

At university I met many like-minded people and I bought into the climbing dream wholesale, to the sorry detriment of my studies. Since then I had been climbing at a high standard. As well as rock climbing, I had learned the skills of snow and ice climbing and mountaineering, and I had made many wonderful ascents of rock faces and high peaks all over the world. Climbing had also led me to my career as a rope access technician. I had heard that there was good money to be made by climbers in abseiling, using ropes to access difficult work sites on tall buildings, bridges, oil rigs and the like. I learned fast and soon progressed to supervisor level. I now worked for an Edinburgh-based firm called the Web, and climbing was part of every aspect of my life.

WE CLIMBED for a couple more pitches up the wide couloir until it brought us to the steeper section and an apparent impasse. But there was a smaller gully, narrow with rocky walls, that sneaked leftwards out of the cul-de-sac. It was steeper than the previous pitches and the strain on arms and shoulders was great, but before long we were both standing in awe at the foot of the great ice field.

An expanse of blue-white ice about 500 metres high and 400 metres wide, sloping upwards at about sixty degrees, the field is too vast to suffer significant melting during the summer, and survives to cloak the foot of Les Droites season after season. Looking up at this ocean of ice and the menacing headwall above made us feel small.

We paused to drink some water and eat a few biscuits, then Jamie broke the inertia. 'Right, then. Let's deal with it.'

We set off, working hard to cover as much ground as possible before nightfall. Pitch after pitch of fairly repetitive climbing followed, never extremely difficult but never easy. There was no let-up in the slope, the ice field being unbroken by ledges or rocks, and the subsurface ice was so hard that we couldn't cut ledges large enough to be of any relief to aching calves. The best we could do was to cut out small footholds and lean back in our harnesses, hopping from foot to foot in an attempt to rest each leg in turn.

When we passed each other on the belay stances we would exchange a few cheery words, but mostly we remained quiet, each secure in the knowledge that the other was equally invigorated by the fantastic surroundings. Exaltation was unnecessary, superlatives inadequate.

Belaying Jamie up one pitch, I leaned back and listened. Apart from the tinkle of ice falling from Jamie's axes below, the silence was absolute. There wasn't a breath of wind. We were alone.

Then, drifting out of the still air, came a faint, high-pitched buzz. I scanned the valley. Far below us, floating over the glacier, was a tiny single-engine plane, looking like a child's toy. Tourists, probably, enjoying a spectacular sightseeing flight. Later on we saw a pair of ski mountaineers gliding gracefully down the glacier, far below us. Those were the only other people we saw.

We were making good progress, but we would soon have to find a place to spend the night. We had been heading for a rocky spur that protruded from the ice field just below its top. This, we hoped, would offer some level ground on which we could dig a bivvy.

Jamie arrived at the foot of the spur, which was made up of a series of rocky bulges separated by icy terraces, and I led off up it looking for a sheltered spot. Before long I had run out of rope and still hadn't found anywhere suitable.

Jamie began to climb and he too had no luck until, ten metres below me, he stopped. I heard his shout and climbed down to join him. He was at the foot of one of the bulges, at a place where two large lumps of granite met at an angle. In the space between them was an alcove, with a flat surface big enough for half a body. It wasn't exactly a five-star bivvy spot, but it was a start.

First, I made sure we had a really bomb-proof belay. Then I set about extending the level section of ice, chipping away at the slope beside it, while Jamie excavated a separate ledge below and parallel to mine. After about half an hour's chiselling we had created a rather short and narrow pair of bunk beds. Home sweet home.

It was dark now, the temperature was dropping, and we began the tricky procedure of getting ready for bed. Sleeping-mats, bivvy bags and sleeping-bags had to be made ready, equipment stowed and secured—all without letting go of any loose item for a second. Hardest of all was removing our boots, crampons and all. If one of us were to lose a boot we would be in dire straits, but we preferred to sleep with our boots off so that our feet could be kept warm during the night.

Sitting on my freshly hewn bed, I took off each boot gingerly and stuffed them both into my sack, which hung securely in the alcove. Keeping the rest of my clothes on, I wriggled carefully into my pit. I then adjusted my anchor rope to stop me from sliding off the ledge.

Jamie, who took charge of the stove as usual, got on with preparing the meal—Burns Supper, as he called it, this being Burns Night. We enjoyed our frugal meal of cheese, biscuits and a mug of hot chocolate, happy to be safely tucked up on our little ledges, then chatted for a while, reflecting on the day's progress.

'Well, this certainly beats going to work,' said Jamie after a pause.

'That's because it's less stressful than your work,' I replied.

After university, Jamie had done teacher training and then moved into caring for children with special needs. He now lived with Anna and me in Edinburgh, and had taken a job as a care assistant in a Dr Barnardo's home. Every day he came home with some crazy story about what his kids had been up to: throwing tantrums, running away, getting in trouble with the police. Most of them came from broken homes and had fallen through the net of foster care. Many had been abused or had learning difficulties. By comparison, my own job—abseiling off oil rigs in gale-force winds—seemed easy.

However, that all felt a long way off now. The sky was full of stars and the surrounding mountains had vanished into the darkness. We were both tired, so we said good night and sank into our sleeping-bags.

It wasn't exactly a good night's sleep. My legs kept sliding off the narrow shelf and, because a slight breeze had picked up, every so often a rivulet of spindrift poured directly onto my head.

I woke with a start, unaware that I'd been asleep, confused by strange dreams. It was still dark but Jamie was already moving about, getting the stove fired up for the morning brew.

After another continental-style breakfast of bourbon creams and hot chocolate, it was time for another big day out on the mountain. Getting out of our bags and getting booted up was worse than the reverse operation the evening before, our limbs being stiff and clumsy, but by the time it was getting light we were set to go.

It was Jamie's turn to lead and he set off, traversing leftwards, to regain the top section of the ice field. When it was time for me to go, I felt rigid, slow and awkward after our cold night. As I climbed, though, I soon warmed up and relaxed into the familiar movement.

We were approximately halfway up the face now, and would have to move quickly today if we were to reach the summit and complete the most difficult part of the descent by nightfall. The headwall was only about three rope lengths away, and rose above us as a series of steep granite slabs. We had to find a way through the initial steep section, which was breached in places by great smears of white ice, drooling down the rocks. We settled upon the largest and most central of these smears and took a diagonal line in its direction.

It was another clear and windless day, the sky unbroken blue. As on the previous day, the temperature was round about –10°C, but the stillness of the air meant it was easy to keep warm.

An hour and a half later we were at the foot of the ice smear. I led off, eager to leave the interminable field of ice behind. I had to be careful as the ice here tended to shatter off in slabs the size of dinner plates, which would then tumble down towards Jamie below. I reached the end of the ropes before the top of the smear and so had to take an uncomfortable stance, hanging from ice screws. Jamie soon arrived at the belay, took the gear and shot off. Now it was my turn to suffer the barrage of cascading ice.

Above the smear were several grooves offering upward progress. We chose the one that led slightly leftwards. When we reached the top of it we were presented with further choices of route. We continued in this way for many pitches, through icy grooves and runnels and across areas of more mixed, rocky ground. The route-finding was quite intricate and the climbing enjoyable and absorbing.

At about 2 p.m. I suddenly became aware of a few flakes of falling snow. I looked up in surprise to see banks of clouds appearing from behind the summit ridge.

'Jamie!' I shouted. 'The snow's arrived. Better get a move on!'

Snow. No big deal really—we could easily cope. It was just slightly worrying to know that the weather was no longer perfect. Snow had been forecast to pass over quickly. But in the mountains you just never know. I didn't want to get caught out in a storm.

The snow wasn't a problem at first. It was quite light, and whisked around our heads in energetic flurries, barely settling anywhere.

We redoubled our efforts but were already moving as fast as we could manage. At a belay stance, we met for a conference.

'What do you think?' asked Jamie.

'I think this is OK.'

Whirling flakes danced between us, beautiful in the soft afternoon light, yet cold and threatening, too.

'Yes, it is, but don't you think it would be a good idea to head straight to the *brèche*?'

I thought about this for a moment. The Brèche des Droites was a small notch in the summit ridge of the mountain where the descent route down the other side began. It was the gateway to our quickest escape from the face. By heading straight for the *brèche* we would save valuable time. We would also miss out on the summit. The *brèche* is only a few metres lower, but there's nothing quite like standing on the highest point of a mountain. It would be a disappointment not to savour that. Still, our objective was to climb the north face of Les Droites, and it was more important to get down quickly.

'OK,' I conceded. 'We'll save the summit for another time.'

We climbed on. Then, quite suddenly, the snow got worse. Heavy clouds were now rolling over the ridge and down into the valley. The beautiful view was soon gone. Snow fell harder and harder, dumping itself onto our shoulders and rucksacks, heavier than I could ever remember snow falling. *Shit.* A spasm of fear shot up my spine. This was bad news. The weather was now definitely against us.

And the conditions got worse as the snow piled onto the face of the mountain higher up, then funnelled down the grooves we were climbing, sweeping over us in powerful waves, blinding and penetratingly cold. The waves shot past with an ominous hissing sound that only emphasised the utter silence of our surroundings.

There was no choice but to battle on. Retreat would be too slow. The quickest and safest route off the mountain from here was up to the *brèche* and down the other side.

We were now at the foot of the steepest icefall we had yet encountered. As we could find no alternative way round, I launched up it. Avalanches of snow came rushing down the icefall. As each wave hit, it was the most I could do to hold on tight. The snow thundered down on my back and shoulders, trying to force me off. It penetrated the crevices in my clothing, forced its way up my sleeves, down my neck. I couldn't see my hands and axes in front of my face.

After about ten seconds, the wave would pass and I would climb as quickly as I could before the next one hit a few seconds later. The placement of ice screws was out of the question, and I climbed on without protection, driven by pure fear, until I reached the top of the pitch.

I shouted, but there was no way Jamie could hear me, so I gave a couple of sharp tugs on the ropes. I stood hunched on the stance, belaying Jamie, as torrents of snow swept over me. The weight of it kept threatening to push me off.

Jamie arrived, his face set in an expression of determination.

'This is grim,' he admitted.

'Let's just keep going, shall we?' I replied.

We reckoned that we couldn't be more than five or six pitches from the top, so we struggled on, picking the line of least resistance. Visibility was down to about fifteen metres between snowstorms, zero during them, so route-finding became difficult.

I fought my way to the top of one groove and found myself at a dead end, separated by a steep drop from the Ginat route, which followed a different gully all the way to the *brèche*. It would be a good route, but there was no way into it from here.

I brought Jamie up until he was in shouting distance, and explained that I had reached a cul-de-sac. Instead of coming up to join me, he made a traverse leftwards. Crossing some difficult mixed ground, he was soon level with my stance, then he disappeared up and out of sight.

When the ropes came tight, I attempted to climb back down the groove. I couldn't get very far, as the ropes were pulling me upwards.

'Slack!' I shouted, but no response. I dithered, not knowing what to do. Unless I took some action, I was stuck there.

Eventually I decided to let myself pendulum across the slabs. I didn't like the look of the swing at all but I was wasting valuable time. I leaned my weight onto the ropes and, praying that Jamie had a good hold of them, stepped out of the groove.

My crampons clattered and scraped on the rocks as I swung, accelerating out of control, across the icy slabs. Snow and rocks rushed past me in a blur until I eventually ground to a halt on the far side. I got my feet established on some holds and breathed a sigh of relief. I could now regain Jamie's route and climb up to join him.

When I reached him I cursed him for not paying me out any slack. Apart from the continuing snowstorm, there was now a gloominess in the air and we realised the light was failing.

'We could stop here for the night,' Jamie suggested. 'Those rocks over there. We could dig out some sort of ledge.'

I couldn't see us getting any shelter in the hopeless spot Jamie was indicating, nor creating a ledge big enough for the two of us.

'I think we should press on for the *brèche*,' I argued. 'We've more chance of a decent bivvy spot there.'

Jamie agreed, so we carried on. Fortunately the climbing was easier now, although the snow was building up on the surface of the ice, and clearing it before each axe placement was time-consuming. We found a ramp line that led up and right and followed this for a couple of miserable pitches. Before long we were climbing by torchlight.

The snow danced eerily in the beams of our head torches. All I could see as I stood on my belay stance was Jamie's bobbing light fading in and out of view. I felt very vulnerable.

Leading up the next pitch, I suddenly felt a rattle in one of my axes and discovered that the bolt that held the pick had come loose. To lose an axe now would be a disaster. However, there was nothing I could do in the middle of a pitch, so I carried on, trying to rely on the other axe as much as possible.

Thankfully, I got to the top without further incident and retightened the bolt. I felt very tired now.

'I've had enough of this,' I moaned. 'Surely we're nearly there.'

'Don't worry,' said Jamie. 'We'll get there soon.'

His next pitch brought him to the end of the ramp, then his head torch vanished from sight. When I followed, I found that the ramp finished at a short drop that was easy to descend, and I joined Jamie in a wide couloir that disappeared upwards into the darkness.

'The *brèche* must be at the top!' he said excitedly.

I led on upwards, too cold to stop and too tired to care. I climbed blindly on until, disappointed once again, I reached the end of my ropes before coming to any *brèche*. Without a word, Jamie joined me, took the gear and set off into the darkness. This time, before running out the full fifty metres of rope, he gave a muffled shout and halted.

Soon there was tug on the ropes, and I began climbing again. As I climbed, the couloir became narrower and steeper until suddenly I saw that the beam of my torch no longer picked out the slope above, but disappeared into inky blackness. My heart leapt. A few minutes later I was beside Jamie on the Brèche des Droites, whooping and cheering with joy. We embraced, grinning with relief.

This was no time for congratulation, though, and we curtailed our celebration to take stock. Unfortunately, although the *brèche* was the gateway to our descent from the mountain, it was a bitter disappointment in terms of space and comfort. The place was a notch in the razor-back ridge that forms the crest of Les Droites. To the south, a steep gully, similar to the one we had just fought our way up, disappeared into the darkness. We were sitting astride the place where the two gullies met—a knife-edge crest of snow and ice about three metres in length. There didn't appear to be anywhere for us to rest.

We discussed the possibility of climbing the west wall of the *brèche* to where we could see a snow slope that offered a glimmer of hope. But the climb looked difficult, we were already very fatigued, and the snow slope would probably turn out to be iron hard. We decided to make the most of the spot where we were.

Digging away at the snow and ice with the adzes of our axes, we attempted to cut down the knife-edge to form a level platform. It took about half an hour of hard work, but eventually we made ourselves a surprisingly acceptable ledge on which the two of us could just lie, side by side. There was no shelter from the elements, and nothing to keep us from rolling off the edge on either side, but at least we would be able to lie down. If we could get a little rest, the snow should stop by the morning, and we would be able to make a quick descent.

We began the laborious business of getting the bivvy ready, unavoidably jostling each other on the tight, icy ledge—sleeping-mats down, bags out, trying to avoid letting the fast-falling snow get in. Equipment was stowed, boots safely tucked into rucksacks.

As soon as we were both organised, we drank the last mouthful of our water then zipped ourselves into our cocoons, to dine privately on a few squares of chocolate and wait for the night to pass.

During the night the wind got up. I lay awake, too uncomfortable to sleep, listening to it battering my bivvy bag. I could feel the weight of Jamie's body pressing against my side. As I lay there, I reflected on the previous day. Perhaps we had been foolish to venture out on this kind of climb in the winter with a less than perfect forecast. Then again, mountaineers have to take risks. Everyone has to decide which risks are acceptable. We all have to draw the line somewhere. Perhaps I would draw it a little earlier in future. Assuming we got ourselves down from this awful place. Once again I felt thankful that I was climbing with Jamie. He was a survivor. The previous two winters he had made attempts on the Eiger and survived severe storms. Two summers ago he had climbed through the most appalling storm on Mont Blanc, in which several other climbers perished. He was as tough as old boots, and could always be relied upon to pull through.

The storm didn't let up. I dozed on and off, my consciousness never far from the cramped ledge where my body lay shivering.

I WOKE to see daylight filtering through the fabric of my bivvy bag, and hurriedly unzipped it to survey the day. My heart sank when I emerged to discover snow falling every bit as thick and fast as the previous night, driven by a strong north wind.

I gave the body next to me a nudge and presently a tousled mop of ginger hair appeared. Jamie grimaced towards the heavens.

'This isn't looking good,' I said.

'Well, what are our options, then?'

'Either we attempt to go down, or we sit it out here, I suppose.'

It was a hard decision to make, whether to go or stay. More than anything, I just wanted to be off the mountain, back in the comfort of the chalet with Anna, laughing and relaxing, and then the glorious luxury of a soft, warm bed. Instead I was freezing cold, zipped into a body bag, unable to move, being buried alive by incessant snow.

To attempt a descent now, though, would be foolhardy. Conditions in the gully would be at best extremely dangerous, at worst downright suicidal. The most sensible course of action was to wait for the storm to pass. Perhaps we would be able to make the descent this afternoon.

So we whiled away the morning, lost in thought. We had to shout to make ourselves heard through the bivvy bags and snow, and over the noise of the wind, so we kept communication to a minimum.

By 2 p.m. it became apparent that we would be going nowhere that day. Our morale was low and sinking further. Time for something to eat. I suggested that we do a stock check of provisions. We'd already eaten any sweets that we'd had in our pockets, so we emerged from our bags to look in the rucksacks. Both were completely buried and it took Jamie some time to excavate them. Meanwhile, I attempted to clear the snow that had worked its way down either side of us and was building up beneath us, threatening to force us off the ledge.

Jamie announced that he had located all the food and listed the inventory. Food: one bag of pasta and dried soup (useless till we got to the hut and could cook it); one large bar of chocolate; one packet of biscuits. Liquid: none.

We were both parched. If we didn't take in liquid we would soon become dehydrated and weak. As getting the stove going was impossible, the best we could do was to nibble small pieces of snow. This eased the pain in our mouths but did little to rehydrate our exhausted bodies.

Jamie passed one half of the chocolate bar over to me. We enjoyed the sticky, sweet squares that were our breakfast, lunch and dinner for the day. Then there was nothing left to do but wait for night to fall, and hope for a let-up in the vicious weather.

Eventually, darkness fell. The storm raged on.

I was by now excruciatingly uncomfortable. The little ledge wasn't long enough for me to lie full length so I lay on my side with my knees up towards my chin. I couldn't turn over for fear of pushing

Jamie from his equally precarious perch, and so I spent most of my time in the one position. The snow that was working its way underneath us gradually thawed with our body heat and refroze to form a layer of solid ice. My hips were getting bruised, and the ice was slippery, making staying in position a constant struggle.

Staying warm was also a struggle. I was wrapped up in all my clothes and my sleeping-bag, but each time I poked my head outside, clouds of spindrift billowed into my bivvy bag. The uninvited snow soon melted, so my prison cell was becoming damp. In an attempt to stay warm, I wriggled and shivered, working on one limb at a time. I also massaged my feet to keep the circulation going in my toes.

Jamie, I knew, was suffering as much as me, but it wasn't his habit to complain.

I tried to imagine how Anna was feeling now. I had said that we might be back as late as Thursday and it was still only Wednesday night, but she knew we hadn't been expecting weather like this. I wondered if she had alerted the rescue services yet. I hoped she had.

THE NIGHT AFTER we'd parted at the cable-car station, Anna had found the note I'd left on her pillow. She slipped the paper into her wallet, vowing to keep it until I'd kept my promise to return. In the small hours of the morning, she found herself awake with a racing heart. Tiptoeing downstairs to get a glass of water, she came across Jamie's father, Stu Fisher. Stu, a doctor, reassured Anna that her thumping heart was just due to anxiety. He also told her how he had lain awake, time after time, waiting for Jamie's return from difficult Alpine peaks or extended Himalayan expeditions. To love Jamie was to accept the risks that formed part of his way of life.

After a while, Anna padded back upstairs to try to sleep.

On Monday, after another day of excellent skiing and boarding, a traditional Burns Supper took place around the chalet's large dining-room table, and the assembled party made a round of toasts. When Anna's turn came, she proposed a toast 'to absent friends', choking on the lump in her throat. A murmur of agreement rippled round the table and everyone raised their glasses.

Tuesday dawned fine once again and it wasn't until noon that Anna noticed a vast bank of clouds marching in from the southwest. Soon the cloud had enveloped the whole of the Mont Blanc Massif and, shortly afterwards, snow began to fall.

Later in the afternoon Anna descended to Chamonix with a couple of the others and bumped into Stu. He was obviously concerned about the deteriorating conditions too, and they went back to the chalet to discuss the situation with our friend Julian Cartwright, Jamie's regular climbing partner and a work colleague of mine.

Jules was concerned but upbeat. He argued that by now we should have completed the climb, and that as long as we could reach a hut or find somewhere to dig in, we would be absolutely fine. The three agreed that if there was no news and no improvement in the weather first thing in the morning, they would alert the rescue services.

On Wednesday morning the weather had indeed deteriorated, so Anna, Stu and Jules went to report their concerns to the PGHM, the Peloton de Gendarmerie de Haute Montagne, a division of the French police force that provides rescue cover in the high Alps. Its officers are fully trained policemen, but they are also qualified guides and talented climbers.

Anna, Jules and Stu walked into the austere PGHM building and explained to a grey-haired officer in uniform that Jamie and I had gone to climb the North Face of Les Droites and that they were worried we might be in trouble. The officer carefully took down the details. This matter would be taken very seriously, he said. Please wait.

After half an hour or so, the grey-haired man returned, accompanied by another officer. They had radioed all the huts in the area, they explained, but there was no response from any of them. The weather was too bad to fly a helicopter. An attempt to find the climbers on foot was also out of the question, but a search and rescue mission was being prepared and they would be ready to scramble as soon as the weather improved. They took a contact number and said they would call as soon as there was any news.

After leaving the PGHM, Anna, Jules and Stu decided to make the most of the snow and head for the slopes at the village of Le Tour. By the time they arrived at the top chair-lift station, Anna was freezing cold. She could see nothing in the raging blizzard and could barely move in the waist-deep powder snow that covered the piste. She got about a hundred metres down the slope before tumbling into the cold, suffocating powder. It was too much. Tears rolling down her cheeks, she took the chair lift down to the café, and sat waiting for the others.

THE LONG NIGHT wore on. Drifting in and out of sleep, I began to imagine I was elsewhere—on another mountain, or in a snow hole in Scotland—anywhere else. Then I couldn't remember where I was. I thought that perhaps this was what it was like to slip into hypothermia, and I shook myself awake in a panic.

No. I'm not hypothermic. Body temperature fine. Back to sleep.

When I opened my eyes again it was light. A powerful north wind was tearing through the narrow gap where we lay, bringing thick snow with it. My despair deepened. When would we leave this hell hole?

Jamie was awake too and we met for a debate, docking together our bag openings, so that we could speak without letting the snow in.

'I think we should try to descend,' said Jamie. 'It would be better than just lying here, freezing to death.'

'Yeah, but at least we're safe here. If we wait till the weather clears then we can get down no problem.'

'The weather might never clear.'

'Don't say that. It's got to.'

We eventually decided to go, both of us wanting to do something proactive rather than suffer any longer where we were.

So we began to move, emerging fully dressed from our frosty cocoons. We attempted to get our equipment together, struggling against the force of the gale. The attempt lasted about five minutes.

'This is hopeless,' screamed Jamie, the wind tearing the words from his lips. 'We can't do this.'

Sixty seconds later we were zipped up in our bags again. I lay huddled in my customary position, beginning to despair of ever getting off this terrible mountain. The longer we waited, the weaker we were becoming. We hadn't drunk, eaten properly or even moved for almost two days. It seemed to me that our only chance now would be a rescue, though I hated the thought of the ignominy involved.

'What's for lunch?' I asked, some time later.

'Well, unless you fancy uncooked pasta, we've got dry biscuits.'

I tried to eat a biscuit but it was hopeless. My mouth was just too dry, so I gave up.

Some time in the afternoon, I sensed a commotion going on next to me. I stuck my head out of my bag to see Jamie frantically digging his rucksack out of the snow.

'Emergency!' he gasped as he dug. 'Is this an emergency?'

'I suppose so.'

'In that case we should have our emergency Kendal mint cake!'

With a flourish, he produced a large bar from his sack.

'Genius!' I cried.

We'd both completely forgotten that Jamie always had an emergency supply of mint cake stashed away. Each Christmas, his granny would present him with a bar 'just in case', and Jamie would obediently carry it on his travels until it disintegrated.

He opened the wrapping to reveal more of a mint mush than a cake. We divided it roughly into two halves, shouted out our thanks to Granny Winder, then wolfed down the wonderful minty pulp. I couldn't remember a sweet bar ever tasting so good.

There was no hint of any mitigation in the weather that day, and we resigned ourselves to a third night in that bitter place.

The nights were the worst. It was colder and the ceaseless wind seemed more savage. Time dragged. It was at night-time that my thoughts turned to the world going on in the valley. How warm everyone down there must be, and how wonderful to be able to eat and drink and curl up in a cosy, soft bed. I promised myself I would never again take the simple pleasures of life for granted.

Some time in the small hours I was woken by a nudge in my back. 'What's wrong?' I responded.

'Do you think it would be a good idea if we got into the same bag?'

It would certainly make sense. It would mean we'd be even more cramped, but warmth was our first priority.

'What if I get into yours?' I suggested. 'It's bigger.'

We put our head torches on and emerged. This was going to be difficult. Rather like trying to get into the same pair of trousers as another person. I wriggled out of my bivvy bag, leaving my wet sleeping-bag behind, and brought my legs over to Jamie's side of the ledge. He opened his bag, which had a zip along half of its length, and I got my feet in. Then came a lot of wriggling and kicking and squirming about. Try as we might we couldn't bring the sides of the bag, which were flapping madly in the wind, together to close the zip. We were struggling away when, suddenly, the bottom fell out of my world.

I felt myself sliding over the icy surface of the ledge. Before I could react, there was no more ledge and I was falling into the abyss. I was aware of the ice accelerating past my face, and I opened my mouth to scream. Snow and space and darkness whirled around my head, swallowing up the scream before it could be uttered. I had a brief vision of a body lying lifeless at the foot of a frozen mountain.

Then the falling stopped, and I was left hanging in my harness, brought to a halt by the rope.

Disorientated, rigid with fear, I looked around to see what had happened. Thankfully, Jamie was still sitting safely on the ledge above me. I had fallen off, down the gully that we had climbed up, and was now hanging from my anchor rope, a few metres below the ledge. Jamie's bivvy bag was still wrapped round my legs, threatening to fall off at any moment. The wind howled around me.

I looked up at the light of Jamie's torch. 'Help me!' I screamed.

'Don't panic,' yelled Jamie. 'You've got to climb the rope.'

'I can't! Help me!'

'Yes, you can. Come on. Try.'

I'd taken my gloves off to wrestle with the bivvy bag zips and was barehanded. I grabbed the icy rope in front of me and heaved with all my might. I tried to lock off with one hand while making a grab for the rope higher up with the other, but my grip failed.

'I can't fucking do it!' I shouted. My fingers were numb with cold and I was almost vomiting with fear.

'Yes, you can!' screamed Jamie. 'Just try again.'

This time I felt a monstrous wave of adrenaline course through me. With a stream of curses, I hauled myself up hand over hand, clutching the frozen rope for all I was worth. I reached Jamie's outstretched hand and made a lunge for it. Clinging on to his arm, I heaved myself back onto the ledge.

'Quick,' barked Jamie. 'Get into the bivvy bag!'

I allowed Jamie to reorganise my anchor so that I couldn't slide off again, and meanwhile I wriggled into Jamie's bivvy bag, which I'd managed to hang on to. Jamie had already got into mine.

Once I was safely wrapped up in the bag I began to calm down. Gradually my breathing slowed and my pounding heart settled.

My worries weren't over, however. My fingers were white with cold and there was no sensation in them. I rubbed them and blew on them but the circulation wouldn't return. If I couldn't warm them up I would be in big trouble. Frostbite in the mountains is a killer.

After several minutes, I felt a warm tingle growing in my fingertips. Slowly the sensation increased, and before long I was suffering the excruciating but reassuring hot aches that always accompanied the return of blood to my hands after a spell of numb cold.

I shook my stinging hands, shouting, 'Ow! Ow! Ow!' until I thought I couldn't stand it any longer. Tears were streaming down my face, and when I caught Jamie's eye, and saw the grin on his face, I couldn't contain my emotion any longer and choked out a strangled cough that was half laugh, half sob. Before we knew it we were both laughing out loud at the ridiculousness of the night's episode.

We came to a compromise with regard to bivvy bag sharing. Jamie lay in the smaller bag up to his waist and I had my legs in the big bag. We kept the top half of the big bag unzipped and managed to wrap it round both of us so that we could huddle together to share body heat.

This was awkward, making it difficult for either of us to move without letting in a blast of cold air, but on the whole we were able to stay significantly warmer. And being face to face we could chat to one another, which helped to pass the time and kept our spirits up.

We settled down to rest for the remainder of the night. I was still cold and frightened but Jamie helped me to warm up and did his best to reassure me that we were going to be OK.

THE MORNING brought no sign of a change in the weather. The north wind still blew, ripping through our notch in the ridge, and the snow still fell. There was no question of attempting a descent.

'How much of a lull in the weather do you suppose they'll need to get to us in a helicopter?' asked Jamie, admitting that a rescue was now realistically our best chance of getting out.

'There'll have to be a clearing in the clouds, or else they won't find us, but these modern helicopters can fly in pretty strong winds.'

'Not as strong as this, though?'

'Uh . . . No. I don't suppose so.'

I had been rubbing my hands together when I suddenly noticed that blisters had formed all over the backs of my fingers and on my knuckles. They were bluish-yellow, taut with liquid and numb to the touch. My instinct was to panic, but Jamie was reassuring.

'Frost nip,' he diagnosed dismissively. 'It'll heal.'

I would have to take greater care of my hands now. The damaged skin would be at more risk, the circulation of blood reduced and the chances of them freezing again would be higher. I was lucky it hadn't been worse. If my fingers had become frozen down to the flesh or even to the bone, the tissue might have been destroyed. I would then be helpless, unable to take care of myself. I carefully replaced my mittens over my blistered hands.

'I spy with my little eye,' announced Jamie all of a sudden, 'something beginning with . . . S.'

'Snow,' I said with a sigh.

'Yes. Your go.'

'Um . . . I spy with my little eye something beginning with . . . BB.'

'Bivvy bag?'

'Yes.'

Thus we passed the time, intermittently dozing, chatting and playing games to keep ourselves sane.

Early in the afternoon I was attempting to have a nap when I was roused by Jamie, shaking me vigorously.

'Look!' he exclaimed. 'It's clearing!'

I shoved my head into the open air. Sure enough, on the north side of the ridge the clouds were beginning to part. For the first time since Tuesday afternoon we could see glimpses of other mountains.

'Yes!' I shouted, willing the clouds to disappear.

We watched, tense with anticipation. At first there were just holes in the swirling clouds, opening for a moment then closing quickly, but as we watched the holes grew larger and more frequent and eventually we could see long chains of snowy peaks stretching into the distance as far as the eye could see. Below us, a long, long way down, we could see the glacier, gleaming white.

The clouds were gone now, but the wind remained powerful.

'I bet we'll see the chopper within an hour,' I shouted excitedly.

In fact we didn't have to wait that long. It was only fifteen minutes before we heard the unmistakable deep throb of a helicopter.

We waited with bated breath.

'There it is!' shouted Jamie.

Far below, at the bottom of the face, we could see the small machine rising towards us. Within a few minutes it was thundering spectacularly overhead and Jamie leapt to his feet, giving the international distress signal—outstretched arms waved up and down at his sides. The helicopter acknowledged us, circling round several times before rolling sharply to the right and shooting off back down towards the glacier, and out of sight.

We looked in horror as the agents of our salvation disappeared.

'Where have they gone?' asked Jamie.

I thought about it. 'I suppose they had to find us first. Now they'll have gone off to prepare the rescue. They'll be back soon.'

We settled down and waited patiently for the return of the cavalry, chatting longingly about steaming baths and hot meals.

About fifteen minutes later we heard the beating of rotor blades once more. We quickly spotted the chopper, racing towards us. Hanging below it we could see a tiny figure, dangling like a spider from the threadlike winch rope.

Jamie and I cheered. 'We're going to be rescued!' we screamed at each other, and embraced with relief.

As the helicopter approached our gap in the rocks, we could see that the machine was being severely battered by the wind. It pitched and rolled, desperately trying to find its balance, but the buffeting gale tossed it about like a plaything. Several times the man hanging below swung dangerously close to the rocky walls on either side. Slowly, the helicopter eased its way into the narrow gap, the blurred tips of its blades inches away from the rock. Then came a monstrous gust of wind and the pilot was forced to abort. The helicopter lurched upwards and its helpless passenger was jerked after it.

Several times, the helicopter crew tried to land their man in the *brèche*, but each time they were beaten back. For a while, the brave man on the end of the wire was hanging only five metres from us. Once again, however, he was wrenched out of reach as the helicopter shot upwards. And this time it disappeared from sight.

Jamie looked at me. 'They'll come back. They've got to.'

After a tense wait they did come back, this time with a smaller helicopter. As before, a rescuer was hanging from the winch line. The new helicopter battled for some time to bring the man in to land, but it too was forced back by the wind. Eventually the man was hanging only metres away from us. I felt sure I could make out his expression of pity as, for the final time, the helicopter pulled back. We watched in dismay as it vanished behind the shoulder of the mountain.

The clouds were now rolling back in, closing the curtains on our hopes of being rescued that day. We were alone on the mountain once more. Neither of us said a word. I felt a lump rise in my throat.

Jamie broke the silence. 'Fancy a cup of tea then?'

I looked at him, incredulous. 'Are you being serious?'

'We're here for another night, so we may as well give it a go.'

So we buried our disappointment and attempted to make a brew. We got everything we needed out of the rucksacks as quickly as possible: stove, fuel, pan, lighter, mug, tea bags. Then we retreated swiftly to the shelter of the bags. Once inside we devised an arrangement whereby I raised myself up on my left elbow and Jamie raised himself on his right, creating a small space for the stove between us. We each then had one arm spare to tend to the stove, although it was tricky keeping the top of Jamie's bag, which formed our roof, from flapping in the wind. One of us would then hold the stove while the other held the pan, packed full of snow, over it.

It was awkward work and we had a couple of eyebrow-singeing incidents, but we started to make progress. It took several loads of snow to make just a mugful of water, and once we had the water it took an age to boil. Eventually, though, we managed to produce a steaming mug of wonderful hot tea. We shared it appreciatively, dunking a few of our dry biscuits, which slid gloriously down our throats, in great contrast to the undunked version.

I still felt like crying with disappointment, but this unexpected supper went a long way towards providing consolation.

Once our nectar was finished we relit the stove, and prepared another brew, which we drank with equal gusto, and then a third, until the biscuits were all gone, and the stove sputtered out, the fuel all burnt. The heat that the stove had provided soon faded away.

It was growing dark now and we settled down for our fourth night at the *brèche*, our fifth out in the open, drawing the bivvy bag round us tightly for protection from the wind.

'They'll be back for us in the morning,' I said. 'Let's just hope that the wind drops in the night.'

Jamie grunted.

That night was much the same as the previous three, but with less snow. We lay side by side, shivering the hours away and praying for the dawn. Our situation was indisputably dire. Jamie and I never talked about the possibility of not making it, of never being rescued. I was sure we were both thinking about it, though.

I wondered what it might be like to die. Whether it would be a gentle drift into oblivion, or something more spiritual, some kind of afterlife. Impossible questions, which I'd pondered many times before but which now seemed so much more immediate. And what about the people left below to mourn our passing? Our friends. Our families. Our girlfriends. How great a hole would we leave in their lives if we never came down from this mountain?

I shook myself back to reality. The helicopter would come for us tomorrow. There was bound to be another break in the weather and this time they'd be ready with a plan to get us out. We'd suffered enough. Now it was time for the happy ending. The eleventh-hour rescue and a tearful welcome at the helicopter pad. Surely it was time for us to go home.

THE MORNING BROUGHT a terrible wind, stronger than any so far, a wind that tore the clouds from the mountains, leaving them exposed to its shocking force, and that sent plumes of spindrift streaming from the summit in great white streaks across the sky. With it came a bone-chilling drop in temperature. We had no thermometer, but the air temperature was certainly well below $-25°C$, which, combined with a wind speed of at least 120km/h, created conditions of the utmost severity. We were at the full mercy of the elements, with only our puny bivvy bags for shelter. And there would be no rescue that morning. Not until the wind dropped.

Jamie and I huddled together to conserve warmth. We tried to sleep, in the hope that on waking we would find it was all over.

Then Jamie spoke. 'What hill are we on?'

'What?' I asked, mystified.

'What are we doing here?' he continued, his voice slow.

It dawned on me what was happening. 'Jamie!' I shouted. 'Come on Jamie! You remember. Where are we, Jamie?'

'I don't know. I can't remember,' he said dreamily.

'Yes, you can!' I insisted, shaking him and rubbing his body with my hands. 'Come on, Jamie! Tell me where we are!'

I was petrified. If Jamie wouldn't respond to my questions and I couldn't help him to warm up, his hypothermia would quickly get worse. He would become unconscious and die within hours.

'What hill are we on, Jamie? Where are we?'

'Oh. We're on the Droites. I remember.'

I carried on questioning Jamie while rubbing him vigorously and soon I was getting quite sensible answers out of him.

'You frightened me,' I chastised him.

'I was just asleep,' he protested, 'and woke up a bit confused.'

'Yeah, right,' I said, but let it drop.

We huddled together as tightly as possible after that, wrapping our arms round each other, and chatted as best we could, lest one or other of us should slip unnoticed into the insidious grip of hypothermia.

We tried to cheer each other with memories of happier times, but there was to be little happiness for us that day, and there was no respite whatsoever from the evil storm.

Eventually the light of day abandoned us once more to the mountain. Lost in the fury of the elements, we clung to each other, our lives inconsequential to the colossal forces of nature.

BY THE THURSDAY morning, back down in the valley, many of our friends were finding the weather conditions too unpleasant to contemplate venturing onto the slopes, so Anna and a friend spent the morning at the swimming baths, enjoying the luxury of the warm water, the steam room and the sauna—a great contrast to the cold and inhospitable world outside, visible through large picture windows. The heat forced Anna to relax properly for the first time in days.

As she floated in the water and watched the snow driving past the windows, she tried to imagine what it must be like for Jamie and me. Were we shivering in a snow hole in the middle of some glacier? Or battling towards a mountain refuge? Or had we already frozen to death? Worst of all, had we disappeared down some hidden crevasse, never to be seen until decades later, when our ice-mangled corpses were found? Two years previously, Jamie himself had discovered the body of some unfortunate climber from Leeds, whose fate had remained unknown since the 1970s, his relatives left to wonder for nearly thirty years.

Anna shook herself from her morbid reverie and swam a length of the pool. She knew it would do no good for her to worry herself into a state. She should think positively. Still, she couldn't help feeling that she should be preparing herself for the worst.

That evening, the increasingly unsettled group of friends went to a bar to unwind. Anna tried to join in, but she wanted to remain sober to be able to deal with any news that might arrive. The others tried to get her to participate but couldn't draw her out of her shell. After a while she decided to go home, and one of the lads walked her back to the chalet. As they marched down the snowy road he tried to offer some words of comfort, but there was nothing he could say.

By Friday morning, over a metre and a half of snow had fallen in the valley since Tuesday. Anna, Stu and Jules went into Chamonix to see if there was any news from the PGHM. There was none, although they were still hopeful of getting a break in the weather.

The three went back out into the streets of Chamonix, aimless and listless. They wandered into a cinema and whiled away an hour or two absorbed in some mindless movie before installing themselves in a café to drink the day away with coffees, teas and beers.

Towards the end of the afternoon, a tall, bespectacled, grey-haired gentleman rushed into the café in a state of excitement. He obviously knew Jules and immediately started talking ten to the dozen. When he was able to get a word in, Jules introduced him to Anna and Stu. John Wilkinson was an Oxford don and mountaineer who had moved to France so he could spend his retirement writing, skiing and doing the odd bit of climbing. His wife was the French author Anne Sauvy. Because she had written a documentary about the work of the PGHM, Anne was the only civilian in the valley permitted to possess a radio tuned to the mountain rescue frequency. John had news.

The PGHM had located Jamie and me, on the top of Les Droites, and we were both alive. However, it had been too windy to rescue us, so now the PGHM were waiting for another chance and were hopeful for tomorrow, although the forecast was cold and windy.

Anna felt a confusing mixture of emotions. We were alive! That was the best news she'd had all week. But the forecast for tomorrow wasn't good. How much longer could Jamie and I last? The idea of us being trapped up there in that horrendous weather didn't bear thinking about.

Jules pointed out that, having survived so far, we must have a reasonable bivvy spot and there would be no reason why we couldn't continue to survive. The others were glad to accept this analysis.

John suggested that the three of them should join him and his wife for dinner that evening. Anna, Stu and Jules accepted, and later arrived at John and Anne's beautiful chalet, which offered unrivalled views across to the stunning Aiguilles.

Anne Sauvy was no stranger to the dangers of the mountains, having herself made many difficult climbs in her younger days, and having spent her life writing about the successes and failures of mountaineers. She promised to keep Anna posted if there were any developments in the PGHM's attempts to reach Jamie and me.

Resigned now to a sixth night of waiting, Anna sat down with the others to a fine meal. Conversation drifted on, but every now and then she would catch herself staring out of the window into the blackness and willing us, with all her heart, to hang on.

ON SATURDAY MORNING the sun was shining, and Anna's hopes leapt. Then, when she noticed the enormous plumes of spindrift streaming across the sky from every mountain summit, she realised how windy it must be and her hopes sank again.

She and Stu took the familiar bus journey to Chamonix, and once more entered the sombre vestibule of the PGHM building. This time the officers drew diagrams of the mountain, detailing the *brèche* where Jamie and I were stranded. They explained how it had been too windy yesterday for their Alouette helicopter so they had enlisted the help of a private helicopter company, whose machine, a Lama, was lighter. The Lama had got close to the *brèche* but had been unable get directly overhead. Their plan now was to land a man on the ridge, who would then be able to descend to reach us.

However, the wind was still the problem. One of the men pointed to the spindrift plume trailing from the summit of the Verte, over a kilometre long. The wind speed at that altitude was estimated to be 130km/h. As things stood, their helicopters were grounded.

Anna emerged from the PGHM nursing the last remnants of a fragile hope. This new weather was even more awful than the endless snow. The air temperature had plummeted, and even in the valley Anna could feel her exposed flesh beginning to freeze. She couldn't begin to imagine how life could be sustained up on the mountain.

She decided to phone my parents and let them know. She had held off in the hope that all would turn out well, not wanting them to worry.

But the story was obviously becoming newsworthy and they would hear sooner or later. Better to hear from her than from the television.

She caught my mother and father just as they were leaving to go to a wedding. The news that their son was stranded on a mountain top, feared dead, caught them from behind like a rugby tackle.

My father sounded quiet and scared, his replies limited to 'Uh-huh', 'Yes', and 'OK'. There was, of course, nothing they could do. Anna left them to cope as best they could.

The chalet rental was ending that day, so Stu and Anna arranged to stay in an apartment up the road. In the afternoon they hugged and said goodbye to all those in the party who were leaving, and spent the rest of the day shifting their stuff, plus Jamie's and mine, to the apartment.

Anna went to bed that night with a heavy heart.

AFTER STU AND ANNA left the PGHM headquarters, Capitaine Blaise Agresti had gathered his men together in the briefing room, and the team had planned a strategy for their next attempt to reach the two stranded climbers. The greatest difficulty with their previous attempts had been the depth of the *brèche*, preventing the helicopter from getting close enough to the climbers. A longer winch line would be too unmanageable and heavy. It was therefore proposed that the winch line be extended with a climbing rope. The rescuer could then be dropped off at the west summit to make his way to the climbers and, hopefully, the helicopter would be able to bring the extended winch line close enough to lift them off.

The mission was planned for first light. Until then all they could do was pray that the two climbers could hold out through the night.

On Sunday morning, the wind had dropped sufficiently for the helicopters to fly. The team held another briefing during which Daniel Poujol, the pilot who had made the earlier rescue attempts in the Alouette, persuaded Agresti that the best man to pilot the smaller Lama helicopter was Corrado Truchet, an extremely experienced pilot and alpine guide. The only trouble was that Truchet was currently in Italy, enjoying a weekend off. The Mont Blanc Tunnel was closed, the roads all blocked, so Poujol and Agresti made an illegal flight to pick him up.

The men hurriedly made their final preparations, aware that the clock was ticking. With every passing minute the climbers' chances were diminishing.

When all was ready, Truchet, his winchman, and rescuer Alain Iglesis, set off in the Lama to carry out a recce.

I KNOW NOW that we're going to die. Ever since our hands froze I've known that we're not going to make it through the night.

I can't get sense out of Jamie any more. He keeps shouting at me, 'It's time to go! We've got to go now!'

I don't understand what he's talking about, and I don't seem to be able to think straight. All I know is the wind, screaming in my ears. And that Jamie's bivvy bag is gone. I don't know what happened to it. It's just gone. Now we are sitting in the open, exposed to the wind, and Jamie is looking at me and shouting, 'We've got to go now!'

As I look in his eyes I see no recognition. Just darkness. Then he looks down at the snow and he doesn't shout any more.

I realise now that the mountain has won and there isn't going to be a happy ending. The hope that kept us going for so long has blown away in the wind, leaving behind only the certainty of death.

I'm sitting on the ice, face into the wind. I've lost my mittens. Both my hands are frozen like meat. I've got no boots on either, and my feet are frozen too. But I feel no pain. Just numbness.

Jamie lies beside me, face down across the *brèche*, like a culled deer on a horse's saddle. At first he fights and struggles, tries to escape. But soon he slows down and just lies there. I shout to him but he doesn't respond. I can't reach him. I can do nothing.

I sit in the snow and watch, feeling detached. I have the strange feeling that I'm no longer on the ledge, but floating high above it.

I didn't expect this. I'm still less than thirty and I'm about to die and I'm not prepared. I think about Anna. I can't believe I won't see her again. I promised her I'd come back. I've let her down. And my parents and everyone else, I've let them all down.

I look across at Jamie. I think he's dead now. I've never seen a dead person before. I wonder how long before I join him. I just want to drift off and join him. It occurs to me that if I unzip my jacket the end will come quicker. I try to grasp the zip but my hands are useless blocks of ice. If I could, I would stand up to face the full force of the wind and meet my fate head on, but the rope that tethers me has become frozen. I am chained to the mountain, so beaten by the forces of nature that I can only sit and wait. I close my eyes, feeling drowsy now. Gradually I slip into the waiting arms of sleep.

Then I'm awake again. I look about. Jamie's lifeless body still lies there. I notice the mountains in front of me becoming lit by the diffuse light of dawn. The light grows stronger and the peaks grow out of the darkness, luminous like ghosts. One by one, the summits catch fire, struck by the first rays of the sun. I gaze on, mesmerised, as the burning red light spreads across the whole of the savage landscape. I am convulsed by the violent beauty and awesome power of it all.

Gradually I become aware that the primal din of the gale is accompanied by another noise. A heartbeat. Faintly, a fast and constant pulse—getting louder. A helicopter.

I am long past surprise, relief or joy. I watch with indifferent interest as the machine thunders into view and swoops overhead. It wheels round in the sky and makes two more passes above me. I wave a frozen hand, rigid as a garden fork. The helicopter retreats.

When the helicopter returns, it carries a man, hanging by a thread. This time the machine heads for the ridge above the *brèche*. With difficulty it hovers, kicking up clouds of billowing spindrift, and sets the man down on the ridge. It then flies off, leaving the man behind.

The man moves fast. He has soon set up an abseil, which brings him to our bivouac. He reaches Jamie first and checks for signs of life.

Something revives inside me, and I find the will to speak, miraculously in French. '*Il est mort,*' I say.

The man leaves Jamie and strides across to where I sit. He is a small man, lean and wiry with steely blue eyes, and his movements are quick and efficient. He wears the blue uniform of the PGHM.

He squats down beside me and fetches a steel flask from his pack. He pours a cup of steaming liquid. '*Buvez du thé!*' he orders.

I sip the hot sweet tea as he brings the cup to my lips. It tastes wonderful but scalds my mouth. '*C'est chaud,*' I complain.

'*Oui. Buvez!*' he insists.

I finish and he pours out another cupful. '*Encore!*' he says, so I drink some more.

He then puts the flask away and gets out a rescue harness. I help him by shifting my weight as best I can while he pulls it underneath me. Then he takes out a knife, locates the frozen rope that binds me to the mountain, and slices through it with one swift stroke.

He takes a radio handset from his jacket and shouts into it. We wait for a minute or two. Suddenly the helicopter appears again, trailing the winch line. It makes no attempt to hover over the *brèche*, but flies straight over. As the pilot makes the pass, the end of the winch line swings precisely towards us. My rescuer deftly catches the karabiner as it swings past and in one movement clips it to my harness.

I have only about two seconds to brace before the stomach-lurching jerk, and I am whisked, spinning into space. The walls of the *brèche* rush past me, then I'm flying through air, high above the glacier, free from the prison of ice that has incarcerated me for so long.

As I am flown away, I look back. The last thing I see is the man in the blue, crouching over the inanimate body of Jamie—my friend.

The helicopter soon sets me down. Everything becomes a confusion of noises and blurred faces. I feel a lot of hands lifting me. A hard metal platform. Loud voices. Another helicopter. A gentle voice says something about oxygen. A gas mask on my face. A kaleidoscope of coloured stars. Then black.

ON SUNDAY MORNING the rest of our party were due to return to Britain, and Stu and Anna were forced to move again. This time, to be closer to the centre of things, they took rooms in the Hôtel Le Chamonix in the middle of the town. The pair were sitting in the bar, drinking coffee, when the television attracted Anna's attention. It was on the news! There was a rescue going on!

Anna and Stu raced up the hill to the PGHM, and the duty officer confirmed that two climbers had been evacuated from the mountain.

Were they alive? implored Stu. The officer was vague. Stu and Anna had difficulty understanding his French. Both had been taken to hospital. One was definitely alive. The other may have been unconscious or have sustained a serious injury.

Then Miles Bright, the man who had arranged the chalet for us, rushed into the building. He told Stu and Anna that he had just come down from Lognan Station, where the climbers had been brought for immediate treatment before being ferried to the hospital. There was no doubt, he said, as to the condition of the two climbers. One was alive. The other was dead. He didn't know which.

Silence fell. Anna and Stu were completely derailed. This was an outcome which neither of them had prepared for. They had been through this whole nightmare together, bolstering each other up, united by their common concern. They had urged each other to keep hoping for the best. Neither of them had thought for one moment that one climber might be rescued alive and the other not. How could one of them get their Jamie back and the other not? How could they look each other in the eye ever again? Were they both, at that moment, wishing with all their hearts for it to be their Jamie who was alive, loathing themselves for wanting the other to be dead?

Anna thought about the crumpled note in her pocket. '*See you soon. xxxx*'. Was it true? Or was she to be reunited with a lifeless corpse?

The PGHM gave Anna and Stu a lift to the hospital.

They were asked to wait and sat silently side by side as the fateful moment bore down on them.

Part Two: Two Hospitals

First I hear a clamour of urgent French voices, issuing instructions. Then I am aware of scissors cutting through my clothes and I am naked, on a hard bed. I am wrapped in wonderful warm blankets and I feel the heat soak into me like water into a sponge.

I feel hands under my arms and legs. I hear, '*Un. Deux. Trois!*' and I am lifted and quickly set down again, this time in a sitting position.

The fuzzy white shapes that surround me resolve themselves into people: doctors and nurses. I am in a small, bright hospital room, sitting in a brown plastic reclining chair. A nurse holds a plastic cup, with a lid like a baby's mug, to my lips. She tips the cup and I drink the warm, sweet liquid.

Two other nurses are filling buckets with hot water and disinfectant, and I wonder if they're going to wash the floor. However, the buckets are placed on stools around my chair, and my hands and feet are immersed. I am being defrosted like a Christmas turkey.

A doctor approaches, a tall man with impossibly long, thin limbs. His gaunt face wears a kind expression.

'I am Docteur Marsigny,' he says, 'chief of the department of resuscitation and traumatology. Can you please tell me your name?'

'Jamie Andrew,' I reply meekly.

'Good. Now, I need to insert a tube into your chest.'

He injects an anaesthetic, then inserts a large needle under my collarbone. Several times he fails to find the vein, explaining that I am very dehydrated and my blood vessels have partly collapsed. Finally the central line goes in and I am hooked up to a drip. The doctor leaves.

I don't know whether it's the rehydration, the warmth, the drugs or a combination of all of these, but I feel a rush of vitality. I am soon buzzing like a man on speed. I chat to the nurses, babbling in the best, most fluent French I have ever spoken. I think the nurses are surprised to find their frozen patient suddenly so lively. They are a cheerful bunch, and I feel that I'm in good hands.

Dr Marsigny strides back into the room, a telephone in his hand. 'Monsieur Andrew, it is your father.' He holds the phone to my ear.

'Jamie?' My father's voice sounds distant and brittle. 'How are you?'

'My hands and feet are in buckets of water.' This is the best description I can come up with. 'Jamie's dead,' I add.

'We know. We're so sorry. Your mother and I have been so worried about you. We're so glad you're alive. I'm flying out to Geneva in the morning. I'll see you tomorrow.'

We say goodbye and Dr Marsigny takes away the phone.

I am pronounced fully defrosted and wheeled into another room where a large steel bath is filling with hot disinfected water. I am lifted once more and lowered into the tub. Bliss.

I wallow in the hot water while a nurse sits beside me, feeding me tea. How strange it seems to be snatched from the living hell of the mountain, to find myself surrounded by friendly people who will look after me. I feel soothed. I am aware that there are matters of gravity that I will have to confront, but right now I am too shattered to care. I am in a dream from which I have no desire to emerge.

Some time later, Dr Marsigny announces it is time for me to go to bed. 'It is important that you rest. I think you are very tired and you are going to have a hard struggle ahead.'

'What's going to happen to my hands and feet?' I ask.

'It is too soon to say. You have very serious frostbite.' In his strong accent he pronounces this last sentence, 'You 'ave very serioz frozbite.' It is to become his catchphrase.

I am put on a trolley and wheeled through blue-walled corridors into a room, also blue walled, which contains a bed, a reclining chair, a sink and various pieces of electronic equipment. This is to be my home for a while. I am lifted onto the bed and slid between smooth, fresh sheets. Two nurses wrap my hands and feet in loose, dry dressings, then hook me up to an automatic temperature and blood-pressure machine. The nurses depart, wishing me a restful sleep.

I look around me and notice the window. Outside, heavy snow falls.

I AM LOOKING pensively out at the snow later that day when I hear a noise at the door. I look round and there stands Anna. Her face is pale, she wears an uneasy smile and I can see red rings round her eyes, but she is the most wonderful sight I have ever seen. I don't suppose I'm looking particularly great myself.

She sits down on my bed. 'Hello,' she says, uncertainly.

'Hello,' I reply. 'We've lost Jamie.'

'I know.' Then the tears begin to flow from both of us. I can't move to embrace her but she leans down and hugs and kisses me.

'I thought you'd never come back.'

'I know, baby,' I say as I weep, 'but I did come back.'

We remain there for a few moments, wrapped in each other. Her smell is so sweet, and her hair and skin are so soft. I no longer care about all the pain and suffering I've been through. All that matters is that we are together again.

Anna draws back. 'The doctor says that I've to leave you to sleep. You're going to need all your strength. I'll see you tomorrow.'

She kisses me on the forehead then backs out of the room,.

My head has no room left for any thoughts. I settle back on the soft pillow and fall swiftly into a deep and dreamless sleep.

I WOKE GRADUALLY on the Monday morning and for a few moments felt secure and content. Then reality returned and my heart sank as I opened my eyes to face my new world. The recollection hit me like a brick wall. Jamie was dead. As for me, I was alive, but God knows what was going to become of me. It seemed pretty obvious that I wasn't going to recover intact. What would I lose? Fingers? Toes? Hands? Feet? The only thing that seemed certain was that my life would never be the same again.

I felt like I had the most ferocious hangover of my life. My head throbbed, my mouth and lips were dry and sore and my whole body ached. My hands and feet were still numb, and because of the drip lines and monitoring equipment I couldn't shift position. Although snow and ice had been exchanged for sheets and blankets, my sentence of enforced immobility was far from over. I had some relief only when a couple of nurses came in to hoist me into a sitting position.

One of the nurses sat down to feed me my first proper meal in a long time, and I had my first experience of what was to become the most hated of all the trials that lay ahead. When being spoonfed, the natural rhythm of eating is lost. A mouthful always arrives too early or too late, or is too big or too small. I couldn't help but rush my chewing, knowing that the person at the other end of the spoon, no matter how tolerant, would prefer to be doing something else. The joy of food was lost. Eating was a chore rather than a pleasure.

After breakfast came a bed bath, followed by a change of bedclothes. After they had changed my various drips and collecting bags, the nurses left me in peace.

Not long after, however, Dr Marsigny came in, accompanied by a squad of white-coated physicians, who got down to the business of undressing and examining each of my limbs.

My hands and feet had turned black and blue overnight, and horribly swollen. Also blackened were my right knee and my right ear. I begged Dr Marsigny to tell me what the outlook was.

Marsigny took a deep breath. 'You 'ave very serioz frozbite,' he said. 'I think . . .' He paused for a moment. 'I think we will have to cut off something, but I don't know what. We first have to wait for the necrotic tissue to separate from the living tissue.'

'How long will that take?' I demanded, reeling at the thought of it all.

'I think several weeks. Right now, the most important thing is to prevent infections from here,' he said, pointing at a blackened hand, 'from travelling up here.' He ran his finger up my arm. 'We are worried you may then have poisoning of the blood and of the kidney. So we will wait, and we will give you some strong antibiotics to control the infections.' He peered down to inspect my right hand. 'I want you to try to make a fist with your hand,' he said.

I strained the muscles of my right arm and watched as the swollen digits made the merest flicker of movement. I knew enough to realise that this slight response was most likely caused by the pull of tendons from further up the arm. The hand itself appeared devoid of life.

Marsigny explained that it was the circulation of blood he was interested in. If the circulation continued, there was hope of saving at least part of the hands. He took photographs of my useless appendages, then the doctors departed.

So, barring miracles, it seemed I was definitely going to lose parts of my body. However, the doctors couldn't, or wouldn't, say what, and so I settled down to the unattractive prospect of waiting.

At first it all seemed too much to take in. I suppose I was in a state of shock. The grotesque monstrosities at the end of each arm and leg held no horror for me. The prospect of spending my life as a cripple in a wheelchair elicited no fear. I was a motionless rock in a world that had suddenly turned itself on its head. My mind was as numb as my inert hands and feet.

Soon, though, the full weight of my concerns began to sink heavily upon me. I thought back over the events of Jamie's death and my salvation and couldn't make sense of it. We had shared everything equally, our food, our drink, our shelter, our hopes. Neither I nor Jamie had suspected that one of us might make it down without the other, that destiny would inexplicably split us apart.

Why had he been taken and not me? Jamie was so much tougher than me. Had he perhaps worn one less layer of clothing? Was his blood circulation less efficient than mine? I couldn't figure it out.

I found it difficult to believe that he had gone. I felt sure that he was holed up in some bar in the town, haranguing an eager audience with the fantastic tale of our latest escapade. Or perhaps he was here in the hospital, tucked up in bed being tended to by lovely nurses.

But no. I'd been with him as he died. I'd sat with his unmoving corpse, waiting for my turn to die. He was gone and I knew that nothing would ever fill the space he'd left behind. I felt like a traitor, that I'd waited for him to die before callously hitching a ride out in a helicopter. I hated myself for having survived when Jamie had not. I felt like I oughtn't to smile or laugh ever again.

I knew, though, that I had to, and my smiles and laughs I saved for the many visitors who arrived at my bedside, some of whom appeared more traumatised than me.

MY FIRST VISITOR that first afternoon was Stu Fisher. He marched into my room with a broad smile and gave me a bear hug, exclaiming how relieved he was that I'd pulled through. I don't know how he found the strength to do that, knowing that his own son hadn't made it, but somehow he found room in his big heart to mourn for Jamie and to celebrate for me at the same time.

I didn't know what to say to Stu. I couldn't express the shock and confusion I felt, and I certainly couldn't relate the events of the previous days, but I told him feebly how very sorry I was and that Jamie hadn't suffered when he died. Stu smiled at me and I saw the red rings round his eyes. But he went a long way to cheering me up with his simple resolve to let life go on.

Jules Cartwright arrived soon after. Jamie's death had upset him greatly, but he was determined that it would not shake his determination to continue mountaineering. He knew that if it had been him that had been taken, Jamie would continue to climb.

Anna came to see me too that afternoon. She sat with me as I drifted in and out of sleep, exhausted from the effort of talking. That evening my father arrived, looking tense. He brightened visibly on seeing me, and was soon chattering away about how worried he and my mother had been and how there'd been a barrage of journalists camped outside their door. I lay and listened, rueful about the amount of trouble I'd caused. Outside, darkness fell and the storm continued.

DURING THE NIGHT my back started to hurt. I was unable to move to alleviate my discomfort and slept little. I was feeling sick and slightly feverish, and I lay awake, turning the events of the previous days over in my mind. What had gone wrong? What had been our fatal error?

If only we hadn't set out with a less than perfect weather forecast. If we had gone lighter and climbed faster, we might have made it off the mountain before the storm struck. Or if we had stuck to the original plan and climbed to the summit and bivvied there, the helicopter might have reached us earlier. Perhaps we should have attempted the descent. It would only have been ten or twelve abseils to the glacier. Perhaps we'd have made it, even in those conditions.

As my head began to construct endless combinations of events, I realised I was getting nowhere. 'If-onlys' don't alter the facts. We can't change time. It runs like a river through our lives and we are powerless to swim against its current or alter its course.

I resolved to cast out my doubts, to convince myself that I had to accept what had happened. But for many days, weeks, even months, I was unable to prevent thoughts of regret and contrition creeping into my head, sinking me into a pit of depression.

I woke that night in a cold sweat, the bedclothes twisted round my legs. I was unable to untangle myself and felt helpless and afraid. I shouted until the night nurse came running. Whispering soft words of comfort, she straightened out my bed and mopped my brow.

AT 10 A.M. ON TUESDAY morning, the team of doctors marched in and had another look at my hands and feet. I say 'my' hands and feet, but they didn't really feel like mine any more. They were now completely black, dry and withered in parts, especially the digits. They looked for all the world like the leathery limbs of an Egyptian mummy, preserved in some museum case. Looking at the wizened little pegs that were once my fingers, I realised that it was unlikely many of them could be saved. I tried to imagine a life without fingers, but couldn't.

Dr Marsigny seemed more concerned about my left leg. The sharp delineation between pink and black flesh was well up my ankle, and the foot was looking quite swollen and putrid.

'You have an infection,' explained Marsigny. 'We are trying to fight it with antibiotics, but if you get more sick we will have to cut this foot. You 'ave very serioz frozbite,' he added, in case I had forgotten.

The good news was that my frozen knee had made a miraculous recovery, and I now had mobility and sensation in it. The top layer of skin was dead, however, and over the following weeks it became grey, wrinkled and leathery. '*Peau d'éléphant*,' the nurses called it— elephant skin—and it peeled off in large, satisfying strips.

The dead tissue in my right ear was also separating off nicely. This was what they were hoping would happen in my limbs. The body's natural healing mechanism creates a barrier between living and dead flesh, allowing the living flesh to repair itself and the dead to shrivel harmlessly. Until that happened the living material was at risk of infection from the dead. Hence all the antibiotics.

After the doctors left I spent the morning, as usual, trying to kill time. Through the window, beyond the staff car park, was a steep wooded hillside. Occasionally a cable car would float into view. As it climbed and vanished in the enveloping mist, I would count the seconds till its counterpart appeared, making the downward trip, and imagine the people inside. I wondered if I'd ever ride in that cable car again. It seemed part of another world now.

My boredom was relieved by the comings and goings of hospital staff. I liked to practise my French, and most of the nurses and doctors took a few minutes out of their routine to chat to the crazy Scottish climber. Everyone was relaxed and friendly. I began to feel at home.

The greatest blessing was that nobody was at all disapproving of the circumstances of my accident. Many of the staff were mountaineers and understood what Jamie and I had been doing. They realised that we weren't foolhardy, suicidal idiots and it was generally accepted that we had been competent but unlucky. This was a great help to me in rebuilding my self-esteem.

After lunch that day I waited impatiently for my visitors. When Anna came through the door, my spirits rose. She had brought a bundle of mail with her, and we spent an enjoyable hour opening cards and reading faxes. I received messages of condolence and encouragement from more friends than I ever realised I had. They would send me long, rambling letters, jokes and stories that kept me entertained. It began to dawn on me that, whatever happened over the coming weeks, I would have the support of an awful lot of people.

I also received cards and letters from complete strangers. The most interesting of these were from people who had suffered in similar circumstances in the mountains, or who were themselves amputees. In particular, I remember one short note in a spidery hand:

Dear Jamie,

When I was sixteen I lost both hands. Since then I've enjoyed an interesting, varied, full life, achieved independence, and a qualification which enabled me to earn a living, to marry and bring up two daughters. I wish you as much good fortune as I have enjoyed, because I'm sure you will meet as many good-hearted people as has been my happy lot.

Yours sincerely, Cyril Wire

P.S. I'm now 82 years old.

Later in the afternoon, my dad arrived with the newspapers from home. My story had created quite a sensation in the press, and all of Monday's front pages had been plastered with headlines like 'ALIVE!' and 'FIVE DAYS IN ICE TOMB WITH DYING MATE'. I didn't bother to read the hopelessly inaccurate stories. My parents, our neighbours and Jamie's mother had all been inundated with journalists. Here in France, the hospital and the Hôtel Le Chamonix were under siege. Anna found this upsetting, and sorely resented being snooped on from behind pot plants in the hospital foyer.

Towards the end of the afternoon, a call was put through to the phone by my bed and I spoke to my mother for the first time. She was understandably emotional. She had always been concerned about her only son being involved in the dangerous activity of mountaineering. Finally her worst fears had come true—or almost come true.

In the evening Anna returned to sit with me. She was my constant companion throughout those troubled times. She was my shoulder to cry on, my psychologist and counsellor. In return, I tried to be all these things for her. As we sat and talked through those long quiet evenings, I realised that she faced the same difficulties as me, that she had lost a close friend too, and that she, too, faced the prospect of living with disabilities. Then I didn't feel quite so sorry for myself.

BY WEDNESDAY, my fourth day in hospital, my general well-being was deteriorating and I was having to be fed by drip as I could hold down little food.

Dr Marsigny announced that he wanted to send me to another hospital nearby, in Bonneville, to run tests that would establish which parts of my hands and feet might be saved. He went on to explain how new techniques were being developed whereby plastic surgeons could rebuild the flesh around living bone. I could see I was going to be in hospital for a long, long time.

Thursday came and it was time for my big trip out. I was gently rolled off my bed and onto a trolley, wheeled down the corridors to the ambulance bay and loaded into the back of a tiny ambulance. A young doctor climbed in and the nurses waved us off.

The bumpy journey wasn't much of a distraction. Lying flat on my back, all I could see from the windows was the sky and the falling snow. Fortunately Bonneville was only forty minutes away, and I was soon being wheeled into the hospital.

The first stage of my test, called a bone scintigraphy, was to have a quantity of radioactive tracer fed into my central line. We then had to wait for a few hours to give the tracer time to travel throughout my system. My hands and feet could then be scanned to see which areas had been reached by the tracer and might, therefore, still be alive.

While we were waiting, the doctor and I were left to have some lunch. The doctor had to spoonfeed me himself and was quite self-conscious and awkward about it. He tried to cheer me up by telling me about a woman he'd seen on television who had an artificial arm with which she could do all sorts of things. Even pick up an egg.

I smiled, but privately I was thinking, Pick up an egg? I want a whole lot more out of my life than to be able to pick up a measly egg! I wondered if that was the best I could hope to achieve.

When the time came to have the scan, I had to lie still on a cold, hard bench for a long time while a huge machine was manoeuvred into position over each limb in turn. For what seemed like an age, the great eye of the scintillation counter peered minutely at my hands and feet, while I willed the blood to trickle back into my bones.

An hour later I was back in the comfort of my own room, where Anna and my dad were waiting for me. They'd had another day of being harassed by the press. In order to lance the boil of media attention, my dad suggested giving them a little of what they wanted. I agreed to let one paper come in and do a five-minute interview, on the condition that a sizeable donation was made to the PGHM.

A short while later, I found myself attempting to answer questions of the 'How sorry are you to have lost your friend?' nature. I was unable to speak about the climb and the rescue but I managed to talk in general terms about how devastated I was but how I was determined to rebuild my life. The three of us then grinned inanely for the cameras. The story ran in all the national papers, and after that the attentions of the press diminished.

I said goodbye to my dad, who was returning to the UK, sure that I was in good hands, and spent the rest of the afternoon with Anna.

The uncertainty of the fate of my hands and feet was preying heavily on my mind now. I was therefore eager for news, good or bad, when Dr Marsigny and the two surgeons, Rik Verhellen and Guy Allamel, came to see me that evening. They all had a very serious demeanour, so I knew that it wasn't good news.

Dr Marsigny showed me the printouts from the bone scintigram. The grey, blotchy images meant little to my untrained eye, but Dr Marsigny explained that there was a slight indication of circulation in the bones but little to strengthen the hope of saving them. To make matters worse, my infection wasn't responding to antibiotics and the doctors now had grave concerns for my health. The bottom line was that they wanted permission to remove my left foot.

I can't say I exactly reeled with shock. Marsigny had consistently expressed his concern that my left foot was the cause of the septicaemia polluting my blood. But it still felt strange to be faced with the reality. I was actually going to be an amputee. In a strange way I didn't feel entirely bad about this. It would be a relief to have the useless piece of rotting meat removed from my otherwise healthy leg. I immediately gave my consent to the amputation.

The operation was set for first thing the next morning. I sneaked one last look at the condemned foot, thought about all the miles it had walked, all the balls it had kicked, the mountains it had ascended, and found it strange to think that it soon wouldn't be there any more.

WHEN I CAME ROUND after the operation I became aware of a dull pain in my left leg. I tried to shift position to alleviate it, but found I couldn't. I turned my head and saw Anna sitting by the bed. She smiled and told me that the operation had gone fine. I wasn't able to move because my leg was in traction.

Gradually I began to sober up from the anaesthetic and the pain became intense. I was in traction, it seemed, because they hadn't closed the wound over my freshly cut bones, and were attempting to stretch the skin to cover them. The alternative to this would have been to cut the bones shorter, but the surgeons had been anxious to leave the residual limb as long as possible to aid the fitting of a prosthetic leg in the future.

That night was my most uncomfortable to date. I'm ashamed to say I spent most of it badgering the night nurse for attention and painkillers. By morning, however, I was able to eat some solid food for the first time in thirty-six hours. I was released from the traction machine and, with the assistance of good old morphine, almost began to feel cheerful.

When Dr Marsigny came to examine me I begged him to tell me what he thought were the chances for my hands.

'Look at them,' he said. 'You tell me what you think.'

I stared down at the pathetic remnants. The stench of rotting flesh filled the room.

'I think this one's dead,' I admitted, nodding towards my desiccated left hand, 'but perhaps there is some hope for this one?' I indicated my right hand, which still had areas of reddish flesh.

'Perhaps,' conceded Marsigny with a gentle smile, but I knew that he was probably allowing me to cling to a few final remains of hope because he realised I had little else left. I knew that the infections were getting worse and that Marsigny was deeply concerned.

Later, a surprise visitor was Alain Iglesis, my rescuer. I felt flattered that he had come to see me and tried to express my gratitude. Alain brushed all compliments aside, and laughed when I told him that his tea had been the best tea in the world. As he left, he explained that he would return to take down details for his report.

On that occasion I didn't glean from Alain many facts of the mission to save Jamie and me, but eventually I did learn the whole story of the brave and desperate attempt to get us down.

It had been one of the most difficult rescues in the history of the Alps. Many in the team were disappointed with its outcome, but to label the mission a failure would be to do a great disservice to all who participated. For my part, I owe my life to the PGHM, and for that I am eternally grateful. Iglesis was given a medal in recognition of his role, although he insisted that any of his fellow rescuers would have done the same had it been their turn.

ON MONDAY, my ninth day in hospital, things took a turn for the worst. Sometime in the afternoon I recall a shiver running down my spine. A few seconds later the shiver returned and before I knew what was happening my whole body was trembling uncontrollably. I managed to shout for a nurse, and the last thing I remember is people rushing all around me, and an oxygen mask coming down over my face.

When I opened my eyes I couldn't work out what was happening. My breathing felt strange. I became aware of the tubes running through my nostrils and down my throat and realised that a machine was breathing for me.

Sitting beside my bed with tears in her eyes was my mother. I opened my mouth to speak but no sound came out. I was prevented from speaking by the tubes in my throat.

My mother was saying, 'We love you so much, Jamie.'

Then I looked down at my arms sticking out of the bedclothes. To my horror I realised that where my hands had been there were now only neatly bandaged stumps. So it had happened. I looked down the bed and judged by the lack of any bump that my right foot had gone, too. I didn't feel any grief or shock—only relief. It was all over. Look Mum, no hands. Sleep dragged me under again.

When I next came round, my dad, my mum and Anna were sitting round the bed. I allowed myself to regain consciousness slowly, during which time I decided that having those horrible tubes stuck in my windpipe was the most intolerable torment. My left arm was trussed to various drips and machinery, but my right arm was relatively free. I waved it frantically at my uncomprehending visitors.

'What is it? What's wrong?' asked my dad in concern.

I pointed the stump in the direction of my nose and made an expression that I hoped said, 'Take these horrible tubes out of me!'

Eventually Dad cottoned on. 'I'll see if I can find a doctor.'

He returned shortly with Dr Marsigny. 'We will have to keep you intubated today,' he explained, 'but hopefully we can take you off the ventilator tomorrow morning.'

As Marsigny left I realised that I had no idea what time it was. How long was it until tomorrow morning? I desperately wanted to know how long I would have to wait, but there was no clock on the wall. I returned to waving my arm about. Somehow I conveyed the concept of time by making a pendulum motion with my arm.

'You want to know what time it is! It's almost four o'clock.'

I sank back exhausted. At least it wasn't long till tomorrow. It then occurred to me that I wasn't sure what day tomorrow was.

IT WASN'T FOR SOME TIME that I learned how many days I had been unconscious and what great danger I had been in. I had passed out on Monday and I woke up on Friday. Later on I was filled in on the events of those missing four days.

By the Monday morning I was being given just about every antibiotic known to man in the attempt to control my septicaemia. The uncontrollable shivering that had overtaken my body was an immune system reaction caused by my fever. I then started to fall into septic shock, a condition that is often fatal. To make matters worse, my lungs began to fill with fluid and became incapable of drawing breath.

The doctors had to act fast to save my life. They sedated me in order to take over control of my vital functions, and intubated me so that a ventilator could breathe for me.

Anna found this latest turn of events almost too much to deal with. She'd had to be so strong for so long, and now things were getting worse. Fortunately, her mother flew out to take care of her. My mother and father came out to Chamonix the following day.

I remained in a critical condition, and on Tuesday the decision was taken to operate. It was the only way to decrease the amount of toxic material entering my bloodstream. The surgeons deliberated for hours before admitting that the complete removal of both hands and the remaining foot was the only way of saving my life. If it was any consolation, when the amputated hands and the foot were examined they were found to be completely dead.

Everyone involved in my case was severely disappointed. They had fought to save what they could of my hands and feet, but in the end they lost everything. Not being able to conceive how an active person could enjoy a life without limbs, some felt that they had failed me.

To make matters worse, the exhausted surgical team had barely finished stitching up my stumps when a disaster occurred that was to require their expertise for the rest of the night and the next morning.

Far up the valley, at the little village of Le Tour, snow had been falling on the slopes for weeks, building up into a vast unstable pack. Finally the pack slipped under its own weight, causing a monstrous avalanche that swept down the hillside. When it struck the outskirts of the village, all buildings in its path were flattened. Thirty-five people were killed and dozens more injured. All the rescue services in the valley spent the night and the whole of the next day digging for survivors. At Chamonix Hospital, the emergency department and surgery teams were treating the injured for shock, hypothermia and broken bones. It was a bad time for the people of Chamonix.

All this time, I slept on regardless.

THE OTHER MAJOR EVENT that I slept through was Jamie's funeral. Stu had arranged for Jamie's body to be taken home to Oxfordshire. The crematorium was packed and overspilled with Jamie's friends and relations. Afterwards a huge party was held in Jamie's honour.

The next day, Alice Brockington, Jamie's girlfriend, flew out to Chamonix. She wanted to see the mountain that had taken Jamie away from her, to understand better what had happened.

On Friday morning, Alice and Anna took the *téléférique* up to the Aiguille du Midi, from where they could see Les Droites, an insignificant peak among the chains of mountains all around. It was the first clear day since I had been rescued, and very cold. Anna was shocked by the biting air and tried to imagine what it had been like for Jamie and me, trapped on that distant mountain ridge, in such conditions.

Anna had been spending hours sitting by my bed while I lay unconscious, willing me to get better. And I did improve quickly after my amputations. The infections died back and my wounds began to heal. On Friday morning I was taken off the drugs that were holding me under sedation. And when the two girls arrived back at the hospital, they learned that I was waking up.

Above: Jamie Andrew rock-climbing on local outcrops near his home in Edinburgh.
Left: Jamie Fisher, in his element, in the Himalayas.
Below left: the steep slope of the ice field, part of the ascent of the north face of Les Droites, required many hours of difficult climbing.
Below right: Jamie Fisher climbing steep ice at the head of the couloir leading to the ice field.

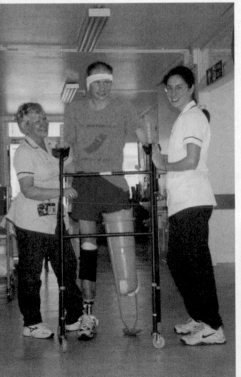

Above left: the north face of Les Droites. A: the bergshrund; B: the ice field; C: the first bivouac; D: the point reached when the storm struck; E: the brèche; F: the planned descent route; G: the summit.

Top right: an uncomfortable bivouac on the first night.

Above right: the weather breaks. Before long the snow storm prevented any futher photos.

Left: learning to walk with Doreen (left), Joy and the PPAM Aid.

Below: surrounded by nurses in Chamonix Hospital.

THE REMOVAL OF THE TUBES from my trachea was a very unpleasant experience, but as soon as they were out I felt like I'd been freed from a straitjacket. I took deep breaths, savouring the rise and fall of my chest under my own volition. I tried to speak but my throat felt like cardboard and I croaked like a frog. I was given a drink of water and started to feel a little better.

I spent the rest of Saturday morning in contemplation. So this was my fate. I was to spend the rest of my life with no hands and no feet. I almost felt like laughing at the ridiculousness of it. I mean, losing fingers or toes is a common hazard of mountaineering. I'd heard of climbers who'd lost a whole hand or a foot to frostbite, but to lose all four just seemed beyond belief.

It was clear I had a lot of readjusting to do. I thought about the physical adaptations I would have to make. Apart from being able to spell prosthetics, I knew nothing about artificial limbs.

I remembered my friend Pete Jennings, whose girlfriend, Juliette Snow, had an artificial leg. I had seen her rock climbing once and thought, Wow, that's impressive, but the leg had been hidden beneath her trousers. It must be possible to lead an active life with one artificial leg. With two, though, would it be possible even to walk? I didn't know. What could you do with prosthetic hands? Would I have to pay for my artificial limbs? Were they fixed directly to the bone?

So many questions. For now I had no answers, and no one in Chamonix Hospital seemed to have any either. None of the doctors had had any experience of prosthetic treatment. Nor were any of my visitors able to provide facts, only odd anecdotes. But all the stories I was told about other amputees were encouraging. The more I heard, the more I realised that there were people out there with similar problems who led as full a life as anybody else.

To add to all the doubt I was going through, I was also struggling with my grief for the loss of Jamie, and the difficult emotion of guilt. Guilt at having survived when Jamie was dead. Guilt at having the opportunity to carry on living life and loving and being loved.

So I made a resolution to myself. Whatever happened to me from then on, the main thing was that I was alive. The loss of Jamie would teach me that. I was alive and it felt good. In fact, it felt wonderful. The loss of my hands and feet was insignificant when one considered the alternative. I resolved to get on with my life and live it to the full, free from regret and guilt. That day, when the tubes were pulled from my nose, must be the low point. From then on I would improve in some way every day, and slowly rebuild the life that I had lost.

ALICE CAME TO SEE ME that afternoon. She sat on the edge of my bed for a while, the tears streaming down her face. I knew how bad I felt about Jamie, but I couldn't even begin to imagine how she felt. Right then, I was unable to talk to her about what had happened on the mountain. The thought of forming the words seemed to drain all the energy out of my body. Alice realised it was too soon to talk and, after a while, gave me a big hug and left.

My next visitor was Alain Iglesis, this time for an official interview. Because there had been a fatality, there had to be a full report on the accident. Iglesis needed to know every last detail of our climb: when we started, how fast we climbed, where we slept, what we ate and why we made the decisions we did. I could picture answers to all the questions in my head, but I just couldn't make the words. Iglesis realised how exhausted I was and gave up. My dad sat with him and answered as best he could. For those questions he couldn't answer, Dad coaxed the information out of me. In the end Iglesis left satisfied.

OVER THE COMING days I started to get better. The infections receded, the aching in my freshly cut bones gradually died away and the pain in my back lifted. Above all my mood improved, and I began to feel that I still had a life that was worth living.

For the short term, however, I resigned myself to an institutional life. My dad bought me a cassette player and people brought or sent me talking books. Some of the nurses gave me music tapes to listen to. Obviously I had to get someone else to put the tape in and press play, but I found I could stop the player at will by giving the row of buttons a clout with my stump, which pleased me greatly.

Visitors continued to arrive. I wondered how it felt for them to see me lying there so helpless and incapacitated. My muscles had wasted away, my ribs were showing and my eyes were sunk deep into my drawn face. I must have been a pathetic sight. I wondered what my guests said to each other after they'd left. I felt excluded from the happy world to which they would return. I longed to be able to go skiing, to swim, to go out for a large drunken meal in a restaurant. One day, I promised myself. Right now I had to be patient.

During the night, the sound of a small boy crying drifted through from the room next door into mine. The crying went on and on until eventually I asked a nurse what was wrong. The boy had a broken leg, the nurse replied, but he was crying because his parents were dead. His entire family had been buried in the avalanche at Le Tour and he was the only survivor. Suddenly my own problems seemed trivial.

ON THE FOLLOWING THURSDAY I had to have another operation, to attempt to close up the ends of my two left stumps. But the surgeons had left the bones as long as they could and the remaining skin wouldn't quite close over. I might have to have plastic surgery, they said. I was impatient to get the stumps sewn up so that my body could get on with the process of healing. I felt that I had reached a stage where, although I perhaps hadn't come to terms with what had happened to me, I was ready to accept the challenge that lay ahead. Until the wounds were closed, though, I was still in limbo.

I spent many waking hours mulling over the ways in which my disability would change my life. On a basic level, I was entirely reliant on other people for my most simple human needs: eating, drinking, washing, going to the toilet. In the fullness of time I would become capable of some of these tasks, but at the moment I had no idea how. Mobility alone would be a problem. Would I ever walk again, or would I be confined to a wheelchair? Would I have to move to a specially equipped ground-floor flat? Writing, cooking, driving, shopping—I had no idea if I would be able to do any of these things again. What about earning a living? My work was entirely physical. Would I be able to get another job? Anna might be able to support us, but what if she needed to be at home to take care of me?

Then there was the greater question of quality of life. It would be all very well to survive on a day-to-day basis, but would I be able to make my life worth living? Would I be able to cope without doing all the things I loved—hillwalking, skiing, sailing, climbing? Most of all climbing. For thirteen years, climbing had defined my life. I'd had so many plans. Every day I remembered mountains I had always assumed I would climb. Now I never would.

I pondered these issues until my case just seemed too desperate. So I decided that I had to throw out my old life and start again. All my preconceptions of myself, who I am and what I do, and all my hopes, dreams and ambitions would have to be discarded and replaced. I would have the assistance of my friends, my family and Anna, who would provide continuity from the old me to the new. From now on, life was going to be a series of challenges and I resolved to draw as much satisfaction as possible from achieving each one.

I set myself long-term goals. On my wall was a picture of Anna and me at a wedding the previous year. We had received invitations to a couple more in the coming summer, and I determined to go to them and hold my own drink and eat my food myself. I spent a long time gazing at that photo. We looked so happy together.

DR MARSIGNY, aware that I was anxious to go home to Scotland, finally declared that I was fit enough to travel. My insurance company sorted out the travel arrangements, and it was arranged for me to go to the Princess Margaret Rose Hospital in Edinburgh, one of the best institutions in the UK for orthopaedics and prosthetics.

I looked forward to going home but I realised I was going to miss Chamonix Hospital. I had been there only three weeks, but I had been through so much that it felt very much a part of me, and I had become close to many of the staff. On the day before we left, Anna and I said goodbye to our new friends as they went off shift. I made a promise to Dr Marsigny that I would return. This time, I said, I would walk into his hospital and shake him by the hand.

The nurses bought me a T-shirt as a souvenir of my stay and Anna got them some chocolates and a card, bullying me into writing the card myself. Gripping the pen carefully between my two stumps I slowly managed to scrawl, *Merci pour tout. Grosses bises, Jamie.*

The travel was being handled by a private company with the fantastic name of International Rescue, and Anna and I were driven to Geneva Airport in a neat little estate-car style ambulance. An impossibly small, sleek jet was waiting for us on the runway. Beside it stood two German pilots and a German female doctor who fussed over me with Teutonic efficiency.

The flight to Edinburgh took a mere two hours, during which time Anna, a nervous flyer, had time to get anxious about the airworthiness of such a tiny plane.

Later, when we got a chance to speak to the pilot, he explained. 'Zis is ze Lear jet. It is used to fly celebrities all round ze world.' He went on to list the names of people who had sat in Anna's seat: Pierce Brosnan, Claudia Schiffer, Boris Becker, King Juan Carlos of Spain. I shuddered to think how much the flight was costing.

Predictably, when we landed at a dank Edinburgh airport, the expected ambulance was nowhere to be seen. Eventually, after a couple of phone calls, a battered old patient-transfer wagon carted us all off round the bypass towards the hospital. As we drew up alongside the dingy entrance, my German escorts looked horrified.

'This is not a hospital; this is a farm!' the doctor protested.

Fortunately the outward appearance of the Princess Margaret Rose Hospital belies the quality of its care. It is actually a centre of excellence. The German medics left me in the robust hands of some Scottish nurses, and I began my new life in my home country, relieved to be released from the land of constant snow.

BUILT IN THE 1930s, in a fine location looking out towards the Pentland Hills to the south of Edinburgh, the Princess Margaret Rose had the atmosphere of a hospital in decline. When I arrived there, many wards were already closed and the rest were due to be relocated to Edinburgh's super new hospital at Little France in two years' time. The remaining in-patients were mostly elderly people having hip and knee operations. Most amputees were treated at the Astley Ainsley Hospital, but because of the severity of my case I was to remain at the PMR, which had Edinburgh's prosthetic service on site. I got the impression, too, that as a high-profile case I was quite a catch. 'To us, you're manna from heaven,' as one of my consultants put it.

I passed the early afternoon settling in and being introduced to all the nurses. Then visitors started arriving. Before long there were about fifteen or twenty people gathered round my bed. This was a trend that was to continue for many weeks, as every day upward of a dozen people would squeeze into my room. I was delighted to be the centre of so much attention and it cheered me up no end. Almost every person I knew made the effort to come and see me, making me realise just how many friends I had.

The next morning I learned that there would be two consultants looking after me, both orthopaedic surgeons. Mr Colin Howie, a tweed-clad Scot with a bushy moustache, was to provide general help and advice but took little active role in my treatment. On that first morning he looked out of the window at the hills on the skyline and promised me that I could be back up there by the summer. I doubted it.

He also took a look at my medication list. 'I see you've been taking a sleeping pill,' he said. 'Don't you think that a draught of whisky would do the trick better? And once you're up and about, a trip or two down to the pub would help things feel more like normal.'

I readily agreed, and in my mind I conjured up the image of a glass of twelve-year-old malt. That night, when the nurse fed me cheap whisky from a plastic cup, my dream was shattered as the rough alcohol just about floored me in my weakened state. But at least I began to sleep well after that.

Mr Roddy MacDonald was to be more directly involved in my treatment. He had a close look at my stumps. The two right stumps were healing up nicely but the two left ones still hadn't been closed. Mr MacDonald explained that I had the option of having the bones trimmed back further, or having plastic surgery. He was in favour of trimming as, in his opinion, they would still be long enough for the successful fitting of prostheses.

Anxious for my stumps to heal as quickly as possible, I was happy to go along with his suggestion. A date later that week was set for the revision of my stumps. Mr MacDonald reckoned on a minimum of six weeks from the operation to the fitting of prosthetic legs—six weeks that I was impatient to see swiftly through.

Other people who arrived at the foot of my bed were of more immediate assistance. Doreen Falls, an experienced physiotherapy assistant, was to oversee the various issues regarding my mobility. Later on she would help me learn to walk on my prosthetic legs; at this stage she taught me to get about on my bum. So far, I had mostly lain or sat in whatever position the nurses put me, helpless as a rag doll. Doreen showed me how I could 'walk' on my bottom, by shifting first one cheek then the other. I soon became an expert at this bum-walking. She also showed me how to bum-walk backwards off my bed into a wheelchair, which gave me a great deal of freedom.

The person who was able to give me the greatest amount of freedom on my first full day, however, was my occupational therapist, Helen Scott, who had a vast amount of experience in helping people with upper-limb deficiencies. When she asked what I most wanted to do for myself, I had no hesitation in replying, 'Feed myself.'

Helen took a measurement of my right stump and went off. She came back at dinner time, with a small nylon strap into which the handle of a spoon could be inserted. Helen fastened the strap with Velcro round my forearm and slotted in a spoon. With a little practice I found I could scoop up a spoonful of soup and bring it to my mouth. I was absolutely delighted as, unassisted, I slurped my way through the rest of the soup.

Over the coming days I practised my strap technique. Using my left stump, I could fiddle the strap into position on my right arm. With my teeth, I could then fasten the Velcro. Holding the bowl of the spoon with my left stump, I eventually managed to push the handle into the sleeve on the strap. It worked equally well with a fork. If I used my left stump to control the fork, I found I could manipulate my food effectively. Soon I was eating all by myself, only getting help to have my food cut up. Consequently I began to eat a lot more.

I naively considered my strap to be a stopgap solution before I got my hands. To this day, though, I still eat with a strap, which I carry in my pocket. It's small, reliable, it doesn't run on batteries, and if I forget it I can always use one of Anna's hairbands or an elastic band.

My mailbag was still bursting every day and I soon had cards and pictures covering every available space on the walls of my room. My tape player from Chamonix was reinstalled, a television set appeared from somewhere and a friend brought in a video recorder. Life in the hospital was pretty easy, my every need being taken care of. It was not fulfilling, though, and while I could easily have filled my days with books, television and videos, I was keen to get on with the business of learning how to live all over again.

I had the operation to trim back my two left limbs on Friday, February 25. Beforehand, a young female doctor came to give me my preoperative anaesthetic.

'When you wake up from the op you'll be on morphine,' she said. 'The flow of the drug is controlled by a machine that delivers a dose each time you press a button, so we need to figure out a way for you to push the button.'

Together we examined several different operating mechanisms and the one we judged the best for me was a rubber bulb that I could squeeze between my two stumps. When I struggled woozily into consciousness after the operation, I saw the bulb hanging over me as arranged. The only trouble was that my left arm was hooked up to the drip and I couldn't move it. As the pain grew, all I could do was bat at the bulb with my right stump before shouting for a nurse.

BEFORE TOO LONG I was once again free from drips and machines, and I soon became quite mobile. The hospital supplied me with an electric wheelchair and my horizons expanded to include the whole of the building, although I quickly discovered there wasn't much to see.

Another benefit of my increased mobility was that I could begin physio. My body was by now shockingly feeble and I was going to have to work hard if I was to ever get fit. My physiotherapist, Joy, did her best to motivate me.

At first, she got me to lie on my back and push down hard with my knees to get my quads working again. That and a few other static exercises, such as buttock clenches, I could do on my own. Other dynamic exercises I could only do during my daily physio sessions.

As soon as my stumps were well enough to take a little rough treatment, Joy would strap physio weights—nylon bags filled with lead shot—to my stumps using crepe bandages. I could then do various arm and leg-raising exercises. We did other exercises with an elastic physio band. Joy attached one end of the elastic to my bed and the other to my stumps. I could then pull against the stretch of the elastic.

At first I found this light physio work quite exhausting, and my muscles would be left quivering after each session. After a while, however, I got used to it and looked forward to my daily workouts.

When I was mobile enough to get into the wheelchair, we had sessions in the physio room, where we did ball rolling and throwing games on the floor to improve my upper-body strength and coordination. I soon learned to catch the balls between my two stumps. One of my favourite exercises was the wobble board, a circular board supported by a half-ball underneath. The idea is to stand or kneel on the board and gently rock back and forth. All the muscles in your legs, abdomen and lower back have to work together as you struggle to find your balance. With practice, you can balance without letting the edges touch the floor. At first I just sat on the board, but as my stumps healed I managed to stand up on my knees. Then Joy would throw balls for me to catch while I tried to remain in balance, feeling like a performing seal.

On the whole, I enjoyed life at the PMR. All the staff were friendly and my room was pleasant. However, one aspect of hospital life I didn't take to was the food, which was bland and mass-produced.

To make matters worse I was visited by a dietician, who poked and prodded and told me I was dangerously underweight. 'I want you to eat as much fatty food as possible,' she said. 'I'm going to give you a carton of cream every day to put on your breakfast cereal and puddings.'

Every slimmer's dream, I thought, to be given these instructions but I couldn't work up the appetite for it. Forcing the cream down made me feel sick.

The dietician also wanted to add build-up drinks to my diet—three a day. I detested these milkshake-like drinks and after a while rebelled completely and stopped eating all of my food supplements.

Fortunately, our flat was only ten minutes' drive away, so a couple of times a week Anna would cook me a fantastic meal at home then drive it to the hospital in an insulated bag. Anna's meals on wheels, plus the occasional takeaway pizza, helped supplement the regular hospital food, and I slowly began to gain weight.

IN THE EARLY DAYS, one of the major limitations to my rehabilitation was the fact that my limbs were swaddled in bandages, making the manipulation of objects difficult. However, I could push things about, and even accomplish fine-control tasks such as turning the pages of a newspaper, although usually not without a good deal of frustration.

Most task learning was driven by simple necessity. If I wanted my drink moved closer or my pillows rearranged and there was no nurse available, I would have to do it myself. I even found I could operate the remote control for the television. The buttons were small but a few carefully aimed stabs would usually produce the desired audio-visual adjustments.

These skills were a great help to me, but it was clear that things could only start properly once the bandages came off. Fortunately I was a fast healer and my scars quickly began to seal up. One by one, my stumps had their stitches removed and I began the process of becoming accustomed to my new arms.

Helen was also intent on seeing that my new arms became accustomed to me and to whatever I might do with them. This was called desensitisation, she explained, and was very important. She began to rub a piece of cotton wool over one of my stumps. I pulled my arm back, cringing as every nerve fired in confusion. Tingling pulses shot down my forearm, sending a shiver down my back. Helen grabbed my arm again and continued with her bizarre torture. It felt like fingernails were being scraped down a dozen blackboards all at once.

Eventually Helen put away the cotton wool and produced a rubber mallet. She then proceeded to rap the most sensitive part of my stump in short sharp blows. Shock waves pulsed down my arm, sending it jerking about uncontrollably. Just when she knew I could take no more, Helen dropped my arm and moved across to the other one. Only when she had left me a quivering wreck, did she relent.

As a parting shot she set me some homework. 'I want you to rub your stumps on any surface that's available,' she said, 'to toughen them up. Your bedclothes, the edge of your table, anything to help them get used to everyday life.'

Helen arrived the next day with her little box of toys, and the day after that. Gradually the sensations in my stumps lessened, although Helen graduated from cotton wool to towelling to dimpled rubber, until she was eventually rubbing sandpaper on my unfortunate limbs. Nowadays my stumps are as tough as my elbows.

With my stumps free from bandages, I was able to try a greater variety of tasks. Helen got me to pick up a jug from the table and pour out a glass of water. This I did, carefully clasping the jug between my shaking stumps.

'Again!' said Helen, and the water-pouring continued until she was satisfied that I had mastered that task, then we moved on to the next.

I tried dressing myself. It didn't take an inordinate amount of practice before I was able to pull on simple loose-fitting clothes like T-shirts, boxer shorts and jogging bottoms. As soon as I was able to, I sacked the nurses from this particular task, pleased to have taken another small step on the road to self-sufficiency.

Helen wheeled me into the bathroom to have a look at the challenges that faced me there. I didn't have an electric toothbrush, so I thought I might as well try my manual version. It seemed pretty impossible to grip the small plastic handle between my stumps and vibrate it in a satisfactory manner, but Helen encouraged me to continue. I found that with a bit of fumbling I could bring it to more or less any desired angle and hold it fairly steadily between my stumps. Then, by shaking my head up and down and from side to side, I managed to give my teeth a slow but rigorous scrub. It seemed unworkably awkward at first and, to begin with, the whole business, including squeezing the paste onto my brush, would take over ten minutes. Every day, though, the task became a fraction easier, until one day I found that it took me no more time than anyone else. I sacked the nurses from this task too.

Flushed with the success of the toothbrush, Helen and I turned our attention to shaving. We thought at first that I might be able to manage a normal razor, but soon found that I couldn't manoeuvre it to all areas of my face at the correct angle.

From a catalogue containing products designed for people with reduced limb function, Helen ordered a razor mounted onto a universal joint that strapped into the user's palm. When it arrived she removed the existing strap and replaced it with one that would fit my stump. As with the tooth-brushing, shaving seemed impossible at first. I would shave a small patch of beard, only to find that none of the rest of my face was in reach. I got there eventually, however. So the nurses lost another job.

Since I had been able to get into the shower chair, I had been having a shower every morning, the nurse on duty washing me in the chair. When I felt confident enough, I asked the nurses to put the soap, shampoo and flannel next to me, turn on the shower, and leave me alone. I would then have plenty of fun juggling with the soap and trying to reach every part of my body with the flannel. I was soon managing quite well. I could reach my left armpit with my right stump but, frustratingly, not my right armpit with my shorter left stump. So, holding the flannel in my teeth, I swung it into my armpit and clamped my arm over it. Still with my teeth, I would then pull the flannel out, giving the armpit a good wash on the way.

It embarrasses me somewhat to write about going to the toilet, but I know that's the question to which everyone wants an answer. I was anxious to find an answer myself, not wanting to spend the rest of my life having my bum wiped for me. Mr MacDonald and Mr Howie had both vaguely reassured me that there were 'ways round the problem', and had left it at that, leaving the nitty-gritty to the occupational therapists.

Helen wasn't so reserved. 'What about the bottom, Jamie?' she would enquire. 'Any progress?'

Luckily my right stump is long enough to reach the crucial area so it was a case of finding some way of attaching toilet paper to my stump, and being able to release it once finished.

Helen came up with the idea of using an elastic band, which I would put onto my wrist with my teeth. Then, holding the band out with my teeth, I would push a corner of my length of toilet paper under it. This would hold the paper in place until the job was done.

As time went by, I was able to dispense with the elastic band, so now I can use any loo without need of special equipment.

It took many weeks to master all these self-care issues, but once I had I was almost completely independent in the bathroom. I began to feel for the first time that I might lead a relatively normal existence.

Helen was keen to see that I could manage all the other little operations one comes across day-to-day. Opening and closing doors was a great favourite. I found I could manage most door handles so long as they weren't too stiff, and pulling the door open wasn't much of a problem. A key in a lock was trickier. I could manage only if the key was quite big and the lock well oiled.

We also spent a lot of time in the department's kitchen, trying to operate kettles and tin-openers, wash dishes, and that sort of thing. I must admit that I had less enthusiasm for this kind of chore.

Anna, too, was struggling to adjust to the changes in her life. Before the accident, she, Jamie and I had lived together. Now Anna was in the flat on her own, the door to Jamie's room firmly closed, the rest of the flat cold and empty. Often Anna would go round to her parents' house, not wanting to sleep on her own.

She worked for a software-testing company in Edinburgh. After we returned from France she was signed off work by her doctor on grounds of stress. Eventually she did return part-time, going into work in the mornings and coming to the hospital in the afternoons. She came to see me every day, which was fantastic.

On the days I felt I was making no progress, Anna would always manage to cheer me up. On the days when she felt that everything was black, I would try to do the same for her. Together we found we were stronger and life didn't seem quite so hard. But we were worried about financial difficulties. I obviously wasn't able to work, Anna was only working part-time, and of course we no longer received rent for the spare room. The bills still had to be paid, however, so we were relieved when my insurance company paid out a lump sum big enough to tide us over for a while.

My two bosses, Gordon and Alan, also helped. It was obvious that my career as a rope access worker had come to an abrupt end, but they were good enough to keep me on full pay for as long as I was in hospital and assured me that there would always be a job available for me in the Web office. This was a great weight off our minds.

IT WAS A red-letter day when my fold-up wheelchair arrived. The hospital chair was too big to fit into Anna's car and too heavy for her to lift, but the new model was much more manageable, opening up the possibility of trips outside the hospital.

On our first trip we decided to go to the recently opened Museum of Scotland. It felt strange driving through the streets of Edinburgh on a normal Saturday morning. I found myself staring at people as they went about their business. It was as if I'd been away for years on a long journey, returning home to find nothing altered, but discovering that it was myself that had changed beyond recognition.

In fact, Edinburgh was a greatly changed place when viewed from our new perspective. I was shocked by how poorly facilitated the city is for something as fundamental as a wheelchair. Pavements are uneven, kerbs rise up like brick walls and public buildings are guarded by staircases. Fortunately, the new Museum of Scotland was an excellently built modern building, and I thoroughly enjoyed whizzing round the polished concrete floors.

We made an effort to go on excursions every weekend, and wherever we went I was surprised to discover that people in the street knew who I was. One lad came up to me and said, 'You're that boy off the moontain, int ye? You're doin' magic, pal!' before swaggering off with a grin.

It was at this stage that I started having to deal with the reactions of strangers. I noticed people staring at me, and small children would often embarrass their parents by asking in a loud voice, 'Mum, why's that man got no hands?' Others would turn to Anna and ask her if I needed any help. I'd heard of this 'Does he take sugar?' reaction to disabled people, but was quite shocked by the reality. I concluded that the best thing I could do was to try not to be embarrassed. In general I found people to be incredibly generous and willing to bend over backwards to help me out. It was quite spiriting to receive all this support and it helped me to feel a little better about myself.

Now that I was more mobile, I thought back to what Mr Howie had said about going to the pub. It sounded very attractive, so Anna and I put the word round that evening visiting time on Wednesdays would be held at the new venue of the Steading Inn. This was a runaway success—the Steading didn't know what had hit it.

On my first visit I was bought a pint and was immediately confronted with the problem of how to drink it. Someone fetched a straw and I tried that, but did not enjoy being compared to a fifteen-year-old who'd heard you could get drunk quicker that way. So I discarded the straw and tried to pick the pint up between my stumps. I was terrified that the glass would slip at any moment, but I managed to bring it to my lips, take a sip and place it carefully down again. I have been drinking beer like this ever since. It is, of course, a technique that requires plenty of regular practice.

I had all of two pints that first night and I was feeling quite drunk when Anna delivered me back to the hospital. My drunkenness on Wednesday nights increased as I built up to three or even four pints, and in my dishevelled state I was a great amusement to the night nurses. On several occasions, on leaving the wheelchair to get into bed, I toppled hopelessly onto the floor. Once, I managed to bring Anna down with me. One of the nurses walked into the room to find the two of us rolling on the floor in fits of laughter.

TWO GENTLEMEN knocked on my door one morning and introduced themselves as Rob Farley and Bill Douglas, biomechanical engineers. It was their job to modify or design any nonstandard items of equipment that might be useful to me in my rehabilitation.

I had been experimenting with pushing myself about in my wheelchair. I couldn't reach the wheel rims, with which a user would normally propel the chair, but I could get some purchase on the rubber tyres with my forearms. The trouble was, the skin on my arms would get raw and I needed something to protect it. Rob and Bill made me a pair of leather driving gloves that slipped over my stumps and fastened with Velcro, thus extending my range in the chair.

I was also keen to operate a computer so I could get on with some correspondence. The solution was fairly simple: Helen made a couple more Velcro straps, one for each stump, and the biomechanics made rubber-tipped, steel-wire probes, which slotted into the straps and stuck out like index fingers. I could then manage two-fingered typing as well as I ever had. I could operate a normal mouse reasonably with my stumps, the tracker-ball type even more so. All of a sudden I was computer-capable and, once Anna had installed an old laptop in my room, I began the huge task of writing letters of thanks to everyone who had written to me.

I was still having difficulty turning keys in locks, and had the idea of a lever with a slot in it, which might be fitted over the head of any key. I described my idea to Rob and Bill and they made it for me out of stainless-steel wire. When I received my key lever, Helen whisked me off on a tour of the hospital to unlock and relock every cupboard and storeroom we could find. Another success for the bio boys.

NOW THAT MY ARMS were well enough healed, I started receiving treatment from my upper-limb prosthetist, Malcolm Griffiths. Malcolm, it turned out, was a keen hillwalker, so we had something in common, and he was encouraging about my chances of getting back into the hills one day.

First, though, we looked at my immediate requirements. I had been expecting Malcolm simply to make me some fully functioning prosthetic hands and so was surprised when he looked to me to tell him what I required. Obviously I wanted a pair of computer-controlled robotic arms, but Malcolm was quick to rein in my science-fiction fantasies. It would, he said, be better to create something simpler.

I was still getting to grips with feeding myself with my strap and a fork, and wondered if Malcolm could come up with a way for me to use a knife. He began work on my first prosthesis right away by taking a plaster-cast mould of my right arm, and the next day returned with a laminated plastic socket, which fitted snugly over my stump. Together we then estimated the correct angle at which a knife should be fitted, and Malcolm went away to add a further lamination with a slot that would accommodate a knife handle. He also fitted a slot on the underside that would take a fork or a spoon.

The knife worked well and I could awkwardly cut up meat or toast with it. I never got into the habit of using it much, however, the whole device being so much less portable than my little strap.

Helen had learned that I was destined for an office job and was keen to develop my stationery-handling skills. So I was whisked back to the occupational therapy department, where filing cabinets were opened and closed, papers were shuffled, folded and stapled and stamps were licked and stuck, until I began to think I didn't fancy working in an office after all.

Another skill I had to remaster was handwriting. Helen and I soon found that my feeding strap could be put to the purpose. I rotated it round my wrist and put a pen—one with free-flowing ink—in the sleeve. Then, by moving my arm across the paper, I could write. The results were illegible at first, but after Helen had made me write my lines a few hundred times I could produce a decipherable scrawl.

As my scrawling improved, my handwriting took shape in exactly the same form as before my accident. Some people even reckoned that it was slightly improved. It just goes to show that handwriting style is a function of the brain, not of the hand.

I WAS NOW surpassing my wildest expectations in relearning everyday skills that I was certain I had lost for ever. Who would have believed that, so soon after such a debilitating accident, I would be feeding myself, washing, dressing, shaving and even going to the pub? I still felt frustratingly immobile, though. More than anything I wanted to be able to walk.

Morag Marks, my lower-limb prosthetist, threw herself into the task with enthusiasm. With me, she was faced not only with the usual difficulty of producing comfortable and functional legs, but also with the additional problem of finding a way for me to put the legs on and take them off. Contrary to my initial speculation, it transpired that prosthetic limbs are not screwed directly into bones, but designed to be attached and removed at will.

Morag reckoned that the Iceross system, manufactured by an Icelandic company, might do the trick. The Iceross is a silicone rubber sleeve that fits tightly onto a stump. It is stored inside-out and is donned by rolling it onto the user's leg. Morag was hopeful that I would be able to roll the Iceross on and off using my arms.

Protruding from the bottom end of the sleeve is a two-inch ratchet pin that holds the prosthetic leg on. The leg consists of a pressure-moulded carbon-fibre socket that encloses the stump up to just below knee level, attached to the bottom of which are the various foot components. When the stump is pressed into the socket, the ratchet pin engages, locking the whole assembly into place. The pin is released by depressing a small button on the outside of the socket.

At this stage Morag just wanted me to get used to the Iceross on its own, wearing the sleeve for only an hour at a time. She left me with my Iceross and Doreen took charge of seeing that I practised with it. In the beginning, it was distinctly uncomfortable, and when it was pulled off pools of sweat would trickle out. My skin became red and irritated, and I began to feel depressed about having my legs wrapped in plastic every day for the rest of my life. Gradually, however, the discomfort grew less until I found I could wear my sleeve for hours at a time. Eventually I found I could roll the sleeve on and off if Doreen got it started for me, but it was to be many months before I could manage by myself.

The next stage in getting me up and walking again was the use of early walking aids, called PPAM (Pneumatic Post Amputation Mobility) Aids. The idea is to get the patient using their walking muscles as soon as possible after amputation, before the muscles atrophy and the sense of balance deteriorates. It is not really possible to walk far on early walking aids, but at least they get you moving about.

The PPAM Aid consists of a large inflatable rubber sock that envelops the whole leg and, as the sock is inflated round the leg, expands into a metal frame that gives the device its rigidity. On the base is a rocker acting as a simple foot.

For the first couple of sessions, Doreen insisted that I just sit with the inflatable balloon on my right leg. Then we put the complete device on my right leg with just the balloon on my left. Eventually, Doreen got the tallest, widest Zimmer frame she could lay her hands on and fitted it with arm gutters. She jacked my bed up so I could place my stumps in the gutters, bound them in place with crepe bandage—and I was ready to stand up.

I took a deep breath and heaved. It was a huge struggle, but suddenly I was upright and looking around from a new perspective. After two months spent lying or sitting, it felt very strange. All the ward staff who crowded in to see the spectacle were amazed to discover how tall I was. They were used to a skinny wee wretch and had assumed I was quite short, but now I towered over all of them.

Soon, the pressure on my stump grew too much and I was forced to sit down. The next day I managed a few short hops and the next I hobbled out into the ward, pushing my Zimmer in front of me. I was jubilant that I was starting to walk again.

At about the same time, I discovered while doing physio that I could also walk about on my knees. This was all very well on the soft physio mats, but I couldn't do it on the harder carpet and lino in my room. I needed to find a way of cushioning my knees.

Weeks before, Doreen had given me a pair of elbow muffs, to protect my elbows when getting in and out of wheelchairs. I didn't use them much, so I got one of the nurses to strap them onto my knees, then lowered myself onto the floor and gingerly took a couple of steps. The muffs offered just enough cushioning to allow me to walk.

Suddenly I could get about my room, and I felt a lot more independent. I also discovered I could go up and down stairs.

One Sunday Anna and I visited Edinburgh's Dean Gallery, which had just opened its doors to the public. Unfortunately they hadn't yet opened their wheelchair access doors to the disabled minority. Determined not to be defeated, I slid out of the chair, and crawled up the half-dozen stairs on my knees, much to the shock of the extremely apologetic entrance staff.

I subsequently asked Rob and Bill if they could make me knee-pads that were more heavy-duty. They duly obliged and I was then able to cover even greater distances on my knees.

ONE AFTERNOON Juliette Snow came to visit me. She was the only person I'd ever met who wore an artificial leg and I was very keen to hear her experiences of using it. Juliette had lost her right leg to cancer as a teenager and had been ill for a long time. Consequently, she had been relatively inactive as an amputee for several years. Now she regularly went hillwalking, rock climbing, canoeing and sailing. I was particularly impressed with her hillwalking exploits as, at that stage, even the thought of walking to the far end of the ward made my knees feel weak.

Juliette showed me her leg and I was surprised how much it resembled a well-used piece of sporting equipment. Multi-coloured and decorated with stickers, its carbon-fibre, plastic and titanium components were covered in scuffs and scratches, the scars of the tough life through which Juliette obviously put it. I hadn't expected something that looked quite so cool.

I received another surprise visitor one day—Cyril Wire, the 82-year-old who had lost his hands. I had recently written to thank him for his letter and to let him know how I was getting on. He was so impressed he had driven from Glasgow to meet me in person.

Cyril had lost both arms in a railway accident when he was sixteen, but this hadn't stopped him leading a full life. He was married with children, had studied painting at the Glasgow School of Art and had gone on to become an art teacher. Tall, thin and smartly dressed, he might have appeared like any other old man, were it not that his right arm was completely missing, and where his left hand should have been he had a fearsome-looking metal hook. With this one hook, Cyril managed every task in his life.

He was keen to show me how the hook worked and I was just as keen to learn. The hook itself was split down its length into two halves. One half was fixed and the other was hinged at the base to form a gripper, which was attached by a nylon wire running under

Cyril's arm onto a harness secured to his opposite shoulder. By a subtle combination of movements of his shoulders and his arm, Cyril could open and close the split hook at will. Using it, he could tie his shoelaces, button his shirt, hold a cup, paint, drive and do a hundred other tasks. I was extremely impressed.

That night, as I went to sleep, I thought about Cyril and Juliette. Cyril seemed to manage, I thought. No, more than manage—he did incredibly well for himself. He had significantly less upper-limb function than me and yet he still got on with it and lived his life. And Juliette—she had to live with one artificial leg, but she didn't let that stop her. I was just going to have to do the same. Everything I wanted to do was possible—they and hundreds of other amputees had already proved that. I just had the task of learning to overcome all my difficulties at once. It would take time, but, for the first time, I felt truly confident that I could get there.

Compared to the difficulties so many thousands of others cope with, I really had little to complain about. I could be paraplegic, or blind, or suffering from some incurable degenerative disease. So many handicaps can afflict the human body and mind. I merely had to cope with the loss of my hands and feet.

People seemed impressed with the way in which I had learned to write on the computer. Jean-Dominique Bauby, completely paralysed by a stroke, wrote an entire book, *The Diving-Bell and the Butterfly*, by blinking one eyelid. What I had to do was easy.

MALCOLM DECIDED that it was time for me to have my first mechanical arm. We got messy with the plaster of Paris one morning, and he went away with a perfect cast of my left arm. It took several fittings of the plastic socket he made from the cast, but a week later I was presented with my very own arm, complete with super-shiny titanium split-hook. Eagerly, I tried it on. First, a thin sock went over my stump, then the socket itself. Finally I had to don the shoulder harness that operated the hook. By swinging the harness behind my back, I found I could catch the harness loop with my right stump and shrug it on like a jacket. Now I was ready to go.

At rest, the hook was closed. If I pushed the prosthetic arm forward, holding the opposite shoulder still, the hook opened. With more complex combinations of movements of my arms, shoulders and back, I discovered I could open and close the hook at will. The motion quickly becomes intuitive, like steering a bike or catching a ball.

I was immediately able to complete simple operations like picking things up. With more care, I found I could manage delicate tasks such as turning the pages of a book. Malcolm explained how the split-hook tool had been developed over many years by generations of amputees, and was considered to be the most versatile device available. He left me to practise with my new arm.

Helen came back to see me. If anything, she was even more excited than I was. She began gathering up assorted objects and scattering them over the bed and floor. Diligently I retrieved the discarded books, tumblers and playing cards, and put them back in their proper places.

Then we turned to more complex tasks—holding cutlery, drinking from a glass, unwrapping sweets. I managed these operations, but all of them I could do already, with my bare stumps. With the prosthetic arm they felt more awkward, less secure. To give an example: with my two stumps I could now pick up and pour from my water jug. If I held the jug in my hook, however, it would slip when I tried to pour.

The main difficulty was perception. The sense of touch plays a crucial role in the subtle art of holding and manipulating. Millions of nerve endings, just below the surface of the skin, are constantly feeding back information to the spinal cord and the brain, allowing the muscles to react instantly to each infinitesimal shift in balance and weight. My prosthetic arm had no nerve endings in it, hence the slips. My stumps, while perhaps not possessing nerve endings in the same concentration as fingertips, were still very sensitive, which was why I was enjoying success in my efforts to relearn many delicate tasks.

As time passed, I found I tended to put my arm aside while doing a difficult task, and I gradually used it less and less. I asked both Helen and Malcolm what they thought. Perhaps I wasn't trying hard enough? They gave the same advice: just do what comes naturally. Every amputee has different needs and finds different ways of doing things. There are no hard and fast rules.

I felt happier once I'd grasped that I didn't have to use my artificial arm. I realised also that the progress I was making with my stumps wasn't just a temporary measure; it would stand me in good stead for the rest of my life. I began to take pride in all the things I could do with just my stumps. If a normal person could do something with their hands, I wanted to do it too.

Helen showed me various devices that helped to open jam jars. All of them were complex, unwieldy things, except for one: a sheet of sticky rubber. You press the rubber onto the lid of the jar and it gives you all the grip you need. I found that, by pressing down on the lid with the flesh of my stump and twisting, I could open even the stiffest of lids. Eventually I dispensed with the rubber and can now open jam jars as easily as anyone else.

Similarly, with corkscrews and tin-openers, I have learned to use the normal mechanical items found in anyone's cutlery drawer.

Throughout this period of relearning everyday tasks, I found myself re-examining the very nature of how we pick objects up and hold them. I hadn't thought about it before, having just left my hands to get on with it, but now I realised that many other parts of my body could be put into service. Obviously my stumps, as a pair, were doing the bulk of my object-manoeuvring work, but singly, too, I found them to be useful. Items could be held in an armpit or between stump and chest, thus freeing up the other stump. I was delighted one evening in the Steading when someone bought me a glass of champagne and I discovered that the stem fitted neatly into the crook of my elbow, allowing me to hold the glass and drink with one arm.

My mouth was now an indispensable tool, my teeth being excellent grippers, and my lips very expert at manipulating small objects. My knees, too, proved useful for holding objects firmly. In fact any part of the body that can be opposed against another part, or a surface, can be useful in picking up, holding and manipulating objects. Fingers are not indispensable. They are just a luxury.

AT EASTER, Anna and I were invited to Perthshire. I felt nervous and excited about spending my first night out of hospital in ten weeks.

We enjoyed a fine, relaxing Saturday evening with our friends Chris Pasteur and Jane Herries, during which I demonstrated at great length my new-found confidence with a stemmed wineglass.

After breakfast on Sunday we went for a walk in the countryside, and my chair wallahs had a great time wheeling me through all sorts of unsuitably rough terrain. It was so nice being out with friends, just doing normal things. But by the time Anna dropped me back at the hospital that evening I was utterly exhausted.

Helen came to see me one morning soon after with the good news that I was to be taken on a 'home visit'. She and two other occupational therapists wanted to accompany me on a tour of my flat to ascertain whether I would have any special requirements.

A couple of days later I was picked up by ambulance and driven across town to my flat, where Anna and the OTs were waiting. The ambulance men lifted me upstairs on a special carrying chair. I was supposed to go round the flat in my wheelchair, but I immediately shunned that and hopped down onto my knees.

It felt strange to be home again. I shuffled into each room, poking into every corner in search of changes, but everything was the same. The place even smelt warmly familiar.

The OTs wanted to see me open every cupboard door, flick every switch, turn on the oven, operate the taps. Anna took the opportunity to cook me a proper quality fry-up, and I sat down at the kitchen table to enjoy it, leaving the OTs to discuss anti-slip mats in the bathroom.

After the success of our Perthshire trip, Anna and I received a flood of dinner invitations. It was great to get out of the hospital in the evenings and it was even better not to have to eat hospital food. Most places were on the ground floor, but when we went to have dinner with Ruth and Ulric Jessop, who live in a second-floor flat, Ulric simply picked me up and carried me up the stairs. I felt slightly embarrassed about being lumped around like a sack of coal, but it was worth it in order to get out and about.

I wanted to spend more time at home now, but not having a pair of ambulance men at my disposal and with Anna not being of quite the same build as Ulric, the stairs were a major obstacle. Resourcefully, she borrowed a spare carrying chair from the hospital and arranged for friends to help cart me up and down the two flights of stairs.

I arrived home triumphantly one Friday, for the weekend, feeling like royalty in my sedan chair. Anna certainly treated me like a king, spoiling me rotten with all my favourite food. She made sure I wasn't short of company, and invited friends for dinner on Saturday.

On Sunday, with some chair-carrying help from the neighbours, we went out to the cinema. On entering the darkened theatre, Anna parked me at the edge of the central aisle and took a seat beside me. Halfway through the film an usher said I was an obstruction. I was furious, but we couldn't make a fuss in the middle of the film, so we allowed the woman to direct us to a space at the back of the theatre where there was room for my chair but no seat for Anna. We did our best to enjoy the rest of the film and saved our complaint for later.

When I returned to my hospital room that evening, I felt odd. I'd had an excellent weekend but I was glad to be back in my nice, safe room. It felt so much more secure than the outside world. I realised I was getting institutionalised. I would have to leave hospital soon.

THROUGHOUT THIS TIME, I was being troubled by phantom limb sensation. It had started back in Chamonix some days after I'd been amputated. As the numbness of the operations wore off, I began to feel strange sensations in the ends of my stumps. To be more precise, I began to feel them *beyond* the ends of my stumps. It seemed bizarre, but in the air where my hands and feet used to be, I could feel the missing appendages. My hands were clenched into tight hot fists, and I occasionally panicked because I couldn't unclench them. The more I willed the invisible fingers to uncurl, the more acutely aware of their paralysis I became.

My feet, also, were apparently still in place, because I had pins and needles in my toes. Worse still, I would have shooting pains, as if I'd been stabbed with a knitting needle. I could always tell exactly where I'd been stabbed—sometimes in my big toe, sometimes under the arch of my foot. The stabbing would set me flinching uncontrollably for a few seconds until the pain subsided.

Dr Marsigny had assured me it was quite normal. These were phantom pains, the severed nerves in my limbs sending confused messages back to the brain. How long would it last? I asked him. He had shrugged. Perhaps for ever.

Having treated many amputees, Mr MacDonald had more experience of phantom sensations. He explained how they could take many different forms. Some people had the clear sensation of the missing limb, floating in the space where it should have been. Others felt sensations of hot and cold, tingling and prickling. Worse still, some people suffered constant pain—pain made worse by the fact that it had no tangible source and so could not be treated.

I asked Mr MacDonald if there was anything that could be done. Lots of things had been tried, he said. Some surgeons attempted to trim back the offending nerves, but invariably it just shifted the trouble elsewhere. Nerve pain isn't treated effectively with normal painkillers, but other drugs give some relief. However, the most important weapon in the battle against phantom limb sensations, Mr MacDonald insisted, was the mind. While I was stuck in a hospital bed, with little else to focus on, it was easy for the pain to become amplified out of proportion. Once I was up and about, thinking about other things, it would become less significant.

Some sensations I didn't particularly mind. I would often sit on the edge of a chair and swing my legs just above the floor, which gave me the peculiar feeling of moving my feet through solid matter. If someone sat down on the end of my bed where I thought my feet were, I would yelp with the anticipation of a pain that never arrived. My hand sensations developed in a different way, however. At first I imagined hands beyond the end of my stumps, and would often miss when reaching for something. Gradually, though, the tight fists of my

Top left: the long hard slog up Ben Nevis—the first hard test of Jamie's new legs and specially adapted equipment.
Top right: ice climbing with prosthetic ice axes.
Above: with Anna, triumphant on the summit of Ben Nevis.
Bottom left: setting out with Manu Cauchy to climb the Cosmiques Arête on the Aiguille du Midi.

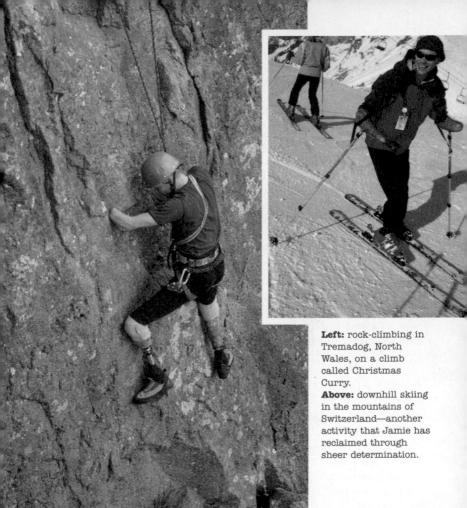

Left: rock-climbing in Tremadog, North Wales, on a climb called Christmas Curry.

Above: downhill skiing in the mountains of Switzerland—another activity that Jamie has reclaimed through sheer determination.

Left: Anna and Jamie, enjoying a holiday in the mountains of northern Spain.

phantom hands receded, until eventually they were actually inside my stumps, shrunken into little balls. When I was tired or hot they would throb intolerably, and there was nothing I could do except shake them above my head to relieve the pressure of the blood.

These distractions were trivial, however, compared to the pain I felt in my leg stumps. The tingling I had originally felt grew into severe needling, punctuated with regular stabs of pain, especially in the left leg. I found the best way to alleviate this was to elevate the stumps and keep them moving, and I developed the peculiar habit of lying on my back and jiggling my legs about like an upturned beetle.

I was certain the pain was mind-based rather than physiological, because it seemed to disappear at night when I went to sleep, but in the daytime I couldn't seem to defeat it mentally. None of the drugs I tried had any effect either. So Mr MacDonald suggested electric current therapy. He brought me a TENS machine, a small battery-powered box with a couple of flat electrodes on wires, which sends an electric current through the skin to interrupt the signals between the nerves and the brain. With the electrodes taped close to the source of pain and the current turned up high, the machine genuinely eased the discomfort for a while, but it always crept back.

I began to think the pain was something I would have to live with.

IN EARLY APRIL Morag made me my first leg, using a pressure-casting system called Icex. It was quite an entertaining business.

First Morag helped me into the Iceross. Then a stump sock went on, for comfort, and the whole leg was wrapped in cling film. Next, a black Lycra sleeve was pulled on, and cushioned pads stuck to all the bony and sensitive areas of my stump.

The Icex comes vacuum packed and rolled up like a giant black condom. Apart from the circular metal base to which the foot components are attached, it is made of a braided carbon-fibre fabric impregnated with an epoxy resin that softens in warm water. Morag took a deep breath, then plunged the Icex into the steaming basin of water. She had three minutes to get everything just right. She frantically unrolled the gently fizzing fabric onto my stump, before hurriedly cutting off the excess material above my knee with a large pair of scissors. Next she rolled a giant rubber balloon over the fabric and, with a fancy-looking bicycle pump, furiously inflated it to the correct pressure. Finally she propped my enormous leg up on a stool.

Inside the balloon I could feel the gentle warmth of the resin setting rock hard. Ten minutes later it was ready, and Morag removed the balloon. Underneath was a perfect grey socket moulded precisely round my stump. The hard part was now to remove the Icex. It took a lot of huffing and puffing before the thing eventually came flying off, sending Morag shooting across to the other side of the room.

She then took the leg off to the workshop to be finished and fitted with a foot. As she left she said, 'What shoe size are you?'

'You can make me any size you want,' I replied smartly.

'I could,' said Morag, 'but I presume you have several pairs of shoes at home that you don't want to have to replace?'

'Oh, yes,' I said sheepishly. 'Size eight.'

The next day Morag brought me my new right leg, with a simple foot attached. It had no moving parts but was slightly springy at the heel and the toe. Morag levered one of my old trainers onto the foot, then helped me put on the Iceross and the new leg. Doreen arrived with the PPAM aid and inflated it over my left stump. With the help of Morag, Doreen and the Zimmer, I cautiously stood up. I carefully transferred my weight from side to side, between the PPAM Aid and the new leg, but found my right stump was still too tender to take all my weight for more than a second.

I tried to put the leg on to show my mum and dad the day after, but I couldn't get it on. It seemed too tight. The following week I cancelled most of my walking sessions because I couldn't get the leg on.

Morag had explained that over the first twelve months an amputee's stumps gradually shrink, as the postoperative swelling subsides and the unused muscle tissue contracts. My stump, however, was expanding, not shrinking. Morag was mystified.

Eventually we realised it must be because of the physio I was doing, which was slowly allowing my muscles to recover their original volume. So, it was back to square one.

A couple of weeks later, Morag decided that my stumps had stabilised and I was ready for another leg. In fact, I was ready for two legs. We paid another couple of visits to the casting room with the inflatable balloon and all the other paraphernalia, and soon Morag had produced a fine-looking pair of legs.

It took a lot of fumbling to get the unfamiliar objects on, but it was immediately obvious that the new right leg was a lot more comfortable than the previous one. The left leg seemed pretty comfortable too.

With Doreen's help, and with my arms in the gutters of the Zimmer frame, I heaved myself onto my new feet and stood there swaying slightly. For the first time I was standing upright on two prosthetic legs. Carefully I eased my body across to the right and allowed the right leg to bear all my weight. Then I did the same with the left leg. Good. Both were capable of supporting me. A bit sore, but bearable.

Slowly, I lifted my right leg an inch or so and brought it forward, placing the foot just in front of the other. I then lifted my left leg. First steps. I rattled the Zimmer forwards a little and repeated it. Before I knew it I was out into the ward and the nurses were gathering to watch.

Doreen said, 'Why don't we take the Zimmer away?'

'I'm not sure I'll manage,' I replied. 'I feel very high up.'

'Nonsense,' insisted Doreen, and she removed the walking frame.

Suddenly I was standing on my artificial legs, with no other support apart from Doreen's hand on the small of my back. I paused a few moments and took a minuscule step forward. Then another.

This was it. I was walking! A big grin spread across my face. It was Tuesday, April 27, three months since I'd last walked upright, ten weeks since I'd woken from a black sleep to find my hands and feet gone, sixty-one days since I'd last gone under the knife, and here I was on my own two feet. I couldn't believe it had happened so quickly.

Fortunately Anna arrived before I tired and was able to watch the spectacle for herself. She took a few photos before I carefully turned round and headed back for my room. By the time I reached my bed I was tired and sore, having walked all of twenty yards.

The following day I made it out of the ward and halfway down the corridor towards the canteen. That evening, I wore the legs to the pub and felt extremely proud of myself when I walked up to the bar and ordered drinks. It was about time I got a round in.

The next step, literally, in learning to walk again, was mastering stairs. Doreen showed me the safe way and I was surprised how easy it was. Facing the rail of a staircase near the ward, I hooked my arms round the steel banisters and stepped sideways up the first step with both feet, before moving my arms up the banister and climbing the next. In this way I crab-walked all the way to the top.

Every day when Anna arrived I was bursting with news of fresh achievements. I spent another weekend at home, and although I couldn't wear my legs for more than about two hours, whenever we went out I put them on so I could walk down the stairs. We took the wheelchair with us, and Anna would push me about for most of the time. We were no longer dependent on anyone else's help.

We spent a lot of time that weekend discussing the future. I could wash, dress, feed and generally look after myself quite well now. My stumps were perfectly healed and I needed no regular medical care.

There seemed to be no reason why I couldn't move back home. The thought of leaving my sheltered bedsit in the hospital scared me, though—which meant it was definitely time for me to go.

I requested an audience with all parties concerned, and Mr Howie, Mr MacDonald, Helen and Doreen gathered in my room. I was prepared to argue my case, but didn't need to. They told me that as far as they were concerned I could go home and attend the limb centre as an outpatient. They would all be available to see me whenever I liked.

I hadn't thought it would be so straightforward. For a minute I toyed with the idea of leaving there and then, but settled for the coming Friday to give myself time to prepare.

I began saying my goodbyes to various nurses and other members of staff who had taken such good care of me over the previous months. I would be sad to leave. The PMR had been my home for ten weeks, and in that time I had made some good friends.

On Friday morning I was summoned to the staff room for a surprise tea party. The nurses had clubbed together and bought me the present they considered most appropriate—a keg of beer. I promised to drink their health in style.

The ambulance turned up early to collect me, and Anna hadn't yet arrived, so I was on my own as the vehicle headed down the road to my flat. I wasn't wearing my legs, and when we got there the ambulance men started unpacking their carrying chair.

'It's all right,' I said. 'I'll manage the stairs on my knees.'

The two men looked slightly shocked, but I was determined not to be carried up my own stairs again and set off on my knees.

The ambulance men left my bags outside the front door and, because I didn't have a key, offered to wait. But I thanked them and sent them on their way. Sitting there, I waited for Anna to return and open the door to the next chapter of our lives.

Part Three: Life On the Outside

On June 16, 1999, twenty or so close friends and family of Jamie Fisher travelled to the Cuillin Hills on the Isle of Skye, where his parents had chosen to scatter his ashes.

We plodded along the coast to an exposed promontory jutting out into the stormy sea, a place where Jamie and I used to come when the mountains were hidden in cloud, to explore the inlets, crags and caves. We gathered in a circle and held a simple service, our voices all but drowned by the crashing of the waves and the roaring of the wind.

We remembered Jamie in silence for a minute, then Jamie's mother produced the casket and we took it in turn to throw handfuls of the ashes into the wind. I watched the stream of fine grey powder as it was carried away through the air and had difficulty relating it to the flesh-and-blood Jamie, so full of laughter and kindness, that I once knew.

That evening I talked with Jamie's older brother, Mat. He and his wife Ayala were living in California, and the first time I had seen them since the accident was on the previous Monday. They had come round to the flat with their newborn son, who had been born two weeks after Jamie died. In honour of the uncle he would never meet, Mat and Ayala named their child Joseph Jamie—JJ for short. JJ was now a beautiful four-month-old little boy, and I could swear he had the same twinkle in his eye that his uncle did.

Jamie's father Stu, his younger brother Robbie and his girlfriend Alice also came round that Monday, and together we went through the sad business of clearing out Jamie's room. He hadn't amassed a great deal in his short life. The most precious items were his library of mountaineering books, and his superb collection of slides, taken throughout his climbing career. We spent a nostalgic couple of hours browsing through them.

In July, Anna and I returned to the Isle of Skye. I was very excited because it was the first trial of my new legs. Morag had made me another pair of Icex sockets, and decided it was time to move up from the simple feet I had been using to a more dynamic pair of 'Flexfeet', made of carbon fibre to allow the user a more active lifestyle.

The first morning on Skye I went with a group of friends on a short walk out to a small tidal island. Things went well to begin with and it was pleasant walking for a couple of kilometres. We descended, with difficulty, a rocky path to the shingle spit that joins the island to the mainland of Skye, and at that point I decided I'd had enough.

Anna and I sat down to eat our lunch while the others explored the island. When they returned, we set off back. Foolishly, I waved the others on, telling them I'd see them in the pub, but as I climbed the rocky path my stumps started screaming with pain. I had to sit down and take the legs off. I could walk no further.

Meanwhile our friends were disappearing into the distance. We shouted, but it was no use. So Anna set off in hot pursuit, and caught them up as they were sitting down to their beers in the pub garden.

Three of the lads abandoned their drinks and kindly jogged all the way back to where I sat, stranded on a rock. They took it in turns to carry me all the way across the moor back to the pub.

In retrospect, I realise I was trying to do too much too soon with my new legs. Fortunately, however, my progress from then on was swift, and I was soon walking better than ever.

In consolation, that evening I got someone to duct-tape a table tennis bat to my right arm and managed to play a very credible game of table tennis. As I had already discovered, simple solutions are nearly always the best—although I might not have agreed with this philosophy while I was having the tape removed from my arm.

WHEN I FIRST LEFT hospital I was able to wear my prosthetic legs for maybe two hours at a stretch and walk no further than 100 metres. Now I could wear the legs all day and walk three or four kilometres before my stumps became too sore. In the car or on the train I took the legs off, and Anna still took the wheelchair with us, but in general I was becoming very mobile and we were out and about all the time.

I was also quite confident with day-to-day life in the flat. Without help, I was able to get up, put on my legs, get dressed, use the bathroom, negotiate the kitchen, use the phone, and generally cope without being a constant demand on Anna.

I was even managing a few household tasks, including hanging up the laundry and wrestling with the vacuum cleaner. One day, I hoped I might even manage washing the dishes. Since turning my back on the prosthetic arms, I had become zealous in my quest to find a way of doing every task with my bare stumps, keeping the amount of specialised equipment to a minimum. We did eventually replace our bath with a shower to make life easier, but on the whole I learned to live in an unadapted environment. As a consequence, I was soon able to cope in any other house or hotel room. This made a big difference when it came to visiting friends, going on holiday, travelling about—activities that were important to me as I continued to rebuild my life.

While in Chamonix we had received invitations to a couple of weddings, and going to them had been a big target for me. I had imagined I would go along in a wheelchair, and had hoped I might manage to hold my own drink and eat my own food. But by the time the weddings arrived, eating and drinking were easy, walking was no longer a problem and, proudly wearing my kilt, I showed off my new legs and even joined in the ceilidh dancing.

Mr MacDonald was right about the phantom limb pains. The day I left hospital they disappeared and never came back. I was so busy I didn't give them a thought. As I got used to wearing artificial legs I mentally projected my phantom feet into the prosthetic ones. The first time I accidentally stood in an icy pool of water, watching the water soak into my shoe, I swear I actually felt the cold liquid oozing between my toes.

As SOON AS I left hospital I decided I wanted to go back to work. Anna was wary. 'Don't you think it's a bit soon?' she asked.

'What would I do with myself at home?' I replied. 'Gordon and Alan said they'll take me back as soon as I want. They're paying me anyway so I might as well make myself useful.'

Anna consented, and the Monday after leaving hospital I began work. I wasn't much help at first. Quite apart from my physical limitations, I was unused to working in an office, I had lost touch with what was happening in the company and I had no defined job. I gradually began to establish myself, though, by shadowing my boss Alan. The office manager taught me the computer systems and I soon became competent with data bases, spreadsheets and web design.

I still couldn't wear my legs all day, so the hospital delivered my electric chair and I was soon tearing around the large open-plan room, being a regular hazard to my colleagues.

The Web was not a rigidly structured company, so in changing roles from site worker to office worker I was more or less free to create whatever job I wanted. I christened myself Training Manager and took over the administration of the company's training services wing, which had been badly falling behind. To my surprise I really enjoyed my new job. Business picked up, the courses ran smoothly and profits began to improve. Soon I was confident that my position was no longer just a charity job. In fact, when Anna decided to retrain as a landscape architect, I became the household's main breadwinner.

In HOSPITAL I had longed to go swimming, but now that I was out I felt a little shy about going to a public pool. Fortunately Morag put me in touch with a wonderful man called John de Courcy who ran a swimming club for the mentally and physically disabled.

The Tuesday evening sessions were pandemonium. There were people with a huge range of disabilities, including blindness, cerebral palsy, Down's syndrome, arthritis and paraplegia. There were also a few amputees. For the full hour the pool was a riot of shouting, laughing and splashing, over which John and his helpers maintained rudimentary control. Everyone had a thoroughly enjoyable time. If it wasn't for John, most of them would probably never go swimming.

My first attempt didn't go quite as expected. John had arranged for me to be coached by Lara Ferguson, a single lower-arm amputee and Paralympic swimmer. I got myself to the edge of the pool on my knees and plunged in confidently. I made all the motions of treading water— only to find myself pitching helplessly onto my back and sinking.

Lara pulled me upright. I hadn't realised quite how important hands and feet are as paddles. My stumps had no purchase in the water and were as useless as round oars. It seemed I was back to square one with swimming as well.

With Lara's patient tuition, however, it didn't take long before I found my balance in the water and discovered, after a lot of floundering about, that I could make my arms into paddles by clenching my elbows. Doggy-paddling with these, I could propel myself slowly through the water. On my second session I swam a length of the pool.

Swimming led me back to another sport—running. I used to love running, and would have given anything to be able to go for long runs in the country again. John de Courcy thought that I might have potential so he introduced me to Peter Arnott, who ran a group for disabled athletes at the Don Valley Stadium in Sheffield. I had never been involved in track athletics before but was keen to learn. The first time I went to a training weekend, I was still only learning to walk, but I was able to join in the fitness sessions and the pool session.

It was an inspiration to watch the other athletes. There were arm amputees who ran about as fast as mainstream athletes, and a one-legged guy who could hop almost as fast as the runners. And of course there were the wheelchair athletes, whose shoulders were as wide as two of me side by side.

At dinner, I chatted to a single amputee called Jamie Gillespie who had lost a leg in a motorbike accident while serving in the army. Now he was a Paralympic athlete and training to be a prosthetist.

He said to me, 'Sometimes I think losing my leg is the best thing that ever happened to me. Before my accident I had a career with limited prospects. Now, I've represented my country in the Para-lympic Games, I'm studying a profession I love, and life's great.'

I was amazed by this positive attitude and I wondered if I could ever feel that way about what had happened to me.

The next time I went to Sheffield I was on my Flexfeet, and I joined the other runners in their walking drills. The session finished off with a quick sprint down the track. I set off in pursuit and to my complete surprise found myself lumbering into a slow run. It wasn't exactly Linford Christie speed, but it was definitely a run.

Beside myself with excitement, I wanted to do it again and again, but realised that I was too tired. Over the next couple of days I paid for my spurt of exercise with cripplingly stiff quadriceps. If I was to make any progress I needed to get fitter.

John de Courcy helped me out with an exercise programme that I could do at home, and with the swimming and the exercises I slowly improved to an acceptable level of fitness.

At the December Sheffield meet, Peter encouraged me to run in my first race. It was a mainstream event, a local club indoor sixty metres, and although I had nothing to lose I was nervous as hell. When the gun went off, however, I just ran as hard as I could until the finish line came rushing past me. I came last, of course, the other able-bodied runners easily outstripping me, but I got a massive cheer from the spectators when I crossed the line.

THAT SUMMER, on a lovely, breezy day, my friend Pete Jennings took me sailing on Loch Rannoch. I could handle the tiller, pushing and pulling with my arms, and with enough time to prepare I could wrap the jib sheets round my stumps and pull them in as directed by Pete.

A month or two later Anna and I were invited for a weekend's sailing off the west coast of Scotland. We had a great time exploring the islands and inlets, watching out for seals, whales and dolphins, and I made myself useful on the tiller as much as possible.

Eventually I had a go at sailing single-handed (if you'll forgive the pun). Edinburgh's local sailing school at Port Edgar had a small trimaran called a Challenger. Although it was developed with able-handed wheelchair users in mind, I found I could handle it reasonably well. I sat in the middle hull with the tiller between my legs, and all the ropes that controlled the single sail and lifted the dagger board were accessible from my position. Although I wasn't fast, I could manoeuvre the little craft confidently back and forth across the water.

THE MILLENNIUM drew to a close. Like most people, I had often wondered what would be happening in my life as we passed from one century to the next. Never in a million years could I have guessed.

What a bizarre year 1999 had been for me, a year of tragedy, disaster, tears and despair. But it hadn't all been bad. I had found out more, in twelve months, about my physical and emotional limits than I had throughout all my years of climbing. I had learned much about myself, and hoped that in some ways I was now a better person.

I was gradually getting used to what had happened to me. My heart no longer sank each morning when I woke up and remembered, but I would still catch myself out. Often I would go for hours at a time, blissfully unaware that I had no hands and feet. Then I would suddenly catch sight of my stumps and think, I'm an amputee! I'm disabled! It felt like a kick in the stomach every time.

Slowly, however, I was beginning to feel secure once again about who I was and what I looked like. My friends, too, were familiar with my new appearance and treated me no differently from anyone else.

For Anna, who had stood by me through thick and thin, who suffered when I suffered and celebrated when I celebrated, it had been a hell of a year, too. In many ways, it had been a lot harder for her. Everything I went through, good or bad, Anna went through it with me. Yet she received little of the credit and none of the attention that I got; her role was often sidelined. A situation like that could easily tear a couple apart, but right now we were closer than we'd ever been.

On New Year's Day, Anna and I decided to get married and I was the happiest man in the world.

The year 2000, we were certain, was going to be a good one.

I HAD PROMISED Dr Marsigny and all the other hosptial staff in Chamonix that I would return, so that they could see how I was getting on. Now that I had made so much progress I was keen to keep my promise. The opportunity came in March 2000, when Manu Cauchy, the head of the A&E department, arranged for Anna and me to visit.

For both of us the trip was certain to be a difficult one. By returning to Chamonix, we would revisit the harrowing memories of the previous winter. Yet only by confronting those memories could we learn to accept what had happened and put it behind us.

So it was with some trepidation that Anna and I pushed our luggage trolley into the arrivals hall of Geneva Airport late one evening. Manu was there to greet us, with many other familiar faces, and we embraced our old friends warmly. I felt very proud when everyone expressed their amazement at how well I was walking.

We had arranged to stay with John Wilkinson and Anne Sauvy for a couple of nights. When we arrived at their chalet, all was dark outside the large picture windows. It wasn't until the morning that I saw, for the first time since my accident, the incredible mountains where my life had changed its course so dramatically just over a year ago.

Looking up at those savage peaks, I felt something stir inside me. Of course I felt horror, regret and pain. At the same time I couldn't help feeling a surge of desire at seeing those beautiful, challenging peaks. Deep down I knew I was still the same person, and my love of the mountains was still there.

First thing in the morning, Manu arrived to drive us the short distance across town to Chamonix Hospital. Despite having been there for three and a half weeks, I had seen very little of the hospital—only my own room and the ceilings of a few corridors—and so was unfamiliar with the building. I was surprised by how big and stylish it was.

Manu led the way through the double doors that led into the intensive care department at the rear. I picked out the door of my old room. Fortunately it was vacant, and I was able to go in. Nothing had changed. The same bed, the same sink, the same pieces of equipment, the damaged paintwork on the walls where my pictures had been pulled off. Even the smell of the place was shockingly familiar.

I went back out into the hall to meet the staff, and was soon hugging and kissing and shaking hands with all the doctors and nurses who had played such an important role in my treatment. It was thrilling to see them all again. I got so excited I started showing off by running up and down the corridor.

Then I heard the familiar sound of a pair of outsized shoes flapping along the corridor, and turned to see Dr Marsigny.

'I promised I'd walk into the hospital and shake you by the hand, and now I have,' I said proudly as we greeted one another.

He smiled and said, 'We are all very 'appy to see you here, Jamie. You are a very special patient to us.'

I half expected him to add, 'And you 'ad very serioz frozbite.'

Then we all went off to the common room to drink wine and chat about old times. Afterwards, we went for lunch with Marsigny and the two surgeons, Guy and Rik. Finally, in the evening, we had yet another meal out, this time with all the nurses and nursing assistants. Anna and I were feeling bloated and exhausted by the time we staggered back to the chalet that night.

The next day Manu had yet another emotional rollercoaster ride lined up for me. We were going to visit Corrado Truchet at Chamonix Mont Blanc Helicoptères, and he was willing, if I wanted, to fly me up to Les Droites and the scene of last year's tragedy.

Did I want to do that? One of the main reasons I had come back to Chamonix was to confront the memories of last year. But wasn't returning to Les Droites taking things a little far? I didn't really need to go back up there to dispel my phantoms. Still, a certain fascination urged me to visit that tiny piece of mountain one more time.

In a small wooden shack in the forest above Argentière, Corrado was waiting to meet us. He gave us a quick tour round his helicopter, the same one that had plucked me off the mountain, then we squeezed into the cockpit and in a matter of minutes were lifting gently off the ground.

The climb up into the mountains was spectacular. We hurtled into the narrow gorge that issues from the snout of the Argentière Glacier, and Corrado guided the machine round its twists and turns. Higher up we passed a couple of ice climbers, who were inching their way up the crystal cascades that tumble down the steep gorge walls.

As we rose out of the gorge, we passed into a bank of cloud. A fractured landscape of tumbled blocks, poised *séracs* and black fissures loomed out of the mist. Then, suddenly, we were over the glacier, shining white in the dazzling sunlight. Higher up stood the familiar mountain peaks, proudly propping up a beautiful blue sky. In a few seconds we were over the foot of the North Face of Les Droites.

It was amazing to see the climb, which had taken Jamie and me two days, flash by so quickly. In an instant we had panned up, past the *bergshrund*, to the start of the ice field. I picked out the area of rocks where we had taken our first bivouac. Then we were up into the headwall and I made out the ice smear where it had first started snowing. I recognised the upper runnels that had seemed to go on for ever, and then the final gully that had led us in darkness to the *brèche*. It all looked so different today—bright, non-threatening.

Suddenly we were hovering over the knife-edge summit of Les Droites. And there below us was the *brèche*. It looked so insignificant now. Just a small notch in a ridge riven with small notches. The place appeared untouched by human hand. There wasn't even a ledge to mark the spot where we had lain, side by side for all those days.

How could I hate this place? It was so beautiful. The fault lay with us, not with the mountain. The mountain was proud, savage and innocent of malice, as were the wind, the cloud and the snow. I couldn't hold a grudge against the mountains.

We circled the *brèche* a few times, then made a tour of all the peaks before making the stomach-lurching descent back down the glacier to the launching pad.

I was relieved that Manu had no more traumatic experiences organised. Anna took the opportunity to show me the Chamonix she had inhabited while I'd been stuck up on the mountain or in hospital. We visited the Hôtel Le Chamonix and paid our respects to the woman who had looked after the avalanche of mail and faxes that had arrived for me. We walked past the apartment block where everyone had stayed, checked out Anna's favourite patisserie and explored the back streets and markets of the town. We were also taken by Blaise Agresti and Alain Iglesis on a tour of the PGHM facilities, and were wined and dined in style at the officers' dinner table.

Soon it was time to leave, but this time our parting was much happier. Anna and I left knowing that Chamonix was no longer a place we needed to feel nervous of. We promised Manu and all our friends that we would return again.

BY NOW I WAS doing quite a lot of hillwalking, and gradually getting up bigger hills. My pair of specially adapted walking poles helped a great deal. Rob had taken a normal pair, cut the handles off and fixed them to stump sockets that Malcolm made for me. It made a big difference to my balance on steep ground. I found I could walk further as I was using less energy, and began to manage ascents of about 500 metres.

It wasn't all plain sailing, though. At the end of a long day in the hills of Glencoe, I was trudging wearily behind Anna when my way was blocked by a large, evil-looking bog. In an attempt to get across, I stepped onto a firm-looking tussock and, to my horror, my leg sank up to the knee in the foul black mire. As I pitched forward my stump parted company with the leg, and I left it behind as I plunged head-first into the muddy pool.

It took Anna about fifteen minutes to extricate me and my leg from the bog, and to help me put the leg back on. By the time I was upright again, we were both black from head to toe.

Partly because of episodes like this, I was quite cautious, never venturing far from a main road. It might have been many more months before I accomplished hills of any significance had it not been for Ali Brown, an ex-RAF serviceman who had lost his leg in a climbing accident and had heard about me through John de Courcy.

Ali explained that he was involved in a mammoth RAF Mountain Rescue Association charity walk from Land's End to John O'Groats. He was organising a subsidiary event to encourage disabled people to get onto the hills, and asked if I would join him on Ben Nevis in June. At 1,343 metres above sea level, Ben Nevis is, of course, Britain's highest mountain. At that stage of my rehabilitation I could barely manage 500 metres, but on a whim I agreed to give it a go.

As June approached, I got down to some serious training. As it was a charity event, I wrote a short email asking for sponsorship and sent it out to all my friends. They forwarded the email to their friends, and so on, until my little note seemed to be spreading like a virus. I was soon receiving replies, offering money and encouragement, from all over the world. The response I received was overwhelming, and I now realised I was well and truly committed to climbing Ben Nevis.

The big day finally arrived, and early on Sunday morning my dad, Anna and I drove up from Glasgow. Nervous tension gnawed at my gut. I had not yet climbed a hill even half the height of Ben Nevis and was utterly unconfident. I'd arranged to meet everyone at the Milton Hotel, although I had no idea who 'everyone' might be. By the time we pulled into the car park I was simply dreading the whole thing.

And there they all were. Television crews, satellite broadcast vans, photographers—the works. For the first time I realised how it must feel to be a pop star. I was ushered from camera to camera, doing several interviews in the space of a few minutes, and a bacon roll was shoved into my stumps. Then I was taken under the wing of Al Sylvester, the leader of the RAF Mountain Rescue Association, and bustled up the road to the start of the walk.

It seemed to take ages but eventually, after several more interviews, we were off, the RAF lads setting the pace. Following us were a crowd of journalists, cameramen, presenters, friends and family. All of creation seemed to be labouring up the hill, and I hobbled along in the midst of it all.

The weather was looking doubtful and a smudge of rain began to fall. As we gained altitude, however, the clouds lifted and the sun made an occasional appearance. The photographers puffing alongside me jostled for position. I found myself constantly being asked to pause for photos at choice vantage points. My patience began to wear thin and I started to get snappy.

Forty-five minutes into the walk and already I was starting to feel it. My thighs ached and my stumps were beginning to feel the strain. This kind of stuff used to be so easy for me. I couldn't believe it had come to this—picking my way slowly uphill, stepping aside to let old ladies and schoolkids overtake me. To cap it all I had about a dozen journalists buzzing round me like flies.

I paused to catch my breath—and to get my head together. In those grim first days after the accident I had quickly discovered that a negative attitude led to nowhere but despair. If I was going to make it up this hill I would have to adopt a more positive attitude.

Fortunately my support team provided plenty of entertainment and conversation to divert me. Anna was never far from my side. My dad and a friend, two old men of the mountains, had plenty of tales to tell, and my sister Louise and her partner Neil had come out for a rare trip into the hills. With the help of this fine support I trudged wearily on, ignoring the circus around me.

Finally I came over a slight rise and there, ahead of me, was an aluminium bridge spanning a small ravine. It was the landmark for which I'd been aiming for the last hour or so, the first rung on a mental ladder stretching ahead of me to the distant summit. Unfortunately the Ben Nevis tourist path is not the most exciting climb in the world, and I was having difficulty in remembering suitable milestones along the way. My ladder was woefully short of rungs.

It's not that I hadn't been that way often enough. I couldn't even begin to count how many times I'd trudged up the Ben, bound for another climbing trip on the north face. But I had never paid much attention to the boring old tourist path. Now, since my world had been turned on its head, the mundane had become a challenge, and the tourist track up Ben Nevis had become an aspiration.

Five and a half hours after setting out, I arrived on the familiar summit plateau that was still partially covered by lingering snow. Helicopters, courtesy of the RAF and the BBC, flew overhead. A huge crowd was waiting to cheer my arrival, champagne corks popped, and another deluge of interviews began. I hugged Anna and posed for the cameras, looking elated and feeling overwhelmed.

Al Sylvester had a surprise arranged for me. The RAF helicopter was going to take me for a tour of the mountain. The big yellow machine was able to touch down long enough to allow me to scramble aboard, and I was whisked off for a ten-minute view of Ben Nevis as I'd never seen it before. I thought for a sneaky moment that I could be spared the long walk down, but the RAF boys were not so unscrupulous and set me down again in precisely the same spot.

When the celebrations were over, I suddenly realised how weary I was. I had been on the go for a long time and I hadn't had a chance to rest. For the press, the event was over: the quadruple amputee had reached the summit of Ben Nevis. For me, the hard part—descending 1,300 metres on my tired and painful legs—was still to come.

The descent was an exhausting grind, by the end of which I was leaning heavily on my sticks and wincing with every step. Eventually, the welcome sight of the pub at Achintee loomed out of the gathering gloom. A small crowd waited to greet me, and I waved gratefully at them as I carried on up the steps to slump into the largest armchair I could find, where the most appreciated pint of beer ever was waiting for me.

As a footnote to the story of my Ben Nevis ascent, which raised many thousands of pounds for charity, it's worth mentioning that by forcing many not very fit ladies and gentlemen of the press to climb the hill, I helped introduce them to the joys of hillwalking. Several of them told me afterwards they'd had a fantastic day and wanted to go out in the hills again. Mention must be made, however, of one poor photographer, on commission for a broadsheet paper, who made the long journey for the all-important summit shot. Suffering terribly with exhaustion, sciatica and blisters, he reached the summit only to discover that I had left and he'd missed the shot. Next morning the paper ran with a photo purchased from Reuters.

BY MOST STANDARDS I was very mobile now. I had climbed Ben Nevis, I could run about twice round a running track without stopping, and I was rarely forced to use the wheelchair any more.

In one respect, though, I still felt handicapped. Wherever we went, Anna drove, and I was reliant on her, or taxis, for transportation. All that changed in August, however, when I got a brand-new car.

When I first considered how I was going to manage to drive, I had assumed that a fairly serious conversion would be necessary. I discovered, however, that the difficulties weren't as great as I had imagined. Gear stick and handbrake I could manage. Indicators, lights and windscreen wipers too. The steering wheel I found difficult. The accelerator and footbrake I could control quite accurately with my right leg, but I couldn't operate the clutch with my left.

So if the car was automatic, I thought, the biggest difficulty would be the steering wheel. Malcolm's solution to this was a steering ball that could be fixed onto any car, and a corresponding steel cup, which he laminated into a socket for my right arm. Wearing this steering arm, I pushed the cup onto the ball, which produced a sort of universal joint with which I could turn the wheel.

Armed with my new equipment I went down to my local driving assessment centre, where I was put through my paces. My assessor gave me a clean bill of health and I was free to drive an automatic.

When my car arrived I immediately took to the streets. It felt peculiar at first, steering with this strange contraption on my arm and accelerating and braking with my artificial foot, but I gradually got used to it, and now find driving no more difficult than I did before my accident. The best part is that the car is almost unaltered. This means that anyone can drive it, and I can drive any other automatic simply by fixing on the steering ball.

One more step on the road to living a normal life.

THAT SUMMER, Anna and I were married at a small private ceremony near Edinburgh. Anna looked absolutely stunning, I did my best to look smart in my kilt, and our closest family and friends joined us for what was one of the happiest days of my life.

Then we headed down to the Lake District, where we'd hired the largest marquee we could lay our hands on, and threw an extravagant party. We invited all the friends who had played such a special part in what had been a very difficult year and a half for us. Manu even managed to make it over, representing our new Chamonix friends. Anna and I danced until we could keep our eyes open no longer and were forced to stumble, delirious with happiness, off to bed.

BY SPRING 2000 I was achieving so much that I could hardly keep pace with myself. Apart from leading a fairly normal life at home and at work, I was now capable of hillwalking, sailing, running, caving, snowboarding and many other sports. However, there was still one thing I yearned to do—and there are no prizes for guessing.

I wanted to go climbing again.

The morning after I returned home from hospital, Anna and I had driven down to the Lake District and checked into a hotel for the night to spend some proper time together. We went for a boat trip on Derwent Water and on nearby crags we spotted climbers, inching their way up sunny rock faces. I watched the tiny figures for a long time and said, 'I want to climb again.'

'I know you do,' said Anna, 'and I know you will.'

I suppose it was inevitable. As a teenager I used to think that climbing, with its heady blend of adventure, beauty and danger, was the only thing that gave my life meaning. As I grew older, I realised that it wasn't the be all and end all. It was, however, the special ingredient that helped shape my personality. I no longer needed climbing to define who I was. But I still wanted to climb again to show that I hadn't been beaten, and because I still loved it. And I was certain that Jamie would have wanted me to return to the mountains, just as he would have done himself if he was in my position.

Gradually I formulated a plan for getting back into rock climbing. I didn't foresee my feet as being too great an issue. In a pair of sticky rubber rock shoes I imagined I would be able to stand on small footholds quite securely. My lack of hands was another matter. Without them, hauling myself up a steep rock face seemed impossible.

In my head I devised some equipment that might help me. I was going to ask Malcolm and Rob to make me a pair of hooks that could be attached to my arms. I would try out and develop these hooks at the local indoor climbing wall, then venture onto an outdoor crag.

The plan went out of the window one evening when our friends Chris Pasteur and Jane Herries gave us a call. They were going to Northumberland the next day for a bit of climbing and asked if we'd like to join them. The forecast was good, so we thought, why not? Out of habit, I packed some climbing gear.

The strangely named Bowden Doors is a beautiful crag that stretches across the crest of the lonely moors west of Belford. The rock is a wonderfully compact, golden sandstone, and it's always been one of my favourite places to climb.

That day was sunny, despite it being early in the season, and the sun soon warmed the chilly rock. Chris and Jane did a couple of routes, while Anna and I walked along the foot of the crag and I dug up old memories of the climbs I'd done there. I stopped beneath a route called His Eminence. I never did manage that one. I'd been trying for years. Dozens of times I had made the beautiful series of moves up the bulging wall and reached that crucial set of finger pockets—like the holes in a bowling ball—only to come flying off. I never got frustrated because I always assumed that one day I would manage it. Not now though. It was to be added to the long list of climbs I would never do.

We rejoined Chris and Jane, who were back on the ground.

'What's it to be then, Jim Jam?' prompted Chris.

'I really don't think there's much point. It's all too steep.'

'Well, what have you got to lose?'

'Nothing, but I'll be very slow.'

'We've got all day.'

So I decided to give it a go, and Chris, Jane and Anna set about getting me into a harness and levering my uncooperative feet into a tight-fitting pair of rock shoes. After a ten-minute struggle, I stood up, ready for action, and turned my attention to the rock.

Introductory Staircase, at the end of the crag, is the easiest route at Bowden Doors and seemed the obvious choice for my first attempt. Chris swiftly led up the climb and settled himself down on the top of the crag to belay me up. Anna tied me into the rope and wished me luck. Instantly, that familiar feeling of complete focus took over. Chris, Jane, Anna, my surroundings, all receded and the rock absorbed the whole of my concentration. That part of the crag runs to a lot of flat edges, and I found that I could balance on them, even though I could feel very little through my feet.

I couldn't pull up with my arms, but where I could get them onto a good flat surface below shoulder level, I could push down effectively. Using a combination of leverage with my arms and careful footwork, I inched my way slowly upwards, taking great care over every single move. Eventually I was able to pull over onto the first of several large ledges. The next ledge was at over head height and it took some cunning manoeuvres, bracing my back against the side wall, to gain it.

The top was now just above me but the last couple of metres proved the hardest. It was another ten minutes or so, doing some very tricky bridging, before I pulled over onto the flat top of the crag to join Chris.

'Nice one,' said Chris. 'Want to do another?'

I had taken over forty minutes to climb ten metres, my stumps were rubbed raw by the rough sandstone, and I was completely exhausted.

'Yeah, all right then.'

I made my way back down, while Chris set up a rope on the second easiest route, Second Staircase. And I completed the climb.

I went home that night absolutely elated. I was shattered and sore, but I didn't care because I'd been rock climbing again. Against all the odds I had realised my dream. In the end it was a case of just putting on a pair of rock shoes and having a go.

AFTER BOWDEN I started visiting our local climbing wall, where I began to develop and expand upon the new techniques I had learned in Northumberland. Over the months I got more proficient until I was climbing things that I would never have dreamed possible. I devised all sorts of ways to hold myself on and pull myself up, coming to realise that both are not so much about fingers but about friction. My stumps soon got very tough and I learned how to hook them over small holds, jam them into holes and crevices, lever them behind flakes, anything to get some all-important purchase on the rock. I also learned how to handle the ropes, taking them in and paying them out using my elbows for grip.

The day I satisfied myself that I had really made my comeback was in August that year, when I made an ascent of a well-known climb in the Lake District, appropriately called Little Chamonix. The last time

I had done Little Chamonix was with Jamie. Now the route proved a good deal more time-consuming. Ten minutes solo climbing for a couple of fit lads translated into three difficult roped pitches for a party of four including a quadruple amputee.

The first pitch took me a long time but the second was a lot more fun. A groove leads beneath a series of overhangs that block access to the final, steep wall. Directly under the overhangs, a large block forms a ledge on which climbers can rest. Sitting on this block I peered nervously at the way ahead. A step off the block, down and across another groove, led to a rib leading round the side of the overhang. But without the security of a couple of fingerholds in an obvious crack, the move was going to be precarious. Eventually, after dithering for a long time, I slithered off the block and found a purchase in the groove. A few further difficult moves and I heaved my way onto the tiny saddle of rock below the spectacular final pitch.

I launched myself up the steep wall. I didn't make fast progress, but soon found that the holds were big enough to enable me to cling to the rock. The difficulty was moving from one hold to the next. Fortunately my training on the climbing wall paid off and I worked out ways of levering my body up the face. Meanwhile, Chris climbed behind me, pointing out footholds that I couldn't see.

When I reached the chimney flake, I jammed first my shoulders, then my hips, my knees and my feet thankfully behind it. There followed an almighty struggle, during which my helmet got wedged completely, until I eventually emerged, gasping, on top of the flake. A few further moves and it was all over—I was sitting on top.

I looked out at that familiar view and savoured the much-missed feeling of being at the top of a difficult climb. I had completed my first real multipitch climb. What's more, I hadn't fallen off once. And I had needed no special equipment. I felt justified in telling the world that I was a climber once more.

MALCOLM PALED. 'I knew this was coming,' he said quietly.

'But do you think you can do it?' I implored.

'I'm sure we could,' he replied. 'But we have to make sure there's no liability if there's an accident. Ice climbing is a risky activity.'

'Hazardous,' I corrected him. 'The activity is hazardous and it's the climber's job to limit the risk. That's why I've come to see you.'

'We'll have to undertake a fairly serious risk assessment.'

'Does that mean you'll do it?' I asked, picking up on Malcolm's use of the future tense.

Malcolm shrugged and sighed. 'Why not?' he conceded. 'But we'll have to get Rob on board too.'

Rob was enthusiastic. 'We're here to facilitate your rehabilitation,' he reasoned. 'If ice climbing is what you did before your accident, then it's our job to help you do it again.'

So the three of us began designing a pair of prosthetic ice axes.

We started in February 2001, but in March the job became more urgent when Manu Cauchy invited me to Chamonix in a couple of months' time to attempt some climbing. Rob and Malcolm pulled out all the stops to get the axes ready in time for my departure.

A Scottish manufacturer kindly supplied the components for the type of axe I wanted. Rob cut the shafts down and designed an additional component that would attach the axe shaft into the top of a prosthetic stump socket. Meanwhile, Malcolm took a cast of my right arm and began laminating a socket. Using carbon-fibre strips he laminated in the junction component Rob had made. The axe shaft and head were fixed to this and the first prototype was almost ready.

The difficult part, however, was holding the socket onto my arm. Malcolm had made it clear from the outset that none of the standard methods of prosthetic arm suspension would be strong enough to hold my full weight when hanging from an ice axe. His socket, therefore, would rely on me providing my own method.

With the help of colleagues at the Web, I designed a harness that secured the ice axe socket to my elbow. This harness was attached to a standard climber's chest harness, guaranteeing that even if the axe slipped, it wouldn't come off my arm entirely. Finally, the prototype axe was ready to use the day before I left for France.

CHAMONIX IN MAY 2001 was warm and foggy. Manu and I skulked about in the valley for a couple of days, visiting friends and getting fat on good food and wine. I was starting to think I might be going home without even seeing the mountains, when the weather cleared.

Manu and I, together with Philippe 'Poutsy' Pouts, one of the PGHM rescuers, took the rattly old funicular railway up to Montenvers above the great glacier, the Mer de Glace. It was a difficult twenty-minute walk down to the glacier. Free of the snows of winter, the ice was iron hard. The sun baked down and meltwater lurked in every hollow.

Manu and Poutsy strapped my crampons to my artificial feet, over my shoes, and we marched up the glacier, heading for a series of crevasses that provided ideal conditions for an ice-climbing school. It was possible to walk in to both the tops and the bottoms of them, making it easy to set up top ropes and practise ice climbing in safety.

As I only had the one axe, we selected an ice wall that wasn't too steep and, while Manu set up the rope, Poutsy helped me into a harness and helmet and strapped me into my ice axe. I felt distinctly ungainly, and was certainly a strange sight to behold with my bizarre cramponed legs and half arm, half ice axe.

I was ready for action, though, and as soon as I was tied into the end of the rope I tackled the ice wall ahead of me. The axe swung well and the pick bit the ice nicely, sinking halfway to the hilt. When I tried to pull myself up on it, however, something in the angle between the shaft and the prosthesis caused the pick to rotate out and I fell backwards. I tried again, taking more care as I pulled up, and kicked my crampons one after the other into the ice. Again, the pick slipped, but I kept my balance this time, removed it carefully from the ice and knocked it in higher up.

This was working! I was making progress.

Poutsy shouted encouragement from below and Manu gave instructions from above. Ignoring them both, I concentrated on placing my axe carefully and pulling up on it without pulling it out. The wall was only six metres high and it wasn't long before I teetered my way to the top, heart pounding with excitement. I lost no time in getting Poutsy to lower me down so I could do it again. I felt extraordinarily privileged to be back climbing in the Alps once more.

Some time later, Rob redesigned his junction component, Malcolm made two more prosthetic sockets, one for each arm, and I made some design modifications to my harnesses. In time for the winter of 2002, both axes were ready.

This time I trialled the equipment in Scotland, on an icy gully below the summit of Aonach Mor. The new axes were a great improvement, and I found I could heave myself up the ice with confidence, relying on the others who were with me for help with rope work, adjustments to clothes, eating and so on. This seemed a small price to pay for the freedom of being able to climb in the Scottish mountains again.

BACK IN THE SUMMER of 1999, Anna and I had gone along to watch the Edinburgh Marathon. I recall watching those crowds of athletes flood past and finding the whole event so inspiring that I longed to take part. Now, two years later, even though the prospect of running over twenty-six miles seemed a little daunting, I vowed to myself that I would run the London Marathon.

At the beginning of December, with four and a half months to go, I began my training. To begin with it all felt pretty futile. My thrice-weekly jogs around the block were broken by frequent stops to sort out my legs. If I didn't stop about every half-mile to take them off and dry the sweat off the silicone liners, they were likely to come flying off, leaving me literally without a leg to stand on. This meant I couldn't get into any sort of a rhythm. By the time I'd staggered a mile and a half I was exhausted and couldn't imagine running any further.

Out of pure stubbornness, however, I continued, and after a few weeks I managed to up my distance to about three miles, stopping as often as five times to fix my legs. I asked Morag if there was anything to be done about the sweat problem, but she said it was common and there was little I could do. However, as I got fitter, she said, the sweating in my legs should reduce.

Then, over Christmas, a muscle strain in my lower back kept me from running for a few days. Just as the back pain got better, I developed a nasty abscess in the flesh of my left stump, setting the running programme back another two weeks. I eased myself back into it as the sore got better, but I couldn't imagine running twenty-six miles.

One grim day at the end of January, I reached a turning point. I had been mooching about the flat trying to work up the enthusiasm to go for a run when I glanced out of the window to check the weather. The air was heavy with swirling snow and already a thick white layer was blanketing the road and pavements. My heart sank. Obviously I wasn't going out in that. But I kept thinking to myself, Come on, Jamie. Don't be a wimp. It's only a bit of snow. You're supposed to be a hard man, for God's sake.

And suddenly I made up my mind to go for it.

Once I was outside, the snow didn't feel so bad. In fact it felt great. It kept me cool and sweat-free, and the inch-thick carpet beneath my feet gave me pleasantly soft running. The streets were eerily deserted. I was so happy to be running out on such a day that I felt unstoppable. In fact, when I arrived back at the flat having completed my usual four-mile circuit, I felt so good I did it all again!

A fortnight later I managed my first half marathon, along the banks of the Water of Leith, running ten miles, then walking three, and the prospect of completing a full marathon looked like a real possibility.

Another week later, however, I developed a strange sharp pain in the end of my right leg. I made appointments to see Morag and my consultant, Mr Macdonald, and both thought it was bursitis—an inflammation of a protective fluid-filled sack that had developed around the end of my tibia. There was no treatment apart from rest.

With only three weeks to go, my leg was still no better. I was beginning to consider pulling out, but with a substantial amount of sponsorship money riding on me I felt under pressure to carry on. In desperation I visited Mr MacDonald and persuaded him to X-ray the leg. The X-ray revealed a spur of bone that had continued to grow from the end of my tibia since it was amputated. It was interesting to know the reason for the pain, but little consolation as there was nothing Mr MacDonald could do about it. He reassured me, however, that it was nothing serious and that there was no reason why I shouldn't run on it, so long as I could take the pain!

In the corridor of the hospital I bumped into my other consultant, Mr Howie. When I explained my problem to him, he looked at me and shook his head. 'You're running twenty-six miles on prosthetic legs and you're complaining about sore stumps? It's no bloody wonder!'

Over the following week I continued my routine in the gym, feeling despondent. I was just about to pull the plug on my attempt at the marathon that year when my leg suddenly stopped hurting. Not knowing whether I would be wise to resume training, I called Peter Arnott from my disabled training group in Sheffield.

Peter's advice surprised me. 'Never mind the training,' he said, 'it's too late for that now. Do just a couple of short runs to keep yourself in shape. Then go out on the day and enjoy yourself. Remember, it doesn't matter how long it takes you to finish. And if I know you, Jamie, you'll finish if it's the last thing you do.'

Encouraged by Peter's faith in me, I decided to go for it.

I WOKE AT 6.30 a.m on Marathon Day, with butterflies in my stomach. Sick with nerves, I caught the train to Blackheath Park, where I met Jamie Gillespie, my amputee friend who was running his first marathon since losing his leg.

The incredible mass of runners pushing to get to the start was quite overwhelming, and despite having left plenty of time I was rushing to get changed. There's really nothing to compare with the feeling of being one of 32,000 runners, preparing to run the race of your life.

At 9.45 the starting gun boomed, there was a roar from the crowd, and my nervous tension evaporated into the excitement of the race. The first six or seven miles were fantastic. Carried along with the thrill of the event, we jogged along, while people clapped and cheered. We chatted to other runners and took plenty of water as we passed through the frequent drinks stations. All the way we were running alongside rhinoceroses, clowns, pram-pushers, a man carrying a canoe, and thousands of more ordinary-looking runners.

At Mile 9 we stopped so Jamie and I could make adjustments to our legs. The strain was beginning to show, but we carried on at our regular pace until we'd clocked up nearly thirteen miles at Tower Bridge. There was a big boost for me when I spotted Stu Fisher, Mat Fisher and JJ in the crowd on the bridge. Further on I saw Anna and rushed over to give her a big sweaty hug.

During the leg to the Isle of Dogs we walked for long sections. The break in my training plan was starting to show. At Mile 20, my sister Louise jumped out of the crowd. I was really suffering now and had slowed right down.

Over the next few miles, various friends appeared along the route giving much-needed support. I was very slow now and beginning to feel demoralised.

I was really struggling by Mile 23 but I knew then that I was going to do it. Nothing was going to stop me now. The last three miles were hell. Every muscle, every bone, every joint in my body screamed for submission, but I wouldn't relent.

Finally I came round the bend from Birdcage Walk onto the Mall and there it was, still an elusive 200 yards away—the finish. Somehow I found the energy to put on a final spurt of speed and crossed the line with a time of 5 hours and 56 minutes.

I'd done it. For so long I had doubted myself, but I stuck to my guns. Running a marathon is something that nobody can ever take away from you. You might never run another step in your life, but you'll always know that you're one of that special group of people who has run the magic distance of 26.2 miles. I am privileged to be one of the first quadruple amputees, perhaps even the first, to ever achieve that feat.

I'VE RETURNED to the Alps again since that first climb with Manu. And every time I return, I find myself asking questions about why what happened, happened. Questions about how it might have been prevented. Questions about the meaning of life, death and fate.

I know now that I'll never find answers—not in this life, anyway— but perhaps it's important to ask, nevertheless. By asking those fundamental questions I learn something about myself, learn how truly remarkable and mysterious this world is, and how incredibly lucky I am to be alive and able to experience it.

JAMIE ANDREW

Since running the London Marathon in 2002, Jamie Andrew has pushed himself on to even greater achievements. In 2003 he achieved his goal of climbing Mont Blanc, prevented only by bad weather from reaching the very summit, but getting to within 300 metres of it. In January this year, he and three other disabled climbers set out to climb to the summit of Kilimanjaro in Tanzania by its most difficult northern route. The other members of the team were Paul Pritchard, an Englishman who was paralysed after a fall during a climbing accident in Australia, Paul Lim, a climber from Singapore who was left paralysed after contracting Guillain-Barré Syndrome, and Pete Steane, a teacher from Tasmania who punctured his spine when he fell in a serious climbing incident in 1982.

To some extent, the group had to learn as they went along, compensating for their disabilities by focusing on their strengths, such as perseverance. 'We wanted to show that disabled people can do things in their own right,' Jamie says of the trip. 'There have been other expeditions with able-bodied *and* disabled people, but this one we were doing by ourselves without help.' Money raised through the climb will go to found a leprosy centre in Tanzania, and the three hope to make a film of the expedition. Already Jamie has received a five-figure donation from one of Scotland's most successful entrepreneurs, who has described him as 'inspirational'.

Would he encourage young people to take up climbing? 'Of course. It's a fantastic sport. And it doesn't have to be dangerous, if you do it within the context of a local climbing wall or simple rock climbs. It's totally life-enhancing, and I'd recommend it to anyone.' And what advice would he give to anyone trying to overcome a huge setback in life? 'Just don't try to overcome all your hurdles at once. There's plenty of time.'

Jamie says that his family are very supportive of his efforts to climb again. 'They know better than to try to discourage me. I would do it anyway; it is part of me.' And he adds that of all his recent achievements the one of which he is most proud is the recent birth of his baby daughter, Iris.

THE LAST JUROR. Original full-length edition © 2004 by Belfry Holdings, Inc. British condensed edition © The Reader's Digest Association Limited, 2004.

THE VARIOUS HAUNTS OF MEN. Original full-length edition © 2004 by Susan Hill. British condensed edition © The Reader's Digest Association Limited, 2004.

THE CODEX. Original full-length edition © 2004 by Splendide Mendax, Inc. British condensed edition © The Reader's Digest Association Limited, 2004.

LIFE AND LIMB. Original full-length edition © 2003 by Jamie Andrew. British condensed edition © The Reader's Digest Association Limited, 2004.

The right to be identified as authors has been asserted by the following in accordance with sections 77 and 78 of the Copyright, Designs and Patents Act, 1988: John Grisham, Susan Hill, Douglas Preston and Jamie Andrew.

ACKNOWLEDGMENTS AND PICTURE CREDITS: *The Last Juror*: pages 6–8: illustration: Getty/Stone and Photodisc; page 155 Sam Abell. *The Various Haunts of Men*: pages 156–158: photomontage Rick Lecoat @ Shark Attack/Photodisc. *The Codex*: pages 306–308: photomontage Curtis Phillips-Cozier/Corbis; page 437: Christine Preston. *Life and Limb*: pages 438–440: Anna Wyatt; page 488 (top) Al Matthewson, (left) Jules Cartwright, (below left) Jamie Fisher; page 489 (top right and above) Jamie Fisher, (left) Anna Wyatt, (below) Catherine Andrew; page 512: (top right) Chris Pasteur; page 513 (left) Roger Payne, (above) Chris Pasteur, (left) Anna Wyatt.

DUSTJACKET CREDITS: Spine from top: Getty/Stone and Photodisc; photomontage Rick Lecoat @ Shark Attack/Photodisc; photomontage Curtis Phillips-Cozier/Corbis; Anna Wyatt.

Printed by Maury Imprimeur SA, Malesherbes, France
Bound by Reliures Brun SA, Malesherbes, France

231/04